INSIGHT GUIDE

THAILAND

Sk
A J L8
✓ S21
523

 APA PUBLICATIONS **L**
Part of the Langenscheidt Publishing Group

ABOUT THIS BOOK

Editorial
Project Editor
Scott Rutherford
Editorial Director
Brian Bell

Distribution
UK & Ireland
GeoCenter International Ltd
The Viables Centre,
Harrow Way
Basingstoke, Hants,
RG22 4BJ
Fax: (44 1256) 817988

United States
Langenscheidt Publishers, Inc.
46–35 54th Road
Maspeth, NY 11378
Fax: (1 718) 784-0640

Worldwide
APA Publications GmbH & Co.
Verlag KG Singapore Branch, Singapore
38 Joo Koon Road
Singapore 628990
Tel: (65) 865-1600
Fax: (65) 861-6438

Printing
Insight Print Services (Pte) Ltd
38 Joo Koon Road
Singapore 628990
Tel: (65) 865-1600
Fax: (65) 861-6438

© 1998 APA Publications GmbH & Co.
Verlag KG Singapore Branch, Singapore
All Rights Reserved
First Edition 1978
Thirteenth Edition 1999

CONTACTING THE EDITORS
Although every effort is made to
provide accurate information in
this publication, we live in a
fast-changing world and would
appreciate it if readers would
call our attention to any errors or
outdated information that may
occur by writing to us at:
**Insight Guides, P.O. Box 7910,
London SE1 8ZB, England.
Fax: (44 171) 620-1074.
e-mail:**
insight@apaguide.demon.co.uk

Anyone who travels as a lifestyle or a calling ends up in Thailand, either for its world-class beaches or perhaps for the northern hill tribes. Whatever the reason, most visitors leave Thailand mumbling the words that they are coming back.

The first European visitors returned home with descriptions of an amazing civilisation with the most beautiful of cities and art. Those in Europe who doubted the returning travellers dismissed the stories as enterprising but fanciful lies. The vivid descriptions, however, were completely true. The cities of Sukhothai and Ayutthaya, for example, were amongst the world's greatest urban centres during their time, and today seduce with their splendour.

How to use this book
For over two decades, *Insight Guide: Thailand* has used the proven format of informative, entertaining and well-written text paired with an evocative approach to photography.

The guide is carefully structured both to convey a thorough understanding of the

915·93

011216

Wat Sri Mongkran,
Mukdahan.

◆ The Travel Tips listings section provides a convenient point of reference for information on travel, hotels, restaurants, shops and festivals. Information may be located quickly by using the index printed on the back cover flap.

The contributors

This edition was supervised by **Scott Rutherford**, who oversees Apa's Asian and Pacific titles. A considerable amount of the destination updating was done by three associates of CPA in Chiang Mai: **Andrew Forbes** has a doctorate in Asian history and has been involved in Thai studies for over 20 years; **Simon Robson** lives in Mae Sa, north of Chiang Mai; and **David Henley** has lived in Thailand for over a decade.

Updating Bangkok were **Susan Cunningham**, who has worked on previous editions and also updated Ko Samui and Nan, and **Paul Hicks**, who has also contributed to Apa's Hong Kong guide. **Jerry Hopkins**, who contributed to the original *Insight Guide: Hawaii* and is a best-selling author, wrote on architecture, arts, and the *Ramakien*.

Ken Scott updated Phuket and Krabi, while Bangkok-based **Sandy Barron** covered the Gulf Coast and western Thailand. Overhauling the extensive Travel Tips was **Katja Thomas**, who also updated areas just outside of Bangkok. **Clare Griffiths**, in Apa's London office, wrote the text for the "Insight On" features.

country and its culture, and to guide readers through its sights and activities.
◆ Understanding the nation requires that one know something of its past. The first section covers Thailand's history and culture in authoritative essays.
◆ The main Places section provides a full run-down of all the attractions and destinations worth seeing. Places of major interest are coordinated by number with full-colour maps.

Map Legend

—··—	International Boundary
⊖	Border Crossing
—•—	National Park
– – –	Ferry Route
✈	Airport
🚌	Bus Station
P	Parking
ⓘ	Tourist Information
✉	Post Office
∴	Archaeological Site
∩	Cave
𝐈	Statue/Monument
★	Place of Interest

The main places of interest in the **Places** section are coordinated by number with a full-color map (e.g. ❶), and a symbol at the top of every right-hand page tells you where to find the map.

Contributors

Forbes   *Robson*

Cunningham   *Rutherford*

INSIGHT GUIDE
THAILAND

CONTENTS

Maps

THAILAND
Bangkok

Thailand **132**

Bangkok **138**

Grand Palace **143**

Central Bangkok **146**

Bangkok Surroundings **179**

Central Thailand **192**

Ayutthaya **196**

Northern Thailand **216**

Chiang Mai **227**

Chiang Mai Surroundings **231**

Golden Triangle **236**

Northeast Thailand **252**

Eastern Gulf **277**

Northern Isthmus **297**

Ko Samui **309**

Phuket **313**

Phang Nga/Krabi **319**

Deep South **327**

Introduction

Kingdom of Thailand **15**

History

Decisive Dates **20**
Rise of Sukhothai **25**
Ayutthaya **34**
Era of the Chakri Monarchy **44**
Contemporary Thailand **53**

Features

Natural History **63**
People **69**
Hill Tribes **78**
Religion **87**
Performing Arts.....................**97**
Arts and Crafts **102**
Architecture **109**
Cuisine **117**

Limestone formations,
Phuket area.

Travel Tips

Insight on....

Customs and Festivals **82**
Images of the Buddha **92**
Temple Art and Architecture ...**112**
Hill-tribe Crafts and Clothing **248**
Feast of Fruits **288**

Information panels

The King **59**
The *Ramakien* **101**
Sweets **121**
Waterways **157**
Prostitution **166**
Culture of Rice **205**
Khmer Legacy **258**
Gems: Crystal Power **284**

Getting Acquainted **338**
Planning the Trip **339**
Practical Tips **347**
Getting Around **351**
Where to Stay **356**
Eating Out **363**
Attractions **370**
Culture **375**
Festivals **377**
Shopping **380**
Sport **385**
Language **387**
Further Reading **388**
◆**Full Travel Tips index
is on page 337**

Places

Introduction **131**
Bangkok.............................**137**
The Old Royal City **141**
Mae Nam Chao Phraya **154**
Beyond the Royal City...........**161**
Outside of Bangkok **177**
Far to the West.....................**186**
Central Thailand **193**
Ayutthaya and Lopburi **195**
Central Plains **202**
Sukhothai **207**
The North **217**
Towards Chiang Mai **219**
Chiang Mai **225**
Chiang Rai/Golden Triangle ..**233**
Mae Hong Son.....................**240**
Nan Valley **244**

The Northeast....................**253**
Khorat Plateau **255**
Northern Khorat **263**
The Gulf Coast **273**
South to Pattaya **275**
Eastern Gulf.........................**281**
The South **293**
Northern Isthmus **295**
Ko Samui and Pha Ngan **307**
Phuket **313**
Phang Nga and Krabi **318**
The Deep South **325**

KINGDOM OF THAILAND

Imagine a place that defines graciousness, tolerance, and aesthetic ideals. You've just imagined Thailand

L and of the free, land of smiles. The former is a literal translation of *Thailand*, while the latter is a promotional slogan that carries considerable truth. Both define the Thai people. Beneath their graciousness, the Thai have a strong sense of self and a humanity without subservience. It is this pride in themselves, and in their monarchy, that underlies the Thai sense of identity and an ability to smile at the vicissitudes of life.

The Kingdom of Thailand – ruled by an elected government but inspired by the world's longest-reigning monarch, who celebrated 50 years on the throne in 1996 – has a population of over 60 million. It is nearly the size of Central America or France, or is twice that of England. Its climate is tropical, with three seasons: hot (March–June), monsoonal (July–November) and cool (December–February). The capital city of Bangkok, called Krung Thep in Thai, has at least 10 million people (accurate estimates are by definition dubious) and lies at the same latitude as Khartoum, Guatemala City and Manila.

Just inland from the apex of the Gulf of Thailand, Bangkok is the country's international gateway, and its seat of government, business and the royalty. It is almost a city-state unto itself and bears little similarity to the rest of the nation. When a Thai says that "I'm heading upcountry tomorrow," she or he could mean anywhere outside of Bangkok's city limits. Anywhere is upcountry. Indeed, the second-largest city in Thailand is perhaps one-fortieth the population of Bangkok. Most of Thailand is rural, a patchwork of rice fields, villages, plantations and forests.

Thailand is commonly divided into four regions: the central plains, of which Bangkok is a part; the north, including Chiang Mai and Chiang Rai; the northeast; and the south, extending from Bangkok down to the Malaysian border. Each region has its own culture and appeal.

Since the East first encountered Siam a millennium ago and the West began trickling in during the 16th century, Thailand has been a powerful magnet for adventurers and entrepreneurs. An abundance of resources, a wealth of natural beauty, a stunning cultural tradition revealed in dazzling architecture and art, and a warm, hospitable people have proved irresistible lures.

Thailand's traditional charms form only one side of the picture, of course. It is a country in transition, rapidly changing from a developing to a developed country in a roller-coaster of a ride. In the 1990s, it went from being one of the fiercest of Asian economic tigers to nearly becoming an economic disaster, a precursor of the economic doldrums that hit Asia at the end of the 1990s. But true to the peo-

PRECEDING PAGES: centuries-old illustration of elephants from a temple mural; architectural detail from Bangkok's Grand Palace; *nang yai*, the shadow-puppet; young girl and her father, protected from evil and misfortune by body tattoos and amulets. **LEFT:** Buddha images of Wat Mahathat, in Phetchburi, south of Bangkok.

ple's spirit, consistent throughout the country's history, Thailand reversed course quickly and regained stability.

Throughout its history, Thailand has shown a stubborn maverick streak and a sense of pragmatism, both of which have created a determination to chart its own course. The result is a country that has never been colonised by a foreign power, has never sought to conquer a neighbour, and one that has intentionally retained its past while moving ahead into the future.

It is hard to ignore the changes taking place, yet there is much that sets Thailand apart from nations on similar paths. The natural beauty is still there in superb beaches, seas of green rice, and forested hills, somewhat safe now that logging is illegal (although it still happens). And even in the most modern towns, the past continues to shine through as temples, palaces and cultural presentations. This uniqueness is not always apparent, especially in a chaotic city like Bangkok that pounds on the senses, all of them, unceasingly. *This is not the exotic Thailand I was promised,* the visitor whines. *This is a nightmare.* Well, Bangkok is a nightmare. It is also a repository of some of the world's most exquisite architecture and historical artifacts. But it is a city that is vibrantly alive.

The Thai enjoys life. Something that fails to give personal satisfaction, whether in work or in play, is not worth doing. Any activity must have something of this quality within it, something that gives value to life. Part of this is distilled from holding on to one's traditions. This may change in Thailand, but for the moment, it is firmly intact in Thailand. The traveller can't help but notice it.

About spellings of place names

The transliteration of Thai pronunciation into a roman alphabet has proved to be a quagmire of phonemes and good intentions. The traveller will encounter several, not just one or two, possible spellings for a single place name. Leaps of linguistic creativity are in order as one negotiates street signs (often romanised), maps and guide books, including this one. As much as possible, this book has sided with common sense and common usage, along with a dose of consistency.

When the letter *h* follows a consonant, it makes the consonant's sound less explosive, softer. Just as Thailand is pronounced *tai-land,* not *thigh-land,* so too with the *ph* sound. The pronunciation of *Wat Po* is the same as *Wat Pho,* and, in fact, they are the same temple in Bangkok. Similarly, the wonderful island of *Phuket* is always spelled thusly, but it is pronounced, always, like *poo-ket,* not *foo-ket* or in other less gracious ways. Other common variations of place-name spellings include *ratcha* and *raja,* and *chom* and *jom.*

The rule of thumb regarding spellings is to be like a Thai when in Thailand: adaptable and tolerant, and with a sense of humour. ❐

RIGHT: the canals in and around Bangkok are still vital to commerce.

Decisive Dates

Pre-Thai civilisation

3600–250 BC: Ban Chiang culture flourishes in north-eastern Thailand.

circa 250 BC: Suvannabhumi trading with India

4th–8th centuries AD: influence of Mon and Khmer empires spreads into Thailand.

9th–13th centuries: Khmer Empire founded at Angkor. Thai peoples migrate south from Yunnan Province of China into northern Thailand, Burma, and Laos. Lopburi becomes an important provincial capital in Khmer Empire, later tries to become independent.

Sukhothai era

1238: Khmer power wanes. Kingdom of Sukhothai founded under Intaradit.

1281: Chiang Saen kingdom founded in north.

1296: Lanna Kingdom founded at Chiang Mai. Mangrai controls much of northern Thailand and Laos.

1280–1318: Reign of Ramkamhaeng in Sukhothai. Often called Thailand's "Golden Age," the period saw the first attempts to unify the Thai people, the first use of the Thai script, and flourishing of the arts.

1317–1347: Lo Thai reigns at Sukhothai. The slow decline of the Sukhothai kingdom starts.

1438: Sukhothai is now virtually deserted; power shifts to the Kingdom of Ayutthaya, to the south and along the Chao Phraya River.

Kingdom of Ayutthaya

14th century: Area around Ayutthaya settled by representatives of the Chiang Saen kingdom.

1350: City of Ayutthaya founded by Phya U-Thong, who proclaims himself Ramathibodi I. Within a few years he controls the areas encompassed by the kingdoms of Sukhothai and the Khmer empire.

1369: Ramesuen, son of Ramathibodi, becomes king.

1390: Ramesuen captures Chiang Mai.

1393: Ramesuen captures Angkor in Cambodia.

1448–1488: Reign of King Trailok, who finally unites the Lanna (Chiang Mai) and Ayutthaya kingdoms.

1491–1529: Reign of King Ramathibodi II.

1549: First major warfare with Mon Kingdom of Pegu.

1569: Burmese capture and destroy Ayutthaya.

1590: Naresuen becomes king, throws off Burmese suzerainty. Under Naresuen, Ayutthaya expands rapidly at the expense of Burmese and Khmer empires and flourishes as a major city.

1605–1610: Ekatotsarot reigns, begins significant economic ties with European traders and adventurers.

1610–1628: Reign of King Songtham. The British arrive and obtain land for a trading factory.

1628–1655: Reign of Prasat Thong. Trading concessions expand and regular trade with China and Europe is established.

1656–1688: Reign of King Narai. British influence expands. Reputation of Ayutthaya as a magnificent city and a remarkable royal court spreads in Europe.

1678: Constantine Phaulkon arrives at Narai's court and gains great influence; French presence expands.

1688: Narai dies, Phaulkon executed.

1733–1758: Reign of King Boromakot. Ayutthaya enters a period of peace, and of arts and literature.

1767: Burmese King Alaungpaya captures and sacks Ayutthaya, destroying four centuries of Thai civilisation. Seven months later General Phya Tak Sin returns and expels the Burmese occupiers. He moves the capital from Ayutthaya to Thonburi, near Bangkok.

Beginning of the Chakri dynasty

1767: Phya Tak Sin crowned as King Taksin.

1779: Generals Chao Phya Chakri and his brother Chao Phya Sarasih conquer Chiang Mai, expel the Burmese from what is now Thailand and so adding most of the Khmer and Lao kingdoms to the Thai kingdom. The Emerald Buddha brought from Vientiane, Laos, to Thonburi.

1782: The now-erratic Taksin deposed and executed, and Chao Phya Chakri is offered the throne, founding the Chakri dynasty and assuming the name Ramathibodi and later Rama I. Capital is moved across the river to the city that becomes known to the west as

Bangkok. Under Rama I, the Siamese Kingdom consolidates and expands its strength. Rama I revives Thai art, religion, and culture.

1809–1824: Reign of Rama II; best known for construction of Wat Arun and many other temples and monasteries. Rama II reopens relations with the West, suspended since the time of Narai.

1824–1851: Reign of Rama III, who left as his trademark the technique of embedding Chinese porcelain fragments as decorations on temples.

1851: King Mongkut (Rama IV) ascends the throne. He is the first Thai king to understand Western culture and technology. Before becoming king he spends 27 years as a monk, studying Western science.

1868: Chulalongkorn (Rama V) ascends the throne, reigning for the next four decades, the second-longest reign of any Thai king. Chulalongkorn ends the custom of prostration in royal presence, abolishes slavery, and replaces corvee labour with direct taxation. Schools, infrastructure, military and government modernised.

1910–1925: Reign of Vajiravudh (Rama VI), Oxford-educated and thoroughly Westernised.

1925–1932: Reign of Prajadhipok (Rama VII). Economic pressures from the Great Depression encourage discontent.

End of the absolute monarchy

1932: A coup d'etat ends the absolute monarchy and ushers in a constitutional monarchy.

1939: The name of the country is officially changed from Siam to Thailand, "Land of the Free." King Ananda (Rama VIII) ascends the throne.

1942: Japan invades Thailand with the acquiescence of the military government, but a spirited if small resistance movement thrives.

1946: King Ananda is killed by a mysterious gunshot, and Bhumibol Adulyadej (Rama IX) ascends the throne. The tireless royal family quickly becomes a symbol of national spirit and unity.

1973–1991: Bloody clashes between army and demonstrating students brings down the military government; political and economic blunders brings down the resulting civilian government just three years later. Various military-backed and civilian governments come and go for almost 20 years.

1991: Another clash between military forces and civilian demonstrators brings the unusual sight of the leaders of both factions kneeling in contrition in front of the king; as a result, the military leaves government to the civilian politicians.

1992: Thailand begins five years of unprecedented economic growth. The face of Bangkok changes, much of it climbing skyward in skyscrapers and middle-class condominiums. Growth reaches 9 percent annually.

1996: King Bhumibol Adulyadej celebrates his golden jubilee of 50 years on the throne, the longest-reigning monarch in the world.

1997: Thailand's banking system and economy begin a free-fall as the baht loses half of its value. Other regional economies also falter.

1998: While other Asian economies continue to wallow in crisis, Thailand follows guidelines established by the International Monetary Fund to resuscitate its financial systems and economy.

LEFT: Ayutthayan general mounts battle elephant.
RIGHT: portrait of King Chulalongkorn, or Rama V.

CHAKRI MONARCHY	
Since 1782, a single royal dynasty – known as Chakri – has lorded over Thailand.	
Rama I (Chakri)	1782–1809
Rama II (Phutthalaetia)	1809–1824
Rama III (Nangklao)	1824–1851
Rama IV (Mongkut)	1851–1868
Rama V (Chulalongkorn)	1868–1910
Rama VI (Vajiravudh)	1910–1925
Rama VII (Prajadhipok)	1925–1935
Rama VIII (Ananda)	1935–1946
Rama IX (Bhumibol)	1946–

THE RISE OF SUKHOTHAI

Sukhothai, the "dawn of happiness", was the first independent Thai kingdom.
Many consider it to be the golden era of Thai history, and of Thai culture

The Thai people have fiercely defended their country's independence for more than 800 years, and can boast the distinction of being the only country in Southeast Asia never to have been a European colony. Nor has the country been divided by serious civil war, as tumultuous as modern Thai politics can be. Indeed, Thai shrewdness in international diplomacy has won them the admiration of nations far more powerful and influential.

The name *Thai* means "free." Although the country was called *Siam* by foreigners from the 12th to the 20th centuries, to its citizens it always carried the name of its capital – Sukhothai and Ayutthaya, for example. In the l9th century. Siam was adopted as the official name of the kingdom, but this was changed to Thailand in 1939.

In the beginning

The origin of the ethnic Thai has been hotly debated for decades. Popular tradition claims that the first people fled to Siam from China to escape the depredations of Kublai Khan's hordes sweeping southward out of Mongolia. The theory might explain Thai empathy with later immigrants. Other theories suggest they originated in Thailand a millennium or two ago; Thais found in today's China are said to have emigrated north from Thailand about 1,000 years ago. Whichever conjecture is correct, it is accepted that the Thais' first home in Thailand was in the northern hills. As the centuries passed, they shared the country with ethnic Laotians, who populated the northeast, bringing a similar language and culture. The southern isthmus linking Thailand (from Bangkok south) with the Malay Peninsula became the home of Muslims. Over the centuries, the population was augmented by Hindu and Sikh Indians, who arrived as merchants, and by Chinese.

PRECEDING PAGE: two terracotta figures from the Sukhothai period. **LEFT:** sculpture from Sukhothai of a Hindu deity. **RIGHT:** illustration of two early indigenous Thai men.

Ban Chiang culture

But long before the Thai people migrated into today's Thailand, the Chao Phraya valley was inhabited by a high civilisation. The first discovery of their prehistoric relics was made during World War II, by a Dutch prisoner of war forced to work on the Siam–Burma "Death

Railway." He uncovered Stone Age implements at Ban Kao, in the western province of Kanchanaburi, which led to the discovery of Paleolithic and Neolithic caves, and to cemeteries containing pottery, tools and other artifacts.

The most important site, however, is the tiny village of Ban Chiang, near Udon Thani in the northeast. Excavations have uncovered painted pottery, jewelry, and bronze and iron tools. If thermoluminescent dating is correct, the Bronze Age in Thailand corresponds to – and according to some, may even predate – that of the Tigris-Euphrates Valley civilisation, which preceded the Bronze Age in Europe. The idea remains controversial, however.

The identity of the Ban Chiang people is a mystery. According to archeological timetables, the existence of pottery normally suggests a culture already 2,000 years along the road to civilisation; Ban Chiang's pottery dates from about 3600 BC. Settlement seems to have lasted until 250 BC, after which the people mysteriously faded from history. While they thrived, they farmed rice, domesticated various animals, and developed highly original pottery-decorating skills, with each design unique to that pot alone and not

OTHER ORIGINS

The Ban Chiang findings illustrate a high level of culture and technology. They also suggest, but not without debate, that China may not be the sole origin of East Asian civilisation.

fied as Southeast Asia. By the beginning of the Christian era, maritime trading between India and the south of Thailand had begun. Hindu statues found at settlements in southern Thailand suggest habitation from about the 4th century. In later centuries, Buddhism and Hinduism – along with Indian ceremonial rites, iconography, law codes, and cosmological and architectural treatises – were adopted *en bloc* by the Southeast Asian ruling elite and modified to suit local requirements and tastes. Sanskrit became the court lan-

repeated in others. Their red-painted jars, decorated with fingerprint whorl patterns, were buried in funeral mounds as offerings. Glass beads and semiprecious stones were also included in the mounds.

Indian influence

Archeological evidence is scant, but ancient texts discuss the presence of people in the region from India around the 3rd century BC.

The Sinhalese Buddhist chronicle, the *Mahavamsa*, relates that India's great Emperor Ashoka (ruled 268 to 232 BC), the first royal patron of Buddhism, sent two missionaries to Suvannabhumi, the "land of gold" now identi-

guage, while Pali was the language of the Buddhist canons. Native chiefs wanting to consolidate power and increase their prestige may have been responsible for this diffusion of culture, calling in Brahman priests (Indians of the priestly caste) to validate and consecrate their rule.

This transmission at court level had a vital and permanent impact, especially in nearby Cambodia. The Mons and Khmers were the first Indianised peoples to form settlements in present-day Thailand. Mon influence is evident in the Buddhist art of the Dvaravati period (6th to 11th centuries); the Khmers, famed as the builders of Cambodia's Angkor Wat, left many temples in Thailand's northeastern provinces. There is also archeological evidence of Mon religious settlements at Lopburi and Nakhon Pathom, from the 7th century onwards.

Arrival of the Thais

As noted earlier, there are several theories to explain the early habitation of Thailand. The most persuasive one says that from perhaps as early as the 10th century, a people living in China's Yunnan region migrated down rivers and streams into the upper valleys of the Southeast Asian river system. There, they branched off. The Shans, also known as Thai Yai (Great

Mai, in 1296. Long after the main group of Thais moved farther down the peninsula to establish more powerful states, Chiang Mai continued to rule more or less autonomously over the northern region, maintaining a distinctive culture of its own. By the 13th century, the Thais had begun to emerge as the dominant rulers of the region, slowly absorbing the weakened empires of the Mons and Khmers. Their rise to power culminated around 1238, when (according to inscriptions) the Khmers were expelled from Sukhothai.

The history of peninsular Thailand is lesser known than that of the north. It was once under

Thais), went to Upper Burma. The Ahom Thais established themselves in Assam. Another group settled in Laos, and yet another occupied the island of Hainan, off the Vietnamese coast.

The greatest number of Thai Noi (Little Thais) first settled in the north of modern Thailand, around Chiang Saen and valleys to the south. They formed themselves into principalities, some of which later became independent kingdoms. The first was in 1238, at Sukhothai, at the southernmost edge of Thai penetration. Then came Chiang Rai, in 1281, and Chiang

LEFT: perhaps from India, terracotta figures found in central Thailand. **ABOVE:** Sukhothai stone engraving.

the control of the mighty empire of Srivijaya, which existed from the 7th to 13th centuries. Ancient chronicles state that in the Srivijayan capital, "a man at noon cast no shadow". This suggests an equatorial location, but there is serious disagreement where that might be. There are competing schools of thought, each claiming Palembang in Sumatra, or Chaiya in southern Thailand. A site in Borneo has also been postulated. The proof of claim forwarded for Chaiya is the discovery of an 8th-century inscription of a Srivijayan king, at Chaiya, near the Kra Isthmus. The empire disintegrated during the 13th century and its dependencies were absorbed by Sukhothai.

Dawn of Sukhothai

The name *Sukhothai* translates into "the dawn of happiness", and if early inscriptions are to be believed, its people enjoyed considerable freedom to pursue their livelihoods. This first independent Thai kingdom is considered the golden era of Thai history, and is often looked back upon with nostalgia as the ideal Thai state. It was a land of plenty, governed by just and paternal kings who ruled over peaceful, contented citizens. Sukhothai represented early Thai tribal society in its purest form.

Siamese tradition attributes the founding of the kingdom to Phra Ruang, a mythological hero. Prior to his time, according to historical legend, the Thai people were forced to pay tribute to the Khmer rulers of Angkor. This tribute was exacted in the form of sacred water from a lake outside Lopburi; the Khmer god-king needed holy water from all corners of the empire for his ceremonial rites, a practice later adopted by Thai kings.

Every three years, the water tribute was sent by bullock carts in large earthenware jars. The jars inevitably cracked en route, compelling the tribute payers to make second and third journeys to fill the required quota. When Phra Ruang came of age, he devised a new system of transporting water in sealed woven bamboo containers, which arrived in Angkor intact. This success aroused the suspicion of the Khmer king. His chief astrologer said the ingenious Thai inventor was a person with supernatural powers who constituted a threat to the empire. The king at once dispatched a gifted general – who had the magic ability to travel swiftly underground – to eliminate the Thai menace.

Phra Ruang perceived the danger and went to Sukhothai, where he concealed himself at Wat Mahathat as a Buddhist monk. The Khmer general, who coincidentally surfaced in the middle of the *wat*, was turned into stone by Phra Ruang. From then on, Phra Ruang's fame spread far and

wide. He left the monkhood, married the daughter of Sukhothai's ruler, and when that monarch died, he was invited to the throne by popular mandate. He assumed the title Sri Indraditya, sovereign of the newly-independent Kingdom of Sukhothai. Fact and fiction are inseparable in this popular account.

Rule of Ramkamhaeng

The most famous king of Sukhothai was the founder's second son, Ramkamhaeng. He was the first Thai ruler to leave detailed epigraphical accounts of the Thai state, beginning with his own early life. He earned his title at age 19 on a campaign with his father against a neighbouring state, in which he defeated the enemy leader in a Thai form of medieval jousting: hand-to-hand combat on elephant-back. As a result, he was named Phra Ramkamhaeng (Rama the Brave) by his father.

Around the time of Ramkamhaeng's accession, the Sukhothai kingdom was quite small, consisting only of the city and surrounding areas. By the end of his reign, he had increased its size tenfold – from Luang Prabang in the east, in modern-day Laos, through Thailand's central plains to the

BUDDHIST BEDROCK

Since the ancient days of Sukhothai, Buddhism has been deeply rooted in the Thai way of life. Together with the monarchy, it provides a continuity for both Thai society and the individual.

bition of slavery and guaranteed inheritance. However, some experts now doubt its authenticity and believe the inscription to be a much later work.

The king was a devout and conscientious Buddhist of the Theravada school that was practiced in Sukhothai. Exchanges were initiated with Sri Lankan monks that resulted in a purification of texts and an adoption of Sinhalese influences in *chedi* design.

There remained, however, a trace of animism in Thai Buddhism. Ramkamhaeng wrote

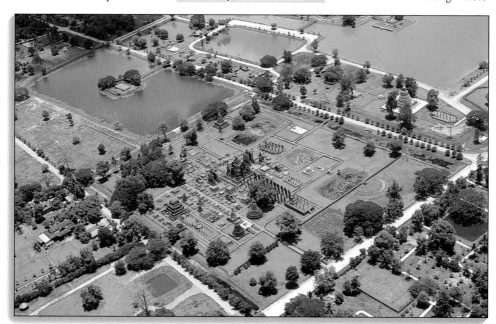

southern peninsula. The Mon state in lower Burma also accepted his control.

Ramkamhaeng was noted as an administrator, legislator and statesman – and sometimes as an amorous king. He is credited with the invention of Thai script, which he achieved by systematising the Khmer alphabet with Thai words. A stone inscription bearing the date 1292 and employing the new script has been attributed to Ramkamhaeng. In the inscription, he depicted the idyllic conditions of his kingdom: fertile land and plentiful food, free trade, prohi-

LEFT: detail of Khmer ruins, Prasat Phanom Rung.
ABOVE: Wat Mahathat, in old Sukhothai.

about a mountain-dwelling ghost named Phra Khapung Phi, a spirit "above all others in the land." If correctly propitiated, he would bring prosperity to the country. The idea of a superior spirit looking after the Thai nation survives today, in the image of Phra Siam Devadhiraj, Siam's guardian angel.

One of the keys to Ramkamhaeng's success lay in his diplomatic relations with China. The Mongol court in northern China pursued a "divide-and-rule" policy and supported the Thais' rise, but at the expense of the Khmers. Ramkamhaeng was said to have gone to China himself in 1299, and the *History of the Yuan* records seven missions from Sien (Sukhothai) between 1282 and 1323. Chinese craftsmen came to teach the Thais their secrets of glazing pottery, resulting in the production of the famous ceramic ware of Sawankhalok, whose kilns still remain and whose products were shipped to China aboard Siamese junks.

In the same year, 1287, that Pagan fell to the armies of Kublai Khan, Ramkamhaeng formed a pact with two northern Thai princes, Mangrai of Chiang Rai and Ngam Muang of Phayo. The three agreed not to transgress, but instead to protect each others' borders against common enemies. The alliance was maintained throughout their lifetimes.

Founding of Chiang Mai

Mangrai completed Thai political ascendancy in the north by annexing the last Mon kingdom of Haripunjaya, in about 1292. He first sent an agent provocateur to sow discord, and when the time was right, his army "plucked the town like a ripe fruit."

Wishing to found a new capital, Mangrai invited his two allies to help him select a site. The location they agreed upon as truly auspicious was one where two white sambars, two white barking deer, and a family of five white mice were seen together. On that spot by the river Ping, Mangrai laid the foundation of Chiang Mai (New Town) in 1296, supplanting his former capital at Chiang Rai and giving him a more centralised location from which to administer the southern portion of his newly-expanded kingdom. Thus, Chiang Mai became the capital of the Kingdom of Lanna, which translates as "Land of the Million Rice Fields."

Tradition says Ramkamhaeng drowned in the rapids of the Yom River at Sawankhalok. His son, Lo Thai (ruled 1318–1347), preferring religion to war, lost the feudatory states as fast as he had gained them. He was called Dharmaraja, the Pious King, an epithet his successors also bore. The relationship between Sukhothai and Sri Lanka, the centre of orthodox Buddhism, intensified during his rule; Lo Thai recorded that he built many monuments to house sacred relics of the Buddha obtained from Sri Lanka.

Lo Thai's son, Li Thai, was as pious as his father. As heir to the throne, he composed a famous treatise on Buddhist cosmology, the *Traibhumikatha,* or *Tales of the Three Worlds.* When he became king in 1347, he ruled according to the ten royal precepts of Buddha. He pardoned criminals, for example, as he wanted to become a Buddha, "to lead all creatures beyond the oceans of sorrow and transmigration."

The prioritising of religion over military affairs might have permitted the meteoric rise of one of Sukhothai's former vassal states, Ayutthaya. This kingdom expanded rapidly, extending its control over the Chao Phraya valley, until Li Thai was forced to acknowledge its hegemony. Deprived of his independence, the pious king took deeper refuge in religion, eventually assuming the yellow robe.

His family ruled for three more generations, but in 1378, power shifted to Phitsanulok, and Sukhothai's population followed. By 1438, Sukhothai was nearly deserted.

The Sukhothai period saw the Thai people, for the first time, develop a distinctive civilisation with their own administrative institutions, art and architecture.

Sukhothai Buddha images, characterised by refined facial features, linear fluidity, and harmony of form, are perhaps the most beautiful and the most original of Thai artistic expressions. Many authorities and Thais say that the Sukhothai aesthetic has been the high point of Thai civilisation. ◻

LEFT: Sukhothai Hindu deity. **RIGHT:** ruins of Wat Chetupon, Sukhothai.

AYUTTHAYA

Ayutthayan kings adopted Khmer cultural influences from the very beginning. Unlike those of Sukhothai, the rulers of Ayutthaya were absolute and inaccessible monarchs

History is ignorant regarding the ancestry of Ayutthaya's founder. But Thai folklore fills the lacuna. The king of Traitrung unhappily discovered that his unmarried daughter had given birth to a child after eating an eggplant, which a vegetable gardener had fertilised with his own urine. The culprit – Nai Saen Pom,

kings. During the reign of Phya U-Thong, a cholera outbreak forced the ruler to evacuate his people to the site of Ayodhya (Ayutthaya), an ancient Indianised settlement named after Rama's legendary kingdom in India.

The location of Phya U-Thong's new capital was blessed with several advantages. Situated

or Man With a Hundred Thousand Warts – was summoned and promptly banished from the city, along with the princess and her new son.

The god Indra, with his divine eye, saw the misery of the trio and decided to grant the gardener three magic wishes. Saen Pom first asked for his warts to disappear. Next, he prayed for a kingdom to rule over. And lastly, he wanted a cradle of gold for his son. The child was known as Chao U-Thong, Prince of the Golden Crib.

Rise of Ayutthaya

Historically, U-Thong was an independent principality in today's Suphanburi. Its rulers were members of the prestigious line of Chiang Saen

on an island at the confluence of the Chao Phraya, Lopburi and Pasak rivers, not far from the sea and surrounded by fertile rice plains, it was an ideal centre of administration and communications. Phya U-Thong officially established the city in 1350, after three years of preparation, when he assumed the title Ramathibodi I, King of Dvaravati Sri Ayodhya. Within a few years, the king united the whole of central Siam – including Sukhothai – under his rule, and extended control to the Malay Peninsula and lower Burma. He and his successors pursued expansionist campaigns against Chiang Mai and the Khmers in Cambodia. No longer the paternal and accessible rulers that the kings of Sukhothai had been, Ayutthaya's sovereigns were absolute monarchs whose positions were enhanced by trappings of royalty reflective of a Khmer *devaraja* (god-king).

The devaraja concept was, however, tempered by the tenets of Theravada Buddhism, wherein the king was not actually divine, but was the protector and supreme head of the religion. Nevertheless, Khmer court rituals and language were emulated at the Ayutthaya court. Brahmans officiated with Buddhist monks at state ceremonies.

KHMER INFLUENCES

Although the Thais were responsible for the decline and eventual collapse of the Angkor empire, the Ayutthayan kings adopted Khmer cultural and artistic influences from the very beginning.

Angkor three years later, and according to the *Pongsawadan*, the Annals of Ayutthaya, some 90,000 prisoners of war were taken. Given the economics of the time, people for labour were more precious than gold.

The death blow to the Khmer capital was delivered in 1431 when forces entered Angkor. The Khmer king abandoned his ancient capital in favour of Phnom Penh. The Siamese army returned from the campaign with booty and many prisoners, including artists and Brahmans.

Ramathibodi I divided his administration into ministries of royal household, finance, interior and agriculture. This, and his subsequent legislation, provided a strong foundation for the kingdom, which survived for 417 years, with Ayutthaya as its capital.

Ramathibodi died in 1369. His son, Ramesuen, captured Chiang Mai in 1390, reportedly with the use of cannon, the first recorded use of this weapon in Siam. Ramesuen's army sacked

PRECEDING PAGE: 17th-century adventurers immortalised on a lacquer cabinet. **LEFT:** crypt mural detail, Wat Ratchaburana, Ayutthaya. **ABOVE:** Ayutthayan royal jewellery found at Wat Ratchaburana.

Reign of King Trailok

Two centuries of wars between Chiang Mai and Ayutthaya reached a climax during the reign of King Boroma Trailokanath, more popularly known as Trailok, who ruled from 1448 until 1488. In his campaigns against Maharaja Sutham Tilok, guile and the occult complemented military might.

Envoys sent from Ayutthaya to Tilok were discovered to have buried seven jars containing ingredients which, it was feared, would magically bring doom upon Chiang Mai. The jars were cast into the river, followed by the envoys themselves, their feet tied to rocks. The fighting between these rival kingdoms led to the transfer of Ayutthayan power, from the capital to Phit-sanulok during the last 25 years of Trailok's reign. The war, however, ended in a stalemate.

Trailok is important for having introduced reforms that shaped the administrative and social structures of Siam up until the 19th century. He brought Ayutthaya's loosely controlled provinces under centralised rule, and regulated *sakdi na*, an ancient system of land ownership that stratified society, dictated responsibilities of both overlord and tenants, and determined salary levels of the official hierarchy.

Trailok also defined a system of corvee labour, under which all able-bodied men were required to contribute labour during part of each working year to the state. This system indirectly heightened the status of women, who were responsible for the welfare of their families in the absence of the men.

Portuguese and Burmese

The 16th century was marked by the first arrival of Europeans, and by continual conflict with the Burmese. The Portuguese had conquered Malacca in 1511, and soon thereafter their ships sailed to Siam. King Ramathibodi II (ruled 1491–1529) granted the Portuguese permission to reside and trade within the kingdom, in return

PALACE PROTOCOL

Trailok's Palace Law of 1450 spelled out the relative ranks of members of the royal family, prescribed functions of officials, and regulated official ceremonies.

It also fixed punishments: death for "introducing amatory poems" into the palace and for whispering during a royal audience, and amputation of the foot of anyone kicking a palace door.

Royalty was not spared punishment, although no menial hands could touch royal flesh. It was therefore the executioner's task to beat the condemned royalty at the nape of the neck with a sandalwood club.

for arms and ammunition. Portuguese mercenaries fought alongside the king in campaigns against Chiang Mai and taught the Thais the arts of cannon foundry and musketry.

But this did nothing to stem the rising tide of Burmese aggression against Ayutthaya, already weakened by wars with Chiang Mai. In 1549, the Burmese laid siege to Ayutthaya. The Ayutthayan king, Mahachakrapat, led a sortie against them. Not only his sons, but his wife and daughter accompanied him into battle mounted on elephants. The queen, disguised as a warrior, galloped her mount between the king and his Burmese foe when she saw her husband in trouble, saving his life, but losing her own.

The Burmese invasion of 1549 was doomed to failure. They withdrew, and Ayutthaya's defenses were fortified with Portuguese help. Three hundred wild elephants were captured and trained for further wars against Burma.

Seven of the new war elephants were white ones. When Burma's new king heard about this, he launched another invasion of Ayutthaya.

In 1569, Ayutthaya fell to Burmese forces. The invading Burmese thoroughly ransacked and plundered the city, and forcibly removed much of Ayut-

> **WHITE ELEPHANTS**
>
> Buddhist kings of Southeast Asia treasured white elephants, considered to be auspicious, thus enhancing royal prestige and ensuring the country's prosperity.

Naresuen had gained an insight into Burmese armed strength and strategies during his formative gears in Burma. He trained his troops in the art of guerrilla warfare; their hit-and-run tactics earned them the nicknames of Wild Tigers and Peeping Cats. Naresuen's opportunity to restore Siamese independence came following the death of the Burmese king in 1581. Revolts in the Burmese empire were tying down the new king at home when Naresuen declared Ayutthaya's freedom, in 1584. During the following nine years,

thaya's population to Burma. The king was among the captives of the Burmese; he died before arriving in Pegu.

The defeated king's leading deputy was appointed by the Burmese to rule Siam as a vassal state. His eldest son, Naresuen, was brought to Burma by the Burmese king as a guarantee for the new vassal's good conduct. Naresuen was repatriated to Siam at the age of 15. Together with his younger brother, Naresuen began to gather armed followers.

LEFT: mural image of a 17th-century European adventurer. **ABOVE:** European impression of Ayutthaya in the 17th century.

the Burmese made several attempts to resubjugate Siam, but Naresuen had taken thorough defensive measures and repulsed all invasions. On one of these occasions, he killed the Burmese king in single combat, both of them mounted on elephants.

Naresuen assumed full kingship upon his father's death in 1590. He reconsolidated the Siamese kingdom, then turned the tables on Burma with repeated attacks that contributed to the disintegration of the Burmese empire. The Khmers, who had been whittling away at Siam's eastern boundary during Ayutthaya's period of weakness, were also subdued. Under Naresuen, Ayutthaya prospered.

Door to the east

The reign of Naresuen's brother, Ekatotsarot, between 1605 and 1610, coincided with the arrival of the Dutch in Siam. Ekatotsarot was not interested in pursuing Naresuen's militaristic policies. Instead, he sought to develop Ayutthaya's economy. To these ends, he decreed several measures to increase state revenue, among them the introduction of taxes on commerce. This gave him a reputation as a "covetous man" among Europeans.

The Dutch opened their first trading station at Ayutthaya in 1608. Keen to promote commercial relations, Ekatotsarot sent emissaries to a demand in Thai society for luxury items like porcelain and silk. The Japanese, who already had established a sizable community of traders at Ayutthaya, paid in silver for local Siamese products such as hides, teak, tin and sugar.

The Dutch established maritime dominance in the Far East when they drove the Portuguese out of Malacca, in 1641. Seven years later, they made a show of naval force in the Gulf of Siam, thereby persuading the Thai court to agree to certain trade concessions and giving the Dutch virtual economic control in Siam. A new king, Narai (ruled 1656–1688), despised the Dutch and welcomed the English as a European ally to

The Hague, the first recorded appearance of Thais in Europe. Later, during the reign of Songtham (ruled 1610–1628), the English arrived bearing a letter from King James I. Like the Dutch, they were welcomed and allotted a plot of land on which to build.

Europeans were primarily attracted to Siam as a door to the China trade. The nature of seasonal monsoons made direct sailing to China impossible, so Ayutthaya and its ports became entrepots for goods travelling between Europe, India and the East Indies, and China and Japan.

The Siamese home market was also quite substantial. The peace initiated by Naresuen had given rise to a surplus of wealth, which created

JAPANESE MERCENARIES

Under the Japanese adventurer Yamada Nagamasa, who earned himself an official rank in the Thai court, many Japanese gained employment as the king's guards.

In 1628 they helped the future king Prasat Thong establish himself as regent to a boy-king, and subsequently to depose the rightful ruler. Unfortunately, the shogun in Edo (modern-day Tokyo) refused to recognise him as the Thai monarch, prompting Prasat Thong to take his revenge on the Japanese settlement in Ayutthaya. Several of the Japanese residents were killed, while the remainder made their escape into Cambodia.

counter Holland's influence. But another Dutch blockade, in 1664, this time at the mouth of the Chao Phraya River, won them a monopoly on the hide trade and, for the first time in Thai history, extraterritorial privileges.

Greek favourite

It was the French who gained greatest favour in King Narai's court. Their story is interwoven with that of a fascinating character, a Greek adventurer named Constantine Phaulkon.

French Jesuit missionaries first arrived at the court of Ayutthaya in 1665. The king's friendliness and religious tolerance were taken by the bishops as a sign of his imminent conversion. Their exaggerated accounts excited the imagination of Louis xiv, who hoped that the salvation of Siamese heathens could be combined with French territorial acquisition. Narai was delighted to receive a personal letter from the Sun King in 1673.

Enter Phaulkon. Son of a Greek innkeeper, he began his career with the East India Company as a cabin boy. He worked his way east with the British, arriving in Siam in 1678. A talented linguist, he learned the Thai language in just two years, and with the help of his English benefactors, he was hired as interpreter within the court. Within five years, Phaulkon had risen through Thai society to the rank of *Phya Vijayendra*. In this powerful position, he had continual access to the king, whose confidence he slowly and surely cultivated.

The previous year, Phaulkon had fallen out of favour with the British East India Company. As Phaulkon moved firmly into the French camp, so did Narai. He sent two ambassadors to Louis's court, and the French reciprocated with a visit to Ayutthaya in 1685. Phaulkon, of course, served as interpreter during the French visit. He secretly outlined to visiting Jesuit priests his plans to convert the entire country of Siam to Catholicism. To effect this, he said, he would need civilians and troops from France. Following another exchange of embassies between the courts of Louis and Narai, a French squadron accompanied French and Thai delegations aboard warships to Siam. The small, but disciplined and well-equipped, French force of 500 soldiers was given landing rights by Narai,

under Phaulkon's advice. For his pains, Phaulkon was created a Count of France and a Knight of the Order of St Michael.

Then the tables began to turn against Phaulkon. A number of high-ranking Siamese officials had become increasingly alarmed by the influence of the "Greek Favourite" on the king. Phaulkon's extravagant lifestyle was considered proof of his blatant robbery of the country. His unpopularity was fuelled not only by the ominous French military presence, but also by a rumour that Phaulkon had converted King Narai's adopted son to Christianity, intending to secure succession to the throne.

When Narai fell gravely ill in 1688, a nationalistic, anti-French faction took immediate action. Led by Phra Phetracha, a commander of the Royal Regiment of Elephants, the rebels confined the ailing king to his palace. Phaulkon was arrested for treason, and in June was executed. Narai died the following month, and Phra Phetracha mounted the throne, declaring as his top priority the immediate withdrawal of French troops. The French eventually removed their soldiers from Thailand.

The presence of Europeans throughout Narai's reign gave the West most of its early knowledge of Siam. Voluminous literature was generated by Western visitors to Narai's court.

LEFT: Naresuen engages the Burmese in a sea battle.
RIGHT: Thai manuscript showing royal parade, 1600s.

Their attempts at cartography left a record of Ayutthaya's appearance, though few maps exist today. Royal palaces and hundreds of temples crowded the area within the walls around the island on which the capital stood. Some Western visitors called it "the most beautiful city in the east."

The kings who succeeded Narai ended his open-door policy. A modest amount of trade was maintained and missionaries were permitted to remain, but Ayutthaya embarked on a course of isolation that lasted about 150 years. This left the rulers free to concentrate mainly on religious and cultural affairs.

Burmese invasion succeeded in capturing Ayutthaya after a siege of 14 months.

The Burmese killed, looted and set fire to the whole city, thereby expunging four centuries of Thai civilisation. Showing complete disregard for their common religion, the Burmese plundered Ayutthaya's rich Buddhist temples, melting down all the available gold from Buddha images. Members of the royal family, along with 90,000 captives and the accumulated booty, were taken to Burma.

Despite their overwhelming victory, the Burmese didn't retain control of Siam for long. Attacks on Burma's northern borders compelled

Ayutthaya's golden age

The reign of King Boromakot (1733–1758) began with a particularly violent struggle for power, but Boromakot's 25-year term was an unusually peaceful one and became known as Ayutthaya's Golden Age. Poets and artists abounded at his court, enabling literature and the arts to flourish as never before.

The tranquil days proved to be the calm before the storm. Boromakot's son Ekatat ascended to the throne in 1758, surrounding himself with female company to ensure his pleasure. Meanwhile, the Burmese empire had regrouped, but invading Burmese armies were repelled in 1760. But seven years later, a second

the Burmese to withdraw most of their forces, and Thai tenacity shortened the period of Burmese domination.

Giving meaning to an ancient proverb that "Ayutthaya never lacks good men," a young general named Phya Tak Sin gathered a small band of followers during the final Burmese siege of the Thai capital. He broke through the Burmese encirclement and escaped to Chanthaburi, on the southeast coast of the Gulf of Thailand. There, Phya Tak Sin assembled a large army and navy. Seven months after the fall of Ayutthaya, the general and his forces sailed up the Chao Phraya to Ayutthaya and expelled the Burmese occupiers.

Move to Bangkok

Taksin, as Phya Tak Sin is popularly known, immediately moved the capital. A site nearer to the sea would facilitate foreign trade, ensure the procurement of arms, and make defence and withdrawal easier.

In the 17th century, a small fishing village downstream had become an important trade and defence outpost for Ayutthaya. Known as Bangkok, "village of wild olive groves," it contained fortifications built by the French. The settlement straddled both

DREAMY ORDERS

Taksin told his troops that the old kings had appeared in a dream and told him to move the capital. Strategic considerations were probably more important than those of the supernatural sort.

Taksin ruled until 1782. In the last seven years of his reign, he relied heavily on two trusted generals, the brothers Chao Phya Chakri and Chao Phya Sarasih, who were given absolute command in military campaigns. They liberated Chiang Mai and the rest of northern Thailand from Burmese rule, and brought Cambodia and most of present-day Laos under Thai suzerainty. It was from the victorious Laotian campaign that the Thai kingdom obtained the famous Emerald Buddha.

banks of the Chao Phraya, at a place where a short-cut canal had widened into the main stream. On the west side of the river, called Thonburi, Taksin officially established his new capital and was proclaimed king.

Taksin's reign was not an easy one. The lack of central authority after the fall of Ayutthaya had led to the rapid disintegration of the kingdom, and it fell upon Taksin to reunite the provinces. At the same time, he contended with a number of Burmese invasions that he resolutely repulsed.

LEFT: King Narai, and Constantine Phaulkon.
ABOVE: wat mural of foreigners.

At Thonburi, Taksin's personality underwent a slow metamorphosis from strong and just to cruel and unpredictable. He came to consider himself a *bodhisattva* or future Buddha, and flogged monks who refused to pay obeisance to him. He tortured his officials, his children, and even his wife to make them confess to imaginary crimes. When a revolt broke out in 1782, Taksin abdicated and entered a monastery. A minor official who engineered the revolt offered the throne to Chao Phya Chakri, who assumed the kingship on 6 April and established the still-reigning Chakri dynasty. Taksin, regarded by a council of generals as a threat to stability, was executed in a royal manner. ❑

ERA OF THE CHAKRI MONARCHY

For a century and a half, Thailand was under the rule of an absolute monarchy.
A coup d'etat ended it in 1932 while the king was at the royal beach in Hua Hin

U pon assuming the throne, General Chakri took the name of Ramathibodi. Later known as Rama I, he ruled from 1782 until 1809. His first action as king was to transfer his administrative headquarters from the marshy confines of Thonburi to the more spacious Bangkok, east across the river.

Understanding the value of traditions and symbols, he set about restoring the confidence of his war-shattered people. Buddha images were transported to Bangkok from Sukhothai and Ayutthaya, architects were instructed to design buildings in the Ayutthayan mode, and even bricks from ruined Ayutthaya were floated by barge to Bangkok for the city's new wall.

He assembled surviving master craftsmen from the old city and had them design the first permanent building in the new capital: Wat Phra Kaeo, constructed to house the Emerald Buddha. An elaborate ceremony marked the movement of the Buddha image from Thonburi to the new temple.

One of Rama I's chief concerns was to secure the borders of his kingdom. Early in his reign, King Bodawpaya of Burma had launched a series of military expeditions involving the largest number of troops in the history of Thai-Burmese wars. Siamese troops boldly counter-attacked the invaders at strategic border points, routing the Burmese before they could do serious harm. After Bodawpaya, Burma became embroiled in British colonial conflicts and Thailand was left more or less in peace.

Modern Thailand is indebted to Rama I for his assiduous cultural revival program. He appointed experts to review and assemble fragments of historical and religious treatises, few of which had survived the destruction of Ayutthaya in 1767.

Rama I perpetuated another Ayutthaya tradition by appointing his brother as *Maha Uparaja*, a "second" or deputy king, with powers almost equal to his own. The deputy king's home, the Wang Na or Palace at the Back, now houses the National Museum and once extended across the northern half of Sanam Luang.

Because the royal regalia had been destroyed with everything else during the siege of Ayutthaya, Rama I had a new crown and robes commissioned for his coronation. Similarly, in his old age, he commissioned a golden urn to be prepared for his body, in accordance with ancient court protocol prescribing that the bodies of high-ranking royalty be placed in urns between the times of death and cremation.

Rama II and Rama III

Rama I's successors, Rama II and Rama III, completed the consolidation of the Siamese kingdom and the revival of Ayutthaya's arts and culture. Best remembered as an artist, Rama II (ruled 1809–1824) was responsible for building and repairing numerous Bangkok monasteries. His most famous construction was Wat Arun, the Temple of Dawn on the opposite bank from the Grand Palace, and which was later enlarged to its present height by Rama IV. He is said to have carved the great doors of Wat Suthat, throwing away the special chisels so his work could never be replicated.

During his father's reign, Rama II had gained renown as a great poet. His classic version of the *Ramakien*, the Thai interpretation of the Indian classical saga *Ramayana*, was completed during his reign, with large sections composed by the king himself. At his court, Rama II employed *khon* and *lakhon* dance-drama troupes to enact his compositions, just as in the courts of Ayutthaya. Rama II reopened relations with the West and allowed the Portuguese to

PORCELAIN LEGACY

Virtually any temple with porcelain-decorated gables, such as Wat Arun, can immediately be ascribed to the reign of Rama III.

Mongkut (Rama IV)

With the help of Hollywood, Rama IV (ruled 1851–1868) became the most famous king of Siam. Commonly known as Mongkut, he was portrayed in *The King and I* as a frivolous, bald-headed despot. But nothing could have been further from the truth. He was the first Thai king to understand Western culture and technology, and his reign has been described as the bridge spanning the new and the old.

The younger brother of Rama III, Mongkut spent 27 years as a Buddhist monk prior to his

open the first Western embassy in the Bangkok capital.

Rama III, who ruled from 1824 to 1851, continued to open Siam's doors to foreigners. The ready availability of Chinese porcelain led him to decorate many temples, including Wat Arun, with ceramic fragments. This vogue did not survive his lifetime. An extremely pious Buddhist, Rama III was considered to be "austere and reactionary" by Europeans. But he encouraged missionaries to introduce Western medicine.

PRECEDING PAGE: procession of royal barges at Prajadhipok's 1925 coronation. **LEFT:** early map of Bangkok. **ABOVE:** Bangkok khlong, late 19th century.

accession to the throne. This gave him a unique opportunity to roam as a commoner among the populace. He learned to read Buddhist scriptures in the Pali language; missionaries taught him Latin and English, thus enabling him to read European texts. As a monk, Mongkut delved into many subjects: history, geography and the sciences, especially astronomy.

Even as an abbot, he established himself as a reformer, ridding the Buddhist scriptures of their superstitious elements and founding a sect, the Dhammakaiya, which stressed strict adherence to Buddhist tenets. Today, these monks can be recognised by their brown robes. Mongkut realised that traditional Thai values would not save his country from Western encroachment. On the contrary, he believed that modernisation would bring Siam in line with the West and reduce hostilities with foreigners.

England was the first European country to benefit from this policy, when an 1855 treaty – not gained entirely without coercion by the British – granted extraterritorial privileges: a duty of only three percent on imports, and permission to import Indian opium duty-free. Other Western nations, including France and the United States, followed suit with similar treaties. And when Mongkut lifted the state monopoly on rice, that crop rapidly became

Siam's leading export. Mongkut wanted his children to gain the same benefits from the English language as himself. For this purpose, he engaged Anna Leonowens as an English teacher. The self-elevated governess greatly exaggerated her role in the Thai court in her autobiographical writings, misrepresenting the king as a cruel autocrat permanently involved in harem intrigues.

In fact, her five years in Siam are hardly mentioned in Thai chronicles. The book, as well as the movie and play based on it, are regarded as insulting to the deeply revered institution of the monarchy and are seldom mentioned by most Thais nowadays.

Mongkut's beloved hobby, astronomy, was the indirect cause of his death. From observatories at his favourite palaces, the Summer Palace at Bang Pa-In and the Palace on the Hill, at Phetchburi, he successfully calculated and predicted a total eclipse of the sun in 1868.

European and Asian sceptics joined him on the southeastern coast of the Gulf of Thailand to await the event. As the moon blocked the sun's light, both the Europeans and the scoffers among the royal astrologers raised an exclamation of admiration, raising the king's esteem among both parties.

But his triumph was short-lived. The king contracted malaria during the trip, and died two weeks later from it.

Chulalongkorn (Rama V)

Mongkut's son, Chulalongkorn, was only 15 years old when he ascended the throne. But he reigned over Siam as Rama V for over four decades – longer than any Thai king until the present King Bhumibol, who has been on the throne for over half a century.

The farsighted Chulalongkorn immediately revolutionised his court by ending the ancient custom of prostration, and by allowing officials to sit on chairs during royal audiences. He abolished serfdom in stages, giving owners and serfs time to readjust to the new order, and replaced corvee labour with direct taxation.

His reign was truly a revolution from the throne. When Chulalongkorn assumed power, Siam had no schools and few roads, railways, hospitals, or well-equipped military forces.

To achieve the enormous task of modernisation, he brought in foreign advisors and sent his sons and other young men abroad for education. He also founded a palace school for children of the aristocracy, following this with other schools and vocational centres for the common people. Until then, the only previous schools in Siam had been the monasteries.

Chulalongkorn's brothers were leading figures in his government, especially Prince Devawongse, the foreign minister, and Prince Damrong, the first interior minister and a historian who has come to be known as the father of Thai history. Chulalongkorn's elder children returned home from their European schools in the 1890s, contributing to the modernisation of the army and navy. The first hospital, Siriraj, was opened in 1886 after years of unrelenting opposition. Most of the Thai common people preferred herbal remedies to *farang* (foreign) medicine. Besides, there was a shortage of doctors. Eventually, the obstacles were overcome.

In foreign relations, Rama V had to compromise and give up parts of his kingdom to protect Siam from foreign colonisation. When France conquered Annam in 1883 and Britain annexed upper Burma in 1886, Siam found itself sandwiched uncomfortably between two rival expansionist powers. Border conflicts and gunboat diplomacy forced Siam to surrender

WESTERN-FREE ZONE

Thailand is the only nation in Southeast Asia that has never been subjected to Western colonial rule.

during his reign, in 1897 and 1907. These led him to seek more spacious surroundings than those of the Grand Palace, so he built a palace on the site of a fruit orchard to the north, in Dusit. It was directly connected to the Grand Palace by the wide Thanon Ratchadamnern. At the Dusit palace, he held parties and even fancy-dress balls, often cooking the food himself. No doubt the food was royal.

The many reforms of Chulalongkorn bore fruit within his lifetime. The economy of the country flourished, and Thai peasantry – by comparison with

to France its claims to Laos and the western part of Cambodia. Similarly, certain territories on the Malay Peninsula further south were ceded to Great Britain in exchange for renunciation of British extraterritorial rights in Siam.

By the end of Chulalongkorn's reign, Siam had given up 120,000 square kilometres (50,000 sq mi) of fringe territory. But that seemed a small price to pay for maintaining the peace and independence of Siam.

Chulalongkorn made two European tours

its counterparts in French Indochina and British Burma – were very well-off. It is no wonder that Chulalongkorn was posthumously named *Piya Maharaj*, the Beloved Great King.

As Rama V, Chulalongkorn was conscious of worldwide democratic trends, not to mention the implications of technology, but he judged his country as yet unprepared for such rapid change. It is said that he brought progress to Siam through the judicious exercise of his absolute power.

Today, there is considerable adulation for King Chulalongkorn and his efforts at reform and innovation, not to mention his down-to-earth attitude.

LEFT: Rama IV (Mongkut) and his queen. **ABOVE LEFT:** Rama V (Chulalongkorn) and his entourage in Europe. **ABOVE RIGHT:** a son of Chulalongkorn.

Vajiravudh (Rama VI)

King Chulalongkorn's successor, Vajiravudh, began his reign (1910–1925) with a lavish coronation. Oxford-educated and thoroughly anglicised, his Western-inspired reforms to modernise Siam affected modern Thai society.

One of the first changes was a 1913 edict commanding his subjects to adopt surnames. In the absence of a clan or caste system, genealogy was virtually unheard of in Siam. The law generated much initial bewilderment, especially in rural areas, and Vajiravudh personally coined patronymics for hundreds of families. To simplify his forebears' lengthy titles for foreigners, he invented the Chakri dynastic name, Rama, to be followed by the proper reign number. (A common name is also used, such as Chulalongkorn.) Primary education was made compulsory throughout the kingdom; Chulalongkorn University, in Bangkok and the first in Siam, was founded, and schools for both sexes flourished during his reign.

Rama VI's most significant political contribution was to promote the concept of nationalism. An accomplished author, he used literature and drama to foster nationalism by glorifying Thai legends and historical heroes in plays. Under a pseudonym, he also wrote essays extolling the virtues of the nation.

At the outbreak of World War I, Siam remained neutral, but late in the war, Vajiravudh joined the Allies in 1917 by sending a small expeditionary force to fight in France, thereby securing Siam's admittance to the League of Nations. The flag of Thailand, a white elephant against a red background, was flown with others at Versailles, but the pachyderm was unfortunately mistaken for a small domestic animal. The incident greatly discomfited the king, who then changed the flag to red, white and blue stripes to represent the nation, the religion and the monarchy – elements regarded by Thais as essential to the structure of modern Thailand.

Vajiravudh preferred individual ministerial consultations to summoning his appointed cabinet. His regime was therefore criticised as autocratic and lacking in coordination. Members of his family were dissatisfied because he rarely saw them, enjoying more the company of his courtiers. His extravagance soon emptied the treasury built up by Chulalongkorn. Towards the end of his reign, the national treasury met deficits caused by the ruler's personal expenses.

> **FIND ANOTHER NAME**
>
> Before the reign of Rama VI, Vajiravudh, most Thais had used only first names, a practice that the king considered uncivilised.

Vajiravudh married late. His only daughter was born one day before he died in 1925. He was succeeded by his youngest brother, Prajadhipok, who reaped the consequences of his brother's brilliant but controversial reign.

Prajadhipok (Rama VII)

The early death of his elder brother propelled Prajadhipok to royal succession, although being an old Etonian, he would have preferred a soldier's career to that of a ruler. Once king, however, he stressed economy and efficiency within the government. Unlike his brother, he tried to cut public expenditure by drastically reducing

the civil service and royal household expenses. Prajadhipok's economic policies, combined with the blessings of increased revenue from foreign trade, amply paid off for the kingdom.

In the early years of his reign, communications were improved by a wireless service, and the Don Muang Airport began to operate as an international air centre. It was also during his reign that Siam saw the establishment of the Fine Arts Department, the National Library and the National Museum, institutions that continue

LEFT: Chulalongkorn's widow and family; Vajiravudh and Prajadhipok are at centre top and lower right.
ABOVE: Prajadhipok delivers the new constitution.

today as important preservers of Thai culture.

Hard-working and conscientious, Prajadhipok was personally concerned with improving the welfare of his subjects. He was aware of the rising demand for greater participation in government by a small foreign-educated faction, but felt that the Thais were, on the whole, not ready for democracy. In 1927, he publicly commented that the people must first be taught political consciousness before democracy could effectively be introduced.

The worldwide economic crisis of 1931 affected Siam's rice export. By the time Prajadhipok dropped the gold standard, linking the Thai baht to the pound sterling, it was too late to stem the financial crisis. The government was forced to implement further economies by cutting the salary of junior personnel, and by resorting to a retrenchment of the armed services. Discontent brewed among army officials and bureaucrats, who felt promotions were due.

Coup d'etat

Rumours and speculation were rampant during the 150th anniversary celebrations of the Chakri dynasty in 1932. Prajadhipok was the last regal representative of traditional Thai kingship to preside over grand pageantry, which featured a royal barge procession.

Two months later, a coup d'etat ended the absolute rule of the Thai monarchs. The coup was staged by the People's Party, a military and civilian group masterminded by foreign-educated Thais. The chief ideologist was Pridi Panomyong, a young lawyer trained in France. On the military side, Capt. Luang Pibulsongram (Pibul) was responsible for gaining the support of important army colonels. With a few tanks, the 70 conspirators sparked off their "revolution" by occupying strategic areas and holding the senior princes hostage. Other army officers stood by as the public watched.

At the time, the king was in Hua Hin, a royal beach retreat to the south. Acknowledging the writing on the wall and to avoid bloodshed, he accepted a provisional constitution by which he "ceased to rule but continued to reign."

Since then, the Thai constitutional monarchy has nevertheless become a beloved institution and a symbol of continuity and stability, not to mention a moral anchor, while civilian and military governments have come and gone with great frequency. ❏

CONTEMPORARY THAILAND

Thailand's modern history has been peppered with intrigue and punctuated with
violence. The monarchy, however, has provided a stabilising anchor

Originally motivated by idealism, the People's Party soon succumbed to internal conflicts. A National Assembly was appointed, but universal suffrage was postponed while the public was to be tutored in the rudiments of representative democracy. The Thai people didn't show much interest, however, and they wouldn't voluntarily attend the party's educational rallies. Other parties were outlawed.

The party's military factions quickly outmanoeuvred the civilian factions. They had greater cohesion and more extensive connections with traditional royal power brokers. The officers exercised their influence when Pridi presented a vague and utopian economic plan in 1933. It called for the nationalisation of land and for the creation of peasant cooperatives. When his opponents attacked the plan as communistic, Pridi slipped into his first overseas exile. The power of Pibul and the army was further strengthened in October of 1933 by the decisive defeat of a rebellion led by Prince Boworadet, who had been Prajadhipok's war minister.

The king had no part in the rebellion, but he had become increasingly dismayed by quarrels within the new government. He moved to England in 1934 and abdicated in 1935. In a farewell message, he said that he had wished to turn over power to the entire people and not to "any individual or any group to use in an autocratic manner." Sadly, a subsequent history of coups, aborted coups and blood-baths has caused the king's words to be often quoted.

Ananda Mahidol (Rama VIII), a 10-year-old half-nephew, agreed to ascend the throne, but he remained for some time in Switzerland to complete his schooling.

The governments of the 1930s had some achievements. Most notably, public primary education, totalling four years, was extended to many rural areas. Indirect and, later, direct elec-

tions to the lower house meant that for the first time representatives from provincial areas had a voice at the national level. After a series of crises and an election in 1938, Pibul became prime minister. His rule grew authoritarian.

While some Thai officers favoured the model of the Japanese military regime, Pibul admired

and sought to emulate Hitler and Mussolini. Borrowing many ideas from European fascism, he attempted to instill a sense of mass nationalism. With tight control over the media and a creative propaganda department, Pibul whipped up sentiment against Thailand's Chinese residents. Chinese immigration was restricted, Chinese were barred from certain occupations, and state enterprises were set up to compete in industries dominated by Chinese firms.

By changing the country's name from Siam to Thailand in 1939, Pibul intended to emphasise that it belonged to Thai (or Tai) ethnic groups and not to Chinese, Malays, Mons or any other minorities.

PRECEDING PAGE: Royal Barges on Bangkok's Chao Phraya; their last appearance was in 1996 for the king's grand jubilee. **LEFT:** King Bhumibol's coronation. **RIGHT:** book showing coup d'etat leaders.

World War II

When Hitler invaded France in 1940, French hold over its Indochinese colonies was seriously weakened. Anticipating that Japan might make a claim, Thailand made its own by invading southern Laos and parts of western Cambodia, in November 1940. Then on 7 December 1941 (8 December in Asia) the Japanese bombed Pearl Harbour and launched invasions throughout Southeast Asia. Thailand was invaded at nine points. Resistance lasted

> **DEMOCRATIC FOCUS**
>
> Bangkok's Democracy Monument was built in 1939 to commemorate the 1932 revolution. In the 1970s, 1980s, and 1990s, it was the focus of numerous pro-democracy protests, and of bloodshed.

reached the stage of operating a guerrilla army.

By 1944, Thailand's initial enthusiasm for its Japanese partners had evaporated. The country faced runaway inflation, food shortages, rationing and black markets. The assembly forced Pibul from office. When the war ended in 1945, Britain demanded reparations and the right to station troops in Thailand. The Thais argued that due to the work of Seri Thai, they were in fact allies. The United States supported the Thai position, partly

less than a day. Pibul acceded to Japan's request for "passage rights," but Thailand was allowed to retain its army and political administration.

Popular anecdote has it that the Thai ambassador to Washington, Seni Pramoj, single-handedly prevented war between Thailand and the United States by hiding the declaration in a desk drawer. Thailand in fact declared war against the Allies. But it is also true that Seni immediately offered his services in Washington to set up an underground resistance movement, Seri Thai.

Starting with overseas Thai students, Seri Thai linked up with a network in Thailand headed by Pridi. The resistance supplied Allied forces with intelligence, but it never quite

because it was then trying to blunt British and French efforts to repossess their Asian colonies.

The next three years were marked by a series of democratic civilian governments. Pridi served behind the scenes, drafting a constitution, and briefly served as prime minister. In 1948, under threat of military force, Pibul took over once again. In the early years, his power was contested. Two coup attempts, supported by the navy, resulted in fierce battles on the streets of Bangkok and along the Chao Phraya River. In the 1950s, Pibul's grip grew tighter. Police power was abused, newspaper editors were beaten, critics disappeared. Pibul had also rid himself of Pridi. After attempting a coup in

1949, Pridi fled into exile. (After years in China, he died in France in 1983.) Pibul sealed Pridi's fate by convening an inquiry that implicated him in the death of King Ananda.

In 1946, on a visit to Thailand from school in Europe, the young Ananda was found dead of a gunshot in his palace bedroom. Pridi believed that the king accidentally shot himself. The charge now seems absurd. Ananda was succeeded by his younger brother, Bhumibol Adulyadej (Rama IX), the present monarch. However, he returned to Switzerland to complete law studies and did not take up active duties as monarch until the 1950s.

enterprises. Private firms were als to appoint officers to their boards .

In 1957, a clique of former proteges over threw Pibul. These generals ran the government until 1973. While Pibul had retained some trappings of democracy, such as a constitution and legislature, the generals employed martial law.

Unadorned dictatorship did not hinder official relations with the United States. By the end of the 1960s, the war in Vietnam was raging and Thailand was America's staunchest ally. American funds built the first roads in the northeast of the country, where air bases and other military facilities proliferated. From here, U.S. air-

Vietnam War

In addition to renewed anti-Chinese campaigns, Pibul vigorously hunted out Communists. Many of the leaders of the small, outlawed Communist Party of Thailand were Sino-Thais. Pibul's anti-Communist credentials helped win both economic and military aid from the United States. The resulting American largess, with too few strings, has been blamed as cause for the corruption that permeates the police and military to this day. Another cause was Pibul's practice of placing military officers to run state

Left: coronation of King Bhumibol Adulyadej.
Above: Bhumibol at crown prince's investiture.

ROYAL SUCCESSION

In the 15th century, King Trailok decreed that the king's eldest son, then brother, is heir apparent. The current king and queen have three daughters and one son. Thus, Crown Prince Maha Vajiralongkorn, born in 1952, is heir to the throne. If for some reason he can't ascend the throne, the oldest daughter, Princess Ubol Ratana, born in 1951, is technically next in line. However, after marrying an American and settling down in the U.S., it's doubtful she'd rule. The popular choice is Princess Sirindhom (b. 1955), a woman of considerable academic and social accomplishments, and highly respected.

craft bombed Vietnam and Laos. The northeast was also the Thai base for forays into Laos.

Meanwhile, Thai Communists had turned to armed conflict in 1965. The original strongholds were in the impoverished northeast, but by the early 1970s, there were Communist areas throughout, including the Muslim south, and especially along the northern frontiers. It would be some time before they were not a threat.

The ruling generals used their power to accrue enormous personal fortunes, but they also improved health standards. Construction boomed, while the business sector expanded. A middle class began to emerge.

The October revolution

In a mystifying burst of generosity, the government issued a constitution and held elections in 1969. The ruling party naturally won most seats, but the generals nonetheless quickly bored of slow parliamentary processes. In November 1971, parliament was dissolved and the generals reverted to their old ruling habits. Many Thais felt betrayed, but only students kept up low-key protests, despite grave personal risk.

With reasonable demands for a constitution and popular elections, students were able to harness public support. The final straw against the government was the arrest of 13 student leaders and professors who had made demands for pop-

ular elections. On 13 October 1973, a demonstration to protest the arrests attracted 400,000 people to Bangkok's Democracy Monument. The next day, the protest turned violent and at least 100 students were shot by riot police. Discovering that their army had deserted them, the ruling generals fled to the United States.

Political parties, labour unions and farming organisations sprang to life with very specific grievances. The press has never again been so unfettered as then. Right-wing and paramilitary organisations sprang up in response. The middle class was originally strongly supportive of the student revolution, as were parts of the upper class. But they came to fear that total chaos or a Communist takeover was at hand.

The 1976 return of one of the previously exiled generals, ostensibly to become a monk, sparked student protests.

On 6 October, police and paramilitary thugs stormed Thammasat University, in Bangkok just north of the Grand Palace. Students were lynched and their bodies burned on the spot. A faction of army officers seized power. Self-government had lasted three years.

The civilian judge appointed to be prime minister, Thanin Kraivichien, outlawed political parties, unions and strikes, and he ordered arrests of anyone "endangering society." A curfew was strictly enforced. Teachers suspected of left-wing leanings were required to attend anti-Communism indoctrination. Many students and other dissidents joined the Communists in the countryside. Yet another military coup took control in 1977. For the next decade, two comparatively moderate generals headed the government, endorsing amnesties for Communists.

Fragile democracy

The prospects for any sustained democracy remain uncertain, especially given the stormy economic situation of the late 1990s.

A former general was elected in 1989, but deposed two years later in a bloodless military coup. The junta, the self-dubbed National Peacekeeping Council, installed a businessman and ex-diplomat, Anand Panyacharun, as a caretaker premier, but were startled when he exhibited an independent streak and earned Thais' lasting affection for running the cleanest government in memory.

As expected, the junta's new party won the most parliamentary seats in 1992 elections.

Unexpected, however, was the public discontent when the coup leader, Gen. Suchinda Krapayoon, assumed the prime minister's post without having stood for election. In the following weeks, students, professors, social workers, maverick politicians, entertainers and the curious public convened in a series of outdoor rallies. On 17 May, more than 70,000 gathered at Sanam Luang, the grassy expanse near the Grand Palace and Democracy Monument. Late in the evening, soldiers

THE KING'S POWER

While avoiding the free-for-all of Thai politics, the king of Thailand retains an immense amount of moral authority, and power. Even the most ruthless of bickering generals and politicians yield to his authority, as in 1992.

erage. Unrepentant, Suchinda stepped down.

The Democrat Party and other prominent junta critics prevailed in September elections. A rarity in Thai politics, newly elected Prime Minister Chuan Leekpai was not personally corrupt and lived modestly. He prevailed for three years, setting a record for a civilian, elected government. He can be credited with diluting the power of military officers in many state enterprises, such as Thai Airways and the Tobacco Monopoly. But by the end,

fired on the unarmed demonstrators assembled there. The number of casualties is uncertain.

Shootings, beatings, riots, arson and mass arrests continued sporadically for three days. Broadcast media, which were controlled by the government or military, enforced a nationwide news blackout. But owners of satellite dishes, in Thailand and around the world, were glued to footage of "Bloody May." At Democracy Monument, vendors began hawking pirated news videos of the international television cov-

Chuan had lost much of the goodwill of the democracy forces that had lifted him to office. For many, he was too passive and reactive.

No one was prosecuted, punished or held responsible for carrying out the May crackdown. As with the massacres of 1973 and 1976, the numbers and identity of those who died or disappeared in May 1992 are still in dispute. Corruption flourished. Most disappointing, Chuan had been deflected in his efforts to push through a law that would have relegated more power to local governments. The final coalition collapsed in 1995 when wealthy members of Chuan's own party were discovered profiting from the latest land reform program.

LEFT: remembering pro-democracy protesters killed by the army, 1992. **ABOVE:** waiting for national election results in Bangkok.

Two subsequent elections brought a provincial businessman, Banharn Silpa-archa, and a former general, Chavalit Yongchaiyudh, to the highest office. Both had unsavoury reputations for their business dealings and campaign expenditures. And both were lambasted by the public and the press for their incompetent handling of the economy. In fact, the rot had set in much earlier. Kick-started by a massive influx of Japanese assembly plants in the late 1980s, for almost a decade Thailand had been one of the fastest growing economies in the world. Per capita income doubled, to US$ 2,000 per year. More than 4 million rural people migrated to

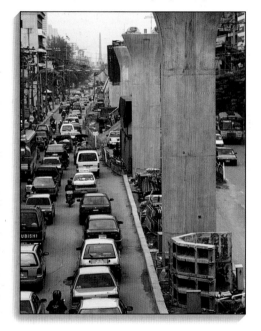

urban jobs. Thailand seemed on the course to becoming an industrialised nation.

Even as economic growth was slowing down, liberalisation of the financial sector in the early 1990s enabled Thai companies to borrow cheap money. Property firms in particular went on a borrowing binge. Visitors today can readily spot the empty hotels, apartments and office blocks that, together with abandoned construction sites, stand as monuments to profligacy.

The first cracks opened in mid-1996 when two officials at the venerable Bangkok Bank of Commerce fled after embezzling more than US$ 2 billion. The central bank stepped in with bail-outs that eventually extended to cash-strapped finance companies. More than US$ 16 billion later, the central bank had covertly carried out the biggest bank bail-out in world history. There was no end in sight.

IMF rescue

Faced with capital flight, currency speculation and a deteriorating balance of payments, in the summer of 1997 the baht was floated from its dollar-weighted peg. It quickly dropped 25 percent in value, dropping even more later.

The Thai government finally sought the help of the International Monetary Fund (IMF). In the following days, on IMF advice, 42 more finance companies were ordered to suspend operations. In sum, 56 of the nation's 91 finance companies were declared insolvent. IMF loans and credit guarantees came only after stringent conditions were met. Chavalit and finance officials reluctantly agreed to halt bail-outs of shareholders, raise income and value-added taxes, cut the state budget, practice strict monetary discipline and accelerate the privatisation of a large number of state enterprises.

As the economy ground to a halt in Thailand, the IMF was blamed for just about every problem in the country. Expensive European automobiles were pawned at bargain prices. Bankers and corporate managers found themselves driving taxis and waiting in restaurants.

Numerous public works projects have been suspended or cancelled. Bangkok has a half-completed rapid-transit system cluttering up its boulevards; overhead tracks and supporting pylons remain uncompleted. There is no guarantee that they will ever be finished.

Chuan Leekpai, who had been prime minister in the early 1990s, returned to office in 1998. More pro-active this time, he appeared to have learned the lessons of the heady 1990s and made internationally applauded moves to resuscitate Thailand. While many Asian economies continued to falter in the late 1990s, Thailand's economy was held up as an example of an economy that was diligently working its way out of the abyss, but still ever so slowly.

Symbolically if not pragmatically, Prime Minister Chuan continued to live in his modest house, in the shadow of an overhead expressway in central Bangkok. ❐

LEFT: suspended construction projects litter Bangkok.
RIGHT: the king and queen at a ceremony.

The King

In a cynical world, it is difficult to imagine the depth of respect that the Thai people have for their monarch, King Bhumibol – Rama IX in the Chakri line. Sceptical outsiders may think it contrived or quaint, but Thais have a profound respect for the king – no mere ceremonial figurehead – and for his moral authority that has offered sanctuary during Thailand's turbulent past 50 years.

Originating in the distant past, in the ancient city of Sukhothai, the royal symbol has endured through wars, revolutions, the fall of dynasties, the smashing of traditions and governments – both dictatorial and democratic – and through times of tribulation and prosperity. During the political turmoil in 1992, Bhumibol ended a political crisis between the prime minister and his chief political opponent, which had threatened civil war. The two men prostrated themselves at the king's feet, on live television, where they stayed silent as the king instructed them on how to bring the country back to a peace. Violence in the streets, which killed dozens, ceased, and there were free elections.

King Bhumibol was born in Cambridge, Massachusetts, in 1927, where his father, Prince Mahidol of Songkhla, was studying medicine at Harvard University, and his mother, nursing. His father, a son of King Rama V and later regarded as the father of modern medicine in Thailand, was a minor member of the royal family. At his birth, there seemed little chance of Prince Bhumibol becoming king. Between him and the throne, according to the laws of succession, stood Bhumibol's own father and Bhumibol's elder brother, Prince Ananda. (Rama VII had borne no sons to take the throne.)

Bhumibol came to the throne in 1946, the latest monarch in the Chakri dynasty, which has produced several enlightened monarchs in the 19th and 20th centuries. The abolition of the absolute monarchy in 1932 had exerted unprecedented strain on the system; the royalty seemed to lose contact with the people, along with their confidence. There were doubts if the monarchy could survive the turmoil of World War II, when 18-year-old Bhumibol ascended the throne unexpectedly after the fatal shooting of his elder brother, King Ananda, in the Grand Palace, in Bangkok. The king's death was never fully explained publicly, but much later, two royal servants were executed for his murder.

In the 50 years since his coronation, the king has proved himself a worthy successor to his celebrated ancestors. With Queen Sirikit, he has travelled to every part of Thailand, the first monarch to visit some parts of the country. He rarely travels outside of Thailand.

He has also turned over his palace grounds to agricultural purposes. Behind the walls of Chitralada Palace, where the king lives (the Grand Palace is for ceremonial and state occasions), the king has transformed gardens into an agricultural research station, with a dairy farm, rice fields, and orchards. His involvement with agriculture began with a concerted effort to find new crops for the hill tribes in order to wean them from opium cultivation. He then focused this experience into farm programs.

The monarchy costs the Thai treasury nothing, at least directly, since the royal family pays its own way with income from vast property holdings and investments. The king's mother, who died in 1995, founded the Flying Doctors program to provide medical and dental services in remote areas. Queen Sirikit works to preserve the arts and crafts, and the techniques of the ancient crafts, and to provide skills and income for rural people.

In addition, the king and queen take part in the numerous royal ceremonies that punctuate the year – the seasonal robing of the Emerald Buddha, the various Buddhist holy days, the opening of Parliament. A skillful musician, King Bhumibol plays jazz on clarinet and saxophone. ∎

NATURAL HISTORY

Although Thailand's wild lands have diminished from excessive logging over
the past couple of decades, it is still endowed with some unique flora and fauna

Thailand's biological treasures and diverse land forms derive from its geographical position as the crossroads of Southeast Asia. Just as the nation has accommodated many peoples and cultures, so it has served as a conduit dispersing plant and animal life.

Roughly the size of France, Thailand covers 513,115 square kilometres (198,115 sq mi). The overall shape resembles an elephant's head with the southern peninsula forming the trunk. The most conspicuous landscape features are striated mountains enclosing cultivated valleys, but there are great contrasts in six geographical regions. In the north, extending along the borders of Burma and Laos, parallel mountains run north to south, generally reaching over 2,000 metres (6,500 ft) in height. The valleys have been cultivated for centuries, but until 50 years ago – with the proliferation of slash-and-burn farming – there was considerable forest cover in the higher altitudes.

To the south, the vast valley called the Central Plain stretches 450 kilometres (300 mi) to the Gulf of Thailand. The overflowing tributaries traditionally deposited rich silt that created an agricultural rice bowl. The farms nowadays are supported by intensive irrigation, courtesy of a network of highly controversial big dams. The western region consists mostly of mountain ranges, the source of tributaries of the Mekong, Chao Phraya and Salween rivers. Sparsely populated by humans, this region is the richest repository of wildlife.

The northeast encompasses the broad and shallow Khorat Plateau, which lies less than 200 metres (650 ft) above sea level. This is a land of poor soils, little rain, too many people, and a bit of grass and shrub. The sandstone base has weathered into strange shapes.

The small, hilly southeast coast is bordered on the north by the Cardomom Range, which protrudes from Cambodia. It includes 80 rocky,

PRECEDING PAGE: bats take flight as a setting sun takes the day. **LEFT:** yellow bittern fishing from lotus leaf. **RIGHT:** waterfall in Khao Yai National Park.

forested islands. Intense heat and violent underground pressures created the rubies and sapphires mined here. Endowed with the heaviest rainfall and humidity, the south covers the isthmus down to the Malay peninsula. Coastal forests were cleared for rubber and palm plantations. But 275 islands, especially in the west-

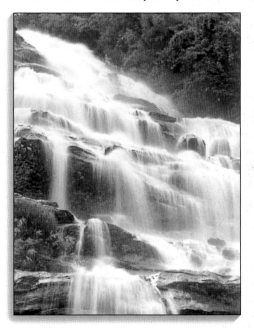

ern Andaman Sea, support unique species and are surrounded by coral reefs.

The limestone rock so common on the Andaman side was once seabed. Soft and easily eroded, it is limestone that is the basis of the crumbly mountains and jutting islets. Underground streams in limestone also created the many spectacular caves.

Flora

Sixty years ago, forests covered about 70 percent of Thailand's land area. In 1960, the figure had dropped to 50 percent. Today, probably only about 15 percent of undisturbed forest remains, although perhaps another 15 percent of it has been replanted, often with non-indigenous species, or else turned into plantations growing the likes of palm-oil trees or eucalyptus. Aside from tiny Singapore, the scale and rate of forest loss in Thailand is the greatest in Southeast Asia. Following fatal landslides, logging was finally outlawed in 1989, but trucks ferrying contraband logs are still a common sight.

The nation's forests can be classified as either evergreen or deciduous; the latter shed leaves seasonally. There are many sub-categories, and a single habitat may contain both types of trees. Evergreen forests, of course, are green year-round. They are most abundant in the uplands

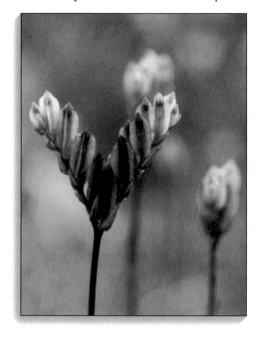

of both the south and southeast, where rainfall is plentiful and the dry season brief. Rain forests are classified as evergreen forests.

Contrary to many preconceptions, all tropical forests are not evergreen, and all evergreen forest is not rain forest. A rain forest is a four-layered forest harbouring the world's densest concentration of species. Herbs, shrubs, ferns and fungi form the bottom layer. A relatively open layer of palms, bamboos and shrubs is above ground level. Mid-level trees, festooned with vines, mosses and orchids, create a 25-metre-high (80 ft) canopy. The well-spaced trees of the upper-most canopy soar as high as 60 metres (200 ft). Healthy rain forests can be

found in the Khao Luang, Koh Surin, Tarutao and Thale Ban national parks, all in the south.

More common than rain forest is the broad-leaved evergreen forest, which is found at higher elevations. Here are found temperate-zone laurels, oaks and chestnuts, along with ferns, rhododendrons and the yew-like podocarps. Varieties of orchids proliferate. Usually the ground level consists of shrubs and grasses that attract larger mammals. The leaves of the taller dipterocarps turn yellow and red before shedding in the dry season. A few weeks later, they burst into purple, pink, orange and red flowers.

One hundred years ago, deciduous forests of the north were thick with teak trees, but virtually all were cut long ago.

Fauna

Of the world's 4,000 species of mammals, 287 can be found in Thailand: 13 species of primates, 18 hoofed species, nine of wild cats (including tigers and clouded leopards), two of bear, two of wild dogs and eight of dolphins. Bats are abundant, with 107 species identified so far. Tigers and the larger deer could soon join the list of mammals that have vanished this century – rhinoceros, several species of deer, two otter species, and the *kouprey,* wild cattle that were discovered in Thailand in the 1930s.

Declared the country's first protected species back in 1921, the Asian elephant is the national mascot, but nonetheless is perilously close to extinction. From well above 20,000 a century ago, fewer than 8,000 survive in Thailand today. Most of these are domesticated, many begging on Bangkok's hard streets. Khao Yai National Park offers the best chance of observing some of the few thousand remaining wild elephants.

Thailand also harbours four types of reptiles and three types of amphibians. Among 175 species of snakes are deadly cobras, kraits and vipers. No doubt most of the insect species haven't been identified yet, but there are 1,200 variegated butterflies. Beetle species may number in the tens of thousands, but have been so little studied that amateurs occasionally discover a new one.

Visitors of national parks and sanctuaries may not see any large animals, but they will be compensated with sightings of birds. There are around 900 species that are permanent residents of the region. In the north are the colourful montane birds with Sino-Himalayan affinities. The birds of the south are similar to those of Malaysia. There are also about 240 wintering and non-breeding migrants that pass through.

Marine life

Off the west coast, the flora and fauna of the Andaman Sea are characteristic of the Indian Ocean. Off the east coast, in the Gulf of Thailand, they are characteristic of Indo-Pacific seas. Coral reefs off both coastlines have been little surveyed, but they support at least 400 species of fish and 30 of sea snakes. The corals them-

LITTLE ENFORCEMENT

The country in fact does have environmental and wildlife protection laws, but they are poorly enforced.

habitats, be they forests or coral reefs, so could disappear many more species of flora and fauna, not only from Thailand, but from the world.

The Forestry Department, which includes the Parks Service, is underfunded and understaffed. In the past few decades, at least 40 rangers have been murdered in the line of duty. Earning less than a factory worker, many rangers also collude with poachers of logs and animals. The country's poorest people inadvertently contribute to the degradation by farming on protected lands. The demands of Chinese-Thais and Chinese vis-

selves come in almost 300 species, with the Andaman Sea boasting a far greater diversity. Intact reefs survive only in areas far from human habitation, such as the vicinity of the Surin and Similan islands.

Environment at risk

As many of the aforementioned remarks concerning habitats and wildlife indicate, Thailand's ecology is an environment in danger of irreversible damage. With the destruction of

LEFT: *Burmannia disticha*, a flower endemic to Khao Yai National Park. **ABOVE:** decreasing in numbers, the Asian elephant, such as this youth, can still be seen.

itors, for both medicinal purposes and gourmet "jungle" dining, further threaten the endangered populations of tigers, bears and deer.

Tourism undoubtedly plays a part in the degradation of Thailand's ecosystems, most visibly when seaside hotels spew untreated sewage. There are also signs that tourism might conceivably become a positive force in the preservation of what remains of Thailand's ecology. There are encouraging signs that a few Thais – among them trekking guides and local green groups, and even a few progressive politicians – are becoming aware that environmental caretaking will sustain tourism longer than continued destruction. ❏

PEOPLE

It will be readily apparent that the Thai people expect life and its experiences, large or small, to be fun and comfortable. Otherwise, what's the point?

Travelers to Thailand are generally struck by the ubiquity of smiles, warmth and friendliness. There are always amiable questions – not to be interpreted as nosiness – and an openness seldom found elsewhere. The standard greeting is *pai nai*, or "Where are you going?" But this is not meant to be interpreted literally, but rather it is the approximate equivalent of "Hello" or "How are you?"

The key focus for understanding the Thai is *sanuk*, a word that can be translated as "fun" or "enjoyable." Indeed, the quantity – and quality – of sanuk, whether in work or play, determines if something is worth pursuing. Almost as important is the concept of *sabai*, best translated as "comfortable" or "contented". As far as Thai people are concerned, in the best of all possible worlds life should be both sanuk and sabai, for visitors to the kingdom as much as for its inhabitants. The antithesis of sanuk is *seriat* – a borrowing from the English word serious. Life just isn't meant to be taken too seriously.

Background

Thailand's lifestyle traditionally has been centred on agriculture, an activity that nurtures a sense of community, especially during planting and harvest. All over the country, ethnic Thais inhabit lowland valleys or plains, growing rice in irrigated paddy fields. They leave the hills and mountains to other peoples – the *chao khao*, or hill tribes, like the Akha and Hmong.

Today, most Thais still live in the country or in small towns, although Bangkok, the archetypical primal city, is now home to more than 10 million people, nearly 20 percent of the national population. The demands of city life have changed much of the countryside's casual ways, but even in Bangkok it is a rare Thai who does not enjoy getting together with friends. Indeed, the notion that one might go off solo to a dinner or on a holiday is considered *mai sanuk*, or not

fun. Similarly, office life must contain a certain amount of chatting and passing around of snacks for it to avoid being mai sanuk.

Generally speaking, Thais hate to be alone, and most are puzzled by the average foreigner's need for occasional solitude. There is a sense of family about Thai activities, a gathering that

does not exclude outsiders. For the visitor invited to join, there is no automatic expectation of reciprocation, although it would always be much appreciated. It is not unusual for a visitor to stray into a small city lane and be invited to join a partying group. Such activities are usually accompanied by music, alcoholic drinks and small snacks. Drunkenness is frowned upon, but a certain tipsiness is acceptable in such circumstances.

When a visitor encounters a tense situation, it is usually because of differences of language and custom. In such instances, it is best to adopt another Thai attitude, *jai yen*, or cool heart, to deal calmly with the problem. It is difficult to

---

PRECEDING PAGE: a net fisherman on Ko Lanta, south of Krabi and Phuket. **LEFT:** a woman working on a farm in Thailand's northeast. **RIGHT:** Thai sailor, Chanthaburi.

stir a Thai to real anger. A smile and an apology should deflate almost any tense situation. Anger, demonstrated by physical violence or raised voices, can provoke serious hostility, however, and an angry Thai can be aggressive indeed. For example, touching a Thai (especially on the top of the head), shouting, or threatening the strong feeling of independence that Thais have may effect an immediate and often hostile response.

Visitors should also avoid pointing their feet at Thais, for example, when crossing their legs, as the foot is considered

> **MISTAKEN IDENTITY**
>
> The original Thai flag was replaced by the king when Europeans, during a royal visit to Europe, mistook the elephant for a rodent.

without breaking, then snapping back into place and swaying in the breeze.

The population

Thailand's population is around 60 million. Most people (95 percent) are Theravada Buddhists. About 80 percent of the population are ethnic Thai. There is a small percentage of Thai Malays living in the south who are Muslim. Islam is Thailand's second religion, accounting for perhaps 5 percent of the population, and Thai-speaking Muslims may be

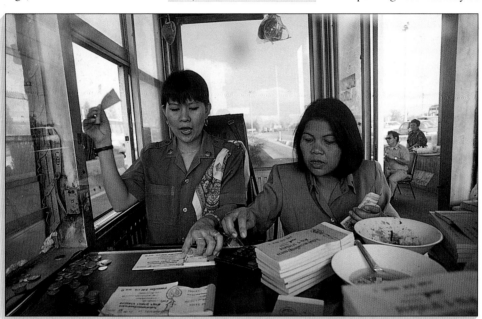

unclean, and pointing it at someone is thought to be a great insult.

Closely allied with jai yen is a concept that provides the answer to all of life's vicissitudes: *mai pen rai,* a phrase best translated as "never mind." Most Thai would rather shrug their shoulders in the face of adversity than risk escalating a difficult situation. Solutions that contribute to restoring or maintaining calm are welcomed. In fact, one reason the Thais have survived intact as a sovereign nation is by adopting a superb sense of compromise, putting trifling or trivial matters in perspective, or else ignoring them. Truly, this aspect of the Thai character may be likened to a bamboo, bending

found in every province of the country, from Chiang Rai in the north to Yasothon in the far northeast. The 2 percent of the population who are Confucianist or Mahayana Buddhist are mainly urban, living in the Chinatown areas of cities like Bangkok, Khorat, Hat Yai and Nakhon Sawan. Some 10 to 15 percent of Thailand's total population are of Chinese descent.

Hill-tribe people living in the north and west total about half a million, and many of the tiny group of Christians in Thailand are concentrated among them. Catholicism made some inroads in Chanthaburi in the south-east, due mainly to French influence. Christians in the north have been strongly influenced by the Protestantism of American Presbyterian missionaries. The main hill-tribe groups include Lisu, Lahu, Akha, Karen, Hmong and Mien (Yao). The smallest and least known peoples living in Thailand are the Mlabri, or "Spirits of the Yellow Leaves", about 250 of whom survive in the Phrae-Nan borderlands, and the Moken, or sea gypsies, who live on islands in the Andaman Sea between Phuket and Ranong

Bangkok's population is thought to exceed 10 million; an accurate census is virtually impossible due to the semi-permanent migrant population. The city functions as the epicentre of the country's political, business and religious life.

The Thais

Whilst all Thai-speaking, Buddhist inhabitants of Thailand consider themselves part of the Thai family, considerable regional differences exist. Basically, Thailand can be divided into four regions – central plains, north, northeast and peninsular south. All educated Thais – and literacy is estimated to run as high as 96 percent – can speak and understand Central Thai, the language of Bangkok, and of the radio and television. Yet Central Thai is far from being the mother tongue of the other three regions. In the northeast, people speak Lao at home, whilst in the north the people speak *kham muang*, or "the language of the Principalities".

Southern Thai is closer to the Central variant, but is spoken much faster and with an economy of terms. Thus, the simple word "tasty" or "delicious" is pronounced *aroi* in Central Thai, *roi* in the snappy southern dialect, *sep* in northeastern Lao, and *lam* in the kham muang of the north. In Central Thai, "Do you speak Thai" emerges as *khun pud phasa tai dai mai?* In kham muang it's *oo kham muang zhang ko?* Quite a difference, but the visitor has no need to worry, as Central Thai is universally spoken and understood throughout the country.

There are also considerable differences in regional cuisine. The Thai restaurants of London and Los Angeles – indeed all over the world – generally serve central Thai cuisine, which has become justly famed internationally.

Northeastern cuisine, by contrast, favours sticky rice (*khao niu*) instead of the more common long-grain rice, which is eaten with the fin-

gers rather than a spoon or chopsticks. Northerners are unique in Thailand in serving cooked tomatoes. The cuisine of Chiang Mai owes much to the culinary influence of neighbouring Burma and Yunnan, in China. Southerners like to use the ubiquitous coconut in their dishes, and the creamy effect of coconut milk helps to tame the otherwise fiery heat of the dishes found in the deep south.

The Chinese

Like every country in Southeast Asia, Chinese merchants have been active in Thailand since the earliest days of commerce. When King

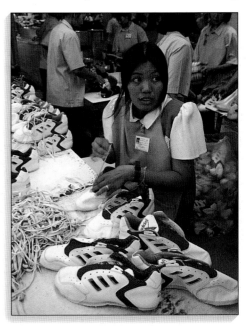

Rama I selected Bangkok as his new capital, the site upon which he wanted to build the Grand Palace was occupied by Chinese shops. He asked the owners to move a kilometre down the riverbank to Sampeng, where they settled in what is today Bangkok's Chinatown.

Throughout the 19th century and the first half of the 20th, immigrants from China poured into the country. As in other Asian countries, these immigrants were denied ownership of land and participation in government, so they naturally drifted towards trade and commerce. One thing, however, has long distinguished the Thai Chinese from their counterparts in most other Asian countries: they have assimilated to a remarkable

LEFT: expressway toll-booth workers, north of Bangkok. **RIGHT:** Thai sneaker factory, near Bangkok.

degree into the life of their adopted land. In part this has been due to government policy.

All children, Chinese or otherwise, are required to learn the Thai language in primary school. (The Chinese language was not even taught at the university level until a few years ago.) Moreover, the Chinese were encouraged, sometimes pressured, into taking Thai names when they wanted a passport, a government scholarship, or an official document. As a result, Chinese and Thais have intermarried freely, so that today, especially in the cities, it is dif-

> ### UBIQUITOUS UNIFORMS
> The wild card in modern Thai politics has always been the military, involved in business and banking as well.

has been, and still is, some jealousy over the ethnic Chinese command of the Thai economy, but the Thai response has been to intermarry with, rather than to isolate, the Chinese. It's a policy that has worked, resulting in little racial tension.

Flag, royalty and Buddhism

At eight o'clock each morning, the Thai national flag is ceremoniously raised in every Thai town and city. The modern flag – introduced in 1917 to replace an earlier red flag emblazoned with a white elephant, the flag of the

ficult to point to anyone and say with assurance that he or she is "pure" Thai or Chinese.

There is no deep-rooted anti-Chinese bias in Thailand, nor have there been any of the serious racial conflicts marring the recent histories of neighbouring countries. Only among the older generation are there people who think and speak of themselves specifically as Chinese. The younger generation thinks of itself as Thai, speaks the language, voices loyalty to Thailand, and has only cursory interests in affairs in China – though pride in Chinese origins remains strong amongst Sino-Thais.

All Thais consider Chinese to be canny businessmen – not without reason. To be sure, there

absolute monarchy – is composed of five horizontal bands of white, red, and blue. The white symbolises the purity of Buddhism; red, the land and its people; and blue, the monarchy as the force that binds the other two together. The central elements of the Thai polity – what makes Thailand Thai – have traditionally been perceived as the Buddhist religion, the Thai language and the monarchy. In recent years, this has changed somewhat, as recognition of other constituent elements of the Thai people, most notably the Malay-speaking Muslims of the deep south, have been brought into the equation. Still, to most Thai, religion, language and king still constitute a unique definition of being Thai.

The three colours, and the flag itself, are revered as symbols of enduring qualities amidst changes, values that were evoked in 1992 when Thais rose up against the military's grip on political power. For the first time, Thailand's burgeoning middle class exerted their influence on political issues; extensive civil unrest, if not civil war, loomed.

Using the moral authority that the monarchy possesses in Thailand, King Bhumibol lectured the prime minister and his primary opponent on live television, as the two men prostrated themselves silently at the king's feet. The crisis immediately evaporated. Since that historical turning point, the changes in government and politics have been enormous, and are continuing to this day.

Since the constitutional revolution of 1932, the king does not govern the country, but he retains considerable influence in government and in society, serving as a beacon of high moral standards and a bellwether in troubled times.

Thais regard the royal family with a reverence unmatched in other countries, and people will react strongly if they consider any member of royalty to have been insulted. Ill-considered remarks or refusing to stand in a cinema for the royal anthem before the start of a movie will earn some very hard stares, or even knocks.

A similar degree of respect is accorded the second pillar of society, Buddhism. Disrespect towards Buddha images, temples or monks is not taken lightly.

Such insults may be unintentional – for example, climbing or clambering about on Buddha images for purposes of photography – so visitors should exercise discretion at all times, remove shoes before entering temples (or also mosques in the south), and behave politely, including the wearing of proper dress. When visiting a temple, it is acceptable for both sexes to wear long pants but not shorts. Unkempt persons or those wearing what might be considered immodest clothing are frequently turned away from major temples.

Monks observe vows of chastity that prohibit their being touched by women, even their mother. When in the vicinity of a monk, a woman should try to stay clear to avoid accidentally brushing against him.

LEFT: walking under an elephant for good luck.
RIGHT: amulets protect from misfortune and evil.

Public behaviour

From the Hindu religion has come the belief that the head is the fount of wisdom and the feet are unclean. For this reason, it is insulting to touch another person on the head, or to point one's feet at or step over another person. Kicking in anger is worse than spitting.

When wishing to pass someone who is seated on the floor, bow slightly while walking and point an arm down to indicate the path to be taken. It is also believed that spirits dwell in the raised doorsills of temples and traditional Thai houses, and that when one steps on them, the spirits become angry and curse the building with

bad luck. Remember this especially in temples.

The Thai greeting and farewell is *sawasdee*, spoken while raising the hands in a prayer-like gesture called the *wai*, with the fingertips touching the nose while bowing the head slightly. It is an easy greeting to master and one which will win smiles.

Thais believe in personal cleanliness. Even the poorest among them bathe daily and dress cleanly and neatly. Thailand is a hot country, and the Thai people very fastidious. They frown on those who do not share this concern for hygiene. The lax care that some foreign travelers bring with their backpack ramblings win few points. Shower and change often, for your own comfort and to receive respect. Toilet paper is not generally provided except in hotels, airports and other tourist-oriented institutions. Look for the tap and water bowl, or a spray-hose.

Twenty years ago, Thai couples showed no intimacy in public. That has changed due to Western influence on the young, but intimacy still does not extend beyond holding hands. As in many traditional societies, displaying open affection in public is a sign of bad manners.

Old people in Thailand are treated with great respect, as are teachers, doctors and other professionals. Mishaps or accidents – such as a small traffic crash – are best met with smiles

but sometimes confusing way of saying "no".

As noted earlier, jai yen, or "cool heart," an attitude of remaining calm in stressful situations, is a trait admired by Thais. Getting angry or exhibiting *jai ron* (hot heart) is a sign of immaturity and lack of self-control. Reacting to adversity or disappointment with a shrug of the shoulders and saying "mai pen rai" (never mind) is the accepted response to most situations.

Thais converse readily with any stranger who shows the least sign of willingness. They may be shy about their English language ability but they try nonetheless: speak a few words of Thai and they respond even more eagerly. Be pre-

and apologies. Violence or rude language should be avoided at all times. The average Thai driver will respond positively to a smiling apology which defuses any delicate situation.

Thais strive to maintain equanimity in their lives and go to great lengths to avoid confrontation. The concept is called *kriengjai* and suggests an unwillingness to burden someone older or superior with one's problems. In many cases, it means not giving someone bad news until too late for fear it may upset the recipient.

Thais don't liking saying "no" too directly for fear of causing offense. In a common manifestation of kriengjai, giving no answer to a question, or evading a direct answer, is a considerate

pared, however, for questions considered rather impolite in Western societies, such as: How old are you? How much money do you earn? How much does that watch (camera, etc.) cost? Thais regard these questions as part of ordinary conversation and will not understand a reluctance to answer them.

If, however, one is reticent about divulging personal information, a joking answer delivered with a smile will usually suffice; for example, to the above question of "How old are you?", answer with "How old do you think?"

Be warned, however, that Thai people can be extraordinary flatterers. Speak a few words of Thai, and you will likely be pronounced *geng*, or "excellent", not to mention handsome or pretty, as the case may be. Smile, appreciate the compliment, and respond in kind. Remember that life is meant to be sanuk.

Government

Executive power is wielded by a prime minister selected by the majority party or a coalition of parties. He or she formulates and executes policies through a cabinet of 13 ministers.

While the prime minister and the parliament might seem far removed from the population,

> **GETTING ALONG THE THAI WAY**
>
> Although there is a significant Chinese population, not to mention the hill tribes, Thailand has little racial tension.

protests. In part, it reflects the sense of family that constantly appears in Thai conversations, and in exhortations to stand together against common enemies. Although Thai leaders are regarded paternalistically, they are increasingly held accountable for their actions.

Provincial governors are still appointed by the government in Bangkok, but most other local officials must now be elected for a fixed term, a change made to the constitution in 1995. Previously, they were elected for life, or else obtained posts through dubious means.

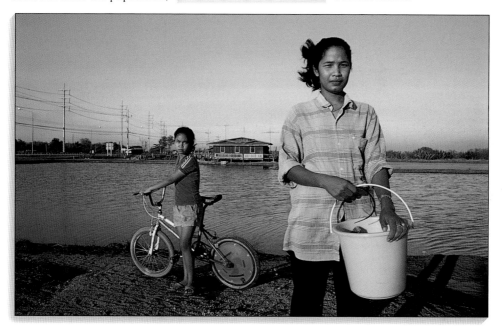

except perhaps at election time, they are, in fact, usually quite responsive to the electorate. It is not unusual for a delegation of disgruntled citizens to rent a fleet of buses to personally lodge a noisy protest in front of the parliament building or local government office against officials or a decree with which they disagree.

Ministers, even the prime minister, often talk with these delegations to remedy problems, although with the clamour generated by the surprisingly vocal and independent local press, it would be difficult for leaders to ignore their

LEFT: getting around in a set of modern wheels.
ABOVE: sisters along a canal (*khlong*) in Bangkok.

Military

For the first time in recent memory, the elected parliament has moved to the peak of political power in Thailand. After the turmoil of 1992, the constitution was changed to make it mandatory for the prime minister to be an elected member of parliament.

Previously, Thailand had generally been governed by generals, who traditionally had seized power by force or had been appointed to office by some of their fellows. Changes in the constitution since 1992 have weakened the political role of the military, but how the military will accept its diminished status over the long run has yet to be seen.

The military's role is vastly different from that in the West, but it is a role that has its roots in Thai history by which rulers and leaders rose out of the ranks of the military. In fact, the traditional avenue for advancement in all sectors of society has been the military. The Thai soldier, like the civil servant, belongs to a sprawling and complex organisation whose activities have most often gone beyond national defence. Thai conscripts serving obligatory two-year terms fill most of the lower ranks and perform duties of defending borders. The upper ranks, however, have been intimately involved in the business and government of Thailand.

SIZE MATTERS
Bangkok is over 35 times larger than the country's second- and third-largest cities, Khorat and Udon Thani.

High-ranking military officers sit on the boards of banks, own hotels, and take part in business even as they actively pursue military careers. It is one of the few occupations in which a bright but poor young man can achieve advancement on merit.

The military establishment is now such an integral part of Thai society that it is difficult to imagine life without it. Its meddling in government over the years, however, has been problematic and increasingly unpopular with the Thai people. Since 1992, the Thai military has promised to stay out of government, and its role has been further weakened by the financial crisis and currency devaluation that enveloped Thailand in 1997.

Women

The constitutional changes of 1995 also spelled out the equality of men and women. The constitution also says that a woman may now be the monarch, previously a forbidden possibility. Granted, true equality is by no means the norm in daily life, as in any society. But the improved status of women, and their greater share

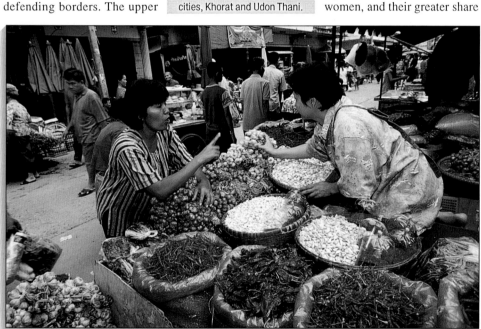

of power in society, has been one of the most remarkable changes of the past few decades. However, Thai women still suffer discrimination in land ownership, marriage, and citizenship. (In fact, however, women obtained the vote at the same time as men, in 1932.)

But in many ways, Thai women have generally been powerful and influential behind the scenes. A 15th-century Chinese visitor reported that "it is their custom that all affairs are managed by their wives, both the king and the common people. If they have matters that require thought and deliberation... all trading transactions great and small, they all follow the decision of their wives."

In big business, women have been at the top for generations, as it has been customary for men to go into government and the military. Today, women are particularly prominent in the hotel business, tourism, real estate, advertising, export trade, banking, and law. Women helm major companies and own several of the largest hotels in Bangkok. Women also head villages and occupy top positions in the civil service and medicine. The university population is almost equally male and female. If renting a house in Thailand, the rent is paid to a woman, no matter whose name is on the title to the property.

In Thailand, lower-class women have less power but often control the family purse strings and moral upbringing of the children. Women with lower levels of education can be found on construction sites, cleaning offices, running small businesses, and driving buses. On the other hand, lapses in enforcement combined with years of tradition have contributed to the exploitation of women in the sex industry.

Sexual attitudes

Most unfairly, Thailand has acquired a something of a reputation as a sexual playland in the West. Much emphasis has been placed on the exploitation and degradation of women and especially children.

To be sure, prostitution exists and to some extent has been established for many centuries. But less than 1 percent of the female population is involved in the commercial sex business, and child prostitution is in fact a rare phenomenon. Most Thais – the overwhelming majority of Thais – are conservative and indeed almost puritanical where sex is concerned. Outside of a few urban venues like Bangkok's Patpong, Soi Cowboy and Nana Plaza, or the Russian- and German-dominated bar scene of Pattaya, Thai society is usually the epitome of respectability and propriety where sex is concerned.

This said, Thai people are generally open-minded and sympathetic in their attitude towards people's sexuality. Sex is seen as a normal human function and, if practiced between consenting or married adults, it is definitely sanuk – who could doubt it? Attitudes towards consensual adult homosexuality are sympathetic, and this extends to a peculiarly Thai (or

Southeast Asian) phenomenon: transvestism. Thailand has more than its share of *katoeys*, or "lady men", transvestite men who are accepted for what they are, treated with understanding and respect, and generally addressed as women. In fact, the most popular nationally-ranked kickboxer in 1998 was a transvestite.

Terms of address

Thais are addressed by their first, rather than their last, names. The name is usually preceded by the word *khun*, a term of respect. Thus, Silpachai Krishnamra would be addressed as Khun Silpachai when someone speaks to him. You

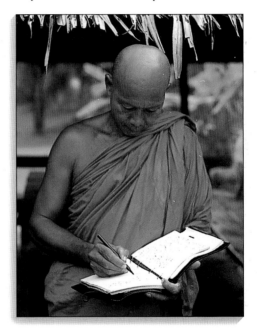

will find some Thais referred to in newspapers with the letters M.C., M.R. or M.L. preceding their names. These are royal titles normally translated as "prince" or "princess." The five-tier system reserves the highest two titles for the immediate royal family. After that comes the nobility, remnants of the noble houses of old. The highest of these three ranks is Mom Chao (M.C.), followed by Mom Rachawong (M.R.) and Mom Luang (M.L.). The title is not hereditary, thanks to a system that guarantees Thailand will never become top-heavy with princes and princesses. Each succeeding generation is born into a lower rank. Thus, the son or daughter of a Mom Chao is a Mom Rachawong. ❏

Left: bargaining in a Nonthaburi market.
Right: saffron-robed monk, near Surat Thani.

HILL TRIBES

One of Thailand's prime tourist draws, the hill tribes of the north – less than 2 percent of the population – have both benefited and suffered from this attention

The tribal people of Thailand make up less than two percent of the total population, but account for a significant degree of interest with visitors to Thailand. (This is in striking contrast to neighbouring Laos and Burma, where the shares are at least 30 percent and 15 percent, respectively, but without the

tice slash-and-burn (swidden) agriculture. In March, at the height of the dry season, they set massive fires to burn the undergrowth on the mountain sides. (Unfortunately, there's no longer much forest left to burn.) The ashes at first provide a rich fertiliser, but over the years the process depletes the soil. Villagers used to

tourist obsessiveness.) Thousands of foreigners annually trek to the tribal people's mountain villages. The average Thai views tribal people as foreigners, if not illegal aliens, and thus not entitled to the same rights as Thais. Most tribal immigration – from Burma or Laos – has occurred only in the past 100 years. In fact, only in the past decade have significant numbers of tribal people been granted Thai citizenship. They cling to the bottom rung of the steep Thai economic and social ladder.

Thailand is home for up to 20 tribes, but there are six principal groups: Karen, Hmong, Mien, Lahu, Lisu and Akha. Living in villages at higher elevations, most hill tribe farmers prac-

then move their villages to a new site, but there's no place to move nowadays. With poorer soil and less of it, villagers often rely on the opium poppy as a cash crop.

Karen

The 265,000 Karen form by far the largest tribe. In Thailand, they comprise two sub-groups, the Sgaw and Pwo, whose dialects are not mutually intelligible. (The karenic language belongs to the Tibeto-Burman linguistic group.) Karens have settled in Thailand since the 18th century and they are still (illegally) trickling in. In Burma, there are between 3 million and 4 million Karens, a Karen rebel state, and a Karen rebel army that has been fighting the Burmese government for over four decades.

Karens were early converts to Christianity when Burma was a British colony. Some Thai Karens are Baptists or Seventh-Day Adventists. But whether of Christian, Buddhist or animist beliefs, the Karens place a great emphasis on monogamy, look down on premarital sex, and can trace ancestry through the mother. Unlike other Thai tribes, they have long practiced lowland wet-rice farming.

NORTHERN HOMES

With the exception of the Karen, who extend down to Kanchanaburi and Tak provinces, most hill tribes live in the three northwestern provinces of Chiang Mai, Chiang Rai and Mae Hong Son.

Opium use is somewhat common. Kinship is patrilineal and polygamy is permitted. Like Thai, Hmong is an Austroasiatic language, meaning that its roots have been traced to southern China. In fact, four million Hmong live today in China's Yunnan Province. The White Hmong and Blue Hmong can be identified by their dialects and clothing: Blue Hmong women wear indigo, pleated skirts and their hair in huge buns. White Hmong women wear white hemp skirts and black turbans.

Hmong

The most recent arrivals in Thailand, Hmong are the second-largest hill tribe, numbering about 80,000. The majority immigrated in the 1950s and 1960s, fleeing from the long civil war in Laos. Ever on the alert for communists, the Thai military then regarded Hmong as subversives, and Hmong relations with Thai officialdom still remain edgy. Ironically, Hmong are renowned for their fierce independence and, in Laos, for anti-communism. Indeed, they were American allies during the Vietnam War.

Left: hill-tribe textile, and a White Hmong woman.
Above: Hmong with clothing of heavy black cotton.

Mien

Like Hmong, most Mien (Yao) probably came to Thailand from Laos, but there are large numbers in Burma, Vietnam and China's Yunnan Province – as well as Laotian Mien refugee communities in San Francisco and Seattle. Many Chinese elements, such as ancestor worship and Daoism, are evident in their animist religious beliefs. Kinship is patrilineal and polygamy is practiced. Mien place great emphasis on the peaceful resolution of conflict. Of all the hill tribes, they probably have the smoothest relations with Thais. Mien, including women, are often outgoing. Mien have also taken to the Thai dress of T-shirts, sarongs and jeans, but traditionally women wear black jackets and trousers, red fur-like collars and large blue or black turbans. Their dense, intricate embroideries are valued on bags and clothing. The language is Austroasiatic.

Lahu

Like the Karen, some of the 60,000 Lahu are Christian. Also like the Karen, traditional Lahu mix animism with millennial myths that have led them to be receptive to messianic movements; some hope for the return of a man-god called Geusha. Besides the usual opium, corn and rice, Lahu have successfully cultivated

chilli peppers as a cash crop. The traditional dress of the four groups – Red Lahu, Black Lahu, Yellow Lahu and Lahu Sheleh – is slightly different, but red and black jackets are common. Lahu are skilled makers of baskets and bags. Lahu languages are Tibeto-Burman.

Lahu are famed for their hunting prowess with both rifles and crossbows. Although leopards and tigers no longer roam the northern hills, Lahu continue to hunt bear, wild pigs, deer, squirrels, birds and snakes. Several hundred thousand Lahu live in Burma, where a small Lahu army, aligned with the Karen separatists, has fought the Burmese government since the 1970s.

Lisu

Although there are only about 25,000 Lisu, they are easily identified by their penchant for bright colours. Women wear long green or blue cotton dresses with striped yokes. Men wear baggy loose pants of the same colours. Lisu are good silversmiths and make jewelry for Akha and Lahu. Lisu are regarded by other tribal people as sharp businesspeople. Animist beliefs are combined with ancestor worship.

Lisu have a strong sense of self-esteem and will eagerly cite the reasons for the pre-eminence of their family, clan or village. Yet unlike other tribes, Lisu have an organisation that extends across villages. Lisu are a sub-group of the Kachins, a large minority group in the Kachin state in the far north of Burma. The Kachin languages are Tibeto-Burman.

Akha

Probably the poorest and the shyest of the hill tribes, the Akha have been the most resistant to assimilation by the Thais. Ironically, the 34,000 Akha are the people that most tourists want to see. The draw is the heavy ornate head-dress worn by the women. It consists of silver disks festooned with old coins, beads and feathers. And unlike other tribal women, who save their finery for ceremonies, Akha wear this even while tending the fields. Animists beliefs are mixed with ancestor worship; Akha can recite their ancestry back 20 generations.

An Akha village is extended by one of two gateways, which separate the domain of people and rice from that of spirits and wild animals. Akha neither farm nor consume opium. The language is Tibeto-Burman.

Other minorities

Strictly speaking, they are not Thai hill tribes, but two other groups, the Shan and Kayan, deserve mention, as their villages are frequent stops on trekking tours.

In their settled communities, rice-growing practices and Theravada Buddhism, the Shan are very similar to Thais. In fact, they are an ethnic Tai (Thai) group, also known as Thai Yai (Big Thai). Their language is similar to the northern Thai dialect, although not intelligible to central Thai speakers. Many Shans have immigrated to Thailand in recent times to escape the upheavals in Burma, but Shans may have been the first Tai inhabitants of northern

Thailand, in the 9th or 10th century. In the large area of Burma bordering the northern tip of Thailand is the home of 4 million Shans and several armies battling for autonomy. One of these was headed by the notorious opium trafficker, Khun Sa.

The Kayan (Padaung) are a Karennic people residing in the southern Shan areas. Until a few years ago, tours from Mae Hong Son would ferry tourists across the border to view Kayan women whose necks had been elongated by layers of heavy

DEADLY NECK RINGS

As successive rings are added to the necks of the so-called Kayan "giraffe women", the collar bone is pushed down and the neck muscles weaken. Removing the rings can thus be fatal.

Loss of culture

The cultures of Thailand's hill tribes are very much in danger of extinction. The chief culprit is not tourism. Greater threats are posed by a shortage of land, loss of land, resettlement, lack of land rights and citizenship, illiteracy and poor medical care. Official Thai hill-tribe policies have been shaped by the desire to discourage swidden farming and the cultivation of opium. Some of the crop substitution programs sponsored by the Thai government, United Nations and

brass rings. Kayan leaders, many of them Catholic, had long discouraged the practice and it had virtually died out. But the tourist attraction was so great that Thai officials allowed three villages to set up west of Mae Hong Son. Many Kayan women have since donned the rings and initiated girls beginning at age five. Tours to view the "Giraffe Women" have been heavily promoted in Bangkok. The 1,000 tourists daily are thus responsible for the reintroduction of a barbaric practice.

LEFT: distinctive headdress of an Akha woman, which are worn even in the fields. **ABOVE:** Mien women in their traditional – and daily – attire.

foreign governments have been very successful. Tribal people are marketing coffee, tea and fruit. But as trekkers amongst the hill tribes can observe, such projects have not penetrated to villages distant from roads and transport.

Some farmers have also resisted switching to non-opium cash crops because of the capital investment involved. They already know how quickly one can get into a crippling debt with (the usually Chinese) moneylenders.

According to development experts, wiser policies would attempt to ensure that villagers can grow enough to feed themselves. If they could do that, they wouldn't need to grow and sell opium to buy rice. ❐

CUSTOMS AND FESTIVALS THROUGHOUT THAILAND

Many festivals and feasts are held throughout the year and visitors should be able to attend at least one celebration during their stay. Loy Krathong, Bun Bang and Songkran are especially worth seeing.

Songkran, one of the most important festivals in the Thai calendar, comes from the Sanskrit and means the beginning of a new solar year. During this festival, people wear new clothes and visit their local *wat* to offer food to the monks. Housewives clean their homes on the eve of the festival and throw out anything old or broken so it will not bring bad luck. On the afternoon of April 13, Buddha images are bathed as part of the ceremony. Young people pour scented water into the hands of their elders and parents as a mark of respect and ask for their blessing. The Songkran custom of throwing water is thought to derive from a rain-making ceremony. According to myth, *naga* (mythical serpents) brought rain by spouting water from the seas. The more seawater they spouted, the more rain there would be, which is why, apart from it being good fun, Thai people throw water at this time of year.

   Another custom during this time is the releasing of caged birds and live fish, which are sold in the markets for this occasion. This part of the festival remembers the time when the central plains of Thailand were flooded during the rainy season. After the earth had dried, little pools of water were left which often trapped young fish. Farmers caught the fish and then released them back into the water on Songkran, thereby gaining merit and preserving a food source.

FESTIVAL OF LIGHTS

Loy Krathong is one of the most beautiful Thai festivals. *Loy* means "to float" and a *krathong* is a leaf cup traditionally made of banana leaf. The festival is not strictly Buddhist, but the floating of krathongs is thought to bring good luck. When the full moon rises, the krathongs are taken to the banks of waterways, and small candles and incense sticks inside them are lit. A prayer is said as they are launched into the water. Children often swim out to collect coins that are put inside the krathongs.

PLANTING TIME ▷
The Royal Ploughing Ceremony takes place in the Sanam Luang at the time of rice planting, in May. Monks bless rice seeds that are scattered over the fields.

◁ **WINTER FESTIVALS**
Nearly all of the country's temples and provinces have festival days, which tend to occur during the cool season.

SPRING FLOWERS
The Chiang Mai flower festival takes place on the first weekend in February. The town has a parade of floral floats and marching bands, holds beauty contests, and produces beautiful displays of the town's cultivated flora.

▽ AUTUMN CANDLES
Loy Krathong is held on the night of the full moon in the 12th lunar month (usually mid November). Small leaf boats contain candle, incense, and often a coin.

WHEN THE MOON SHINES BRIGHT

As Thailand is a Buddhist country, several religious holidays are attached to the lunar calendar and held on nights of the full moon. Visakha Puja (above) is a nationwide public holiday. It falls on the 15th day of the waxing moon in the sixth lunar month, which is May. This is the date of Buddha's birth, enlightenment and entry into *nirvana*.

On this night, devout Thais and their families gather at *wat* to hear a sermon on the life of Buddha given by the chief monk. As the moon rises, they hold a candle, incense stick and flowers between their hands, which are placed in a position of prayer. The monks of the wat then lead a procession three times around the temple *bot* (ordination hall), and the candles and incense are placed in a tray at the front of the bot. It is a solemn and moving ceremony that only a few foreign visitors will be invited to attend.

Visakha Puja has been celebrated in Thailand since 1300 AD. The ceremony was revised in 1817 and its observance was strengthened by Rama IV. During his reign, three nights were devoted to reading the *Life of Buddha*. Today, reading from this text is limited to one evening; however, several temples hold religious ceremonies that last until the dawn of the following day.

◁ NEW YEAR SPLASH
Songkran is the Thai new year festival, celebrated from 13 to 16 April. It involves lots of good-natured water throwing – so be prepared to get rather wet, if not drenched.

MAY MAYHEM ▷
The Bun Bang Fai or rocket festival is celebrated in the northeast, especially in Yasothon. Rockets are fired into the sky to bring rain at the end of the dry season.

RELIGION

A sense of spirituality sifts through most every aspect of Thai daily life.
At its foundation is Buddhism, with a distinctly Thai texture

*I*n the pale light of early morning, a young saffron-robed monk walks with grave dignity along a city street, a cloth bag over one arm, a metal alms bowl cradled in the other. Silently, he opens his alms bowl to receive the offerings – not handouts – of rice and curries placed in it by ordinary Thais, who have stood for a long while before their homes awaiting his arrival. He says not a word of thanks, because, according to Buddhist tenets, he is doing them a favour, providing them a means to make merit so they can be reborn in the next life as higher beings. Turning, he continues to walk on bare feet to the next set of alms givers, following the steps of monks before him for 2,000 years.

Buddhism – a philosophy, rather than a religion – has played a profound role in shaping the Thai character, particularly in the people's reactions to events.

The Buddhist concept of the impermanence of life and possessions, and of the necessity to avoid extremes of emotion or behaviour, has done much to create the relaxed, carefree charm that is one of the most appealing characteristics of the people. Tension, ulcers, nervous breakdowns and the like are not unknown in Thailand, at least not in places like Bangkok. But they are still fairly uncommon, in no small way due to the influence of Buddhism.

Buddhism first came to Southeast Asia from India as early as the 4th century, and was passed to the Thais by way of the Mon and Khmer kingdoms between the 10th and 12th centuries. King Ramkamhaeng introduced Theravada Buddhist influence to Thailand from Sri Lanka (Ceylon) in the 13th century, after he invited Ceylonese monks to reform the Khmer-influenced Buddhism then being practiced in his Sukhothai kingdom.

The basic form of Buddhism now practiced

PRECEDING PAGE: nearly every Thai male spends time as a monk, at any age. **LEFT:** lighted candles and lotus buds at Bangkok's Wat Benchamabophit. **RIGHT:** the golden glow of a temple's Buddha image.

in Thailand is Theravada, sometimes also called Hinayana, or "lesser vehicle". Originating in India, Theravada is also practiced in neighbouring Burma, but even a casual visitor to temples in both countries will quickly perceive differences between them. As they have done with most outside influences – Khmer temple

decorations and Chinese food, for instance – over the centuries the Thais have evolved a Buddhism of their own.

In addition to Theravada Buddhism, there is the Mahayana (Greater Vehicle) Buddhism practiced by those of Chinese descent. Their shrines can be found throughout Bangkok, and in most towns of Thailand. To the visitor stepping into a *sanjao,* or shrine, it is immediately evident that Mahayana is observed with more vigour. Incense smoke clouds the air, sticks are shaken out of canisters to tell fortunes, paper money is burned for use by deceased ancestors, bells are rung and the din of piety permeates every corner.

Temple life

Thailand's 300,000 monks typically live in a *wat,* practicing and teaching the rules of human conduct laid down by the Buddha more than 2,500 years ago. There are literally hundreds of Buddhist wat in the cities and suburbs, usually sited in serene pockets of densely-packed neighbourhoods and serving as hubs for spiritual and social life.

The term wat defines a large walled compound made up of several buildings, including a *bot* or hall where new monks are ordained, and one or more *viharn* where sermons are delivered. It may also contain a belltower, a *ho trai* (library), and *guti,* or monk meditation cells, as well as stupas, called *chedi* in Thailand. Chedi contain the ashes or relics of wealthy donors, or of important persons, emulating the Buddha whose ashes and relics were placed, by his instruction, in a mound of earth.

There may even be a school on the premises to educate the local children. And if there is any open space in temple the grounds, it is a sure bet that it will be filled with happy kids playing soccer or *takraw.*

The total number of monks in residence at Thailand's 28,000 wat varies from season to season, swelling during the rainy season, the

normal time for a young man to enter the priesthood. Thai tradition requires that every Buddhist male enter the monkhood for a period ranging from seven days to six months, or even a lifetime. Regulations require that government offices and the military give a man time off to enter the monkhood; companies customarily grant leave time with pay for male employees entering the monkhood.

The entry of a young man into monkhood is seen as repayment to parents for his upbringing, and as bestowing special merit on them, particularly his mother. Since women cannot be ordained, it is the son, as monk, who also makes merit for his mother and other female relatives.

That merit advances her along the road to *nirvana*, which is attained for her, as for all Buddhists, when she acquires so much merit that she vanishes from the painful cycle of earthly death and rebirth.

Prior to being ordained, the would-be monk is shorn of all his hair. He then answers a series of questions put to him by the abbot to assure that the newcomer is in good mental and physical health. He then moves to a monks' dormitory, or to a small *kuti* or meditation house.

SIGNIFICANT NAMES

Wat that were founded by Thai royalty, or perhaps hold a special sacred status because something revered is kept within, often have names that begin with *Maha-*, *Rat-*, or *Ratcha-*.

in a group separate from the men, and receive whatever food has not earlier been consumed by the monks. A Buddhist monk must not only abstain from stealing, lying and idle talk, taking life, indulgence in sex, intoxicants, luxuries and frivolous amusements, he must also obey no fewer than 227 rules that govern the minutiae of daily conduct and manners. Except amongst the Dhammakaiya sect, in practice the monk usually observes ten basic rules. He can have no possessions except the yellow robe, the

While in the temple, he listens to sermons based on the Buddha's teachings, studies the *Tripitaka,* or *Three Baskets* (the teaching of Buddha in Pali), practices meditation, and learns the virtues of an ascetic life. He shares in the work of the monastery: washing dishes, keeping the quarters clean. He goes out at dawn to receive his daily food.

There are nuns who wear white robes, but they do not share the same rights as the monks, as there is no provision for the ordination of women. They live in side areas of the wat, chant

alms bowl and a few personal necessities. He eats two meals a day, the first early in the morning and the second before noon. A monk is forbidden to touch money, sleep on a comfortable bed, sing or dance.

Communal centre

For all its Spartan life, however, a Buddhist wat in Thailand is by no means isolated from the real world. Most wat have schools of some sort attached to them; in fact, for centuries, the only schools in most of Thailand were those run by monks. The wat has traditionally been the centre of social and communal life in the villages, with monks serving as herbal doctors, psycho-

LEFT: monk's quarters at Wat Arun, Bangkok.
ABOVE: morning offerings, Wat Benchamabophit.

logical counsellors, and arbitrators of disputes. Monks also play an important part in daily life, such as the blessing of a new building, or a birthday or funeral.

Except during the period of Buddhist Lent, from July to October, monks are free to travel about from one temple to another at will. Moreover, the wat are open to anyone who wishes to retire to them.

On *wan phra,* a day each week determined by the lunar calendar, Thais go to the wat to listen to monks chant scriptures

> **FOOLISH BELIEFS?**
>
> King Mongkut (Rama IV), who welcomed Christian missionaries to Siam and learned English from them, said to them: "What you teach us to do is admirable, but what you teach us to believe is foolish".

as are many funeral rites. The rites of statecraft pertaining to the royal family are presided over by Brahman priests. One of the most popular and impressive of these, the Ploughing Ceremony, takes place each May in Bangkok to signal the beginning of the rice planting season. A team of sacred oxen is offered a selection of grains. Astrologers watch carefully, as the grains that the oxen choose will determine the amount of rainfall and the degree of success or failure of the year's crops. Afterwards, the

and deliver sermons. In addition to providing monks with food, the laity earns merit by making repairs on the temple or, even better, replacing an old and derelict building with a new one. At the end of the Lenten season, groups of Thais board boats or buses and travel to distant villages to make donations, an occasion filled with as much riotous and festive celebration as solemn ceremony.

Brahman influences

Many of the Thais' non-Buddhist beliefs are Brahman in origin, and even today Brahman priests officiate at major ceremonies. The Thai wedding ceremony is almost entirely Brahman,

oxen draw a gilded plow around the field and seeds are symbolically sown (and afterwards eagerly collected by farmers to bring them luck). The head priest, after complex calculations, makes predictions on the forthcoming rain and bounty of the next harvest.

Spirits and spirit houses

The variety of *phi* (spirits) in Thailand is legion, outnumbering the human population many times over. A seductive female phi, believed to reside in a banana plant, torments young men who come near. Another bothersome one takes possession of her victims and forces them to remove their clothes in public. (The most destructive spirits apparently are only female.)

A very common sight in any town in Thailand, including sophisticated Bangkok, is a small house, generally set atop a post on a site selected after complex astrological consideration. In ordinary residences, the house may resemble a Thai dwelling; in hotels and offices, it may be an elaborate mini-temple, made of cement and painted and gilded.

In either case, these spirit houses serve as the abodes of the locality spirits. It is within their power to favour or plague the human inhabitants, so the spirit house is regularly adorned with placatory offerings of food, fresh flowers and incense sticks. If calamity or ill luck befalls the compound, it may be necessary to call in an expert to consult the unhappy spirit to determine what is wrong.

One of the most famous spirit houses in Bangkok is the Erawan Shrine, at the intersection of Ratchadamri and Ploenchit roads, adjacent the Hyatt Regency. This shrine, honouring the Hindu god Brahma, was erected by the owners during the construction of the original hotel in the 1950s, after several workers were injured in mysterious accidents. The shrine soon acquired a widespread reputation for bringing good fortune to outsiders as well.

A less well-known shrine sits in the compound of the Hilton Hotel. Its offerings consist entirely of phalluses, ranging from small to gargantuan, sculpted from wood, wax, stone or cement with full fidelity to life. They are left by women hoping to conceive a child.

To the average Thai, there is nothing inconsistent about the intermingling of such practices and beliefs with Buddhism. In the end, although deeply founded on Buddhism, Thai beliefs are both pragmatically and spiritually harmonious with the needs of the Thai people.

Protective amulets

Nearly every Thai male, and a large number of women as well, carry some sort of amulet, usually on a chain around their necks. Some wear as many as half a dozen charms to protect them from automobile accidents, gunfire, snakebite and almost any other disaster. In the provinces,

tattoos ward off evil. Astrologers are consulted regularly to learn auspicious times for weddings, important journeys, moving into a new house, and even the promulgation of a constitution or other governmental action.

Religious tolerance

A little over 90 percent of the Thai people are Buddhist, but religious tolerance is (and always has been) extended to other religions. Around 6 percent of Thais are Muslim, with the remainder Christian, Hindu and Sikh. Indeed, the national constitution declares that the king is the "upholder" of all religions.

Islam is the second largest religion in Thailand, and all over the country, but especially in the south, there are hundreds of mosques. The Thai government contributes to the repair and construction of these mosques, as well as to the Buddhist temples.

Christian missionaries have struggled for more than a century for converts in Thailand, without great success. Today, there are around 500,000 Christians in Thailand. King Mongkut suggested that Christianity had succeeded only where the indigenous religion was weak. There are pockets of Christians – notably protestants in Chiang Mai and Catholics in Chanthaburi – but few steeples amidst the chedi spires. ❐

LEFT: an extravagant and large spirit house. **RIGHT:** a *malai*, made of jasmine flowers; while beautiful at first, as it finally withers and decays, the malai reflects the impermanence of things and life.

IMAGES OF THE BUDDHA

From the gigantic seated Buddha at Wat Si Chum to tiny Buddhas worn as amulets, Thai artists have produced religious icons that rank among the world's greatest expressions of Buddhist art.

Images of the Buddha are devotional objects and are not considered to be works of art by their makers. When artists make an image of the Buddha, they follow specific rules – the Buddha is defined by a set of peculiar characteristics, a particular monastic garb and a series of *mudra* (attitudes, postures or gestures). The 32 bodily marks, evident at the time of the Buddha's birth, include hands that reach the knees without bending, a lion-like jaw, and wheel marks on the base of the feet. Buddhist artists have interpreted these marks according to the era in which they were working and the school of interpretation they chose to follow.

SUKHOTHAI SCHOOL

Thai Buddhist imagery was at its artistic height during the Sukhothai period (late 13th to early 15th centuries), when the smoothness and sheen of cast metals perfectly matched the graceful, elongated simplicity of the basic form. During this era, the Buddha was usually represented sitting cross- legged or with one foot forward in the "striding" position. One hand is raised in *abhayamudra* (dispelling fear). Slightly androgynous in appearance, the images also feature a flame-like *ketumula* on the crown of the head, protruding heels, flat soles and toes all the same length.

◁ **SPIRITUAL DETAILS**
Thai artists simplify anatomical details in their images of the Buddha to emphasise the spiritual qualities of Buddhism and to convey enigma and serenity.

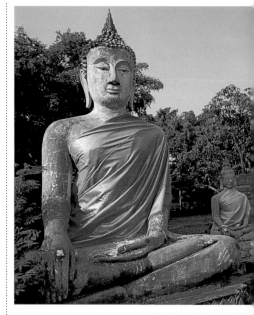

COLOSSAL CHEDI ▷
This standing Buddha in Phra Pathom Chedi, Nakhon Pathom, is said to be the world's tallest monument of its type. The relic chamber was raised to its present height of 125 metres (410 ft) in 1860.

▽ **FASTING FIGURE**
This statue of a fasting Buddha is in the grounds of Wat U Mong, in Chiang Mai. The wat was founded in 1371 by King Ku Na.

SYMBOLISM OF MUDRAS

The Buddha can be seen either sitting, standing, lying or, in Thailand, walking. Every image of the Buddha is represented in a particular *mudra* or attitude. Hand gestures in particular are key iconographical elements in representations of the Buddha:

• *Abhayamudra* is the mudra of dispelling fear or giving protection: the Buddha is usually in a standing position, the right hand raised and turned outwards to show the palm with straight fingers.

• *Bhumisparcamudra* or calling the earth as witness: this is made by a seated figure, with the right hand on the knee and the fingertips touching the ground.

• *Dharmacakramudra* means spinning the Wheel of Law: both hands are held in front of the body, with the fingertips of the left hand resting against the palm of the right hand.

• *Dhyanamudra* is the meditation mudra: the hands rest flat in the lap, one on top of the other.

• *Varamudra*, giving blessing or charity: made by the seated or standing Buddha with the right arm pointing downwards, the palm open and fingers more or less straight.

• *Vitarkamudra* is the preaching mudra: the end of the thumb and index finger of the right hand touch to form a circle, symbolising the Wheel of Law.

SUKHOTHAI SCHOOL

Buddha images at Wat Phra Si Sanphet, Ayutthaya, are seen in the attitude of *Bhumisparcamudra* (calling the earth as witness). The images date from the 13th and 14th centuries.

▽ WHEEL OF LAW

This Chinese-style Buddha can be found in Chiang Rai, at Wat Phra Singh. The Buddha is represented in the *Vitarkamudra* (preaching mode). The gesture of the right hand symbolises the Wheel of Law.

△ RECLINING GIANT

Phra Phuttahatmongkol in Wat Hat Yai Nai is the world's third largest reclining Buddha (attaining *parinibbana* – nirvana – in death). It measures 35 metres (115 ft) from head to toe. Visitors can climb inside the Buddha's chest.

▽ SEATED IMAGE

The Temple of the Big Buddha, Ko Samui, contains a modern 12 metre (40 ft) Buddha in the attitude of *Bhumisparcamudra*.

PERFORMING ARTS

In Thailand, performances of dance and drama are nearly one and the same.

Many performances are derived from an epic tale, Ramakien

The Thai people have combined a lively imagination, a superb aesthetic sense and a fine hand to produce some of the most detailed and arresting visual arts found in Asia. In the performing arts, Thai dance-dramas are among the world's most dazzling, with elaborate and colourful costumes, and graceful, enchanting movements.

When discussing Thai theatre, one cannot use the word "drama" without uttering the word "dance" immediately before it. The two are inseparable, the dancer's hands and body expressing the emotions that the silent lips do not. In effect, the actor is a mime, with the story line and lyrics provided by a singer and chorus to the side of the stage. An orchestra creates not only the atmosphere, but an emotive force.

It is thought that the movements of dance-drama originated in *nang yai* (shadow puppet) performances of the 16th and 17th centuries. Huge buffalo hides were cut into the shapes of characters from the *Ramakien*. Against a translucent screen, which was back-lit by torches, puppeteers manipulated these figures to tell complex tales of good and evil. As they moved the hide figures across the screen, the puppeteers danced the emotions they wanted the stiff figures to convey. It is thought that these movements evolved into an independent theatrical art.

The most popular form of dance-drama is the *khon*, performed by dancers wearing brilliantly-crafted masks. An evening's entertainment comprises several episodes from the *Ramakien*. (The entire *Ramakien* would take 720 hours to perform, slightly longer than even the most feverish theatre-goer is prepared to endure.)

The expressionless masks focus the viewer's attention on the dancers' movements, where one sees grace and control of surpassing beauty – a dismissive flick of the hand, a finger pointed in

accusation, a foot stamped in anger. The favourite character is Hanuman, in his white monkey mask, whose dance movements would tax even the strongest viewer. Only the characters of Rama, Sita and Phra Lak appear without masks, but features are kept stiff, looking very much like masks.

The most graceful of the dramatic arts is the *lakhon*. There are two forms: the *lakhon nai* ("inside" lakhon), which was once performed only inside the palace walls, and then only by women, and the *lakhon nawk* ("outside" lakhon), performed beyond the palace walls by men. Of the two, lakhon nai is the more popular entertainment.

Garbed in costumes as elaborate as their movements, the performers glide slowly about the stage, even in the most emotional moments, their faces impassive and devoid of smiles or expression. The heavily stylised movements convey the plot and are quite enchanting, though for most foreign visitors, 30 minutes is

PRECEDING PAGE: young classical dancers at the royal court. **LEFT:** a painted screen depicting *nang yai*, or shadow puppets. **RIGHT:** young dancers in traditional dance costumes.

sufficient to absorb the essentials of the play. Lakhon's rich repertoire includes the *Ramakien* and tales that have romantic story lines.

There have always been two cultures in Thailand: palace and village. The village arts are often parodies of the palace arts, but more like burlesques with pratfalls and heavy-handed humour. *Likay* is the village form of lakhon. Broad, bawdy humour is its mainstay, played out against gaudy backdrops to an audience that walks in and out of the performance at will, eating and talking and having a good time, regardless of what takes place on stage. It is possible to glimpse likay at a *wat* (temple) fair, or at Bangkok's Lak Muang, when a resident troupe is hired by a worshipper to give thanks for a wish granted. Another venue for hired performances is the Erawan Shrine, in Bangkok. A variant often seen in markets is *lakhon ling*, the monkey theatre in which the roles are played, oddly enough, by monkeys.

Bangkok's *ngiew* or Chinese opera theatres have closed their doors forever, victims of television with its unending *qong-fu* programs. Wandering in a market at night, however, one may come across a performance that has been arranged as part of the entertainment during a funeral. (Grief is experienced privately; what

INDIAN EPICS

One of the two great Indian epics informing Thai theatre and dance is the *Ramayana*. (The other is the *Mahabharata*.) From the Sanskrit meaning "romance of Rama", the *Ramayana* is the basis for many regional epic tales, including the *Ramakien* in Thailand. It's a moral tale, full of instructions and examples for leading the ethical life. In its homeland, India, the *Ramayana* has been told for 3,000 years. With the spread of Indian culture throughout Southeast Asia, the *Ramayana* has become part of the mythology of Burma, Laos, Cambodia, Indonesia, and Thailand. (See page 101 for more on the *Ramakien*.)

one shares with friends is happiness.) They may also be seen at wat fairs during the winter.

Puppet theatre has also lost most of its Bangkok audiences to television, but a few troupes remain. *Hoon krabok* puppets, similar to Punch and Judy puppets, tell the story of Phra Aphaimani. Delicately crafted, they are charming to watch. Performances are often arranged by major hotels for their guests during the year-end holiday season.

Modern Thai drama has yet to come into its own in a major way. Leading hotels produce stage plays, but they are primarily for popular entertainment – soap operas, comedies, and translations from Western plays.

Rural performances

The counterparts to the grace and beauty of classical dance are the more traditional and less structured dances performed in rural villages by farm families. Each region has a special form unique to it.

Harvest, fingernail, candle and fishing dances are performed by groups of women in village costumes. In flirtation dances, they are joined by male dancers attempting to weave romantic spells on unsmiling but appreciative partners.

> **MOOD MUSIC**
>
> Listen to Thai music as one would jazz, picking out one of the instruments and following it, then switching to another instrument as the mood moves one.

regard to how others are playing it. (Some say the same about Thai politics.)

Seldom does an instrument rise in uninterrupted solo; it is always being challenged, cajoled by the other instruments of the orchestra. In a sense, it is the aural counterpart to Thai classical painting, with every space filled and a number of separate strands woven together, seemingly at random but with a distinct pattern. A classical *phipat* music orchestra is made up of a single reed instrument, the oboe-like *phinai*, and a vari-

Music

Classical Thai music eludes many finely-tuned Western ears. To the uninitiated, it sounds like a mishmash of contrasting tones without any pattern. To aficionados, it has a very distinct rhythm and plan.

Thai music is set to a scale of seven full steps, but it is normally played as a pentatonic scale (the scale of *Auld Lang Syne*). The rhythm is lilting and steady, with speeds varying according to section. Each instrument plays the same melody but in its own way, seemingly without

---

LEFT: dance-drama students learning the moves.
ABOVE: *phipat* ensemble, with oboe-like *phinai*.

ety of percussion instruments. The pitch favours the treble, with the result that the music sounds airy rather than stentorian. The pace is set by the *ching*, a tiny cymbal, aided by the drums beaten with the fingers. The melody is played by two types of *ranad*, a bamboo-bar xylophone and two sets of *gong wong*, tuned gongs arranged in a semicircle around the player. Another type of orchestra employs two violins, the *saw-oo* and the *saw-duang*. It is usually heard accompanying a Thai dance-drama.

The *ja-kae*, a stringed instrument similar to a Japanese *koto*, sits flush with the floor and is often played as a solo instrument in the lobbies of some of Bangkok's larger hotels and restaurants. A separate type of orchestra performs at a Thai boxing match to spur the combatants to action. It is composed of four instruments: the ching, two double-reed oboe-like flutes, and a drum. It plays a repertoire entirely its own.

Originating in the countryside, but having found a permanent home in the city as well, are the *klawng yao* or long drums. They are thumped along with gongs and cymbals as accompaniment to group singing. Never played solemnly, they lend an exuberant note to any occasion – and for a Thai, it doesn't take much of an excuse to have an occasion. It may be a procession on the way to ordain a new monk, a

bus trip upcountry, or a *kathin* ceremony in the late autumn, when groups of Buddhists board boats to travel upriver to give robes to monks at the end of the three-month lenten season.

Literature

Thais have always placed a heavy emphasis on oral tradition, and it's a good thing, too, because most of its printed classical literature was completely destroyed by the flames of Ayutthaya's destruction in 1767.

Moreover, as tropical insects have a particular relish for the palm-leaf paper on which manuscripts were traditionally written, books are manifest examples of the Buddhist tenet that

nothing is permanent. The classical works existing today came from late-night sessions during the reigns of Rama I and II, when scholars delved into their collective memories and, on breeze-cooled palace verandas, recreated an entire literature.

At the heart of Thai literature is the *Ramakien*, the Thai version of the Indian classical tale, *Ramayana*. This enduring story has found a home in the literature of every Southeast Asian nation. In Thailand, it forms the basis of a dance-drama tradition. Understanding it allows one to comprehend a wide variety of dramatic forms, its significance for Thailand's monarchs who have adopted the name Rama as their own, and its role as model for exemplary social behaviour.

The *Ramakien* is the vividly told tale of the god-king Rama and his beautiful wife, Sita, paragon of beauty and virtue, and a model for all wives to follow.

Sita is abducted by the nasty 10-headed, 20-armed demon king Tosakan, who imprisons her in his palace on the island of Longka (Sri Lanka), importuning her at every turn to divorce Rama and marry him. With his brother Phra Lak, Rama sets off in pursuit, stymied by mammoth obstacles that test his mettle. Along the way, he is joined by the magical white monkey-god, Hanuman, a mischievous but talented general who is one of the Thais' favourite characters. Hanuman and his army of monkeys build a bridge to Longka. After a pitched battle, Tosakan is killed, Sita is rescued, and everyone lives happily ever after.

Another classical work, pure Thai in its flavour and treatment, is *Khun Chang, Khun Phaen*, a love triangle involving a beautiful young woman with two lovers – one a rich, bald widower, and the other, a poor but handsome young man. This ancient soap opera provides a useful insight into Thai customs, manners and morals of the Ayutthaya era.

Written by Sunthorn Phu, the poet laureate of the early 18th century, *Phra Aphaimani* is the story of a rebellious prince who refuses to study to be king, instead playing the flute, much to the disgust of his father. After numerous exciting adventures, this prodigal son returns home to don the crown and rule his father's realm. ❐

LEFT: traditional *nang yai* performance of *Ramakien*.
RIGHT: masked characters from *Ramakien*.

The Ramakien

If Thai literature has a long tradition and a short history, there can be no better illustration than the *Ramakien*, the Thai version of the Indian legend *Ramayana*, an epic tale that arrived in what later became Thailand some 1,000 to 2,000 years ago, with the first wave of Buddhist missionaries from Sri Lanka.

As was true for many early cultures around the world, in Southeast Asia there were few written languages, or limited literacy, and the history, myths and stories of the various peoples were passed down orally by skilled storytellers from generation to generation. In retelling the *Ramayana*, the characters and tangled plot remained, but the tale changed, becoming identifiably Thai as character names were changed and various Buddhist ceremonial elements were added to what was, originally, a Hindu text. It was not until when the Thai capital was in Ayutthaya – named for the primary city in the *Ramayana* – that the work was finally transcribed. Sadly, only fragments of that version of the epic story remained following the sack of the city in 1767 by the Burmese, who burned virtually all of the written literature. Today, it is a required part of the school curriculum, so it is an allegory of the triumph of good over evil that is familiar to virtually every Thai.

The story opens in India with a demon, who was given great physical strength by Shiva, the Hindu lord of the universe. Betraying the trust, the demon rolled up the surface of the Earth like a carpet, removing all signs of life so he could be the sole survivor. Shiva called on the powerful god Vishnu the Preserver for vengeance, who turned himself into a white boar, decapitating the demon with his tusks and restoring life to the planet.

Upon returning to his celestial home in the Cosmic Ocean, Vishnu meditated until a lotus appeared, unfolding to reveal a young man who was taken to Shiva as the future king. Shiva dispatched the god Indra to find a new city for the king, travelling on a white elephant named Erawan, leading a host of angels to Earth. A city called A-Yu-Da-Ya was founded, named for four hermits who resided there, praying for 4,000 years, a paradisiacal metropolis with a bejeweled palace, sumptuous gardens, and 56,000 maidens to cater to the king's every whim.

And this is merely the start of the story. Immodest or subtle the *Ramakien* is not, and in this lush and exuberant excess lay much of its popularity.

Battles were of such cosmic proportion that a collaboration between Steven Spielberg and Walt Disney would be required to convey them properly. Fire streamed from a god's third eye to vaporise demons caught debauching celestial maidens. A magical snake arrow was sent to coil itself around an enemy and elevate him into a fearsome thunderstorm. Hanuman was able to levitate and fly, aiding his beloved master, Phra Ram, the king of Ayutthaya (and a reincarnation of Vishnu), to defeat the dreaded King Thotsakan of Longka (Sri Lanka), the 10-headed villain who had kidnapped Phra Ram's wife. It is an imaginative and captivating tale that blends romance, high adventure, and fantasy,

three key elements that some say are essential to understanding life in Thailand today. In fact, in the earliest written Thai version, there were 60,000 verses, 25 percent more than were in the Sanskrit original transcribed in Sri Lanka. A performance of the 138 acts, or episodes, involving more than 300 characters, lasted longer than 700 hours. Today, popular episodes may be seen in briefer performances of Thai classical dance, *khon*.

Artistic representations of the plot and characters may also be seen in murals and bas-relief throughout the country, from stone carvings at Prasat Hin Phimai and other Angkor-period temples in northeastern Thailand to wall paintings at Bangkok's oldest temple, Wat Po. ■

Arts and Crafts

With numerous cultural and aesthetic influences from around Asia, it's no wonder
that Thailand's creative arts and crafts have nearly a universal appeal

As is true of its architecture, music, religion, and cuisine, the handicrafts of Thailand are the clever result of outside ingredients being stirred by skilled practitioners over centuries to form something clearly and uniquely Thai. Someone with some knowledge in the field may say, "That bit's Chinese...and

that bit's Indian...and that bit's European," yet it must also be concluded that the effect, the end-product, is entirely home-grown.

Thailand is renowned worldwide as a centre of flourishing arts and crafts – one of the reasons it's a shopper's delight – and the best-known arguably are the textiles, most notably the colourful, shimmering silk. Villagers in the northeast had woven and worn silk for centuries, but it wasn't until after World War II – when the leading silk industries in Japan, China, Italy, and France were destroyed – that Thailand emerged as a primary source. Credit is given to an American expatriate, Jim Thompson, who organised provincial weavers, introduced long-

lasting chemical dyes and improved looms, and took samples of the gleaming cloth to New York. There, the costumes were made from his silk for a new Broadway musical, *The King and I*. *Vogue* magazine followed along and within a short time, a world market had been created. Most of the raw silk is still being produced on northeastern silkworm farms and manufactured by a number of companies, in addition to the prominent Jim Thompson stores. Thailand also produces excellent cotton garments and, from the hill tribes in the north, skirts and other items with remarkable embroidery. The best are from the Lisu tribe.

Thailand is equally famous for its gold and silver jewellery and gemstones, now the country's sixth-largest export category (behind the far less glamourous computer parts, garments, integrated circuits, rubber, and sugar). It commands a part of the global jewellery market rivalled only by Sri Lanka and India. In the Ayutthaya and early Bangkok eras, gold's use in a variety of royal household items, such as cosmetic jars and tableware, as well as on thrones and ceremonial objects, brought honour to the owners and to the artisans who were commissioned by royal and other wealthy families. Today, most of the gold jewellery sold is less imaginative, taking the form of heavy chains purchased as a hedge against a fluctuating currency and as a status item.

More affordable items in great variety are fashioned from silver. Not so long ago, the silver used came from melted-down Indian, Burmese and French coins from Indochina. Nowadays, most of it is imported and then pounded into delicate and ornately crafted trays, boxes, bowls, and other containers noted for their raised designs. The finest work is done in the north and usually sold in shops in Chiang Mai and Chiang Rai.

Most of the gems sold in Thailand today are imported from neighbouring Burma and Cambodia, the bulk arriving in Thailand by sometimes questionable means. A hundred years ago, gems were set in gold and silver jewellery noted more for the artistic fittings than for the stones themselves. Precious stones also played a prominent role in the decoration of crowns and other royal implements. The Nine Gems of the Brahman faith – diamonds, rubies, emeralds, yellow sapphires, blue sapphires, garnets, moonstones, zircons, and the cat's eye – were thought to have special powers.

Contemporary Thai jewellery, some of it adapted from traditional Thai motifs, still utilises a variety of stones, but more and more, they are being purchased

CRYSTAL POWER

In the Ayutthaya period, generals rode into battle on elephants, wearing sashes encrusted with jewels the generals believed would give them protection and strength.

mainly in the north – is fashioned by highly skilled and patient artists who laboriously apply layer after layer of a resin to containers most often made from wood or woven bamboo. Some of the finest work may require several weeks or months. This art form also is used to decorate temple and palace doors, which are further illuminated by paintings depicting Buddhist legends and tales from the epic *Ramakien*.

Still another craft from China, related to lacquering, is mother-of-pearl decoration. Most of the

without settings and resold by the buyers in the west. The Khmer gem market in Trat, near the Cambodian border, and Burmese markets in Mae Hong Son offer an exciting alternative to the high-pressure Bangkok "factories", where quality is often poor and the prices are ridiculous. Unless you know gems, beware. The Tourism Authority of Thailand warns visitors not to buy gems from a source recommended by anyone they have just met.

Lacquerware is another Burmese-Chinese import, and much of that made today – again,

iridescent shell comes from the Gulf of Thailand and adorns lacquered boxes, furniture, musical instruments and statuary. One of the more stunning examples is on the soles of the feet of the huge reclining Buddha figure in Bangkok's Wat Po, but displays may also be seen in Chinese restaurant tables and chairs.

Clay pots found in the northeast have been carbon-tested back to 3600 BC. Yet even with that long history, ceramic handicrafts generally don't get the attention they deserve. Best known, perhaps, is the pale-green celadon used for everything from ash trays to dinner settings to large vases, and the enamelled terracotta ware with floral and Buddhist decorations, called

LEFT: finely woven silk is sold in countless hues and colours. **ABOVE:** lacquer hats on Royal Barge oarsmen.

bencharong, another imported Chinese art improved upon.) Realistic reproductions of those early clay pots from the Bronze Age may also be found in antique stores and at a museum shop at Ban Chiang, and replicas of old stone sculpture are offered in Ayutthaya.

A word about antique stores. Real antiques cannot be taken out of Thailand without a permit from the Department of Fine Arts. In recent years, the government has been going after museums and private collectors around the world, demanding – and getting – many old religious artifacts back. Buddha images are sold widely, but they are for local use, and unless you

can wear it around your neck, its export is strictly forbidden, even if it was manufactured last week. Also, Thai craftsmen are ingenious when it comes to copying something, from a Versace shirt to a Rolex watch. Many of the "antiques" offered are no such thing.

Another handicraft, distinctly Thai, is ornamental woodcarving. In this, the Thais have no peers, developing over time traditional motifs such as the lotus and other flowers, mythological creatures from India, serpents and dragons from China. Usually this decorative work is found on furniture and in the adornment of religious and royal buildings, royal barges and carriages, and in a modest style even in the humblest homes. When visiting a *wat*, look up toward the eaves and don't just pass through an open door, stop to examine it; some what you see will surprise. When Thailand was covered by forest, such carving was at its peak and much of this painstaking carving has survived the wicked Thai climate. However proficient the product, it is unfortunate that most of the woodwork sold today is made from rattan and bamboo. Teak is now an endangered plant.

A category of handicrafts that never really went away and now is attracting attention are the objects of everyday rural life. Baskets whose origins were strictly utilitarian – to winnow, store, cook and carry rice to the table, to transport crops from the fields, even to tote small children – are now regarded by many as "folk art." Some of the woven containers, using thinly cut bamboo and other plants, are lightly lacquered for strength. Others are given modern handles and serve Western women as purses.

Brightly painted wooden "bells," or clappers that are hung around the necks of water buffaloes, baskets used to catch fish in the flooded rice paddies, kitchen implements made from coconut shells and carved wood, machetes used in the fields, coconut graters, large earthen water jars, even the worn wood and bamboo yokes used by villagers and street vendors to carry their heavy baskets of food to market – everything "authentic" is now in great demand. Poor northern hill-tribe villages, induced by the government and international organisations to stop growing opium, are now supplementing their meagre subsistence economy with the production of embroidered shoulder bags and native silver jewellery. There is even a market for the crossbows and old-style flintlock rifles with which the mountain tribesmen once hunted small game. Because so much is being produced quickly to satisfy the new demand, much of the quality is slipshod. A visit to the National Museum or the Jim Thompson House in Bangkok – Thompson was an avid collector blessed with impeccable taste – will reveal appropriate guidelines. The present Queen of Thailand, under her self-help organisation called SUPPORT, also sponsors a number of provincial workshops, with the product so identified and sold in many stores. ❑

LEFT: cooking items have both utility and simple elegance. **RIGHT:** silver working near Chiang Mai.

ARCHITECTURE

The temples of Thailand are top on most visitors' agendas. Beyond the temple, the
traditional Thai house reflects a nearly perfect adaptation to the environment

If culture is an expression of the best of a society, architecture must occupy society's zenith, for it is defined by the designs and spaces created for home life, worship, and work. As is true in much of Thailand's artistic expression, many of the finest temples, palaces and other buildings in the kingdom show the influences of several cultures, yet all are identifiably and unquestionably Thai.

Indian, Khmer, Burmese, and Chinese architectural styles have had substantial effect through the centuries, but there is no mistaking the swooping multi-tiered roof lines, the distinctly ornamental decorations and blinding colours, the stunning interior murals and lovingly crafted and gold-adorned Buddha images, and the miles of interlocking waterways.

Sadly, many of those canals, called *khlongs*, have been replaced with traffic-jammed roadways, but thousands of the classical Thai structures may still be seen. There are approximately 30,000 temples in Thailand, and hundreds of these compounds established for the veneration of Buddha are worth visiting. So, too, the several royal residences, some blending western neoclassical features, the result of visits to Europe by early Thai kings and the European expatriate's presence in Thailand.

The temple

Any study of Thai architecture begins with the temple, or *wat*, whose traditional role was as a school, community centre, hospital, and entertainment venue, as well as the place where the lessons of Buddha were taught. Every part of a Thai wat has symbolic significance. The capitals of columns are shaped either like water lilies or lotus buds; the lotus symbolises the purity of Buddha's thoughts – it pushes through the muck to burst forth in extraordinary beauty.

Some of these compounds like Wat Po in Bangkok are vast, while others in rural villages

are quite modest. They generally include an assembly hall, or *bot*, where monks perform ceremonies, meditate, and sermonise. A second assembly hall, or *viharn*, is where lay people make offerings before a large Buddha figure. Dome-shaped *chedi* are where relics of the Buddha may be housed. There may also be tower-

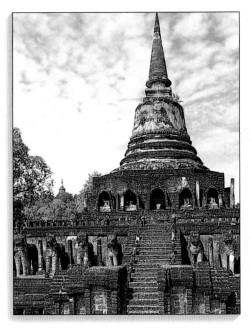

ing, phallic spires, called *prang*, epitomised by the Wat Arun on the banks of the Chao Phraya in Bangkok, opposite the Grand Palace.

As different as the wats may be, there are similarities, or themes. Symbolism abounds in the ornate decoration. Bots are bounded by eight stones, believed to keep away evil spirits, an example of how animist beliefs coexist with Buddhism. Roof peaks are adorned with *chofa*, the curling, pointed extensions at each end that represent the *garuda*, the vehicle of Vishnu. In its claws it holds two *naga*, mythical serpents that undulate down the eaves.

The garuda is a royal symbol, imported from India. Companies bearing it on their building

PRECEDING PAGE: traditional house, Nonthaburi, north of Bangkok. **LEFT:** from a mural at Wat Bowon Niwet, Bangkok. **RIGHT:** Sri Lankan-style temple stupa.

facades operate "by royal appointment". At the top of a chedi may be a stylised thunderbolt sign of Vishnu, ancient Hindu lord of the universe.

The various outside influences are evident in other ways. Most of the ancient remains in northeastern Thailand reveal a heritage shared by the more famous Angkor Wat in neighbouring Cambodia, as this region was once a part of the sprawling Khmer empire. In the north, many of the older chedi are Burmese in style, constructed during that country's occupation of what was then the kingdom of Lanna.

Window panels and murals in Bangkok dating to the early 18th century cross many cultural

and international boundaries, and are decorated with mythological figures from the Indian *Ramayana*, Chinese dragons, Indian nagas (or serpents) and foreign merchants wearing distinctly European garb.

"They are gorgeous," summarised Somerset Maugham, the British novelist and traveller who frequently visited Southeast Asia in this century and wrote extensively about both Thailand and Southeast Asia. "They glitter with gold and whitewash, yet are not garish; against that vivid sky, in that dazzling sunlight, they hold their own, defying the brilliancy of nature and supplementing it with the ingenuity and playful boldness of man."

Traditional dwellings

Homes for ordinary people share the same sensitive treatment as those for the exalted. Thai-style teak houses, with their inward-sloping walls and steep roofs, seldom fail to charm with their airiness and their marvellous adaptation to tropical climates.

Like the wat, the Thai house has gone through a centuries-old evolution. Some trace the style to southern China, origin of today's Thai population and where many ethnic Thais still live. Steep roofs, sometimes multi-layered like the wats that dominated village life, with only a few rooms or one large, divided room elevated on

---

DOMESTIC DESIGNS

The design of the traditional Thai dwelling is well suited for Thailand's tropical weather: often on stilts to rise above flooding, steep roof lines for shedding rain, materials that retain coolness, and ventilation that takes advantage of breezes.

The architectural styles of traditional homes vary depending upon region, although the characteristics noted above are common throughout. In the flat central plains north of Bangkok, an open verandah is often the focus of home life as an outside living space. To the north, where the temperatures are cooler, design of ventilation and living spaces often retains warmth. In most traditional homes, the central, innermost room is both sleeping area and home for ancestral spirits.

Outside most Thai homes and commercial buildings is the spirit house, a miniature dwelling intended for the natural spirits that are found on the land. These spirit houses can be plain and modest, or gaudy and quite large.

---

pilings distinguished the earliest homes. The structures were positioned to take advantage of prevailing winds, and many of the components were prefabricated, then fitted together with wooden pegs.

In time, the elevation above the ground increased to protect the home from flooding and unwanted animal visitors, while producing a space beneath the house for keeping livestock or to be used for daily work such as weaving. Such homes are common in villages throughout Thailand today, although in urban areas, nearly all homes are now more western in design and steadfastly anchored to the ground. Most of the early homes were made of native woods such as teak and bamboo, materials that are still used today, although teak is now on the nation's endangered list. The Jim Thompson House is a good example. Numerous other examples line the banks of the silvery network of canals that crisscross the Thonburi suburbs.

In Thailand's southern provinces, a different design evolved, reflecting the warmer, wetter climate. Here, the pillars were shorter, there was no exterior verandah, and windows had hinged shutters that closed from the top during torrential monsoon rains. With the arrival of Western traders and missionaries in the 18th century, and with early trips to Europe by Thai monarchy in the 19th, Western-style buildings joined the traditional Thai structures along both sides of the Chao Phraya River, the centre of Bangkok's government and commerce.

Much of this early architecture remains today, including a part of the Oriental Hotel and the original French embassy next door, both designed by European architects. Shophouse architecture in the Sino-Portuguese style uses stout walls and often ornate window and roof treatments that were the hallmark of a type of housing once preferred by Chinese shopkeepers. As in yesteryear, the downstairs serves as a place to market one's goods; the upstairs is the family home. Shophouses at Tha Chang boat landing on the Chao Phraya, to the northwest of the Grand Palace, are good examples.

The Vimarnmek, in Bangkok's Dusit district and built entirely of teak but appearing decidedly more Western than Thai, and the Italianate palace built by King Chulalongkorn at Bang Pa-In near Ayutthaya offer ample evidence of Thailand's passionate embrace of Western styles that continues to this day. (The present king and queen live in a modern palace with satellite dishes on the roof.)

Most contemporary architectural efforts show little regard for the past, as hundreds of new high-rises go up each year in the cities, while tract homes and look-alike rows of townhouses are erected for the country's growing middle class in the suburbs and small towns. During the building boom of the 1980s, many architects seemed to be trying to outdo each other. See the "robot building" on Bangkok's Sathorn Road, its sides decorated with outsized nuts and bolts,

and also the headquarters for *The Nation* newspaper in Bangkok's Bang Na district, looking like two stylised grand pianos turned on their sides. At the same time, Corinthian columns and curvilinear banisters appeared on the balconies of virtually every new townhouse, appearing not only incongruous but in many cases ridiculous.

Seeing the past

Nothing beats seeing the surviving traditional structures in their natural settings, of course, but for the traveller with limited time, a visit to the Ancient City, half an hour south of Bangkok, is a must. (See *Outside of Bangkok*, page 177.)

Here, arranged over 80 hectares (200 acres) set out in roughly the shape of Thailand itself, are more than 100 full-sized and reduced-scale replicas of the country's most important monuments, temples, and palaces, as well as a typical turn-of-the-century commercial street, a floating market, and khlong-side village. Visitors in Bangkok should also consider hiring a long-tailed boat for a tour of the Thonburi khlongs and visits to the Jim Thompson home, which was constructed from three traditional homes moved from Ayutthaya, and the Kamthieng House on the grounds of the Siam Society, a simple but elegant home transported from Chiang Mai. ❑

LEFT: ornate ceiling of a wat, or temple. **RIGHT:** traditional architecture depicted in a temple mural.

TEMPLE ART AND ARCHITECTURE

The wat *plays a vital role in every community, large and small. They are also home to the country's 300,000 monks. For many visitors, they are one of the most memorable sights of Thailand.*

A typical Thai *wat* (loosely translated as monastery or temple) has two enclosing walls that divide it from the secular world. The monks' quarters or dormitories are situated between the outer and inner walls. This area may also contain a bell tower (*hor rakang*). In larger temples the inner walls may be lined with Buddha images and serve as cloisters or galleries for meditation. This part of the temple is called *buddhavasa* or *phutthawat* (for the Buddha).

Inside the inner walls is the *bot* or *ubosth* (ordination hall) surrounded by eight stone tablets and set on consecrated ground. This is the most sacred part of the temple and only monks can enter it. The bot contains a Buddha image, but it is the *viharn* (assembly hall) that contains the principal Buddha images. Also in the inner courtyard are the bell-shaped *chedi* (relic chambers), which contain the relics of pious or distinguished people. *Salas* (rest pavilions) can be found all around the temple; the largest of these areas is the *sala kan parian* (study hall), used for saying afternoon prayers.

POPULAR TEMPLE ICONS

During the 10th century, the Thai Buddhist and Khmer-Hindu cultures merged, and Hindu elements were introduced into Thai iconography. Popular figures include the four-armed figure of Vishnu; the *garuda* (half man, half bird); the eight-armed Shiva; elephant-headed Ganesh; the *naga*, which appears as a snake, dragon or cobra; and the ghost-banishing giant Yak.

SINGHA HEAD ▷
Fierce-looking bronze *singha* (mythical lions) stand guard outside the ordination hall of Wat Phra Kaeo in Bangkok.

△ **WAT PHRA KAEO**
The Temple of the Emerald Buddha is one of the most impressive examples of Thai temple art, and one of the world's great religious buildings.

THE ART OF MURAL PAINTING

△ SYMBOLIC ROOF DECOR
The *bot* (ordination hall) roof of Wat Po in Bangkok is adorned with a carving of a mythical *garuda* (bird-man) grasping two *naga* (serpents) in its talons.

CHEDI ▷
Wat Po has 95 *chedi*. They contain the ashes of royalty, monks and lay people. The four large chedi are memorials to Thai kings.

◁ THE CLOISTERS
The cloisters of Wat Po are lined by 394 seated bronze Buddhas dating from the reign of Rama I.

THE LIBRARY ▷
Phra Mondop (the library), Wat Phra Kaeo. Libraries or scripture repositories *(hor trai)* are built high up above the ground in order to protect the religious scriptures from flood damage.

Thai murals are found on the interior walls of *bot* (ordination halls) and *viharn* (assembly halls). Usually painted in solid colour without the use of perspective or shading, the murals are used by monks as meditation and teaching aids. Not many murals over 150 years old remain intact in Thailand, as they were painted straight onto dry walls and therefore could not survive the ravages of the Thai climate.

The mural above comes from Wat Phumin in Nan, northern Thailand. It was painted in the mid-19th century as part of restoration carried out by Thai Lu artists. The murals depict *jataka* (Buddha's birth) tales and also illustrate aspects of northern Thai life.

Murals dating from this period commonly contain scenes from everyday life, local myths, birds, animals and plants, as well as religious themes.

Mural painting was at its height during the reign of Rama III of Thailand (1824–51), who encouraged a huge program of construction and restoration of Buddhist temples. Of special note from this period are the fine murals in Wat Thong Thammacht in Thonburi, painted in 1850.

CUISINE

You bet it can be quite hot. It can also be cool. There is nothing apathetic about Thai cuisine, which most likely explains its appeal around the world

Good food in Thailand is found in fascinating places, from seafood markets to floating restaurants to hawker stalls. Wherever one travels in the country, aromas and attractive food presentations are very appealing.

Thais take time over their meals, talking and making an entire evening of the affair. Since dishes are placed in the middle of the table and shared by all, it makes sense to take several friends so that one can order more dishes and sample more tastes.

While it's true that there are very spicy regional dishes – certain southern Thai curries are notable – not all Thai food is hot and spicy. Generally, an authentic Thai meal will include at least one very spicy dish, a few that are less hot, and some that are comparatively bland, flavoured with only garlic or herbs.

Usually, purely Siamese creations will take their place alongside adapted Chinese and Indian dishes, influences easy to spot.

Thai food is eaten with rice. Traditionally, rice has always been the most important dish in any Thai meal. In times past, Thais would eat rice with just a few condiments, or in times of hardship with nothing more than fish sauce.

Curries and sauces have become more sophisticated and more important as Thailand has become more affluent, and now it is commonplace for the central rice bowl to be accompanied by a selection of other dishes, often including chicken, pork and fish.

At the start of the meal, heap some rice onto a plate and then take a spoonful or two of curry. It is considered polite to take only one curry at a time, consuming it before ladling another curry onto the rice. Thais eat with the spoon in their right hand and fork in their left, the fork being used to push the food onto the spoon for transport to the mouth. Chopsticks are used only for Chinese noodle dishes.

PRECEDING PAGE: the cuisine of Thailand is known for both taste and aesthetics. **LEFT:** only the freshest of produce is used. **RIGHT:** grinding fresh chillies the traditional way with a mortar.

There seems to be some confusion among those who have sampled their first Thai meals abroad regarding the proper condiments to add to the food. Contrary to popular belief, peanut sauce, an "indispensable" addition to nearly every dish in Thai restaurants found in Western countries, is really of Malayan and Indonesian

origin and is used in Thailand only for *satay.* Similarly, instead of salt, Thais rely on *nam plaa,* or fish sauce, for their salt intake, often serving it with chopped chilli peppers to make a spicy dip.

Spicy and hot dishes

Kaeng means curry. The group includes the spiciest of Thai dishes and forms the core of Thai cooking.

Among the green curries is *kaeng kiaw wan kai,* a gravy filled with chunks of chicken and tiny pea-sized eggplants. A relative, *kaeng kiaw wan nua,* has slices of beef in it. *Kaeng luang,* a category of yellow curries, includes *kaeng karee*, an Indian-style curry which is made with chicken or beef. *Kaeng pet* is a red curry with beef or pork. A close relative is *penaeng nua*, a southern-style "dry" curry with a characteristic coconut flavour. *Kaeng som* is cooked in a hot-sour soup generally filled with pieces of either fish or shrimp.

Among the fiery favourites is *tom yang kung*, a lemony broth teeming with shrimp. It is served in a metal tureen that is wrapped around a mini-furnace heated by charcoal, so that it remains piping hot throughout the meal. *Po taek* (The Fisherman's Net Bursts) is a cousin of *tom yang kung*, containing squid, mussels, crab and fish.

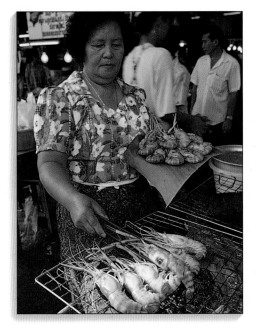

Yam is a hot and spicy salad combining meat and vegetables. Particularly popular in northern and northeastern Thailand, it is one of the hottest dishes available.

Mild curries

Tom kha kai, a thick coconut-milk curry of chicken chunks with lemon grass, is milder than the average Thai dish and a great favourite with foreign visitors.

Plaamuk tawt kratiem phrik tai is squid fried with garlic and black pepper. When ordering, ask that the garlic (*kratiem*) be fried crispy (*krawp krawp*). The dish is also prepared with fish. *Kaeng joot* is a non-spicy curry, a clear

broth filled with glass noodles, minced pork and mushrooms. *Nua pat nam man hoi* is beef fried in oyster sauce garnished with chopped shallots and green vegetables.

Muu pat priaw wan – sweet and sour pork – is probably of Portuguese origin and may have arrived in Thailand via Chinese émigrés. It is also possible to order it in most restaurants with red snapper (*plaa krapong*), beef (*nua*) and shrimp (*kung*).

Ho mok talay is a seafood casserole of fish and shellfish chunks in a coconut mousse, steamed in a banana-leaf cup.

Kaeng matsman is a southern-style curry. It consists of pieces of beef or chicken, combined with potatoes, onions and peanuts in a mildly-spiced curry sauce flavoured with coconut milk.

Of Chinese origin but having secured a place in Thai cuisine is *plaa jaramet nung kiem bueh*, steamed pomfret with Chinese plum and bits of ginger. *Pu paat pong karee* is pieces of unshelled, steamed crab smothered in a curry sauce laden with shallots.

Hoi maleng pu op moh din is a thick, savoury coconut milk gravy filled with mouth-watering mussels cooked in a clay pot.

Noodles and others

Most noon-time dishes are derived from Chinese cuisine, and noodle dishes, a Chinese invention, have been adopted by the Thais. Those served at street-side, open-front shops come in two varieties: wet and dry. When ordering either, specify the wetness by adding the word *nam* (wet) or *haeng* (dry) to the dish's name. Thus, a soupy *kuay tiaw* would be *kuay tiaw nam*.

Kuay tiaw is a lunchtime favourite, a soup of noodles with balls of fish or slices of beef. *Baa mii* is egg noodles with pieces of meat and vegetable. Some rice-based lunchtime dishes are also Chinese and include *khao man kai*, boiled rice topped with slices of chicken and chopped ginger; *khao moo daeng*, a similar dish with red pork slices; and *khao kaa moo*, stewed leg of pork with greens on rice.

Then, there are the variants using noodles. *Kuay tiaw rat naa* is broad white noodles boiled and served in a dish with morning glory. *Pat tai* is noodles fried in a wok with tofu, chopped vegetables and dried shrimp. *Pat siew* is of white noodles cooked with thin slices of beef, fresh greens and soy sauce. Served late at night and early in the morning are two soup-like dishes filled with boiled rice. The rice in *khao tom* is watery and augmented with minced pork and shallots.

A close relative is *jok,* in which the rice has been cooked until the liquid becomes viscous like a porridge. Into this mix is tossed ginger, coriander, slices of meat and generally a fresh egg.

Each of Thailand's four primary regions has its own cuisine. Northern and northeastern dishes are related to Lao cooking, which is eaten with gluti-

The sausage is roasted over a fire fuelled by coconut husks, which impart an aroma to the meat. Generally prepared hygienically, it is best to buy it only at better restaurants. Beware the *phrik kii nuu* chilies that lurk inside waiting to explode on the tongues of the unwary.

Khao soy originated in Burma. This egg noodle dish is filled with chunks of beef or chicken and is lightly curried in a gravy of coconut cream, and then sprinkled with crispy noodles and served with chopped red onions and lime.

Nam phrik ong combines

SPOON SHOCK

A surprise to some visitors is that most Thais use a spoon and fork, not the chopsticks found in Thai restaurants in Europe and North America.

nous rice. Southern food is flavoured with the tastes of Malaysian cooking. Central cuisine corresponds closely to the food in Thai restaurants abroad.

Northern cuisine

Northern specialties are generally eaten with *khao niaw* or sticky rice, which is kneaded into a ball and dipped into various sauces and curries. *Sai oua* (also called *naam*) is an oily, spicy pork sausage that epitomises northern cooking.

minced pork with chilies, tomatoes, garlic and shrimp paste. It is served with crisp cucumber slices, parboiled cabbage leaves, and pork rind.

Laap is a minced pork, chicken, beef or fish dish normally associated with northeastern cuisine. While northerners traditionally eat it raw, northeasterners cook it thoroughly. It is served with long beans, mint leaves and other vegetables that contrast with its pungent flavour.

Kaeng hang lay, another dish of Burmese origin, is a relatively mild northern dish which is popular with foreign visitors. Pork and tamarind flesh give this curry a sweet-and-sour flavour. The curry is especially suited to dipping with a ball of sticky rice.

LEFT: cooking giant prawns in a street market.
ABOVE: like many Asian foods, Thai meals are a balance of spicy and cool, *yin* and *yang*.

Northeastern cuisine

Northeastern food is simple and spicy. Like northern food, it is eaten with sticky rice, which *Isaan* (northeastern) diners claim weighs heavily on the brain and makes one sleepy.

Kai yang, or northeastern roasted chicken, has a flavour found in no other chicken. Basted with herbs and honey, it is roasted over an open fire and chopped into small pieces. Two dips, hot and sweet, are served with it.

Nua yang is beef dried like a jerky. One can chew for hours on a piece and still extract flavour from it. *Som tam* is the dish most associated with the northeast. It is a spicy salad

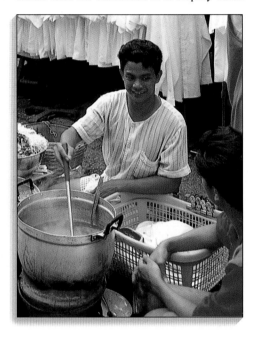

made from raw shredded papaya, dried shrimp, lemon juice and chilies.

Southern cuisine

Khao yam is rice with *kapi* (a paste made of fermented shrimp). *Pat pet sataw* looks like a lima bean but has a slightly bitter yet pleasant flavour. This dish is cooked with shrimp or pork, together with a sprinkling of chilies.

Khao mok kai, essentially a Thai *biriani,* lays roasted chicken on a bed of saffron rice and mixes it with ginger, which has been fried lightly to make it crisp.

Khanom chin is found throughout Thailand but is thought to be of Mon origin. Tiny bits of

minced beef are stewed in a red sauce and then served atop rice noodles. It is generally sold in markets in the early morning.

Nam phrik kung siap, or dried prawn on a stick, is grilled and served with chilies, *kapi* (fermented shrimp paste) and lime.

Kaeng tai plaa was created by bachelor fishermen who wanted a dish that would last them for days. Fish kidneys, chilies and vegetables are blended in a curry sauce and stewed for up to seven days. *Ho mok khai plaa* is made from fish roe that are stirred into a coconut mousse, wrapped in leaves and steamed.

Chinese

Most Thai Chinese are of Teochow descent, so the typical Thai Chinese restaurant serves Teochow dishes with a distinct Cantonese flavour. Teochow is famed for dishes such as thick shark's fin soup, goose doused in soy sauce, and roasted duck with fresh green vegetables. Fruits and teas are integral parts of every meal. Poultry, pork and seafood are essentials, as are a huge variety of fungi and mushrooms.

Other Chinese cuisines are well represented in Thailand. Shanghai food is typified by dishes that are fried in sesame or soy sauce for a long time, making them sweeter and oilier than the other cuisines.

Libations

The local beer is Singha, which is quite strong and, if taken to excess, can cause a fearsome hangover. Western beers such as Carlsberg, Kloster and Heineken are also widely available The local cane whiskey is called *mekhong* and packs a wallop for the unsuspecting. A bit sweet, it is drunk neat, or more popularly, mixed with club soda and lime.

Thailand has its own special coffee, made with a thick black melange of coffee, chicory and who knows what else, strong enough to set a dead person's heart beating. In the markets, Thais fill the bottom of the glass two fingers high with sweetened condensed milk and pour the coffee over it. Ask for it black (the iced version is called *oliang*) in order to gain the full flavour of this exotic mixture. Tea is usually served with a considerable amount of condensed milk, and thus is quite sweet. ❐

LEFT: cheap and ready offerings. **RIGHT:** some of Thailand's hearty sweets are of Portuguese origin.

Sweets

In Bangkok, desserts and sweets (*khanom*) come in a bewildering variety – from light concoctions through to custards, ice creams and cakes, and an entire category of confections based upon egg yolks cooked in flower-scented syrups. Bananas and coconuts grow everywhere in Thailand, and if they were to be removed from the list of ingredients available to the khanom cook, the entire edifice of Thai dessert cookery would come crashing down.

The heavier Thai confections are rarely eaten after a big meal. Desserts, served in small bowls,

Many of these sweets are made amazingly inventive, putting familiar ingredients in surprising surroundings. You may finish off a rich pudding, for example, before realising that its tantalising flavour came from crisp-fried onions.

Excellent khanom of various types can also be bought by the bag-full from roadside vendors, who prepare them fresh on portable griddles. One such sweet is the **khanom beuang**, or "roof-tile cookie", which consists in one version of an extremely thin crispy shell folded over taco-style, and filled with coconut, strands of egg yolk cooked in syrup, spiced and sweetened dried shrimp, coriander and a sugary cream.

are generally light and elegant. **Kluay buat chii**, a popular after-dinner sweet, consists of banana chunks stewed in sweetened, slightly salted and scented coconut cream, and served warm. Another favourite, **thap thim krawb**, is made from small balls of tapioca flour, dyed red and shaped around tiny pieces of water chestnut. These are served in a mixture of sweetened coconut cream and ice.

Anyone walking through a big Bangkok market is bound to come across a sweets vendor selling anything from candied fruits to million-calorie custards made from coconut cream, eggs and palm sugar. They are generally sold in the form of three-inch squares wrapped in banana leaves. Such snacks are good for a quick boost of energy.

Sangkhya maphrao awn is a magnificent custard made from thick coconut cream, palm sugar and eggs, then steamed inside a young coconut or a small pumpkin. **Khao laam** is glutinous rice mixed with coconut cream, sugar and either black beans or other goodies, and cooked in bamboo segments, then slit open and the rice eaten. **Taeng thai nam kati** consists of a Thai melon cut into small cubes and mixed with ice and sweetened, flavoured coconut cream. **Khanom maw gaeng** is a custard-like sweet, again made with coconut cream and eggs, but this time with soybean flour to thicken it. **Kluay khaek** uses bananas sliced lengthwise, dipped in coconut cream and flour, and deep fried until is crisp. Try **katit**, a rich coconut ice cream. ■

PLACES

A detailed guide to the entire country, with principal sites cross-referenced by number to the maps

Diversity and contrast characterise both Thailand's people and its geography. Within an area of 514,000 square kilometres (199,000 sq mi) – roughly the size of France – are tropical rain forests, broad rice plains and forest-clad hills that lie between 5 degrees and 21 degrees north of the equator, in the centre of the geographical jigsaw puzzle of Southeast Asia.

There is an abundance of natural resources. Under the canopies of its rain forests, a wide variety of flora and fauna abound: iridescent kingfishers, parakeets, pheasants, hornbills, flying squirrels and lizards, gibbons, hundreds of species of butterflies, and nearly a thousand varieties of orchids. A cornucopia of fruit grows as well, wild in the jungles, or tended carefully on small family holdings and in larger plantations. Nearly 30 varieties of fruit are here: banana and plantain, coconut, durian, orange, lime, mango, papaya, breadfruit, jackfruit, mangosteen, rambutan, lychee and lamyai abound.

Elevations of the terrain run from sea level along the 2,600-kilometre-long (1,600 mi) coastline to a peak of 2,596 metres (8,517 ft) in the north, a region of hills clad in teak forests and valleys carpeted in rice, fruit trees and vegetables, and bordered by Burma and Laos.

The northeast is dominated by the arid Khorat Plateau, where farmers struggle to cultivate rice, tapioca, jute and other cash crops. With strong cultural affinities with neighbouring Laos and Cambodia, the region is rimmed and defined by the Mekong River.

In the central plains, monsoon rains transform the landscape into a vast hydroponic basin, which nourishes a sea of rice, the country's staple and an important export. Through this region flows the Mae Nam Chao Phraya – *mae nam* means river – carrying produce and people south to Bangkok, washing rich sediment down from the northern hills, and during the monsoons, flooding the rice fields.

The south of Thailand runs down a long, narrow arm of land leading to Malaysia. An area strongly influenced by Malay culture and Islam, this southern isthmus is peppered by rubber and palm-oil plantations that alternate with rice and fruit trees. ❑

PRECEDING PAGES: monks on a northern road; Silom area, Bangkok; dusk near Chiang Rai; limestone islands, Krabi. **LEFT:** Wat Prathat Chom Kitti, Chiang Saen.

BANGKOK

A city of wild plums or angels it is not. Bangkok is rather a city of uncanny chaos anchored by the grandest of palaces

The Thai people call Bangkok, which means City of Wild Plums, Krung Thep, or the City of Angels. To be correct, however, Bangkok's full name is Krungthepmahanakhon Amonrattanakosin Mahintharayutthaya Mahadilokphop Nopphosin Ratchathaniburirom Udomrathaniwetmahasa Amonphiman Awatansathit Sakkathatiya Witsanukamprasit, or in English, City of Angels, Great City of Immortals, Magnificent City of the Nine Gems, Seat of the King, City of Royal Palaces, Home of the Gods Incarnate, Erected by Visvakarman at Indra's Behest.

Bangkok began as a city of canals and elephant paths. When motor vehicles redefined urban transportation, the old thoroughfares were simply filled in or paved over for the new wheels.

The population of Bangkok has grown nearly ten-fold since World War II. Today, about one out of every eight Thais live in Bangkok. The second-largest city in the country is just one-fortieth its size. Growth in Bangkok seems out of control, an impression most substantiated by the city's world-class traffic snarls. At first glance, the greater metropolitan area of over 15 million people appears as a bewildering melding of new and old and indeterminate, and of exotic and commonplace and indescribable, all tossed together into a gigantic urban fuss. This, in fact, is what Bangkok is. If Bangkok seems to lack order, it is because it never has had such, save for Rattanakosin, the royal core of the city where the kings built their palaces. Moving outwards from this artificial island, defined by canals and the Chao Phraya, the city becomes increasingly less and less organised.

Chaos in construction began in earnest during the late 1950s, and a large part of what assaults the eye today started then – the lofty office buildings, the air-conditioned supermarkets and shopping centres, nearly all the broad streets and international hotels, the endless blocks of shophouses following what one critic called the egg-crate principle of design. Before this boom, the now-fashionable residential streets on either side of Thanon Sukhumvit and Thanon Phaholyothin were rice paddies.

Yet despite the growth, large areas around the old Grand Palace, the Chinese district, and across the river in Thonburi (Thailand's capital before Rattanakosin and now included in the Greater Bangkok Metropolitan Area) were, for the time, hardly touched by the building fever. But the pause was momentary, of course. New construction between Chinatown and Lumpini Park, for example, is replacing the squat buildings with towering glass ones, some of them seeming to take forever to complete. ❐

PRECEDING PAGE: Grand Palace and Wat Phra Kaeo, Bangkok. **LEFT:** the never-ending journey of life in Bangkok.

THE OLD ROYAL CITY

Map, page 143

At the centre of Rattanakosin, the old royal city, is the Grand Palace and the mystical Emerald Buddha of Wat Phra Kaeo. Just outside the palace grounds are the sacred Wat Po and Lak Muang

Although it's difficult to perceive from ground level, a bird's eye view would reveal that the old royal city occupied an oval island, part natural, part artificial. The western bank of this island is formed by Bangkok's defining river, **Mae Nam Chao Phraya**, and the eastern side by an artificial canal or moat, Khlong Lot. After a brief sojourn across the river in Thonburi, in the early 1780s Rama I set out to construct a protected city on the Ayutthayan model by using the artificial canal to create an island at a bend in the river, what is called **Rattanakosin**. Until the 1932 revolution, this district housed all the royal quarters, governmental administrative offices and most royal temples.

A bird's eye view would also reveal that this inner island, Rattanakosin, is only the western half of a larger oval island. Outer Rattanakosin is bordered on the east by yet another canal, Khlong Ong Ang, which is renamed Khlong Banglampoo north of the Rathadamnoen intersection. Long settled by merchants and artisans, this outer part of Rattanakosin still holds reminders of old Bangkok.

Grand Palace

The southern side of Thanon Na Phra Lan is lined by the white crenellated walls of the **Grand Palace ❶** (open daily; admission fee). The only entrance and exit to the complex is in the middle. On the right are the Royal Household offices. To the left is the ticket booth.

The first stop within the palace grounds is **Wat Phra Kaeo Ⓐ** (Temple of the Emerald Buddha), a shrine for Thai Buddhists that is comparable in religious importance to Mecca or St. Peter's. Passing though the gate, you will confront 6-metre-tall (19 ft) demon statues inspired by the *Ramakien*, the Thai version of the Indian epic *Ramayana*. You must walk the glittering length of the *bot* to reach the entrance to it. In front are scattered Chinese-style statues, which function as stand-ins for incense offerings to the **Emerald Buddha** inside. The small, clothed, 75-centimetre-tall (30 in) jadeite Emerald Buddha is perched high on an altar, shielded by a nine-tiered umbrella and enclosed in a glass case.

Non-Buddhists may be disappointed by the small size of the Emerald Buddha, but its power and importance stems from the image's mystique, which should be instantly apparent from the demeanour of the pilgrims inside the bot. (Don't wander around. Sit down promptly with toes pointed behind.) Supposedly made in Sri Lanka, the image apparently was discovered in Chiang Rai in the early 1400s. Credited with miraculous powers, over the centuries it shifted to many locations as a prize of war. While still a general, the future Rama I spirited the image away after sacking Vientiane in 1779 and placed it here in 1784. The removal is still fresh in the minds of Laotians.

OPPOSITE: Wat Phra Kaeo and the Emerald Buddha.
BELOW: the Emerald Buddha.

Exiting the bot, note three buildings to the north aligned on a broad, raised marble terrace. On the far left is the golden **Phra Si Ratana Chedi ⓑ**, erected by King Mongkut (Rama IV) to house a shard of the Buddha's breastbone. At the centre, tiled with green glass and topped with a crown-like tiered roof, is the **Phra Mondop ⒞**, a library of Buddhist scriptures. Always closed, it is surrounded by statues of white elephants. On the right is the **Prasad Phra Thep Bidom ⒟** (Royal Pantheon), which is open on some religious holidays. Inside are life-sized bronze and gold statues of all the Bangkok kings.

From this terrace are good views of the royal mausoleum, bell towers and eight *prang*, or Khmer-style towers. The walls of the cloister surrounding the temple courtyard are painted with vivid and detailed scenes from the *Ramakien*. The story begins in the middle panels of the northern wall and proceeds counterclockwise. Even if unfamiliar with the saga of Rama and Sita, it's enjoyable to examine the slices of ordinary life depicted, such as puppet shows, household chores, children playing ancient games, opium smokers and gamblers.

Wat Phra Kaeo's exit in the southwest wall leads to the Grand Palace's temporal sector. Although the royal family decamped to the more modern Chitralada Palace to the north in the Dusit district in 1946, most of the Grand Palace's labyrinth of structures and gardens remains closed to the public. Some official ceremonies are still held here.

What visitors can glimpse of the Grand Palace is a little of the complex's northern fringe. Directly in front is the unassuming **Amarin Vinitchai Throne Hall ⒠**, the northern-most of a three-building group. The three-roomed throne hall served as the bed-chamber for Rama I and as a residence for Rama II and Rama III. In the early days of Bangkok, it also served as a court of justice, where

The Emerald Buddha is graced with three costumes, which change with the seasons: a crown and jewelry in summer; a gilded robe during the rainy season; and a golden cloak in winter. The change is done in a ritual ceremony by the king.

BELOW: Dusit Maha Prasad, and throne in Chakri Maha Prasad.

Map,
page 143

cases were judged by the king or his ministers. Each new king has spent his first crowned night here. The gold-topped red poles standing at the entrance once tethered the elephants of visiting dignitaries. Inside, a throne sits atop a boat-shaped base. In the old days, this throne and base were hidden by a screen of curtains. At the appointed time, conch shells blew and the curtain was drawn back to reveal the seated king.

To the right (or west) is the grander, perhaps incongruous **Chakri Maha Prasad** ⓕ. An audience and reception hall, it was designed by an English architect on neoclassical lines on the request of King Chulalongkorn. Court elders were disturbed by this strong dose of Westernisation and persuaded the king to add the three Siamese-style towers to the roof. The top floor contains ashes of Bangkok kings.

On the left-hand side of this building is a door – always closed to the public – that leads to the Inner Palace. This was once the domain of the king's scores of concubines, and no adult male, save the king, could enter it. Nowadays, the modern king sometimes hosts receptions here for high-ranking diplomats. A cooking school for upper-class Thais also operates here.

To the far right, on the western side of the courtyard, the building with the four-tiered roof and nine-tiered spire is the **Dusit Maha Prasad** ⓖ. Dating from 1789, it is a splendid example of classical Thai architecture. The balcony on the north wing contains a throne once used for outdoor receptions. Traditionally, deceased kings and queens lie here in state until their cremations on Sanam Luang. The exquisite pavilion in front of Dusit Maha Prasad was built to the height of the king's palanquin, so that he could alight from his elephant and don his ceremonial hat before proceeding to the audience hall.

Dusit Maha Prasad holds Rama I's teakwood throne, adorned with inlaid mother-of-pearl.

Detail from Wat Po.

Wat Po

Exiting from the Grand Palace, turn left on Thanon Maharat and walk south past Thanon Thai Wang (which runs into the Tha Tien river-taxi dock, after passing a fresh market surrounded by turn-of-the-century shophouses). Turn left (that is, east) onto Soi Chetuphon and head to the entrance gate of **Wat Po ❷** (open daily; admission fee), Bangkok's largest and oldest temple, predating the Chakri dynasty. Its first buildings were constructed in the 16th century. If the Grand Palace seemed a preserved museum piece, these sprawling grounds are a living, breathing organism that is still the home to several hundred monks.

Most tours only tarry at the temple housing the **Reclining Buddha** in the western courtyard. Virtually filling a chapel, the brick-and-gold-plated statue is 46 metres (150 ft) long and 15 metres (50 ft) high. It depicts the dying Buddha on his side, awaiting his escape to *nirvana*. Observe the soles of his feet, which are inlaid with intricately wrought mother-of-pearl. The 108 designs are the ancient symbols by which an enlightened one can be identified.

In the eastern courtyard, screened by cloisters, is the large beautiful bot, Wat Po's principal praying and ordination hall. Girdling its base are sandstone panels with 152 superbly carved scenes from the *Ramakien*. Nearby vendors sell rubbings of them. Yet more *Ramakien* tales are depicted in mother-of-pearl on the teak doors.

The courtyard is strewn with chedi and stone statues in strange positions. They are *rishi*, or Hindu hermits, and they were once used to instruct illiterate people on the nature of illnesses and the massage methods for treatment. Wat Po still runs an herbal medicine school. Continue to the far eastern wall to find the massage hall, where an expert, vigorous one-hour massage costs foreigners a couple

BELOW: feet of the Reclining Buddha, Wat Po.

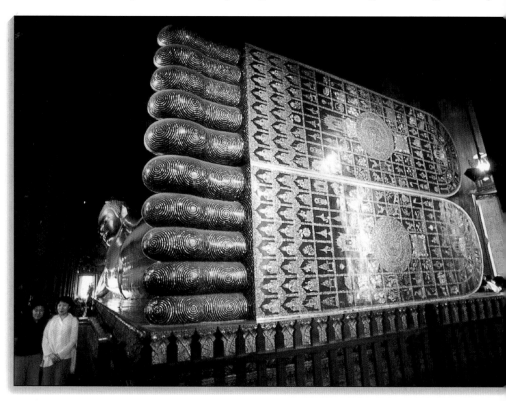

of hundred baht. Those who wish to study can take 30-hour courses, which are regularly offered in English.

Rejoining Thanon Maharat and walking south past the Ministry of Commerce and police station, you'll shortly find yourself at the very southern tip of the inner Rattanakosin oval. The landmark here is the Charoen Rat Thirty-One Bridge, built in 1910. While the reinforced concrete structure itself is nothing special, note the monkeys holding up the plaster balustrade. This was the first, but certainly not the last, bridge with *Charoen* in its name. A favourite Thai word, it means "growth" or "development". The new King Vajiravudh (Rama VI) was 31 years old the year it was built. Follow the road as it turns north and becomes Thanon Rachini. On the other side of Khlong Lot, Thanon Atsadang runs parallel. Shophouse fans may want to cross the canal at Phra Phitak Road to peer at the canal-side Atsadang structures, which were probably built late in the 19th century. Note the European style of pediments and doorway decorations. Early in this century, this was a fashionable precinct of car showrooms and boat-engine shops. As is apparent, it is still a thriving market area, but the run-down shophouses now house truck-transport companies and warehouses.

Lak Muang, the foundation pillar.

Lak Muang

If one heads on Thanon Na Phra Lan in the opposite, or easterly, direction, at the far edge of Sanam Luang is an enclosed, gilded tree trunk that is the official centre of Bangkok. Erected by Rama I in the late 1700s, this is **Lak Muang ❸**. Similar to the Shiva *lingam* that represent potency, the Lak Muang is the capital's foundation stone, where the guardian deity lives and from where the city's power emanates. (Many Thai cities have such a spiritual anchor.)

BELOW: vendors at Wat Po, and exterior of Lak Muang.

Map, page 146

Sheltered by a graceful, recently renovated shrine, Lak Muang and its attendant spirits are believed to have the power to grant fertility and other wishes. Floral offerings are piled high around the pillar, and the surrounding air is laden with incense. Devotees bow reverently before pressing a square of gold leaf to the monument. In an adjoining *sala*, classical dance and music are usually underway by a resident troupe hired by supplicants whose wishes have been granted.

Retracing your steps back to the inner island, turn northward and walk to the Ministry of Foreign Affairs, formerly the **Saranrom Palace**. This entire area was once the site of the "palaces" of members of the much extended royal family. Most were torn down during the Chulalongkorn era to make way for useful office buildings. Built in 1868, Saranrom is one of the few to survive.

Once a royal mini-zoo and crocodile garden, the front the palace today is a soothing, monument-studded public garden. The memorial at the centre honours one of Chulalongkorn`s 92 concubines. On a boat journey to the summer palace in Bang Pa-In, she fell into the river and drowned before scores of peasants. They were unable to save her because commoners couldn't touch royalty.

In early May, Sanam Luang is the site of the Royal Ploughing Ceremony, which is the official start of Thailand's rice-growing season. Sanam Luang's use as a kite-flying field began when King Chulalongkorn, an avid kite-flyer, okayed using the royal field for kites.

Sanam Luang

Directly north of the Grand Palace is a disk of clipped lawn, **Sanam Luang ❹** (Royal Field). Another by-product of the destruction of the "second king's" palace, it was established as a cremation ground for royalty. In a city so short of green spaces, it now provides desperately needed space for impromptu soccer games, jogging, kite flying and children's games. It is also the natural venue for public protests. Massacres during pro-democracy demonstrators in 1973, 1976 and 1992 took place in and around Sanam Luang.

Turn right onto narrow Thanon Phra Chan (which runs into the Tha Prachan/Wat Mahathat river-taxi dock). The sidewalk becomes progressively denser with vendors of new and antique amulets, featuring Buddha, famous monks and occult objects. The amulets are guaranteed to fend off bullets, create fortunes, or induce potency or fertility. The vendors' trail eventually leads to the entry to **Wat Mahathat ❺** (open daily). The buildings here are undistinguished, but one of two universities for monks is in the wat. It is also an important meditation centre. On Buddhist holidays, it blooms with herbal medicine vendors and stalls.

Just south are former royal office buildings that belong to the government Fine Arts Department and **Silpakorn University**, Thailand's first fine-arts school. Silpakorn sometimes sponsors art exhibits of both Thai and foreign artists. But if wanting to be certain to see some contemporary art, turn right where Thanon Na Phrathat ceases at Thanon Na Phra Lan. The Na Phra Lan Cafe has art on the walls, pretty food and a handsome, artsy clientele.

Continue along Thanon Na Phra Lan to discover two groups of 19th-century shophouses. The L-shaped Tha Chang group, near the end of the road at the Tha Chang cross-river ferry jetty, is the better-preserved. A century ago, there were about 10,000 shophouses on Rattanakosin; today there are probably fewer than 1,000. Thai builders were inspired by the Sino-Portuguese models of colonial Singapore and Malaya. Bangkokians were smitten with the stucco and cement materials as much as the idea of harmonious facades. Tha Chang's 33 two-storied units have sloped roofs with pediments, pilasters and balconies at the end units. Walls and windows are adorned with Chinese Baroque touches. Like shophouses elsewhere on the island, these do not have the ground-floor open colonnades characteristic of Singapore and Malaysia.

Not coincidentally, **Thammasat University ❻** monopolises much of the western stretch of Sanam Luang. It was founded as a law university in 1932 by Pridi Panomyong, an architect of the revolution and star-crossed figure of modern Thai history. Thammasat retains a radical reputation, and its students are always at the forefront of popular protests. Foreign visitors are welcome to stroll the grounds, although they may be shocked by the dilapidated buildings and ill-supplied libraries. Bear in mind that, after Chulalongkorn University, this is the second-oldest and second-most prestigious university in the country.

A treasure house of both Thai and Southeast Asian riches is the **National Museum ❼** (open Wednesday–Sunday; tel: 224 1370; admission fee), comprising a half-dozen old and new buildings.

One of oldest is at the rear of the compound, the Wang Na, dating from 1782. The name refers to the palace of the "second king". His vast palace once extended across to Khlong Lot and up to the Grand Palace. It was occupied by the second-in-line to the throne. When his heir-apparent attempted a violent overthrow, however, King Chulalongkorn abolished the office in 1887 and tore down most of the buildings. The Wang Na today is one of the remnants; it houses *khon* masks, gold and ceramic pieces, weapons, musical instruments and an elephant riding-seat of ivory.

Map, page 146

BELOW: Buddha image from the National Museum.

TIP

While Bangkok's National Museum is the finest of them all, there are nearly three dozen branches of the National Museum throughout Thailand, in most of the urban and cultural centres.

In front of the Wang Na's entrance is the similarly aged **Buddhaisawan Chapel**, once the second king's private place of worship. Today it shelters the bronze, Sukhothai-style Phra Buddha Sihing. Like the Emerald Buddha, it has a tangled history as one of the spoils of war and is reputed to have miraculous powers. On the day before the Songkran festival every year, it is paraded through the streets. Note the chapel's beautiful, well-preserved murals of Buddha's life. The two modern buildings in the rear of the complex cover an awesome chronological spectrum of Thai and Asian art. The southern building has the oldest pieces, representing the Dvaravati and Srivijaya periods, as well as examples of Khmer, Lopburi and Chaiya sculpture. Later periods are represented in the northern building. Besides ceramics and sculpture from Sukhothai and Ayutthaya, there are articles from the Lanna and Chiang Saen kingdoms.

One of the museum's most valuable possessions, familiar to every student of Thai history, is located elsewhere: a black, stone stele that is controversially accredited to King Ramkamhaeng and which is believed to bear the oldest sample of Thai script. If true, it would date from 13th-century Sukhothai. The stele's message describes or prescribes a kingdom of peace and prosperity. It's located in the same building with the ticket office, formerly an open-sided audience hall. Here can also be found some bronze tools from Ban Chiang, the archeological site in the northeast that indicates humans settled there 5,000 years ago. The museum has guided tours on several mornings a week in English and one day each week in French, German and Spanish. Check with the Tourist Authority or the museum for times.

The **National Gallery ❽** (open Wednesday–Sunday; admission fee), on the northern tip of Sanam Luang on Thanon Chao Fa, was once the national mint.

BELOW: Buddhai-sawan Chapel.

Today, the National Gallery shelters a few gems of 20th-century Thai art and the Thai film archive. It occasionally hosts shows of foreign and Thai artists. If time is limited, however, it's more rewarding to visit the National Museum immediately south.

Map, page 146

East of the Grand Palace

To the east of the Grand Palace is the first of Rattanakosin's canals. Before crossing over the canal, notice immediately to the north what, yes, appears to be a golden pig lording over a construction site. The Pig Memorial was built in 1913 as a birthday present from friends to Queen Saowapha, Chulalongkorn's favourite wife. (She was born in the Year of the Pig.) The construction site is part of an on-going archeological search for city walls built by Rama I.

Wat Ratchabophit ❾ (open daily) is easily recognisable by its distinctive doors, carved in relief with jaunty soldiers wearing European uniforms. Built in 1870, the design was intended to meld Western and Thai art forms. Note the unusual layout, with a tall, gilded chedi at the centre of the courtyard and enclosed by a circular cloister. Built into the northern side of the yellow-tiled cloister is the bot, itself covered in brightly-patterned, multi-hued tiles.

Exterior detail of Wat Ratchabophit.

The bot's windows and entrance doors are works of art. Tiny pieces of mother-of-pearl have been inlaid in lacquer, in an intricate rendition of the insignias of the five royal ranks. In a recess beside one of the doors is a bas-relief of a god named Khio Kang – or Chew Hard, meaning "the one with long teeth" – who guards this sanctuary. Four chapels, connected to the central gallery by small porticoes, further enlarge this colourful temple. The doors open into a startling temple interior. Instead of murals and the customary shadowy interior of Thai temples, this has been rendered like a Gothic chapel, with all the light and delicacy of a medieval cathedral if it were infused with a Versailles salon.

BELOW: gilded stucco decor, Wat Ratchabophit.

Since the temple was begun before King Chulalongkorn's visits to Europe, he may have been inspired by his visit to the British colonial city of Singapore. The outside garden is studded with memorials, many modelled after pint-sized Christian churches. These enclose the ashes of Chulalongkorn's numerous concubines and children. The wat occupies the corner of Ratchabophit and Fuang Nakhon roads.

Continue north up Thanon Faung Nakhon and turn right at the second corner onto Soi Sukhat. Two short blocks east is **Wat Suthat ❿** (open daily), built at the turn of the 18th century. The outdoor compound is populated by pagodas and statues, mostly brought from China as ship ballast in the early 19th century. The statues include bronze horses, Chinese scholars and homely *farang* (foreign) sailors wearing goofy hats. Wat Suthat's fame stems from the enormous dimensions of its *ubosot* and *viharn*, respectively the ceremony and main halls. Both have galleries of gilded Buddha images. Dominating the viharn is an 8-metre-tall (26 ft) meditating Buddha cast in 14th-century Sukhothai. Brought to Bangkok down the Chao Phraya on Rama I's orders, the statue is now surrounded by well-preserved 19th-century murals tracing the last 24 lives of Buddha. Note the depictions of fabulous sea monsters and foreign ships on the columns of the viharn. The doors are one of the wonders of Thai art. Carved to a depth of five centimetres (2 in), they follow the Ayutthayan tradition of floral motifs, with tangled jungle vegetation hiding small animals. Accounts vary as to whether Rama II designed or carved the doors himself. When they were completed, he ordered the chisels thrown into the river so that the fine carving could not be duplicated.

Immediately north of Wat Suthat is a giant red wooden structure. This is the 200-year-old **Giant Swing**, once the centrepiece of an annual ceremony honouring the Hindu god Shiva. A bench bearing teams of two to four standing young men was suspended from the crosspiece. When the swing was swung, the men would attempt to catch with their teeth a bag of gold suspended from on high. Accidents were so common that the ceremony was abandoned in 1933, although lately city officials have considered reviving it as a tourist attraction.

Self-explanatory rule at all temples.

Just northwest of Giant Swing is the city's only Brahman temple. The three holy halls are about the same age as the swing and are still used. Although Thailand is a devoutly Buddhist state, Hindu Brahman rituals accompany many ancient royal ceremonies, with Brahman priests always at hand.

The stretch of road running eastward from this very busy intersection is called Bamrung Muang. It was one of the first paved roads in Bangkok. Today it is noisy, polluted, traffic-choked and frequently bereft of sidewalks. It can be hell to negotiate if not nimble-footed and quick of reflexes; the cautious may think it wise to take this route only on Sunday or holiday. Still, those who toss caution to the winds and venture a few blocks east to a cluster of alleys on the right called **Ban Bat** will note that many shops here make or sell monks' alms bowls and other religious articles for monks and laity.

BELOW: Wat Suthat and Giant Swing.

Golden Mount

Until the 1960s, the **Golden Mount** ⑪ (open daily) was the highest spot in the city. Although Rama III was never able to achieve the desired height because the soft earth underneath kept sinking, King Mongkut (Rama IV), his successor, firmed matters up in the mid-19th century by placing a thousand teak logs in the boggy soil. His son, Chulalongkorn, finally completed the task.

The Golden Mount is still an excellent viewing and photographic perch. Standing 78 metres (256 ft) high, the top level is reached by a stairway that ascends around the base of the hill. The gilded chedi on top is believed to contain Buddha relics. During World War II, sirens here warned of Allied air raids.

From the Golden Mount, it is easy to spy **Wat Saket** (open daily) to the east on the same grounds. Long before the arrival of the Bangkok kings, a temple stood here during the Ayutthaya period. Rama I built Wat Saket just outside the city walls to serve as a commoners' crematorium. In the late 19th century, it became a dumping ground for the corpses of the poor felled by cholera epidemics. Dogs and vultures waited to feast on them.

Back towards the east

At the northwestern corner of the Golden Mount's grounds is the intersection of two canals holding three names: Khlong Banglamphoo, which turns into Khlong Ong Ang, and Khlong Mahanak. During daylight hours, one can catch a boat traversing eastward on the Mahanak canal and get off at Jim Thompson's House, the World Trade Centre, Soi Asoke or beyond. The much smaller motorised long-tails on Khlong Mahanak originating from Banglampoo canal veer southward to the Hua Lamphong Railway Station in less than 15 minutes.

Map, page 146

The spire atop the Golden Mount, like atop many of Thailand's sacred Buddhist structures, symbolises Mount Meru, a mythical mountain.

BELOW: the swing ceremony, and making a monk's alms bowl.

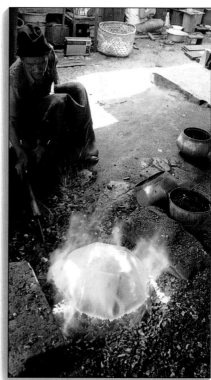

Map, page 146

Murals at Wat Bowon Niwet were painted by Krua In-khon, who had never been outside of Thailand. Look for southern America antebellum mansions, race tracks and people dressed in the fashions of 19th-century America.

OPPOSITE: Golden Mount, late 1800s.
BELOW: Golden Mount at sunset.

Just north of the Golden Mount is an intersection where six roads converge. Thanon Ratchadamnoen Klang, the broad western avenue leading to Democracy Monument, was inspired by Paris's Champs d'Elysees, and until 1941 it was lined with mahogany trees. To reach it, take the Mahathai Athit Bridge across the Mahanak canal – Thais call it the Weeping Bridge because of its bas reliefs of sobbing figures. Or else take a little detour back across Ong Ang canal via the larger Phanfalilat Bridge. This leads to **Mahakan Fort**, originally built at the turn of the 18th century, but much restored since. It is one of only two remaining watchtowers of the old city wall.

If strolling south along the busy, canal-side Thanon Mahachai, some of the other remnants of the city wall that encircled Rattanakosin in the 19th century are visible. Go through the very first archway to reach "dove's village", a calm refuge specialising in antiques, bird cages, bird accessories and birds themselves. This is where connoisseurs purchase doves for competition in singing contests. A silver-tongued dove may be worth more than US$ 10,000.

Directly behind, to the west, is **Wat Ratchanadda** ⑫ (open daily), a thriving centre for amulet vendors. The best-selling amulet depicts a monkey holding a phallus in its hands. Sunthorn Phu, the greatest Thai poet, once resided in the monks' cloisters. You can't miss the large, multilayered metal pagoda: **Loha Prasad** ⑬, recently opened after 150 years of sporadic construction. Visitors can roam ground-floor corridors lined with Buddhas.

Backtrack or pick any lane northward to arrive at **Democracy Monument** ⑭ – or at least a view of the 24-metre-tall (78 ft) wings in the middle of a hectic traffic circle. A major city landmark, the monument was built in 1939 to commemorate the overthrow of the absolute monarchy in June 1932. The 75 cannons around the base are symbolic of the Buddhist year 2575, equivalent to AD 1932. Plaster reliefs at the base represent the revolutionaries.

The resemblance to fascist architecture is not coincidental. The monument was designed by the Italian-born Corrado Feroci, who took the Thai name Silpa Bhirasi and is much honoured today as the founder of Silpakorn University, and as the father of the modern Thai art movement. As evident in some of this other works, Silpa was much taken by Italian fascist ideas concerning art, if not the political philosophy. Regardless, the monument is a potent symbol of democracy. The avenue between here and Sanam Luang to the west is a natural site for public demonstration. It was in this vicinity that the massacres of 1973, 1976 and 1992 took place. The monument also serves as a memorial place for making offerings to those who died in those violent years.

To the northwest is **Wat Bowon Niwet** (open daily) on the southern corner of Thanon Bowon. It was built between 1824 and 1832 by Rama III. His son, the future king Mongkut, spent many of his 27 years as a monk here, attempting to purge Thai Buddhism of superstitions and aberrant practices. Subsequent kings have served their brief monkhoods here.

The buildings are undistinguished, except for the murals inside the bot. They display a knowledge of Western perspective that is startling compared to the traditional, two-dimensional Thai mural scenes. ❏

Map,
page 146

MAE NAM CHAO PHRAYA

It was the river of kings, and is now the river of commerce. Dividing old Bangkok and Thonburi, the Chao Phraya is the most splendid part of Bangkok, lined by hotels, temples and eclectic architecture

The Mae Nam Chao Phraya, Thailand's celebrated River of Kings, snakes 365 kilometres (225 mi) south from Nakhorn Sawan in the central plains, past the ancient city of Ayutthaya, down to Bangkok and finally out at Samut Prakarn into the Gulf of Thailand. Nowadays, this historic river (*mae nam* means "river") appears at first glance as a rather murky flow of water, buzzing with industrial-looking tugs, express-boat taxis, and noisy *rua hang yao*, or long-tailed boats. Nonetheless, exploring this famous river and its intricate network of *khlong*, or canals, is one of Bangkok's more appealing highlights. Besides the towering modern apartments and the luxurious riverside hotels, there are ancient temples and the fairytale spires of the Grand Palace. And along the smaller connecting canals are rustic wooden houses, floating markets and smiling children diving unselfconsciously naked into the muddy waters – an appealing glimpse of life away from the city's pollution and congestion.

For centuries, the Chao Phraya has been the lifeblood of Thailand. It was along this river that the Thais fled from their ancient stronghold of Ayutthaya (an excellent river-cruise excursion from Bangkok) after defeat by Burmese invaders in 1767 to establish their new kingdom briefly in Thonburi, before moving to the more protected Bangkok on the opposite bank. To this day, Mae Nam Chao

BELOW: old house and spirit house on the river, and speeding along a back canal.

Phraya remains a working river, the means by which rice and a whole host of other supplies from the fertile central plains are transported to the capital.

For travel writers and other visitors, the Chao Phraya is central to the romance of Bangkok. In 1888, a little-known 30-year-old Polish seaman, Teodor Konrad Korzeniowski, wrote: "There it was, spread largely on both banks, the Oriental capital which had yet suffered no white conqueror. Here and there in the distance, above the crowded mob of low, brown roof ridges, towered great piles of masonry, king's palace, temples, gorgeous and dilapidated, crumbling under the vertical sunlight, tremendous, overpowering, almost palpable, which seemed to enter one's breast with the breath of one's nostrils and soak into one's limbs through every pore of the skin."

Bangkok's venerable **Oriental Hotel** ⓯, established in 1876, named a suite in its author's wing after this scribe, who later changed his name to Joseph Conrad. Today, the grand hotel that overlooks the banks of the Chao Phraya and operates its own luxury river cruises upstream to Ayutthaya is also where most visitors embark for their first taste of the Chao Phraya. Two minutes' walk from the hotel is the **Tha Orienten Pier**, where one can hop a 7-baht ride on an express river taxi and get off at any of the stops along the route, to as far north as Nonthaburi. Alternatively, charter a long-tail boat for a faster, private, but considerably more expensive glimpse of river life. Remember to bargain fiercely for the boat hire; expect to pay at least 300 baht an hour.

There are several pier stops south of Tha Orienten, but most of the highlights of the river are to the north, and also to the west along Khlong Mon. As the express boat noisily chugs off, filled by a mix of local commuters, tourists and saffron clad monks, take a glimpse of the old colonial buildings on the Bangkok

Oriental Hotel swimming pool and Chao Phraya.

BELOW: Wat Arun and cross-river ferry during flooding of the Chao Phraya River.

**Map,
page 146**

*In the mid 1800s,
perhaps 90 percent of
the city's half-million
population lived
along the city's
khlong, or canals.*

OPPOSITE: driver of
rua hang yao, or
long-tail boat.
BELOW: river pier at
the Oriental Hotel,
with the Sheraton in
the distance.

side of the river: the **French Embassy**, the crumbling **Old Customs House** and the **General Post Office**. On the Thonburi side are the new and as yet unfinished Peninsula and Sofitel hotels. On the right side of the river is the **River City Shopping Complex** , and a patch of rather tatty warehouses and shacks fronting the Chinatown area by the Tha Ratchawong pier. Just beyond a singularly tacky modern high-rise with a mock St Paul's Cathedral dome are two bridges: **Phra Pok Klao Bridge** and the **Memorial Bridge ⑰**, the first to span the Chao Phraya and opened by King Rama VII (Prajadhipok) in 1932 to commemorate the 150th anniversary of the Chakri dynasty. The bridges mark the beginning of the royal district of Rattanakosin.

On the left and directly opposite the Grand Palace is **Wat Arun ⑱** (open daily), unmistakable and one the river's oldest and most distinctive landmarks, dating back to the Ayutthayan period before King Taksin moved the Thai capital south to Thonburi and later to Bangkok. The temple's 82-metre-high (270 ft) *prang*, which is featured on the 10-baht coin, is bedecked with millions of tiny pieces of Chinese porcelain donated by average Thai citizens during the reign of King Mongkut (Rama IV).

Named after Aruna, the Hindi god of dawn, Wat Arun is a spectacular sight from the river. The central prang, which symbolises Mount Meru, the mythical Buddhist peak, is surrounded by four minor prangs at the corners of the *wat*. In between the minor prangs are four *mondop*.

Just beyond Wat Arun, also on the Thonburi side of the river, is **Wat Rakang**, the bell wat and which has a lovely collection of bells that are rung each morning. In the library, superb murals dating from 1788 depict scenes from the *Ramakien*. Further is **Khlong Bangkok Noi** and the **Royal Barge Museum ⑲** (open 8.30am–4.30pm daily; admission fee). The Royal Barges are a fascinating collection of superbly crafted and regal river vessels, which are kept housed in a rather nondescript warehouse. The most famous of the Royal Barges is the 46-metre (150 ft) *Subanahongsa*, constructed in 1911, and which normally conveys the king during a Royal Barge procession. The craft requires a crew of 54 oarsmen, two steersmen, two officers, one flagman, one rhythm keeper and one singer, who chants to the cadence of the oars. Two seven-tiered umbrellas are placed in front of and behind the golden pavilion that shelters the king. On the prow of the barge is a gilded *hong*, or sacred swan.

Should you have the opportunity to witness this rare event, which only happens once every few years, do not miss it. Oarsmen in traditional costumes propel the mighty vessels in a lengthy procession, chanting ancient barge songs called *bot heh reua*. Instruments play and thousands cheer. It is a sight that evokes the pomp and splendour of the early kingdom that gave the Chao Phraya its old name, River of Kings.

Further upstream on Khlong Bangkok Noi is **Wat Suwannaram**, built by Rama I on the site of an earlier temple and extensively renovated since. Within the *viharn* are well-preserved murals from the early 1800s depicting, among other events and scenes, the ten lives of Buddha. Commissioned by Rama III, they are thought by many to be Bangkok's best temple murals. ❏

Waterways

For centuries, the river and *khlong*, or canal, served as the transportation arteries of Thailand. In a land that flooded whenever the monsoon-swollen rivers overflowed their banks, it made little sense to build roads that would be washed away. Rivers and canals also provided natural defenses as moats against invaders.

In the central plains, and especially at Ayutthaya, master engineers diverted a river to turn Ayutthaya into a fortified island. Later, in Bangkok, engineers dug a canal across a neck of land between the present site of Thammasat University and Wat Arun, thereby eliminating a long roundabout route to the mouth of the Chao Phraya. Erosion eventually widened the canal, which has now become the river's main course. The original river loop became the khlong of Bangkok Noi and Bangkok Yai. When King Rama I established Bangkok, he had three concentric canals constructed, turning the royal city into an island. Other canals were dug to connect them. In the 19th century, it was estimated that more than 100,000 boats plied Bangkok's canals.

The most extensive rural canal expansion came during the reign of King Chulalongkorn. His engineers mapped the central plains, and the monarch gave farm land to those who would dig a section of canal passing through his property. In a few years, thousands of kilometres of canals crisscrossed central Thailand. The magnitude of this enormous project can only be appreciated from the air.

In the mid 20th century, Bangkok shifted from boats to cars. Canals were filled in to create roads, and houses were built on solid ground. The result is evident: congested and noisy streets in the hot season, flooded streets in the monsoon season.

Zipping along at water level in a *rua hang yao*, or long-tailed boat, is one of the coolest ways to tour the city. The rua hang yao is a particularly Thai invention, born of necessity. In engineering terms, it is simplicity itself: A car or truck engine is mounted on a pivot at the stern of a long, low and narrow boat. A long shaft, or "tail", extends from the back of the boat, the small propeller spinning furiously in the water, spitting a rooster tail and propelling the boat at quite rapid speeds. In the narrow canals, the pivot allows the boatman to turn the craft in a very tight radius.

A lovely 90-minute route zips upriver to Khlong Bangkok Noi. A short way beyond the Bangkok Noi Railway Station is the Royal Barge Museum. If asked, the driver will stop for a few minutes for a tour of the museum. Continue up the canal, turning left into Khlong Chak Phra, which soon changes its name to Bang Kounsri and eventually to Bangkok Yai.

One of the most scenic khlong in the eastern section of Bangkok is Khlong Saen Sap, dug to carry troops to Chachoengsao to fight invaders from the east, and to join the Bangpakong River for a journey into the sea. The canal begins at Pratunam, but the water is filthy and fetid there.

Better to start at the Ekamai Bridge or at Phrakanong Khlong Tan Bridge. The canal is straight and unshaded, so it's less attractive than the twisting and convoluted Thonburi canals, but nevertheless it passes through lovely rice country. In any case and on any khlong, take a look. ■

BEYOND THE ROYAL CITY

To the north of the royal city is Dusit, with the modern palace and Thailand's parliament. South is Chinatown and the old foreigners' district. West are the clutter and high-rises of a modern city

Map, page 138

The royal district of old Bangkok – with its brightly coloured exotic temples, saffron-clad monks and the stately allure of the magnificent Grand Palace – rightly draws the first attentions of most visitors to Thailand. But it is the less picturesque, more chaotic contemporary Bangkok that gets its tenacious grip on travelers, overloading the senses with an intoxicating mixture of sunbaked petrol fumes, the hot steam of stir-fried noodles, the screech of *tuk-tuks* and the sing-song haggling of night-market hawkers and go-go bar touts. It's a city that doesn't so much appeal to the senses as bludgeon them with striking, vivid, noisy and contrasting images. One night in Bangkok, or even one day of wandering through the sweltering heat, is not for the fainthearted, but it is certainly a memorable experience. Still, there are quiet escapes within the city.

Dusit, north of the royal city

To the north of Rattanakosin, the old royal city, is the much more serene and dignified Dusit area. Just past the railway line on the north side of Thanon Sri Ayutthaya is a huge leafy set of grounds surrounded by a moat and high railings. Within these grounds are grazing cattle, milk churns and fishponds. It would be easy to think this was a farm, but in fact it is the **Chitralada Palace ⓴**, where the king and queen live. The current king, Bhumibol Adulyadej, has lived here throughout his reign. Chitralada Palace was built in 1913 by King Rama VI (Vajiravudh), who at the time still lived in the Grand Palace but wanted a quiet retreat from the pomp and grandeur of the court. The villa itself is a low-rise structure obscured by the greenery, but the grounds are put to good use for experimental farming projects. Chitralada Palace is not open to the public.

Just past the Chitralada compound, on the other side of Thanon Sri Ayutthaya, is **Wat Benchamabophit ⓴** (open daily), or the Marble Temple. The last major temple built in Bangkok, it was started by Rama V (Chulalongkorn) in 1900 and was finished 10 years later. Through the rear entrance of the courtyard is a huge *bodhi* tree approaching a century in age and said to be derived from a tree that came from Buddha's birthplace in India.

Just past Wat Benchamabophit is Thanon Ratchadamnoen, a pleasant, tree-lined boulevard that leads past a huge square dominated by a **statue of King Chulalongkorn ⓴** on horseback. Chulalongkorn was responsible for much of this part of Bangkok. On the anniversary of his death on 23 October, the square is crowded with students and government officials honouring him by laying wreaths at the base of his statue.

To the left of the square is **Suan Amporn ⓴**, a spacious park with fountains and trees. It is the setting for

PRECEDING PAGES: downtown looking west. **OPPOSITE:** dusk over Silom, near the Chao Phraya. **BELOW:** Bangkok's traffic.

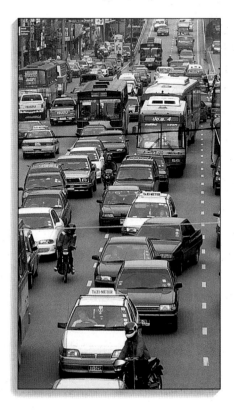

many royal social functions and fairs. Directly behind and north of the square and statue stands **Ananta Samakom** ❷ (Royal Throne Hall), an Italianate hall of grey marble crowned by a huge dome. It was built in 1907 by King Chulalongkorn as his throne hall, later becoming the National Assembly (Parliament) building. Special permission is required to go inside the building, decorated with huge murals depicting famous events in Thai history. In 1974, Parliament moved to new premises a short distance north.

East is **Dusit Zoo** ❷, the city's main animal park and one of the most popular places in Bangkok for family outings. A lake with boats for rent is surrounded by an aviary and enclosures containing the exotic wildlife of Asia: gibbons, Sumatran orangutans, snakes and elephants.

Vimarnmek.

Behind the old National Assembly building is **Vimarnmek** ❷, billed as the world's largest golden teak-wood mansion. As much a work of art as the treasures it holds within, Vimarnmek, or Cloud Mansion, was built by King Chulalongkorn as a residence for his family in what was, in 1900, the suburbs of Bangkok. The airy, 100-room home is filled with crystal, Faberge jewellery and other objets d'art brought from Europe. It demonstrates as well as any museum in the country the extent to which the royal family were influenced by European culture in the latter part of the 19th and early part of the 20th centuries.

Chinatown

South of the Dusit area, east of the old royal city and on the north side of the winding Chao Phraya, is Bangkok's Chinatown.

Chinese merchants originally settled the area that now comprises the old royal city, but were asked to move to the present **Sampeng Lane** ❷ (Soi Wanit 1)

BELOW: studio in Vimarnmek.

when construction began on the Grand Palace in the 1780s. In 1863, King Mongkut built Charoen Krung (New Road), the first paved street in Bangkok, and Chinatown soon began to expand northwards towards it. Charoen Krung runs over 6 kilometres (4 mi) from the Grand Palace southward to where it terminates at the river, just south of the Krung Thep Bridge. Chinatown was followed at Khlong Krung Kasem by a Muslim district that, in turn, was followed by an area occupied by *farang* (foreigners) where the Oriental Hotel now stands. Later, a third road, Thanon Yaowarat, was built between Charoen Krung and Sampeng, becoming the principal road of Chinatown and the name by which this area is frequently known, **Yaowarat**.

The area has had a somewhat rowdy history. What began with mercantile pursuits soon degenerated into a lusty, earthy entertainment area. By 1900, alleys led to opium dens and houses whose entrances were marked by green lanterns (*khom khiew*). A green-light district was like a Western red-light district, and while the lanterns have disappeared, the term *khom khiew* still signifies a brothel. Eventually, Sampeng was tamed into a sleepy lane of small shops selling goods imported from China. Sampeng Lane begins on Thanon Maha Chai and is bound at either end by Indian and Muslim shops. The western end, Pahurat, has a warren of tiny lanes filled with Indians and Sikhs selling cloth. Across the canal is Sampeng proper, with shops selling inexpensive jewellery, tools, cloth, clothes, toys, shoes and novelties.

After leaving the old royal city and crossing Thanon Chakrawat, turn right a short distance to the entrance of **Wat Chakrawat** ㉘, an odd amalgam of buildings. Dating from the Ayutthaya period and thus predating Chinatown, it has a small grotto with a statue of a laughing monk. Myth says that it is the likeness of

Map, page 138

Thailand's first Chinese immigrants were merchants in the 1500s. In the centuries since, the kingdom's Chinese population has become strongly integrated in Thai society.

BELOW: shy girl in Chinatown.

Street sign for a palm-reading expert, Chinatown.

BELOW: paper images are burnt for the ancestors.

a monk who was once slim and handsome, so handsome he was constantly pestered by women. His devotion to Buddhism led him to the unusual remedy of eating until he grew so gross that the women lost interest. Near the end of Sampeng the shops bear Muslim names. The merchants here trade gems. Marking the eastern end of Sampeng is **Wat Pathuma Kongkha ㉙**, another temple from the Ayutthaya period. It was here that criminals of royal birth were executed for crimes against the state.

At places, Thanon Yaowarat looks like a somewhat dowdier version of a Hong Kong street with its forest of signs. It is best known for its gold shops, all of which seem to have been designed by a cookie cutter, so alike they look. Daily prices are scrawled on the windows of shops painted red for good luck. Mirrors and neon lights complete the decor.

Yaowarat is also an old entertainment area. Halfway down on the north side of the street is the famous "Seven Storey Mansion" that flourished well into the middle part of the 20th century. It was designed so that those interested only in dining could do so on the ground floor. As the evening progressed and one relaxed, one would ascend the stairs, floor by floor, to more Sybaritic delights. Unrepentant hedonists headed straight for the top floor. Between Yaowarat and Charoen Krung, near the western end of Chinatown, is **Nakhon Kasem ㉚** (Thieves Market). A few decades ago, it was the area a householder searched after being robbed, a likely place where one might recover stolen goods for a very reasonable price. It later became an antique dealer's area, but now handles mainly more prosaic household items.

Near the eastern end of Charoen Krung is Chinatown's biggest Buddhist temple, **Wat Mangkon ㉛**. From early in the morning it is aswirl with activity and incense smoke reminiscent of old China. The most interesting lane nearby is Isara Nuphap, which runs south from Thanon Phlab Phla Chai. Around the entrance to Isara Nuphap are shops selling paper effigies of houses, Mercedes-Benzes, household furniture and other items. These are burnt in the Chinese *kong tek* ceremony, a ritual that, it is believed, sends the material goods to the afterlife for use by deceased relatives.

Just east of the point where Thanon Yaowarat meets Thanon Charoen Krung (not far from Hua Lamphong Railway Station, which connects Bangkok to the rest of the country by rail) is **Wat Traimit ㉜** (open daily) and the famous Golden Buddha. Found by accident in the 1950s at a riverside temple when a construction company was extending its dock, the huge stucco figure of the Buddha was too heavy for the sling. It snapped and, to the horror of all, smashed to the ground, breaking one corner. A close examination showed a glint of yellow through the crack. Further investigation revealed that the stucco was only a thin coat, and that inside was an image of solid gold weighing over five tons. Like many similar statues, it was probably made elsewhere in Thailand during the Ayutthaya period. To preserve it from Burmese invaders, it had been covered in stucco to conceal its true composition and rested undetected for centuries.

Bangkrak and Silom

Further south and just east of the Chao Phraya is **Bangkrak**, a vibrant modern district that has risen in just the past decade. This area has long been a neighbourhood of *farang*, the expat foreigners. Anchoring the western end is the grand **Oriental Hotel**, right on the bank of the Chao Phraya. From the Oriental, stroll past the gaggle of *tuk-tuk* drivers, long-tail boat touts and "copy-watch" sellers

Map, page 138

Wat Traimit's Golden Buddha may be the world's largest solid-gold Buddha at 4 metres in height. Of Sukhothai style, it may date from the 13th century.

BELOW: wholesale market, Chinatown.

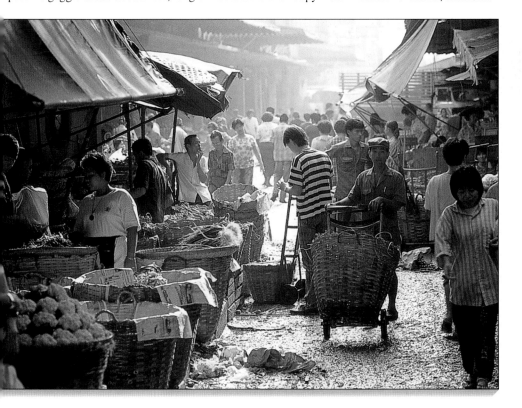

Fate or Choice?

Thailand has a prostitution problem. It is of neither recent nor imported vintage. Contrary to the impression of many foreigners, prostitution has been illegal for over 30 years. Social scientists and non-governmental organisations estimate that there are between 300,000 and 2 million Thai prostitutes in Thailand and overseas in places like Japan. In Thailand, no truck stop or town with a population of 20,000 would be complete without a few ramshackle brothels.

According to a Thai newspaper editor, except for the area surrounding the Grand Palace, there is not a single neighbourhood in Bangkok where sex is not for sale, mostly to Thai men. The venues include brothels, hotels, nightclubs, massage parlours, bars, barber shops, parks, karaoke lounges and even golf courses. At the top are private-member clubs, advertised in the glossiest magazines. At the bottom are locked brothels, where the women – and young girls – are virtually enslaved. As measured by compensation and working conditions, the tawdry bars serving foreign men in Patpong are somewhere in between.

There is no single reason why Thailand has more prostitutes than many poorer countries. The traditional explanation of poverty, however, carries less and less weight. While most patrons of Thai prostitutes are Thai men, foreigners also contribute to the demand. Besides the infamous sex tours from Japan, Germany, Australia and elsewhere, there is also a sizable community of Western men, notably in Pattaya and Phuket, who live in Thailand solely because of the cheap sex, child sex or teenage wives.

Agents kidnap young girls or trick them with offers of factory jobs from remote provinces. These girls may end up in locked brothels, from which they may eventually be smuggled to other Asian countries.

It's hard for poor families to resist the blandishments. Particularly at April "harvest time", when 12- and 13-year-old girls finish the customary 6 years of schooling, agents flock to villages, where they offer parents hundreds of dollars or electric appliances in exchange for pretty daughters. A girl typically has to work off a debt that is twice her sale price, although she may have to start over if she is resold before reaching her goal.

When asked why she became or remains a prostitute, a young woman will usually talk about luck or fate. Yet true Buddhists believe in neither, and don't subscribe to predestination. Buddhism, of course, doesn't sanction prostitution at all.

Feminist NGOs don't focus their primary efforts on extricating girls and women from prostitution. They have found that regardless of how women were originally lured into prostitution, few are strongly motivated to get out. The work is easy, the money is too good, and the family pressure overwhelming. Instead, the advocates concentrate on prevention, teaching marketable skills.

Prostitution is probably the principal reason why the AIDS epidemic is so extensive in Thailand. Random blood testing indicates that just under 1 million men, women and children are now infected with AIDS in Thailand. It is neither a Thai nor a *farang* (foreigner) problem. It is a human problem. ■

to the end of the *soi* (alley or lane), turn right and you'll soon be at the less exciting end of one of Bangkok's most exciting streets, Thanon Silom. Cross over and start walking down Silom and you will quickly pick up the flavour of the city – the end-to-end gridlock of cars, the small clusters of motorcyclists with gaudy numbered vests who act as a taxi service (if you're in an adventurous mood, take one to the end of the street as they weave skillfully among the cars, buses and tuk tuks). On either side of the street are jewellery and handicraft stores, banks and restaurants, offices and shopping malls. There are some big brash eateries popular with tourists such as Silom Village, but much more appealing are the elegant restaurants for the locals tucked discreetly away in the lanes off Silom, especially Thanon Pramuan, near a Hindu temple, **Maha Uma Devi**, founded in the 1860s. In the neighbourhood is Thanying, a Thai restaurant in the style of an aristocratic Thai home, set in leafy gardens and run by a Bangkok socialite who is also closely related to the Thai royal family.

Silom really comes to life at night. The Silom night-market begins about half way down on the left side of the street, crowding the narrow pavement with a colourful array of stalls on both sides. Here you must bargain fiercely for the fake watches, jeans, T-shirts, shirts and luggage on offer. Most bargaining is done with the aid of calculators, though if you can get the hang of Thai numbers, it'll probably help bring down the price. About half way along the night-market, the stalls curve off to the left along a noisy neon-lit street. Love it or hate it, and few have any other opinion, the notorious **Patpong** ❸❸ (which is actually two streets – Patpong I and Patpong II) has an electric, sinful arrogance that any visitor ought to experience at least once. It's hard to imagine a starker contrast to the serene temples and palaces and the gracious smiles and *wai* of

Map, page 138

Map, page 138

TIP

In November, Maha Uma Devi is the centre of the Hindi festival of lights, Deepavali.

OPPOSITE: Patpong dancer. **BELOW:** transvestites in Patpong.

TIP

The tranquil airs of Lumpini Park give way to Thai boxing, or muay thai, *which dates to the 1400s. Bouts are staged at Lumpini Stadium (east of the park) on Tuesdays and Fridays, and at Ratchadamnoen Stadium, south of Dusit, on Mondays, Wednesdays and Thursdays.*

BELOW: morning *tai chi*, Lumpini Park.

hotel staff than the raucous touting and outrageous sex shows of Patpong. Nowadays, there seem to be as many curious middle-aged couples as die-hard sex tourists in and around the bars of Patpong, and the atmosphere is sometimes more racy fun than unrelenting sleaze. There are more bars on Thanon Suriwong, which runs parallel to Silom, and on Silom Soi 4, which runs parallel to Patpong and Patpong II. The bars in Soi 4 attract a very different kind of crowd, generally younger. Some are gay bars while others are trendy bar/cafes popular with resident expatriates. The long-running Rome Club has a decadent transvestite cabaret show every night around midnight and is well worth a visit.

At the end of Silom is a huge and busy intersection that can take a good fifteen minutes to cross. But to the northeast across the intersection lies respite from the relentless dust and petrol fumes of the city. **Suan Lumpini 34 (Lumpini Park**), which Bangkokians call the lung of the city, is a tranquil and tropical oasis of greenery with boating lakes, open-air exercise areas, and outdoor cafes. In the morning, people jog, practice *tai chi* exercises, lift weights, even dance under the trees. Along the park's lakes, kiosks rent rowboats or paddleboats. In the afternoons, boys play *takraw* and soccer, or during the hot season, fly kites. Everything stops, momentarily, at 6pm, when the Thai national anthem is played in the park and people stand rigidly to attention in a moving and sincerely felt display of patriotism.

Directly west along Thanon Rama IV is the **Saowapha Institute 35** (open Monday–Friday 8.30am–4.30pm, Saturday and Sunday 8.30–noon; admission fee), or as it is better known in English, the **Snake Farm**. Operated by the Thai Red Cross, its primary function is not to entertain tourists (though it does) but the more serious business of producing anti-venom serum to be used on snakebite

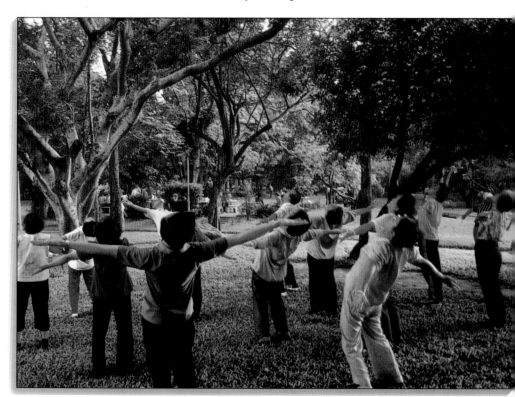

victims, of which there are many every year throughout the country. The Snake Farm, the second oldest of its kind in the world, produces serum from seven types of snake: the king cobra, Siamese cobra, banded krait, Russell's viper, Malayan pit viper and the green and Pope's pit viper. This snake farm is professionally run, informative and well worth a visit. Adjacent is a respected clinic for sexually-transmitted diseases.

Core of modern Bangkok

Coming out of Lumpini Park at the northwestern end onto Thanon Ratchadamri, head north along Ratchadamri, which eventually reaches Bangkok's prime shopping district. Along the way on the left is another section of greenery, the **Royal Bangkok Sports Club**, a private club with sports facilities, golf course, swimming pool, tennis courts and horseracing on Sundays during all but the rainiest months. The club is closed to non-members, but the racecourse is open to the public. There is no off-track betting, so you'll have to wait till other people put their baht on the line to get any idea of the winning odds. These are then displayed on a huge computerised board and the prices change dramatically as everyone places their bets at the last minute.

Access to the racetrack is from the other side along the parallel Thanon Henri Dunant. (Thais still use its old name of Sanam Ma, or Racecourse Road.) Across this road stands the temple-like buildings of **Chulalongkorn University** ㊱, the country's oldest and most prestigious institution of higher learning. Built in a mixture of Thai and Western styles, with spacious yellow-roofed pavilions, an open gallery and an assembly hall, the university was founded by King Vajiravudh, who reigned from 1911–1925 and named the university after his father.

Map, page 138

BELOW: Lumpini Park, and downtown twilight.

Heading north along Thanon Ratchadamri towards the intersection with Thanon Rama I, one passes two of the city's most opulent hotels, The Regent and the Grand Hyatt Erawan. At the intersection, the **Erawan Shrine** ❸ draws visitors and locals. To improve their fortunes or to pass exams, believers make offerings at a statue of a four-faced deity. To repay the god for wishes granted, supplicants place floral garlands or wooden elephants at the god's feet. On most days, dancers in traditional costume and paid by worshippers add to the colourful scene. Outside are little stalls where people sit all day making floral garlands that worshippers purchase as offerings. This attractive corner is, however, now somewhat marred by the ugly elevated transit rails overhead – forever under construction and dwarfing the intersection.

This intersection also marks the centre of Bangkok's prime shopping district. In the future there are plans for a series of air-conditioned walkways that will link the main shopping malls within a one-kilometre radius. East of the intersection is Thanon Ploenchit, either side of which are ritzy malls, including the international-designer showcase Gaysorn Plaza, complete with a Planet Hollywood; adjoining Thanon Chitlom has the largest branch of Thailand's Central Department Store. This was burnt down in 1995 but has now been rebuilt.

Thanon Rama I turns into Thanon Ploenchit heading east. Beyond the British Embassy, the boulevard eventually turns into Thanon Sukhumvit – an area known simply as **Sukhumvit** ❸ – and stretches virtually as far as the resort town of Pattaya. Sukhumvit is a very busy commercial and residential district, with many restaurants and bars that cater to locals and expats, but relatively few tourists, as the area is not rich in cultural attractions. There are, however, the enormous **seafood market** on Soi 24, and the **Kamthieng House**, a lovely 130-

BELOW: Erawan Shrine.

year-old Thai-style house in the Siam Society compound on Sukhumvit Soi 21.

To the northwest of the Erawan Shrine – kitty-corner across the intersection – is the World Trade Centre, yet another huge shopping mall. If feeling trapped by malls and commerce, duck into **Wat Pathum Wanaram** ㊴, a quiet temple tucked in behind the World Trade Centre. The temple was built by King Mongkut in a large park that also held a palace and a lotus pond (after which the temple was named), so that he could escape the summer heat of Rattanakosin. The palace is gone, the trees have been cut and the ponds filled in to build the World Trade Centre complex. Wat Pathum Wanaram is the most popular temple in Bangkok among taxi drivers, who drive here to have their vehicles blessed against accidents. The temple also holds regular meditation classes.

Opposite the World Trade Centre is the government's handicrafts store, **Narayana Phand** ㊵. It has an excellent selection of Thai-made goods on several floors and is worth exploring, if for no other reason than to learn about the wide variety of Thai crafts. Along the way up Ratchadamri to Ratchadamri Arcade and Bangkok Bazaar are numerous small shops crammed into a small space and vendors spilling off the pavements. One can often find some good handicraft bargains at small shops in Ratchadamri Arcade. The pair serve as a link between the chic shops of Ratchaprasong and the bazaar atmosphere of the vast, sprawling **Pratunam** ㊶, a little further to the north and a favourite shopping place for many Thais and budget travellers. Pratunam means "water gate" and refers to the lock at the bridge to prevent Khlong San Sap, to the east, from being flooded by the one to the west, which leads to the Chao Phraya.

North is **Suan Pakkad** ㊷ (open Sunday–Thursday 9am–4pm) also known as the Cabbage Patch Palace, at 352 Thanon Sri Ayutthaya. The splendid resi-

Map,
page 138

Two high-rise towers loom near Pratunam: a tall one and a short one. For nearly a decade, the short one was Thailand's tallest building. The taller skyscraper, 90-storey Baiyoke Tower, has been under construction for nearly an eternity.

BELOW: tourist police ready to help.

Map, page 138

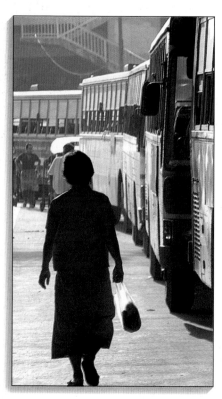

Store offerings of silk.

OPPOSITE: garden outside Jim Thompson's house. **BELOW:** looking for a bus.

dence belonged to the late Princess Chumbhot, one of Thailand's leading gardeners and art collectors. The beautifully landscaped grounds (*suan* means garden, *pakkad* means cabbage) contain numerous plants the princess brought from all over the world, as well as varieties found in the Thai jungle. One probably would not wish to wander much further north than here, except perhaps by taxi to **Chattuchak** weekend market, one of the biggest outdoor markets you are ever likely to see and a real highlight for both casual and serious shoppers.

Continue west along Thanon Rama I to yet more shopping. The intersection of Rama I and Phaya Thai roads is one of the best areas to shop, especially for those who like a little local colour and confusion. On the southwest corner next to the **National Stadium** 🕒 is the air-conditioned Mahboonkrong or MBK Centre, one of Bangkok's biggest complexes. It's more like an indoor market than a mall, with five crowded floors of cheap local clothes, stalls, supermarkets, boutiques and fast-food joints.

To the east across Phaya Thai is the Discovery Centre, a plush air-conditioned mall comprising mainly international brand names at extravagant international prices. Of more interest to visitors is the adjacent Siam Centre, a mecca for young Thai trendies looking for locally made international labels. Across the road (don't even try walking through the endless traffic – take one of the walkways across the street) is one the oldest shopping areas in Bangkok, **Siam Square** 🕒. Inside are movie theatres, bookstores and a wealth of restaurants. There is also the British Council, with its excellent library, and the Hard Rock Cafe. Chinese visitors, including movie stars from Hong Kong, frequently flock to this area for its shark's-fin and bird's-nest soup restaurants.

But there are other attractions besides shopping and eating in this area. On Khlong Maha Nag at the north end of Soi Kasemsan II is the **Jim Thompson House** 🕒 (open daily 9am–5pm; tel: 215 0122; admission fee). This Thai-style house is, in truth, a collection of seven Thai houses acquired from central Thailand, disassembled and brought to Bangkok, and then joined together by the remarkable American. Thompson came to Thailand at the end of World War II as an intelligence agent and later revived the Thai silk industry. In 1967, while on a visit to the Cameron Highlands in Malaysia, Thompson mysteriously disappeared; despite an extensive search, no trace has ever been found of him. Some say he simply died of a heart attack, while others suggest CIA shenanigans. Nonetheless, his sumptuous traditional Thai-style home remains and is open to the public. The silk business he founded continues to flourish, and if you are looking for expensive and tasteful souvenirs to take home, Jim Thompson silks are a good value.

Inside the houses and throughout the grounds are 14 centuries' worth of Southeast Asian antiques. If looking to invest in antiques, come here first to see the best. There are, for example, a limestone torso of a Buddha image, said to be one of the oldest existing Buddha figures in Southeast Asia. Throughout the house are carved images, in wood and stone, of Burmese spirits and Buddhas. Superb paintings from the 1800s fill the master bedroom, while blue-and-white Ming-dynasty porcelain is displayed elsewhere in the house. ❐

OUTSIDE OF BANGKOK

Escaping the fuss of Bangkok is easier than might be imagined. Crocodiles, roses, immense Buddhas, World War II relics, wild tigers and elephants, waterfalls, and markets await on day-trips

Map, page 179

THAILAND

Bangkok

Located near enough to Bangkok for a comfortably paced day-trip, the eastern province of Nakhon Nayok offers waterfalls and a pretty park. The most scenic route to this province is Route 305, which branches off Route 1 just north of Rangsit, 30 kilometres (20 mi) north of Bangkok. A wide road runs northeast along a lovely canal, passing rice fields and small rivers to **Nakhon Nayok ❶**, about 140 kilometres (90 mi) northeast of the capital. From the town, Route 33 heads northwest and then, within a few kilometres, Route 3049 leads off to the right towards two waterfalls, including Sarika Falls. Near the parking lot are pleasant outdoor restaurants and stalls selling fruits and drinks. Sarika Falls itself is impressive around the end of the rainy season, from September to November. Wear good shoes; the stone paths are slippery.

Nearby is **Wang Takrai National Park**. Along the way is the temple of Chao Pau Khun Dan, named after one of King Naresuan's advisers whose spirit is believed to protect the area. Prince Chumbhot, who established Suan Pakkad in Bangkok, also established the 80-hectare (195 acre) Wang Takrai Park in the 1950s; a statue of him stands on the opposite bank of the small river flowing through the park. His wife, Princess Chumbhot, planted many varieties of flowers and trees, including some imported species. Cultivated gardens sit among tall trees, which line both banks of the river flowing through the park. Bungalows are available.

Khao Yai National Park ❷, the nearest highland escape to Bangkok, lies 200 kilometres (125 mi) northeast of the capital and covers 2,170 square kilometres (840 sq mi). Established in 1962, it is the oldest national park in Thailand. With its proximity to Bangkok, visitors are approaching one million in number annually. It takes about three to four hours to drive to Khao Yai from Bangkok, via one of two routes.

Several years ago, extensive accommodation was available within the park, as well as a restaurant and an 18-hole golf course. These facilities, however, have been closed in an effort to reduce the environmental damage of development. Presently, there are a campsite and some simple dormitories within the park, and camping out on one of the observation towers may be a possibility as well. (Inquire at the TAT office or the forestry department in Bangkok, or at park headquarters.) Outside of the park and on the main road from Pak Chong to Khao Yai, resort hotels and guesthouses have proliferated in recent years.

Khao Yai's highest peaks lie on the east along a land form known as the Khorat Plateau. **Khao Khieo** (Green Mountain) is 1,351 metres (4,433 ft) high and **Khao Laem** (Shadow Mountain), 1,328 metres (4,357 ft).

Khao Yai is comprised of broad-leaf evergreen forests and mixed deciduous trees, with grasslands and scrub

PRECEDING PAGES: white-handed gibbon, Khao Yai. **OPPOSITE:** school lunch. **BELOW:** Khao Yai National Park.

as secondary growth. Even on a short walk through the park, unusual palms, lush ferns and tenacious vines abound and provide a welcome respite. In the cool season, many trees and shrubs come into flower, and numerous wild orchids may be seen, including *Bulbophyllum khaoyaiense*, native only to the park.

Pig-tailed macaques and white-handed and pileated gibbons are among the most commonly seen small mammals. Larger mammals including bears, wild pigs, guars, leopards and other large cats, and various species of deer are occasionally spotted. Khao Yai is also home to about 200 elephants and perhaps 40 tigers, but these are rarely seen. In addition, over 300 species of migrant and resident birds have been identified.

The visitor's centre, adjacent to park headquarters, has somewhat disjointed but interesting displays. It is a good place to begin a tour of Khao Yai. Guides are sometimes available at the headquarters, but you'll have a better chance of getting an English-speaking one if you organise a tour of the park through one of the guesthouses in the area. A dozen or so trails, from 2 to 8 kilometres (5 mi) in length and of varying degrees of difficulty, snake through the park to waterfalls, and to grassy areas and salt licks. In several clearings there are observation towers to watch animals feed.

In the late afternoon, several guesthouses offer trips to a limestone cave at **Khao Rub Chang**, just north of the park and where, at dusk, a massive exodus of wrinkled-lipped bats darkens the sky for more than an hour.

After dark, night safaris can be arranged in which powerful halogen spotlights are used to illuminate night-feeding animals such as barking deer, sambar and civet. At night, winter temperatures may drop to below 15°C (60°F); warm clothes are handy.

TIP

At certain times of the year, the State Railways of Thailand may offer weekend day-trips to Khao Yai; however, the bus is more reliable and often faster.

BELOW: tiger cubs in Khao Yai, a rare sighting.

South of Bangkok

The **Crocodile Farm** ❸ (open daily; admission fee) is located in Samut Prakarn Province, near the river-mouth town of Samut Prakam, half an hour's drive (30 kilometres/20 mi) southeast of Bangkok on the old Sukhumvit Highway (Route 3). Started in the 1960s with an initial investment of about 10,000 baht (less than US$500 back then), the owner now has three farms (two in the northeast) worth 100 million baht. At present, this farm has about 30,000 fresh- and saltwater local crocodiles, as well as some South American caimans and Nile River crocodiles. They are hatched and raised in tanks. The young are protected from mosquitoes, which can blind them by biting their eyes, with netting.

The highlight of a visit to the farm is a show in which handlers enter a pond teeming with crocodiles and toss them about rather roughly. While this sounds dangerous in print, the lethargic beasts are less likely to bite because of innate viciousness than because their noon nap has been interrupted. After the crocodiles are skinned, incidentally, their meat is sold to restaurants in Samut Prakarn and Bangkok. The farm also has a zoo and amusement park with rides. The irony of all this is that the owners have succeeded in preserving the animal; nearly all the wild Asian species have been hunted to extinction.

Also in Samut Prakarn, a few kilometres from the Crocodile Farm, is **Muang Boran** ❹ (**Ancient City**; open daily 8am–5pm; admission fee), which bills itself as the world's largest outdoor museum. The brainchild of a Bangkok millionaire with a passion for Thai art and history, it took around three years to construct. In what used to be 80 hectares (200 acres) of rice fields, designers sketched an area roughly the shape of Thailand and placed the individual attractions as close to their real sites as possible. There are replicas (some full-size,

Map, page 179

Crocodile Farm.

Bangkok Surroundings

most others one-third the size of the originals) of famous monuments and temples from all parts of the kingdom. Some are reconstructions of buildings that no longer exist, like the Grand Palace of Ayutthaya, and some are copies of real places, like the Phimai sanctuary northeast of Nakhon Ratchasima, and the huge temple of Khao Phra Viharn on the Thai-Cambodian border. Experts from the National Museum in Bangkok worked as consultants to ensure the historical accuracy of the reproductions. At present, there are more than 60 monuments covering 1,500 years of Thai history. The monuments are spread out over a large area; it may be most convenient to drive between them. However, the grounds are beautifully landscaped with small waterfalls, creeks, ponds, rock gardens and lush greenery; deer graze freely amongst the many interesting sculptures representing figures from Thai literature and Hindu mythology. In addition to the monuments, Ancient City also has a model Thai village, in which artisans work on handicrafts such as lacquerware, ceramics and paper umbrellas.

For those with time, Paknam is a bustling fishing town with an interesting market along its docks. Cross the river by ferry to the famous **Wat Phra Chedi Klang Nam**, which, contrary to its name ("the chedi in the middle of the river"), is now on solid land, the result of the river shifting its course. Thai kings used to stop at this temple on their way in and out of the country on state visits, praying for success in their journeys or offering thanks on their return.

West of Bangkok

Less than an hour's drive due west from Bangkok, **Suan Sam Phran ❺ (Rose Garden**; open daily; admission fee) is the brainchild of a former lord mayor of the capital. The garden lies 30 kilometres (20 mi) west of the capital on Route 4,

BELOW: Ancient City.

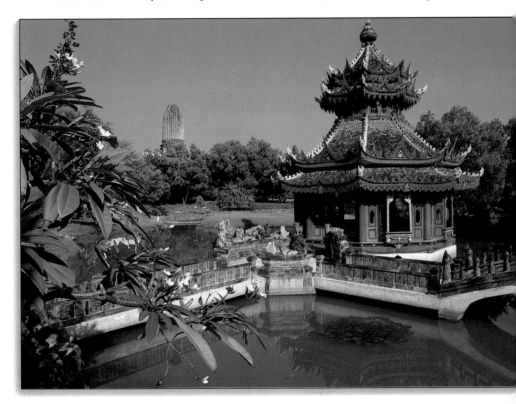

en route to Nakhon Pathom. Its large area of well-landscaped gardens contains roses and orchids, and includes accommodations, restaurants, a golf course reputed to be among the 25 best in the world, paddle boats on an artificial lake, and a children's playground. Its premier attraction is a daily Thai cultural show.

In a large arena, beautifully costumed Thai actors demonstrate folk dances, Thai boxing, a wedding ceremony, cock-fighting and other rural entertainment. Outside after this show, elephants put on their own show, moving huge teak logs as they would in the forests of the north. The elephants then carry tourists around the compound for a small fee.

Just 50 kilometres (30 mi) west of Bangkok, beyond the Rose Garden on Route 4, is the town of **Nakhon Pathom** ❻, famous for **Phra Pathom Chedi**, which rises majestically over the surrounding countryside. At just over 125 metres (410 ft) in height, it is the tallest Buddhist monument in the world, a few metres taller even than the Shwedagon in Rangoon.

Nakhon Pathom is believed to be Thailand's oldest city. The name derives from the Pali for "first city." According to legend, it was the capital of Suvannabhumi, the "land of gold," and it was to here that King Ashoka (268–232 BC) sent two missionaries from India to introduce Buddhism. The first archeological records date from the 6th century when the area was populated by the Mons, Dvaravati-Buddhists who flourished in the Chao Phraya basin from the 6th to 11th centuries. The original chedi is believed to have been constructed by the Mons in the late 10th century. In the early 11th century, Nakhon Pathom and the surrounding area fell to the Khmers, who built a Brahman (Hindu) *prang* some 40 metres (130 ft) tall, which enclosed the original Buddhist structure.

In 1057, King Anawratha of Pagan besieged the city, leaving the chedi in

Map,
page 179

TIP

Southeast of the Phra Pathom Chedi is the Phra Pathom Chedi National Museum, with a nice collection of artefacts excavated from the area. Open Wednesday–Sunday. Admission fee.

BELOW: Nakhon Pathom's Phra Pathom Chedi.

ruins. Although the city regained brief importance in the 16th century as a defensive position against the invading Burmese, it wasn't until 1853 that repairs were begun in earnest to the chedi. King Mongkut, who had spent time in the area as a young monk before gaining the throne, was impressed with the age and history of the edifice, and believed it to contain a relic of the Buddha. The final structure was completed during the reign of King Chulalongkorn in the early 20th century. Set in a huge square park, the massive chedi, covered with golden-orange tiles imported from China, rests upon a circular terrace, the perimeter of which is accented with sacred trees. Walking up the enormous main staircase leads to the North Viharn and the Sukhothai-style standing Buddha, the stone head, hands and feet of which were discovered in Sawankhalok in 1900. King Vajiravudh commissioned a bronze body cast to match the stone pieces; the statue was enshrined in 1915 and is greatly revered by Thais. The king's ashes are buried at the base of the statue.

After investigating the chedi, wander around the grounds for a few moments. Have your palm read for a small fee (there's at least one fortune teller who speaks enough English to make it entertaining), enjoy a delicious iced coffee made fresh on the spot and served in a small plastic bag with a straw, and peruse the startling selection of skin magazines that are sold just at the base of the chedi.

In former times, a royal visit to Nakhon Pathom was more than a day's journey, so it is not surprising that a number of palaces and summer residences were built there. One of them, **Sanam Chand Palace**, 2 kilometres west of Phra Pathom Chedi, has a fine *sala*, a meeting pavilion now used for government offices, and a building in a most unusual Thai interpretation of English Tudor architecture, used appropriately as a setting for Shakespearean drama. In front

BELOW: riverside laundry washing.

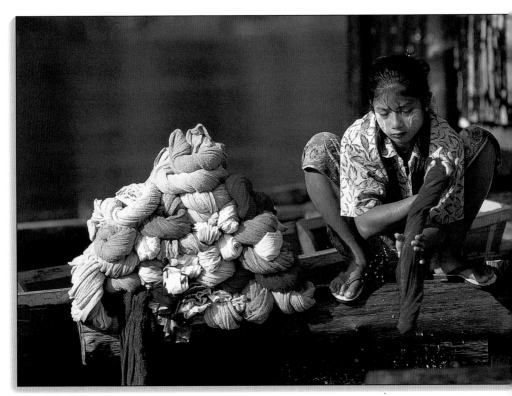

stands a statue of Yaleh, the pet dog of King Vajiravudh, who commissioned the palace. The fierce dog, unpopular with the court, was poisoned by the king's attendants. Even as a statue, Yaleh looks insufferable. Although most of the palace buildings are closed to the public, one of them serves as a small museum and contains memorabilia of Vajiravudh.

Map, page 179

A good way to approach the coastal port of **Samut Sakhon ❼** is by a branch railway connecting it with Thonburi, on the other side of the Chao Phraya from central Bangkok. The line, called the Mae Khlong Railway, runs at a loss, but it is subsidised because of its usefulness to the population of the three provinces west of Bangkok. The 40-minute journey first passes through the suburbs, then through vegetable gardens, groves of coconut and areca palms, and rice fields.

A busy fishing port, Samut Sakhon lies at the meeting of the Tachin River, the Mahachai Canal and the Gulf of Thailand. The main landing on the riverbank has a clock tower and a restaurant serving excellent seafood. Nearby, fishermen at the fish market unload fish, crabs, squid and prawns from their boats. At the fish-market pier, it's possible to hire a boat for a round-trip to Samut Sakhon's principal temple, Wat Chom Long, at the mouth of the Tachin River. Most of the buildings are modern except for an old viharn, which dates back about a century, immediately to the right of the temple's river landing. The extensive grounds overlooking the water are charmingly laid out with shrubs and flowering trees. There is also a statue of Chulalongkorn. His homburg hat does not in the least detract from his immense dignity.

From Samut Sakhon, cross the river to the railway station on the opposite side. Here, board a second train for another 40-minute trip to **Samut Songkhram ❽**, on the banks of the Meklong River. The journey goes through

BELOW: harbour at Samut Songkhram.

broad salt flats, with picturesque windmills revolving slowly in the sea breezes. Samut Songkhram is another pretty fishing town; wandering its wharf is both an olfactory and a visual experience. Return to Bangkok along the same rail route or hire a long-tailed boat for a trip up the Meklong River to Ratchaburi.

Eighty kilometres (50 mi) southwest of Bangkok, near Samut Songkhram, lies the town of **Damnoen Saduak ➒**, famous for its daily floating market. Beginning before dawn, women in traditional straw hats manoeuvre flat-bottomed boats laden with produce, fish and flowers into position along the canals. They hawk their wares in a colourful spectacle lasting most of the morning, but be there early (the majority of tourists arrive on buses around 9am) for the most authentic experience. Air-conditioned buses depart the southern bus terminal for Damnoen Saduak every half hour beginning at 6am.

Kanchanaburi and the River Kwai

Established in the early 1800s, thus making it a young city by Thai standards, **Kanchanaburi ➓** is about 120 kilometres (75 mi) northwest of Bangkok, past Nakhon Pathom and not far from the Thai border with Burma. It prospers from gem mining and a teak trade with Burma. The world's smallest species of bat, about the size of a bumblebee, was discovered near an odd-looking railway bridge crossing the Meklong River, also known as the Kwai Yai, a few kilometres outside of Kanchanaburi. The bridge is contoured with a series of elliptical spans, with an awkwardly rectangular centre.

This bridge is often called the "Bridge on the River Kwai". In fact, it's not. The bridge that spanned the mightier Kwai River and inspired the novel and film was farther north. Of course, the original bridge no longer exists.

Seeking to shorten supply lines between Japan and Burma in preparation for an eventual attack on British India, the Japanese began work on a railway between Thailand and Burma in 1942. For a large part of its 415 kilometres (260 mi), the railway followed the river valley. Although the logistics of doing so were often nightmarish, following the valley allowed construction of the railway simultaneously in different areas. At the end, there were nearly 15 kilometres (9 mi) of bridges completed. The Japanese forced 250,000 Asian labourers and 61,000 Allied prisoners-of-war to construct 260 kilometres (160 mi) of rail on the Thai side, to Three Pagodas Pass on the border. It is estimated that 100,000 Asian labourers and 16,000 Allied prisoners lost their lives from beatings, starvation, disease and exhaustion. In Kanchanaburi, graves mark 6,982 of those Allied soldiers. There are two cemeteries in Kanchanaburi. The larger is on the main road nearly opposite the railway station; the second, Chungkai, is across the river on the banks of the Kwai Noi. Both hold the remains of Dutch, Australian, British, Danish, New Zealander and other Allied prisoners-of-war; American dead were removed to Arlington Cemetery, outside Washington, D.C.

An appreciation of the enormous obstacles the prisoners faced is provided by the **JEATH Museum** (open daily; admission fee), near the end of Lak Muang Road. (The name derives from the first initial of those nationalities involved in the construction.) Established in 1977

TIP

In late November and early December, Kanchanaburi has a week-long fair that features a nightly sound-and-light show celebrating the Allied attack on the bridge over the Kwai River. Make reservations well in advance – it's popular with locals.

BELOW: sound-and-light show over the Kwai Yai bridge.

by the monks of **Wat Chaichumpol** (Wat Chanasongkhram) next door, the museum was constructed like the bamboo huts in which the war prisoners lived. Utensils, paintings, writings and other objects donated by prisoners who survived share some of the horror of their hellish existence.

Don't confuse the JEATH Museum with the newer **World War II Museum** that is located beside the bridge; the signs can be misleading. The World War II Museum is a curious hodge-podge of exhibits including prehistoric village life, Thai proverbs, stamps, currency, animal skeletons, and one notable display in the rear courtyard of exceptionally poor taste.

In spite of the fact that the memorial bridge is often mistaken for the one made famous in print and film, it is worthwhile visiting from an historical point of view. It can be reached by boat or samlor from Kanchanaburi. Visit at 11am or 4.30pm if you want to see the train passing over the bridge.

The bridge has lost some of its artificial mystery with commercialisation, but walking across it is a sobering experience. (Niches between the spans provide an escape in case a train passes by.) A steam locomotive used shortly after the war is displayed beside the tiny station platform, along with an ingenious Japanese supply truck that could run on both roads and rails. Floating restaurants and hotels line the banks of the river, which is attractive and peaceful despite its grisly history.

Today, most of the old tracks have been removed, except for a section running peacefully from Kanchanaburi to the terminus at Nam Tok, a 50-kilometre (30 mi) journey taking about one-and-a-half hours across one of the shakiest bridges in the world; the wooden pillars and sleepers creak and groan as the train moves slowly across them. ❏

Map,
page 179

Detail from
Wat Chaichumpol.

BELOW: crossing on the modern bridge over the Kwai Yai.

Map,
page 179

THAILAND

Bangkok

FAR TO THE WEST

Beyond the day-trip to Kanchanaburi are some of Thailand's wild lands. Keep going, and one reaches the border with Burma. Unfortunately, only Thais can continue onward beyond the frontier

To head out from Kanchanaburi towards the lush, mountainous west is to take a road to nowhere. Or so it seems. Remote Three Pagodas Pass has little to show beyond the modest markers that give it its name, a military checkpoint and a small thriving market. Nearby Sangkhlaburi is a somnolent, spacious outpost perched between lake and jungle. Beyond the peaks and clouds lies southern Burma, as inaccessible as it is close.

The highway out of Kanchanaburi winding northwest towards the Burmese frontier may be going nowhere much – no border crossings are permitted – but there is no shortage of natural and historical diversions along the way. An appropriate beginning, one which gives context to this jungled area's ancient origins, is the prehistoric burial site at the village of **Ban Kao ⓫**, on a side road about 30 kilometres (18 mi) into the 250-kilometre (150 mi) stretch from Kanchanaburi to the Burmese border. Neolithic remains discovered near the village may date as far back as 10,000 years, archaeologists believe. At a small museum near the site are pottery and human remains that date from 3,000 to 4,000 years ago.

Seven kilometres (4 mi) and a few millennia further on, the 13th-century remains of a Khmer city associated with the Angkor empire have been turned into an historical park. **Prasat Muang Singh ⓬**, situated prettily on the Kwai

BELOW: woman from near the Burmese border.

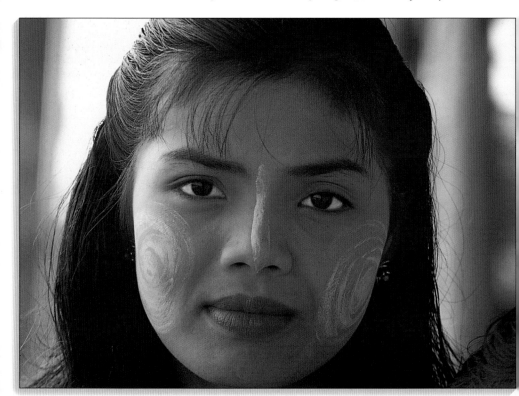

Noi, covers 70 hectares (170 acres) and encompasses four groups of ruins. Sculptures of deities, laterite brick shrines, and the remains of an elaborate water system can be seen.

Jumping centuries ahead again, the tendency of jungle and time to erase the evidence of history has been energetically tackled at a World War II site 80 kilometres (50 mi) beyond Kanchanaburi on Route 323. **Hellfire Pass** ⓭ is the largest of many mountain cuttings carved out of rock in atrocious conditions by Asians and Allied prisoners-of-war forced to build the so-called Death Railway, intended by the Japanese to link Singapore and India. The pass has been turned into a memorial for the thousands who died, mainly of malaria and dysentery. The prisoners worked with hammers, picks, shovels, steel tap drills and dynamite. Close examination of the sheer walls of Hellfire Pass reveals the marks of the old drills and blast holes. Most of the railway was abandoned or dug up soon after the war ended. A portion that remains takes visitors from Kanchanaburi to Nam Tok, a small touristy market town not far from the pass.

About 20 kilometres (12 mi) further up Highway 323, and also reachable by boat from Nam Tok, **Sai Yok National Park** ⓮ evokes a light-hearted atmosphere with picnickers and swimmers – in stark contrast to the gory Russian roulette scenes filmed here for the movie *The Deerhunter*. Sai Yok is quieter than **Erawan National Park** ⓯, with one of Thailand's most popular waterfalls and about 80 kilometres (50 mi) from Kanchanaburi along a different road. Beyond Erawan to the northeast are two limestone caves, Tham Phra That and Tham Wang Badan, as well as Huay Khamin Falls, with large, deep pools.

Back on Highway 323, the **Hin Dat** hot springs make a restful stop. Just yards from the freezing and rushing river water, bathers soak quietly in calm, steam-

TIP

Within the 500 square kilometres of Sai Yok National Park, accommodations available include simple bungalows and houseboats.

BELOW: clouded leopard, and black-throated sunbird.

**Map,
page 179**

*Parts of Burma
beyond Three
Pagodas Pass were
taken from ethnic
groups by Burma's
army in the 1990s.
Several refugee
camps on the Thai
side, most of them
well off main roads,
hold thousands of
Mon and Karen
refugees.*

OPPOSITE: deciduous
forest north of
Sangkhlaburi.
BELOW: on the lake
near Sangkhlaburi.

ing, mineral-rich hot springs. Food stalls, shrines and pleasant walking areas add to the gently festive atmosphere. Just beyond, the Phatat waterfall is a short drive to the right from the main highway. Slightly further on, one of a number of elephant camps along this route is open to the public.

Thong Pha Thum, nestled under the mountains, is the last village before the winding, climbing ascent to Sangkhlaburi, where the combination of steep limestone mountains and a huge lake created by the Khao Laem hydroelectric dam make for dramatic views. At about the half-way mark along this stretch, high in the mountains, the **Sunyataram Forest Monastery** is a meditation retreat affiliated with the charismatic Phra Yantra Bhikku, one of Thailand's most famous and revered monks – at least until he was associated with a series of personal and financial scandals in the mid 1990s and defrocked.

The monastery, quiet now for perhaps less happy reasons than its original meditative purpose, is an attractive, slightly ramshackle collection of wooden buildings spread out over a section of old forest. Small fish pools and winding trails add to the charm. Devotees here haven't given up on the disgraced monk; the former Phra Yantra's posters still adorn some wooden walls and his sermons and books are for sale. Two other pleasant stops close by include the Dar Thongthong and Kroenkrawia waterfalls.

Sangkhlaburi ⑯, which may well be one of Thailand's prettiest towns, is still relatively undiscovered. Perched around the large Khao Laem reservoir, surrounded by high peaks and practically untouched by the kind of ugly concrete shophouse development that has spread throughout most of Thailand, it is a fascinating cultural meeting point. Thai, Burmese, Mon and Karen all live here, most involved in one way or another with border trade, legal and otherwise. Tourism is slowly but steadily increasing here in low-key fashion. The town has no real hotels, but a growing number of guesthouses cater to hardy travellers. The attractions include unbroken tranquillity, river rafting and hiking.

A stroll across a part of the lake, over Thailand's longest wooden bridge, leads to an attractive Mon village. Villagers, who built the bridge themselves, are experts at speedily negotiating on motorcycles the steep, bumpy lane that leads from the bridge to the main town. Just past the Mon village, the towering **Chedi Luang Phaw Utama**, which has fine vistas over the countryside, is topped by about 6 kilograms (13 lbs) of gold. The striking **Wat Wangwiwe Karam** nearby is built in an amalgamation of Thai, Indian and Burmese styles. In front of the chedi, a well-organised market sells Burmese and Mon handicrafts, textiles and other general goods.

Three Pagodas Pass ⑰, 16 kilometres (10 mi) beyond Sangkhlaburi at an elevation of 1,400 metres (4,600 ft), has been the main trade link between western Thailand and southern Burma for centuries. It was also the entry point into Thailand for invading Burmese troops on elephants during the Ayutthaya period. The fairly nondescript pagodas are less a draw for tourists than the busy marketing that goes on here. Beyond the checkpoints, the Burmese town of Paythonzu is generally open only to Thai day-trippers. ❐

Central Thailand

0   25 km

0   25 miles

CENTRAL THAILAND

*Here in the plain defined by the Mae Nam Chao Phraya,
Thailand's rice culture blossomed, as did its great empires*

The traditional source of Thailand's wealth is rice. Intricately diked and irrigated rice fields have fed its people for more than 700 years. The central plains are the fertile heart of Thailand, towards which the early Thais steadily migrated from the mountains and valleys of the northern mountains.

Towards the end of the dry season, in May, the fields are alive with farmers turning the earth. A month or so later, when the rains have come, water covers the shallow paddies sprouting with young rice plants. In November, the rains fall off, and the grain turns golden. Harvest time. Afterwards, there are the festivals that coincide with the burning of the harvested fields, as the earth is prepared for another cycle of cultivation.

Several major rivers water this fertile heartland – notably the Ping, Wang, Yom and Nan, which eventually combine to form the majestic Chao Phraya, emptying into the Gulf of Thailand below Bangkok. Thai history has followed these rivers with the establishment of great empires, all found in the central plains: the Angkor-style towers of Lopburi, where the Khmers once ruled to reap the bounty of the plains, and the sprawling ruins farther south, near Bangkok, of once-great Ayutthaya. To the north, the flower of Sukhothai bloomed, perhaps the finest highlight of Thailand's past.

The wooden houses of the central plains, more than any other part of the country, reflect the classic style of Thai architecture. The paneled walls slant slightly inward to achieve an oddly graceful effect, the steep roof seeming to strain toward the sky. The faces of the people here in the central lowlands are less likely to reveal the imprint of Chinese, Lao, Burmese or Malay ancestry, as these races have intermingled with the Thai in both the cities and in the border regions.

Like the heartland of many countries, the central plains are often ignored by travelers on their way elsewhere, to Chiang Mai and the north, for example. Yet for those who stop here, perhaps more than anywhere else in Thailand, the foundations of Thai culture and society are best uncovered, and most readily understood. ❐

PRECEDING PAGES: a water buffalo feeds in the cool of a central plain dawn.

AYUTTHAYA AND LOPBURI

For four centuries, Thailand's capital city was at Ayutthaya, north of today's capital, Bangkok, and on the Mae Nam Chao Phraya, the great river through Thailand's central plains

Map, page 192

THAILAND

Bangkok

Were one ignorant of the importance and history of **Ayutthaya ❶**, one would nonetheless be impressed by the beauty and grandeur of this city built by 33 monarchs over 400 years. From the ruins, it is easy to appreciate the genius of the kings who built this great city. Located 85 kilometres (55 mi) north of Bangkok, Ayutthaya was laid out at the junction of three rivers: Chao Phraya, Pa Sak, and Lopburi. Engineers had only to cut a canal across the loop of the Chao Phraya to create an island. Canals were also constructed as streets; palaces and temples were erected alongside.

To approach the city as 17th-century visitors did, travel up Mae Nam Chao Phraya from Bangkok. Several deluxe boats make a pleasant voyage of the journey. Once in Ayutthaya, a river tour around the island in a long-tail boat can be arranged on the landing stage close to Chan Kasem Palace. Not only is this an excellent introduction to the ruined city, it is also the most convenient way to reach some of the more isolated sites on the mainland side of the river. Despite the claims of some Bangkok tour operators, there is modern accommodation here, as well as several clean, inexpensive Chinese hotels.

OPPOSITE: chedi of Wat Phra Ram, Ayutthaya. **BELOW:** canal-side homes in Ayutthaya.

Foundations of Ayutthaya

Ayutthaya was founded around 1350 by a prince of U-thong. Thirty years later, the kingdom of Sukhothai passed under Ayutthayan rule, which then spread as far as Angkor in the east and Pegu, in Burma, to the west.

It was one of the richest cities in Asia by the 1600s – exporting rice, animal skins, ivory – and with a population of one million, greater than that of contemporary London. Merchants came from Europe, the Middle East and elsewhere in Asia to trade in its markets. Ayutthayan kings engaged Japanese soldiers, Indian men-at-arms and Persian ministers to serve in their retinues. Regular relations with Europe began in the early 1500s, first with the Portuguese and later with the Dutch, British, and especially the French. Europeans wrote awed accounts of the fabulous wealth of the courts and of the 2,000 temple spires clad in gilded gold.

As fast as it rose to greatness, it collapsed, suffering a destruction so complete that it was never rebuilt. Burmese armies had been battering at its gates for centuries – its strong fortifications, with ramparts 20 metres (65 ft) high and five metres (20 ft) thick, were generally effective – before occupying it for a period in the 16th century. Siamese kings then expelled the Burmese and reasserted their independence. In 1767, however, the Burmese triumphed again. In their victory, they burned and looted, destroying most of the city's monuments, and enslaving, killing, or scattering the population. Within a year, Ayutthaya had become a ghost town, its population of over one million reduced to a few thousand. Today, the ruins stand by themselves on the western half of the island, with modern Ayutthaya a bustling commercial town concentrated in the eastern part of the island.

Start close to the junction of the Nam Pa Sak and Chao Phraya rivers, passing by the imposing **Wat Phanan Choeng A**. Records suggest that the *wat* was established 26 years prior to Ayutthaya's foundation in 1350. The temple houses a huge seated Buddha, so tightly crowded against the roof that he appears to be holding it up. Wat Phanan Choeng was a favourite with Chinese traders, who prayed there before setting out on long voyages; it still has an unmistakably Chinese atmosphere.

Ayutthaya was at one time surrounded by stout walls, only portions of which remain. One of the best-preserved sections is at **Phom Phet**, across the river from Wat Phanan Choeng.

Upstream from Wat Phanan Choeng, the restored **Wat Buddhaisawan B** (Phutthaisawan) stands serenely on the riverbank. Seldom visited, it is quiet, and the landing is an excellent place to enjoy the river's tranquillity in the evenings. Farther upstream, the restored **Cathedral of St Joseph** is a Catholic reminder of the large European population that lived in the city at its prime.

Where the river bends to the north is one of Ayutthaya's most romantic ruins, **Wat Chai Wattanaram C**, erected in 1630. Perched high on a pedestal in front of the ruins, a Buddha keeps solitary watch. The stately *prang* with its surrounding *chedi* and rows of headless Buddhas make a fine contrast to the restored **Queen Suriyothai Chedi D** on the city side of the river. Dressed as a man, the Ayutthaya queen rode into battle, her elephant beside that of her husband. When she saw him attacked by a Burmese prince, she moved between

TIP

Vendors sell ceramics they claim were dropped overboard by 17th-century sailors, only recently recovered. Given the volume of the wares and length of time they have been on sale, the sailors must have been very butterfingered.

them with her elephant, receiving a lethal lance blow intended for her husband.

Chan Kasem Palace , known as the Palace of the Front, was originally constructed outside the city walls, close to the junction of the rivers and the new canal. King Naresuan built it as a defensive bastion while he was engaged in wars against his northern rivals from Chiang Mai. In 1767, the Burmese destroyed the palace, but King Mongkut later resurrected it in the 19th century as a royal summer retreat for escaping Bangkok's heat. Now housing a small museum, the palace looks out on the busiest part of the modern town.

The old royal palace, **Wang Luang**, apparently was of substantial size, if the foundations for the stables of 100 elephants are any indication. It was later razed by the Burmese. The bricks were removed to Bangkok to build its defensive walls, so only remnants of the foundations survive to mark the site. Close by stands the three stately chedi of **Wat Phra Sri Sanphet** , a royal temple built in 1491 that honours three 15th-century kings. The identical chedi have been restored and stand in regal contrast to the surrounding ruins.

For two centuries after Ayutthaya's fall, a huge bronze Buddha sat unsheltered near Wat Phra Sri Sanphet. Its flame of knowledge and one of his arms had been broken when the roof, set afire by the Burmese, collapsed. Based on the original, a new building, the **Viharn Phra Mongkol Bophit**, was built in 1956 around the restored statue. The resulting shrine works remarkably well, the giant black-coloured Buddha exuding a genuinely numinous feeling of power.

Across the river from the old palace stands another restored temple, **Wat Na Phra Meru** . Here, a large stone Buddha is seated in the "European fashion" on a throne – a sharp contrast to the yoga position of most seated Buddhas. Found in the ruins of Wat Mahathat, the statue is believed to be one of five that

An elephant-mounted Ayutthayan general prepares to lead his army against the Burmese.

BELOW: Ayutthayan jewelry, and Lopburi sculpture.

originally sat in a recently-unearthed Dvaravati-period complex in Nakhon Pathom. The bot contains an Ayutthaya-style seated Buddha on the altar. Across a bridge from Wat Na Phra Meru are the ruins of **Wat Konthi Thong**.

Back on the island and across the road from Phra Mongkol Bophit, **Wat Phra Ram ❽** is one of Ayutthaya's oldest temples. Founded in 1369 by the son of Ayutthaya's founder, its buildings dating from the 1400s have been completely restored twice. Elephant gates punctuate the old walls, and the central terrace is dominated by a crumbling prang to which clings a gallery of stucco *naga*, *garuda* and statues of the Buddha. The reflection of Wat Phra Ram's prang shimmers in the pool that surrounds the complex. Once a marshy swamp, the pool was dug to provide landfill for the temple's foundations.

In 1957, looters removed much of the gold from Wat Ratchaburana. Only some was recovered.

Two of Ayutthaya's finest temples stand side by side northeast across the lake from Wat Phra Ram. Built in 1424 by the seventh king of Ayutthaya as a memorial to his brothers, the well-known **Wat Ratchaburana ❶** dominates its surroundings. Excavations during its restoration in 1958 revealed a crypt containing gold jewelry, Buddha images and other objects, among them a charming, intricately decorated elephant – property of the interned brothers. These treasures are kept in the **Chao Sam Phraya National Museum** (open daily; admission fee) to the south. Some of Thailand's finest ancient paintings cover crypt walls.

Across the road, **Wat Phra Mahathat ❶** is one of the most beautiful temple complexes in Ayutthaya, and one of its oldest, dating from the 1380s. Its glory is its huge prang, which originally stood 46 metres (150 ft) high. The prang later collapsed, but it was rebuilt four meters higher than before. Stone Buddha faces, each a metre in height, stand silently around the ruins. Together with the restored chedi that ring the prang, these combine to make this one of the most impres-

BELOW: the restored Wat Phra Ram.

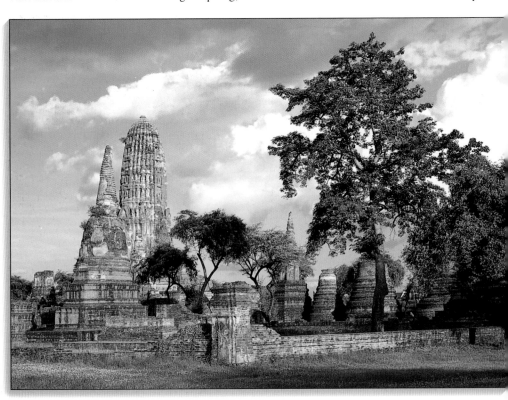

sive sites in Ayutthaya. Next door, the government has built a model of how the royal city may have once looked.

Wat Suwan Dararam , to the southeast and constructed near the close of the Ayutthaya period, has been beautifully restored. The foundations of the *bot* dip in the centre, in emulation of the graceful deck line of a boat. This typical Ayutthayan decoration is meant to suggest a boat that carries pious Buddhists to salvation. Delicately-carved columns support the roof, and the interior walls are decorated with brilliantly-coloured frescoes. Still used as a temple, the atmosphere of the wat is magical in the early evening when the monks chant their prayers. East is **Wat Yai Chai Mongkol**, originally established in the mid 1300s. In single-handed combat on elephant-back, King Naresuan slew the crown prince of Burma in 1592. The immense chedi, built to match the Phu Khao Thong Pagoda just north of Ayutthaya, was erected in celebration of the victory. Buddha statues line the courtyard.

Just north of Ayutthaya, the **Wat Phu Khao Thong**, better known as the **Golden Mount**, stands with its 80-metre-high (260 ft) chedi alone amidst the rice fields, its upper terraces commanding a panoramic view of the countryside. While the wat dates from 1387, the chedi was built by the Burmese after their earlier and less destructive conquest in 1569. It was later remodelled by the Siamese in their own style. In 1957, to mark 2,500 years of Buddhism, a 2,500-gram (5.5 lb) gold ball was mounted on top of the chedi.

In the opposite direction from the Golden Mount, the road runs to the only **elephant *kraal*** left in Thailand. This 16th-century kraal is a reminder of the days when elephants were not only caught and trained to work in the jungles, but were also an essential requisite for a strong army. The last elephant roundup

Map, page 196

BELOW: Wat Ratchaburana.

In 1688, as Narai lay mortally ill in his palace, an army officer seized the throne. The king called in a Buddhist abbot to ordain his loyal attendants as monks, to save them.

BELOW: elephant round-up at Ayutthaya's kraal, 1895.

was in 1903. Standing at the edge of the restored stockade with its huge teak columns, one can imagine the thunder of the mighty beasts.

Bang Pa-In ❷, a charming collection of palaces and pavilions once used as a royal summer retreat, lies a short distance downriver from the ruins of Ayutthaya. The rulers of Ayutthaya used Bang Pa-In as long ago as the 17th century, but the buildings one sees today date from the late 19th- and early 20th-century reigns of Rama V and Rama VI, who used to come up from Bangkok.

Lopburi

The former summer capital of Siam, **Lopburi ❸**, lies 10 kilometres (6 mi) north of Ayutthaya. Here, the hills of the Khorat Plateau appear on the horizon, the first break in the flatness of the central plains.

Artifacts from the neolithic and bronze ages have been found in large quantity in Lopburi, testifying to the great antiquity of the city. In the Dvaravati period, from the sixth to 11th centuries, it was a major religious centre thought to have attracted savants from around the region. At the height of the Angkor empire in the 11th and 12th centuries, it was a provincial capital. Then came the Thais, who put their imprint on most of the old buildings that now survive. It was not until the mid 1600s that Ayutthaya became a bustling international city with upwards of three dozen nationalities represented. Some French architects even ventured to Lopburi, where Narai retreated in summer to escape the heat.

The grounds of **Narai Ratchaniwet**, or **Lopburi Palace** (also called King Narai's Palace), built between 1665 and 1677, are enclosed by massive walls, which still dominate the centre of the modern town. The palace grounds have three sections enclosing its governmental, ceremonial and residential buildings.

Moving inward, the middle section once enclosed the Dusit Maha Prasat Hall, Chantra Paisan Pavilion, and Phiman Mongkut Pavilion. The inner courtyard was that of the king, where his residence, Suttha Sawan Pavilion, was nestled amidst gardens and ponds.

Map, page 192

Of King Narai's buildings, the only one that has substantially survived is the **Dusit Maha Prasat**. This was built for the audience granted by the king in 1685 to the ambassador of Louis XIV. Near the Dusit Maha Prasat is the **Phiman Mongkut Pavilion**, a three-storey mansion in the colonial style and built in the mid-19th century by King Mongkut. The immensely thick walls and high ceilings show how the summer heat was averted most effectively before air-conditioning arrived. The mansion, small but full of character, displays a mixture of bronze statues, Chinese and Sukhothai porcelain, coins, Buddhist fans, and shadow-play puppets. Some of the pieces, particularly the Ayutthaya bronze heads and Bencharong porcelain, are superb.

King Narai had a Greek adviser, Constantine Phaulkon, who had come to Asia years earlier on a merchant ship as a cabin boy. Although not officially the foreign minister, by the mid 1680s Phaulkon was managing Siam's relations with the European powers. However, his ambition also led him to meddle in domestic matters, making him unpopular with the Buddhist clergy and with officials of Narai's government. When the king lay dying, Phra Phetracha seized power and had Phaulkon tortured, then hacked to pieces.

The remains of a grand palace in Lopburi, said to have belonged to Phaulkon, rival those of the royal palace. Located just north of Narai's residence, the buildings show strong European influence, with straight-sided walls and pedimental decorations over Western-style windows. ❏

BELOW: Phaulkon's palace, Lopburi.

Map,
page 192

THE CENTRAL PLAINS

For most foreign travelers, Thailand's central plains is a fly-over or drive-through zone on the way to the north. Yet, culturally and agriculturally, it is one of Thailand's most important regions

Nakhon Sawan ❹, 250 kilometres (150 mi) north of Bangkok, has long been an important commercial centre because of its location as the hub of roads and rivers connecting north and central Thailand. The Ping and Nan rivers, already swollen by their tributaries, meet the Wang and the Yom at Nakhon Sawan, forming the Chao Phraya. Route 1 divides here, sending a branch, Route 117, due north to Sukhothai and Phitsanulok, while itself continuing northwest towards Tak. Reaching one's destination in the central plains, as in most other parts of Thailand, is generally quick and comfortable. The main cities in the centre are linked to Bangkok by road, rail and air. Of these three modes, the most common is by coach.

Under its old name of Paknampoh, Nakhon Sawan played a vital role in the teak trade. It was here that the great teak rafts, which had sometimes been travelling for two or three years from the northern forests, were broken up into smaller rafts for floating down to Bangkok on the Chao Phraya River. Teak rafts may still occasionally be seen on the river below Nakhon Sawan, but since the government's banning of logging in Thailand, they are not nearly as numerous as they were in the heyday of Thailand's teak trade. Today, there are few traces of Nakhon Sawan's historic past in the modern commercial town.

BELOW: central-plain smile, and a face at a local fair.

The most notable shrine is outside the town, across the bridge over the Chao Phraya. Here on a small hill stands **Wat Chom Kiri Nak Phrot**. On a clear day the views from the top of the hill are stunning. The main structure dates from the 14th-century Sukhothai period, but the Buddha image, seated on a throne supported by demons, is of the Ayutthaya period. Behind the main shrine is a massive, finely-adorned bronze bell about a century old, supported aloft on tall brick pillars.

A favourite outing for those living in and around Nakhon Sawan is a trip to **Bung Boraphet ❺**, a large lake a few kilometres to the east. Until they were hunted to extinction, crocodiles used to bask on its shores. This low-lying area acts as a catchment during the rainy season. At the height of the monsoon in September and October, the swollen lake covers an area of some 120 square kilometres (50 sq mi). A good time to visit is on a moonlit night, in the cool season, for a picnic on the island.

The "new" city of **Kamphaeng Phet ❻** lies three kilometres off Route 1, about 120 kilometres (75 mi) northwest of Nakhon Sawan and on the east bank of the Ping River. This city was built by King Li Thai (1347–1368), of the Sukhothai dynasty, to replace the older town of Chakangrao on the opposite bank. Both served as garrison towns for the Kingdom of Sukhothai.

Along the road to Kamphaeng Phet are the remains of a fort, **Phom Seti**, built to defend the former city of Chakangrao. Farther along the road is the well-restored *chedi* of **Wat Chedi Klang Tung** – the "Chedi in the Middle of the Fields" – another relic of the earlier city.

With its numerous rice and noodle houses, the modern part of town is on the other side of a bridge over the Ping River. The well-designed **Provincial**

Found in the northern part of the Central Plains, this terracotta depicts Davaravati, 10th–11th century.

BELOW: ruins of Kamphaeng Phet.

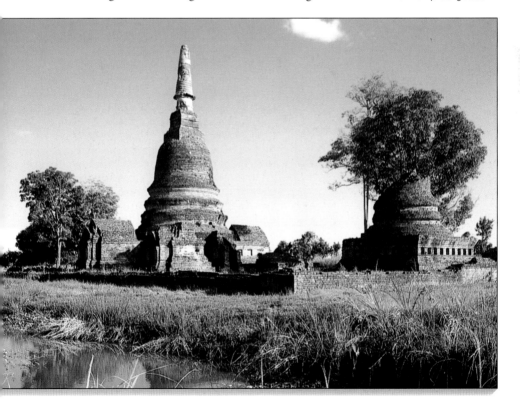

Map, page 192

Museum contains one of Thailand's finest bronze statues of the Hindu god Shiva. This life-sized image was cast on the orders of the governor of Kamphaeng Phet in the first quarter of the 16th century.

Early during the reign of King Chulalongkorn, a German visitor removed the image's head and two hands. Too afraid to arrest a *farang* (Westerner), the governor quickly sent word to Bangkok that the priceless fragments were on their way by boat. Officials in Bangkok detained the German, who declared that he was going to give them to the Berlin Museum.

King Chulalongkorn, a skillful diplomat, found a way to placate the German as well as keep the cultural treasures for his country. He promised to send an exact copy of the whole Shiva image to Germany, so that the authentic fragments could remain in Thailand. And so it was done. The copy of the bronze is still in Berlin. Other exhibits in the museum include pre-Sukhothai bronzes, stucco Buddha heads from local monuments, and some ceramics.

A car or coach is necessary for a tour of the fortifications and temples, as they are some distance from the modern town. A visit to King Li Thai's fortifications reveals why the town was called Kamphaeng Phet, or Diamond Walls: the massive ramparts of earth are topped by laterite rising 6 metres (20 ft) above the outer moat, once overgrown with water hyacinths but now in the midst of an extensive restoration.

The chief monuments of Kamphaeng Phet lie northwest of the walled city. The monks who built them were of a forest-dwelling sect, strongly influenced by teachers from Sri Lanka. Their temples, constructed of laterite, are thought to show Ceylonese influence. Most of them, however, underwent major changes during restoration in the Ayutthaya period.

The familiar themes of Buddhist architecture, *viharn* and chedi, are repeated in the ordination halls of two temples. These two temples are of special interest and should be seen even on a rapid tour.

The first, **Wat Phra Si Iriyabot**, derives its name from Buddha images that are depicted in four postures (*si* meaning four, and *iriyabot*, postures) on the central square *mondop* (sanctuary): walking, standing, sitting and reclining. The standing image is largely intact, with the original stucco coating on its head and lower part of the body. This is an impressive and unaltered example of Sukhothai sculpture. Unfortunately, the other images are in very poor condition. The whole temple stands on a platform that is encircled by the original laterite railing and walls. The other temple, **Wat Chang Rob**, or Shrine Surrounded by Elephants, consists of the base of a laterite chedi surrounded by elephant buttresses, a theme borrowed from Sri Lanka that claims the universe rests on the backs of these beasts.

The row of elephants on the south side is almost complete, but several are missing on the other flanks of the stupa. Unfortunately, the spire of the great monument has vanished, but the ruins of a crypt on the upper level of the stupa can still be inspected. The pillars of the former viharn also remain.

Repair work was completed in the late 1990s, restoring much of the original form without – luckily – robbing the elephants of their appeal. ❑

OPPOSITE: planting rice seedlings.
BELOW: Wat Phra Si Iriyabot.

Culture of Rice

The Thai expression *kin khao* is translated as "to eat," but it actually means "to eat rice." Indeed, here where rice has been a staple for centuries, the two are synonymous.

The rice-planting season begins in May, when the king presides over the ancient ploughing ceremony at Sanam Luang, in Bangkok. This Brahmanic rite symbolises the attention that the spirits give to the prospects for the forthcoming rice harvest.

Cultivating rice is by necessity a cooperative effort, tightening the bonds of family and community. According to tradition, a farmer can ask fellow villagers to help with the work, and without having to pay for their labour. All that is expected from the host is a meal during the day, and perhaps some rice liquor at the end of the day's work. In the countryside, nearly everyone is a farmer as they put aside normal jobs to help with the preparation of paddy fields and the sowing of seed. Children are on holiday from school, as they will be when harvesting begins later in the year.

The social importance of this cooperation can hardly be exaggerated. It has a direct influence on individual behaviour, because if there are problems between individuals, families and communities, the work will not get done. Moreover, it is believed that quarrelling will upset the rice spirit and the crop may fail. Soon after the rice seedlings are transplanted into the paddy fields, villagers leave token packets of rice and other food in the fields as offerings to the rice spirit.

A ceremony important to the crop is the Bun Bang Fai, or skyrocket festival, which assures abundant rains. The festival that takes place as the monsoon rains begin has Buddhist origins, although it also contains elements of Brahmanism and animism. Buddhists say it began at the death of the Lord Buddha, when one of his grieving disciples, unable to touch his torch to the top of the funeral pyre, hurled it up to the top in a manner similar to the appearance of skyrockets being shot off. Villagers make their own rockets with gunpowder, launching them from a ladder-like structure, or from a very tall tree. Monks are involved, and if the rockets do not go off properly, the monks will lose prestige.

The cooperative effort given to the rice crop continues through the growing months. One of the most onerous tasks is keeping birds away from the ripening grain. By early December, rice is ripe enough for harvesting in Thailand's rice bowl, the central plains, and in the north, but the harvest comes later in the south. Harvesting schedules are fixed by common consent within each village.

Finally, when the rice is in the barns, the farmers at last relax and enjoy themselves. And it is then that they celebrate Songkran – the most joyous festival of the year, which marks the beginning of the traditional Thai new year, in April.

Big commercial farmers and agribusiness companies produce rice on a mammoth scale. Chemicals have now supplanted the powers of the rice spirit. Former farmers have left their fields altogether, and instead work on roads, drive trucks, and maintain tractors. Rice is no longer the top Thai export, but it is still a vital one – Thailand continues to remain the world's top rice exporter, earning about US$ 1.5 billion annually. ■

SUKHOTHAI

Map,
page 192

Sukhothai, the first independent Thai kingdom, is considered to be the golden era in Thailand's history. Some of ancient Sukhothai, at the northern extent of the central plains, enchants today

The route towards the ancient city of **Sukhothai ❼** (Dawn of Happiness) passes through "new" Sukhothai, a bustling modern town of concrete shophouses. About 10 kilometres (7 mi) farther on, the road enters the limits of old Sukhothai through the **Kamphaenghak (Broken Wall) Gate**. The authorities chose to run the road directly through the ruins, rather than around them.

The Sukhothai Kingdom began around 1240, when King Intradit asserted his independence from the Khmers. Sukhothai, which grew to include most of modern-day Thailand and parts of the Malay Peninsula and Burma, is synonymous with some of the finest artistic endeavours in Thai history, including perhaps the most exquisite Buddha images. Unfortunately, the golden age was relatively short-lived, just two centuries and nine kings long. The upstart Kingdom of Ayutthaya absorbed Sukhothai in 1438. The most notable Sukhothai king was Ramkamhaeng, who developed the Thai script, promoted Theravada Buddhism and established links with China, among other accomplishments.

The remains of ancient Sukhothai's massive walls reveal that the inner city was protected by no fewer than three rows of earthen ramparts and two moats. The city was begun by the Khmers, who left behind three buildings and the beginnings of a water system, similar to that of Angkor Wat. After the Angkorian empire began to contract, the Khmers abandoned Sukhothai and the Thais moved in, building their own structures. They eschewed the intricate Khmer irrigation system, installing a much less complex one of their own. It is suggested that water, or the lack of it, in part contributed to the city's demise. It is possible that the city was originally served by the Yom River, which later shifted course and deprived Sukhothai of a dependable source of water.

Exploring the ancient city

A short distance from Kamphaenghak Gate is the **Ramkamhaeng National Museum** (open daily, 8.30am–4pm; admission fee), a good starting point for a tour of the enclave. The museum contains a fine collection of Sukhothai sculpture, ceramics and other artifacts, as well as exhibits from other periods. The entrance hall is dominated by an impressive bronze image of the walking Buddha. This style of image is regarded as the finest sculptural innovation of the Sukhothai period (1230–1440). There had been earlier essays in high and low relief, but the Sukhothai sculptors were the first to create statues of the walking Buddha. It also displays the elements that typify the Sukhothai style, including fluid lines, a somewhat androgynous figure, and strict interpretation of the 32 *raksana,* or characteristics by which a Buddha would be recognised: wedge-shaped heels, arms hanging to the knees, fingers and toes of equal length, amongst other distinguishing features.

In this period, the Thais definitively embraced Theravada Buddhism and invited monks from Sri Lanka to clarify points of scripture. While Buddhism was blossoming, Hindu influence remained strong, indicated by the two bronze images of Hindu gods flanking the walking Buddha in the museum. The one on the right, with the combined attributes of Vishnu and Shiva, is especially fine. Also worth noting is a stone torso of an *apsara,* or celestial maiden, in the Khmer style. An important object proudly displayed on the mezzanine floor is a copy of

Walking in Sukhothai.

OPPOSITE: Wat Mahathat during Loy Krathong.

the famous stone inscription of King Ramkamhaeng; the original is the most prized exhibit of the National Museum in Bangkok. It was at the **Non Prasat** (Palace Mound), now merely a slightly raised terrace of earth and brick, that the inscription was found. In 1833, the future King Mongkut, then a monk, discovered the stone, which had been inscribed in 1292. On it, King Ramkamhaeng had recorded his conquests in surrounding kingdoms, and the fact that in 1283 he devised the Siamese alphabet. However, some experts now doubt its authenticity and believe the inscription to be a much later forgery.

Once situated on the Non Prasat was the stone throne of Ramkamhaeng, and although there is little to be seen now, apart from the walled terrace, this was the numinous centre of old Siam. Alexander Griswold notes: "The political significance of the throne can scarcely be exaggerated, for the king sat on it when he discussed affairs of state… and when he received his vassals who came to do homage". The stone throne, called the Manangasila, is now in the Temple of the Emerald Buddha in Bangkok.

Over the centuries, until the 16th century, kings added to Wat Mahathat until there were 200 or so chedi.

Within the walls of Sukhothai are the ruins of some 20 temples and monuments. The greatest of them is **Wat Mahathat**, west of the museum. It is not known with certainty who founded this temple, which Griswold called "the magical and spiritual centre of the kingdom", but it is presumed to have been the first king of Sukhothai. Wat Mahathat owes its present form to a remodelling completed by King Lo Thai, around 1345.

BELOW: Wat Mahathat at sunset.

The original design, discovered a few years ago during repairs, was a quincunx of laterite towers based on a laterite platform. The four axial towers, which can still be seen, are of the Khmer style but with stucco decorations added by Lo Thai. The central tower is now hidden in the basement of Lo Thai's "lotus bud" tower. The axial towers were linked to the central tower by laterite buttresses, which are still visible. The principal Buddha image, cast in bronze by King Lu Thai (1347–1368), is now in Bangkok, at Wat Suthat. The stucco frieze of walking monks around the base of the main tower is unusual.

Amongst the 20 other shrines within the walls, and some 70 more in the neighbourhood, many repeat familiar architectural themes. The following short-list reflects the monuments of special interest.

Wat Sri Sawai, southwest of Wat Mahathat, was originally a Hindu shrine that contained an image of Shiva. Triple towers remain, built in a modified Khmer style; the stucco decoration, added to the towers in the 15th century and showing mythical birds and divinities, is particularly fine.

Wat Chana Songkhram and **Wat Trakuan**, located immediately north of Wat Mahathat, have especially nice Sri Lankan-style chedi, of which only the lower parts still stand. Wat Trakuan has revealed many bronze images of the Chiang Saen period.

Wat Sra Sri, north on the other side of the highway and on the way to the southern gate, has a chedi of the Sri Lankan type. The ordination hall (*bot*) lies on an island to the east of the spire. The ruins of the main shrine consist of six rows of columns, which lead to a well-restored, seated Buddha image. Achille Clarac comments: "The detail, balance and harmony of the proportions and decoration of Wat Sra Sri, and the beauty of the area where it stands, bear witness to the unusual and refined aesthetic sense of the architects of the Sukhothai period".

Leaving the walled city by the northern San Luang, or the Royal Shrine gate, and travelling about a kilometre, one arrives at the important shrine of **Wat Phra Phai Luang**. It originally consisted of three laterite towers covered with stucco,

Map, page 192

BELOW: bullock cart decorated for Loy Krathong.

TIP

Perhaps the most exquisite time of the year to see Sukhothai is during Loy Krathong, during the November full moon. This festival celebrates the end of the rainy season.

BELOW: ruins of Wat Chetupon.

probably built in the late 12th century, when Sukhothai was still part of the Khmer empire. This shrine might have been the original centre of Sukhothai, since Wat Mahathat is of a later period. A fragmentary seated stone Buddha image, accurately dated to 1191 and the reign of the Khmer King Jayavarman VII, was found here and is now in the grounds of the town's Ramkamhaeng Museum. During restoration in the mid 1960s, a large stucco image of the Buddha in the central tower collapsed, disclosing numerous smaller images inside. Some date these images to the second half of the 13th century.

To the east of the main shrine lies a pyramidal brick chedi that originally contained seated stucco Buddha images dating from the late 13th century. Later, the niches were walled up with bricks, which were removed during a restoration started in 1953.

When heads of the stucco images began appearing on the antique market in Bangkok, authorities realised that the stupa was being pillaged. A team from the government was dispatched to the site, but most of the damage had already been done. Those heads – in the Chiang Saen style – that have not left the country are in private collections elsewhere in Thailand, or else in the custody of the National Museum in Bangkok.

Beyond Wat Phra Phai Luang to the west is **Wat Si Chum**, with one of the largest seated Buddha images in Thailand. The *mondop*, or enclosing shrine, was built in the second half of the 14th century, but the image itself, called Phra Achana, or The Venerable, is believed to be the one mentioned in King Ramkamhaeng's inscription. There is a stairway within the walls of the mondop that leads to the roof. The ceiling of the stairway is made up of more than 50 carved slate slabs with scenes from Buddhist folklore. Their function is to turn

Map,
page 192

the ritual climbing of the stairs into a symbolic ascent to Buddhahood. Partly because of the precarious nature of the stairway, and partially to avoid people standing above the Buddha's head, it is no longer permitted to climb the stairs.

There is a story that troops gathered here before an ancient battle were inspired by an ethereal voice that seemed to come from the Buddha itself. Some suggest a cunning ploy by a general who hid one of his men on the stairway and instructed him to speak through one of the windows concealed by the body of the image; the effect was inspiring, however, and the soldiers routed the enemy.

South of the walled city is another group of shrines and monasteries. One of the most interesting is **Wat Chetupon**, where the protecting wall of the viharn is made of slate slabs shaped in imitation of wood. The gates are also formed of huge plates of slate mined in the nearby hills. They somewhat resemble the megaliths of England's Stonehenge, but on a smaller scale. The bridges across the moat that surround the temple are also made of stone slabs. On the central tower of Wat Chetupon are Buddha images in the standing, reclining, walking and sitting postures. The walking Buddha here is regarded as one of the finest of its kind.

"To the west of the city of Sukhothai", says King Ramkamhaeng's inscription, "is a forested area where the king has made offerings. In the forest is a large, tall and beautiful viharn which contains an 18-cubit image of the standing Buddha". This is now identified as **Wat Saphan Hin**, Monastery of the Stone Bridge. It is so called because it is approached by a stairway of large stone slabs. The image is situated on the crest of a low hill and can be seen at a considerable distance. It is 12 metres (40 ft) high, with its hand raised in the attitude of giving protection, and is almost certainly the image described by King Ramkamhaeng.

Many other monuments are to be found in this western area. They were probably built by monks from Sri Lanka, who preferred to locate their monasteries in the forest. Another monument worth visiting, near the road and not far from the western gate of Sukhothai, is **Wat Pa Mamuang**, Shrine of the Mango Grove, where King Lu Thai installed a famous monk of the Theravada sect in 1361. Still standing are the shrine foundations and the ruins of the main chedi.

Outside Sukhothai

About 50 kilometres (35 mi) north of the modern town of Sukhothai, along a concrete highway, lies the venerable city of **Si Satchanalai ❸** on the banks of the Yom River. Founded in the middle of the 13th century, as was Sukhothai, it served as the seat of the viceroys of Sukhothai and was always mentioned as the twin city of the capital. Whereas restoration, removal of trees, and the installation of lawns have removed some of the grandeur of Sukhothai, Si Satchanalai's setting gives it an aura few other ancient sites have. It is a pleasure to wander through the wooded complex, rounding a corner and being surprised by a new wat or monument.

The first and most important monument to visit in Si Satchanalai is **Wat Chang Lom**. There can be little doubt that this is the "elephant-girdled shrine" described in King Ramkamhaeng's stone inscription. The great king records that he started to build it in 1285 to house

BELOW: standing Buddha at Wat Saphan Hin.

**Map,
page 192**

*East a kilometre or so
of Si Satchanalai is
Chalieng, an earlier
Khmer site from the
late 1100s and early
1200s. It is thought to
have been an outpost
for travelers.*

Opposite: Wat Chedi
Chet Thaew.
Below: Phra Bud-
dha Chinaraj is ven-
erated throughout
Thailand.

some exceptionally holy relics of the Lord Buddha, and that it was finished six years later. It is the only surviving stupa that can be attributed with virtual certainty to King Ramkamhaeng. Built of laterite and stucco, it is a large bell-shaped spire in the Sri Lankan style standing on a two-storey, square basement. The upper tier contains niches for Buddha images, now mostly empty, while the lower level contains 39 elephant-shaped buttresses built of laterite blocks.

South of the Elephant Shrine are the ruins of **Wat Chedi Chet Thaew**, which include seven rows of chedi believed to contain the ashes of the viceroys of Si Satchanalai. One of the stupas has a stucco image of the Buddha sheltered by the *naga* (divine serpent), which is in unusually good repair.

Farther south still, and close to the massive walls of the city, are the remains of **Wat Nang Phya**, Temple of the Queen. This has fine stucco decoration on one of the external walls. Dating probably from the 16th century, this stucco work has some affinities with European baroque.

Other temples worth visiting include **Wat Khao Phanom Pleung** and **Wat Khao Suwan Kiri**, set on two scenic hills linked by a walkway. **Wat Phra Si Ratana Mahathat** in Chalieng, one of the most beautiful temples, lies a couple of kilometres southeast of the old city in a setting overlooking the Yom River.

Si Satchanalai is also associated with the famed Sawankhalok ceramics, which were among Thailand's first export products. The brown bowls and their distinctive double-fish design were sent to China aboard junks; remains of them have been found in the Gulf of Thailand. It is still possible to buy genuine antique Sawankhalok ceramics in the area; most, however, are copies.

Fifty kilometres (30 mi) east of Sukhothai, **Phitsanulok** ❾ now has only a few mementos of the past; a fire over three decades ago razed most of the old town. The new city is a rather dull collection of concrete shophouses. However, nothing can detract from its superb location along the Nan River, with its quays shaded by flowering trees and its houseboats and floating restaurants moored beside the steep banks. The great fire fortunately spared **Wat Phra Sri Ratana Mahathat**, the principal shrine in Phitsanulok.

The **Phra Buddha Chinaraj**, the image in the main bot, is venerated throughout Thailand. This has given rise to a busy traffic in religious objects and souvenirs. The seated image was cast in the Sukhothai style.

The bot that enshrines the Phra Buddha Chinaraj comprises a three-tiered roof that drops steeply to head-high side walls, focusing attention on the gleaming image at the end of the nave. Flanking the image are two wooden pulpits of superb late-Ayutthaya workmanship. The large one on the left is for monks, who chant the ancient, Pali-language Buddhist texts. The smaller pulpit on the other side accommodates a single monk who translates the chants into Thai (since few of the congregation would understand Pali). Note the main doors inlaid with mother-of-pearl, dating from the late 18th century. The *prang* (spire) in the centre of the temple complex was rebuilt in the Khmer style by King Boromatrailokanat. The cloisters surrounding the prang contain Buddha images from several periods, some of them of great artistic value. A repository of art objects includes Thai and Chinese ceramics. ❐

much of Mae Sot's character. Shops advertise in Thai, Chinese, Burmese, and English. With its confusion of narrow streets, sidewalk stalls, bicycles, and pedestrian shoppers, it has the air of a frontier boom town.

From Mae Sot, it is a five-kilometre (3 mi) drive to the Burmese border. Worth a visit is an ornate Burmese temple with tiers of red-tiled rectangular roofs fringed with silverwork that are piled heavenward into a tower. Within the sanctuary are four Buddha images, one of which has gold jewelry distending its earlobes. Continue to the **Mae Nam Moei**, which forms the border with Burma. A new road bridge across the Moei to the Burmese town of Myawaddy has recently been completed, but has yet to open because of political disagreements.

North of Tak to Chiang Mai

Bhumibol Dam.

Return to Tak and continue north on Route 1 and then onto Route 106, which describes an "S" and twines itself about Route 1. On the left, about 20 kilometres (15 mi) past Tak, the village of **Ban Tak** lies on the banks of the Ping River. In the days when the river offered the only passage north, Ban Tak was a village of boat builders. Today, it is quiet but picturesque, with houses on stilts that teeter on the riverbank and a rickety bamboo footbridge overlooking children swimming. Opened in 1964 and named after Thailand's current king, **Bhumibol Dam ❸** (also called Yanhee Dam), sits 30 kilometres (20 mi) north of Ban Tak, on the left of Route 1. The dam, Thailand's largest, generates enough power to light Bangkok and a large number of Thailand's rural provinces. With permission, it's possible to drive across the 154-metre-high (505 ft) cement retaining wall to view the reservoir stretching 120 kilometres (75 mi) northwest.

BELOW: moving cattle on the open highway.

About 60 kilometres (40 mi) north of the Bhumibol Dam turn-off, Route 1

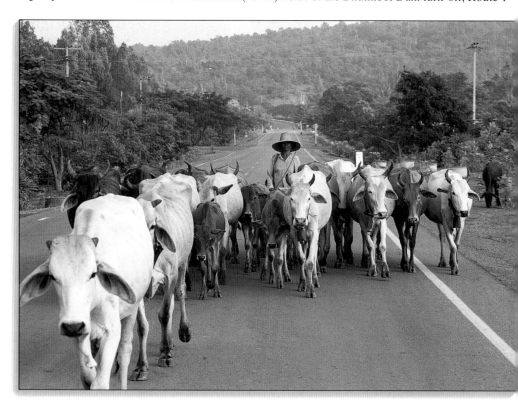

arrives at **Thoen**. Although Thoen can be passed through rapidly, it does enjoy a small claim to fame as the home of lucky *pohng kham* stones. Each pohng kham contains a variety of colours and encapsulated "scenes". Some of the clear pieces hold strange, crystalline formations resembling wisps of blue hair, jungle moss, or even a city skyline.

From Thoen to Lampang, Route 1 undulates over teak-covered hills and a mountain pass sprinkled with spirit houses before dipping into the broad, cattle country of the Yom River Valley, dominated by the former kingdom of Lampang. Approximately 18 kilometres (12 mi) before Lampang is the junction with the road to **Ko Kha**.

Turn left past the town and cross the Wang River, bearing left for one kilometre, to reach one of the greatest treasures of the north: a revered temple, **Wat Lampang Luang ④**. Cherished by scholars for its antiquity and delicate artwork, the temple compound is all that remains of a fortress city that flourished more than a millennium ago. It is said to have been founded by a 7th-century princess, Chama Dewi, who bore two sons; one became king of Lampang, the other, king of Lamphun. The wat, entirely rebuilt in the 16th century, played a key role in the golden period of the northern kingdoms. Nearly 200 years ago, Burmese invaders occupied the temple. According to legend, Lanna patriots sneaked into the temple through a drain, surprising and routing their enemy. Monks will point to a hole in the balustrade; it's said that the hole was caused by the cannon ball that killed a Burmese general.

The temple's museum features lacquered bookcases, jewelled Buddhas, and wooden *tong* banners that hang from poles like stiff flags. Most revered is a small Emerald Buddha believed to have been carved from the same stone as its

Map, page 216

The main chedi at Wat Lampang Luang has taken on a bluish-green hue because of its copper covering oxidising from centuries of rain. Inside the chedi is said to be a relic of the Buddha, a strand of hair.

BELOW: teak viharn of Wat Lampang Luang.

Map, page 216

Phra Keo Don Tao.

OPPOSITE: Buddha, Wat Kukut.
BELOW: Wat Prathat Haripunchai.

famous counterpart in Bangkok. It is displayed each November during the annual temple fair. The most important structures are the copper-plated chedi and the huge viharn with its low roofs.

About 20 kilometres (12 mi) north past Ko Kha, Route 1 enters the provincial capital of **Lampang ❺**. Half the size of Chiang Mai, it has been developed almost to the level of its northern cousin. While much of its bucolic tranquillity has disappeared, it retains one relic of the past found in no other Thai city: horse-drawn carriages. These can be hired by the journey or by the hour. There are few more romantic pursuits to be found in Asia than clip-clopping down a moonlit back street.

Two Burmese-style temples in the town are worth visiting. Seven chapels, one for each day of the week, stand at the base of the chedi in **Wat Pha Sang**, located on the left bank of the Wang River. On the right bank, **Wat Phra Keo Don Tao** is a lovely fusion of Burmese and northern Lanna architecture. In the pavilion, columns soar to ceilings covered in a kaleidoscope of inlaid enamel, mother-of-pearl, and cut glass depicting mythical animals. North of town stand the 20 chalk-white spires of **Wat Chedi Sao Phra**, set in the rice fields.

Straddling the Ping River and once an influential centre of the Mon culture – until King Mangrai overran the city in 1281 – **Lamphun ❻** is just 25 kilometres (15 mi) south of Chiang Mai via an attractive, tree-lined highway.

Lamphun is said to date from the mid 6th century and is famed for two elegant temples, attractive and confident women, and succulent *lamyai* fruit. Located on the banks of the Mae Kuang River, the provincial town was once on the main road from Lampang to Chiang Mai. A highway now bypasses Lamphun, making for a quiet and peaceful atmosphere. The town has managed to preserve a mellow upcountry quality, appropriate to its historical dignity.

To gain the best perspective on **Wat Prathat Haripunchai**, enter it through its riverside gate, where large statues of mythical lions guard its portals. Inside the large compound, monks study in a Buddhist school set amidst monuments and buildings, which date as far back as the late 9th century, thus making the wat one of the oldest in northern Thailand. The base of the 50-metre-high (165 ft), gold-topped chedi in the centre of the courtyard is the oldest structure in the temple.

Ten centuries younger, but still respectably old, the gilt-roofed library stands to the left of a *sala* that shelters one of the world's largest bronze gongs. The somewhat disorganised temple museum contains a representative sampling of several styles of old Buddhist art.

A kilometre west of Lamphun's old moat stands **Wat Kukut**, dating from the 8th century. (It's also known as Wat Chama Devi.) The temple has a superb pair of unusual chedi. Erected in the early 1200s, the larger chedi consists of five tiers, each of which contains three niches. Each niche holds a Buddha statue, making an impressive display of 15 Buddha images on each side.

South of Lamphun, beyond the cotton-weaving town of **Pasang** – commonly believed by Thais to have the loveliest females in the country – is the hilltop pilgrimage centre of **Wat Phrabat Tak Pha**. A Buddha footprint on the hill is reached up a flight of 469 steps. ❏

CHIANG MAI

*Hill tribes lure travelers to the Chiang Mai area, although many
hill villages and treks evoke commercialisation. Still, Chiang Mai's
hospitality and the area's diverse offerings are reason enough to go*

Map,
page 216

It has become commonplace in many guidebooks to bemoan the supposed demise of **Chiang Mai ❼**, Thailand's once fabulous "Rose of the North". Noisy *tuk-tuk*s are said to have replaced silent *samlor* pedicabs, concrete commercial buildings to have ousted traditional wooden housing, and high-rise condominiums to have marred the serene northern skyline. Happily, this is far from being the case. Chiang Mai has grown, it is true, and the volume of traffic has certainly increased along with urbanisation.

But high-rise buildings are a thing of the past, at least in the beautiful and historically important old city, where all new construction is strictly limited to three-storey buildings. In recent years, the city streets have been attractively cobbled in red brick, concrete lamp standards replaced by ornate Parisian-style lanterns, and the city walls and moats excavated and restored.

Despite its increasingly rapid urbanisation, 700-year-old Chiang Mai remains prized as a pleasant, cool-season escape from the sticky humidity of Bangkok. Situated 300 metres (1,000 ft) above sea level in a broad valley divided by the picturesque 560-kilometre-long (350 mi) **Mae Nam Ping**, the city reigned for seven centuries as the capital of the Lanna (Million Rice Fields) Kingdom. The city's northern remoteness kept the region beyond the close control of Bangkok – 700 kilometres (400 mi) south – well into this century.

In its splendid isolation, Chiang Mai developed a culture quite removed from that of the central plains, with wooden temples of exquisite beauty and a host of unique crafts, including lacquerware, silverwork, wood carvings, ceramics and umbrella-making. Although hospitality of both the hill tribes and the northern Thais is sometimes strained by the sheer numbers of visitors, they remain more gracious than in many other cities.

OPPOSITE: northern farming.
BELOW: modern Chiang Mai.

Origins

Chiang Mai's story begins farther north, in the town of Chiang Rai. Its founder and king, Mangrai, ruled a sizable empire that ran as far north as Chiang Saen, on the Mekong River. He founded Chiang Rai in 1281. But when the Mongol ruler Kublai Khan sacked the Burmese kingdom of Pagan in 1287, Mangrai feared that his realm might be threatened and so formed an alliance with the rulers of Sukhothai, then Siam's capital. With his southern boundaries secure, Mangrai captured the old Mon kingdom at Lamphun. To centralise his rule, he established a new base in the Ping River Valley in 1296. This new capital he named Chiang Mai, or New City. The location was chosen by the auspicious sighting of white deer, and of a white mouse with a family of five, all at the same time, or so the story has it. Rather than building on the banks of the Ping, which often floods, he built his city with the help of 90,000

TIP

Be careful on the
streets on April 13, and
for several days there-
after. Songkran, the
traditional Thai new
year, is when one
sprinkles water on
friends to bless them.
In Chiang Mai, espe-
cially, it rapidly degen-
erates into a deluge of
cascading proportions.

BELOW: grounds of
Wat Chiang Man.

labourers half a kilometre to the west and surrounding it with stout brick walls.
Less than a century after Chiang Mai's founding, however, Ayutthaya replaced
Sukhothai as the capital of Siam. This new kingdom had its own expansionist
dreams and ambitions, including designs on its neighbour to the north. For the
next 400 years, there was fierce competition and sometimes open warfare. In
the 16th century, Ayutthaya crushed an invasion by Chiang Mai, and Chiang
Mai's power waned. To compound its troubles, the region was invaded in the
early 1700s by the same Burmese enemy who was laying siege to Ayutthaya.

Although the Burmese were finally defeated, the people of Chiang Mai were
so exhausted and discouraged by the constant conflict that they abandoned the
city. It remained deserted until 1796, when the Burmese army was finally
defeated; new nobles began restoring the city to its former prominence. It continued to enjoy autonomy from Bangkok, at least until the railway brought meddling central government administrators. In 1932, following the death of the last
king of Chiang Mai, the north was finally fully incorporated into the Thai nation.

Old Chiang Mai

The commercial centres of downtown are along Thanon Tapae, with numerous
hotels, shops and guesthouses. Hotels have sprung up along Huai Kaeo Road,
which leads out to Doi Suthep. Red *songtao* pick-ups may be hailed all over
town; fares are a fixed five baht for most journeys. More expensive, but still
quite cheap, tuk-tuk noisily carry passengers to any point around town. A few
pedal samlor still offer a more leisurely way of travel.

The city's history began with **Wat Chiang Man Ⓐ**, which translates as
"power of the city". In the northern part of the old city, it was the first temple to

be built by Mangrai, who resided there during the construction of the city in 1296. Located in the northeast part of the old walled city, it is the oldest of Chiang Mai's 300-plus temples. Two ancient, venerated Buddha images are kept in the abbot's quarters and can be seen on request. The first image, Phra Sae Tang Tamani, is a small 10-centimetre-high (4 in) crystal Buddha image taken by Mangrai to Chiang Mai from Lamphun, where it had reputedly resided for 600 years. Apart from a short sojourn in Ayutthaya, the image has remained in Chiang Mai ever since. On Songkran in April, it is paraded through the streets.

The second image, a stone Phra Sila Buddha in bas-relief, is believed to have originated in India around the 8th century. Both statues are said to possess the power to bring rain and to protect the city from fire. The only other important structure in Wat Chiang Man is Chang Lom, a 15th-century square *chedi*, buttressed by rows of stucco elephants.

Imperiously positioned at the head of the city's principal thoroughfare is **Wat Phra Singh Ⓑ**, Chiang Mai's most important temple and also its largest. Founded in 1345, it dominates the quiet heart of the old, walled city, near the western gate of Suan Dok. Wat Phra Singh is noted for three monuments: a library, chedi and the Viharn Lai Kham. The magnificent Lanna-style wooden library, on the right side of the compound, is raised on a high base decorated with lovely stucco angels. Behind the main *viharn,* built in 1925, is a beautiful wooden *bot,* and behind this, a chedi built by King Pha Yu in 1345 to hold the ashes of his father. Wat Phra Singh's most beautiful building is the small Phra Viharn Lai Kham, to the left of the bot. Of all of Chiang Mai's temple buildings, it is perhaps the most outstanding. Built rather late in the Lanna period, in 1811, the wooden building's front wall is decorated in gold flowers on a red lac-

Map, page 227

Carved and gilded door, Wat Phra Singh.

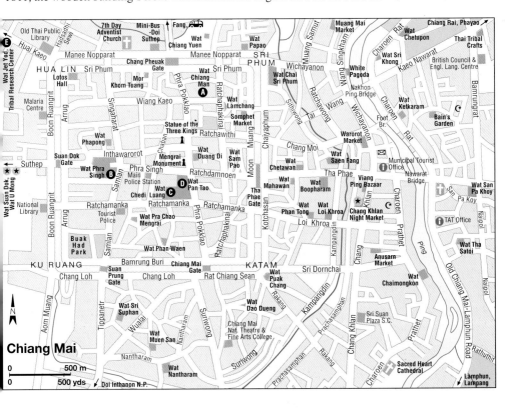

quer ground. Intricately carved wooden window frames accent the doors. The interior walls of the Viharn Lai Kham are decorated with murals commissioned by Chao Thammalangka, who ruled over Chiang Mai between 1813 and 1821. Although focusing on the Buddhist stories of Prince Sang Thong (north wall) and the *Tale of the Heavenly Phoenix* (south wall), they also record in fascinating detail aspects of early 19th-century Lanna society and exhibit clear indications of persisting Burmese cultural influence.

Calamity is associated with **Wat Chedi Luang C**, built in 1401 to the east of Wat Phra Singh. A century and a half later, a violent earthquake shook its then 90-metre-high (295 ft) pagoda, reducing its height to 42 metres (140 ft). It was never completely rebuilt, although recently it has been impressively restored. Even in its damaged state, the colossal monument is majestic. For 84 years the Emerald Buddha, now in Bangkok, was housed in this wat before being moved to Vientiane. King Mangrai was reportedly killed nearby by an untimely bolt of lightning. Close to the wat's entrance stands an ancient, tall gum tree. When it falls, says a legend, so will the city. As if serving as counterbalance, the *lak muang,* or city boundary stone, in which the spirit of the city is said to reside, stands near its base. The viharn of **Wat Pan Tao D**, adjacent to Wat Chedi Luang, formerly a palace, is a masterpiece of wooden construction. Its doorway is crowned by a beautiful Lanna peacock framed by *naga*, or mythical serpents.

Located one kilometre northwest of the city walls, **Wat Jet Yod E** was completed by King Trailokaraja in 1455. As its name "Seven Spires" suggests, it is a replica of the Mahabodhi Temple, in India's Bodhgaya, where Buddha gained enlightenment while spending seven weeks in its gardens. The beautiful stucco angels that decorate its walls are said to bear faces of Trailokaraja's own family.

BELOW: chedi of Wat Suan Dok hold ashes of Chiang Mai's royal family.

Although similar to a temple in Burma's then-capital of Pagan, it did not stop the Burmese from severely damaging it during the Burmese invasion of 1566.

One of the most impressive city temple complexes is **Wat Suan Dok ⒡**, one kilometre west of the wall's western gate. At its northwest corner are white-washed chedi that contain the ashes of Chiang Mai's royal family; the huge central chedi is said to hold no fewer than eight relics of Buddha. A short way out of town to the north, towards Doi Suthep, is **Wat U Mong**. With a honeycomb of underground cells used for meditation, the restored site lies amidst beautiful teak trees, and is one of the many quiet spots still left in Chiang Mai.

Map, page 231

Beyond the old city

A steep series of hairpin curves rise up the flanks of **Doi Suthep ⒢** – 15 kilometres (9 mi) northwest of the city – to Chiang Mai's best-loved temple, **Wat Doi Suthep**. The site was selected in the mid 1300s by an elephant that was turned loose with a Buddha relic strapped to its back. It climbed half-way up Doi Suthep, then stopped and would climb no more. Doi Suthep was built at the spot where it halted.

The architecture of Wat Doi Suthep is considered to be very representative of Lanna culture.

The ascending road passes the entrance to the Huai Kaeo Falls, where a minibus goes to the top. The scenery en route is spectacular, with the road winding its way to a large car park beneath Wat Doi Suthep. Seven-headed naga undulate down the balustrade of a 290-step stairway that leads from the parking lot to the temple. For the weary, a funicular makes the same ascent for a few baht. From Wat Doi Suthep, Chiang Mai is spread out below at one's feet.

From the upper terrace, a few more steps lead through the courtyard of the temple itself. In the late afternoon light, there are few sights more stunning than that which greet one at the final step. Emerging from cloisters decorated with murals depicting scenes from the Buddha's life, one's eyes rise to the summit of a 24-metre-high (80 ft) gilded chedi, partially shaded by gilded bronze parasols. The chedi is surrounded by an iron fence with pickets culminating in praying *thevada*, or angels. Appearing in the east and west ends of the compound are two viharn. At dawn, the eastern one shelters chanting nuns in white robes. At sunset, the one on the west holds robed monks chanting their prayers.

BELOW: covered children.

From the parking area of Wat Doi Suthep, a road ascends 5 kilometres (3 mi) to **Phuping Palace ⒣**, the winter residence of the royal family. Constructed in 1972 and situated at 1,300 metres (4,265 ft), the palace has audience halls, guest houses, dining rooms, kitchens and official suites. It also serves as headquarters for the royal family's agricultural and medical projects, carried on among hill tribes and in nearby villages. When the royal family is absent, the public may stroll – Fridays through Sundays, and on holidays – through the well-tended gardens.

Commercialised hill tribes

From the palace entrance, the road continues through pine forests to the commercialised Hmong hill-tribe village of **Doi Pui**. The village has been on the tourist track for some time, but recent improvements have brought material benefits to its inhabitants, including a paved

TIP

The area around
Chiang Mai is perhaps
best visited during
winter, late November
through early Febru-
ary, when it is abloom
with an astounding
variety of beautiful
flowers. Each February
the annual Flower
Festival fills the streets
with floral parades.

street lined with souvenir stands. Once subsistence farmers, the tribespeople have learned that visitors come bearing gifts, and a camera automatically triggers a hand extended for a donation. Hmong are itinerant farmers here, and in Burma and Laos. They once depended upon opium cultivation for their livelihoods. Despite government efforts to steer them towards more socially acceptable crops, many still cultivate patches deep in the hills.

An interesting insight into opium farming is provided by Doi Pui's Opium Museum, which describes in detail the process of cultivation and harvest. For those who lack the time to go deeper into the northern hills, this Hmong village offers an example of hill-tribe life, though one doubts it retains much of its original personality.

Once an agricultural region, the **Mae Sa Valley** ❶ cultivates a new money-earner: tourism. Waterfalls, working elephant camps, butterfly farms, orchid nurseries and a charming private museum called Mae Sa House Collection (with prehistoric artifacts and Sukhothai ceramics, among many things) vie for the visitor's attention. The valley also has quiet resorts along its river.

North of Chiang Mai

To reach the northern town of Fang, take Route 107 north from Chiang Mai (beginning at Chang Puak Gate) towards Chiang Dao. The road passes through rice fields and small villages, then begins to climb past Mae Taeng into the Mae Ping Gorge, which forms the southern end of the Chiang Dao Valley. Ahead, on the left as one follows the river's right bank through scenic countryside, is the massive outline of Chiang Dao mountain.

At the 56-kilometre marker is the **Chiang Dao Elephant Camp** ❶, on the

BELOW: umbrellas
made in Chiang Mai
are famous.

bank of Mae Nam Ping. Twice daily, a line of elephants walk into the river to be bathed by *mahout* for the amusement of tourists, who reward the baby elephants with bananas. The elephants then move to a dusty arena to demonstrate how to make huge logs seem like toothpicks, picking them up or dragging them with great ease across the teak-shaded open space. After the show, one can take a short elephant ride, and then hire a small bamboo raft for a 45-minute trip down the Ping River.

About 60 kilometres (40 mi) from Chiang Mai on Route 107, a dirt road branches left and goes to **Doi Chiang Dao** ⓚ, which at 2,186 metres (7,175 ft) is Thailand's third-highest peak. A jeep or a trail bike is needed to negotiate this 9-kilometre-long track, which leads up the mountain to the Hmong village of Pakkia. Entry to the sanctuary is restricted and permission must be obtained from the wildlife headquarters near Wat Pa Bong at the foot of the mountain.

The government's agricultural aid on Doi Chiang Dao is aimed at eradicating opium cultivation. From the government station here, officials trek out to assist hill tribes living on the slopes of Doi Chiang Dao and on the neighbouring mountains. At the nearby nursery, horticulturists experiment with new strains of tea that are gradually being introduced throughout the region.

Farther north, Route 107 enters the town of **Chiang Dao** ⓛ, located 70 kilometres (45 mi) from Chiang Mai. Chiang Dao is a quiet wooden town supplying surrounding villages, but its cafes and general stores are interesting. At the far end of town, a simple road leads off west and to the left for 5 kilometres to caves. Guides with lanterns lead visitors deep into high caverns containing several Buddha statues. Further down in a deeper section of the cave is a large, reclining limestone Buddha. ❑

**Map,
page 231**

Elephant training.

BELOW: April's Songkran festival in Chiang Mai.

CHIANG RAI AND THE GOLDEN TRIANGLE

Map, page 216

Just the mention of "Golden Triangle" suggests uncertain frontiers and illicit smuggling. And, indeed, both are found here. But the area north of Chiang Rai also offers escapes for the adventurous

Like other cities of the north, Chiang Rai has undergone rapid development, not only in the town itself but also in the surrounding hills where vacation homes for affluent Thais are rising. Indeed, for travellers seeking the exclusively historical, Chiang Rai has little of its rich past extant. Capital of Thailand's northernmost province, Chiang Rai lies only about 65 kilometres (40 mi) to the east of Fang. But for most visitors the trip to Chiang Rai begins in Chiang Mai, the focal point for the northern part of the country.

From Chiang Mai

Out of Chiang Mai, Route 107 heads due north past Chiang Dao to **Fang ❽**, located 150 kilometres (100 mi) from Chiang Mai. Fang is another town where development has dulled a reputation for wildness. Established by King Mangrai in the late 1260s, Fang was levelled by the Burmese in the early 1800s and remained uninhabited until the 1880s. During the 1950s, the district witnessed a "black-gold rush" following a minor discovery of crude oil. Production never matched expectations, but "nodding donkey" pumps still groan and grind in the fields to the west of the town.

Fang enjoys a reputation for opium smugglers, although nothing in its seemingly-benign appearance would suggest such. Straddling both sides of the road in a flat valley, Fang is home to remnants of Chiang Kai-shek's Guomintang (Nationalist) army; these Chinese-speaking soldiers fled China's Yunnan province after the 1949 Communist takeover, settling in Chiang Mai and Chiang Rai provinces.

Dressed in distinctively embroidered clothing, Mien hill tribes live in the mountains east of Fang. The women wear black hats decorated with red or magenta woolen balls, while babies carried on their mothers' backs sport little embroidered caps. Young girls may spend an entire year embroidering large pants for their weddings. The government has worked extensively with the Mien, promoting crops as substitutes for the more lucrative opium.

A few kilometres south of Fang, Route 109 cuts east towards Chiang Rai. North from Fang, a rough road leads 25 kilometres (15 mi) to **Thaton ❾**, on the banks of the Mae Kok. Here, rent a boat for an exciting 3-hour journey down the Kok to Chiang Rai. It is now also easy to continue north to the hill town of **Mae Salong ❿**.

The road is dusty but wide and has been paved since 1991. It swiftly climbs a ridge along the Burmese border, emerging at a small town clinging to the hillsides. At first, it seems one has taken a wrong turn and ended

OPPOSITE: ferry on the Mekong. **BELOW:** opium poppy.

Northern Akha child.

up in a Chinese village. The walls of the houses are decorated by red banners covered in gold Chinese characters; everyone speaks Chinese, while only the young speak Thai.

It quickly becomes apparent that these, too, are the descendants of Guomintang soldiers who were given refuge in Thailand. Unfortunately, many soon became involved in the opium trade and were not pacified until quite recently by the Thai army. Here, many of the inhabitants tend tea plantations and brew some rather potent wines.

Of more recent vintage is Baan Hin Taek, a few kilometres north. It was only in 1988 that the opium warlord Khun Sa was ousted from this mountain stronghold. A 13-kilometre paved road leads to the village, allowing visits by outsiders. Beyond Hin Taek lies Burma and heavily-armed soldiers man bunkers labelled with the unreassuring sign, "Tourist Security Post".

The road east drops off the ridge, eventually entering the Chiang Rai Valley just above Mae Chan.

From Lampang to Chiang Rai

The standard routes to Chiang Rai are Route 1, which continues north from Lampang, or Route 118, which leads northeast from Chiang Mai via Doi Saket, cutting travel time by half over the older route via Lampang.

Route 1 twists around and over mountains on its way to Ngao, 80 kilometres (50 mi) northeast of Lampang. At the highest point in the road, below twin rocky peaks, drivers usually stop – or if in a hurry, blow their horns – to pay respects to the *phi* (spirits) believed to inhabit the pass. Spirit houses, some simple, others as elaborate as small palaces, cluster along the side of the road.

BELOW: lush
northern landscape.

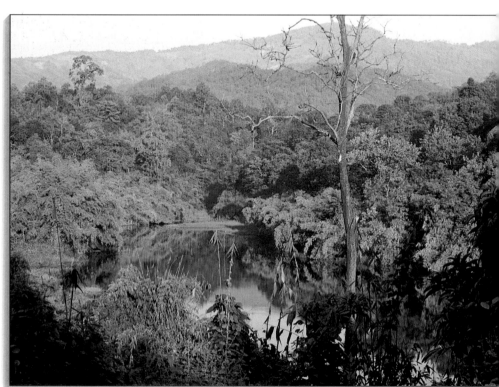

Teak saplings line Route 1 between Lampang and Ngao, thanks to the Forest Industry Organisation (FIO), which also runs the **Young Elephants Training Centre ⓫** (open daily; admission fee). Here, 50 kilometres (30 mi) northeast of Lampang and a kilometre west of the highway, behind Pang-la village, visitors can watch elephant keepers put their young pachyderms through mounting, marching and log-dragging drills until around noon. If made to train beyond noon, the elephants stamp their feet in protest, until they are allowed to lumber off to their stalls for a snack of sugar cane.

About 20 kilometres (15 mi) before Ngao, a left turn leads in less than one kilometre to a small grove of teak trees and a refreshment stand that mark the entrance to **Tham Pha Thai ⓬**, probably the most interesting cave in Thailand. Climb the 283 concrete steps up the hill, then drop down into the huge arched entrance to the grotto, above which stands a gleaming white *chedi*.

Inside the main cave is a large bronze Buddha, an object of great veneration judging from the number of garlands and candles. Most striking, however, is the colossal stalagmite rising like a white explosion from a sea of limestone. Often a young novice monk will lead visitors down into the cave and point out bizarre limestone formations, which, with a little imagination, can resemble a throne, a rabbit or a turtle. Within the cave, slithering green snakes wrap themselves around electric wires or coil up in crevices. The guide explains that these snakes are protected and have never bitten anyone. The 400-metre (440 yd) walk into the cave ends at a small mound of bat guano. Light streaks down from a jagged opening in the cave roof, silhouetting flying bats onto the cavern walls.

About 10 kilometres (6 mi) before Ngao, on the left of Route 1, the Burmese-style **Wat Chong Kram** exudes charm in the face of alarming decrepitude. The

Map, page 216

Cave entrance.

BELOW: carrying a load, and entrance of Tham Pha Thai.

ceiling is gradually becoming crooked as its supporting pillars sink into the mud.

Route 1 continues through **Ngao** , another typical northern Thai town, and then 50 kilometres (30 mi) farther north to **Phayao** ⓮. Although quite small and apparently undistinguished, Phayao holds great interest for archaeologists, as the town was rebuilt in the 11th century on a more ancient site. Judging from the remains of a moat and eight city gates that enclose an area of about 2 square kilometres, scholars believe the older site may predate the Bronze Age. **Wat Li**, on the left of the road, has a fine collection of terracotta Buddha heads from Phayao's own early, distinctive and unique school, which were unearthed in the surrounding fields and land near the *wat*.

The cultivation of opium was first introduced to northern Thailand in the late 1800s by hill-tribe people from southern China.

Between the lake and the road, leaving Phayao, sits **Wat Si Khom Kham**, considered by scholars to be the area's most important temple because of its 400-year-old, 16-metre-high (55 ft) Buddha image inside a *viharn*. In a new *ubosot* on the edge of the lake, modern Thai artist Angkarn Kalayanapongsa has created a beautiful set of murals.

Chiang Rai

From Phayao, Route 1 continues north 100 kilometres (65 mi) to the provincial capital of **Chiang Rai** ⓯, located in Thailand's northernmost province at an elevation of about 580 metres (1,900 ft). King Mangrai, who also established Chiang Mai as a walled city, founded Chiang Rai in the late 1200s.

Legend claims that the king, then ruler of Chiang Saen, decided to conquer regions to the south after his favourite elephant ran away in a southerly direction. The search for the elephant led to the banks of Mae Nam Kok, where the king decided to build Chiang Rai. A much-venerated statue of King Mangrai stands in northeastern Chiang Rai, by a reconstructed stretch of the old city wall.

Like much of northern Thailand, lengthy wars with Burma inflicted suffering on the town and its residents; for much of the 1800s, it was almost uninhabited. In recent years, in large part due to both drug money and tourism, Chiang Rai has regained some of its prosperity, reflected in the existence of new hotels and shops.

Despite its exotic location, the city itself lacks both ambiance and historical ruins. Near the busy streets are two of the town's most important temples: Wat Phra Singh and Wat Phra Kaeo. Both share the distinction of having once sheltered famous images. The chedi and viharn at **Wat Phra Singh**, where legend holds that an important Buddha image was located, have been restored too many times to allow accurate dating, but documents suggest the 15th century or earlier.

Founded sometime in the 13th century, **Wat Phra Kaeo**, behind Wat Phra Singh, is believed to have been the original residence of the Emerald Buddha that is now in Bangkok at the royal temple of the same name. (Apparently the chedi in Chiang Rai was struck by lightning, revealing the Buddha in the 1430s.) To the west of Wat Phra Kaeo rises Ngam Muang. Atop the hill, **Wat Ngam Muang** is believed by local people to contain remains of King Mangrai.

From Chiang Rai, Route 110 continues 30 kilometres (20 mi) north to **Mae Chan** ⓰. Formerly a centre for silverwork, the tiny district town serves mostly as a trading post for hill people, especially members of the Akha and Mien tribes.

Map, page 236

Northern border and Golden Triangle

The **Mekong River** – the name conjures up images of another time, another place, another world. It is the 12th-longest river in the world at 4,000 kilometres (2,500 mi) in length, passing through six countries on its way to the South China Sea. It is also defines much of the border between Thailand and Laos, only now a border that is significantly opening to trade and travel.

The ancient capital of **Chiang Saen** ⑰ nestles near where Burma, Laos and Thailand meet. This area, known as the Golden Triangle, has for years produced around half of the world's opium supply. Thailand's contribution has dropped to almost zero in the past 20 years, but both Laos and especially Burma continue to produce opium in major quantities.

Scholars believe Chiang Saen was founded around the end of the 13th century and strongly fortified about 100 years later by a grandson of King Mangrai. The Burmese captured it in the 16th century, but Rama I of Thailand recaptured it in the early 1800s. Fearing history would repeat itself with another Burmese invasion, however, Rama I ordered the town abandoned. It remained deserted for nearly a century. In 1957, the revived town became a district seat.

Chiang Saen's lovely setting on the Mekong River strongly enhances the charm of its old temples. Moreover, it is one of the few ancient towns in Thailand to have retained most of its lovely old trees, giving it a rare claim to tranquillity. The remains of its stout wall and moat can clearly be seen at its perimeter, and ruins of ancient monuments are scattered everywhere, popping up when one least expects them.

Just west of town stands **Wat Pa Sak**, whose name derives from the use of 300 teak, or *sak*, trunks for the original enclosure. The temple's foundation was laid in 1295 during the reign of King Mangrai. Earlier Srivijaya and Dvaravati influences, along with the then-prominent Sukhothai style, are evident in the *that* (reliquary), the clothing worn by the deities and the walking Buddhas.

Located about one kilometre west of the town gate, **Wat Prathat Chom Kitti** occupies a hill commanding a good view of Chiang Saen. Chronicles suggest that the old reliquary, with a leaning top, was first built around the 10th century and subsequently restored at least twice. Below this temple lies a ruined chedi in **Wat Chom Chang**. From here, a staircase leads farther downhill and back towards the town.

Close to the main street stand **Wat Chedi Luang** and a branch of the **National Museum**. The 60-metre-tall (200 ft), 13th-century chedi stands out in style as well as size; its bricks rise from an octagonal base to a bell-shaped top. In the grounds of the museum, one can see a good assortment of bronze Buddhas and other Chiang Saen art.

The most scenic return trip from Chiang Saen to Chiang Rai is via water in a long-tail boat down the Mekong River, as far as **Chiang Khong** ⑱, a three-hour trip after the rainy season when the river is high.

BELOW: limestone landscape.

The river follows an approximately S-shaped course, first flowing southeast to the mouth of the Kok River, then curving north between beautiful hills and mountains, then finally south again for a thrilling 20 kilometres (12 mi) down deep and narrow sections, through stomach-churning rapids and swirling eddies beneath steep, jungled mountainsides.

At Chiang Khong, the river widens slightly. Set on left-bank hills, the Laotian town of **Ban Houei Sai** lies opposite the Chiang Khong district seat. Lao government officials still work in Fort Carnot built by the French. When relations between Thailand and Laos are cordial – nearly always nowadays, especially since the opening of the Friendship Bridge in the northeast at Nong Khai – a ferry boat carries visitors across the river to the customs post on the Lao side. Day visits by non-Thai nationals are not yet possible, however. A visa to enter Laos must be obtained beforehand.

Heart of the Golden Triangle

Returning to Chiang Saen and heading north for around 9 kilometres (6 mi) brings the visitor to the small town of **Sop Ruak**, which proudly promotes itself as the "Heart of the Golden Triangle". In recent years, the town has heavily cashed in on the wild mystique of the area that most Westerners hold, and now Sop Ruak is home to several high-quality resorts and hotels, which entice people to stay longer than they would have a few years ago. The main street of Sop Ruak is lined with souvenir shops that sell a variety of local textiles and plastic kitsch, as well as numerous food stalls and sit-down restaurants providing welcome refreshment to those passing through the town; the quality of culinary offerings is rather variable, however.

BELOW: black giant squirrel aloft.

In reality, the town of Sop Ruak has little to hold the traveller's attention, aside from the views of neighbouring Burma and Laos. Worth a visit, though, is the unprepossessing yet informative **House of Opium** at the southern end of town. This small museum houses displays relating to the history, cultivation and trade of the *Papaver somniferum* – the opium poppy from which heroin is extracted, and for which the area of the Golden Triangle is famous.

Several boat trips are currently available from Sop Ruak, including ferries to Chiang Saen and Chiang Khong, as well as round trips on the Mekong and Ruak rivers skirting the Burmese and Lao frontiers. Occasional trips depart for the long journey to China's province of Yunnan, but these are not yet regular.

Continuing north and east from Sop Ruak, the road finally reaches **Mae Sai**, the most northerly town in Thailand. This busy border town, with Tachilek clearly visible on the Burmese side of the small Sai River, has a real frontier feel to it. In the shops and stalls along the main streets, Burmese, Thai, Shan and hill-tribe traders sell a heady mix of gems, lacquerware and antiques – both new and old – along with imported whisky, cigarettes and medicinal herbs.

Visitors are usually allowed to cross the small bridge to Burma for up to three days, for a quick stroll around **Tachilek** – which like Sop Ruak really has little to offer except for the claim of visiting Burma – or for a longer journey as far as Kengtung, midway between Thailand and China. Frontier regulations between Thailand and Burma are prone to change, so check before crossing. And note that the bridge closes in the evening, so be sure not to be stranded on the wrong side of the river.

In the mid 1990s, the area around Tachilek was a site of the Burmese army's campaign against the Shan guerrilla movement, which was concentrated around here. As many as 3,000 refugees fled into Thailand near Mae Sai to escape the fighting. (Later, the infamous drug warlord Khun Sa, long the kingpin of the opium trade in the Golden Triangle, surrendered to the Burmese junta, only to take up residence in Rangoon.) The Shan are ethnically related to Thais and Laos, and have long had considerable autonomy from the Burmese government. Opium cultivation has financed the Shan independence movement against the Burmese government.

To the west of the main street, close to the border, there is a flight of steps ascending a small hill to **Wat Phra That Doi Wao**. This temple was purportedly constructed in memory of several thousand Burmese soldiers who died in battle against Chiang Kai-shek's Guomintang army, which was fighting against Mao Zedong's Communists for control of southern China here in 1965. The temple grounds afford splendid views over Mae Sai and Burma.

About 6 kilometres (4 mi) south of town, **Tham Luang** (Great Cave), on a turn-off to the west of Route 110 heading back to Chiang Rai, burrows for several kilometres into the hills. Gas lanterns are available for hire at the entrance. The first cavern is impressive in its size alone. Thereafter, a series of short, sometimes fairly restricting passages lead to caverns of varying magnitude, where the roof formations and crystalline deposits become more magnificent. ❏

Map,
page 236

BELOW: Lisu women in traditional attire.

Map,
page 216

MAE HONG SON

Perhaps long the most ignored part of Thailand, Mae Hong Son's isolation leaves it feeling rather unfettered by modern contrivances. Still, people have lived here for over 10,000 years

Mae Hong Son

THAILAND

Bangkok

Secluded by jungle ridges and framed on the north and west by Burma, the Mae Hong Son area has benefited from years of benign neglect by the outside world. (Access was difficult until the mid 1960s, when a paved road opened up the town.) Mae Hong Son's years of human occupation, however, are rather lengthy. In a cave, an archaeologist found tools and seeds from betel nut, cucumber and black pepper, all apparently cultivated by early people. Analysis dates these between 10,000 and 6,000 BC. Later items include cutting tools from around 7,000 BC.

To reach Mae Hong Son by road, head south from Chiang Mai on Route 108. Just before the 57-kilometre marker, turn right and drive 10 kilometres (7 mi) past the entrance of **Doi Inthanon National Park ⑲**, a popular retreat named after its prime attraction, Doi Inthanon, the highest mountain in the country at 2,596 metres (8,517 ft). Girls rush out to visitors to sell bead necklaces, whilst cold beer and soft drinks are served in small shops along the river's edge, below Mae Klang Falls.

From the shops, walk up a bit to see this powerful cataract and its spectacular fusion of muddy brown water and white spray. Clearly marked footpaths branch into the rocky hills; one leads around a corner of boulders to a full view of a wider fall, Pakauna, which slides over its broad, craggy slopes for 120 metres (400 ft) like a liquid carpet.

The road continues to climb a further 25 kilometres (16 mi) to the peak of **Doi Inthanon**, whose summit is dominated by an off-limits radar station. Another spectacular waterfall, Mae Ya, is in the southern part of the park, dropping more than 250 metres (820 ft).

The limestone mass of Doi Inthanon is a comparatively modest foothill in the southern extension of the Himalayan range, which stretches southeast from Yunnan in southern China. Although less than a giant, Doi Inthanon has a majesty of its own conveyed by its steep, forest-clad slopes and mist-enshrouded summit. Karen and Hmong tribespeople still live nearby in isolated villages but are slowly being relocated, as the mountain is now a national reserve. On its summit the ashes of Chiang Mai's last king are enshrined.

By making prior arrangements with park authorities in Chiang Mai, it is possible to take a 3- to 5-day hike on foot or by pony up the mountain. Several campsites afford simple accommodation for trekkers. During the climb, one can observe rare birds and enjoy nature under a broad canopy of trees.

At the 58-kilometre marker on Route 108, one kilometre south of the park turn-off, is **Chom Thong ⑳**. The town's pride is the elegant **Wat Phra That Si Chom Thong**, where glints of subdued light accentuate a beautiful collection of bronze Buddhas. The

BELOW: Shan child.

monastery creaks with old age, as do the slumping boughs of trees scattered about its courtyard. The brilliantly gilded *chedi* dates from 1451, and the sanctuary, only 50 years later.

A large cruciform *viharn* built in 1516 – deeply incised with a profusion of floral patterns entwined with birds and *naga* serpents – dominates this temple compound. Four standing Buddhas, clothed like celestial kings, flank the viharn. Although much of the decoration in the temple reflects the Burmese penchant for elaboration, the central Buddha image, with its protective naga, seems eminently Thai and resembles the famed image at Wat Phra Singh Luang in Chiang Mai. On either side of the viharn are enshrined miniature gold and silver Buddha images, some bejeweled and metallic, others carved of crystal.

Further south on Route 108 are many northern touches: rambling, stylised elephants carved on the backs of bullock carts; *lamyai* trees and green bean-patches; giant plaited baskets, in which farmers thresh harvested rice; and shady, thatched-roof *sala* dotting the extensive rice fields.

Hot ㉑, 90 kilometres (50 mi) southwest of Chiang Mai on Route 108, once lay 15 kilometres farther south at the mouth of the Ping River, until the rising reservoir behind the Bhumibol Dam submerged it. Today, it has evolved into a fully-fledged town that seems to have been there forever. Farther south on Route 1012 lies the original site of ancient Hot. Cracked, rain-washed chedi dot the landscape – dignified relics from the time when Hot was part of the early kingdoms of the north. Excavations have unearthed gold jewelry, amulets and lively stucco carvings, which are now on display in Chiang Mai.

Route 1012 continues south to **Wang Luang**, a tiny village that earns its keep by selling dried fish caught in the catchment area created by Bhumibol Dam.

TIP

A boat can be hired at Wang Luang for an hour's voyage among the islands at the estuary of the Ping River, and out onto the expanse of water at the upper end of the reservoir. Reflections of ruined chedi and strange, eroded cliffs enliven remote mountain scenes.

BELOW: falls at Mae Klang, Doi Inthanon National Park.

Karen people have settled much of this area. Their necks hidden by a profusion of black beads and their bodices covered with thick, coloured patchwork, Karen tribeswomen walk into the tiny town to buy provisions.

From Hot, Route 108 strikes out west across the Chaem River, following its right bank toward Mae Sariang. About 20 kilometres (15 mi) from Hot, the road passes **Ob Luang Gorge**, sometimes referred to as Thailand's version of the Grand Canyon, though this requires a considerable stretch of the imagination. Stop at the sala for a look into the deep, ragged incisions in the rock.

Hill-tribe farming

Most of the area's villages belong to the largest hill-tribe group in Thailand, the Skaw Karen, who have settled along the Thai-Burmese frontier as far south as Chumphon. In the moist valleys they plant wet rice on steep terraces. On the slopes, black tree stumps stand out like whiskers on a green background of rice sprouts; nomadic Karen burn away the forest to make clearings to plant new crops. This slash-and-burn technique has scarred the mountain sides and caused extensive erosion; today many Karen have taken to sedentary farming.

In places, the road skirts high banks of red earth. Fresh mounds of mud on the asphalt show that landslides are not uncommon – the steep banks cannot always hold back the run-off. A solution to this problem may be the pine tree. Though it is not a tree one normally associates with tropical Thailand, the pine is well suited to rebuilding the soil. Its roots form an extensive earth-holding network, and its seeds are not easily destroyed by fire.

The drive towards Mae Sariang is more exciting than the town itself. The road runs like a roller coaster over the mountains. Not even motorbikes can reach

Because northern Thailand is on a bird migratory flyway, nearly 10 percent of the world's species can be seen here at some time during the year. The Chiang Mai area alone offers around 400 species.

BELOW: hill-tribe woman bottle-feeding cattle.

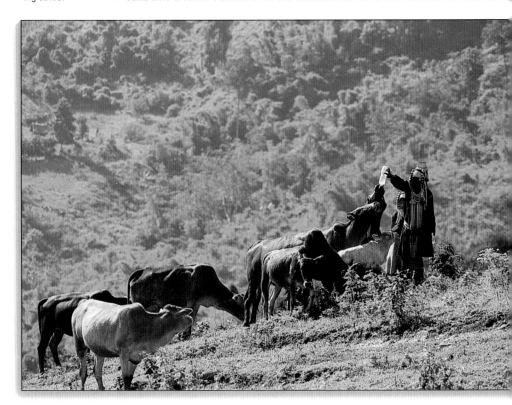

some of the small leaf-and-bamboo huts tucked away in these hills. Hemmed in by mountains, **Mae Sariang** ㉒ itself lies 100 kilometres (65 mi) west of Hot, at the point where Route 108 bends to the north. A few Burmese-style temples, a small, white mosque and a few Karen handicraft shops distinguish this small district administrative centre and border trading post.

Route 108 continues north on a rough track from Mae Sariang, through mountain scenery that is amongst the most breathtaking in Thailand, reaching Mae Hong Son 170 kilometres (100 mi) later.

Mae Hong Son ㉓ lies in a valley between deep-green mountains, which accounts for its early morning fogs. The forest valley is buttressed by mountains that separate Thailand from Burma. Mae Hong Son has for years been a destination for seekers of old-world serenity. (Nonetheless, like most of Thailand, it is gradually being developed, including two major new hotels.) The presence of Karen, Hmong, Lawa, Shan, Lisu, and Lahu, who taken collectively easily outnumber the ethnic Thais, adds intrigue to an ill-kept secret: Mae Hong Son is smack in the middle of border smuggling routes.

A commanding view of the town of Mae Hong Son and the surrounding countryside is afforded from **Doi Kong Mu**, a hill that rises 250 metres (820 ft) above the town. At night, the two tall chedi of **Wat Phra That Doi Kong Mu** atop the hill light up like timid beacons of civilisation in this corner of Thailand. Erected in the 19th century, the wat reflects Burmese influences. A pond and a park at the centre form a core of beauty and peace that few other Thai towns possess. On the edge of the lake, across from a fitness park, are the intertwined temples of **Wat Chong Klang** and **Wat Chong Kum**. These Burmese-style temples, with their pristine, white chedi, look moving when reflected in the lake. ❐

Map, page 216

Unusual chedi of Wat Chong Kum.

BELOW: street front, Mae Hong Son.

Map,
page 216

THAILAND

Bankok

NAN VALLEY

If looking for life unjaded by tourism, along with some superb outdoor activities, seek no further than the area around Nan, once the capital of a small kingdom later to join the first Lanna empire

The Nan Valley may be Thailand's last great undiscovered tourist territory. It has lovely mountain scenery, the full complement of hill tribes, a new national park, and a friendly population not yet jaded by exposure to foreign travelers. The principal roads make for excellent mountain biking and motorcycling, since they are sealed, hilly rather than mountainous, and not often disrupted by traffic. The drawback is that very few people speak English, many signs are not romanised, and there is barely any accommodation outside of Nan.

With its cement-block and egg-carton architecture, the town of **Nan** ㉔ initially appears to be yet another nondescript upcountry town, with a population of around 25,000. A stroll or spin beyond the downtown area, however, will soon reveal plenty of old wooden houses, which come in three upraised styles. There are exhibits of the three styles at the local branch of the **National Museum** (open Wednesday–Sunday; admission fee), which should be a first stop on any tour. Located in the former airy residence of the last two Nan princes, the museum also provides introductions to tribes, textiles, crafts and history. The 300-year-old black elephant tusk on display is reputed to have magical powers.

The first Nan dynasty emerged in the mid 1300s. By the end of the 14th century, Nan was among ten Thai-Lao states that joined to form the first Lanna

BELOW: gilded images facing the four cardinal points, Wat Phumin.

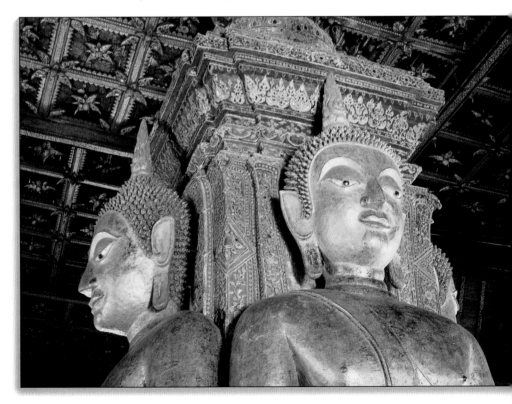

empire. The town was later conquered by the Burmese and the next few hundred years were tumultuous, but in 1788 Nan finally allied with the Rattanakosin, or Bangkok, kingdom. Because Nan's rulers fully cooperated in the drive by Bangkok's King Chulalongkorn to unite a crazy quilt of vassal states into a modern nation, the province was allowed to retain its special status as a semi-independent principality until the death of the last Nan prince in 1931.

The allegiances and influences of the past 600 years are evident in Nan temples, which display the styles of Lanna, Sukhothai, northern and southern Laos, the Thai Lu people, and combinations thereof. Styles of the Sukhothai period are prominent at **Wat Chang Kham**, which is across the street from the museum and located within the old city walls. The elephants, seven on each side, supporting the second tier of the square *chedi* are a Sukhothai motif. The standing Buddhas in the 15th century *viharn* are also Sukhothai style and very common in Laos. The *wat* library, with its high ceiling but now empty, was at one time the largest in Thailand.

Next door to the National Museum is the even older **Wat Hua Khuang** with a wooden verandah in the Luang Prabang (that is, northern Lao) style. Although it's often closed, visitors may be lucky to catch the weekend painter who for years has been restoring the murals. The town's most famous murals, however, are found a short walk south at **Wat Phumin**, which was first constructed in 1596. The building in question has a highly unusual cruciform layout that combines viharn and *bot*. If the great carved doors of the viharn wing are fully open, make sure to peek behind them to see the murals that decorate this front wall. There are rowing boats loaded with bearded foreigners, who smoke pipes and wear naval caps. Among them are even a few heavily-dressed *farang* (foreign)

From the 1960s to the 1980s, Nan Valley was a stronghold of communist insurgents, who filtered through the border with Laos. Later, Thai communists took advantage of government amnesties. Still off-limits is a small patch in the north due to "bandits".

BELOW: dragon-boat race in Nan, and mural detail, Wat Phumin.

Map,
page 216

OPPOSITE: Akha
tribeswoman.
BELOW: Sao Din.

women. And there's a great three-masted sailing ship. The murals depict an
episode from the *Jataka* tales, the chronicle of Buddha's previous incarnations.
The scenes of Asian characters engaged in war, torture and all-around mayhem
on the other walls convey one hellish life. Since the murals were painted in the
late 19th century, shortly after the cession to the French, it has recently been
proposed that the murals may also have intended to express how Nan people
regarded their long history of betrayals and abandonment.

Wat Phra That Cha Haeng is located on a hill about 3 kilometres southeast
of town and across the Nan River – where the large "dragon boats" race for a
week every autumn. You'll recognise the wat by the lengthy *nagas* snaking down
the hill in greeting. The square gilded chedi is Lao-style. The bot, however, has
many Thai Lu influences, such as the sweeping, five-layered wooden roof, the
low ceilings and the dog-like dragons guarding the entry. A minority, but not a
hill tribe, Thai Lu are ethnic Thai people that immigrated to the Nan Valley about
150 years ago.

On the return trip to town, turn left before crossing the river and watch how
thick, rough *saa* paper is made from mulberry bark in a factory that resembles
someone's backyard.

One can arrange one- to three-day hill treks in Nan, but it's also easy to visit
tribal (and Thai) villages on the approximately 80-kilometre (50 mi) journey to
Doi Phu Kha National Park ㉕. Few of the tribal villages are long standing.
During the insurgency some decades ago, many people were relocated from the
uplands to remove them from communist temptations. They were joined by
tribal people fleeing war-torn Laos. After a decade or more in refugee camps,
they have been dispersed to new villages throughout the province.

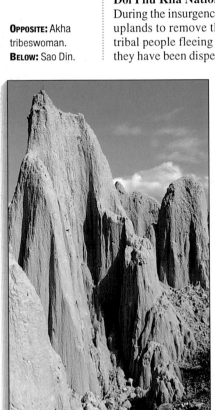

Trails meander through tribal villages. Like most of
the forests that visitors will spy elsewhere in Nan, these
here are the fruit of reforestation projects. The national
park does have some undisturbed areas, but they are not
served by trails. Park rangers or U.S. Peace Corps volunteers can direct you to some pretty spots, such as the
1,300-metre (4,300 ft) peak of Don Khao and Ton Tong
waterfall. Continue for about 20 kilometres (12 mi)
along Route 1256, the windy, steep road running east
of park headquarters, to reach the Htin village of Ban
Bor Kleua, where the salt wells still function.

On the return trip to Nan town, take the eastern
branch of Route 1080, which sprouts off south of the
town of Pua. About a half-dozen kilometres along the
way is **Ban Pa Klang**, a veritable town of Hmong, Htin
and Mien people. Mien make and sell silver jewelry
here. The views of majestic mountains along this route
are stunning, though it's difficult to pick out **Doi Phu
Kha**, the province's highest at 1,985 metres (6,512 ft).

As for the area south of Nan, the top sights are the
eerie Hom Chom and **Sao Din** rock pillars. Carved by
the wind, these bare, pointed projectiles form desolate
canyons. Nan, both the town and the province, are usually entered from the southwest via Route 101, a soothing ride through tobacco, cotton and rice fields and
gently rolling, reforested hills.

The next substantial town south is **Phrae** ㉖, capital
of the like-named province. ❒

CRAFTS AND CLOTHING OF THE HILL TRIBES

Each hill tribe of Thailand has its own customs, dress, language and spiritual beliefs that are reflected in the crafts they produce.

Textiles and silver jewelry play a very important role in the ceremonial activities of Thailand's hill-tribe communities. Hill-tribe women are defined by what they wear, and their choice of clothing and adornment can reveal not only what tribe they are from, but also their social status, age and even where their home town is located. However, the way of life of Thailand's hill-tribe people is changing as they are slowly assimilated into mainstream Thai society, abandoning many features of their traditional culture. This may be sad for visitors in search of traditional hill-tribe culture, but the process is inevitable and has distinct advantages for these ethnic minorities, since they can now benefit from educational opportunities and medical facilities.

Hill-tribe craft items started to be made commercially in the mid-1970s when small craft centres were set up in refugee camps. Authentic items are now rare and expensive, but good quality, modern crafts can be found in craft shops.

BRASS NECK RINGS ▷
Padaung women once wore brass rings around their arms, legs and necks; the tradition has, thankfully, diminished. Still, some Padaung refugees from Burma are forced by tour operators to pose for tourists.

◁ HMONG EMBROIDERY
Women from the Hmong hill tribe used to hand-weave cloth, but today they use ready-made fabrics for their intricately embroidered clothing. The Hmong are skilled in making indigo-dyed batik which is then embroidered with appliquéd layers of geometrically-shaped fabric to make up their skirts.

▽ LISU TEXTILES
Lisu women make distinctive clothing. In the past, the cloth was woven by hand but the Lisu now use machine-made material that they run up on sewing machines.

AKHA COTTONS

Women of the Akha hill tribe spin cotton into thread with a hand spindle, then weave it on a foot-treadle loom. The cloth is dyed indigo and is then appliquéd and decorated with shells, seeds, silver or buttons and made into clothing for the family. The men make a variety of baskets and other items from wood, bamboo and rattan.

LISU CEREMONIAL WEAR ▷

On special occasions, Lisu men wear turbans and the women don large amounts of hand-crafted silver jewelry, chunky necklaces and colourful tunics with silver buttons. Men of the tribe are skilled blacksmiths. The sale of crafts means they no longer need to grow opium poppies to make a living.

▽ **AKHA HEADDRESS**
Married Akha women are famous for their head-dresses decorated with silver coins, which they wear all the time. Unmarried women from the tribe attach small gourds to their head-dresses.

HOW THE KAREN MAKE *IKAT*

The White Karen tribe (above) produce striped warp *ikat* textiles woven on back-strap looms. Ikat is a technique used to pattern cloth that involves the binding of the cloth with fibre or strips of material, so in places it becomes resistant to dyeing.

Before the cloth is dyed, the weft (yarns woven across the width of the fabric) or the warp (lengthwise yarns) is pulled tightly over a frame and then threads are bound tightly together singly or in bunches. The cloth is then dyed several times using different colours. As a result, complex and beautiful patterns are built up with soft, watery edges on the parts of the cloth not completely covered by the binding materials.

The dyeing process is complex, with the dominant colour of the ikat dyed first. Cotton yarns are the most suitable for making warp ikat, and the dyes used to produce these textiles are natural dyes that are easily absorbed by cotton. The most popular colours for warp ikat are indigo and red. Weft ikats use mainly yellow dyes (made from turmeric), diluted indigos and a deep crimson red extracted from the lac insect. Orange, green and purple are created by an overdyeing process.

Northeast Thailand

THE NORTHEAST

To the Thais, the northeastern part of the nation is known as Isaan, a place of historical and natural importance

The northeast does not usually figure prominently on anybody's list of travel destinations in Thailand. This is a pity, for the northeast is a treasure trove of ancient monuments. Parts of the region were ruled by the Khmers, during the great period when they built Angkor Wat and colonised large areas of northeastern Thailand, building temples in key cities. Outside of Angkor itself, the northeast is certainly the best place in Asia to view the remains of the Khmer culture.

The northeast of Thailand is a high plateau upon which about one-third of the country's population lives. Many northeasterners' ancestors migrated from Laos across the great Mekong River, which forms the natural border between Laos and Thailand. Today, Thais of the northeast retain the Lao quality of sweet passivity in the face of adversity. The quality is useful, for the northeast is not always an easy place to live. The soil is often thin and infertile, there is either not enough rain, or too much, and the Mekong can be unforgiving when it floods. So many northeasterners go to Bangkok, filling unskilled jobs in the capital. Small wonder that the northeast also has a tradition of dissident politicians whose demands for social reform have been louder than those from other parts of the country.

The basic agricultural products of the northeast are poor-soil staples like cotton and tapioca. Mulberry trees, too, are grown to feed the worms that spin silk. In the late 1950s, the Friendship Highway, a joint Thai-American undertaking, opened the region. In the 1960s, large American military bases during the Vietnam War pumped money into the region and made boom-towns out of places like Nakhon Ratchasima (also called Khorat), Udon Thani and Ubon Ratchathani. In 1994, the first road bridge from Thailand into Laos, crossing the Mekong River at Nong Khai, opened.

For several years now, there has been a fairly successful effort to develop the northeast. Numerous development projects have been initiated by the royal family and the government to improve production, processing and transport for agricultural products.

Because the northeast isn't on the agenda of most foreign travelers, this reason alone, perhaps, is the major lure of the region. ❐

PRECEDING PAGES: sorting out raw silk, a product of Khorat, that has been spun.

KHORAT PLATEAU

*With Cambodia to the south, it's not surprising that northeastern
Thailand retains a Khmer texture to its history, whether
in the architecture of ancient sanctuaries or in old tales*

Map,
page 252

THAILAND

Bangkok

The good roads of northeast Thailand – an area called *Isaan* by the Thais –
invite travel by car, which undoubtedly is the best way to see the many out-
of-the-way sights in this part of the country. The Friendship Highway, or
Route 2, the main road through the northeast, begins about 100 kilometres (60
mi) from Bangkok, branching off of Route 1 just before the town of **Saraburi**.
About 20 kilometres (15 mi) after the Saraburi turn-off on Route 2, a dirt road on
the right leads to an experimental farm run by the Kasetsart Agricultural University of Bangkok, and then beyond to **Phra Ngam** (Beautiful Buddha Image),
a cave where a Dvaravati-era image may be seen. There are numerous other
caves nearby, many yet unexplored.

Another 15 kilometres (10 mi) leads to **Muaklek**. Once known for malaria,
Muaklek has been transformed from an unhealthy jungle into dairy land that
features a small arboretum garden, where a wonderful variety of roses bloom
along a stream.

About 50 kilometres (30 mi) east of Saraburi is **Wat Teppitakpunnaram**,
where a monumental white Buddha sits on a green mountain, like an alabaster
relic. The countryside in this area belongs to **Khao Yai National Park ❶**, hidden 40 kilometres (25 mi) to the south. (See *Outside of Bangkok,* page 177.)

Route 2 continues northeast up the Khorat Plateau,
passing the reservoir of **Lam Takhong**. Soon the blue
lake disappears and scrub brush, typical of the dryer
areas of the northeast, begins to dominate the scenery.
About 150 kilometres (100 mi) from Saraburi is the
provincial capital of **Khorat**, now officially called
Nakhon Ratchasima ❷.

Richest and largest city in the northeast, and once an
air base for American bombers during the Vietnam War,
Nakhon Ratchasima now serves as a trade, communications and military centre for the entire northeast
region. It is also the capital of the most densely-popu-
lated upcountry province in Thailand, with over 1.5 million residents.

Although a busy and important commercial centre,
Nakhon Ratchasima has not forgotten its past. A statue
of national heroine Khunying Mo (Tao Suranari) presides over the town square and the whitewashed old city
wall, from around the 10th century. Khunying Mo was
the wife of an assistant provincial governor in the early
19th century, when Prince Anu of Vientiane led his
army to Khorat.

After taking the city, the prince threatened to enslave
its residents. Khunying Mo rallied the women of Khorat, who enticed many of the Laotian soldiers to a
drunken revelry and then killed them whilst they slept.
Prince Anu, who meanwhile had gone to attack
Saraburi, was forced to withdraw his depleted forces to

OPPOSITE: Prasat Hin
Phimai. **BELOW:**
young Phimai girl.

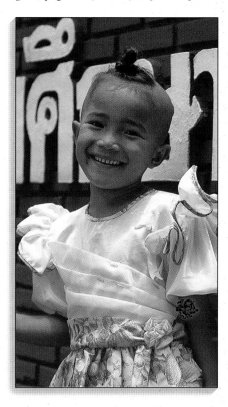

Vientiane, to the north. Outside the walls and moat is the off-beat **Wat Sala Loi**, erected in 1973 in the shape of a Chinese junk. The symbolism is clear – it will convey the faithful believer of Buddha to *nirvana*.

Silk is one of the region's most important industries. To visit a nearby silk production centre, take Route 304 south towards Kabinburi. After 30 kilometres (20 mi) is the town of **Pak Thong Chai**, where the Jim Thompson silk company has established a weaving cooperative to produce Thai silk. It is, in fact, the world's largest hand-woven-silk enterprise.

There are 300-plus Khmer ruins in Thailand, most of them in the northeast. There has been a concerted effort since the 1920s to restore many of them.

Excursions from Nakhon Ratchasima

The main attractions outside Nakhon Ratchasima are two sites created nine centuries ago by Khmer architects, both northeast of town on Route 2.

The peaceful monastery of **Prasat Phanom Wan** ❸ has heavy stone galleries, revealing the Khmer penchant for false windows with stone mullions, a method adopted to compensate for the soft stone. Elaborate zig-zag patterns cover the carved stones.

An uncommon stillness pervades this 11th-century retreat, broken only by the footsteps of resident monks. Unlike the majority of Khmer ruins, this one contains an active temple. Behind its well-preserved vaulted entrance, the original, dark sanctuary is filled with many more recent Buddha images of different styles, most of them covered with patches of gold leaf. Full-grown trees sprout from the oldest chambers. The presence of older monks in residence reminds visitors that donations are needed to help with the upkeep of the site.

BELOW: differing Buddha styles, Prasat Phanom Wan.

Farther north are the ruins of **Prasat Hin Phimai** ❹, 50 kilometres (30 mi) from Nakhon Ratchasima on the Mae Nam Mun, a tributary of the Mekong.

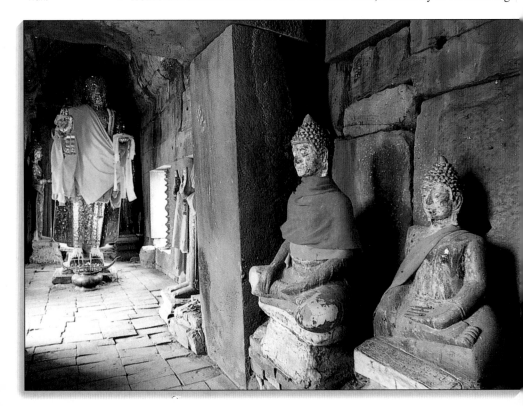

Renovated with the help of the same expert who restored Angkor Wat in nearby Cambodia, it has been suggested that Phimai may have been a prototype for Angkor Wat itself.

Map, page 252

The last of the great Angkor monarchs, King Jayavarman VII, who replaced Hinduism with Mahayana Buddhism as the official religion, could easily travel from his palace along a 240-kilometre (150 mi) road to Phimai, which was at the western extent of his expanding kingdom. A string of 112 rest houses was constructed along the route to shelter pilgrims and government officials making the long journey to Phimai. During the king's reign (AD 1181–1201), Phimai prospered within a walled rectangular area 1,000 metres by 560 metres, on an artificial island created by linking the Mun River and one of its tributaries via a canal. There were four entrances, with serpents, or *naga,* guarding each. The primary entrance faces south. Like the shrines at Angkor, the monuments at Phimai were never inhabited. Shops, libraries and houses were built of wood, and therefore have disintegrated centuries ago.

Detail from Prasat Hin Phimai.

However, the old city gate, most likely the main entrance to the sanctuary, still stands at the end of Phimai's present main street. Near the bridge over the Mae Nam Mun, the government maintains an open-air museum displaying some of the more beautifully carved lintels and statues found in the area.

Before leaving Phimai, visit Sai Ngam, or "Beautiful Banyan Tree", one kilometre east of the temple near an irrigation reservoir. It has an umbrella of dense leaves and roots that locals revere as a shelter for special spirits, and it is claimed to be the largest banyan tree in the world.

From Phimai, one can continue north on Route 2 to **Khon Kaen** and directly to the Mekong River town of Nong Khai. But for a better look at the rural north-

BELOW: old ruins at Phimai.

Khmer Legacy

Between the 10th and 14th centuries AD, a large part of mainland Southeast Asia, from the Mekong Delta in the east to around Phetchburi in the west, lay under the control of the Khmer Empire. Administered at the height of its power by god-kings, the empire's capital at Angkor was connected to the outlying reaches of the empire by a system of highways and religio-political strongpoints such as Khao Phra Viharn, Wat Phu, Phanom Rung, and Phimai.

By the mid-19th century, when the frontiers of present-day Indochina were effectively fixed by French colonialism, the Khmer Empire had long since disappeared, leaving Cambodia much reduced in size. It is true that the crowning glory of the Khmer past, Angkor Wat, still lay within Cambodia's confines, as did the magnificent "lofty sanctuary" of Phra Viharn, albeit only just. Yet many other symbolic relics of the Khmer past now lay outside Cambodia, most notably Wat Phu in southern Laos and

a series of magnificent sites across Thailand's Tung Kula Rong Hai, the "Weeping Plain" of the lower Northeast.

Thailand has long valued these unique historic treasures, yet only very recently have concerted efforts been made to preserve and promote them. Over the past three decades, several of the most important sites have been painstakingly and successfully restored by the government's Department of Fine Arts. Moreover, the Tourism Authority of Thailand has publicised a "Khmer Culture Trail" in lower Isaan which offers the visitor an unparalleled opportunity to explore the glories of the Khmer past.

Khorat and Buriram provinces host the major Khmer complexes: Prasat Hin Phimai, Prasat Phanom Rung and Prasat Muang Tham. All three have been carefully restored, though Phanom Rung is perhaps today the most impressive. Like Angkor Wat itself, these temples were all originally constructed as Hindu temples dedicated to Vishnu and Shiva, and as such the ruins demonstrate, particularly in their carvings, a deistic diversity and Indic sensuality not evident in more recent, Buddhist structures. It was under Jayavarman VII that Hinduism was replaced by Buddhism, and the temples were converted to *wat*. Their significance to Thai Buddhists remains strong, weakened neither by memories of foreign powers on what is now Thai soil nor by the slightly unfamiliar iconography. Phanom Rung is indeed a regular and important place of Buddhist pilgrimage.

As far away as Lopburi, Khmer influence is easily recognisable in the three ruined *prang* of Phra Prang Sam Yot, often attributed to Jayavarman VII. And in the vicinity of Phanom Rung are various Khmer *kuti*, or meditation retreats, as well as several other unrestored temple complexes languishing in the forests and undergrowth. All bear testimony to the fact that this area, far from being an outpost of the Khmer empire, was very much in its heartland. Indeed, as recently as 1976, Democratic Kampuchea's (now Cambodia) despotic regime was staking a claim to the region, promising to "liberate" lost Khmer territories in Thailand. Fortunately, whilst the the local Khmer-speakers are conscious of, and justly proud of, their cultural links with Angkor, they are also loyal Thai citizens. ■

east, Khmer temples, and Isaan atmosphere, journey along Route 24, southeast of Khorat, running roughly parallel to the Cambodian border.

Three full ponds – essential elements of Khmer monumental architecture – and pretty farmland surround **Prasat Phanom Rung ❺**. Historians believe this temple was an important station between Angkor and Phimai during the 11th and 12th centuries. Several generations must have elapsed during its construction, since several of the stone lintels resemble the early Baphuon style, while the naga date from the later Angkor Wat period. A stone inscription in Sanskrit mentions King Suryavarman II, the ruler behind the construction of Angkor Wat.

The temple includes a stolen lintel spirited out of Thailand by art thieves in the early 1960s. Later it surfaced in the United States in a museum collection. After negotiations, it was returned to Thailand in the early 1990s and put back in its original position over a temple entrance. The main *prang* of Phanom Rung, and its galleries and chapels, reflect the geometric precision of Angkor architecture; symmetrical doors and windows face the four cardinal points. The monumental staircase, relieved by landings, exudes a sense of mass and power typical of Khmer design. Look for the sandstone bas-reliefs of elephants and enthroned Hindu deities. Monks of the Dharmayuti sect maintain the temple.

Farther east a couple of kilometres is **Prasat Muang Tham**, or Lower Temple, sitting on a mossy lawn like an art historian's daydream. Older than Prasat Phanom Rung, its cornerstones were laid in the 10th century, with the temple finished about a hundred years later. Thick jungle surrounded Muang Tham until recently, when a group of families moved there from Ubon, cleared the area and established a large village.

Five prang – surrounded by galleries, protected by walls, and now shaded by trees – constitute Muang Tham, which has recently been beautifully restored. Once crazily leaning blocks of masonry and fallen lintels are now back in place, the monumental tank rebuilt and filled with lilies. The huge rectangular stone blocks that form the outer walls contain drilled circular holes, probably used for stone figures shaped like lotus buds. The outer rims of the ponds are lined with naga, whose many heads rise at the corners, marking the outer boundary of the temple.

Surin and Si Saket

Located on an old Khmer site, **Surin ❻** was known primarily for silk production until the government tourism authority began organising an annual elephant roundup each November. The people of Surin are famed for their skill at training elephants. (In the early 1900s, there were around 100,000 working elephants in Thailand; now there are but 4,000.) During the well-publicised roundup, *mahout* put their pachyderms through a variety of acts. Special buses and a train from Bangkok take tourists to the popular event.

A direct rail line connects Surin to the next main town, **Si Saket**, which borders on Cambodia. Travelling by car is less direct.

The province of Si Saket's former main attraction no longer lies in Thailand. In the early 1960s, the World Court awarded to Cambodia the splendid temple complex of **Khao Phra Viharn ❼**, southeast of Si Saket

Map, page 252

Elephants are a common element not only in modern-day Surin, but also in the ornamentation of ancient Khmer ruins.

OPPOSITE: example of Khmer design in Thailand's Khorat.
BELOW: guardian image, Wat That Phanom.

Map, page 252

Khmer image of a garuda, the mythological creature.

about 100 kilometres (60 mi) and easily reached from the Thai side of the border. It is, however, almost inaccessible from Cambodia. Depending upon the political situation, it is sometimes possible to visit Khao Phra Viharn, which sits on a 500-metre-high (1,650 ft) perch and was opened in 1992 after being closed for decades. Nevertheless, it has sometimes closed since then because of danger from the residual Khmer Rouge insurgency in Cambodia. It can be reached from Si Saket by a 60-kilometre (40 mi) drive to Kantharalak, then into the jungle on another 40-kilometre (25 mi) leg to the border.

Its construction starting sometime in the early 11th century, Khao Phra Viharn stretches almost a kilometre in length. Its stairs alternate between hewn bedrock and imported stones placed there perhaps 100 years before the days of Angkor Wat. Each layer is marked by an increasingly large *gopura,* or gate, and ends at the topmost sanctuary that honours the god Shiva.

To the east of the first gopura, a precarious trail descends through the jungle to the Cambodian plains. Before the second gopura, a sacred pond cut in the rock was found to contain a 45-kilogram (100 lb) fish, which is now displayed in Cambodia's National Museum, in Phnom Penh.

The second gopura, shaped like a Greek cross, is superbly carved in the Khmer style of the 11th century. Its lintels show Vishnu in a scene from the Hindu myth of creation. The stairs continue in a symbolic ascent to heaven, past another purificatory basin to the first courtyard with its two palaces and gopura, finally up to the second and third courtyards and the main sanctuary. At the end of the long ridge is a breathtaking precipice, 600 metres (2,000 ft) above the Cambodian countryside, a stunning achievement of turning a natural site into a work of exquisite art.

Far to the east

Ubon Ratchathani ❽, Royal Town of the Lotus Flower, lies 700 kilometres (430 mi) east of Bangkok and about 60 kilometres (40 mi) east of Si Saket. Its size and wealth indicate the increasing prosperity of the region. In fact, much of the town's early growth coincided with the American build-up during the Vietnam War in the 1960s. Office buildings, construction sites, and some of the best-endowed temples in the northeast rise abruptly behind the banks of the Mun, which flows eastward into the Mekong, 100 kilometres (65 mi) away.

In the 1100s, the area surrounding Ubon Ratchathani was part of the Khmer kingdom, until the Ayutthayan empire supplanted the Khmers. Ubon Ratchathani itself is a rather young urban centre, founded in the late 1700s by Lao immigrants. Established by King Rama III, **Wat Thung Si Muang** is noted for its library made of teak wood. The **National Museum** (open Wednesday–Sunday; admission fee) in Ubon Ratchathani is Khorat's finest and is well worth a stop. Housed in the former country residence of King Vajiravudh, the museum displays a number of fine artefacts, including of Khmer, Lao and Hindu origins.

The highlight of Ubon's festival year is the Wax Candle Procession each July, when huge mythical animals and legendary figures are carved from beeswax and paraded through the streets.

A decent excursion out of Ubon is **Kaeng Tanna National Park** ❾, to the northeast near Laos and the Mekong River and noted for its prehistoric cave paintings and a series of rapids where the Mae Nam Mun is squeezed through a gorge before entering the Mekong.

If planning to travel north from Ubon Ratchathani, allow a full day for the trip north from Ubon to Nakhon Phanom. In the dry season the fields along Route 212 look barely arable, but after the rains they produce the rice that turns golden brown in late October. ❑

OPPOSITE: Prasat Phanom Rung.

NORTHERN KHORAT

Map, page 252

In the northeast, there are archeological findings that suggest not all technological advances came south from China. But if not interested in technology, consider the region's expansive lands

THAILAND

Bangkok

The Thais call northeastern Thailand, *Isaan*. It is a poor part of Thailand, but its cuisine, as an off-the-wall example, dismisses any notions of a poverty in creativity or initiative. Typically overlooked by both Thai and foreign travelers, northeastern Thailand makes up for its lack of awesome scenery with a number of fine nature preserves and ancient archaelogical sites.

From just north of Bangkok, Route 2 heads northeast to **Udon Thani ❿** via Khorat (Nakhon Ratchasima) and Khon Kaen. Udon Thani is a town that grew quickly with the arrival of American airmen during the 1960s. Today, instead of military convoys, noisy motorcycles and packed pickup trucks fill city streets that are punctuated by increasing numbers of traffic lights.

From Udon Thani, Route 2 continues north 50 kilometres (35 mi) to **Nong Khai ⓫**, on the southern bank of the Mekong River. In 1994, the 1.2-kilometre-long Friendship Bridge opened, connecting Nong Khai with the Laotian capital of Vientiane, on the other side of the Mekong River in Laos. This first bridge across the lower Mekong may mean Nong Khai's days as a quiet town are numbered. Fancy hotels are opening in anticipation of the increased tourism and business, though this has yet to materialise.

OPPOSITE: Friendship Bridge. **BELOW:** Ban Chiang excavations.

East of Udon Thani

The people of **Ban Chiang ⓬**, long used to encountering fragments of pots, beads, and even human bones when digging around their houses or working on their farms, paid little attention to archeological finds in this area 50 kilometres east of Udon Thani. Then, in 1966, a young American anthropology student showed some of his finds to the archaeology authorities in Bangkok. His discoveries led to more comprehensive analysis of the artifacts found around Ban Chiang, leading to some surprising, if not controversial, conclusions. Not only were the finds older than believed, between 4,500 and 5,700 years old, but bronze artifacts found around Ban Chiang were dated at around 3,600 BC.

If accurate, this would put the appearance of bronze in Thailand centuries earlier than in the Middle East, until then thought to be the earliest location of such bronze manufacture. Equally intriguing is that this dating of Ban Chiang bronze would suggest that bronze manufacture may have been transmitted from Thailand to China, rather than from China to Thailand, which has long been the received wisdom. Still, many experts maintain that the dating of 3,600 BC for the appearance of bronze remains too early, suggesting that 2,000 BC, or even 2,500 BC, is more accurate. This would put the appearance of bronze in Southeast Asia later than the Middle East, but at around the same time as China. Even were the claims of antiquity not authenticated, the

Rock inscriptions found in the northeast reflect Khmer influence over 1,000 years ago.

BELOW: traditional ceremony in the northeast.

beautiful whorl designs of the pottery and the intricacy of the bronze jewelry and implements would earn Ban Chiang culture high marks among the early peoples of the earth. Many of these artifacts can be seen in Ban Chiang's museum, established with the help of the U.S.-based Smithsonian Institution.

Farther east on Route 22 about 120 kilometres (75 mi), **Sakon Nakhon ⑬** is spread out along a low plain that borders Nong Han, Thailand's largest natural lake. (Visitors should avoid going for a swim, however, as the waters are infested with liver fluke.) Although the site was one of the Khmer's important regional centres, the ancient Khmers left monuments whose significance is so minor that only those with keen archeological interest should make a special effort to see them. In the town centre, the white *prang* of Wat Choeng Chum hides a 10th-century laterite prang; you must peer through a crack in the door to see it. West of town is Wat Narai Cheng Weng, built in the Khmer Baphuon style by a princess in the 11th century.

Farther east on Route 22 is **Nakhon Phanom ⑭**. On a fresh morning, a chain of jagged, powder-gray mountains can be seen behind the small Laotian town of Thakhek, across the wide Mekong. Over 25,000 Vietnamese refugees crossed the river during the 1950s and 1960s to settle in this province. Although security precautions long complicated their resettlement, many Vietnamese have prospered financially in the town's markets, perhaps matching the Chinese in business acumen. During the Vietnam War, American rescue and reconnaissance missions flew from the Royal Thai Air Force Base hidden behind grassy mounds west of town. The base was also a listening post filled with sophisticated radios and electronic sensors. Nowadays few signs of the base's past remain. The town is quiet, attractive and relaxed.

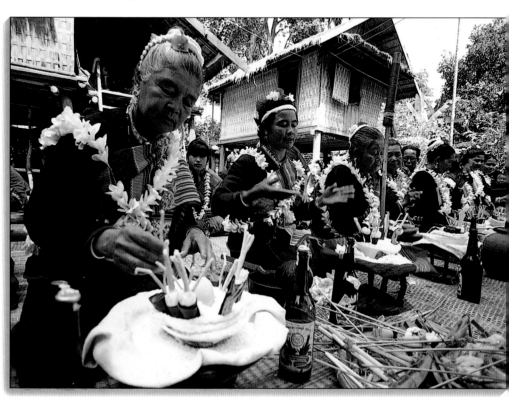

Fifty kilometres (30 mi) south is **That Phanom** ⓯. The route stays close to the Mekong River all the way up to the village and temple of That Phanom. The road is in good condition, straight and flat. Uncultivated brush interspersed with rice fields rushes by. Blue-shirted farmers balance produce-laden baskets from the ends of long poles.

Thousands of pilgrims from northeastern Thailand and southern Laos used to make an annual pilgrimage to Wat That Phanom to make offerings at the base of the spire, which was built around the 9th century and restored several times later. In mid 1975, the spire collapsed after four days of torrential monsoon rains. But in 1979, the temple was restored, again making it well worth a visit for those interested in history or simply seeking a beautiful setting. For a short and pleasant side trip into the countryside, north of That Phanom and inland is **Ban Renu**. Like several small weaving villages in northern Thailand, Ban Renu is famous for textiles. The people are friendly and welcome visiting bargainers.

Continuing south on Route 212 leads to the district town of **Mukdahan** ⓰, on the right bank of the wide Mekong River and opposite the Laotian town of Savannakhet. (Mukdahan is, in fact, a trading centre for Laotian timber, agricultural products and gems.) Take the road to the river, turn right, and visit Wat Sri Nongkran, a temple built by Vietnamese refugees in 1956. The gates present a curious mixture of Thai contours, Vietnamese writing and Chinese-inspired dragons. Southward on Route 212 will lead to Ubon Ratchatani.

West of Udon Thani

Route 210 runs west of Udon Thani 150 kilometres (100 mi) to the ruggedly beautiful province of **Loei** ⓱, and to the town of the same name. Midway en

Map, page 252

BELOW: Phu Kradung National Park.

Map, page 252

TIP

The Thai government prohibits the illegal excavation and sale of artifacts, but near archaelogical sites, villagers may approach offering to sell artifacts, almost always good fakes.

OPPOSITE: typical Isaan headscarf.
BELOW: wreathed hornbills in flight.

route, stop at **Tham Erawan ⑱** (Elephant Cave), about 50 kilometres (30 mi) before Loei and a couple of kilometres off the road. Despite its isolation, the monastery there is well organised. A life-size statue of Erawan, the triple-headed elephant of Thai mythology, marks the steep stairway and rocky path to the cave's entrance. The climb up is rough. Prehistoric artifacts have been found here, but apart from its size and an occasional cobra emerging from the rocks, all that distinguishes the cave is an elephant's skull.

An ongoing agricultural boom is slowly changing Loei's shy simplicity. The usually placid Mae Nam Loei flows through the centre of town. Until the 1980s, Communist insurgents hid amidst the surrounding forests. What is now the traveller's delight was once the civil servant's nightmare. In the Thai bureaucracy, being assigned to Loei was like going to Siberia. In the old days, Loei was a jungle outpost that meant fever, cold weather, little comfort, isolation and poor security. Not so today – Loei has numerous hotels, restaurants, and even a street full of karaoke bars.

Route 203 plunges west into the wilderness to **Phu Rua National Park ⑲**. The road slices through heavy banks of red laterite, past a sawmill and fields of *kenaf* and cotton, the latter being the area's primary source of income. In December, the mountains lie under thick blankets of smoke as farmers burn the forest undergrowth. Phu Rua itself is about 1,370 metres (4,500 ft) high. A rough road to the top affords a view of the national forest.

To reach the Mekong near where it once again becomes the border between Thailand and Laos, drive 50 kilometres (30 mi) north from Loei to the charming riverside town of **Chiang Khan ⑳**. A boat can be hired for the short ride downstream to the Kaeng Khut Ku rapids, worthwhile both for their beauty and for the sheer sense of being in the deep heart of Southeast Asia.

No experience in the Loei area can match the crisp beauty of **Phu Kradung National Park ㉑**, the most memorable escape in northeast Thailand and just 100 kilometres (60 mi) south of Loei. Phu Kradung came to public attention only 50 years ago during the reign of King Rama VI. Phu Kradung, a 60-square-kilometre (24 sq mi) plateau lying between 1,200 and 1,500 metres (5,000 ft) in elevation, beckons the naturalist-at-heart to try some of its 50 kilometres of marked trails.

The entrance to Phu Kradung is on Route 201. About three kilometres from the entrance is the park office, where one can arrange for porters, storage for excess equipment, and parking. The park provides bedding and blankets in cabins that hold up to eleven people. It is by no means an easy climb, but it is well worth the effort. Ladders enable visitors to negotiate the steepest boulders; views of the valley are excellent.

Atop Phu Kradung, clear and mostly level paths crisscross the tableland. Rare birds, including hornbills, woodpeckers and pheasants, may be seen. Even wild elephants and the occasional panther make their homes on the mountain. Most of the wildlife is quite shy, however. The park's cabins and upper offices are located 3 kilometres from a small radar station and helicopter pad. The government closes the park in the summer months to permit the ecology to recover. In the past forests were cut indiscriminately, but times have changed a little. ❒

THE GULF COAST

It was Thailand's eastern gulf coast that first lured travelers to the country's beaches several decades ago. It still does

The eastern coast along the Gulf of Thailand is an almost unbroken stretch of sand that runs to Trat, the narrow finger of land that abuts the neighbouring country of Cambodia. Closer to Bangkok, towns like Si Racha and Chonburi, if somewhat lacking in visual charm, are nonetheless important commercial centres, with factories for processing and canning the region's agricultural produce. Si Racha, in particular, is noted for a fiery hot chilli sauce bearing its name that is a prominent feature of Thai dinner tables.

Few areas in Asia have undergone such a precipitous rise to fame and, some say, a plummet in popularity and integrity, as the beach resort of Pattaya. This huge resort was once a beautiful and quiet beach, a graceful, 4-kilometre-long crescent of golden sand lapped by gentle waves and balmy breezes. By the 1980s, the visitors came flowing in from all directions, making it one of the great success stories in Asian tourism. By the late 1980s, there were dozens of high-rise hotels lining the beach. Pattaya's lustre had begun to dull, however, with a lack of planning that robbed the resort of the very qualities that made it so popular. Too, it gained a reputation as a seaside Patpong of pedophiles and Western men looking for cheap sex.

Nevertheless, tourism brought the Eastern Gulf new prosperity. While mainstream travelers are avoiding Pattaya, islands along the coast like Ko Samet and Ko Chang are luring visitors. Still, tourism is far from being the region's sole source of income. Older industries in the area have long played an important part in the Thai economy. Much of the seafood consumed or exported by Thailand comes from Eastern Gulf ports, and some of the largest fruit orchards are located between Rayong and Chanthaburi. The area around Chanthaburi is also noted for its gem mining, such as for sapphires.

All this industry notwithstanding, the Eastern Gulf's main lures for the average foreign visitor are its sun and sand, and its plentiful tourist facilities. Despite the naysayers, Pattaya and its sisters continue to thrive, and maybe even improve. ❐

PRECEDING PAGES: fruit stand stacked with offerings; boat on gulf harbour. **LEFT:** seller of Southeast Asia's popular durian.

SOUTH TO PATTAYA

Far away and close at the same time, the coastal road southeast of Bangkok along the Gulf of Thailand offers a little of everything to travellers, whether hot beach, hot sex or hot sauce

Map, page 277

THAILAND

Bangkok

The main route from Bangkok to the pretty eastern Gulf Coast is the unappealing Bangna-Trad highway, lined by nondescript concrete buildings. The views pick up when Bangna joins with the older Sukhumvit highway from Bangkok – Route 3 – just outside Chonburi, and the landscape gradually starts to become green and hilly.

Chonburi ❶ is a sprawling and industrious town of about a quarter million merchants, traders and craftsmen. Filled with Bangkok-style traffic, it is also the accident capital of Thailand. Nevertheless, its attractions include **Wat Buddhabat Sam Yot**, Buddha's Footprint Mountain of Three Summits, just outside town. Built amidst green trees by an Ayutthayan king and renovated during the reign of King Chulalongkorn, this hilltop monastery was once used to conduct the water oath of allegiance, when princes and governors drank the waters of fealty, pledging loyalty to the throne.

Near the centre of Chonburi, a colossal gold-mosaic image of Buddha dominates **Wat Dhamma Nimitr**. The largest image in this region and the only one in the country depicting the Buddha in a boat, the 40-metre-high (135 ft) statue recalls the story of the Buddha's journey to the cholera-ridden town of Pai Salee. On the same hill is the local Chinese Buddhist Society, with the burial shrines of prominent members.

Those interested in the historical arts could stop near the old market at the oldest and most important *wat* in the province, **Wat Intharam**, a mix of architectural styles and one of the best examples of Ayutthayan architecture in the southeast. In the 18th century, this wat was the rallying point for soldiers recruited by King Taksin to drive the Burmese from Ayutthaya.

South of Chonburi

Seven kilometres (4 mi) south of Chonburi on a back road is the town of **Ang Sila**. Once favoured by Thai royalty as a resort, the town takes its name of Stone Basin from the chain of rocks that form an oval protrusion into the sea. The roads are lined with shops selling the sculpted wares of local craftspeople. Fishing beds line the shallow waters around the village, and the small pier is full of activity.

Farther south sits an unusual monastery on a hill, **Rua Sam Pao**. Facing seaward and recently expanded, its walls are shaped like the huge hull of a Chinese junk, which some say points to a shipwreck in which emigrants from China were lost. In fact, it represents a vessel carrying the faithful to *nirvana*. The more than 300 meditation cells arranged around the main ship are also in the shape of small boats.

Many of the residents are very old and believe that to die at Rua Sam Pao brings good fortune; many of the

OPPOSITE: waiting for the show, Nong Nooch Village.
BELOW: Pattaya resort.

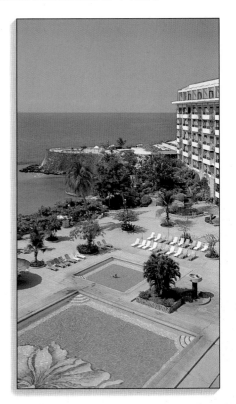

older Chinese women believe that, when they die, their souls will be carried on the sea back to China. Pilgrims share the hill with hundreds of monkeys, and some excellent seafood restaurants make this a popular spot with day-trippers.

On the road past Ang Sila, the long straight beach at the slightly-rundown **Bang Saen** comes alive each weekend as hordes of Thai tourists descend in buses. A profusion of beach umbrellas, inner tubes and wrinkled watermelon rinds quickly cover the sandy beach, the surf filled with bobbing people. Under the casuarina trees lining the sand, picnickers enjoy vendor food and pick up souvenirs. The south end of the beach runs into a messy, garbage-strewn fishing and factory district and is best avoided. Bang Saen's main street on Thanon Sukhumvit is lined with hundreds of stalls selling local produce.

At the Bang Saen Reservoir bird refuge, with permission it is possible to sit in a blind and observe waterfowl. Chinese graves dot the countryside outside the town – the hills and sea make this a favourite burial spot for Bangkok Chinese. Up the hill behind the bird reserve is the **Khao Khieo Open Zoo**. It presents large and small animals in relatively natural settings. A huge aviary built over a natural hill allows visitors to stroll around and relax among plants and water-falls in the company of hundreds of species of birds. On the hill are simple, but comfortable, bungalows that can be reserved from the Dusit Zoo, in Bangkok.

Si Racha ❷, further south, descends from the hills and extends into the sea on tentacle-like piers. Its famous hot sauce can be enjoyed at waterfront restaurants, where fresh shrimp, crab, oyster, mussel or abalone are dipped into the thick, tangy red liquid. An offshore rock supports a picturesque wat with Thai and Chinese elements. A footprint of the Buddha cast in bronze graces the wat, as do pictures of the goddess of mercy, Kuan Yin, and the Monkey God.

There are many spicy if not hot sauces to be tried in Thailand. The town of Si Racha is known for a local version called nam prik si racha.

BELOW: transvestite show and beach high-rise in Pattaya.

From the longest pier at Si Racha, boats ferry passengers to a nearby island, **Ko Si Chang ❸**. On the southern end of Ko Si Chang are deserted beaches and the attractively overgrown remains of a former royal palace once used by King Chulalongkorn as a summer retreat. A few modest bungalows past the Chinese temple overlooking the main town offer good sea and cliff views. Ko Si Chang also has the Yai Phrik Vipassana Centre, a meditation retreat.

Pattaya

A few kilometres south of Si Racha, the busy port of Laem Chabang has seen massive growth since the mid 1990s. Well-known is **Pattaya ❹**. Few areas in Asia have undergone such a precipitous rise to fame and, soon after, a plummet into notoriety as Pattaya.

This huge resort was once a quiet village and beach known only to a handful of foreigners and Thais from Bangkok. By the 1970s, others were starting to discover its charms. Large hotels began to rise along the seashore. By the 1980s, Europeans and American sailors flocked to its beaches, and to those of **Jomtien**, the neighbouring beach just south.

Then Pattaya's lustre begun to dull. There were disturbing signs that problems lurking beneath the surface were surfacing: polluted beaches and water, as well as crime. The town had gained a seedy reputation, a waterfront Patpong-like rest-and-recreation holdover from the Vietnam War. Visitors started going elsewhere, to Phuket and Ko Samui. Pattaya today is still primarily known as a sex resort – the go-go bars are the most noticeable feature of the main tourist areas. Paedophiles pick up boys in a large open bar fronting the street in the main tourism strip, just a few metres from a nearby police box. South Pattaya

Map, page 277

TIP

No matter how much effort some Pattaya businesses have made to make Pattaya respectable, the place has a backdrop of sex tourism, high crime, and drug abuse. It's impossible to ignore.

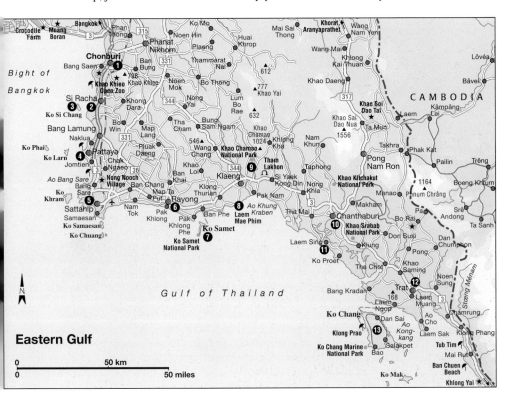

Eastern Gulf

Map,
page 277

*Golf swings south of
urban Bangkok.*

is the main tourist and bar area, though bars and shops are increasingly moving into the quieter north section of town.

Hotels like the Royal Garden have attempted to publicise the resort's family attractions, with limited success. The resort is attracting a new clientele from Russia and eastern European countries. The larger hotels are well equipped with water sports and activities. New things to do include an authentic Ripley's Believe it or Not. A local English-language paper, *The Pattaya Mail*, keeps visitors and foreign residents well-informed about things to do, services and special offers and excursions. But the backdrop of sex tourism, a high crime rate and obvious drink and drug abuse is impossible to ignore in Pattaya.

The angler can test skills at landing grouper and red snapper, mackerel and bonito, sailfish and barracuda. Fishing expeditions can be arranged at Pattaya shops, and at Bang Sare farther down the coast. Off shore, **Ko Larn**, whose name translates as Bald Island, has the wide, soft-sand beaches that Pattaya lacks and it is a pleasant place to spend a leisurely day. The shore is filled with good seafood restaurants, and there are water-sports facilities for those who may be inclined to stir from their beach chairs. The island also has a golf course. Ten kilometres (7 mi) east of Pattaya is the Siam Country Club, which boasts one of the finest golf courses in the kingdom.

South of Pattaya

Excursions can be organised to visit sapphire mines, orchid farms and an elephant *kraal,* and boat trips to local islands are also easily arranged. Year by year, visitors have been exploring farther and farther south of Pattaya, discovering new resort areas with less noise and crowds. One popular resort for Thais is **Nong Nooch Village**, a complex of bungalows situated in park land around a lake and offering a variety of activities, including an elephant show, an orchid nursery and a cactus garden.

Just before Nong Nooch, a quiet resort at the end of Soi Sunset offers wonderful coastal and hill views past a quiet beach, which is almost always deserted. Beyond Nong Nooch are a number of resorts fronting waters known for deep-sea fishing, both commercial and sport. The area is one of the premier spots in the world for marlin and sailfish. The winding, busy streets of the untouristy fishing village of **Bang Sare**, cozily sheltered under a forested hill, are in great contrast to the resorts of the area. Food stalls, school children, motorbikes, dogs and cottage-industry shophouses bump up against each other in a scramble of activity and life.

*Six kilometres past
Sattahip, a broad
road leads to a large
Thai military base,
which once served
the American air
force as its only B-52
airstrip on the Asian
mainland during the
Vietnam War.*

Overlooking a scenic bay sprinkled with small islands, the fishing town of **Sattahip ❺**, about 20 kilometres (15 mi) south of Pattaya, blossomed overnight to become a busy deep-water port. It now acts as a headquarters for the Thai navy, which owns much of the surrounding land and many of the small islands off the coast. In the heart of town, a large and modern temple rests on turquoise pedestals, while in the commercial centre, a boisterous market teems with fish, fruit and vegetables. Sattahip is a place to decompress, offering little more to do than stroll past the shops or sit in an open-front coffee shop sipping an *oliang,* the great sweet iced coffee that originally came from French Cambodia. Enjoy a spicy curry near the market, or browse over teak elephants in the shops.

From Sattahip, the road follows the coastline eastward, but offers only occasional glimpses of the sea. The land is flat and arid, providing little scenic beauty until approaching the town of **Rayong ❻**. This area is being developed as Thailand's newest industrial region. While there are nice beaches popular with local workers at the weekends, the proximity of oil refineries and heavy industry at Maptaput make seafront alternatives further down the road more attractive. ❏

OPPOSITE: motorcycle taxi and young passenger.

EASTERN GULF

Extending down to the Cambodian border, this part of Thailand is rich in both gems and island beaches. Real gems take some knowledge to recognise, but picking the beaches is intuitive

Map, page 277

At the busy market town of **Rayong ❻**, 220 kilometres (140 mi) from Bangkok, an attractive local tourism office is well-stocked with information on the east coast as far as the Cambodia border. A right turn in the centre of town leads to an old, but industrious, fishing village that occupies land between the beach and the estuary. Rayong is famed for its *nam plaa*, or fish sauce, the source of salt in Thai diets and the *sine qua non* of Thai condiments. Nam plaa is made from a small silver fish that abounds in the Gulf; it is decomposed for about seven months to produce a ruddy liquid, which is filtered and bottled on the spot.

About 20 kilometres (15 mi) past Rayong is a turn-off to **Ban Phe**, on the coast. Dressed in weathered black shirts, straw hats and sarongs, women carpet the ground with tangerine-coloured shrimp, drying them in the sun.

This busy fishing port is sheltered on the west by a rocky outcrop, and by the 6-kilometre-long island of **Ko Samet ❼** to the south. The island is remembered by students of Thai literature as the place where Sunthorn Phu, a romantic court poet, retired to compose some of his work. Born in nearby Klaeng, Sunthorn Phu called the island Ko Kaeo Phisadan or "island with sand like crushed crystal". Ko Samet's sand is reputed to be the finest in Thailand. The island has gained popularity as a superb resort for its pristine waters and cosy coves, but not without controversy. Cheap bungalow complexes are being razed to build small hotels. Garbage and noise have increased on the larger stretches of beach. Ko Samet is, in fact, part of a national park, which means that much of the development is actually illegal and is periodically half-heartedly tackled by local authorities.

The coastal road leading east from Ban Phe passes fish mongers and barber shops before entering the kilometre-long pine forest of **Ban Pha Phrae National Park**, a refreshing change in scenery from the scrubland preceding it, and a popular picnicking spot with Thai tourists and locals.

Attractive resorts line the 10 kilometres (6 mi) from Wang Kaew to the peninsula of **Laem Mae Phim ❽**, an underrated part of the Thai coast. Suan Wang Kaew is a landscaped garden on a hill stretching into the sea and a favourite Thai picnic spot. It has bungalows and rooms for rent on the west side. A couple of good restaurants jutting out to the sea provide views of the long stretch of sand in front.

This stretch of coast has seen little of the commercialisation that has developed at most Thai resorts. Vendors offering cheap goods and traditional massage are notable for their absence. It's not unusual for visitors to have the beaches (which could be cleaner) almost to themselves when weekend vacationers from Bangkok

OPPOSITE: popularity threatens Ko Samet. **BELOW:** coral reef off Ko Samet.

have departed. Further on from Laem Mae Phim is a popular Thai resort where excellent seafood restaurants line the top end of the beach. A few kilometres on, the charming, untouristed fishing village of **Ao Khai** is a restful place to watch the loading and unloading of all sorts of fish from old, gaily coloured wooden fishing boats.

Just offshore are a number of jagged islands. Many local resorts offer day-trips to the nearby islands, one of which has been set aside as a reserve for turtles. On the way to Chanthaburi from Laem Mae Phim, the village of Ban Krum has a small park dedicated to the poet Sunthorn Phu, with statues of the poet and some of his most famous characters.

The town of **Klaeng** is quietly busy, its streets lined with numerous and attractive old-style Thai wooden houses. The imposing Wat Saranat Thammaram is located at the market. At Klaeng, a new double-lane highway leads directly to Chonburi and Bangkok.

Khao Chamao National Park ❾, 12 kilometres (8 mi) to the north off Route 3 a few kilometres past Klaeng, has a long waterfall with eight levels. Ascent is relatively easy with the aid of special bridges and walkways. Soro brook carp cluster in the pools by the hundreds. The fish scrabble to grab green leaves that drop from trees overhead or from the hands of helpful visitors to the falls. When eaten, this carp is said to induce stomach aches or a mild "high" due to its diet of a special fruit.

Nearby are the **Khao Wong caves**, about 60 in all, many of which are occupied by Buddhist monks. One cave has been turned into a shrine with a replica of the Buddha's footprints. **Wat Khao Sukim**, a large meditation temple set high in the mountains further down the coast (turn left off Route 3), has stun-

Chanthaburi's history began as much as 6,000 years ago. But historical pages are mostly blank until the 17th century, when Ayutthaya's King Narai moved people from Chiang Mai and Laos to Chanthaburi to defend it against incursions and attacks by Khmer and Vietnamese forces.

BELOW: unloading supplies during a downpour.

ning views, tranquil shady spots and strangely life-like wax figures of Buddhist monks. There are displays of fine jade, furniture and antiques. A funicular takes visitors to the top, or else it's an energetic walk up hundreds of steps on the adjacent stairway lined with two colourfully decorated stone-and-ceramic serpents.

From Wat Khao Sukim to Chanthaburi, the mountain road has few surprises, except for an understated, official-looking sign for "Paradise", which is an invitation that may be hard to pass up. "Paradise" is a Catholic religious retreat, with a church and little bungalows clustered around a small lake and waterfalls.

Chanthaburi

The area between **Chanthaburi** and the Cambodian border lies in a climate pattern somewhat different from the rest of Thailand, receiving the southwest monsoon that makes it wetter, but greener. The rains nurture rubber plantations, a luscious *rambutan* crop, and what are reputedly the best durians in the kingdom. (Try one, but don't bring it back to your hotel.) Gems, delicious fruits, handicrafts, beaches, an air of quiet antiquity, and relics of the past make this area a prime spot.

Chanthaburi itself sits amid rolling hills beside the winding Chanthaburi River. Its residents are a mix of Thai, Burmese, Chinese and Vietnamese faces. The lake in the town centre, built by the French, is a favourite meeting and exercise spot, and is an unusual feature in Thai towns. Motorcycles clog the town's streets. Shops along the river and elsewhere are open in the front, revealing rows and rows of grinding stones upon which artisans patiently cut facets on precious stones that are mined nearby.

Chanthaburi's recent history is contained on a hill, and in a jail. About 5 kilo-

Map, page 277

Khmer lintel from the early 7th century found in the Chanthaburi area.

BELOW: coastal fishing trawlers.

Thailand's Gems: Crystal Power

Thais have turned a national passion for gems and jewellery into one of the country's largest export industries. Rubies, sapphires and jade are among the best bargains, while gold, silver and diamond products, finished by master craftsmen, are also popular buys.

Rubies, the name given to red, gem-quality corundum stones, vary in shade from pinkish or purplish to the brownish-red found in Thailand, depending on the stone's chromium and iron content. A really fine ruby can appear to glow like hot coal. Since prehistory, rubies have been associated with a range of spiritual and supernatural beliefs. The Burmese thought rubies conferred invulnerability, and that they could foretell danger by loss of colour or brilliance. Most of the rubies in Thailand traditionally originated from the Chanthaburi region, and from the Pailin area of

Cambodia, which together account for around two-thirds of the world's supply of rubies. A small number come from Vietnam and parts of Africa.

Thailand's ruby mines were known in early times, with the first known reference coming from a Chinese traveller, Ma Huan, in AD 1408. Now they are close to depletion. At Bo Rai, once the king of Thai ruby-mining towns, abandoned equipment litters the landscape. Where there used to be hundreds of traders, just a few remain. Supplies from the Cambodian side of the border have become more sporadic. Rubies from the remote Moguk and Mong Hsu mines in upper Burma, where primitive, back-breaking extraction methods still apply, are relatively rare and highly sought-after for the international market when they get to Thailand.

An important distinction is made between prime-quality unheated stones, most of which come from Moguk, and less valuable heat-treated samples, originating primarily in Mong Hsu. The latter tend to look like bad garnet before treatment, after which they turn into bright-red gems.

Sapphires, also composed of corundum, come in different colours, from the highly-prized rich-blue to orange, green, yellow, pink and colourless varieties. Sapphire was traditionally believed by Buddhists to produce a desire for prayer, to help ward off negative energies, and to promote calm. Thailand's sapphires now come mainly from Sri Lanka, Australia and Africa. Locally mined sapphires in Kanchanaburi and Phrae, and Cambodian stones from the Pailin area, are increasingly limited in number and quality.

In recent years, Thailand has also become a major centre for processing diamonds, catering to a large foreign as well as thriving domestic jewellery

Shopping for gems and jewellery in Thailand is easy and rewarding, so long as one sticks to reputable stores. (If in doubt, contact the local Tourism Authority of Thailand office for authorised gem and jewelry establishments.) Innumerable scams involving gullible tourists have been reported in the Thai press. They often take the form of an individual with a "special offer", backed up by a convincing story. A polite but firm refusal will deflect the scam. ■

metres south of town stands **Khai Nern Wong**, the "Camp on a Small Circular Hill." King Taksin retreated here after the fall of Ayutthaya in 1767 to regroup his forces, recruit new soldiers and construct a fleet of warships. From this staging point, he returned to Ayutthaya to rout its Burmese occupiers. On the same hill are the remains of a fortress built by King Rama III. At several points around the hill, derelict cannons point at the now-silent jungle. Several of the pieces are of great size; locals claim they protect the mouth of the Chanthaburi River, over ten kilometres away. Today, spirits are believed to keep watch in the ruins.

Across the river is the French-style **Church of the Immaculate Conception**, the largest Catholic church in Thailand. Built around 1880, its congregation is comprised of Vietnamese who migrated to Thailand over the last two centuries. The descendants of these immigrants engage in a number of businesses, foremost of which is the weaving of reed mats, handbags and purses in attractive shapes and patterns. Many items are made in homes. Some excellent products can be ordered from the nuns of the church.

Nearby is **Laem Sing** ⓫, site of a Thai confrontation with European powers. Around the turn of the century, the Thais were embroiled in a territorial dispute with the French occupiers of Cambodia. The French invaded and for 11 years stationed a garrison at Laem Sing. The Tuk Daeng (Red Building) Customs House and the Kook Khi Kai (Chicken Dung Prison) attest to their presence.

Since the 15th century, the area's prime activity has been mining for sapphires and other precious stones, especially rubies. The red soil of the rubber plantations is pitted with holes up to 12 metres (40 ft) deep, each miner staking a claim and hauling out the muck by the bucket-full. It is backbreaking work, with meagre rewards. But occasionally a giant gemstone is found.

Map, page 277

Gem dealer displays a blue-sapphire ring.

OPPOSITE: a precious sapphire find.
BELOW: tattoos protect from evil.

Map, page 277

TIP

If the political situation in Cambodia changes, then one day it may be possible to enter Cambodia from Thailand's gulf border with it. But for now, don't plan on entering Cambodia from here.

OPPOSITE: tattoos can be free-form or detailed. **BELOW:** Nam Tok Praew waterfall.

The nearest gem-mining area is at **Khao Ploi Waen** (Hill of the Sapphire Ring). To reach it, return to Khai Nern Wong, the old fort ruins. Just past it is a junction where the gemstones are traded and purchased. Another kilometre on is Khao Ploi Waen. The open pits in the hillside are up to 10 metres deep.

A side trip to the north for consideration: From **Sa Kaeo**, 200 kilometres (125 mi) to the north of Chanthaburi, drive 60 kilometres (40 mi) east on Route 33 to **Aranyaprathet**. On the border with Cambodia, until a few years ago the area held huge refugee camps. The area still sees occasional influxes of refugees, depending upon the sporadically-difficult situation in Cambodia.

Back in Chanthaburi, head down the road to its waterfalls. At the 324-kilometre marker of Route 3, directly opposite the Chanthaburi turn-off, a small road leads inland for 20 kilometres (13 mi), through orchards of rambutan, durian, oranges and lychees. **Nam Tok Krating** (Bull Waterfall) is a cascade of small falls tumbling 400 metres (1,300 ft) across a granite face.

Farther down Route 3, near the 347-kilometre marker, is another popular waterfall, **Nam Tok Praew**. Beyond makeshift stalls, where women sell sticky rice and durian jam, is an oddity: a pyramidal *chedi* overlooking the falls. The chedi commemorates a consort of King Chulalongkorn who drowned while being rowed up the Chao Phraya River. Her death was particularly tragic, since her attendants could have saved her, had they not been forbidden to touch the body of a royal person. Today, falls and pools are seldom deserted in daylight.

Trat

The road to Trat, 400 kilometres (250 mi) from Bangkok and the last major town before the Cambodian border, passes through rubber plantations, paddies and marshlands. About ten kilometres beyond Chanthaburi, the attractive Chinese temple **Wat Bang Korn** is a peaceful oasis. Further on is **Oasis Sea World**, a breeding and conservation station for dolphins. Humpbacked and Irrawaddy dolphins perform aquatic shows daily here for tourists.

A gem-trading centre, **Trat** ⓬ itself is undistinguished, but it serves as a starting point for trips to beautiful offshore islands. Head from the town clock tower to the port of **Laem Ngop**, about 20 kilometres (15 mi) southwest. There, boats leave in mornings for **Ko Chang** ⓭. Eight kilometres (5 mi) wide and 30 kilometres (20 mi) long, Thailand's third-largest island is famed for wild boar and the Mai Yom Falls. Off the northern tip of Ko Chang, some of the largest sharks in the gulf cruise near a rocky outcrop. Nearby, **Ko Mak** and **Ko Kut** offer clear lagoons and excellent diving. Lodging is of simple bungalows and a few new although modest resorts.

From Trat, drive down the scenic narrow finger of Thailand to the town of **Khlong Yai**, built over the water. From the main street, rows of houses run into the sea. Between them, parked like cars on a side street, are moored fishing trawlers that earn the inhabitants their income. The road, with unspoilt sea views, continues to **Hat Yai**, a fishing (and smuggling) village on the Cambodia border, an interesting spot from which to watch life, and trucks of whiskey and cigarettes, go by. ❒

A FEAST OF FRUITS

There is a sizeable range of fruits in Thailand, many of which may be unfamiliar. As well as bananas and pineapples, there are other brilliantly coloured and strangely shaped fruits for the adventurous traveller.

Thai people love food, and during the afternoon they snack on an incredible variety of fruits. For visitors who are in need of a boost, fruit can be a great source of refreshment and energy. Traditional fruit sellers have glass-fronted carts stacked with blocks of ice and pealed pieces of seasonal fruits. Choose a selection of what you want to eat and the vendor will pop it into a bag for you along with a toothpick for spearing the slices. Some fruits, like pineapple, are eaten with a little salt and ground chilli, a twist of which is supplied separately. Don't be afraid of this combination – the natural sweetness of the pineapple is enhanced by this bitter condiment, surprisingly enough.

One of the best ways to cool down is to drink a delicious fruit juice or *naam phon-la-mai*. To order, say the Thai word for water (*naam*) in front of the name of the fruit, or just point to your selection from the fruits on display. Another favourite drink is fruit juice blended with ice – known as a *naam pon* or "smoothie". You can have syrup mixed in to sweeten your juice (*namm pan*) or salt added (as the Thais like it) to bring out the flavour of the fruit.

CONTROVERSIAL DURIAN

People either love or hate durian. Ask any visitor in Thailand to recall the first time they came across it and they will describe, in detail, its "perfume". To most *farang* (foreigners), the durian's odour is repugnant, but for the Thais the fruit commands the utmost respect.

According to devotees the rewards of eating durian far outweigh any objections to its smell. The only way to enter the great durian debate is to try it for yourself. If you can't face eating the fruit *au naturel* there is durian cake, ice-cream and chewing gum.

◁ **JACKFRUIT *(KHANUN)***
The ripe, rich yellow sections of the jackfruit are waxy-textured and semi-sweet. When green they are used in curries, and the flowers and young shoots are eaten in salads.

RAMBUTAN *(LUUK NGOH)*▷
The hairy rambutan (*rambut* means hair in Malay) is a close relative of the lychee, and its translucent, sweet flesh has a similar taste. There is a technique to squeezing it open to avoid squirting yourself with its juices; any Thai can demonstrate this.

▽ **STAR FRUIT *(MA DUN)***
This sweet, yellow fruit is native to India. It has a thin waxy skin with a crisp texture and sweet-tart juice. It can be found in fruit salads or can be candied and eaten as a confection. The unripe fruit is bright green and is sometimes added to dishes that require an acidic taste.

△ CUSTARD APPLE *(NOI-NA)*
The custard apple looks like a small, light green hand-grenade and can be pulled apart by hand. The pulp is soft, often mushy, very sweet and very tasty. It is best to eat it with a spoon.

▽ MANGOSTEEN *(MANGKHUT)*
Thais believe durian requires the cool, refreshing sweet taste of the mangosteen as a chaser. See if you can guess how many sections your mangosteen has before you break it open.

CROPS: A GROWING CONCERN

Farming and fishing have always been at the centre of Thai life. Despite rapid industrialisation, this is still the case. Thailand is self-sufficient in food, and agribusiness is an important pillar of the Thai economy, claiming nearly a quarter of GDP and making Thailand the only net food exporter in Asia. Thailand is the world's leading exporter of canned pineapple and has big overseas markets in canned logans and rambutans.

Fruit production is expected to increase as available land and labour resources dwindle and farmers switch from producing staple crops, such as rice and cassava, to cash crops like soya beans, fruits, sugar cane and rubber. Large fruit farmers are starting to process their products before they reach the consumer, and many are now applying for loans to invest in equipment to dry and freeze their produce. Although some of this produce will be sold to Thailand's neighbours, much of it will end up in the snack food departments of Japanese supermarkets – Japanese businesses have already set up factories in Thailand to process fruits, vegetables and nuts for their home market.

DURIAN *(TURIAN)*
he most expensive of Thai uits has mushy flesh that stes good with sticky rice d coconut milk. Ignore the nell and you will be rewarded.

APANESE PEAR ▷
his crunchy and slightly y. fruit is usually eaten w. Its semi-sweet flavour n be enhanced by dipping it to slightly salted water.

THE SOUTH

From carefree and warm beaches to the curries and mosques near Malaysia, surprises abound in Thailand's south

Southern Thailand, a long arm of land sometimes likened to an elephant's trunk, consists of 14 provinces and is rich in stunning scenery. Wild jungles alternate with rocky mountains and broad beaches of powdery sand. While a few select areas are increasingly world-class destinations, other parts of the region are still being discovered by the outside world.

Countless islands, large and small, are scattered down this narrow strip of land that leads to Malaysia. The eastern coast of the Isthmus of Kra faces the Gulf of Thailand, while the other shore lies on the Andaman Sea and Indian Ocean. Other than the larger islands like Ko Samui (*ko* means island in Thai) and Phuket, which have been developed for tourism, few of the many other islands are visited.

In many ways, the south of Thailand is a world far removed from the rest of the country, especially in the deep south. A different climate, religion and type of farming make it unique among Thailand's regions. Groves of rubber trees are more common than fields of rice. The gilded dome of a Muslim mosque becomes a more familiar sight than the sloping orange roof of a Buddhist temple. In the provinces near the border, the people speak Malay as well as Thai, and throughout the region, there is a distinctive southern dialect, as well as a cuisine resembling that of Malaysia.

From time to time there is talk – as there has been since 1793 – of building a 100-kilometre-long (60 mi) canal, like the Panama and Suez canals, across the Kra Isthmus, from outside Songkhla to north of Satun. Alternative "land bridge" proposals include from Songkhla to Penang, in Malaysia, and from near Surat Thani to Krabi. Any of these routes would minimise the need to use Singapore as a shipping transit point, but the environmental concerns are monumental.

Rich in natural resources, the south is Thailand's most prosperous region after Bangkok. (And like the north, only in the present century has the south become fully integrated into the Thai kingdom.) Rubber, the country's second-largest agricultural export product after rice, thrives so well that Thailand is one of the world's largest exporters, as with tin, which is mined in southern provinces. And until the government banned logging, so too with teak. Tourism is a fairly new industry in the south, but already it has become a major foreign exchange earner.

For many years, access to the south's secluded areas was a major undertaking. Only the really adventurous attempted it. While getting around the southern areas is easy these days, there is still a sense of adventure and remoteness to one's travels here. ❏

PRECEDING PAGE: isolated beach in northwestern Phuket. **LEFT:** boats at rest in Phang Nga Bay, on the western coast of peninsular Thailand.

NORTHERN ISTHMUS

Looking like the trunk of an elephant, the Isthmus of Kra is Thailand's overland link to the Malaysian peninsula. Both sides of this narrow isthmus offer some of the world's finest beaches

Map, page 297

THAILAND

Bangkok

There is little to distinguish **Ratchaburi** ❶, but in recent years it has become a ceramics centre, manufacturing everything from large brown rainwater storage jars decorated with dragons and known as *ong*, to exquisite *benjarong* wares, small porcelain vessels with intricate, five-coloured designs. One can spend a day wandering from shop to shop in Ratchaburi, contentedly browsing among a wide variety of styles and types. Prices are generally very reasonable, and outlets will be only too pleased to arrange shipping.

Phetchburi ❷, 160 kilometres (100 mi) south of Bangkok, has far more to offer. Approaching the town on Route 4, take the left fork and continue past a rocky hill on the right. Cross the railroad tracks and stop under the shady trees for a visit to the cave at **Khao Luang**. Around midday, huge stalactites and dozens of Buddha images are bathed in a soft light that pours through the cave roof.

Entering Phetchburi, *naga*-topped walls frame the pathway to **Khao Wang**, a palace built by King Mongkut in the 1860s. Ascend by foot or miniature railway the fragrant frangipani-fringed path, past the royal stables, to the restored palace at the summit. The gleaming – sometimes blindingly – white palace is dominated by an observatory, which the king constructed to pursue his favourite pastime of astronomy. The view from the parapet is superb; one can survey the entire city, its river, the rice fields and the mountains along the Burmese border to the west.

Four temples are worthy of a visit. **Wat Yai Suwannaram** is east of the river, and **Wat Kamphaeng Laeng** is just southeast of it. Wat Yai Suwannaram, built in the 17th century, has murals that are among the oldest in the country. Wat Kamphaeng Laeng, a Khmer temple, is thought to delineate the most western frontier of the Angkorian empire. **Wat Ko Keo Sutharam** contains fading, but beautiful, Ayutthaya-period murals dating from 1734. **Wat Mahathat**, in the middle of town, is marked by a huge *prang* that towers over it. Much of the decor is new, but it nevertheless acts as a magnet for Buddhists, and visitors will find that festivals are often in progress there.

About 20 kilometres (15 mi) southeast of Phetchburi is **Kaeng Krachan Dam** (or Ubol Ratana Dam, after the current king's daughter). Visitors may stay at bungalows overlooking the scenic reservoir and take boats up the reservoir to the river.

Forty kilometres (25 mi) south is **Cha-am**, the first of several beach resorts along the peninsula. Better known is the sister resort of **Hua Hin** ❸ further south, Thailand's oldest major beach resort. It was put on the map in 1910 by the brother of King Rama Vl, Prince Chakrabongse, who led a party of European and Thai royalty down the peninsula to hunt game. King Prajadhipok (1925–1935) built a palace here called **Klai**

OPPOSITE: wat and dwellings, Hua Hin.
BELOW: Khao Luang.

A 1932 guide called Hua Hin "the most popular with travellers... longing for a game of golf". In those days, sand traps were assisted by roaming tigers on the links. Today, Hua Hin's well-tended and world-famous 18-hole courses are considerably tamer.

Klangwan, meaning "far from worries". Ironically, he was vacationing here in 1932 when a bloodless coup toppled him, replacing 700 years of absolute monarchy with a constitutional one. Unfortunately, the palace is not open to the public. Remnants of the 1920s and 1930s linger at the **Hotel Sofitel Central**, better known by its former name, the **Hua Hin Railway Hotel**. Renovated, it retains its air of gentility with ceiling fans and gardens filled with a menagerie of animal topiary. The tea room is, in fact, a museum collection of domestic Thai artifacts from the 1920s and 1930s. Because of its old-world atmosphere, this hotel stood in for the French Embassy in Phnom Penh in the film *The Killing Fields*.

A bit further south, the Royal Garden Hotel offers modern amenities amidst luxury accommodations. **Hua Hin Beach** itself is wide, flat, and shelves very slowly. Its regency character lingers in the availability of horses, which can be rented for a gallop, or a trot, along the sand. As a booming weekend resort for Bangkok residents, Hua Hin's modern development generally lacks the charm lingering in the old Railway Hotel. The town nevertheless has a thriving night market with a range of food stalls, international restaurants, and shops that are open late to satisfy the appetite of visitors.

For some lively local colour, stroll down to the pier in the morning, or else in the evening, to watch fishermen unload their catches while women examine and bargain for a wide variety of fresh seafood, including an occasional catch of shark or stingray.

South of Hua Hin

BELOW: white-sand beach, and Hua Hin's train station.

Leave Hua Hin by heading south again on Route 4. About 20 kilometres (15 mi) from the town, the highway crosses a river, then enters **Pranburi**. Children play under stilt-houses while fishermen hang their nets to dry on wooden racks.

Further south, the jagged outline of the **Khao Sam Roi Yot National Park** ❹ comes into view. The gorges and caves here once sheltered bandits who robbed unwary travellers; their haunts were cleared out long ago. Now, deer, monkeys and numerous species of birds roam the park, the coastal areas of which have been badly denuded by prawn farms.

The sky above Khao Sam Roi Yot (300 Peaks Range) is remembered in the annals of the Chakri dynasty. In 1868, King Mongkut, an astute mathematician and astronomer, brought the governor of Singapore and the Bangkok court here to view a total eclipse of the sun, which he had foretold. The king's prediction, to the astonishment of local astrologers, was only four minutes off. News of this event helped to discredit the superstition that an eclipse occurred when a giant swallowed the sun and disgorged it only when impelled by gongs and general noise-making. (Unfortunately, King Mongkut contracted a fever and died a week after his return to Bangkok.)

About 90 kilometres (55 mi) south of Hua Hin, **Prachuap Khiri Khan** ❺ faces a scenic little harbour enclosed by knob-like hills. A natural arch at Khao Chong Krachok frames the sky. Steps – 404 in all – lead up the hill to a small monastery surrounded by frangipani trees. Within the *chedi* are special Buddha relics bequeathed to the state by Rama I and Rama IV and used in the coronation of Chakri kings.

From Prachuap, continue to **Huai Yang**. The waterfall here cascades over 120 metres (400 ft) of boulders in a forest setting not far from the Burmese border. Beyond lies **Bang Saphan** ❻, divided in two by the tracks of the south-bound railway. A wide bay is rimmed by a pretty, 6-kilometre-long beach. A green hill, Khao Mae Pamphung, is to the north; Ko Thalu is to the south. Here, seafood and drinks are served on the beach.

South of Bang Saphan, the countryside eventually becomes lush and mountainous. Rubber plantations spread beneath

TIP

During the swallow
mating season, from
March through August,
collectors climb high
up the cliffs to fetch
the swallows' nests.
Merchants bid for
nest concessions;
gunmen are hired to
guard the claim. Don't
forget if looking for
swallow nests.

BELOW: southern
street market.

limestone cliffs that erupt from the Kra Isthmus and further south down the Malay Peninsula.

Around 500 kilometres (300 mi) south of Bangkok, Route 4 comes to an important junction, where it branches right and heads west to the Andaman Sea, on the west coast. The left branch leads to Chumphon, Lang Suan and the east coast towns of Surat Thani, Nakhon Si Thammarat and Songkhla. Turn left at this junction to reach **Chumphon ❼**, noted for its inexpensive bird's nest soup. East of it lies **Paknam Chumphon**. Situated at the mouth of the Mae Nam Chumphon, this fishing port rents boats by the hour for trips to nearby islands, where swallows build their nests. The island of **Lanka Chio** is especially famous. The island-dotted coastal waters make for exciting sailing, too, for those so inclined.

To the west coast

South on Route 41 is Surat Thani. A longer way, and more scenic, is Route 4, which strikes west across the narrowest point on the Kra Isthmus, then veers south, following the Pakchan River through **Kraburi** on the way to Ranong.

About 12 kilometres (8 mi) beyond Kraburi, turn left just before the 504-kilo-metre marker to reach **Tham Prakayang**, a temple in a cavern. If you lack a flashlight, the monks may lend one for the dark ascent into the image-filled cave. One completely black Buddha gazes upon visitors through mother-of-pearl eyes. A limestone-and-wooden staircase leads up and out of the cave to well-worn paths, trodden by monks who meditate amid the solitude atop the outcrop.

South of Tham Prakayang, the highway winds through jungled hills and crosses a wide river. Punyaban Falls appears next to the road. Truck drivers stop,

Map, page 297

don sarongs, and take a quick dip in the cool water. This is a popular spot for Thai tourists, who stop for snacks at the teahouse near the falls. Climb a path to the left of the falls for a good view of the Pakchan estuary, nearby islands, and the contours of mountains on the southern tip of Burma.

Further down the road, turn right near the Thara Hotel to enter **Ranong ❽**. The hotel itself holds one of Ranong's main attractions: hot mineral water piped from nearby thermal springs. A well encloses the main outlet, which pours forth 500 litres (130 gal) per minute of sparkling mineral water at 70°C (160°F). Cross a suspension bridge to a little park, or climb the hill behind the shrine to a small wat enclosed in a secluded grove.

The road past the hot springs leads to the village of **Hat Supin**. This is tin-mining country; stark landscapes of white silt, bamboo scaffolding, deep and dark pits, and gouged-out cliff faces are everywhere. In open-cast mining, water from high-pressure hoses carves holes in the earth. The mineral-laden water is filtered through a sieve, which separates the tin ore from the mud and sand. One of Thailand's major exports, tin is mined all along the Indian Ocean coast of the isthmus. Much of the ore comes from private holdings, like those around Hat Supin. A small sign with fish painted on it points the way to **Wat Hat Supin**, where children rush up to sell sweet popcorn, which is fed to hundreds of carp that swarm in a pool located by the side of the temple.

Drive back to Ranong, then take the three-kilometre road to **Saphan Pla**, on the sea where boats unload fish at a modern wharf and trucks dump tons of crushed ice on emptied decks. From this port, some boats sail the Indian Ocean as far as Bangladesh in search of fish. Directly opposite Saphan Pla is **Ko Pak Nam**, with its stilt houses and fishing boats. Boats can be rented for trips to the

Spirit house.

BELOW: across the Kra Isthmus.

island. Continuing south past Kapoe and Khuraburi for 160 kilometres (100 mi), the road meets the junction of Route 401, near the town of Takua Pa. From here, the highway heads east towards Surat Thani.

The indifferent appearance of **Takua Pa** ❾ belies its rich past. In the third century BC, Emperor Ashoka of India sent troops to conquer Klingkarach, in the southeast of his country. Natives of that region fled overseas and resettled in Takua Pa and Takua Tung. Later, the area became a significant port for Indian traders, who settled along the Malayan coast when the region was called Suvannabhumi, Land of Gold, over 1,500 years ago. Three statues of Brahma, Shiva, and Vishnu – all four-armed and larger than human size – found in nearby hills, and two 7th-century Dvaravati statues, discovered on an island in the mouth of the yellowish Mae Nam Takua Pa, add to the archeological evidence. By the 16th century, Portuguese merchants were buying and selling goods on this coast, especially at Phuket and Malacca.

Today, Takua Pa has little to claim except as the district centre of a rich tin-mining area. South of Takua Pa, a road branching off Route 4 leads to **Bang Sak**, a beach that rims a scenic, wide bay. It is typical of sparsely-touristed bays along the Andaman Sea coast in Phang Nga. Out at sea, barges engage in small-scale tin mining.

Forty kilometres (25 mi) south of Takua Pa, at **Khao Lak**, about 30 families live most of the year in the natural shelter of this cove. The men do not fish, but rather dive for tin, with the aid of air pumps and goggles. Like nautical prospectors, they stay underwater one or two hours at a time, loading tin-bearing sand into buckets. Workers hoist the full buckets onto bamboo rafts and sieve their contents. Every June, the powerful monsoons churn up the ocean and halt the

Some scholars think Indian traders sought shortcuts across Thailand to the South China Sea. Unearthed statues have traced caravan routes across the Kra Isthmus to Surat Thani. Takua Pa is thought to have been a major centre for the spice trade.

BELOW: coconut-hunting patrol.

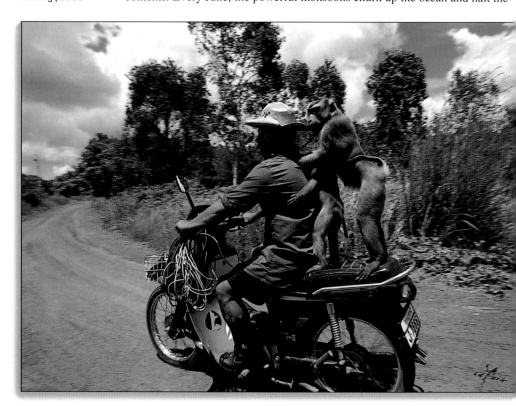

tin diving. The mining families abandon their huts to the destructive lashing of wind and sea until the monsoon relents.

If continuing south from here, one will reach the island of Phuket and the Phang Nga Bay area.

Map, page 297

Return to the eastern seaboard

Back at Takua Pa, Route 401 cuts east across the isthmus, a great drive full of ups, downs and challengingly-sharp corners, zig-zagging over and around the cloud-cloaked limestone pinnacles of the Kra Isthmus. First the road enters the hills, plunging through a remarkable series of streaked limestone precipices and splintered rocks. Then it traverses the wide valley of the Takua Pa River, passing tin mining camps flanked by mountains. For a midway rest, stop at **Wat Thamwaran**, just to the left of a small river. The wat provides a simple shelter for monks who often meditate near a cave.

Nature-oriented travellers have the pleasure of stopping at the well-marked **Khao Sok National Park ❿**. The park, in combination with Klongsang Wildlife Sanctuary and the Ratchaprapha Dam (sometimes called Chiaw Lan), covers 123,600 hectares (300,000 acres) of mostly virgin rain forest, with surrounding peaks rising to over 1,000 metres (3,300 ft). Although poaching is rife, the sheer size of the forest has helped protect sizeable populations of elephant, bison, langur, bear, Asiatic wild dogs, and even brilliant-beaked hornbills, as well as tiger, leopard and other jungle cats. The world's largest flower, the 80-centimetre-wide (2.6 ft) *Rafflesia* (known in Thai as *bua phut*), was recently found in the park, one of the few places in the world where it occurs. A number of Spartan, but clean, bungalow resorts along the Khlong Sok River act as a base

The Rafflesia is a real stinker, with the intent of attracting pollinating insects. Parasitic and lacking leaves, it grows in roots of host trees. Once a year, it surfaces and blooms, smelling foul and hoping for a passing insect. Days later, the flower withers.

BELOW: the banteng, a wild cattle species found in the south of Thailand.

Map, page 297

Ancient votive tablet from the Srivijaya empire.

OPPOSITE: Wat Mahathat, in Chaiya. **BELOW:** Suan Mok art.

for guided treks and canoeing excursions, and for trips to floating villages on the lake. The road leaves the hills and enters dense rubber plantations before entering the town of **Surat Thani** ⑪. This busy shipbuilding, fishing and mining centre lies on the bank of the Tapi River. Surat itself has little worth seeing, but it is a point of departure for several interesting side trips, not to mention a primary departure port for ferries to Ko Samui and beyond.

Ancient empire

Twenty kilometres (12 mi) north of Surat Thani is **Chaiya** ⑫, a small and sleepy town of unpainted wooden buildings, like any small town of south Thailand. But the area is the subject of a debate about whether or not it was the capital of a once-great empire.

Some historians now believe that the capital of the Srivijaya empire – described by the wandering Chinese monk, I Ching, in AD 671 – was not Palembang, in Sumatra, but rather Chaiya. In fact, they claim, the date previously accepted as the founding of the empire in Palembang was actually the date it was conquered by Chaiya. The name Chaiya may be a contraction of Srivijaya.

In any case, only a few traces remain of this mighty empire, which once stretched from Java through Malaysia and into Thailand. Less than two kilometres out of town stands **Wat Mahathat**, one of the most revered temples in Thailand. Its central chedi is thought to be over 1,300 years old, a direct visual link between Chaiya and the Srivijaya period. A small museum adjoining the wat displays some interesting relics found in the vicinity.

Closer to town is **Wat Wieng**, where an inscription from AD 755 is ascribed to a King Vishnu. It was the erroneous attribution of this inscription, 50 years ago, to a different location that led to the hypothesis that Nakhon Si Thammarat was an important local Srivijayan centre.

Two other wats, Wat Long and Wat Kaeo, equidistantly spaced from Wat Wieng, mark the sites of Srivijaya edifices. Today, only Wat Kaeo holds a dim reminder of a forgotten past in the crumbling wall of a once-great chedi. All that's known is that it commemorates a victory in battle.

A few kilometres west of these historic remains, a small hillock rises from the flat countryside. Here stands a Buddhist retreat named **Suan Mok**, as new as Chaiya's past is old. The walls and columns inside the central building are covered with an eclectic series of paintings, which run the gamut from the history of Buddhism in Asia to Aesop's fables from Europe.

Suan Mok owes a surrealistic touch to a wandering Zen Buddhist, Emanuel Sherman, whose search for enlightenment led him from the United States to Japan and Thailand, eventually ending on the island of Pha Ngan, off the Thai coast.

After his death, local artists covered one wall with illustrations to portray Sherman's epigrams. Bas-reliefs telling the story of the Buddha decorate the outer walls. They were modelled locally from photos of the Indian originals. Suan Mok's quirky touch continues into its adjoining structures. The *bot* is a large concrete ship that serenely sails the sea of suffering to eventual *nirvana*. ❑

KO SAMUI AND KO PHA NGAN

*Savvy travelers need little introduction to the appeal of Ko Samui,
once a backpacker's retreat but now an international resort. A few
of the other islands nearby, however, are not as well-known*

Map,
page 309

THAILAND

Bangkok

PRECEDING PAGES:
island silhouette.
OPPOSITE: a boring
Ko Samui beach.
BELOW: waterfall at
Na Muang.

Sometime during your stay in Thailand you will probably meet a few entrenched expatriates or aging tourists who will be unable to resist waxing nostalgically about the Ko Samui they discovered a generation ago. They camped under the stars on powdery Chaweng Beach. They explored coral reefs from fishermen's boats. And they shared the simple meals of coconut farmers by the light of flickering kerosene lamps. That island is long gone.

Nowadays, about 3 million tourists descend upon Ko Samui every year. There are luxury hotels, fancy restaurants, a modern airport, easy transport, and the full panoply of water sports and other diversions. Despite that, the island's 250 square kilometres (100 sq mi) retain much natural beauty. The interior is still the preserve of coconut farmers and forested hills. Unlike high-rise Phuket, buildings are prohibited from surpassing the height of palm trees on Samui. Hire a motorbike or hop on a circulating *songtao* – pick-up trucks with benches in back—and follow the paved, well-fringed rolling road that rings the island.

The choice of beach or diving spots, nonetheless, should take into consideration the monsoonal wind factor. From May to October, the southeast monsoon blows on the western and northern coasts. From October to January, unleashing the heaviest rains in November, the northeastern monsoon can disrupt the eastern coast. Usually you can still swim during these periods, if not lounge and read on the beach.

In addition to all the outlets for water sports, in the island's interior are several waterfalls descending from the heights of **Khao Phlu**, the island's highest point at 635 metres (2,080 ft).

Aside from attendance at the Catholic Church or immigration office, there's no reason to linger among the drab cement blocks of Samui's biggest town, the western port of **Na Thon ❶**. Ferries to Ko Pha Ngan and Ang Thong National Marine Park depart from Na Thon, however.

The original beachcombers and today's tasteful hotels were drawn to Ko Samui by a 6-kilometre-long swathe of soft, silky sand at **Chaweng ❷**. The sand at its half-sized southern neighbour, **Lamai ❸**, is slightly lower grade. Behind each beach runs a treacherous road—pitted, potted and often swamped—that barely supports a sprawl of all the traveler's necessities: post office, e-mail, banks, money exchanges, travel agencies, clothing shops, tailors, gyms and body piercers. Not to mention all manner of restaurants, bars and music clubs, with old rock and reggae prevailing over techno. Samui never approaches the sleazy excesses of Pattaya and Phuket, but Lamai has a conspicuous share of open-air hostess bars, go-go girls and transvestite shows.

South of Lamai, the small beaches of **Ban Hua Thanon ❹** and **Ban Bangkao ❺** are nothing to write home about, but the coral reef is healthy near the former, and the latter is a charming, wooden Muslim village. From either, make a day trip inland and swim at the two-tiered waterfall at **Na Muang ❻**.

Coming up the western side of the island, **Ban Taling Ngam ❼** offers a couple of rather deluxe resort retreats. Further north, just before the road juts east along the northern coast, is Na Thon.

For panorama, head along the north shore to **Maenam ❽**. The sand is coarser than that of the east, but the 4-kilometre stretch is little developed. East of Maenam, **Bo Phut ❾** is much narrower, but relatively protected, whichever way the wind blows. Popular with French and Italian families, it's a short walk from the cute little fishing village of Ban Bo Phut. As for **Bangrak ❿** (better known as **Big Buddha Beach**), it's a mystery why anyone stays here unless they enjoy the din from the adjacent road or the airplanes roaring overhead. Or perhaps it's the view of the indisputably large Buddha statue and its complement of especially garish souvenir shops. Quieter **Choeng Mon ⓫**, on the island's northeastern spur, has decent sand and is within quick access of Chaweng's facilities.

Sprinkled elsewhere around the island are a go-kart track, snake farm, butterfly aviary and lots of snooker parlours. With 10 stadiums and counting, water-buffalo fights are Samui's newest entertainment. The bulls don't draw blood, but the high-stakes betting is fast and raucous. The numerous signs for "monkey shows" are actually opportunities to see pig-tailed macaques engaged in their usual jobs on coconut farms. They twist coconuts from the tree tops, then retrieve and deposit them in burlap bags. Copra, the dried coconut flesh, will eventually be pressed to produce coconut oil.

Last but not least are the attractions of 41 brilliant isles comprising **Ko Ang**

The gold-gilded Buddha near Big Buddha Beach is actually on a small island, Ko Faan. The Buddha statue is 12 metres (40 ft) high.

BELOW: Bo Phut, on Ko Samui.

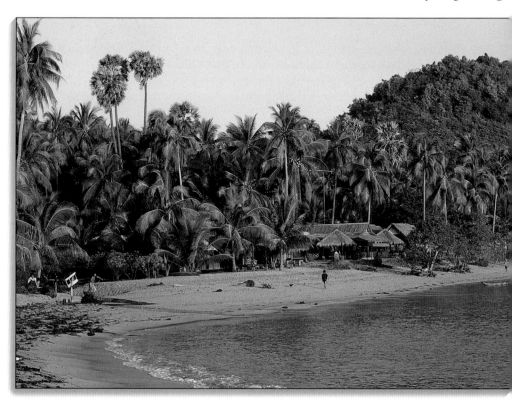

Thong National Marine Park ⑫. Day-long package trips voyage to Ko Wua Talab, park headquarters, and Ko Mae Ko. But these tours allow little time to investigate any more than a viewpoint and a cave on Wua Talab and the clear, pea-green saltwater lake on Mae Ko. On both, the designated swimming spots have negligible coral and fish. It's better to take the standard tour out, but stay a few days on Wua Talab. Visitors can rent park bungalows or tents, or set up their own. The island is teeming with macaques, langurs, otters, birds and other wildlife. Hire one of the fishermen to take you to a smaller isle with virgin coral.

Ko Pha Ngan

If Ko Samui is the land of package tours and brief vacations, its neighbour 15 kilometres (9 mi) to the north, **Ko Pha Ngan**, is a refuge for backpackers on leisurely world tours and Europeans whiling away winter-long holidays. Smaller, rustic and rugged, and with horrible roads, Pha Ngan lacks Samui's spectacular beaches, but has plenty of secluded, craggy bays sheltering small sandy jewels adorned with coral. As of last count, over a dozen of these host a bungalow resort or two (or 40, in the case of Hat Rin), where US$ 5 will get you a sturdy roof, a cold-water bath and electricity at least until midnight.

Ah, yes, about the roads… From the cacophonous southern port town of **Thong Sala** ⑬, a ferry port for Ko Samui and Ko Tao (except for e-mail and mountain bike rentals, there's little call to hang around Thong Sala), there is a newly-paved 10-kilometre stretch that runs due north to the village of **Cha Loak Lam** ⑭, a favourite stopover on the north coast for trawlers. This route is plied by *songtao* "taxis," which can drop you off for the short walk to Pang waterfall, followed by a challenging 400-metre (1,300 ft) climb to the island's stellar view-

Map, page 309

TIP

Many people prefer Chaweng and Lamai in a stiff wind – usually in winter between November and February – because it forces jet-skiing and water-skiing, and the incessant droning of motors, to a halt.

BELOW: statue of Buddha, near Big Buddha Beach.

Another sunset on Ko Pha Ngan.

ing point. The dirt trails branching off to the western coast lead to about a half-dozen beaches and are navigable by motorbike if it hasn't rained recently. These are not Pha Ngan's premier beaches, although there's fine snorkelling coral at Hat Yao (West) and Mae Hat to the north. The rutted trails meandering around the eastern quadrant, however, are always hazardous and should not be attempted by novice cyclists, whether on motorbike or mountain bike.

East of Cha Loak Lam, the justly prized beach of the moment is **Hat Khuat ⓫** (Bottle Beach), which can only be reached by sea. The quickest approach is from Ban Cha Loak. Continuing eastward and down the coast, one could enjoyably argue the merits of **Hat Sadet** (with a waterfall and jumbo rocks bearing the graffiti of Thai royalty) or **Thong Nai Pan ⓰**, with its wonderful cliff viewpoints, a double-barrelled bay and a coral reef. Eventually you will reach the pretty southern cove of **Hat Tien ⓱**, which offers an additional choice of beaches on either side. One of the two bungalow resorts here is The Sanctuary, with an arresting central building constructed amidst enormous boulders and outcroppings. From September through May, it sponsors alternative health and New Age courses. Hat Tien forswears videos, noise and mind-altering drugs.

Not coincidentally, the next sign of habitation, a mere 10 minutes away by long-tail boat, is **Hat Rin ⓲**, better known internationally than Pha Ngan itself. The fame, or notoriety, stems from the monthly all-night "full-moon" party. The biggest bashes of the year take place in December and January, when leading British deejays fly in with cutting-edge sounds and hordes of young clubbers. Together with the island's semi-permanent foreign residents and the charters from Samui, the numbers can swell to 10,000. Even in the slowest months, when the ambience is more akin to a frat party, 3,000 people may dance into the next day. Poopers gripe that the party has become detached from its pagan roots; others say that undercover policemen have put a damper on the chemical enhancements. Of the two beaches that comprise Hat Rin, the eastern side of the headland, known as Sunrise Beach, is far superior with a wide bay of sand, good swimming and a bit of coral. West of the headland, Sunset is scraggy and usually strewn with flotsam, but it's so quiet that you can fall asleep to the waves. Besides, it's only a 10-minute walk to Sunrise. In between, there's a grid of dirt lanes lined with clothing, jewelry and dive shops, as well as two banks, a clinic, post office, pharmacies, tattooists and overseas telephones. Besides the usual video cafes and unusual MSG-free zones, there are genuine Italian restaurants.

There's even a thrice-daily boat connection between Hat Rin and Samui. Nonetheless, the roller-coaster road joining Hat Rin and Thong Sala is now cemented and has further opened up the intervening villages and so-so beaches of Ban Tai and Ban Khai.

An easy stroll up a hill from Ban Tai brings you to **Wat Khao Tham ⑲**. During most months of the year, Australian and American teachers run well-recommended 10- to 20-day Buddhist meditation courses at this temple.

Ko Tao

Alone in the middle of the ocean, flung a good 40 kilometres (25 mi) northwest of Ko Pha Ngan, tiny **Ko Tao** is the third principal island of the 80-strong Samui archipelago. The home of fewer than 800 fisher folk, it was colonised in the past decade by backpackers ever on a tireless search for "somewhere quiet." Ko Tao is quiet. The brief strip of paved road supports only one or two trucks. There's no place to race motorcycles. There are no bars, nightclubs, banks or jet skis. No go-karts. You can fall asleep listening to the waves.

Arriving by boat from either Chumphon or Ko Pha Ngan at **Ban Mae Hat**, the only proper village, you will be greeted by long-tail-boat touts proclaiming the virtues of their often isolated bungalow resorts. Be wary. Those located on the northern and eastern coasts probably do provide fine snorkelling sights surrounding cottage-sized boulders, but there is no beach or sand.

To the left (north) of Ban Mae Hat, the long beach of **Sai Ree** is deceptive, since the water is too shallow for anything more vigorous than the breast stroke. Likewise with Coral Beach on the right. Better to heed the touts from the southern coast. Or walk the few kilometres to **Ao Cha Loak** and **Hai Sai Daeng**.

Once settled, nature lovers can happily explore the island's 21-square kilometres (8 sq mi) on foot. Rough trails criss-cross the uninhabited, thickly forested interior. Although you may never glimpse the gibbons, you will probably hear their distinctive *whoop-whoop* signaling their presence in nearby tree tops.

For a cooling drink and a swim, follow the obvious signs for those boulder-strewn bungalows dotted around the coast. Ko Tao's strongest attraction, though, is its proximity to about 25 excellent scuba diving sites. In fact, these are where many diving trips originating in Ko Samui or Ko Pha Ngan head each day. At Ban Mae Hat, at least a dozen foreign-managed dive shops fiercely compete. Certified instruction is available. ❑

Map, page 309

TIP

Diving services operate year-round, but January through May offers the best visibility, reaching up to 30 metres. Visibility drops markedly from June to September, as well as in November, when the monsoonal winds shift.

BELOW: macaques are often heard, not seen, aloft.

PHUKET

Long before Ko Samui hit the limelight, Phuket was the prime beach destination in Thailand. It still is, and unlike Pattaya, which has sunk into sleaziness, Phuket retains its tropical charms

Map, page 313

THAILAND

Bangkok

Phuket's physical beauty is even greater than its exquisite beaches. This beauty stems from its picturesque villages, coconut groves, and rubber plantations, as much as from its patchwork of wild flowers presented against a backdrop of forested hills. Seaward from the beaches, coral reefs teem with marine life. It can be a dangerous beauty. During the monsoon season, May to October, rough surf and high winds can make swimming unsafe. The eastern shore is comprised primarily of rocky shoals, mud flats and mangroves. Nearly all of Phuket's decent beaches are located on the western side of the island. Landward, Phuket people exude the confidence of islanders who have prospered from an island rich in natural resources.

For centuries Phuket was a backwater. The long road south from Bangkok to reach it, the lack of a bridge across to the mainland, bad roads on the island itself, and a seeming lack of interest in developing it for recreation meant that it languished in relative isolation for decades despite natural resources of tin, rubber and coconut. Indeed, Phuket airport was only upgraded to international status in the 1970s to let tin and rubber merchants travel easily to Penang, Kuala Lumpur and Singapore. No one thought about tourism back in those days.

In the late 1970s, Phuket began appearing on the maps of budget backpackers. They stayed in fishermen's bungalows or camped out on the beach at Patong. Word spread, and developers descended on the island. The airport was expanded to handle long-haul jets from Europe. Dirt roads were paved. As tourist dollars flowed towards the beaches, the island grew to become the richest province in Thailand, second only to Bangkok.

OPPOSITE: yet another typical Phuket sunset.

The lion's share of Phuket's wealth now comes from tourism. The boom has had a social knock-on. Although there are only 10,000 native Phuket inhabitants, an estimated 240,000 migrant Thais, drawn from all 76 provinces in the kingdom, now live and work on the island, mostly in tourism-related activities.

Urban Phuket

The road from Phang Nga crosses the 600-metre (2,000 ft) Thaothep Kasaetri Bridge to Phuket, an island about the same size as Singapore. The sojourn to Phuket town, 30 kilometres (19 mi) to the south, soon reaches the emotional heart of the island. The intersection at **Ban Tha Rua ❶**, leading to Surin Beach and Khao Phra Taeo National Park, is dominated by a bronze statue of two women warriors, swords in hands. The pair are sisters: Chan and Muk. In 1785 they led an army of villagers against Burmese invaders.

Unlike many provincial centres, **Phuket ❷**, a town on the island's southeast coast, has a rich identity of its own. The style is set by the beautiful colonial-style

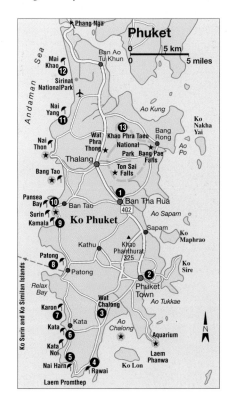

houses built by tin and rubber barons at the end of the 19th century. The construction followed a disastrous fire that destroyed the downtown area. Thanon Thalang, Thanon Phang Nga, and some of the smaller surrounding streets are still lined with Sino-Portuguese-style shophouses. Three storeys high, the rowhouses were built by middle-income Chinese to house their extended families. The ground floor normally serves as a shop and reception hall; the upper floors are the living quarters. Huge signs with large Chinese characters etched in gold are hung over, or alongside, the doors to identify the family residing within. The Chartered Bank building, Thai Airways office and others, with their arched loggias, resemble buildings of colonial Singapore and Penang.

The charm of Phuket's old buildings is complemented by the many Chinese shrines that accent the town with bright splashes of colour. Of note is the brightly painted temple of **Jui Tui** and its smaller companion Put Jaw next door, which sit just past the market on Thanon Ranong. Like many similar Chinese shrines elsewhere in Asia, their central altars are dedicated to Quanyin (Kuan Yin), the goddess of mercy. Jui Tui is the starting point for the five days of colourful and bizarre parades that mark the annual Phuket Vegetarian Festival each October.

Outside of town, the only building worthy of note is **Wat Chalong ❸**. It sits 6 kilometres further south on the Phuket Bypass, a ring road of sorts that runs west of Phuket. The opulently decorated temple is famed for the gilded statue of Luang Pho Chaem, the wat's abbot who gained fame as a lay physician.

Southern Phuket

South along the coast from the town of Phuket is **Rawai ❹**, whose foreshore is a mass of rocks that lie exposed during low tide, when clam hunters venture out,

In 1786, Capt. Light of the East India Company sought to secure Phuket for England. Thai claims and England's desire for a more strategic island to guard the Straits of Malacca led Light to drop the plan. So he founded Penang, which became the chief British colony on the Malay peninsula until the 1819 founding of Singapore.

BELOW: offering at a Chinese temple, town of Phuket.

Map,
page 313

turning over the stones in search of dinner. Rawai offers many tasty seafood snacks sold along the beach. Rawai also holds one of the island's handful of *chao lay* (sea gypsy) villages. The sea gypsies were once nomadic fishing families, roaming from island to island. They are skilled fishermen both above and below the water. From a young age, they learn to dive to great depths in search of lobsters, prawns, and crabs, staying below for up to three minutes. However, diminishing stocks and environmental and tourism concerns have robbed the sea gypsies of traditional fishing grounds.

Because the sea gypsies are not allowed to own the land they live on, they cannot install permanent facilities, such as brick houses or even septic tanks. Their villages are effectively shanty towns, impermanent shacks reflecting their lack of spiritual attachment to terra firma. The gypsies are not materialistic. Even as fish stocks dwindle, they are reluctant to take up waged employment. They fear complicated involvement with government officers or business people. Proposals have been made to enhance the sea gypsies' standards of living, but lacking strong collective will, the placid gypsies are losing their identity. The youngsters speak Thai instead of Urak Lawoi, their indigenous tongue.

From Rawai the coastal road continues over the north-south ridge of hills, offering great views of Ko Phi Phi, 45 kilometres (30 mi) away. Continuing south around the point at **Laem Prom Thep**, you come to one of the island's prettiest beaches. Nestled between two hills, fronted by a calm sea and backed by a lagoon, **Nai Harn ❺** is a serene setting. The surrounding headlands are lashed by a salty breezes that allow only sturdy grasses to grow.

The picturesque bays of **Kata ❻** and **Kata Noi** have a more intimate feel due to their smaller size. There is fine snorkelling at the southern end of Kata Noi

TIP

Prom Thep Cape is a well-visited vantage point for viewing the sunset. The gold-and-green promontory plunges into the hissing sea.

BELOW: Kata Noi.

beach. Relax Bay, with its single hotel, Le Meridien Phuket, offers some snorkelling along its northwestern rocks. **Karon Beach ❼** is a long and quiet strip of sand backed by hotels and restaurants at its top, middle and bottom, with empty plots of former rice paddy in between. Both Karon and Kata are much less frenetic than Patong, but with a growing choice of hotel, dining and water-sport facilities.

The most developed beach is **Patong ❽**, due west of the town of Phuket and north of Karon. In the early 1970s, Patong was little more than a huge banana plantation wedged between the mountains and a wide crescent of sand. The plantation is now a tourist city-by-the-sea, with multi-storey condominiums and hotels rising above night markets, seafood emporiums, beer bars, discos, and tour shops. The beach itself is dotted with colourful parasols.

In the calm weather from November to May, the bay is peppered with visiting yachts. Unlike most other Phuket beaches, Patong has a wide range of water-sports facilities, including scuba diving, windsurfing, waterskiing, parasailing, jetskis, sailing and boogie boards. Dive shops offer trips Racha and Phi Phi islands, or 80 kilometres (50 mi) northwest to the Similan Islands Marine National Park, considered one of the best diving areas in Asia. Patong also has the most developed land-sports facilities on the island. Most large hotels have pools and many have tennis courts. There are four 18-hole golf courses in Phuket, and one 9-hole.

Patong is a gourmet's delight. Seafood is a specialty. The legendary Phuket lobster, however, each weighing up to 3 kilograms (6 lb), is now caught in Burmese or Indonesian waters. Patong is also a great place to eat Western, Indian, Mexican, Italian, Japanese and Korean cuisines.

BELOW: Le Meridian Phuket, one of several world-class resorts on Phuket.

After dark, Patong has many open-air bars along Soi Bangla in the middle of the resort. These barbeers, as they are called, lure customers with a heady mix of female company, rock music, and an ocean of booze. Within a few steps you can eat great seafood, barter your price for a silk shirt, go bungy jumping, join some Thai boxing, or buy real estate. Patong is all things to all people. At any major beach you can rent cars, jeeps or motorcycles to explore the island. A valid driver's license is all that is necessary. The town itself is reputed to have had the first paved road in the kingdom. Phuket also has the highest road fatality statistics in Thailand. Usually only vehicles rented by the large international firms carry insurance, despite signs and verbal promises to the contrary.

Travelling cheaply means relying on the blue-and-white *songtao* – two-row, wooden buses that leave the Phuket town market for every point on the island. Alternatively, small and cramped red vehicles called *tuk-tuk* function as taxis. Barter for the fare before starting off.

Map, page 313

Northern Phuket

Some 3 kilometres (2 mi) north of Patong, quiet **Kamala Bay ❾** retains charm around its Islamic hamlets, with their well-kept gardens against a backdrop of forested hills rising to over 500 metres. The tranquillity won't last. At the northern end of Kamala, a giant Disney-like theme park is being built.

The attractive coastal road north to **Surin Beach** passes mouthwateringly compact Singh Beach, its sandy cape hedged by verdant headlands. Larger Surin Beach with its seafood shacks soon gives way to idyllic **Pansea Bay ❿**, dominated by two proprietary resorts, the Chedi and the Amanpuri. The long beach at **Bang Tao** is dominated by the immense Laguna Phuket Resort, housing five hotel complexes. Much of the land around here used to be a tin mining wasteland. In 1785, the Burmese invaded here, seeking to takeover the island.

Nai Yang ⓫ beach, just south of the airport, is now under the jurisdiction of **Sirinat National Park**. It is a pleasant hangout where local people and tourists come to eat seafood and spicy papaya salad under the casuarina trees. An offshore reef allows year-round swimming in the shallow bay. There are a few Spartan bungalows for rent in the national park. With a good map, it is possible to drive along Phuket's scenic west coast all the way from Nai Yang to the island's southern tip, Laem Prom Thep.

North of Nai Yang is Phuket's longest beach, **Mai Khao ⓬**. The 9-kilometre-long (6 mi) beach is undeveloped, a haven for beachcombers and the giant sea turtles that come ashore December through February to lay their eggs.

The last main outpost of the island's monsoon evergreen forest can be inspected on an organised hike through **Khao Phra Taeo National Park ⓭**. Wild bears and cats still live within the small park, and all of the wildlife is rather keen to avoid all human contact. The park is fringed by two pretty waterfalls: Ton Sai on the west, and Bang Bae on the east.

The sheltered waters off the northeast coast around **Ao Po** contain numerous pearl farms. Organised tours to the farms are informative. ❐

BELOW: pearls.

Map,
page 319

THAILAND

Bangkok

PHANG NGA AND KRABI

*The traveller couldn't ask for a more exquisite, seductive,
and resplendent retreat than the islands and bays of Phang Nga.
Increasingly popular – and threatened – is Ko Phi Phi*

In the waters east of the island of Phuket, the spectacle of towering limestone massifs reaches its zenith with 300-metre (1,000 ft) peaks crowding together in close proximity. The same unlikely topography imposes itself throughout Phang Nga Province, making it the most spectacular and visually opulent province in Thailand. The appeal isn't just physical. The ingenious ways people have adapted to such surroundings makes Phang Nga and its bay one of the wonders of the world.

On the mainland north of the island of Phuket, the town of **Phang Nga ❶** is revealed as a lovely, docile township left behind in Thailand's development surge. The main source of employment seems to be in sleepy government offices. Several small hotels provide simple accommodation.

The main objective of any first-time trip, however, should be to the geological wonderland of **Phang Nga Bay**. A long-tail boat trip from near the Phang Nga Bay Resort Hotel reveals Andaman mangrove culture at its best, with mussel farms, floating fish traps, and Brahminy kites circling overhead looking for scraps. The mangroves are fertile breeding, spawning, and feeding grounds for mud skippers, crabs, prawns, and an assortment of fish such as sea bass. Hungry dolphins penetrate the upper reaches of the channels at high tide. Mangrove

BELOW: one of
Phang Nga Bay's
many caves.

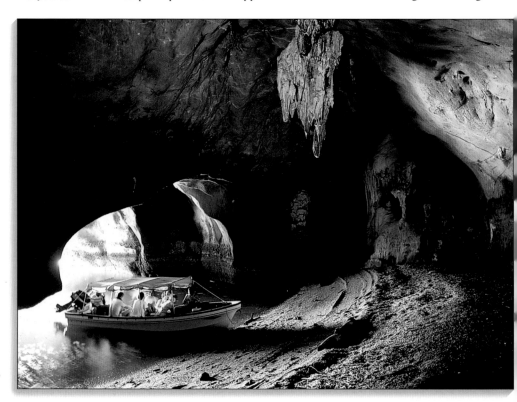

wood also feeds the long-established charcoal-making industry, a feature of the Andaman coast from Ranong to Malaysia.

Just before the mouth of the Mae Nam Phang Nga, an excursion boat approaches the base of the mountain of **Khao Kien**, where a cavern contains primitive paintings depicting human and animal forms. Such cave daubings are quite common in the limestone caves in the area, and were painted by primitive people around 2,000 years ago. The strange forms depicting sea creatures, six-fingered hands, and semi-human shapes are thought to have played a religious-shamanistic role for the cave dwellers. Prior to hunting expeditions or battles, primitive people would make sacrifices to placate spirits in front of the paintings. The floors of many caves in Phang Nga and Krabi are still scattered with the discarded sea shells of prehistoric people. Tide fluctuations have compromised archeological evidence. Forty thousand years ago it was possible to walk to Phi Phi. Five thousand years ago sea levels were higher than at present.

On what seems a collision course with a huge limestone outcrop, the boat then slips into the barely discernible, overgrown cave entrance of **Tham Lod**. For more than 50 metres, the boat slides under giant stalactites. Rocks protruding from the water appear to have been sliced by a sword-wielding god. In **Tham Nak**, a twisted stalagmite at the cave's entrance resembles a *naga* serpent, giving this cave its name. Green stalactites burst from the ceiling like a frozen waterfall. The whole mountain-island drips with streaked limestone.

Ko Talu receives its name from *talu,* meaning to pass from one side to the other – in this case, not over the mountain, but under it as the boat squeezes through a cave filled with stalactites. **Ko Khao Ping Gun** is perhaps the most spectacular of Phang Nga's islands. Behind the beach, the mountain seems to

Ancient cave paintings of the Phang Nga Bay region.

BELOW: limestone, or karst, pillar.

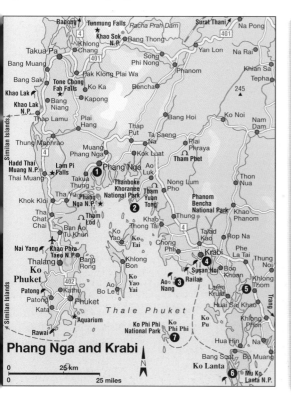

Phang Nga and Krabi

0 ___ 25 km
0 ___ 25 miles

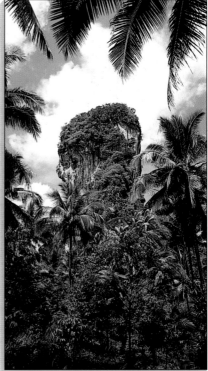

have split in two, the halves leaning against each other. Locals say they are two lovers. This area was the setting of part of the James Bond movie *The Man with the Golden Gun*. A small beach overlooks another island, **Ko Tapoo**, or Nail Island, which looks like a thorny spike driven into the sea.

Further south in Phang Nga Bay, the towering islands hold natural treasures hidden from passing boats. Far from being impregnable, a few of the sheer islands allow cave access by canoe when the tide is right. By squeezing in through minute gaps at the correct tidal window, canoeists paddle into a lost world, an open-top sea chamber, its sheer walls covered with vines and ferns. It's like entering the hole in the middle of a donut through a side door. These are ecological time capsules where eagles, macaques, and other mangrove species have dwelled for millennia unfettered by people. The chambers are caused by acidic rain water percolating into the limestone peaks. The soluble limestone island becomes addled with hidden chasms, causing the roof to cave in.

To the south

South of Phang Nga, the journey southward on the mainland coast takes the traveller further into the heart of limestone country. At times, the horizon resembles the graph line of a seismic tremor, with huge jutting rocks thrusting out of the plantations and forests.

About 50 kilometres (30 mi) southeast of Phang Nga, **Tanboke Koranee National Park** ❷ is one of the most beautiful in Thailand. Like a scene from *Lost Horizon*, the park is dominated by lofty cliffs. In one spot, an underground stream rises amid lush vegetation at the base of a mountain. Foot paths wind beneath cliff faces covered in green vines, punctuated with brilliant hibiscus.

TIP

A small number of sea canoe companies in Phuket arrange superlative day trips into the hidden *hong* of Phang Nga Bay. Of the operators, the pioneering SeaCanoe Thailand has the best safety, service, and environmental track record.

BELOW: rocky retreat near Krabi.

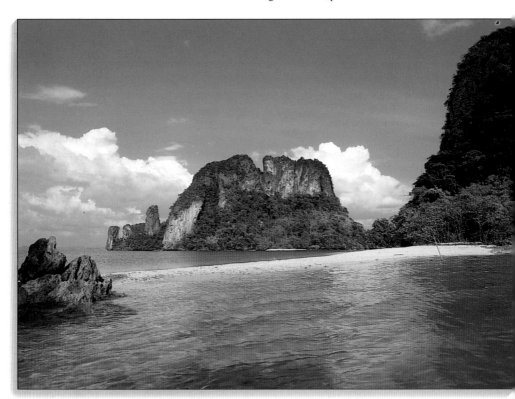

At **Ao Nang Bay** ❸, near Krabi and 3 kilometres eastwards along the coast road, comfortable resorts act as a base for exploring nearby islands and hidden coves. The Ao Nang area, with its low-key bungalow developments, seafood restaurants, scuba diving and sea canoeing and mountain bike options, makes a refreshing alternative to brassier beach resorts on Phuket.

The town of **Krabi** ❹ is a small but bustling service centre built opposite mangrove swamps along the Krabi River. From here, long-tail boats sail out to Railae Beach; larger ones leave for Ko Phi Phi daily, and for Ko Lanta, November to May. From town, the Krabi River mangroves can be explored by renting a long-tail boat, first stopping off to visit the huge cavern inside the Kanab Nam twin peaks, which flank the river. Traditionally, the leaves, bark, fruit and mosses of the surrounding mangroves provided folk cures for the alleviation of lumbago, thrush, kidney stones and menstrual pains. The trees also provided a source of weak alcohol and leaves for wrapping tobacco. Two rare bird species inhabit the mangroves: the mangrove pitta and the brown-winged kingfisher.

Southeast from Krabi the land gradually flattens. Dike-enclosed rice fields appear on both sides of the road. Seemingly-abandoned suitcases and boxes on the roadside designate bus stops; passengers wait under banana trees nearby.

Forty kilometres (25 mi) south of Krabi, a hot spring and nature trail make **Klong Thom** ❺ a rewarding stop. The small museum at Wat Klong Thom displays artefacts such as beads, pots and religious icons, purportedly from the 5th to 7th centuries AD, when the area was a port for traders, monks and diplomats crossing the peninsula. A bumpy laterite trail eastwards from the main intersection leads to a hot spring suitable for bathing. Farther on, the Tung Tieo nature trail starts and finishes at an inviting emerald pool. Southwest of Klong Tom,

Map,
page 319

BELOW: busy beach on Ko Phi Phi.

Map,
page 319

and also accessible by boat from Krabi, quiet **Ko Lanta** ❻ offers some rustic bungalow accommodation along its 19 powdery beaches. At low tide there is as much chance of finding monkey or lizard tracks as human, although one might prefer the former.

Ko Phi Phi

Turquoise waves caress a beach so dazzlingly white it is almost painful to the eye. The water is so crystalline that colourful fishing boats seem suspended in mid-air. With palm-fringed beaches and lofty limestone mountains as a back-drop, **Ko Phi Phi** ❼ arguably surpasses Phuket as one of the most beautiful islands in Asia. Where Phuket is undulating, physically sociable and with a size-able population, Phi Phi, like the karst islands of Phang Nga, is geologically dramatic, its population confined to low-lying sand bars below towering rocks.

The underwater grinding you hear while snorkelling is the sound of hungry parrot fish munching their way through the 12 kilos of coral reef they consume each year. The coral is digested and excreted as fine sand.

Phi Phi lies equidistant, about 45 kilometres, from both Phuket and Krabi. The island is in fact two islands: the smaller **Phi Phi Ley**, a craggy limestone monolith similar to the other shrub-covered peaks of Phang Nga Bay, and **Phi Phi Don**, a national park with an epicentre of anarchic tourism development. Ironically, it is the unprotected Phi Phi Ley which remains environmentally pris-tine. By contrast, the tiny village of Phi Phi Don is now a riot of Kodak signs, T-shirt shops, mini-marts, dive centres, burger joints, tour counters, and hair-braiding shacks – a cheap and cheerful tourist ghetto surrounded by resorts charging from US$5 to $200 a night. Like Thailand itself, Phi Phi is full of con-tradictions. Infuriating one moment, a joy the next. Until 1994, it was the only marine national park in the world with a transvestite cabaret.

If you move out of the village, the grandeur of the island reasserts itself. A 30-minute hike up to a flower-covered viewpoint reveals Phi Phi Don's layout: barbell-like rock massifs connected by a spit of sand covered in coconut trees.

From the village, an easy 40-minute coastal walk leads to **Had Yaow** (Long Beach), with some of the whitest sands and clearest water imaginable. Swim-ming and snorkelling here takes place with a majestic view of Phi Phi Ley's ver-tical north face in the distance.

To enjoy the best of Phi Phi, take a long-tail boat ride around both islands. The boat stops at the so-called Viking Cave on Phi Phi Ley first. The cave is renowned as a site for swallows that build their nests on the ceilings of rocky caverns. A web of bamboo scaffolding reaches up, disappearing into the gloomy upper recesses of the cave. Sinewy young men climb up these precarious lad-ders to collect the swallow nests, which are sold as delicacies to Chinese restau-rants. However, there is no demonstration of nest gathering in any cave that still hosts swallows. The nests are more valuable, ounce by ounce, than pure gold, so no concessionaire is going to publicise the location of a productive site.

Tropical fish find sanctuary in the coral reefs of Ko Phi Phi.

Viking Cave is named after its wall painting of long boats with sails. How old these pictures actually are, and who painted them, remains in dispute. What is certain, of course, is that before the 19th century, no Norsemen ever visited the Andaman Sea. It is likely the cave painting here is of later origin than others in Phang Nga and Krabi.

At **Maya Bay**, the long-tail boat stops for snorkelling in a horseshoe bay of corals surrounded by steep cliffs and a deserted white beach. After circumnav-igating much of both Phi Phi islands, the boat stops at Bamboo Island for more snorkelling. The reefs at Bamboo are bigger, with more branch and seafan forms. Fish life is more diverse, including groupers lurking in the nooks and crannies. Should the diving bug bite, Phi Phi has dive shops where visitors can earn their open-water diving card. The deeper waters of Ko Bida and Hin Muang, with

OPPOSITE: Ko Phi Phi.

their barracudas, manta rays, and whale sharks, can then be explored. ❑

THE DEEP SOUTH

Map, page 327

South of the resort islands of Samui and Phuket, the peninsular character of Thailand takes on subtle changes as it approaches Malaysia. Mosques replace wats, and coconut joins curry

THAILAND

Bangkok ●

Lower peninsular Thailand is where Thai-speaking Buddhism meets Malay-speaking Islam. It's a land of verdant jungle and limestone peaks, azure seas and rich, coconut-flavoured cuisine. Southern peninsular Thailand is criss-crossed by a network of excellent roads that connect the Andaman Sea with the Gulf of Thailand. Once troubled by insurgent guerrillas of the People's Liberation Army of Thailand in the north, and by guerrillas of the Communist Party of Malaysia in the south, the region is now completely safe for the traveller. True, a handful of Muslim separatists still hide in the jungled hills that straddle the Thai-Malay frontier, but these regions are well off the beaten track, and the problem is rapidly disappearing. The deep south is an area of pristine beaches, friendly, predominantly rural communities, and markets overflowing with exotic fruits and other native produce. Amongst Thais elsewhere in Thailand, the people of the deep south have a reputation for quickness of thought and swiftness to anger – though this is far from apparent to the foreign visitor. It's a land where travellers can revel in the sun or explore ancient Srivijayan sites.

Trang ❶ is an industrial town inhabited primarily by the descendants of Teochew-speaking Chinese immigrants, who originally sought work here panning tin but wound up running the region's rubber trade. Trang's Chinese heritage is reflected in monuments at the northern approach to the city. At **Ban Bangrok**, 3 kilometres north on Route 4, a shrine honours Kwan Tee Hun, a red-faced, bearded god believed to have the power to prevent or start war. Farther south, a dragon gate guards the city from intruders. From Trang, there are a number of interesting side trips. The beach at **Pak Meng** lies on the Indian Ocean, a long and rough trip from Trang, but the scenery and sunsets are memorable. **Surin**, which lies a short distance west, has a large and beautiful pond surrounded by well-kept gardens.

The port of Pak Bara, on the opposite coast of the isthmus in Satun Province, around 150 kilometres (90 mi) southwest of Hat Yai, serves as the port for remote **Ko Tarutao Marine National Park ❷**. The 51-island archipelago, with a mixed Thai and sea gypsy population, is known for its extensive corals, unpopulated sandy beaches, and simple beach huts. After the monsoon abates, small tour and supply boats link the islands between November and May each year.

Nakhon Si Thammarat

Continuing northeast from Trang through Huai Yot, a beautiful and winding valley threads its way to **Nakhon Si Thammarat ❸**. Nakhon may well have been the capital of the illusive kingdom Tambralinga, mentioned in Chinese annals. A large hoard of silver coins of a type sometimes attributed to Funan, dating from the fifth or

OPPOSITE: painted prow of Muslim *korlae*, or fishing boat. **BELOW:** Songkhla girl.

sixth century AD, was discovered near Moklan village. Nakhon later became a regional centre of the Sumatra-based Srivijaya empire, at least until the 10th century. Trade and ecclesiastical links between Nakhon and southern India and Ceylon flourished. Around this time, the city's name evolved to the Sanskrit Nagara Sri Dhammaraja, or City of the Glorious Dharma-Observing King, and numerous Indian migrants settled in an area known as Hat Sai Kaeo, or Beach of Crystal Sand, where the city's most sacred site, Wat Phra Mahathat, still stands. Later, the city became an important regional centre whose governors ruled the entire south. From the 16th century it was known to Europeans by the Malay name of Ligor.

The human legacy of Nakhon's rich history is evident in the surviving traditions of the *nang thalung* shadow-puppet play, and also in exquisite classical dance-dramas called *lakhon* and *manohra* performed to acclaim by the city's fine-arts school. At **Suchart House**, on Si Thammasok Soi 3, it is possible to watch puppets for shadow-puppet plays being made from leather, and perhaps enjoy an impromptu performance by a master puppeteer.

The physical aspects of Nakhon's history are extensively displayed in the **National Museum** (open Wednesday–Sunday; admission fee), at the southern end of Thanon Ratchadamnoen and housing one of the most important collections in Thailand outside of Bangkok. **Wat Phra Mahathat** is Nakhon's most revered temple, and one of the country's oldest. The *wat*'s prime attraction is a 77-metre-high (250 ft) *chedi,* the top of which is covered by an estimated 270 kilograms (600 lbs) of gold. To the right of the chedi, a temple museum houses an assortment of delicate gold and silver offerings. South of the chedi, the Viharn Luang, with its inward-leaning columns, is a fine example of Ayutthayan design.

While Wat Phra Mahathat may be up to 10 centuries old, the chedi dates from the 1400s.

BELOW: interior and exterior, Wat Phra Mahathat.

In the city centre, the outdoor **Boworn Bazaar** near the Thai Hotel presents a pleasant environment for Thai dining and drinking, especially at the Ban Lakhon wooden restaurant, built round a mature *takian* tree. Nakhon comes alive, literally, during the Festival of the 10th Lunar Month, usually in October, when spirits of ancestors return in response to donations of food at temples by devotees.

The road north leads to the gulf-coast town of **Sichon**, which offers scenic views and southern-style handicrafts. Nearby, it is also possible to visit the cave that some believe sheltered King Taksin after he was deposed by Rama I. (More orthodox histories hold that Taksin was tied up in a velvet sack and beaten to death with a sandalwood club in the manner reserved for royalty.) Take the road across the railroad tracks to the village of Lan Saka, then right at the first fork and go 9 kilometres (6 mi) to the cave, with a magnificent view of the countryside.

Heading south

The mostly coastal Route 408 links Nakhon to Songkhla, running south through extensive shrimp farms, lime orchards, dusty training arenas for fighting bulls, and the village of Sathing Phra, where many ancient artifacts have been found.

An alternative to the coast road are the inland routes 403 and 41 leading to **Phatthalung ❹**, which offers rather basic hotels, though one may wish to continue without stopping. If so, head back to Route 4 and turn south for Hat Yai.

In Khuan Khanun district, just north of Phatthalung, Route 4048 leads to **Thale Noi**, the largest waterfowl reserve in Thailand. Around 150 species of birds make up a population of about 100,000 during the peak migratory period, from December to April. The average depth of the lake is just 1.5 metres (16 ft).

Westwards from the main Phatthalung intersection along Route 4, motorists

Phatthalung may be where nang thalung – shadow-puppet plays of local folklore – was first performed in Thailand.

Map, page 327

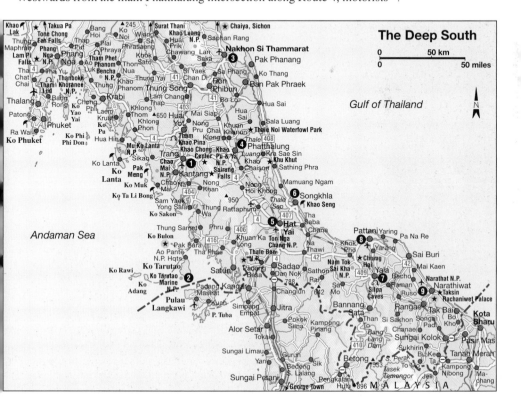

were sometimes relieved of their cash and valuables in the past by highway robbers, but this is no longer the case. You will likely only see Thai soldiers camped in tents between rows of rubber trees.

About 35 kilometres (20 mi) west of Phatthalung, the **Khao Chong Centre of Wildlife and Nature Study** encompasses jungle, a rocky creek, and a number of waterfalls. Drive into the reserve, but do not panic if you encounter soldiers brandishing weapons; the reserve hosts a military camp.

Khao Chong represents part of Thailand's developing conservation and ecology movement. Students at its Nature Education Centre study local flora and fauna in their natural rain-forest environment. The small zoo houses local wildlife such as the *binturong*, Prevost squirrel, Brahminy kite, hog badger and several endangered species, including the white-handed gibbon, which poachers usually capture at a young age by killing the mother.

The hog badger has a curious connection with southern Thai bullfighting, which draws gamblers from far and wide. The long-clawed mammal is occasionally hunted for the fat of its nose. It's claimed that a bull with this wild-smelling fat rubbed on its horns can intimidate and defeat any opponent. The use of this fat is regarded, understandably, as cheating.

From Khao Chong, the return drive to Phatthalung zigzags under towering trees, past pink rocky outcrops, and up and down the mountainous watershed along the spine of the isthmus. About 3 kilometres before Phatthalung, the highway branches south to Hat Yai.

Continue straight, past the provincial administrative offices, and then bear left on a road to Khuan Khanun (Jackfruit Hill) and **Wat Ku Ha Sawan**. This antiquated temple was recently renovated, but behind its yellow buildings, a staircase climbs up to a large grotto lighted by a natural arch. A delightfully obese and laughing Buddha marks the entrance. Around a copper-leafed *bodhi* tree are dozens of Buddha images. Light from the arch glints off the statues' gold leaf.

To the right of Wat Ku Ha Sawan lies another cave, formerly inhabited by a hermit monk. His personal collection of Buddha images is kept there.

To visit another temple and the northern end of the Thale Luang inland sea, take the road leading east from here. **Wat Wang** (Palace Temple) is 8 kilometres (5 mi) from the city. An attractive chedi graces the temple courtyard. Inside the temple proper are unrestored frescoes dating back about two centuries.

Down the road is Ban Lampam, where the waters of the inland sea, 70 kilometres (40 mi) from its entrance to the Gulf of Thailand, are fresh.

A short boat trip from Phatthalung leads to **Tham Malai**, a cave lying between the province's two famous peaks: Broken-Hearted Mountain and Broken-Headed Mountain. Legend says these represent two women turned to stone as punishment for jealousy, perhaps sharing a common and lasting interest in the same man. To reach the cave, best is to catch the boat behind the Phatthalung train station for the 15-minute ride to Tham Malai. A monk caretaker will turn on a generator to light up the stalactites, a useful idea if one has not brought a torch along for the journey.

BELOW: Muslim women at prayer.

Hat Yai

The commercial capital of south Thailand, **Hat Yai ❺** is a boom town. Rubber and tin have been its traditional income earners, but they are rapidly being over-shadowed by an entertainment and commercial centre geared towards thousands of sybaritic Malaysians, who pour over the border each month to enjoy illicit pleasures denied at home. Nightclubs with singers, massage parlors and broth-els are the magnets for some single men, whilst women and families come for the wide range of shopping and reasonably-priced restaurants.

Hat Yai has several cultural points of interest, nonetheless. **Wat Hat Yai Nai**, in the middle of town, has the third-largest reclining Buddha in the world. One can do more than just admire the exterior of this giant atop its 3-metre-high (10 ft) base. Ascend the pedestal and enter the Buddha's innards, where lungs and shrines are displayed side by side.

Sunday is usually the day for bullfights. The TAT office will confirm dates and fight locations, which rotate around the city's handful of arenas. Do not envisage a *corrida* with matadors and picadors; Thai-style bull fighting is a contest that pits one bull against another. Two animals are brought face to face. They lower their heads, clash horns and paw the ground, each pushing against the other like sumo wrestlers. The fight may last minutes or a couple of hours. It ends when one bull "bulldozes" the other to the edge of the ring, or when one simply turns and takes flight.

For those with more gastronomic interests, the shark's fin soup at Hat Yai's restaurants draws people all the way from the reaches of Bangkok and Kuala Lumpur. Other specialties are poached duck and fried pigeon. Several large open-air restaurants serve superb seafood to the accompaniment of live music.

From Hat Yai, there are two rail and three road routes to Malaysia. The more frequently used railway line runs southwest, crossing the border to Alor Setar and But-terworth, the connection port for Penang island.

The second heads southeast through Yala and ends at the border town of Sungai Kolok. From there, it is a short walk and taxi ride to Kota Bharu on Malaysia's east coast.

The **Rubber Research Centre** on the outskirts of Hat Yai, en route to Songkhla, serves all of Thailand. It experiments with new grafting and tapping methods, and with how to induce the rubber trees to be more bountiful in their production of latex. Small-holding farmers study at the centre, where there is a rubber pro-cessing laboratory. Next to the research centre is the **Songkhla Nakharin University**, a splendid complex set on a 120-hectare (300 acres) campus. A pumpkin-shaped building containing the auditorium and labora-tories is surrounded by a moat. Arched windows in the pumpkin-shaped building catch breezes from all direc-tions and funnel them through the building to provide natural air-conditioning. An exhaust pump in the cen-tre sucks the warm air out.

Songkhla

If Hat Yai is brash, then **Songkhla ❻** is discreet, a well-kept secret from the pleasure-seekers who visit Hat Yai. Trains, buses and taxis cover the 25 kilometres (15 mi)

Map, page 327

Tapping the latex from a rubber tree.

BELOW: Songkhla harbour.

between the two towns. Located at the tip of a quiet peninsula, Songkhla is an old city showing clear signs of Chinese influence. Only the seaward (eastern) shore is suitable for sunbathing and swimming. The north portion of the beach is backed with lush casaurina trees, and here one finds monks in saffron robes walking past humpbacked bulls being prepared for the bullfights. The focal point of the beach is a bronze statue of a little mermaid, perched on a rock and looking wistfully seaward.

Immediately northwest of the mermaid, a score of seafood restaurants occupy the sandy strand. Select your ingredients from fresh seafood displayed on ice, including 35-centimetre-long (15 in) tiger prawns.

Across the road from the mermaid is **Khao Noi**, a topiary garden with realistic fighting bulls, birds in flight and an elephant sculpted out of living yew. Around the corner, on Thanon Sukhum, a group of monkeys gathers in the late afternoon to scratch, screech and scowl. They sit, hands on knees, looking like crotchety members of a debating society.

Songkhla boasts two museums. The dusty museum in **Wat Matchimawat** is in marked contrast to the spic-and-span **Songkhla National Museum** (open Wednesday–Sunday; admission fee), set in a beautifully-proportioned Chinese mansion built in 1878. The latter contains an excellent collection of ceramics and documented relics, recovered by scuba divers from an ancient wreck in the Gulf of Thailand. The Wat Matchimawat museum collection ranges from early Thai *bencharong* (five-colour) pottery and 200-year-old shell boxes, to oddities like a gas-powered fan.

The 200-year-old marble Buddha gracing the altar inside the *viharn* is minus its gold lotus crown, which is now preserved in a vault to protect it from thieves.

Image from Wat Matchimawat.

BELOW: fishermen near Songkhla.

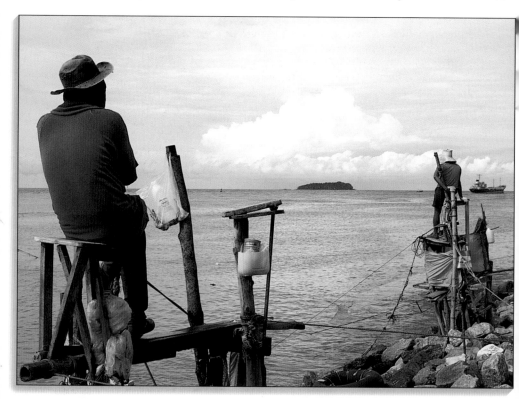

Stone lions, a gift of a rich 19th-century Chinese merchant, guard the doorway that opens onto a set of interesting murals. Some show scenes of Songkhla's history, while others depict European sailors and a steamboat.

Map, page 327

Lift your eyes as you walk along Thanon Nakhon Nawk and Thanon Nakhon Nai; old Chinese families living in these lovely Sino-Portuguese shophouses are reputed to be extremely rich and conservative.

Continue towards the lake to Thanon Vichianchom. A steep path leads, 20 minutes later, to the summit of **Tangkuan** and the ruins of an ancient chedi. The panorama is superb, and the bustle at the wharves along the lake bear witness to Songkhla's status as a busy fishing port.

A pleasant excursion can be made to **Ko Yor**, situated in **Thale Sap** or Songkhla Lake, one of the largest lakes in Southeast Asia. The lake is, in fact, a deep ocean inlet, and its waters are rather brackish. En route to Ko Yor, stop at the fisheries station, where enormous white *plaa kapong* (white snappers) are bred. Ko Yor is renowned for its locally-woven cotton, ancient Buddhist monuments and its simple tranquillity.

The lake is also home to tens of thousands of water birds, which migrate here to settle among the rushes. With special permission, it is possible to take a boat onto the lake to observe their habits. The water, even in the middle of the lake, is no more than one metre deep, making the grassy bottom with its darting fish easy to see.

Another excursion by boat is to the offshore islands of Maew and Nuu (Cat and Mouse). Nuu is the larger of the two and has some pleasant picnic spots and swimming beaches.

Three kilometres south of the town is a small, extremely active fishing village, inhabited mainly by Muslims. It is the fishing boats, rather than the people, however, that are the most colourful. It would be difficult to beat these brightly-painted *korlae* for imaginative themes and execution.

Beyond the fishing village lies the rocky beach of **Khao Seng**, whose fame rests on an apparently precariously poised giant boulder called Nai Bang's Head. Legend says that if you succeed in pushing it over, you will uncover the millionaire's treasure buried beneath it. Inland from the beach is the Banloa Coconut Plantation, where you can watch monkeys trained to climb trees and toss down selected coconuts.

Wat Kho Tham is built among enormous boulders on a nearby hilltop. The cave contains the inevitable Buddha's footprint, and a reclining Buddha sheltered by an overhanging rock. Around the corner is **Wat Mae Chi**, a charmingly sandy spot inhabited by Buddhist nuns. The shaven-headed nuns, often quite young, dress in white robes, grow flowers and, like monks, rise at 4am to meditate before setting out to collect alms.

BELOW: mosque.

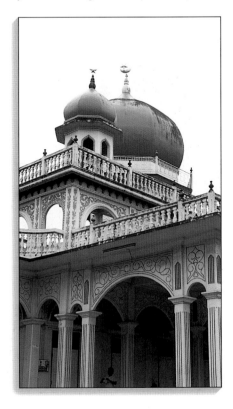

South of Songkhla

Down the east coast from Songkhla are the provincial capitals of Yala, Pattani and Narathiwat. Many of the residents of **Yala ❼** are ethnic Chinese, whilst Pattani and Narathiwat are fascinating centres of southernmost Thailand's Malay Muslim culture. **Pattani ❽** is home to a large fishing fleet and the 400-year-old Kreuse

Map,
page 327

Mosque, built in 1578 by a Chinese settler, To Khieng, who converted to Islam. In fact, construction seems never to have been fully completed. According to legend, this is because To Khieng's sister, Lim Ko Niaw, sailed from China and begged her brother to renounce Islam and return to their ancestral home. When he refused, she cursed the mosque, saying it would never be completed, then hanged herself from a nearby cashew-nut tree.

Today, the mosque is maintained by the faithful in its original state. No attempt is made to complete it, because local Muslims believe lightning will strike anyone who makes the attempt. Meanwhile, Lim Ko Niaw has acquired a certain religious status herself – her shrine at San Jao Leng Ju Kieng is always packed, and in February it is the site of an important ceremony featuring fire walking and a vegetarian food festival.

Of interest near Yala are the Silpa caves. The large cave of Tham Koo Hu Pimuk contains a 25-metre-high (80 ft) Buddha, considered a holy pilgrimage site by southern Thai Buddhists.

Towards Malaysia

Narathiwat ❾ is markedly distinguished by its rural charm, prized songbirds and succulent mangoes. Next stop further south is Malaysia, accessible by ferry from the small town of Tak Bai. Yet before moving on, the traveller should linger a while in Narathiwat, which offers fine swimming at the beach at Narathat, a delightful and pleasant stretch of all-but-deserted white sand shaded by tall casuarina trees.

Wat Narathiwat is reached by walking north along Thanon Pichitbamrung, the town's main street, and towards the green dome of the provincial mosque.

OPPOSITE: climbing for the boss. **BELOW:** Diard's trogon.

Here a bridge leads right across a branch of the Mae Nam Bang Nara to the beach. A fascinating and informative glimpse of the life of southern Thai Muslim villagers can be gleaned at this point by walking through the fishing village at the mouth of the Bang Nara. Brightly painted fishing vessels jostle for space in the clear waters, and everywhere fish of all sizes and species are laid out on racks to dry in the sun. While the people are welcoming to visitors, the people here are conservative and Islamic, and female travellers should take care that their dress does not offend local sensibilities with halter tops or shorts.

Satun is an overwhelmingly rural province with the largest Muslim population – over 80 percent – in Thailand. A tiny, riverside town, it's a pleasant place to overnight if en route to Malaysia by sea. Boats to the Malaysian province of Perlis, just south of Thailand, cost around US$2, departing either from Khlong Bambang, which is directly in the centre of Satun, or at Tammalang Pier, in the estuary just south of the town.

Boats also leave Tammalang three times daily for Malaysia's fabled Langkawi Island, costing around US$5 each way. Travellers exiting Thailand for Malaysia via Satun should remember to get their passport stamped at the immigration office in town; if you forget, there is a distinct possibility of bureaucratic delays and perhaps even a bureaucratic nightmare on arrival in Malaysia. ❑

INSIGHT GUIDES
Travel Tips

FLY SMOOTH AS SILK TO EXOTIC THAILAND ON A ROYAL ORCHID HOLIDAY.

Watching exquisite cotton and silk umbrellas being hand-painted in Chiang Mai. Lazing in the shade in sun-drenched Phuket. This s what holidaying in Thailand is all about. Book the holiday of your choice now, flying Thai. Smooth as silk. **Thai**

Simply travelling safely

American Express Travellers Cheques

- are recognised as one of the safest and most convenient ways to protect your money when travelling abroad

- are more widely accepted than any other travellers cheque brand

- are available in eleven currencies

- are supported by a 24 hour worldwide refund service and

- a 24 hour Express Helpline service provides assistance and information when travelling abroad

- are accepted in millions of shops, hotels and restaurants throughout the world

Travellers Cheques

CONTENTS

Getting Acquainted

The Place 338
Time Zones 338
Climate 338
Economy 338
Government 338

Planning the Trip

What to Bring 339
Electricity 339
What to Wear 339
Entry Regulations 339
Health 340
Currency 340
Public Holidays............341
Getting There 341
Special Facilities 342
Useful Addresses 343

Practical Tips

Emergencies 347
Medical Services 347
Weights & Measures ..348
Business Hours 348
Tipping.......................349
Media..........................349
Postal Services............349
Courier Service...........349
Telecommunications ..350

Getting Around

On Arrival 351
Domestic Travel 351
Public Transport 352
Private Transport 354
On Foot/Hitchhiking 355

Where to Stay

Bangkok......................356
Outside of Bangkok 359
Central Plains..............359
North and Northeast 359
Gulf Coast 360
Northern Isthmus 360
Ko Samui/Pha Ngan 360
Phuket 361
Krabi/Phang Nga 362
Deep South 362
Guesthouses 363

Eating Out

What to Eat 363
Where to Eat 363
Drinking Notes 369

Attractions

Leisure Pursuits 370
Sightseeing 370
Beaches.....................371
Trekking......................372
Nightlife 373

Culture

Culture 375
Museums 375
Art Galleries 376
Concerts 376
Theaters......................376
Movies 376
Libraries......................376
Bookstores 377

Festivals

Festivals & Fairs 377

Shopping

General 380
Export 380
Complaints..................380
Shopping Areas 380
Department Stores 382
What to Buy 383

Sport

Participant Sports 385
Spectator Sports 386

Language

Origins & Intonation 387
Thai Names 387
Phonology 387
Useful Phrases 388

Further Reading

General 388
History 388
People 389
Religion 389
Art and Culture............389
Natural History 389

Getting Acquainted

The Place

Lying between 7 degrees and 21 degrees latitude, Thailand has a total land area of 514,000 sq km (198,000 sq mi), nearly the size of France or twice as large as England. The country is said to resemble an elephant's head with its trunk forming the southern peninsula. Bangkok, its capital, is sited at its geographic center, approximately at the elephant's mouth. The country is bordered by Malaysia on the south, Burma on the west, Laos across the Mekong River to the northeast and Cambodia to the east.

The north is marked by low hills and contains the country's tallest peak, Doi Inthanon, standing 2,590 meters (8,500 ft) tall. A range of hills divides Thailand from Burma and forms the western boundary of the broad alluvial central plains, the country's principal rice-growing area. To the east, the plains rise to the Khorat Plateau, which covers much of the Northeast. The spine of the southern peninsula is the same range of hills that separates Thailand from Burma, sloping down to the Andaman Sea on the west and the Gulf of Thailand on the east. Thailand has a total of 2,600 km (1,600 mi) of coastline.

Bangkok is situated at 14 degrees north latitude. Bangkok is a city divided into halves by a river, the Chao Phraya, which separates central Bangkok and Thonburi. The city covers a total area of 1,565 sq km (605 sq mi) of delta land, of which no natural area is more than 2 meters (7 ft) above any other.

Chiang Mai lies 700 km (435 mi) north of Bangkok. It sits 300 meters (1,000 ft) above sea level,

and is crowned by Doi Suthep, which rises to a height of 1,675 meters (5,495 ft). The city is home to over 150,000 people.

Phuket, an island in the Andaman Sea, lies 890 km (550 mi) or a 70-minute flight south of Bangkok. Measuring 50 km (30 mi) long by 20 km (13 mi) wide, it is approximately the size of the city-state of Singapore.

Time Zones

Thailand Standard Time is 7 hours ahead of Universal Time (Greenwich Mean Time).

Climate

There are three seasons in Thailand: hot, rainy and cool. But to the tourist winging in from anywhere north or south of the 30th parallel, Thailand has only one temperature: hot. To make things worse, the temperature drops only a few degrees during the night and is accompanied 24 hours by humidity above 70 percent. Only air-conditioning makes Bangkok and other major towns tolerable during the hot season. The countryside is somewhat cooler, but, surprisingly, the northern regions can be hotter in March and April than Bangkok.

Hot season (March to mid-June), 27°–35°C (80°–95°F).
Rainy season (June to October), 24°–32°C (75°–90°F).
Cool season (November to February), 18°–32°C (65°–90°F), but with less humidity.

Adding together the yearly daytime highs and the nighttime lows for major world cities, the World Meteorological Organization has declared Bangkok to be the world's hottest city. When the monsoon rains fall, most of the country swelters.

Chiang Mai enjoys a cooler climate. In the cool season, temperatures range between 13° and 28°C (55° and 82°F) and are lower in the hills. Like Bangkok, the heaviest rain falls in September,

and some of the city streets are often flooded.

In Phuket, the monsoon begins in early May, but generally ends late in October. Temperatures range from 34°C (93°F) in the hot season to nighttime temperatures of 21°C (70°F) in the cool season. The water temperature never drops below 20°C (67°F).

Economy

Nearly 70 percent of Thailand's 60 million people are farmers who till alluvial land so rich that Thailand is a world leader in the export of tapioca (No. 1), rice (No. 2), rubber (No. 2), canned pineapple (No. 3), and is a top-ranked exporter of sugar, maize and tin. Increasingly, Thailand is turning to manufacturing, especially in clothing, machinery, and electronics.

Government

Thailand is a constitutional monarchy headed by His Majesty, King Bhumibol. The royalty's power has been reduced considerably from the period before the 1932 revolution. However, the present king can, by the force of his personality and moral authority, influence the direction of important decisions merely by a word or two.

Although he no longer rules as did the absolute monarchs of previous centuries, he is still regarded as one of the three pillars of the society – monarchy, religion and the nation. This concept is represented in the five-banded national flag of Thailand: the outer red bands symbolizing the nation; the inner white bands the purity of the Buddhist religion; and the thick blue band at the centre representing the monarchy.

His dedication over many years in working with farmers to improve their lands and yields has influenced others to follow his example in serving the people. Her Majesty Queen Sirikit and other members of the royal family have also been active in promoting the interests of Thais in the lower economic strata. Thus, the photographs of the king and queen hang in nearly every home, shop and office, placed there, not out of blind devotion, but out of genuine respect for the royal family.

The structure of the government is defined by the constitution and its enabling ordinances. A new constitution, designed to reform the political system, was passed in 1997. Despite its frequent revisions, the constitution has remained true to the spirit of the original aim of placing power in the hands of the people; the exercising of it, however, has often favored certain groups over others, especially the military, which has sometimes abused its power.

Modeled loosely on the British system, the Thai government consists of three branches: legislative, executive and judiciary, each acting independently of the others in a system of checks and balances. The legislative branch is composed of a senate and a house of representatives. The senate consists of 262 leading members of society, including business people, educators and a heavy preponderance of high-ranking military officers. They must be over 35 years of age and must not be members of political parties. Members are selected by the prime minister and approved by the king. The house of representatives comprises 391 members elected by popular vote from each of the 76 provinces of Thailand.

The executive branch is represented by a prime minister, who must be an elected member of parliament. He is selected by a single party or coalition of parties and rules through a cabinet of ministers, the exact number dependent on his own needs. They, in turn, implement their programs through the very powerful civil service. The judiciary consists of a supreme court, an appellate court, and a pyramid of provincial and lower courts. It acts independently to interpret points of law and counsels the other two branches on the appropriateness of actions.

Planning the Trip

What to Bring

Bangkok, Chiang Mai, Pattaya, and Phuket are modern destinations with most of the modern amenities found in similar places in Europe or North America.

Lip balm and moisturizers are needed in the north during the cool season. Sunglasses and hats are useful items to protect eyes and sensitive skin from tropical glare.

Electricity

Electrical outlets are rated at 220 volts, 50 cycles, and accept either flat-pronged or round-pronged plugs.

What to Wear

Clothes should be light and loose; natural blends that breathe are preferable to synthetics. Open shoes (sandals during the height of the rainy season, when some Bangkok streets get flooded) and sleeveless dresses for women or short-sleeved shirts for men are appropriate. Suits are worn for business and in many large hotels but, in general, Thailand lacks the formal dress code of Hong Kong or Tokyo. Casual but neat and clean clothes are suitable for most occasions. Some formality is needed for business appointments.

The cool season in the north can be chilly. A sweater or sweatshirt will be welcome, especially when traveling in the hills.

One exception is the clothing code for Buddhist temples and Muslim mosques. Shorts are taboo for both women and men wanting to enter some of the important temples. Those wearing sleeveless dresses may also be barred from certain temples. Improperly dressed and unkempt visitors will be turned away from large temples like the Wat Phra Kaeo (Temple of the Emerald Buddha) and from the Grand Palace. Dress properly in deference to the religion and to Thai sensitivities.

Entry Regulations

VISAS AND PASSPORTS

Travelers should check visa regulations at a Thai embassy or consulate before starting their journey. All foreign nationals entering Thailand must have valid passports. At the airport, nationals from most countries will be granted a free transit visa valid up to 15 days, provided that they have a fully-paid ticket out of Thailand.

Tourist visas allow for a 60-day stay from the date of entry into the kingdom. A 30-day transit visa may also be issued to some visitors. People who are waiting for a work permit to be issued can apply for a non-immigrant visa which is good for 90 days. A letter of guarantee is needed from the Thai company you intend to work for, and this visa can be obtained from a Thai embassy or consulate at home.

Visas can be extended before they expire by applying at the **Immigration Bureau** on Soi Suan Plu, Sathorn Tai Road, tel: 286 4231, 287 3101, ext. 2271. (8.30am–4pm, Monday–Friday.) Visitors wishing to leave Thailand and return before their visas have expired can apply for a re-entry permit prior to their departure at immigration offices in Bangkok, Chiang Mai, Pattaya, Phuket and Hat Yai. An exit visa is not required.

VISA EXTENSIONS

If planning a longer stay, a transit visa valid for 30 days or a tourist visa valid for 60 days must be obtained from a Thai embassy or consulate abroad by filing an application, supplying three passport-sized photographs and paying a fee. Visas can be extended by applying at the **Immigration**

Bureau on Soi Suan Plu (8.30am–4pm, Monday–Friday) before the visa's expiration date. There is a fee.

CUSTOMS

The Thai government prohibits the import of drugs, dangerous chemicals, pornography, firearms and ammunition. Attempting to smuggle heroin or other hard drugs may be punishable by death. Scores of foreigners are serving long prison terms in Thai jails for drug-related offenses.

Foreign tourists may freely bring in foreign banknotes or other types of foreign exchange. For travelers leaving Thailand, the maximum amount permitted to be taken out in Thai currency without prior authorization is 50,000 baht.

Foreign guests are allowed to import, without tax, one camera with five rolls of film, 200 cigarettes, and one liter of wine or alcoholic spirits.

Health

Visitors entering the kingdom are no longer required to show evidence of vaccination for smallpox or cholera, but immunization against cholera is still a good idea. Before you leave home, check that tetanus boosters are up to date. Malaria and dengue fever persist in the rural areas. When in the hills – especially in the monsoon season – tuck pants legs into socks to deter leeches, and apply mosquito repellent on exposed skin when the sun begins to set.

Most first-time visitors experience a degree of heat exhaustion and dehydration that can be avoided by drinking lots of bottled water and slightly increasing the amount of salt in the diet. Sunblock is essential.

AIDS is not confined to "high risk" sections of the population in Thailand, and visitors are at risk from casual sex if they do not use condoms. It is estimated that almost the entire population of prostitutes in the country are HIV positive.

HYGIENE

Thais place high value on personal hygiene and are aware of the dangers of germs and infections. They do not, however, place such a high priority on keeping the environment clean. Establishments catering to foreigners are generally careful with food and drink preparation and sanitation.

Bangkok water is clean when it leaves the modern filtration plant; the pipes that carry it into the city are somewhat less than new, however, and visitors are advised to drink bottled water or soft drinks. Both are produced under strict supervision, as is the ice used in large hotels and restaurants. Most streetside restaurants are clean; a quick glance should tell you which are and which are not.

PRECAUTIONS

With its thriving nightlife and transient population, Bangkok is a magnet for sexual diseases. The women (and men) in these service industries are aware of the consequences of carelessness and of not insisting that their partners take precautions, but economic necessity, coupled with a Thai reluctance to offend anyone, means that there is a great risk of taking home a souvenir one would rather not share with friends and loved ones. Assume that there is a good chance of picking something up and take appropriate measures. Some massage parlors, mindful of the dangers, now bar foreign patrons and cater only to Thais in the belief that they reduce their risks.

Malaria is still highly dangerous in some regions of Thailand. The best protection is to avoid being bitten. Mosquitoes are most active at night, between the hours of sundown and sunrise. After dark you should wear long trousers, long-sleeved shirts, shoes and socks or stockings. Hands and neck should be protected with an insect repellent, and you should sleep in rooms with adequate mosquito screens on the windows and under a mosquito net. If you decide to

protect yourself with anti-malarial tablets, remember that mosquitoes in many areas are resistant to many of the proprietary brands of medication. Seek advice from a tropical institute before your departure. Should you nonetheless contract malaria, there is a network of malaria centers and hospitals throughout Thailand. It is important to remember that the most dangerous form of malaria often appears disguised as a heavy cold. If you contract what appears to be influenza, you should consult a doctor immediately. This also applies during the weeks after your return from the tropics.

Currency

The *baht* is the principal Thai monetary unit. It is divided into 100 units called *satang*. Banknote denominations include 1,000 (gray), 500 (purple), 100 (red), 50 (blue), 20 (green) and 10 (brown) baht.

While the banknotes are easy to decipher, the coinage is a confusing matter with a variety of sizes and types for each denomination. There are 10-baht coins (brass centre with a silver rim), two different 5-baht coins (silver pieces with copper rims), three varieties of 1-baht coin (silver; usually only the small-size will fit in a public telephone), and two small coins of 50 and 25 satang (both are brass-coloured).

EXCHANGE RATES

The once-stable Thai currency was devalued in mid-1997. Since then, the exchange rate, which for years had hovered at 25 baht to the US dollar, has risen to an average of around 35 to 45 baht to the dollar. There is no currency black market.

BANKING SYSTEM

Thailand has a sophisticated banking system with representation by the major banks of most foreign countries. Money can be imported in cash or traveler's checks and converted into baht. It is also possible to arrange telex bank drafts from one's hometown bank. There is no minimum requirement on the amount of money that must be converted. Both cash and traveler's checks can be changed in hundreds of bank branches throughout the city; rates are more favorable for traveler's checks than for cash. Banking hours are 10am–4pm, Monday–Friday, although some banks near major tourist areas maintain longer operating hours for foreign exchange. Hotels generally give poor exchange rates in comparison with banks.

ATM/DEBIT CARDS

Most banks now have ATM machines, usually outside the bank proper and accessible around the clock. Currency is dispensed in baht only. Note, however, that many banks only accept ATM cards linked directly to Thai bank accounts; for those with ATM cards on the Plus or Cirrus networks who wish to withdraw funds directly from their home bank accounts, Hongkong and Bangkok banks are good bets.

Occasionally, an ATM card may not work at one machine for some unspecified reason; try another branch of the same bank and results may be different. Alternatively, MasterCard and Visa debit cards (as distinct from credit cards; with debit cards, the money is withdrawn immediately from an associated bank account) are also accepted at many ATM machines. Most banks have signs with an array of symbols indicating which cards are accepted at the machine. Periodically, cards are accepted at machines in spite of the fact that no related sign appears out front. When in doubt, give it a try, but be prepared to be flexible.

CREDIT CARDS

American Express, Diners Club, MasterCard and Visa are widely accepted throughout Bangkok. In provincial destinations, it is better to check that plastic is accepted, and not to count on using cards.

Credit Card Warning: Credit card fraud is a major problem in Thailand. Do not leave credit cards in safe deposit boxes. Notification of loss of credit cards can be made at the following offices:

Bangkok
American Express, 388 Phaholyothin Road. Tel: 273 0033 (customer service), 273 0022 (24-hour emergency), fax: 273 0464. Open 8.30am–5pm Monday–Friday. **Diners Club**, Silom Complex, 12th Floor, 191 Silom Road. Tel: 238 3660, fax: 231 3550. Open 8.30am–5pm, Monday–Friday. **Visa Centre**, Bldg. One, 11th Floor, 99/38 Witthayu Road. Tel: 256 7324/9, fax: 256 7151. **MasterCard International**, Sermmitr Tower, 11th Floor, Soi 21 (Soi Asoke), Sukhumvit Road. Tel: 260 8572/3, fax: 260 8574.

Chiang Mai
American Express, Bangkok Bank, 2/3 Prachasampan Road. Tel: 276 816. **Visa and MasterCard**, Thai Farmers Bank, Ta Pae Road. Tel: 270 151. Hours: 8.30am–3.30pm Monday–Friday.

Phuket
American Express, 95/4 Phuket Road. Tel: 218 887. **Visa and MasterCard**, contact any branch of Thai Farmers Bank or Bangkok Bank.

Public Holidays

The following dates are observed as official public holidays:
New Year's Day January 1
Magha Puja February (full moon)
Chakri Day April 6
Songkran (Thai New Year) April 13–15
Labor Day May 1
Coronation Day May 5
Ploughing Ceremony May (variable)
Visakha Puja May (full moon)
Asalaha Puja July (full moon)
Khao Phansa July
Queen's Birthday August 12
Chulalongkorn Day October 23
King's Birthday December 5
Constitution Day December 10
New Year's Eve December 31
Chinese New Year in February is not an official public holiday, but many businesses are closed for several days.

Getting There

BY AIR
Bangkok is a gateway between east and west and a transportation hub for Southeast Asia served by most of the major airlines. In addition to Bangkok, Thailand has three other international airports: Chiang Mai, Phuket and Hat Yai.

Thai Airways International flies to more than 50 cities on four continents. The flying time from the UK is about 12 hours, from the west coast of America, about 21 hours. Flights from Australia and New Zealand take about 9 hours.

BY SEA
The days when travelers sailed up the Chao Phraya River to view the golden spires of Bangkok are long gone. Luxury liners now call at Pattaya and Phuket but have ceased serving Bangkok. Check with a travel agent or shipping company to find those which depart from your city.

A regular cruise ship, *Andaman Princess*, operates between Bangkok and Singapore. Details from Siam Cruise Co., Bangkok. Tel: 255 8950, fax: 255 8961.

BY RAIL
Trains operated by the State Railways of Thailand are clean, cheap and reliable, albeit a little slow. There are only two railroad entry points into Thailand, both from Malaysia on the southern Thai border. The trip north to Bangkok serves as a scenic introduction to southern Thailand.

The *Malay Mail* leaves Kuala Lumpur every day at 7.30am, 8.15am, 3pm, 8.30pm and 10pm, arriving 7 to 9 hours later at Butterworth, the port opposite Malaysia's Penang Island, at 1.35pm, 5.50pm, 9.10pm, 5.30am and 6.40am respectively. A daily train leaves Butterworth at 1.40pm, crossing the border into Thailand and arriving in Bangkok at 9.30 the next morning. There are second-class cars with seats which are made into upper and lower sleeping berths at night. There are also air-conditioned first-class sleepers and dining cars serving Thai food. Prices from Butterworth to Bangkok are US$50 or less, depending upon class of service.

Trains leave Bangkok's Hua Lampong Station daily at 3.15pm for the return journey to Malaysia. A second, somewhat less convenient but more entertaining, train travels from Kuala Lumpur up Malaysia's east coast to the northeastern town of Kota Bahru. Take a taxi across the border to catch the SRT train from the southern Thai town of Sungai Kolok. Trains leave Sungai Kolok at noon and 3pm, arriving in Bangkok at 8.35am and 10.35am the following day.

If you like to travel in style and prefer not to fly, the Eastern & Oriental Express (Tel: 251 4862) is Asia's most exclusive travel experience. Traveling several times a month between Singapore, Kuala Lumpur and Bangkok, the 22-carriage train with its distinctive green-and-cream livery passes through spectacular scenery. It's very expensive, but classically elegant and high-brow.

BY ROAD

Malaysia provides the main road access into Thailand, with crossings near Betong and Sungai Kolok. It is possible to cross to and from Laos from Nong Khai by using the Friendship Bridge across the Mekong River. Visitors need visas. Drivers will find that most Thai roads are modern, paved and usually well maintained.

Special Facilities

LEFT LUGGAGE

There are two left luggage facilities at Don Muang International Airport. One is on the 1st floor on the northern end of the arrival hall after passing through customs. The second is in the departure hall on the 3rd floor near the currency exchange counter. The fee is 20 baht (US$0.60) per bag per day.

RESERVATIONS

Hotel reservations can be made in the airport arrival lounge once you have passed through customs. It is recommended that you book a room in advance during the Christmas-New Year and Chinese New Year holidays and, for destinations outside of Bangkok, during Songkran in mid-April.

CHILDREN

Children may enjoy the unusual animals of **Dusit Zoo** (Ratchawithi Road, off Rama V Road), or paddling boats in the lake at the zoo, or in **Lumpini** or **Chatuchak Parks**. Miniature golf is available at **Yama's Golf Course**, Si Nakharin Road, tel: 721 8888, daily 10am–9pm. **Safari World**, Thailand's only drive-through wildlife park, is at 99 Ramindra Road, Minburi (40 km (25 mi) east of Bangkok). Tel: 518 1000/19. Daily 9am–7pm. In addition to elephants, lions, giraffes and other mammals, look for dolphin and sea lion shows at **Marine Park** and white pandas at the **Panda House**. An exciting day out for the whole family. Alternatively, an afternoon at one of Bangkok's many amusement parks is guaranteed fun.

Adventureland, Seacon Square, 904 Si Nakharin Road. Tel: 721 8888/96. Weekdays: 11am–9pm, weekends: 10am–10pm. Upside-down roller coaster, go-karts, roller blade rink.

Dream World, Nakhon Nayok Road, Rangsit (north of Don Muang Airport). Tel: 533 1152. Weekdays: 10am–5pm, weekends: 10am–7pm. Four different themes, largest water log slide in Asia.

Magic Land, 72 Phaholyothin Road (near Central Plaza). Tel: 513 1731. Weekdays: 10am–5.30pm, weekends: 10am–7pm. Ghost house, roller coasters, ferris wheels.

Siam Park, 101 Sukhapiban 2 Road, Minburi (east of Bangkok). Tel: 517 0075. Weekdays: 10am–4pm, weekends: 9am–9pm. Amusement park and water park, also a small zoo. Note: The park

prohibits the wearing of T-shirts in the swimming areas, so take plenty of suntan oil for tender young skins.

In Pattaya children may enjoy a day at **Water World** at the Pattaya Park Beach Resort or a visit to **Ripley's Believe It or Not** museum at the Royal Garden Plaza. In Phuket head for the **Crocodile Farm and Elephant Land** on Chana Charoen Road. Shows are held at 11am and 3.30pm daily.

GAYS

Gays quickly discover that Thailand is one of the most tolerant countries in the world. In Bangkok, most of the gay bars are on Soi Patpong 3 or the upper end of Silom Road. Transvestites and transvestite shows are common in Bangkok, and also in both Pattaya and Phuket.

DISABLED

To say that facilities for the handicapped in Thailand, even in Bangkok, are underdeveloped is something of an understatement. Sidewalks are uneven, riddled with potholes and studded with obstructions; ramps are non-existent. (It's no accident that on many street corners sit cobblers repairing damaged shoes.) Crossing major streets in Bangkok without making use of the pedestrian bridges (steep flights of stairs on either side of the street linked by an overhead walkway) is to court disaster, even for the non-disabled. Few buildings in Bangkok have ramps, although the various hotels throughout Thailand in the Holiday Inn, Hyatt International, Novotel and Sheraton chains are wheelchair-accessible. While there is no taxi service specifically geared towards the disabled, and ordinary taxis often do not have enough storage room for a wheelchair, some of the newer taxis are modified station wagons with ample room in the back. Hiring a private car, however, may be the most reliable alternative.

In spite of this disheartening picture, disabled travelers can visit and enjoy the wonders of Thailand. Forethought and flexibility are key.

Some organizations to contact for further information include:

Association of the Physically Handicapped of Thailand, 73/7-8 Soi 8, Tivanon Road, Talaat Kawan, Nonthaburi 11000. Tel: (2) 951 0569.

Mobility International, Post Office Box 10767, Eugene, OR 97440. Tel: (541) 343 1284.

Society for the Advancement of Travel for the Handicapped, 26 Court Street, Brooklyn, NY 11242. Tel: (718) 858 5483.

Useful Addresses

DOING BUSINESS

Most hotels have business centers with communications and secretarial services in several languages. Elsewhere in Bangkok, it is possible to lease small offices with clerical staff.

Chambers of Commerce

American, Kian Gwan House, 140 Witthayu Road. Tel: 251 1605, 251 9266, fax: 651 4474. Open 7.30am– noon, 1.30–3.30pm Monday–Friday.

British, 54 Soi 21 (Soi Asoke), Sukhumvit Road. Tel: 260 7288/9, fax: 260 7287. Open 8am–noon, 1–4.30pm, Monday–Friday.

Franco-Thai, Richmond Tower, 10th Floor, Soi 26, Sukhumvit Road. Tel: 261 8276, fax: 261 8278. Open 9am–noon, 1–6pm, Monday–Friday.

German-Thai, Klongboonma Bldg., 4th Floor, 699 Silom Road. Tel: 266 4924/5, fax: 236 4711. Open 8am–4pm, Monday–Friday.

Thai-Canadian, CP Tower, 19th Floor, 313 Silom Road. Tel: 231 0981/2, fax: 231 0893. Hours: 8am–4pm.

SPECIAL CLUBS

Alliance Francaise, 29 Sathorn Tai Road. Tel: 213 2122/3, fax: 213 2064. Open 8am–6.30pm, Monday–Friday; 8.30am–1.30pm, Saturday. Library, bookshop and cafeteria; open to all. In Chiang Mai: 138 Charoen Prathet Road. Tel: 275 277.

American University Alumni (AUA), 179 Ratchadamri Road. Tel: 252

8170/3. Library open to non-members. American films, monthly newsletter, cafeteria. In Chiang Mai: 24 Ratchadamnern Road. Tel: 211 973, 278 407.

Bangkok Cosmopolitan Lions Club, 10 Soi Soonvijai, New Phetburi Road. Tel: 318 1518. Meetings on the last Thursday of the month. Foreign members welcome.

British Council, 254 Chulalongkorn Soi 64, Siam Square, Rama I Road. Tel: 252 6136, 252 6111. Open 8.30am–4pm, Monday–Friday. Library open to members only. British films, monthly newsletter. In Chiang Mai: 198 Bamrungrat Road. Tel: 242 103.

Foreign Correspondents Club of Thailand, Maneeya Centre, 518/5 Ploenchit Road (next to Amarin Plaza). Tel: 652 0580. Non-members may browse in the small library with the purchase of something at the bar or restaurant.

Goethe Institut, 18/1 Soi Ngam Duphli, Rama IV Road. Tel: 287 0942/4. Open 8am–5pm, Monday–Friday; and from 8am–12.30pm on Saturday. German films, restaurant, monthly newsletter. Open to all.

Rotary Club, Bangkok Rotary, Grand Hyatt Erawan Hotel. Tel: 254 1234. Foreign members welcome; English is the medium.

TOURIST OFFICES

Planning a trip to Thailand can be made easier if you contact a travel agent or an office of the **Tourism Authority of Thailand** (**TAT**), the Thai government's official tourism promotion organization. These offices offer promotional brochures, maps and videotapes of the country's many attractions. The head office at 372 Bamrung Muang Road (Tel: 226 0060, 226 0085, fax: 226 0072) will provide you with essential tourist information; for a more complete service, the information office, at 4 Ratchadamnern Nok Avenue (Tel: 282 9775/6), has a wealth of brochures on various attractions and personnel to answer questions.

TAT has its own travel information site on the Internet: www.cs.ait.ac.th/tat/. The TAT's e-

mail address for sending inquiries is tat@cs.ait.ac.th.

Below are some of the offices of the Tourism Authority of Thailand.

Asia and the Pacific

Australia: Royal Exchange Bldg., 7th Floor, 56 Pitt St, Sydney 2000. Tel: (02) 247 7549, fax: (02) 251 2465.

Hong Kong: Room 401, Fairmont House, 8 Cotton Tree Drive, Central. Tel: (852) 868 0732, 868 0854, fax: (852) 868 4585.

Japan: Hibiya Mitsui Bldg., 1-2, Yurakucho 1-chome, Chiyoda-ku, Tokyo 100, tel: (03) 358 06776/7, fax: (03) 358 07808; Hirano-machi Yachiyo Bldg., 5th Floor, 1-8-13 Hiranomachi Chuo-ku, Osaka 541, tel: (06) 231 4434, fax: (06) 231 4337; Hakata Pal Bldg., 2nd Floor, 2-63 Gokushu-machi, Hakata-ku, Fukuoka 812, tel: (092) 262 3031, fax: (092) 262 3032.

Malaysia: c/o Royal Thai Embassy, 206 Jalan Ampang, Kuala Lumpur. Tel: (093) 248 0958, 248 6529, fax: (093) 241 3002.

Singapore: c/o Royal Thai Embassy, 370 Orchard Road, Singapore 0923. Tel: (65) 235 7694, 235 7901, 733 6723, fax: 733 5653.

South Korea: Room 2003, 20th Floor, Coryo Daeyungak Centre Bldg., 25-5, 1-ka. Chungmu-ro, Chung-ku, Seoul. Tel: (02) 779 5417, fax: (02) 779 5419.

Taiwan: Thailand Trade and Economic Office, 2B Central Commercial Bldg., 16-18 Nanking East Road, Section 4, Taipei. Tel: (02) 579 6111, fax: (02) 577 9914.

Europe

France: 90 Avenue des Champs-Elysees, 75008 Paris. Tel: (01) 4562 8656, 4562 8748, fax: (01) 4563 7888.

Italy: Ente Nazionale per il Tourismo-Thailandese, Via Barberini 50 00187, Rome. Tel: (06) 487 3479, 481 8927, fax: 487 3500.

England: 49 Albemarle St, London WIX 3FE. Tel: (171) 499 7670/9, fax: (171) 629 5519.

Germany: Bethmannstr, 58/IV., D-6000, Frankfurt/M.I. Tel: (069) 295 704, 295 804, fax: (69) 281 468.

USA

Chicago: 303 East Wacker Drive, Suite 400, Chicago, IL 60601. Tel: (312) 819 3990/5, fax: (312) 565 0359.

New York: 5 World Trade Centre, Suite 2449, New York, NY 10048. Tel: (212) 432 0433, 432 0435, fax: (212) 912 0920.

Los Angeles: 3440 Wilshire Blvd, Suite 1101, Los Angeles, CA 90010. Tel: (213) 382 2353/5, fax: (213) 389 7544.

Thailand

Bangkok: 372 Bamrung Muang Road. Tel: 226 0060, 226 0085, fax: 226 0072.

Ayutthaya: Si Sanphet Road. Tel: (035) 246 076/7, fax: 246 078.

Cha-am: 500/51 Phetkasem Road. Tel: (032) 471 005/6, fax: (032) 471 502.

Chiang Mai: 105/1 Chiang Mai-Lamphun Road. Tel: (053) 248 604, 248 607, fax: (053) 248 605.

Chiang Rai: 448/16 Singhakhlai Road. Tel: (053) 717 433, fax: (053) 717 434.

Hat Yai: 1/1 Soi 2 Niphat Uthit 3 Road. Tel: (074) 243 747, 238 518, 231 055, fax: (074) 245 986.

Kanchanaburi: Saeng Chuto Road. Tel: (034) 511 200, fax: 511 200.

Khon Kaen: 15/5 Prachasamosorn Road. Tel: (043) 244 498/9, fax: (043) 244 497.

Krabi: Uttarikit Road, opp. Thai Farmers Bank. Tel: (075) 612 740.

Lopburi: H.M. The Queen's Celebration Building, c/o Lopburi Provincial Hall, Narai Mahart Road. Tel: (036) 422 768, fax: 422 769.

Nakhon Nayok: 084/23 Suwannason Road. Tel: (037) 312 282, 312 284, fax: (037) 312 286.

Nakhon Phanom: 184/1 Sunthornvichit Road. Tel: (042) 513 490/1, fax: (042) 513 492.

Nakhon Ratchasima: 2102-2104 Mittraphap Road. Tel: (044) 213 666, fax: (044) 213 667.

Nakhon Si Thammarat: Sanam Na Muang, Ratchadamnern Road. Tel: (075) 346 515/6, fax: 346 517.

Pattaya: 246/1 Moo 9, Beach Road, Pattaya. Tel: (038) 428 750, 427 667, fax: (038) 429 113.

Phitsanulok: 209/7-8 Surasi Trade Centre, Boromtrailokanat Road. Tel: (055) 252 743, fax: 252 742.

Phuket: 73-75 Phuket Road. Tel: (076) 212 213, 211 036, fax: (076) 213 582.

Rayong: 153/4 Sukhumvit Road. Tel: (038) 655 420/1, fax: (038) 655 422.

Surat Thani: 5 Talat Mai Road, Ban Don. Tel: (077) 281 828, fax: (077) 282 828.

Trat: 100 Moo 1, Trat, Laem Ngop Road, Laem Ngop District, Trat (opp. pier at Laem Ngop). Tel: (039) 597 255, 597 259/60, fax: (039) 597 255.

Ubon Ratchathani: 264/1 Khuan Thani Road. Tel: (045) 243 770, fax: (045) 243 771.

Udon Thani: 16/5 Mukkhamontri Road. Tel: (042) 325 406/7, fax: (042) 325 408.

WEB SITES

www.tat.or.th: Tourism Authority of Thailand.

www.thnic.net: Thailand Network Information Centre provides a list of Thailand's major web servers.

www.asiaaccess.net.th/citymap: an interactive map library.

www.bkk.post.co.th: *Bangkok Post*.

www.bkkmetro.com: *Bangkok Metro* magazine.

www.khonkaen.com: Everything you need to know about Khon Kaen, including accommodation, entertainment, events, maps, weather forecast. Excellent links to other parts of the country.

www.kohphangan.com: Sponsored by the merchants and resort operators on Ko Pha Ngan.

www.mahidol.ac.th: Mahidol University.

www.samart.co.th/hps: Although based in Thailand, this site is a directory of New Age information and alternative health care on offer throughout Southeast Asia.

utopia-asia.com: Regional information relevant to gays and lesbians, many hits, voted a "cool site" by Yahoo.

AIRLINE OFFICES

Bangkok

Air France, Vorawat Bldg., 20th Floor, 849 Silom Road. Tel: 635 1199 (reservations & ticketing), fax: 635 1204; airport: 523 7302, 535 2112/3.

Air India, c/o S.S. Travel Service, SS Bldg., 10/12-13 Convent Road. Tel: 235 0557, 236 7188 (reservations & ticketing), fax: 631 0340; airport: 535 2121.

Air Lanka, Charn Issara Tower, 6th Floor, 942/34-35 Rama IV Road. Tel: 236 0159, 236 9292/3 (reservations & ticketing), fax: 236 7617; airport: 535 2331/2.

Air New Zealand, 1053 Charoen Krung (New) Road. Tel: 237 1560 (reservations & ticketing), fax: 267 0300; airport: 535 3981/2.

Alitalia, Boonmitr Bldg., 8th Floor, 138 Silom Road. Tel: 233 4000 (reservations & ticketing), fax: 237 6454; airport: 535 2602.

All Nippon Airways, C.P. Towers, 2nd Floor, 313 Silom Road. Tel: 238 5121 (reservations), 238 5141 (ticketing), fax: 238 5137; airport: 531 8899, 535 2037.

Bangkok Airways, Queen Sirikit National Convention Centre, New Ratchadapisek Road. Tel: 229 3456 (reservations), 229 3434 (ticketing), fax: 229 3454; airport: 535 2497/8; email: bkkair@loxinfo.co.th.

British Airways, Abdulrahim Place, 14th Floor, 990 Rama IV Road. Tel: 636 1747 (reservations), 636 1770 (ticketing), fax: 636 1749 (reservations), 636 1748 (ticketing); airport: 535 2220.

Canadian Airlines International, Maneeya Bldg., 6th Floor, 518/5 Ploenchit Road. Tel: 251 4521 (reservations), 255 5862 (ticketing), fax: 254 8376; airport: 535 2227/9.

Cathay Pacific, Ploenchit Tower, 11th Floor, 898 Ploenchit Road. Tel: 263 0606 (reservations), 263 0616 (ticketing), fax: 263 0622 (reservations), 263 0631 (ticketing); airport: 535 2155/6.

China Airlines, Peninsula Plaza, 4th Floor, 153 Ratchadamri Road. Tel: 253 4242 (reservations), 253

5733 (ticketing), fax: 253 4791; airport: 535 2366, 535 2466.
Dragonair, 37/52 Montri Road, Phuket. Tel: (76) 215 734, 217 300/1, fax: 217 299.
Garuda Indonesia, Lumpini Tower, 27th Floor, Rama IV Road (opp. Lumpini Boxing Stadium). Tel: 285 6470/3, 679 7371/2 (reservations & ticketing), fax: 285 6474; airport: 535 2171.
Japan Airlines, JAL Bldg., 254/1 Ratchadapisek Road. Tel: 692 5151 (reservations), 692 5185 (ticketing), fax: 274 1410 (reservations), 274 1460 (ticketing); airport: 535 2135/6.
KLM, Thai Wah Tower II, 19th Floor, Sathorn Tai Road. Tel: 679 1100 (reservations & ticketing), fax: 679 1415; airport: 535 2191.
Korean Air, Klongboonma Bldg., 699 Silom Road. Tel: 635 0465/72 (reservations & ticketing), fax: 267 0992; airport: 523 7320.
Lao Aviation, Silom Plaza, Ground Floor, 491/17 Silom Road. Tel: 236 9822/3, 237 7139 (reservations & ticketing), fax: 236 9821; airport: 535 3786.
Lufthansa, Q House Bldg., 18th Floor, Soi 21, Sukhumvit Road. Tel: 264 2400 (reservations), 264 2401 (ticketing), fax: 264 2399; airport: 535 2211.
Malaysia Airlines, Ploenchit Tower, 20th Floor, 898 Ploenchit Road. Tel: 263 0565/71 (reservations), 263 0520/9 (ticketing), fax: 263 0577 (reservations), 263 0576 (ticketing); airport: 535 3781, 535 3679.
Myanmar Airways, Jewelry Trade Centre, 23rd Floor, Unit H1, 919/298 Silom Road. Tel: 630 0334/8 (reservations & ticketing), fax: 630 0339; airport: 523 7420, 535 2484.
Northwest Airlines, Peninsula Plaza, 4th Floor, 153 Ratchadamri Road. Tel: 254 0789 (reservations), 254 0771 (ticketing), fax: 254 0741; airport: 535 2413.
Orient Thai Airlines (domestic), Jewelry Centre, 17th Floor, 138/70 Nares Road. Tel: 267 3210/4 (reservations & ticketing), fax: 267 3216; airport: 535 2021.

Pakistan International, Chongkolnee Bldg., 2nd Floor, 56 Suriwongse Road. Tel: 234 2961/5 (reservations & ticketing), fax: 234 2357; airport: 535 2127/9.
Philippine Airlines, Chongkolnee Bldg., 1st Floor, 56 Suriwongse Road. Tel: 233 2350/2 (reservations & ticketing), fax: 234 8455; airport: 531 1021.
Qantas, Abdulrahim Place, 14th Floor, 990 Rama IV Road. Tel: 636 1747 (reservations), 636 1770 (ticketing), fax: 636 1749 (reservations), 636 1748 (ticketing); airport: 535 2220.
Royal Brunei, Charn Issara Tower, 20th Floor, 942/135 Rama IV Road. Tel: 233 0056, 233 0293 (reservations & ticketing), fax: 267 5036; airport: 535 2627.
Royal Air Cambodge (Cambodia), Two Pacific Place Bldg., 17th Floor, Room 1706, 142 Sukhumvit Road. Tel: 653 2261/6 (reservations & ticketing), fax: 653 2267; airport: 535 3781.
SAS, Glas Haus Bldg., 8th Floor, Soi 25, Sukhumvit Road. Tel: 260 0444 (reservations & ticketing), fax: 260 6269; airport: 535 2716.
Singapore Airlines, Silom Centre Bldg., 12th Floor, 2 Silom Road. Tel: 236 0440 (reservations & ticketing), fax: 236 5294; airport: 535 2260.
Swiss Air, Abdulrahim Place, 21st Floor, 990 Rama IV Road. Tel: 636 2160/5 (reservations & ticketing), fax: 636 2168; airport: 535 2371/2.
Thai Airways, head office: 89 Vibhavadi Rangsit Road, tel: 513 0121 (general), 545 1175/6, 280 0060 (reservations), 545 3691 (ticketing), fax: 628 0111 (reservations), 691 5007 (ticketing); Larnluang branch office: 6 Larnluang Road, tel: 280 0100, 280 0119 (general), 628 2000 (reservations), 280 0119, ext. 1766 (ticketing); fax: 628 2486, 628 0111 (reservations), 280 1748 (ticketing); Silom branch office: 485 Silom Road, tel: 234 3100/19 (general), 628 2000 (reservations), 266 8307 (ticketing), fax: 628 0111 (reservations), 237 4114

(ticketing); airport: 535 4646/8 (domestic), 535 2836/7 (international).
United Airlines, Regent House, 19th Floor, 183 Ratchadamri Road. Tel: 253 0558 (reservations), 253 0559 (ticketing), fax: 251 4406; airport: 535 2231/2.
Vietnam Airlines, Ploenchit Centre Bldg., Soi 2, Sukhumvit Road. Tel: 656 9056/8 (reservations & ticketing), fax: 656 9101; airport: 535 2671, 535 5327.

Chiang Mai
Thai Airways, 240 Phra Poklao Road. Tel: (53) 211 541, 210 042.

Phuket
Bangkok Airways, 158/2-3 Yaowarat Road. Tel: 225 033/5, 212 341.
China Airlines, 59/29 Bangkok Road. Tel: 223 939/40.
Dragonair, 37/52 Montri Road. Tel: 217 300/1.
Malaysian Airlines, 1/8-9 Tungka Road. Tel: 216 675, 213 749.
Silk Air, 183/10 Phangnga Road. Tel: 213 891, 213 895.
Thai Airways, 78 Ranong Road. Tel: 212 946, 216 755, 216 678.

EMBASSIES

Australia, 37 Sathorn Tai Road. Tel: 287 2680. Visas: 8am–12.30pm.
Austria, 14 Soi Nantha, Sathorn Tai Road. Tel: 287 3970/2. Visas: 9am–noon.
Belgium, 44 Soi Pipat, off Silom Road. Tel: 236 0150. Visas: 8am–noon.
Brunei, 154 Soi 14, Soi 63 (Soi Ekamai), Sukhumvit Road. Tel: 381 5914/6, fax: 381 5921. Visas: 8.30–11.30am.
Burma, 132 Sathorn Nua Road. Tel: 233 2237, 234 4698. Visas: 8.30am–noon.
Canada, Boonmitr Bldg., 11th Floor, 138 Silom Road. Tel: 237 4126. Visas: 8–11am.
China, 57 Ratchadapisek Road. Tel: 245 7032, 245 7044, 247 7554, fax: 246 8247. Visas: 9am–noon.
Denmark, 10 Soi 1 (Soi Atthakan Prasit), Sathorn Tai Road. Tel: 213 2021/5. Visas: 9am–1pm (Friday: 9am–noon).

France, 35 Soi 36 (Soi Rong Phasi Kao), Charoen Krung (New) Road. Tel: 266 8250. Visas: 8.30am–noon, issued by Consular Section, 29 Sathorn Tai Road. Tel: 287 2585/7.

Germany, 9 Sathorn Tai Road. Tel: 287 9000, fax: 287 1776. Visas: 8–11am.

Indonesia, 600 Phetburi Road. Tel: 252 3135/40. Visas: 8am–4pm.

Israel, Ocean Tower II, 25th Floor, 75 Soi 19, Sukhumvit Road. Tel: 260 4854/9, fax: 260 4860. Visas: 8am–noon.

Italy, 399 Nang Linchi Road. Tel: 285 4090, fax: 285 4793. Visas: 8.30–11.30am.

Korea (South), 23 Thiam Ruam Mit Road, off Ratchadapisek Road (near Thai Cultural Centre). Tel: 247 7537/9. Visas: 8.30am–noon and 1.30–4.30pm.

Laos, 520 and 502/1-3 Soi 39, Ramkhamhaeng Road. Tel: 539 6667, fax: 539 6678. Visas: 9am–4pm.

Malaysia, Regent House, 183 Ratchadamri Road. Tel: 254 1706; fax: 253 8970. Visas: 8.30–11.30am.

Netherlands, 106 Witthayu Road. Tel: 254 7701/5. Visas: 9am–noon.

New Zealand, 93 Witthayu Road. Tel: 254 2530. Visas: 8am–noon.

Pakistan, 31 Soi 3 (Soi Nana Nua), Sukhumvit Road. Tel: 253 0288/90. Visas: 9am–noon.

Philippines, 760 Sukhumvit Road (opposite Soi 47). Tel: 259 0139/40. Visas: 9am–4pm.

Singapore, 129 Sathorn Tai Road. Tel: 286 2111, 286 1434. Visas: 9am–noon.

Sri Lanka, Ocean Tower II, 13th Floor, Soi 19, Sukhumvit Road. Tel: 261 1934/8. Visas: 8.30am–noon.

Switzerland, 35 Witthayu Road. Tel: 253 0156/60. Visas: 9am–noon.

United Kingdom, 1031 Witthayu Road. Tel: 253 0191/9. Visas: 8–11am, (Friday: 8am–noon).

United States, 120/122 Witthayu Road. Tel 205 4000. Visas: 7am–3pm.

Vietnam, 83/1 Witthayu Road. Tel: 251 5836, 251 5838, fax: 251 7203, 254 4730. Visas: 8.30–11am and 1.30–4pm.

BANKS

Bangkok

Banks in Bangkok include Thai institutions as well as branches of foreign banks. Most are equipped to handle telegraph and telex money transfers and a wide range of money services. In the provinces, the services are much more restricted. If you have overseas business to conduct with a bank, it is better to do it in Bangkok.

Thai Banks

Bank of Asia, 191 Sathorn Tai Road. Tel: 287 2211/3, fax: 287 2973/4.

Bank of Ayutthaya, 550 Ploenchit Road. Tel: 255 0022, 255 0033.

Bangkok Bank, 333 Silom Road. Tel: 231 4333.

First Bangkok City Bank, 20 Yukon Road. Tel: 223 0501, fax: 255 3036.

Krung Thai Bank, 35 Sukhumvit Road. Tel: 255 2222, fax: 255 9391.

Siam City Bank, 1101 New Phetburi Road. Tel: 253 0200/9, fax: 208 5489.

Siam Commercial Bank, 9 Ratchadapisek Road. Tel: 256 1234.

Thai Farmers Bank, 400 Phaholyothin Road. Tel: 470 1122.

Thai Military Bank, 3000 Phaholyothin Road. Tel: 299 1111, fax: 273 7121/4.

Overseas Banks

Bank of America, 2/2 Witthayu Road. Tel: 251 6333, fax: 253 1905.

Bank of Tokyo, Harindhorn Tower, 2nd Floor, 54 Sathorn Nua Road. Tel: 266 3011, fax: 266 3055.

Banque Indosuez, 152 Witthayu Road. Tel: 651 4590/2, fax: 651 4574.

Banque Nationale de Paris, Dusit Thani Bldg., 5th Floor, 946 Rama IV Road. Tel: 651 5678/84.

Chase Manhattan Bank, Bubhajit Bldg., 2nd Floor, 20 Sathorn Nua Road. Tel: 234 5992/5, 238 1720/4, fax: 234 8386.

Citibank, 82 Sathorn Nua Road. Tel: 232 2484, fax: 639 2560.

Deutsche Bank, 208 Witthayu Rd. Tel: 651 5000, fax: 651 5151.

Hongkong Bank, Hongkong Bank Bldg., 64 Silom Road. Tel: 233 5995, fax: 236 7687.

Sakura Bank, Boonmitr Bldg., 1st Floor, 138 Silom Road. Tel: 234 3841/8, fax: 236 8920, 634 2383.

Standard Chartered Bank, 990 Rama IV Road. Tel: 636 1000, fax: 636 1198.

Chiang Mai

Bangkok Bank, 53-59 Ta Pae Road. Tel: 272 938. Kiosk open 8.30am–8.30pm.

Bank of Asia, 149/1-3 Chang Klan Road. Tel: 270 029/30. Kiosk open 8.30am–8pm.

Bank of Ayutthaya, 222-6 Ta Pae Road. Tel: 252 446, 252 441. Kiosk open 8.30am–8pm.

Krung Thai Bank, 298/1 Ta Pae Road. Tel: 214 696, 225 738. Kiosk open 8.30am–4.30pm.

Siam Commercial Bank, 17 Ta Pae Road. Tel: 273 171, 274 520. Kiosk open 8.30am–7pm.

Thai Farmers Bank, 194, Chotana Road. Tel: 222 897. Kiosk open 8.30am–6pm.

Thai Military Bank, 207 Chang Moi Road. Tel: 251 058/9. Kiosk open 8.30am–6pm.

Phuket

Bangkok Bank, 22 Phangnga Road. Tel: 211 292/5.

Bank of Ayutthaya, 64 Rasda Road. Tel: 211 577.

Siam City Bank, 33/124 Patak Road, Karon. Tel: 396 095.

Siam Commercial Bank, 66 Rasda Road. Tel: 212 254/5.

Siam Commercial Bank, 89/2-4 Beach Road, Patong. Tel: 321 467.

Thai Military Bank, 76/3 Ranong Road. Tel: 212 123, 212 978.

RELIGIOUS SERVICES

Bangkok

Christian

Assumption Cathedral, 23 Oriental Lane, Charoen Krung Road. Tel: 234 8556. Sunday Mass: 10am.

Calvary Baptist Church, 88 Soi 2, Sukhumvit Road. Tel: 251 8278. Service: 10.45am.

Holy Redeemer Catholic Church,

123/19 Soi Ruam Rudi, Witthayu Road. Tel: 256 6305, 256 6578. Sunday Mass: 8.30am, 9.45am, 11am and 5.30pm.
International Christian Assembly, 196 Soi Ekamai, Sukhumvit Road. Tel: 391 4387. Services: 10.30am.
International Church of Bangkok, Student Christian Centre, 328 Phaya Thai Road (near Asia Hotel). Tel: 258 5821. Service: 9.30am.
St. Louis Church, 215/2 Sathorn Tai Road. Tel: 211 0220. Sunday Mass: 6am, 8am, 10am, 11.15am and 5.30pm.

Hindu
Thamsapha Association, 50 Soi Wat Prok, Charoen Krung (New) Road. Tel: 211 3840. Services: 7am–10pm.

Jewish
Jewish Association of Thailand (Ashkenazi), Jewish Community Centre, 121 Soi 2, Soi 22 (Soi Sai Nam Thip), Sukhumvit Road. Tel: 258 2195, fax: 663 0245. Services: Friday evenings and holidays.
Even Chen Synagogue (Sephardic), The Bossotel Inn, 55/12-14 Charoen Krung (New) Road (near Oriental Hotel). Tel: 630 6120, fax: 237 3225. Services: daily at 8am, Friday at sundown, Saturday at 9am. Shabbat meals at synagogue by advance reservation.

Muslim
Sha-Roh-Tal Islam Mosque, 133 Soi I Sukhapiban Road. Tel: 328 8950.

Sikh
Wat Sirikurusing Saha, 565 Chakraphet Road. Tel: 221 1011. Services: 6am and 5pm.

Practical Tips

Emergencies

SECURITY AND CRIME
If you run into trouble in Bangkok, the **police emergency number is 191**. There are also Tourist Police assigned specially to assist travelers, and who are more likely to speak English.

When in Thailand, avoid:
• Touts posing as Boy Scouts soliciting donations on Bangkok's sidewalks. The real Boy Scouts obtain funds from other sources.
• Touts on Patpong offering upstairs live-sex shows. Once inside, one is handed an exorbitant bill and threatened with mayhem if he or she protests. Pay, take the receipt, and go immediately to the Tourist Police to gain restitution, which may or may not be forthcoming. (If you do venture into one of these establishments, keep track of the number of drinks you order and check your bill carefully.)
• Persons offering free or very cheap boat rides into the canals. Once you are well into the canal, you are given the choice of paying a high fee or being stranded.
• Persons offering to take you to a gem factory for a "special deal." The gems are usually flawed and there's no way to get a refund.
• Persons on buses or trains offering sweets, fruits or soft drinks. The items may be drugged and the passenger is robbed while unconscious. This is unfortunate because Thais are generous people and it is normal for them to offer food to strangers. Use discretion.

The **Tourist Police headquarters** is at 29/1 Soi Lang Suan, Ploenchit Road, tel: 255 2964; another office is at the Tourist Assistance Centre at the Tourism Authority of Thailand headquarters at 372 Bamrung Muang Road, tel: 282 8129; or they can be reached by simply dialling 1699. Tourist police booths can also be found in many tourist areas including Lumpini Park (near the intersection of Rama IV and Silom Roads) and Patpong (at the Silom Road intersection). Most members of the force speak English. Their offices can be found in Chiang Mai, Pattaya and Phuket as well. In Chiang Mai, they are located below the Tourist Authority of Thailand office at 105/1 Chiang Mai-Lamphun Road. Tel: 248 604/5, 248 607. In Pattaya, their office is on Second Road, near Soi 6. Tel: 429 371 or 1699. In Phuket, go to the TAT office at 73-75 Phuket Road. Tel: 212 213, 211 036.

Medical Services

HOSPITALS
First-class hotels in Bangkok, Chiang Mai and Phuket have doctors on call for medical emergencies. The hospitals in these three destinations are the equivalent of those in any major Western city. Intensive-care units are fully equipped and staffed by doctors to handle emergencies quickly and competently. Nursing care is generally superb, because there is a higher staff-to-patient ratio. Many doctors have been trained in Western hospitals, and even those who have not speak good English.

Most small towns have clinics which treat minor ailments and accidents. In the unlikely event that you suffer a criminal attack in Bangkok, you must go to a police hospital, normally the one at Ratchaprasong intersection.

Bangkok
BNH Hospital, 9 Convent Road. Tel: 632 0560, 632 0582/6. All major specialties, several Western doctors, convenient to the Silom Road area.

Samitivej Hospital, 133 Soi 49, Sukhumvit Road. Tel: 392 0010/9, 655 1024/5. Popular with expatriates living in the area.
Thai Nakharin Hospital, 345 Bang Na Trat Road. Tel: 361 2712/61. All major specialties represented by mostly US-trained doctors, excellent ambulance service.

Chiang Mai
Lanna Hospital, off the super highway on the north side of town. Tel: 211 037.
McCormick Hospital, on Kaeo Nawarat Road, on the northeastern edge of town. Tel: 241 311/2.
Suan Dok Hospital, on the corner of Boonruangrit and Suthep roads, across from Wat Suan Dok. Tel: 221 122.

Pattaya
Pattaya International Hospital, Soi 4, Second Road. Tel: 428 374/5.
Phyathai Siracha General, 90 Si Racha Nakorn Road, Si Racha, Chonburi. Tel: 770 200/8.
Pattaya Memorial, 328/1 Pattaya/ Klaeng Road. Tel: 429 422/4.

Phuket
Bangkok-Phuket Hospital, 2/1 Hongyok Utit Road, Phuket town. Tel: 254 421/9. Emergency, ext. 1060.
Patong-Kathu Hospital, Sawatdirak Road, Patong Beach. Tel: 340 444.
Phuket International Hospital, Chalermprakiat Road, Phuket. Tel: 249 400. Emergencies: 210 935.

MEDICAL CLINICS
For minor problems, there are numerous clinics in all the major towns and cities. The **British Dispensary**, located at 109 Sukhumvit Road (between Soi 3 and 5), tel: 252 9179, has British doctors on its staff. In Chiang Mai, go to Loi Kroh Clinic on Loi Kroh Road, tel: 271 571. Most international hotels also have an on-premises clinic or doctor on call.

DENTAL CLINICS
Dental clinics are almost as numerous as medical clinics.
In Bangkok, one clinic with a

long-standing reputation is the **Dental Polyclinic**, at 2111/2113 New Phetburi Road, tel: 314 5070. The **Dental Hospital**, Soi 49, Sukhumvit Road, tel: 260 5000/15, looks more like a hotel than a dental hospital and has the latest imported dental equipment.
In Chiang Mai, there is The **Dental Hospital**, 1/42 Mu 3, Chiang Mai-Lampang Superhighway. Tel: 411 150.
In Phuket town, the **Dental Care Clinic** is located at 62/5 Rasda Centre. Tel: 215 025.

STD CLINICS
Clinics along Ploenchit Road perform tests for sexually transmitted diseases; there are several similar clinics in Patpong. **Bangkok General Hospital**, Soi Soonvijai, New Phetburi Road, tel: 318 0066, is reputed to offer the most reliable tests for the presence of HIV, and **BNH Hospital** on Convent Road is a good source for HIV/AIDS information.

PHARMACIES
Pharmaceuticals are produced to the highest standards, and pharmacies must have a registered pharmacist on the premises. Most pharmacy personnel in the shopping and business areas speak English. Many prescription drugs in other countries can be bought, legally, over the counter in Thailand.
Pharmacies, or chemists, are everywhere in Bangkok; look for a green cross. Some of the more common ones are **Siam Drugs**, **People's Health & Beauty Care**, and **Boots**, an English chain which opened in Bangkok in late 1997.
In addition, many of the larger grocery stores have pharmacy counters with helpful personnel who generally speak passable English. Try branches of **Foodland**, **Central** or **Robinson**.

SNAKE BITES
There is little chance of being bitten by a poisonous snake in Bangkok or its environs, but should it occur, most clinics have anti-venom serum on hand. If they cannot acquire any,

travel to the **Saowapha Institute** (Snake Farm) on Rama IV Road. They maintain sera against the bites of six types of cobras and vipers. Provincial clinics maintain a constant supply of anti-venom serum supplied by the Institute.

OTHER SERVICES
Counseling: Community Services of Bangkok, 15/1 Soi 33, Sukhumvit Road, tel: 258 4998, 258 5652, fax: 260 3563. **CSB** is a volunteer organization made up of foreigners to provide information and assistance to families living in Bangkok. They offer a counseling service, a telephone hotline (662 0979) and are always willing to help travelers with problems who have nowhere else to turn. In addition they offer interesting courses on a variety of subjects.
Group Meetings: Alcoholics Anonymous (AA) meets daily, and Al-Anon meetings are held on Saturdays, at Holy Redeemer Catholic Church, 123/19 Soi Ruam Rudi, Witthayu Road, tel: 256 6305, 256 6157; for information on Overeaters Anonymous (OA) and Narcotics Anonymous (NA) meetings, contact Community Services of Bangkok, tel: 258 4998, 258 5652.

Weights and Measures

Thailand uses the metric system of meters, grams and liters.

Business Hours

Government offices are open from 8.30am–4.30pm on Monday–Friday. Business hours are from 8am or 8.30am–5.30pm on Monday–Friday. Some businesses are open half days from 8.30am–noon on Saturdays. Banks are generally open from 10am–4pm, five days a week, but many operate money-changing kiosks throughout the city, which are open until 8pm, seven days a week.
The **General Post Office** in Bangkok is located on Charoen Krung (New) Road between Suriwongse and Si Phraya roads. It

is open from 8am–8pm Monday–Friday, and from 8am–1pm on weekends and holidays.

Branch post offices are located throughout the city, and many of these usually stay open until 6pm. Kiosks along some of the city's busier streets sell stamps and aerograms and ship small parcels. Hotel reception counters will send letters for their guests at no charge. Most department stores are open 10am–9pm seven days a week.

Ordinary shops open at 8.30am or 9am and close between 6pm and 8pm, depending on the location and type of business. Some pharmacies in the major cities remain open all night. Small open-air coffee shops and restaurants open at 7am and close at 8.30pm though some stay open past midnight. Large restaurants generally close at 10pm. Most coffee shops close at midnight; some stay open 24 hours.

Tipping

Tipping is not a custom in Thailand, although it is becoming more prevalent. A service charge of 10 percent is generally included in restaurant bills and is divided among the staff. A bit extra for the waitress would not go unappreciated.

Do not tip non-metered taxi or *tuk-tuk* drivers unless the traffic has been particularly bad and he has been especially patient; 10 baht would suffice for a long journey over 60 baht. Hotel bellmen and room porters are becoming used to being tipped in urban centres but will not hover with hand extended.

Media

PRESS

The English language morning newspapers are one of the foreigner's lifelines to the outside world. There are two national English-language dailies – *Bangkok Post* and *The Nation*. The *Asian Wall Street Journal* is printed in Bangkok. The *International Herald Tribune* is available at most bookstalls after 4pm. Newsstands

in major hotel gift shops carry air-freighted, and therefore expensive, editions of British, French, American, German and Italian newspapers. Newsagents on Soi 3 (Soi Nana Nua), Sukhumvit Road also offer Arabic newspapers.

In addition, check out *Bangkok Metro*, a lush, well-put-together monthly magazine which features interesting writing; book, film & restaurant reviews; shopping information; and a calendar of Bangkok events, including sports and health pursuits, as well as activities for children. Several pages are devoted to happenings in Phuket and Samui.

In Pattaya, the weekly *Pattaya Mail* contains local news and features, as well as information on events, special offers and new facilities and services in the area.

RADIO

AM radio is devoted entirely to Thai-language programs. FM frequencies include Radio Thailand (92.5 FM) with a variety of English-language programs including a travel show in the late afternoon, and Chulalongkorn University (101.5) which plays jazz from 5pm–6pm and classical music from 8pm–10pm. Other popular stations can be found at 89 FM (Thai rock); 95.5 FM (English-speaking DJs playing hits from the 70s, 80s and 90s); 105 FM (easy listening with hourly international, local and traffic news); 107 FM (hits from the 50s through the 90s with hourly CNN broadcasts).

In addition, Voice of America, BBC World Service, Radio Canada, Radio Australia, Radio New Zealand, Radio France Internationale, Deutsche Welle, Singapore Broadcasting Company and Radio Japan all offer shortwave radio broadcasts in English and Thai throughout the day. Check newspapers for current frequencies and program schedules.

TELEVISION

Bangkok has five Thai language television channels, in addition to a variety of satellite and cable

television services: Satellite Television Asian Region (STAR), International Broadcasting Corporation (IBC), Thai Sky and UTV. BBC World, Australia TV, CNN, HBO, Discovery, TNT and ESPN, as well as other news, sports, music and entertainment programs, are widely available on these networks.

Postal Services

Thailand has a comprehensive and reliable postal service. Major towns offer regular air mail service, as well as express courier service that speeds a package to nearly every point on the globe.

Main post offices in Bangkok, Chiang Mai and Phuket have special facilities where stamp collectors can browse and buy from a wide selection of beautiful Thai stamps. In Bangkok, the General Post Office (GPO), on Charoen Krung (New) Road between Suriwongse and Si Phraya roads, tel: 233 1050/9, 235 2834, is open from 8am–8pm during the week, and from 8am–1pm on weekends and holidays. (Note that it will be easier to conduct business at the GPO in person, rather than relying on telephone service.) At the right side of the lobby is a packing service with boxes in various sizes; charges are nominal and depend on the size of the parcel. A separate building to the right of the main GPO provides telecommunications services (telephone, telegram, fax and telex) around the clock.

Branch post offices are located throughout the country. Hours vary but they generally close at 4.30pm, although some stay open as late as 6pm. Post office kiosks along some of the city's busier streets sell stamps, aerograms and ship small parcels. Hotel reception desks will also send letters and postcards for no extra charge.

Courier Service

A number of international courier agencies have offices in Bangkok: **DHL Worldwide**, Grand Amarin Tower, 22nd Floor, 1550 New

Phetburi Road. Tel: 207 0600, fax: 207 0630.

Federal Express, Green Tower, 8th Floor, Rama IV Road. Tel: 367 3222, fax: 367 3221.

TNT Express Worldwide, 599 Chong Non Si Road, Khlong Toey. Tel: 249 0242/6, 249 5702/6, 671 9300/13, fax: 249 1264.

United Parcel Service, 16/1 Soi 44, Sukhumvit Road. Tel: 712 3090, 254 5066 (cargo only); fax: 712 1818.

Telecommunications

Thailand has a sophisticated communications system, not that it always works; the lines have a way of getting jammed, like the traffic, especially after a heavy rain. Most hotels have telephone, telegram, e-mail, and fax facilities.

TELEPHONE

Most international telephone calls can be dialled direct from Bangkok. International telephone calls can be placed at the General Post Office (GPO) 24 hours a day. Most provincial capitals have telephone offices at the GPO; hours are generally 7am–11pm.

Area Codes
Thailand country code: 66
Bangkok: 02
Chiang Mai: 053
Chiang Rai: 053
Chiang Saen: 053
Chumphon: 077
Hat Yai: 074
Hua Hin: 032
Kanchanaburi: 034
Ko Samui: 077
Krabi/Ao Nang: 075
Mae Hong Son: 053
Mae Salong: 053
Nakhon Ratchasima (Khorat): 044
Pattaya/Jomtien: 038
Phang Nga: 076
Phi Phi: 075
Phuket: 076
Songkhla: 074
Sukhothai: 055
Surat Thani: 077

Note that any telephone number beginning with 01 indicates a cellular telephone, and the zero must be dialled. Note, also, that telephone calls to Malaysia do not require a country code; simply prefix the number, including the area code, with 09.

Operator Assistance
For directory assistance in Bangkok, dial 13; for assistance in the provinces, dial 183. There is a serious shortage of telephone lines in Bangkok, which is being addressed by the installation of an additional two million lines. The modernization has meant that some existing telephone numbers have changed, often with little advance notice. For information regarding changed telephone numbers, dial 233 1199 or 13.

For operator assistance with a **domestic call** (including those to Malaysia), dial 101; for assistance with an **international call** (including collect/reverse charges calls), dial 100. Note that calls to Laos must be operator-assisted; dial 101 for help. Operators at these numbers speak English.

International Telephone Calls
The international prefix from Thailand is 001. Home Direct is a service whereby one can reach an international operator in a number of countries worldwide. Home Direct is accessible from most private telephones, the GPO in Bangkok, many post office telephone offices in the provinces, and at the airports in Bangkok, Chiang Mai and Phuket. It is not, unfortunately, widely available from hotel telephones. To access Home Direct, dial 001 999, and then the following: Australia, 61 1000; Canada, 15 1000; Germany, 49 1000; Italy, 39 1000; New Zealand, 64 1066; United Kingdom, 44 1066; USA, 1111 (AT&T), 12001 (MCI), 13877 (Sprint).

TELEGRAM, E-MAIL AND FAX SERVICES
Main post offices in nearly every city offer telegram, telex and fax services to all parts of the world. Many small shops throughout the country also offer a variety of telephone and fax services, although the prices may be a little steep, particularly for faxes.

On-Line Access
Some of the larger hotels now offer Internet access and/or e-mail services; if this is a requirement for your stay in Bangkok, check in advance to make certain such facilities are available at the hotel of your choice. An option might be one of the Internet cafés and coffee houses which are becoming popular in Bangkok:

Byte in a Cup, Siam Discovery Centre, 4th Floor, Room 401, 989 Rama I Road. Tel: 658 0433/5, fax: 658 0436, website: www.byte-in-a-cup.com. Daily 10am–7pm. Elegant coffee house, convenient location, but busy.

Cyber Café, Ploenchit Centre, 2nd Floor, Sukhumvit Road (between expressway and Soi 2). Tel: 656 8472/3, email: cybercafe @chomanan.co.th; website: www.cybercafe.co.th. Daily 10am–10pm. Spacious, but a little out of the way. Over 20 terminals, non-smoking bar. Several other locations, including one at Don Muang International Airport, Terminal 2 (opposite John Bull Pub). Tel: 535 5671. Daily 24 hours. Note that foreigners are charged more than Thais.

Cyber Pub, Dusit Thani Hotel, 946 Rama IV Road. Tel: 236 0450, ext. 2971. Ten terminals with charges of 5 baht per minute; food and beverages available.

Cyberia, 654/8 Sukhumvit Road (corner Soi 24). Tel: 259 3356/7, fax: 259 3358, email: svars@cyberia.co.th, website: www.cyberia.co.th. Daily 10.30am–11pm. Bangkok's most popular Internet café. Beer, wine, Italian menu.

HelloPub, Hello Guest House, 1st Floor, 63-65 Khao San Road. Tel: 281 8579, email: hellopub@loxinfo.co.th. Daily 10am–10pm. Three terminals, coffee, snacks. Convenient to many inexpensive guesthouses.

Getting Around

BANGKOK AIRPORT

From Bangkok's Don Muang International Airport, the journey along the expressway into the city can take from 30 minutes to one hour or more, depending on traffic conditions. Larger hotels will often send a limousine to meet their guests, if arranged before arrival.

Mini-bus/Limousine Service: Thai Airways runs both a mini-bus (100 baht) and limousine service (350 baht) from the airport to the major hotels. The limousines, while more expensive than any other mode of transport, may be the most convenient way into Bangkok, particularly during rush hour. Because they have to fight traffic to deliver their passengers to various hotels around the city, the mini-buses can take considerable time to get you to your hotel.

Airport Bus: In 1996, a special express bus service began operations from the airport to three areas of Bangkok: **route A1** goes to the Silom Road area; **route A2** goes to central Bangkok, including Chinatown, and **route A3** runs along Sukhumvit Road. Detailed maps of the routes are available at the bus counter (to the left of the taxi counter); the fare is 70 baht.

Taxis: You can book an air-conditioned public taxi at the taxi counter at the left-hand side of the arrivals hall. The fare is determined according to your destination, and should be around 200 baht for most points in the city. The clerk will write down your destination and the price. Give this ticket to the taxi driver, and pay him the price noted on it when you arrive at your destination. Occasionally, someone may approach you in the arrivals hall in an attempt to sell you a similar ticket for a vastly inflated price. Needless to say, he should be ignored.

It's also theoretically possible to get a metered taxi into town from the airport; in practice, however, the drivers often refuse to turn on the meter in favour of seeing how much you're willing to pay for the trip. Note that if you do find a metered taxi willing to take you into Bangkok, you will be liable for the additional 30-baht expressway fee. On the other hand, if you arrange your taxi through the taxi counter for a set fee, the expressway surcharge, if any, should be included in the price.

Public Buses: For economy-minded travelers, air-conditioned buses – Nos. 4, 13, and 29 – stop in front of the airport. The trip into town costs 16 baht. The last buses leave about 8pm.

For the **return trip to the airport**, the Thai Airways limousine service has in-town offices at Montien Hotel, tel: 233 7060, and Asia Hotel, tel: 215 0780. Most major hotels have airconditioned limousines, often available to non-guests if you book in advance. Non-metered taxis make the trip for 150–250 baht depending on traffic conditions. Metered taxis will be less expensive if there are no traffic jams on the way.

International and domestic transfer: The 500-m trip between Bangkok's international and domestic airports is by way of a free shuttle bus at 15-minute intervals from 6am–11pm.

CHIANG MAI AIRPORT

Chiang Mai's airport is a 10-minute drive from the city centre. There is frequent bus service, but it runs a circuitous route, and visitors with a lot of luggage might prefer the following modes of transportation:

Limousines: Major hotels have limousines to ferry guests with reservations (one can make a reservation at the airport) to their premises. They charge about 100 baht per person.

Mini-bus: Thai Airways operates a mini-bus between the airport and its town office on Phra Poklao Road. The cost each way is 20 baht per passenger. You must find your way from the office to the hotel.

PHUKET AIRPORT

Limousines: Thai Airways offers air-conditioned limousines to each beach. The price is computed per vehicle, and each vehicle holds up to four persons.

Mini-bus: Major hotels maintain mini-buses to ferry guests with reservations (it is possible to make a reservation at the airport) to and from the airport. The Thai Airways mini-bus runs hourly between the airport and its Phuket town office on Ranong Road. You must then find your own way from the office to the hotel.

BY AIR

The domestic arm of Thai Airways operates a network of daily flights to 21 of Thailand's major towns aboard a fleet of 737s and Airbuses. From Bangkok, there are daily flights to Nakhon Si Thammarat, Narathiwat, Trang, Nan, Phrae, Nakhon Phanom and Sakon Nakhon; two flights daily to Surat Thani, Lampang, Nakhon Ratchasima and Ubon Ratchathani; three flights daily to Udon Thani; four flights daily to Chiang Rai and Khon Kaen; five flights daily to Phitsanulok; six flights daily to Hat Yai; eight to ten daily flights to Chiang Mai; a dozen daily flights to Phuket; and five flights a week to Buri Ram. Connections to Mae Hong Son and Mae Sot are made via Chiang Mai (four flights daily) and Phitsanulok (four flights a week) respectively. Thai Airways offers a "Discover Thailand" visitor's pass, allowing four domestic flights, for about US$250. Certain conditions apply, notably that this pass must be purchased outside Thailand. Contact a Tourism Authority of Thailand (TAT) office for further details. In addition, Bangkok Airways, Thailand's first privately owned domestic airline, flies from Bangkok to Ko Samui more than a dozen times daily; to Sukhothai and Chiang Mai twice daily; and to Ranong at least once daily.

Note that if you are planning a trip to the tropical island of Ko Samui from Bangkok, you will save much traveling time if you go by air, a journey of less than two hours; the same trip by road and boat may take as long as 14 hours.

BY RAIL

The State Railways of Thailand operates three principal routes from Hua Lampong Station. The northern route passes through Ayutthaya, Phitsanulok, Lampang and terminates at Chiang Mai. The northeastern route passes through Ayutthaya, Saraburi, Nakhon Ratchasima, Khon Kaen, Udon Thani and terminates at Nong Khai. The southern route crosses the Rama VI bridge and calls at Nakhon Pathom, Phetchaburi, Hua Hin and Chumphon. It branches at Hat Yai, one branch running southwest through Betong and on down the western coast of Malaysia to Singapore. The southeastern branch goes via Pattani and Yala to the Thai border opposite the Malaysian town of Kota Bharu.

In addition, there is a line from Makkasan to Aranya Prathet on the Cambodian border.

Another line leaves Bangkok Noi station, in Thonburi, on the western bank of the Chao Phraya River, for Kanchanaburi and other destinations in western Thailand. There is also a short route leaving Bangkok Noi that travels west along the rim of the Gulf of Thailand to Samut Sakhon and then on to Samut Songkram.

Express and rapid services on the main lines offer first-class, air-conditioned or second-class, fan-cooled cars with sleeping cabins or berths and dining cars. There are also special air-conditioned express day coaches that travel to key towns along the main lines. 20-day rail passes are available.

Reservations can be made at the station or with any travel agent within 30 days prior to departure.

In Bangkok, details from: **Hua Lampong Station**: Rama IV Road. Tel: 233 7010, 233 7020 (information), 223 3762, 224 7788, 225 6964 (reservations), fax: 225 6068. **Bangkok Noi (Thonburi) Station**, Arun Amarin Road (near Siriraj Hospital). Tel: 411 3102.

Note that it is often difficult to get through to the train station by telephone; it may prove nearly impossible to get through to anyone who speaks English. A better alternative may be to book your train trip through your hotel or a local travel agency. There will likely be a small additional service charge, but it will save heartburn and headaches.

Also, make certain that you know from which station your train leaves, particularly if you are travelling west to Kanchanaburi.

BY ROAD

Bus service is reliable, frequent and very affordable to most destinations in Thailand. Rest stops are regular, and in some cases limited refreshments are available on the bus.

Fan-cooled buses, painted orange, are the slowest since they makes stops in every village along the way. For short distances, they can be an entertaining means of travel, particularly in the cool season when the fan and the open windows make the trip reasonably comfortable.

Blue air-conditioned buses, however, are generally a faster, more reliably comfortable way to get to your destination. VIP buses are available on some of the longer routes; these usually have larger seats, more leg room and toilets.

Bus Stations

For bus and coach journeys to destinations outside of Bangkok, the major terminals are:

Eastern, Sukhumvit Road, opposite Soi 63 (Soi Ekamai). Tel: 391

2504, 391 9829, 392 2520/1. Departures for Pattaya, Rayong, Chanthaburi.

Northern and Northeastern, Moh Chit, Phaholyothin Road. Tel: 271 0101/5, 279 4484/7, 271 2961. Departures for Ayutthaya, Lopburi, Nakhon Ratchasima, Chiang Mai.

Southern, Boromrat Chonnani Road (western bank of Chao Phraya). Tel: 435 1199/1200, 391 9829, 435 0511, 434 5557/8. Departures for Nakhon Pathom, Kanchanaburi, Phuket, Surat Thani.

To reach a small town from a large one, or to get around on some of the islands, *song taos* (meaning two benches), pick-up trucks with benches along either side of the bed, function as taxis.

Public Transport

BANGKOK
Taxis, Tuk-Tuks & Motorcycles
There are two types of taxi available in Bangkok, metered and non-metered. Both are air-conditioned and reliable, but the drivers' command of English is usually minimal. This might present a problem, not only in conveying your destination, but with non-metered taxis, in bargaining the price.

Do not step into a non-metered taxi without having first agreed on a price, which can fluctuate depending on the hour of the day and the amount of traffic, rain, and the number of one-way streets he must negotiate. The base fare for all journeys is 30 baht. Taxi drivers do not charge you an extra fee for baggage stowage or extra passengers, and there is no tipping. Check with hotels for typical fares.

The metered taxis are a much better choice if you do not know the precise distance to your intended destination. If you know Bangkok well, you might be able to negotiate a price below that which you would pay for a metered taxi. However, taxi drivers are experts at outwitting their less knowledgeable passengers, so if you are just a casual tourist, stick to the metered taxis. The minimum basic fare is 35 baht, and it rises in two-baht increments depending on the length of time and distance involved in the trip. Make sure the driver of the metered taxi does, in fact, turn his meter on after you get in.

Occasionally a driver will try to negotiate a flat fare from you instead of turning on his meter; this practice is particularly common in the area of the World Trade Centre and the Erawan Shrine. Sometimes the fare quoted amounts to thievery; you will nearly always get a better rate from a metered taxi. Note that any trips made along the expressway ("highway" to some drivers) will involve an additional toll of 30 baht, which you will be expected to pay. Also, most taxi drivers do not maintain a ready supply of small change; it's best not to offer anything larger than a 100-baht note in payment of fare.

If the English fluency of taxi drivers is limited, that of tuk-tuk (also called samlor, meaning three wheels) drivers is even less. Tuk-tuks are the brightly coloured three-wheeled taxis whose nickname comes from the noise their two-cycle engines make. They are fun for short trips, but choose a taxi for longer journeys, particularly during the heat of the day. A tuk-tuk driver on an open stretch of road can seldom resist racing, and the resultant journey can be a hair-raising experience. For very short trips, the fare is 20 baht.

As the traffic situation continues to worsen in Bangkok, motorcycle taxis have proliferated; their drivers wear single-colour vests. Passengers are required to wear helmets on the major roads, but the drivers do not always supply them. Be aware that in the case of an accident, not a rare occurrence, the driver will likely not hold any insurance. In spite of the risks, this means of travel is worthy of consideration when the streets are hopelessly deadlocked.

Note that Wireless Road, location of many embassies, a large hotel and several banks, is more commonly known by its Thai name, Thanon Witthayu. Similarly, Sathorn Road, a main thoroughfare

divided into north and south which runs between Lumpini Park and the river, is often referred to as Sathorn Nua (north) and Sathorn Tai (south). A certain amount of confusion can be avoided if you have your destination written in Thai to hand to the driver.

Buses and Mini-buses

Bangkok buses come in four varieties: executive, air-conditioned, ordinary, and the green mini-buses. They operate every two or three minutes along more than 100 routes and are an excellent way to see the outer areas of the city. Bus maps give the routes for all types of city buses.

Buses are especially useful during rush hours when traveling up one-way streets, like parts of Sukhumvit Road, because they can speed along specially marked bus lanes going against on-coming traffic. Conductors prowl through the aisles collecting fares and issuing tickets. Unfortunately, destinations are only noted in Thai so a bus map is needed. Most routes cease operating around midnight, though some run all through the night.

Red executive micro-buses hold 20 seated passengers in air-conditioned comfort; they charge a fare of 30 baht regardless of the destination, but serve fewer routes. Ordinary buses come in two varieties: red and white (more expensive) and blue and white. Aside from the price, there is no difference in service routes. Both can be very crowded. (It is a sight to see one listing heavily to one side while students cling to the open doors.) Their drivers are the cowboys of the road and usually drive in very colourful fashion. Some drivers deck out their buses with stereo sets; others even have television sets, though on bumpy roads the reception is less than perfect. Note that pocket-picking and bag-slashing is not an uncommon occurrence on Bangkok buses. Keep your wallet in a front pocket and your bag in front of you at all times.

Mass Transit Projects

Several mass transit projects are in various stages of planning or construction in Bangkok. Bangkok Metropolitan Authority has plans for a subway and elevated rail system (Hua Lampong-Khlong Toey-Lard Prao) as well as the addition of several more elevated expressways.

Unfortunately, the economic crisis of the late 1990s put many of these projects on hold. When they will be completed is anyone's guess, but visitors will see the half-completed work everywhere in downtown Bangkok

Skytrain, an ambitious elevated rail system, will link Phra Khanong-Bang Seu and Sathorn-Lard Prao initially; other lines will follow. Although this project was first proposed in 1986, construction did not begin until 1994. The **Bangkok Elevated Road and Train System (BERTS)**, a US$3.2 billion project, envisions 60 kilometres (35 mi) of elevated rail lines and nearly 50 kilometres (30 mi) of additional expressways around Bangkok, much of it stacked one on top of the other. Although a certain amount of preliminary construction has been undertaken for this project, serious problems arose with the Hong Kong-based contractor. It is possible that Bangkok's Metropolitan Rapid Transit Authority (MRTA) may assume control of this endeavour. Finally, MRTA has its own plans for a 21-kilometre (13-mi) subway system, encompassing 18 stations and running from Hua Lampong to Bang Seu via Huay Khwang. Other proposals have involved construction of a monorail "beltway" around Bangkok and introduction of a tram system in the heavily congested area of the Grand Palace, Wat Phra Kaeo and the National Museum.

Sadly, each of these projects has suffered from interdepartmental bickering and a lack of central administration. The absence of cohesive oversight resulted in frequent route changes, land expropriation problems and no real solution to Bangkok's traffic.

Boats

Chao Phraya River express boats (white with red trim) run regular routes at 15- to 20-minute intervals up and down the Chao Phraya River, going all the way to Nonthaburi, 10 km (6 mi) north of the city. The service begins at 6am and ceases at 6pm. Fares are 5–10 baht depending on the distance, and are collected on board.

Ferries, often red, cross the river at dozens of points and cost just a couple of baht per journey. They begin operating at 6am and stop at midnight. It is also possible to catch a long-tail taxi to many points along the Chao Phraya or the canals; it helps to be fairly familiar with the waterways before doing so. Fares begin at 5 baht.

CHIANG MAI

Buses: Chiang Mai has red mini-buses known locally as *song tao*. They are prepared to carry passengers almost anywhere within the town.

Tuk-tuk: They charge according to distance, starting at 10 baht. You must bargain for the price before you get in.

Samlor: These pedal trishaws charge 5 baht for short distances. Bargain before you board.

PHUKET

Buses: Picturesque wooden buses ply regular routes from the market to the beaches. They depart every 30 minutes between 8am and 6pm between Phuket town market and all beaches except Rawai and Nai Harn. Buses to Rawai and Nai Harn leave from the traffic circle on Bangkok Road. They prowl the beach roads in search of passengers. Flag one down, 15–20 baht per person.

Tuk-tuk: The small cramped *tuk-tuks* function as taxis. They'll go anywhere. Barter your fare before getting on. For example, Patong to Karon, 120 baht, Patong to airport, 300 baht. Within town is 10–20 baht if shared.

Motorcycle taxis: 10–20 baht per ride. A convenient if dangerous way to get around.

LIMOUSINES

Most major hotels operate air-conditioned limousine services. Although the prices are at least twice those of ordinary taxis, they offer the comfort and convenience of English-speaking drivers and door-to-door service.

RENTAL CARS

Thailand has a good road system with over 50,000 km (31,000 mi) of paved highways, and more are being built every year. Road signs are in both Thai and English, and you should have no difficulty following a map. An international driver's license is required.

Driving on a narrow but busy road can be a terrifying experience; right of way is generally determined by size. It is not unusual for a bus to overtake a truck despite the fact that the oncoming lane is filled with vehicles. It is little wonder that, when collisions occur, several dozen lives are lost. In addition, many of the long-distance drivers consume pep pills and have the throttle to the floor because they are getting paid for beating schedules. One is strongly advised to avoid driving at night for this reason. When dusk comes, pull in at a hotel and get an early start the next morning.

Avis, Hertz and numerous local agencies offer late-model cars with and without drivers, and with insurance coverage for Bangkok and upcountry trips. A deposit is usually required except with credit cards.

In the provinces, agencies can be found in major towns like Chiang Mai, Pattaya and Phuket. These also rent four-wheel-drive jeeps and mini-buses. When renting a jeep, read the fine print carefully and be aware that you are liable for all damages to the vehicle. Ask for first class insurance, which covers both you and the other vehicle involved in a collision.

Bangkok

Although Avis has a desk at the international terminal at Don Muang Airport, and Hertz one at the domestic terminal, the general practice is for car rental agencies to deliver the car to your hotel; you fill out the rental agreement there. Check the brakes and air conditioning, and make certain to read the fine print for insurance terms before accepting the car.

Avis, 2/12 Witthayu Road. Tel: 255 5300/4; airport: 535 4031/2.
Hertz, 1526/40 Patanakarn Road. Tel: 722 6151/61; airport: 535 3004.
Grand Car Rent, 233-5 Asoke-Dindaeng Road (near Rama IX intersection). Tel: 248 2991/2.
Khlong Toey Car Rent, 1921 Rama IV Road. Tel: 251 9856.
Sathorn Car Rent, 6/8-9 Sathorn Nua Road. Tel: 633 8888.
SMT Rent-a-Car, 931/11 Rama I Road, (opposite National Stadium). Tel: 216 4436, 216 8020.

Chiang Mai

Avis, 14/14 Huay Kaeo Road. Tel: 222 013, 221 316.
Hertz, 90 Sri Dornchai Road. Tel: 279 474. Branch at Suriwongse Hotel, tel: 270 051.
Car Rent, 49 Chang Klan Road (opposite the Night Bazaar). Tel: 249 197.

Pattaya

Budget, 333/1 Moo 6, Sukhumvit Road, Naklua, Banglamung. Tel: 726 185, 422 149/50.
Via, 215/15-18 Second Road, South Pattaya. Tel: 426 242.

Phuket

Budget, opposite airport. Tel: 205 396/7. Good for Suzuki Caribians. Free delivery.
Pure Car Rent, 75 Rasda Road, Phuket town. Tel: 211 002.
Via, 70/85 Rata Utit Road, Patong. Tel: 341 660.

MOTORCYCLE RENTAL

Motorcycles can be rented in Chiang Mai, Pattaya and Phuket (just about everywhere, in fact) for economical rates. Remember that when you rent a motorcycle, you must surrender your passport for the duration of the rental period.

Motorcycles range in size from small 90cc models to giant 750cc behemoths. The majority are 125cc trailbikes. Rental outlets can be found along beach roads and main roads in each town.

It is not uncommon for rental motorcycles to be stolen; lock them up when not in use, and only park them in areas with supervision.

On Foot/Hitchhiking

There are not many places one can walk in Thailand, other than national parks like Khao Yai and Phu Kradung. It is possible to hitch a ride on ten-wheel trucks but it is not advisable; if female, you are asking for trouble. It is strongly recommended that you do not travel at night on trucks, as the drivers are often tanked up on amphetamines and cause some of Thailand's horrendous accidents.

Khao Yai Nat'l Park

GETTING THERE

It takes about three to four hours to drive to Khao Yai from Bangkok, via one of two routes. The northern entrance to the park may be reached by following Route 1. Go through Saraburi and Muak Lek, and turn right onto Route 2090 five kilometres (3 mi) before Pak Chong.

The route to the southern entrance of Khao Yai requires driving to Nakhon Nayok. About 25 kilometres (15 mi) beyond the town, turn left onto Route 3077. The park headquarters is approximately 40 kilometres (25 mi) from either of the entrances.

There are frequent buses from Bangkok's northern bus terminal to Pak Chong, a pleasant ride of about three hours, which costs around 70 baht. (Look for the enormous white Buddha on the right hand side of the road on the way out.) In Pak Chong, you can catch a *song tao* in front of the 7-11 market across the street from the small bus station. Alternatively, most of the hotels and guest houses in the area will arrange to pick you up if you plan to

stay with them. At certain times of the year, the State Railways of Thailand may offer weekend day-trips to Khao Yai; however, the bus service is more reliable and, surprisingly, faster.

GETTING AROUND

Most of the guesthouses around Khao Yai conduct tours of the park.

Ko Samui/Pha Ngan

KO SAMUI
Getting There

Air: 14 flights daily from Bangkok, 2 flights daily from Phuket, 1 flight daily from U-Tapao, 4 flights weekly from Singapore. Additional international flights are being considered.

Bus/train/boat: Two overnight and one daytime train run daily from Bangkok to the mainland town of Surat Thani. Train-bus-boat or bus-boat packages (the latter start from Khao San Road in Bangkok) deposit travelers in the early morning hours at Tha Thong pier, 5 km (3 mi) east of Surat Thani. From here, two express boats (sometimes three) take less than three hours to reach Na Thon, Samui's main port. Directly from Surat Thani, at Ban Don pier, a slower boat, with stuffy berths, departs at 11pm daily and arrives at Na Thon six hours later.

Getting Around

Song taos circulate around the island's principal ring road throughout the day and well into the evening. Motorbikes are very popular and can be rented on every beach and at just about every bungalow, starting at about $6 per day. Rental mountain bikes can be found at Chaweng and Lamai beaches. Jeeps and cars can be rented at the biggest hotels and the airport, as well as at shops in Chaweng, Lamai and Na Thon.

KO PHA NGAN
Getting There

Air: Ko Pha Ngan has no airport. See Ko Samui details.

Boat: Two boats per day (three in peak season) travel from Samui's

Na Thon port to Pha Ngan's Thong Sala, a journey of about 45 minutes. Three boats per day take one hour to travel between Bangrak (also known as "Big Buddha Beach" pier) and Ko Pha Ngan's Hat Rin Beach. The 7.30am and 1.30pm express boats departing from Tha Thong near Surat Thani, on the mainland, proceed to Thong Sala after taking on and discharging passengers on Ko Samui. The strangely named "Speed Ferry" is a vehicle ferry that takes between five and six hours to travel directly between Surat's Tha Thong and Thong Sala. It leaves Tha Thong daily at 4pm. All boat schedules may be disrupted by weather conditions, especially between late August and early December.

Getting Around

Song taos regularly ply the cement roads between Thong Sala and Cha Loak Lam, and between Thong Sala and Hat Rin. When sufficient numbers pile on, they depart; they will pick up or discharge passengers anywhere along the way. Arriving by boat at Thong Sala or Hat Rin, passengers will be greeted by touts in long-boats sent from the various resorts. Especially in the rainy season, this is probably the best mode. At other times, long-boat travel to other coastal points will require haggling. If there is a semblance of a trail, motorbikes can be rented from bungalows and small shops, as well as in Thong Sala. Mountain bikes can be rented in Thong Sala.

KO TAO
Getting There

Air: Ko Tao has no airport. See Ko Samui details.

Boat: From Ko Samui and Ko Pha Ngan, one boat per day (sometimes two) travels from Thong Sala on Ko Pha Ngan to Ko Tao's only port, Ban Mae Hat. It departs at 12.30pm for the one-hour journey. The 8am boat from Surat Thani on the mainland, which continues directly on from Ko Samui to Ko Pha Ngan each day, arrives at

Ko Pha Ngan's Thong Sala port at noon. So there is just enough time to transfer to the Ko Tao-bound boat. Day trips to Ko Tao are also common packages vended on the two bigger islands.

From Chumphon: Two daily boats travel directly to Ko Tao from this fishing port 450 km (280 mi) south of Bangkok. The express boat, dèparting at 8am, takes less than two hours. The much slower boat leaves at midnight and arrives at 6am. This boat is a small converted fishing vessel and does not have berths.

Because of Ko Tao's distant and exposed location, between June and November boats to and from the island are often canceled due to inclement weather. Ko Tao boats are canceled more often than boats between Ko Samui and the mainland, or between Ko Samui and Ko Pha Ngan.

Getting Around

Long-boats transport new arrivals to various beaches. But once settled in, one can walk anywhere.

Where to Stay

Hotel accommodation in all the major tourist destinations in Thailand is equal to the very best anywhere in the world. The facilities in the first-class hotels may have as many as 10 or more different restaurants serving Western and Asian cuisine, coffee shops, swimming pools, exercise rooms, business centers, banqueting halls, shopping arcades, and cable & satellite television. The service is second to none. Indeed, most of the moderately priced hotels rival what in Europe would be considered first-class hotels. Even the budget and inexpensive hotels will invariably have a swimming pool and more than one food outlet.

Because of the financial and tourism slumps that plagued Southeast Asia in 1997 and 1998, hotel rates can range widely, even amongst the top-end hotels. Depending upon season and the situation at the moment, discounts can exceed 50 percent or more of the published rack rate. It pays to shop around and try bargaining – even at the best hotels.

Following the Bangkok listing is a selection of regional hotels from among the many available. They have been chosen to show a range of facilities and prices and, in a few cases, because they are different. Note that a resort hotel does not always have the same connotation in Thailand that it might in the West; often it means nothing more than that the hotel is located in the countryside. One might be surprised by excellent service and luxurious accommodations at a resort hotel, but to expect it, particularly in the smaller areas, is to court disappointment in many cases. Hotels also charge a value added tax (VAT) of 10 percent and often, service charges of 10 percent or more.

During peak holiday periods (holidays, Christmas, New Year, etc.), accommodation is at a premium rate, as it is during high season, from November through April. But the rest of the year, it is always worth asking for a discount.

ABOUT ROOM RATES

Rather than using absolute dollar or baht values for room rates, we have chosen to use relative categories of very expensive, expensive, moderate, inexpensive, and budget.

First, rates are highly elastic right now, especially with the economic problems in Thailand. In Bangkok there is a glut of rooms, and rates can often be highly discounted. Moreover, in Bangkok especially, some luxury hotels quote prices in baht, while others, such as the Oriental, quote only in dollars. Even if a room rate is quoted in dollars, it may be billed on the credit card in baht, and so can vary depending upon exchange rates.

Bangkok

EXPENSIVE

Amari Airport, 333 Choet Wutthakat Road. Tel: 566 1020/1, 566 2060/9, fax: 566 1941. Closest hotel to international airport and therefore popular with travelers arriving late and departing early. Connected to airport with footbridge and shuttle bus.
Amari Boulevard, 2 Soi 5, Sukhumvit Road. Tel: 255 2930, 255 2940, fax: 255 2950. Small but luxurious. An oasis in a raucous tourist area filled with street markets, noodle shops and bars.
Amari Watergate, 847 Phetburi Road. Tel: 653 9000/19, fax: 653 9044, 653 9048. Contemporary high-rise hotel in old market area. The roaring expressway in front of it can be a problem for guests.
Arnoma Swissotel, 99 Ratchadamri Road. Tel: 255 3410, fax: 255 3456/7. Good location, and good restaurants and service.
Asia, 296 Phaya Thai Road. Tel:

215 0808, fax: 215 4360. Offers many extra facilities possibly to offset the noisy, non-stop traffic at its doors.

Beaufort Sukhothai, 13/3 Sathorn Tai Road. Tel: 287 0222, fax: 287 4980. Quiet, luxurious, a cool, green hotel favored by diplomats. Near the city's centre on a busy thoroughfare but set well back amid tropical gardens.

Bel-Aire Princess, 16 Soi 5, Sukhumvit Road. Tel: 253 4300/30, fax: 255 8850. One of the small "boutique" hotels offering personalized service. Close to many big business organizations.

Central Plaza, 1695 Phaholyothin Road. Tel: 541 1234, fax: 541 1087. Midway between the airport and city, but a long way from anywhere except the popular weekend market at Chatuchak Park.

Dusit Thani, 946 Rama IV Road. Tel: 236 0450/9, fax: 236 6400. Bangkok's first high-rise hotel. Adjacent to major banks and business headquarters on Silom Road. Close to nightlife on Patpong.

Emerald, 99/1 Ratchadapisek Road. Tel: 276 4567, fax: 276 4555/6. A large establishment in a growing business, shopping and recreation quarter, but a long journey from the centre at peak traffic periods.

Evergreen Laurel, 88 Sathorn Nua Road (intersection with Soi Pipat). Tel: 266 7223, fax: 266 7222. Smallish but elegant, European atmosphere. On a busy thoroughfare but close to big business and foreign embassies.

Grand Hyatt Erawan, 494 Ratchadamri Road. Tel: 254 1234, fax: 254 6308. On a major intersection and home to the famous Erawan Shrine, one of the best known religious symbols in Bangkok. Adjacent to shopping and horse-racing and golf courses.

Hilton International, 2 Witthayu Road. Tel: 253 0123, fax: 253 6509. Set in beautiful garden with pool. Close to embassies. Good access to and from the airport.

Holiday Inn Crowne Plaza, 981 Silom Road. Tel: 238 4300, fax: 238 5289. Between business

centre and river. A choice location with small shops nearby.

Imperial Queen's Park, 199 Soi 22, Sukhumvit Road. Tel: 261 9000, fax: 261 9530/4. With 1,400 rooms, it is Bangkok's biggest hotel. A cavernous place where guests must walk long distances. Interesting shops, bars and restaurants in the vicinity.

Indra Regent, 120-126 Ratchaprarop Road. Tel: 208 0033, fax: 208 0388. Surrounded by old markets and eating places which are gradually making way for Thailand's largest wholesale centre for garments.

JW Marriott, 4 Soi 2, Sukhumvit Road. Tel: 656 7700, fax 656 7711. Opened in 1997. 446 rooms in an excellent location, close to major shopping and business areas, and with direct freeway access.

Landmark, 138 Sukhumvit Road. Tel: 254 0404, fax: 253 4259. Central location, and near airport road. Well-equipped for business travelers. Good shopping in and outside the hotel.

Le Méridien President, 971 Ploenchit Road. Tel: 253 0444, fax: 253 7565. Central location. The hotel has a French flavour and the best hotel coffee shop in town. Elegant shops and restaurants nearby.

Marriott Royal Garden Riverside, 257/1-3 Charoen Nakhon Road. Tel: 476 0021/2, fax: 476 1120. A resort hotel with the conveniences of nearby downtown. On the western side of the river, a bit to the south, but there are fine views of the riverside life from the hotel terraces. Free river shuttle to Oriental Pier.

Monarch Lee Gardens, 188 Silom Road. Tel: 238 1991, fax: 238 1999. In the heart of the banking and insurance district, but conveniently placed for good shops and restaurants. Nightlife is close.

Montien, 54 Suriwongse Road. Tel: 234 8060, fax: 236 5219. Across the street from Patpong and convenient to the business district along Silom Road. Two pleasant restaurants, a coffee shop, and the

only in-house fortune teller in a Bangkok hotel.

Novotel Bangkok, 392/44 Soi 6, Siam Square, Rama I Road. Tel: 255 6888, fax: 255 1824/7. French management. This is a busy quarter of small shops, movie theaters, eating places and traffic chaos.

Oriental, 48 Oriental Ave. Tel: 236 0400/20, fax: 236 1937/9. A visit is a must, even if it is only to have a drink on the river terrace. The Oriental is part of the history of East meeting West. Repeatedly voted one of the world's best hotels because of its riverside location and its superb service.

Regent Bangkok, 155 Ratchadamri Road. Tel: 251 6127, fax: 253 9195. High luxury in the heart of the city. With music and tea in the lobby lounge, there are echoes of the old Orient. The best hotel swimming pool in Bangkok.

Royal Orchid Sheraton, 2 Captain Bush Lane, Si Phraya Road. Tel: 237 0022, 266 0123, fax: 236 8320. One of the big three riverside hotels with high levels of services and exceptional facilities. All have road access difficulties at peak traffic times but guests may travel by river and see little-known areas of Bangkok.

Shangri-La, 89 Soi Wat Suan Plu, Charoen Krung (New) Road. Tel: 236 7777, fax: 236 8579. Every room has a river view. The evening buffet on the riverside terrace is famous. The biggest hotel on the river.

Sheraton Grande, 250 Sukhumvit Road. Tel: 653 0334/8; fax: 653 0400. Opened in late 1996. 445 rooms in a prime location along the Sukhumvit corridor. Four restaurants, including Italian and Chinese. Expect excellent service in elegant surroundings.

Siam City, 477 Sri Ayutthaya Road. Tel: 247 0120, 247 0130, fax: 247 0178. Good facilities near government offices and army headquarters. A prime spot to hobnob and people-watch.

Siam Intercontinental, 967 Rama I Road. Tel: 253 0355, fax: 253 2275. With 10 acres of gardens, tennis courts, jogging paths, swimming pools, golf greens and driving ranges, this is a cool retreat from the roar of the city. Big and small shops, movie houses and restaurants are just beyond the front gates.

Westin Banyan Tree, Thai Wah II Tower, 21/100 Sathorn Tai Road. Tel: 679 1200, fax: 679 1199. Occupying the lower two and top 28 floors of the tallest building in Thailand. The well-equipped and spacious suites are ideal for the business traveler.

MODERATE

Ambassador, 171 Soi 11-13, Sukhumvit Road. Tel: 254 0444, fax: 253 4123. Large complex with over 1,000 rooms, good food court, several fine restaurants and nightclubs. Close to shopping and restaurants.

Maruay Garden, 1 Soi 40, Phaholyothin Road. Tel: 561 0510, fax: 561 0549. Located 20 miles north of the heart of Bangkok, but close to the expressway and well-served by metered taxis. Over 300 rooms, daily dim sum lunch buffet.

Mercure Hotel, 1091/336 New Phetburi Road. Tel: 253 0510, fax: 253 0556, email: mercureb@ksc15.th.com. 650 rooms centrally located, close to expressway and shopping areas, excellent executive services.

Plaza, 178 Suriwongse Road. Tel: 235 1760/79, fax: 237 0746. Part of the Mandarin Group, close to business district, shopping and sights on Silom and Patpong, rooftop tropical garden.

Somerset, 10 Soi 15, Sukhumvit Road. Tel: 254 8500/24, fax: 254 8534. Small, elegant hotel, conveniently close to a variety of restaurants and shops.

Tai-Pan, 25 Soi 23 (Soi Prasanmit), Sukhumvit Road. Tel: 260 9888, 260 9898, fax: 259 7908, website: www.taipanhotel.co.th. 150 rooms situated close to the business, shopping and entertainment areas along the Sukhumvit corridor.

Tartawan Place, 119/510 Suriwongse Road. Tel: 238 2620, fax: 238 3228. Located in a quiet

soi off Suriwongse, in the heart of the business district. Also very convenient to shopping and entertainment. Excellent service. Major European languages spoken in addition to Thai and English.

Windsor Palace, 8-10 Soi 20, Sukhumvit Road. Tel: 262 1221, 262 1234, fax: 262 1212, website: asiatravel.com/embassysuites. This 34-storey Embassy Suites property offers 463 suites, with three non-smoking floors.

INEXPENSIVE

Bangkok Centre, 328 Rama IV Road. Tel: 238 4848/57, fax: 236 1862. Central location; convenient to railway station. Over 200 rooms.

Euro Inn, 249 Soi 31, Sukhumvit Road. Tel: 259 9480/7, fax: 259 9490. Convenient to shopping and entertainment areas.

Golden Dragon, 20/21 Ngam Wong Wan Road. Tel: 589 0130/41, fax: 589 8305. 114 rooms. Close to airport; 20 minutes from centre of Bangkok. Swimming pool. Good service.

Grand Inn, 2/78 Soi 3 (Soi Nana Nua), Sukhumvit Road. Tel: 254 9021/7, fax: 254 9020. 24 rooms. At the lower end of the Sukhumvit corridor.

Jim's Lodge, 125/7 Soi Ruam Rudi, Ploenchit Road. Tel: 255 3100, 255 0190/9, fax: 253 8492. 75 rooms. Convenient to many embassies. Pleasant restaurant. Good service.

New Trocadero, 343 Suriwongse Road. Tel: 234 8920/9, fax: 236 5526. 130 rooms. Popular with Westerners. Coffee shop. Good travel services.

Park, 6 Soi 7, Sukhumvit Road. Tel: 255 4300/8, fax: 255 4309. 140 rooms, most bright and cheerful. Restaurant, coffee shop and bar. Small pool set in peaceful garden.

President Inn, 155/1416 Soi 11, Sukhumvit Road. Tel: 255 4230/4, fax: 255 4235. Conveniently located.

Rajah, 18 Soi 4, Sukhumvit Road. Tel: 255 0040/83, fax: 255 7160. 450 rooms. Near good shopping and restaurants.

Silom Street Inn, 284/1113 Silom Road. Tel: 238 4680, fax: 238

4689. Pleasant restaurants and shopping in the vicinity.

Thai, 78 Prachatipatai Road. Tel: 282 2831/3, fax: 280 1299. Pleasant surroundings, convenient to TAT office, Banglampoo Market and other attractions.

Tower Inn, 533 Silom Road. Tel: 234 4051, 234 4053, fax: 234 4051. 140 rooms. Midway between Patpong and the river. Good shopping in the area.

Viangtai, 42 Rambutri Road, Banglampoo. Tel: 280 5392/9, fax: 281 8153. In central Banglampoo, on the edge of the Khao San Road area. Convenient to the National Museum and Sanam Luang.

BUDGET

A-One Inn, 25/12-15 Soi Kasem San 1, Rama I Road. Tel: 215 3029, fax: 216 4771. Located beside Siam Square and close to World Trade Centre and Chulalongkorn University. Spacious rooms, friendly service.

Atlanta, 78 Soi 2, Sukhumvit Road. Tel: 252 6069, 252 1650, fax: 255 2151, 656 8123. 50 rooms, some without air conditioning, no TV. Excellent restaurant with tea-time classical music and jazz most evenings. Pool. Well regarded by return visitors. Great value.

Bangkok Christian Guest House, 123 Soi Sala Daeng 2, Silom Road. Tel: 233 2206, 253 3353, fax: 237 1742. Despite its name, more expensive than most guesthouses, with pleasant rooms starting at 650 baht, breakfast included. Convenient to nightlife.

Burapha, 160/14 Charoen Krung (New) Road. Tel: 221 3545/9, fax: 226 1723. On the edge of Chinatown and therefore a little noisy. Reasonable service.

Comfort Inn, 153/11-14 Soi 11, Sukhumvit Road. Tel: 251 9250, 254 3559/60, fax: 254 3562. 60 rooms. Convenient location close to shopping and restaurants.

Florida, 43 Phaya Thai Road. Tel: 247 0990, fax: 247 7419. Interesting, rather old building, near the Victory Monument.

Opera, 16 Soi Somprasong 1, Phetburi Road. Tel: 252 4031, fax:

253 5360. Convenient to Pratunam Market and Siam Square. Pool. Coffee shop.

YMCA, 27 Sathorn Tai Road, and **YWCA**, 13 Sathorn Tai Road. Tel: 286 1936, fax: 287 1996. 50 rooms, some cottages, sports facilities, European, Chinese and Thai restaurant. Quiet.

Outside of Bangkok

KANCHANABURI (034)
Moderate

Duen Shine Resort, Kanchanaburi. Tel: 513 611. Bungalows by the river near the bridge.

Felix River Kwai Resort, Kanchanaburi. Tel: 511 184, fax: 511 259. Comfortable hotel in a pretty garden setting near the bridge.

KHAO YAI PARK (044)

A campsite and some simple dormitories are available within the park, and camping out on one of the observation towers may be a possibility as well. Policy changes are not uncommon; inquire at the TAT office or the Royal Forestry Department in Bangkok, or at park headquarters for further details.

Moderate to Expensive

Juldis Khao Yai Resort, 54 Moo 4, Thanarat Road (km 17), Pak Chong. Tel: 297 297, fax: 297 291. In Bangkok, tel: (02) 613 7273/77, fax: (02) 613 7272. A beautifully situated hotel favored by corporate groups and well-heeled Thais. Adequate food; surprisingly inadequate service. No regularly scheduled tours of the park, although arrangements can be made with other tour operators.

Moderate

Khao Yai Garden Lodge, Thanon Thanarat, Kilometer 7, Pak Chong. Tel: 313 567, fax: 312 143. A cozy atmosphere and excellent food are offered by this German-Thai couple. 35 rooms ranging from 100 baht (fan-cooled, shared toilet) to 1,400 baht (air-conditioned, traditional Thai decor, private bath). Spacious grounds include a bird garden, a 40-year old tortoise, and many

botanical wonders; herbal sauna and swimming pool with waterfall available from 1998. Offers a range of tours, not only of Khao Yai, but throughout the Northeast as well. Will pick up from Bangkok with prior arrangement.

Budget

Jungle Adventure Guest House, Kongwaksin Road, Soi 3, Pak Chong. Tel: 313 836. Dormitory accommodation and basic rooms ranging from 70–200 baht per night. One-and-a-half-day tours of Khao Yai at 950 baht per person.

Wildlife Safari, 39 Subsanun Road, Pak Chong. Tel/fax: 312 922. Simple, clean accommodation ranging from 100–400 baht. Note that lodging is limited to those taking the one-and-a-half-day tours of Khao Yai at around 750 baht.

Central Plains

SUKHOTHAI (055)
Moderate

Wang Neua, Singhawat Road. Tel: 611 193, fax: 612 038. A modern provincial hotel with swimming pool.

Inexpensive

River View Hotel, Nikhornkasem Road. Tel: 611 656. As the name implies, with a river view but not much else.

North and Northeast

CHIANG MAI (053)
Expensive

Amari Rincome, 1 Nimmanhemin Road. Tel: 221 044, fax: 221 915. One of the best hotels in Chiang Mai. Elegant, but situated on the edge of town.

Pornping, Charoen Prathet Road. Tel: 270 099, fax: 270 119. Centrally situated tower housing the famous Bubbles disco.

Royal Princess, Chang Klan Road. Tel: 281 033, fax: 281 044. Managed by the Dusit group, this first-class hotel is well known for its service. Located next door to the night market.

Moderate

Chiang Inn, Chang Klan Road. Tel: 270 070, fax: 274 299. Located near the night market, with a pool

and one of the city's most popular discos, The Wall Club.

Galare Guest House, Charoen Prathet Road. Tel: 273 885, fax: 279 088. Attractive and inexpensive location by the river.

Inexpensive

Top North Guest House, Moon Muang Road, Soi 2. Tel: 278 900, fax: 278 485. Quiet, central, cheap and with pool; one of the most attractive offers in town.

CHIANG RAI (053)
Moderate

Dusit Island Resort, Kraisorasit Road. Tel: 715 777, fax: 715 801. The best hotel in town lies on an island in the Kok river.

Wiang Inn, Phaholyothin Road. Tel: 711 533, fax: 711 877. No pool, but a disco and a central location.

CHIANG SAEN (053)
Moderate

Le Méridien Baan Boran. Tel: 784 084, fax: 784 090. Attractive luxury resort directly at the Golden Triangle, with elephant stables on the premises.

MAE HONG SON (053)
Moderate

Holiday Inn. Tel: 612 234/9, fax: 611 524. Ultra-modern and with all amenities. On the edge of town.

Inexpensive

Baiyoke Chalet. Tel: 611 486, fax: 611 533. Friendly little hotel, near lake.

MAE SAI (053)
Moderate

Wang Thong. Tel: 733 388, fax: 733 399. Luxury hotel with Chinese decor and a view of the bridge marking the border.

Inexpensive

Mae Sai Hotel. Tel: 731 462. Directly next to the ruby market.

MAE SALONG (053)
Moderate

Khum Naiphol Resort. Tel: 765 014. Built by General Tuan's family and still run by them.

NAN VALLEY (054)

Inexpensive

City Park Hotel, 99 Moo 4, Yontakakit Koson Road, Tambon Tuu Tai. Tel: 710 376. Air-conditioning, pool, satellite TV. Inconvenient location about 10 km (6 mi) southwest of town.

Dhevaraj Hotel, 466 Sumonthewaraj Road, Amphur Muang. Tel: 710 078, 710 212, 710 803; fax: 771 365. Standard plastic and tile provincial hotel, circa 1980. Air-conditioning, TV, elevator. Central location.

Nan Fa Hotel, 440 Sumonthewaraj Road, Amphur Muang. Tel: 772 640, 771 697. Central location. Air-conditioning, TV, dubious plumbing. Clean, well-maintained old wooden building. For sheer atmosphere, this is it. On ground floor, craft store and Thai restaurant, which features live folk music in early evening.

Papua Bhuka Hotel, 141 Pua-Namyao Street, Moo 4, Tambon Xilalang, Amphur Pua. Tel: 791 156, 791 166; fax: 791 166. About a half dozen kilometers (4 mi) south of the town of Pua on Route 1080, this is the only option outside of Nan town. Air-conditioning, satellite TV, small restaurant. Beautiful views of misted mountains, convenient for jaunts to tribal villages and Silaphet waterfall.

Doi Phu Kha National Park. Budget accommodation (100–200 baht) in bungalows on edge of park. Visitors can set up tents. Small restaurant. Advisable to bring extra supplies.

N. RATCHASIMA (KHORAT) (044)

Moderate

Sima Thani, Mittraphap Road. Tel: 213 100, fax: 213 122. Best hotel in Nakhon Ratchasima with a beautiful lobby dotted with Khmer-style figures.

Royal Princess, 1137 Suranari Road. Tel: 256 629/35, fax: 256 601. On the edge of town. Decorated in northeastern Thai style.

Gulf Coast

CHANTHABURI (039)

Moderate

Maneechan Resort, 110 Moo 11, Plubpla, Chanthaburi. Tel: 343 777/8, fax: 344 123. A complex with private homes and a resort with excellent sports facilities.

PATTAYA/JOMTIEN (038)

Expensive

Dusit Resort, 240 Beach Road. Tel: 425 611, fax: 428 239. Top-class service and all the requisite amenities plus a good range of water sports.

Royal Cliff, 353 Moo 12, Cliff Road. Tel: 250 421/40, fax: 250 511/513. One of Pattaya's top addresses, ostentatiously built into a cliff with a good private beach.

Royal Garden Resort Pattaya, Beach Road. Tel: 412 120/6, fax: 429 926. Operated by the group that owns the Marriott Royal Garden Riverside, in Bangkok, the Royal Garden had led the drive to make Pattaya a family destination. First-class facilities.

Moderate

Amari Orchid Resort, Beach Road, North Pattaya. Tel: 428 161, fax: 428 195. A welcoming beach hotel with a luxuriant garden.

Inexpensive

Cosy Beach Hotel, 400 Moo 12, Pratmnak Road, Pattaya. Tel: 250 800, fax: 250 799. Lush gardens, good facilities, quiet beach.

Diana Inn, 216/6-9 Pattaya 2 Road, Pattaya Beach, Chonburi. Tel: 429 675, fax: 428 239. A pleasant hotel with an attractive pool and friendly service.

Northern Isthmus

HUA HIN (032)

Expensive

Melia Hua Hin, 33 Naresdamri Road. Tel: 511 612, fax: 511 135. An elegant resort hotel on the beach at Hua Hin. Features over-sized ocean-view rooms and a spectacular pool.

Royal Garden Resort, Phetkasem Beach Road. Tel: 511 881, fax: 512 422. A low-rise resort on Hua Hin's long, snow-white beach. Operated by the same group that owns the Marriott Royal Garden Riverside, in Bangkok. Uncrowded retreat with full services. Nearby is the sister hotel Royal Garden Village.

Sofitel Central Hua Hin. Tel: 512 021, fax: 511 014. The former Railway Hotel, this establishment is full of Old World splendour.

CHUMPHON (077)

Moderate

Cabana Resort. Tel: 501 990. A bungalow complex with a famous diving school. Guests will be met in Chumphon on request.

Inexpensive

Jansom Chumphon, Sala Daeng Road. Tel: 502 502, fax: 502 503. Large central business hotel with popular coffee shop and disco.

Sai Ree Lodge, Sai Ree Beach, Pak Nam. Tel: 521 212, fax: 502 479. Pleasant, clean thatched cottages beside the beach linked by elevated wooden walkways. Good sea view.

SURAT THANI (077)

Moderate

Saowaluk Thani, 99/44-46 Surat-Kranchanadit Road. Tel: 283 295/6, fax: 273 977. The best hotel in Surat, located in eastern end of the city and run by the Dusit group from Bangkok.

Wang Tai Hotel, Talad Mai Road. Tel: 283 020, fax: 281 007. On the edge of town, but with a pool. Excellent coffee shop with good food to match the live (Thai) music.

Ko Samui/Pha Ngan

KO SAMUI (077)

Expensive

Baan Taling Ngam, 295 Moo 3, Ban Taling. Tel: 423 019/22; fax: 423 220. Part of the Oriental Hotel chain. The beach on this secluded western coast is mediocre with coarse sand, but the views are stunning from the rooms perched on a hillside. Pools at beachside and hilltop. Ideal when the northwest monsoon is blowing.

Moderate to Expensive

Imperial Boat House, Choengmon Beach. Tel: 425 041, email:

imperial@ksc.net.th. North of Chaweng and a quieter alternative. Luxury rooms in two-storey converted rice barges.

Laem Set Inn, 110 Moo 2, Hua Thanon. Tel: 424 393, 233 299, fax: 424 394, 233 301. Chinese-style hardwood houses have been transplanted and restored to form this boutique hotel. This southeast beach is unremarkable, but good snorkeling. Excellent for children.

Moderate

Chaweng Regent Resort, 155-4 Central Chaweng Beach. Tel: 422 389, 422 008. Three swimming pools, meeting facilities. Smack in the middle of Chaweng Beach, backs onto the nightlife scene.

Poppies Samui, PO Box 1, Chaweng Noi. Tel: 422 419. Twenty-four cottages hidden among greenery, Balinese style. Near the southern end of the beach. Reputed for its restaurant.

The Princess Village, Central Chaweng. Tel: 422 382. South-central location. Pretend you're back in Ayutthaya in these period-style bungalows with traditional furnishings and all mod-cons.

Samui Euphoria Resort, 101/3 Bo Phut Bay. Tel: 425 100/6, fax: 425 107. Tennis, billiards, badminton, putting green, petanque, fitness club, pool. Popular with French and Italian families.

Inexpensive

Spa Resort, North Lamai Beach. Tel: 230 855, fax: 424 126. A hotel and New Age health centre. Fasting regimes, herbal saunas, colonic irrigation as well as traditional Thai massage, hikes and mountain-biking trips. Services also offered to non-guests.

Samui Palm Beach Resort, Bo Phut Bay. Tel: 425 494. Well-appointed cottages. Top of the line for around Bo Phut.

KO PHA NGAN (077)

Inexpensive

Panviman Resort, Thong Nai Pan Beach. Tel/fax: 377 048; Bangkok reservations: 587 8491; fax: 587 8493; email: panviman@ kohphangan.com. The island's most upscale resort straddles a steep

headland that overlooks two fine, secluded northeastern beaches. Excellent snorkeling, fishing, views. Some air-conditioned cottages and hotel-style rooms.

The Sanctuary, PO Box 3, Hat Tien Beach. A low-budget, attractively designed bungalow resort. Four km (2 mi) from Hat Rin Beach. Between September and May, hosts a series of New Age courses ranging from massage and tai chi to past-life regression and "cranial sacral."

KO TAO (077)

Inexpensive

Koh Tao Cottage, Ao Chalok Ban Kao Beach. Tel: (01) 725 0751; fax: (01) 725 0662. The island's poshest resort. Twenty-four bungalows with fan, fridge and window screens. No air-conditioning.

Nang Yuan Resort, Ko Nang Yuan. Tel: (01) 726 0085. These simple bungalows may seem overpriced for these parts, but you're paying for the beaches, coral and exclusivity on this sandbar off Ko Tao.

Phuket

PHUKET TOWN (076)

Moderate

Metropole, Montri Road. Tel: 215 050, fax: 215 099. Modern and elegant high-rise hotel. Staff wear Thai traditional garb. Popular with business travelers as well as tourists. Very good food and beverage outlets, particularly the coffee shop's buffet lunch. This is a four-star hotel at three-star prices.

Inexpensive

Thavorn, Rasda Road. Tel: 211 333/5. One of the first hotels in Phuket. Lobby displays historical pictures of local culture. Rooms fronting Rasda Road are noisy but otherwise comfortable. Central location.

BEACHES (076)

Very Expensive

Banyan Tree, The, 33 Moo 4, Srisoonthorn Road, Choeng Talay District. Bang Thao/Laguna. Tel: 324 374, fax: 324 375. Individual bungalows encircling a larger

lagoon; some are garden bungalows, the more expensive ones come with private outdoor pool. Full range of spa facilities. Low key, discreet, quite romantic and luxurious. The perfect quiet and private getaway.

The Chedi, Choeng Talay. Pansea. Tel: 324 017/20, fax: 324 252. High-class Asian-inspired resort bungalows linked by elevated walkways. Strangely, no tubs, only showers in rooms. Most balconies overlook an immaculate beach. A romantic setting with first-rate cuisine, but isolated setting.

Le Méridien, 8/5 Moo 1 Karon Beach. Relax Bay. Tel: 340 480/5, fax: 340 479. Huge 470-room 5-star hotel filled with activities year-round, including a glitzy variety show every night. Mega- sized swimming pools. Guests have access to what is effectively the hotel's own private beach, in a small bay midway between Patong and Karon.

Phuket Yacht Club, 23/3 Viset Road. Nai Harn. Tel: 381 156/63, fax: 381 164. Deluxe hotel, operated by the Le Méridien group. A beautiful luxury hotel hugging one end of isolated but spectacular Nai Harn beach. Elegant rooms with equally large private sun decks, with classic views of the spectacular Nai Harn Bay and Promthep Cape.

Sheraton Grande Laguna, Choeng Talay District. Bang Thao/Laguna. Tel: 324 101/7, fax: 324 108. A 341-room deluxe hotel built around fresh water lagoons reclaimed from an old tin mining site. Numerous dining outlets. The star attraction is the unique winding swimming pool with piped-in music underwater.

Expensive

Amari Coral Beach, 104 Moo 4, South Patong. Tel: 340 106/10. Well-run remote hotel on its own site, about 10 minutes' walk from the southern tip of Patong Beach. Uninspiring beach front. Trips to nearby Paradise Beach are popular with guests. First-rate Kinaree Thai restaurant.

Boathouse, The, 2/2 Patak Road. Kata. Tel: 330 015/7, fax: 330

561. Situated on the quiet end of Kata, this small and elegant beach-front "boutique" hotel prides itself on attentive and personalized service. Main building built in the Ayutthaya style with steep sloping roofs. Famous for its sophisticated Boathouse Wine & Grill restaurant, and for its wine list.

Club Andaman Beach Resort, 77/1 Thaviwong Road, Patong. Tel: 340 530, fax: 321 527. Large hotel in expansive, manicured gardens close to but not on the beach. Cottage accommodation in addition to hotel wing. Tennis courts, gym, pool. Well-appointed rooms with in-house video, fridge and safe deposit box.

Club Med Phuket, 7/3 Patak Road. Kata. Tel: 330 455, fax: 330 461. Large resort in front of central Kata Beach. Caters to the young-at-heart with lots of organized activities. Excellent French and international cuisine.

Dusit Laguna, Choeng Talay District. Bang Thao/Laguna. Tel: 324 320/32, fax: 324 174. Part of the Dusit chain of deluxe hotels in Thailand, this five-star resort reflects its Thai heritage, apparent in the decor, staff costumes and the acclaimed Ruen Thai restaurant. Broad, sweeping Bang Thao Bay is exposed and unsafe to swim in the monsoon season.

Holiday Inn, Thaviwong Road. Patong. Tel: 340 608/9, fax: 340 435. Right beside the beachfront action. Very popular and large resort hotel that attracts families on long vacations. Swimming pool and the Pirate's Cove minigolf for the children. Superlative steaks at Sam's Chicago Steak House.

Karon Beach Resort, 5/2 Moo 2, Patak Road. Karon. Tel: 330 006, fax: 381 529. Small family-run bungalow resort located at quiet end of Karon beach. There are a restaurant, snack bar, swimming pool and tour counter on site with the facilities of both Kata and Karon beaches a short walk away.

Marina Cottage, South Karon Bay. Karon. Tel: 330 625, fax: 330 516. Thai-style cottages exquisitely landscaped into a hilly coconut

plantation. Dino Park crazy golf appeals to adults as well as kids. Two excellent restaurants: Sala Thai (central Thai cuisine) and On the Rock (seafood mostly).

Inexpensive

Jungle Beach Resort, 11/3 Viset Road. Nai Harn. Tel: 288 264. Fan-cooled and air-conditioned rooms in a tourist-class bungalow resort tastefully melded into its surroundings. Good place for nature-oriented relaxation on the remote southern tip of Phuket.

Krabi/Phang Nga

KRABI (075)
Very Expensive

Dusit Rayavadee Resort, Phra Nang Headland. Tel: 620 740/2. Sumptuous deluxe resort discreetly landscaped alongside Phra Nang and Railae beaches. Water sports, tennis courts, sauna, gym. Two restaurants: Thai/seafood and international.

Moderate

Meritime Hotel, 4 Pipatkul Road. Tel: 620 028, 620 046, fax: 612 992. Krabi town's most luxurious hotel 2 km (1 mile) from the town centre. Each room has a balcony overlooking limestone karsts, mangrove forests and the township. Satellite TV, coffee shop, pool.

Phra Nang Inn, Ao Nang Beach Road. Tel: 637 129. Conveniently located hotel fronting Ao Nang beach. The old wing is more sociable than the new. Owners organize nature and culture tours. Has its own sea canoe facility for guests. Beachside restaurant and sunset bar.

Inexpensive

City Hotel, 15/2 3 Sukon Road. Tel: 611 961. Clean and friendly family-run hotel, with nice touches like fruit basket and TV in each room. Both fan and air-conditioned rooms available.

Gift's Bungalows, Ao Nang Beach Road. Tel: 637 193. Simple but clean jungle huts in a verdant tropical garden. Atmospheric restaurant serves tasty food and homemade breads. Surprisingly good for the price range.

Viengthong Hotel, 155/7 Uttarakit Road. Tel: 611 188, fax: 612 525. Centrally located hotel overlooking the river. Fan and air-conditioned rooms and a popular coffee shop open late.

PHANG NGA (076)
Moderate

Phangnga Bay Resort Hotel, 20 Tha Dan Road. Pansea. Tel: 412 067/70, fax: 412 057. Long-established hotel built right on the mangrove waterside in majestic Phang Nga Bay. Excellent location beside the river, ideal as a base for the exploration of nearby islands. Quality of service and dining fails to match the setting.

PHI PHI (075)
Expensive

Palm Beach Travelodge Resort, Laemthong Beach. Phi Phi. Tel: (076) 214 654 (Phuket town office); (01) 723 0922 (resort). Designer award-winning bungalows on isolated beach facing Bamboo and Mosquito islands. Desert island setting. Varied water sport facilities, including scuba diving. Internationally run.

Moderate

Phi Phi Princess Resort, Loh Dalam Bay. Phi Phi. Tel: 612 188. Comfortable newly built beach-front bungalows with satellite TV and minibar. Faces Phi Phi's most attractive bay. Convenient to village.

Inexpensive

Charlie Beach Resort, Loh Dalam Bay, Phi Phi. Tel: 620 615. Centrally located, quiet set of bungalows with immaculate beach setting. Good room choice. 24-hour security. Restaurant is only good for drinks and satellite TV.

Deep South

HAT YAI (074)
Moderate

Central Sukhotha, 3 Sanehanusorn Road. Tel: 352 222, fax: 352 223. The most upmarket hotel in town, plumb in the centre of city.

The Regency, Prachathipat Road. Tel: 234 101. Modern tower in the middle of the market with a view.

Inexpensive
Laemthong Hotel, Thamamoonviti Road. Tel: 352 301. Large, simple and clean Chinese hotel in a central location.

SONGKHLA (074)
Moderate
Haad Kaeo Princess Resort, Kilometer 5, Tambon Chingkoh, Songkhla. Tel: 331 059/67, fax: 331 058. The only beach resort in Songkhla. Suitable for families. Located 30 minutes' drive from town on the road to Sathing Phra.
Samila Hotel, 1/11 Ratdamnern Road. Tel: 322 448. Ideally situated at the crossing between the two beaches. With garden and pool.
Inexpensive
Lake Inn, 301 Nakhon Nawk Road. Tel: 314 823, fax: 314 843. High-rise with lake views.
Pavilion, 17 Platha Road. Tel: 311 355, fax: 323 716. Good-value hotel with large pool and modern, well-appointed rooms.

Guesthouses

If you are on a limited budget, there are numerous guesthouses offering clean, economical accommodation. Once of primary interest only to backpackers because of their sparse facilities, many have now been upgraded to include fans, air-conditioning and bathrooms in the rooms rather than down the hall. As such, they afford a viable alternative to the frugal traveler. Prices range from 80 to 400 baht.

Generally possessing no more than a dozen rooms, they are more like pensions than hotels, and appeal to travelers who like personalized service, friendly staff and a more relaxed pace.

Their numbers are legion, and to list them would fill several books. In Bangkok guesthouses are found in Banglampoo, particularly along Khao San Road, and in the Soi Ngam Duphli area off Rama IV Road. In Chiang Mai, check along the river and in the area of Chaiyaphum Road. In Pattaya and Phuket, guesthouses are much less common.

In other towns, guesthouses are generally family-run establishments and so are scattered around town. But look in the vicinity of bus and railway stations, and along main streets. The smaller the town, the more likely they are to be found on the main street.

BANGKOK
Apple Guest House, 10 Phra Athit Road. Tel: 281 6838. 70–100 baht. Restaurant.
Bangkok International Youth Hostel, 25/2 Phitsanulok Road. Tel: 282 0950, 281 0361, fax: 281 6834. A range of accommodations from dorm rooms to rooms with bath, choice of fan or air-conditioning. 70–300 baht. Cafeteria. Hostel members only; temporary membership may be purchased.
Chart Guest House, 61 Khao San Road. Tel: 280 3785. 60–100 baht. Some air-conditioned rooms available for 400+ baht.
Lee 4 Guest House, off Soi Si Bamphen, Soi Ngam Duphli, Rama IV Road. 120–180 baht. Said to be the best of the three Lee guesthouses in the vicinity. Clean, large rooms.
P. Guest House, 151-157 Trok Sa-Ke, Tanao Road. Tel: 224 1967. 80–120 baht. Helpful staff.
Peachy Guest House, 10 Phra Athit Road. Tel: 281 6471, 281 6659. 85–150 baht, extra for air-conditioning. Garden restaurant.
Shanti Lodge, 37 Sri Ayutthaya Road. Tel: 281 2497. 50–150 baht. Clean rooms, friendly service, coffee shop.
Tavee Guest House, 83 Sri Ayutthaya Road. Tel: 280 1447, 282 5983. 50–150 baht. Clean. Reasonably quiet.

Eating Out

What to Eat

The dramatic rise in the number of Thai restaurants around the world says something about the popularity of one of the world's supreme cuisines. It is no surprise that when gourmets arrive on these shores fresh from Thai dining experiences at home, they fall into a feeding frenzy that lasts their entire stay.

The base for most Thai dishes is coconut milk. Ginger, garlic, lemon grass and fiery chilies give Thai dishes a piquancy that can set tender palates aflame. While many of the chilies are mild, their potency is in obverse proportion to their size; the smallest, the *prik kii no* or "rat dropping chilies," are guaranteed to dissolve your sinuses and cloud your vision with tears.

For those averse to spicy food, chefs can tone down the curries or serve one of the dozens of non-spicy curries.

Where to Eat
BANGKOK
In Europe, the very best restaurants are not usually to be found in hotels. In Thailand, the reverse is true. There are, of course, exceptions to both these generalities. All the following restaurants contribute to making Thailand a gourmet's paradise.

Thai Dinner and Cultural Shows
Baan Thai, 7 Soi 32, Sukhumvit Road. Tel: 258 5403, 258 9517. Pleasant atmosphere in a group of old Thai houses in a tropical garden. Popular with group tours. Thai dancing begins around 9pm.
Maneeya Lotus Room, 518/4 Ploenchit Road. Tel: 251 0382, 252

6312. Open daily. Lunch 10am–2pm. Nightly 7pm with Thai classical dance performance at 8.15pm.

Sala Rim Nam, Charoen Nakhon Road. Tel: 437 9417, 437 3080, 437 2918. Located in a beautiful, temple-like building across the river from the Oriental – particularly good Thai dancing. Free boat service from Oriental Hotel landing. Book in advance.

Sala Thai, Indra Regent Hotel, 120-126 Ratchaprarop Road. Tel: 208 0033. Attractive reproduction of a classic building on an upper floor of the hotel.

Silom Village Trade Centre, 286 Silom Road. Tel: 234 4448, 233 9447. Open-air and indoor restaurants, traditional food stalls, Thai cultural show presented every Saturday and Sunday from 12.45am and Thai classical dance shows daily at 8pm. Informal atmosphere.

Hotel Buffets

Many hotels in Bangkok vie with each other to prove that their lunch and dinner buffets surpass that of their competitors, both in quality and value for money. The result is an overwhelming choice of prices. You will not be disappointed wherever you choose to go, and even the least-expensive buffets still offer a bewildering variety of dishes. All are highly recommended. In addition, many hotels offer lavish Sunday brunches, with clowns, magicians, games, videos and other diversions to keep children amused.

Thai Cuisine

All Gaengs, 173/8-9 Suriwongse Road. Tel: 233 3301. Elegant, modern decor and delicious Thai cuisine. $$

Baan Kanitha, 36/1 Soi 23 (Soi Prasanmit), Sukhumvit Road. Tel: 258 4181. A good introduction to Thai cuisine with tasteful decor and attentive service. $$

Benjarong, Dusit Thani Hotel, 946 Rama IV Road. Tel: 236 0450/9. Superlative Royal Thai cuisine served on exquisite bencharong ware. $$$

Bon Vivant, Tawana Ramada Hotel, 80 Suriwongse Road. Tel: 236 0361/98. Splendid cuisine with a host of Thai dishes, beautifully prepared and presented. $$

Bussaracum, 35 Soi Pipat 2, Convent Road. Tel: 235 8915. Extremely popular with local connoisseurs of classical Thai cuisine; pleasant, informal atmosphere. $$

Cabbages and Condoms, 8-10 Soi 12, Sukhumvit Road. Tel: 252 7349, 251 5552. Value for money and first-class cuisine. If you are not familiar with Thai food, this should be among your first choices. The profits support various family planning and HIV awareness programs and other charitable projects. Entertaining gift shop adjacent. $

Celadon, Beaufort Sukhothai, 13/3 Sathorn Tai Road. Tel: 287 0222. Exceptional cuisine in the setting of an exotic water garden. $$$

Chilli House, Soi 4, Silom Road (near the Rome Club). Tel: 266 9564. You can enter either via Silom Road or through the Patpong Car Park on Soi Patpong 2. Everything expertly prepared and presented by a top Thai chef, especially the seafood dishes. $

D'Jit Pochana, 62 Soi 20, Sukhumvit Road. Tel: 258 1578. Branches at 1082 Phaholyothin Road (near Chatuchak Park), tel: 279 5000/2, and at Ploenchit Centre, 3rd Floor, tel: 656 8454. A long-established Thai restaurant, diverse menu. Try the wild boar curry. $

Hemlock, 56 Phra Athit Road (opposite River Express Boat entrance). Tel: 282 7507. Excellent food, impressive wine list, many foreign beers. $

Krua Langsuan, 93/12 Soi 5, Soi Lang Suan. Tel: 252 1945. Picturesque venue. Dine on pleasant Thai and Chinese cuisine while listening to Thai folk music. $

Laicram, 120/12 Soi 23 (Soi Prasanmit), Sukhumvit Road. Tel: 258 9616, 238 2337. Branches at 11/1 Soi 49/4, Sukhumvit Road, tel: 392 5864; Thaniya Bldg., Thaniya Road, tel: 231 2117.

Excellent variety of Thai dishes. $–$$

Lemongrass, 5/21 Soi 24, Sukhumvit Road. Tel: 258 8637. Known for its excellent cuisine. $$

Nipa Thai, Landmark Hotel, 138 Sukhumvit Road. Tel: 254 0404. As with all the many restaurants in this hotel, its Thai restaurant is of the highest standard. $$$

Pan Kitchen, Tai-Pan Hotel, 25 Soi 23 (Soi Prasanmit), Sukhumvit Road. Tel: 260 9888. Tasty Thai cuisine. Worth going out of your way to try the inexpensive buffet set lunch which also includes some European dishes. $–$$

Salathip, Shangri-La Hotel, 89 Soi Wat Suan Plu. Tel: 236 7777. Superb Thai dining on the river's edge. $$$

Sidewalk, 855/2 Silom Road. Tel: 236 4496. The owner is French-born Pierre Chaslin, the author of the best selling "Discover Thai Cooking." Superb cuisine, ordinary decor. $

Sorn Daeng (at the Democracy Monument), 78/2 Ratchadamnern Road. Tel: 224 3088. One of the oldest restaurants in town, known for good Thai food. $

Spice Market, The Regent Hotel, 155 Ratchadamri Road. Tel: 251 6127. Beautifully decorated restaurant, with dishes that the chef can adapt to suit Western palates. $$

Thai Pavilion, Holiday Inn Crowne Plaza, 981 Silom Road. Tel: 238 4300. Traditional Thai cuisine in a traditional setting. $$

Thai Room, 37/20-5 Soi Patpong 2. Tel: 233 7920. Serving Thai, Mexican, Chinese and European food. One of the oldest restaurants in the city. $

Thanying, 10 Pramuan Road, Silom Road. Tel: 236 4361. Excellent Thai food in very pleasant surroundings. $$

The Glass, 22/3-5 Soi 11, Sukhumvit Road. Tel: 254 3566. As well known for its food as its live music in the evenings. $$

Isaan/Lao and Northern Thai

Ban Chiang, 14 Soi Srivieng, Surasak Road (off Silom Road). Tel:

236 7045, 266 6994. Pleasant surroundings, comprehensive selection of central Thai and Isaan dishes, good wines. $

Bua Luang, 116 Soi Rambutri, Banglampoo. Tel: 282 2635. A long-standing restaurant with good Northern dishes. $

Khing Klao, Soi 22, Sukhumvit Road (just beyond Washington Square). Tel: 259 5623. Interesting decor, great Chiang Mai sausage dishes. $

Mai Klang Krung, 114/3 Sethasiri Road, Phaya Thai. Tel: 279 2866. Peaceful garden setting serving traditional Northern fare. Chicken wrapped in banana leaves a specialty. $

Panjimhut Isaan Restaurant, Sukhumvit Road, between Soi 51 and 53. Tel: (none). Excellent Isaan food, but not for those with delicate palates. $$

Sara Jane's Larb Lang Suan, 36/2 Soi Lang Suan. Tel: 252 6572. Traditional, spicy Northeastern dishes. $$

Som Tam, Si Nakharin Road, opposite Seri Centre. Tel: 393 5884, 748 0794. Delicious Isaan cuisine, very popular. Will tone down spices if asked. $

Seafood

Dusit Rimtarn Seafood Restaurant, Supakarn Shopping Centre, Sathorn Bridge. Tel: 437 9671. A view of the river. Seafood and other Thai and Chinese cuisine superbly prepared under the supervision of the Dusit Thani Hotel. $$–$$$

For Hor Gor Dor, 15 Soi 4, Soi 63 (Soi Ekamai), Sukhumvit Road. Tel: 391 1326. Quiet location, beautiful decor, generous portions. $$

Lord Jim's, Oriental Hotel, 48 Oriental Avenue. Tel: 236 0400. Top-quality restaurant noted for its good atmosphere, excellent food and service. $$$

Sammuk Seafood, 2140-4 Soi 90, Lard Prao Road. Tel: 539 2466/9. One of many inexpensive Thai seafood restaurants in Bangkok. This particular one has won many accolades for the quality of food. $

Sea Food Market, 89 Soi 24, Sukhumvit Road. (Look for the large

neon lobster sign.) Tel: 261 2071/4. Novel grocery store layout; pick out the seafood of your choice from a vast variety on ice and have it cooked to suit your taste; informal. Great selection of wines. Can be expensive if you succumb to the temptation of ordering too much. $$–$$$

Talay Thong, Siam Inter-Continental Hotel, 967 Rama I Road. Tel: 253 0355. High quality dining, decor and service. $$

Wit's Oyster Bar, 21/10 Soi Ruam Rudi, Ploenchit Road. Tel: 252 1820, 251 9455. A plush English-style oyster bar. $$

Outdoor Thai Restaurants

When giving instructions to the taxi driver, tell him "Suan Aahaan" (garden restaurant) before giving him the name of one of the restaurants below.

Baan Buang, 32/10 Mu 2, Ratchadapisek Road (opposite Nikko Hotel). Tel: 277 8609, 277 7563. $–$$

Buatong, 30 Ratchadapisek Road. Tel: 245 5545. $–$$

Tum Nak Thai, 131 Ratchadapisek Road. Tel: 276 7810. This restaurant has merited an entry in the Guinness Book of Records as the largest in the world. Waiters on roller skates serve food from all regions of Thailand; very popular with tourists. $–$$

Riverside Restaurants

Baan Khun Luang, 131/4 Khao Road (off Ratchawithi Road). Tel: 241 0928, 241 0521, 241 2282. Thai, Chinese and Japanese cuisine in a riverside setting. $

Kaloang Home Kitchen, on the river, behind the National Library (at the end of Sri Ayutthaya, cross Samsen, turn right, then left to the river). Tel: 281 9228, 282 7581. Very popular, generous portions. $$

Rim Naam Terrace, Montien Riverside Hotel, Rama III Road. Tel: 292 2800. Lovely setting with Thai and Vietnamese specialties. $$

Savoy Seafood Restaurant, River City Complex, 23 Yotha Road. Tel: 435 0611. Excellent Thai and Chinese seafood dishes. $$

Chinese

Canton Palace, Evergreen Laurel Hotel, 88 Sathorn Nua Road. Tel: 266 7223. An elegant restaurant with excellent Cantonese cuisine. $$

Chinatown, Dusit Thani Hotel, 946 Rama IV Road. Tel: 236 0450. Less expensive than the Mayflower also within the hotel, but just as delicious. $$

Chiu Chau, Ambassador Hotel, 171 Soi 11-13, Sukhumvit Road. Tel: 254 0444. Delicacies from the Southern Chinese province of Chiu Chau (Guangchao). $$

Coca Noodles, 8 Soi Tartawan, Suriwongse Road. Tel: 236 9323. Branches at Siam Square, 416/3-8 Henri Dunant Road, tel: 251 6337; The Mall 4, 1911 Ramkhamhaeng Road, tel: 318 0997; 1/1 Soi 39, Sukhumvit Road, tel: 259 8188. Cantonese hot pot, sukiyaki and noodle dishes. $$

Dynasty, Central Plaza Hotel, 1695 Phaholyothin Road. Tel: 541 1234. Traditional cuisine with Peking duck, shark's fin and abalone all featured in the extensive menu. $$

Great Wall, Asia Hotel, 296 Phaya Thai Road. Tel: 215 0808. The heart of any good hotel is in the kitchen; at the Asia Hotel there are several different kinds of restaurants, this being one of the best. $$$

Hoi Tien Lao, 762 Laadya Road, (Thonburi bank of river, opp. Royal Orchid Sheraton Hotel). Tel: 437 1121. Cantonese food; one of Bangkok's oldest and most popular Chinese restaurants. $$

Hong Teh, Ambassador Hotel, 171 Soi 11-13, Sukhumvit Road. Tel: 254 0444. A favorite with local gourmets for banquets. $$

Jade Garden, Montien Hotel, 54 Suriwongse Road. Tel: 234 8060. Southern Chinese dishes prepared by Hong Kong chefs in an elegant setting. $$

Lin-Fa, Siam City Hotel, 477 Sri Ayutthaya Road. Tel: 247 0120, 247 0130. An elegant Chinese restaurant in one of Bangkok's most stylish hotels. $$$

Lok Wah Hin, Novotel, 392/44 Soi 6, Siam Square, Rama I Road. Tel:

255 6888. Cantonese and Szechuan cuisine at its best. $$
Mayflower, Dusit Thani Hotel, 946 Rama IV Road. Tel: 236 0450. One of Thailand's best hotel Chinese restaurants. $$$
Ming Palace, Indra Regent Hotel, 120-126 Ratchaprarop Road. Tel: 208 0033. Southern Chinese dishes. $$
New Great Shanghai, 648-652 Sukhumvit Road (near Soi 24). Tel: 258 7042. Popular with local Chinese, especially for Sunday lunch. Tremendous variety of duck, marvelous rice bread. $$
Noble House, Hilton International Hotel, 2 Witthayu Road. Tel: 253 0123. Cantonese cuisine, profuse all-you-can-eat dinner buffet with over 75 items to choose from, tasteful decor. $$–$$$
Nguan Lee, 101/25-26 Soi Lang Suan, Ploenchit Road. Tel: 251 8366, 252 3614. Covered market; real atmosphere. One of the few restaurants where you can eat the famous Mekong giant catfish. $$
Rice Mill, Marriott Royal Garden Riverside, 257/1-3 Charoen Nakhon Road. Tel: 476 0021/2. Built on the site of an old rice mill, this luxury riverside hotel has a splendid Chinese restaurant. $$$
Royal Kitchen, 146 Soi 55 (Soi Thong Lo), Sukhumvit Road. Tel: 391 0252, 391 9634. Excellent food in an elegant setting. $$–$$$
Scala Restaurant, 218/1 Soi 1, Siam Square, Rama I Road (near Scala Theatre). Tel: 254 2891. One of the house specialties is Peking Duck. The adjoining restaurant specializes in shark's fin. $$
Shang Palace, Shangri-La Hotel, 89 Soi Wat Suan Plu. Tel: 236 7777, ext. 1350 & 1358. Superb Cantonese and Szechuan specialties. The lunchtime dim sum is a real treat. $$–$$$
Shangrila, 58/4-9 Thaniya Road. Tel: 234 0861. Branches at 154/4-5 Silom Road, tel: 234 9147/9; 306 Yawarat, tel: 224 5933. Cantonese cuisine. $$
Silom Restaurant, 793 Silom Road. Tel: 236 4442. One of the oldest Chinese restaurants in town; northern Chinese dishes. $$

Silver Palace Restaurant, 5 Soi Pipat, Silom Road. Tel: 235 5118/9. Well known for the variety of its delicious dim sum menu. Cantonese cuisine in opulent surroundings. $$$
Sui Sian, Landmark Hotel, 138 Sukhumvit Road. Tel: 254 0404. Cantonese and regional delicacies to the highest standards. $$$
The Chinese Restaurant, Grand Hyatt Erawan, 494 Ratchadamri Road. Tel: 254 1234. Sophisticated Cantonese specialties prepared by Hong Kong chefs. $$$
The Empress, Royal Princess Hotel, 269 Lan Luang Road. Tel: 281 3088. Delicious lunchtime dim sum. $$
Ti Jing, Monarch Lee Gardens Hotel, 188 Silom Road. Tel: 238 1999. A dazzling array of dim sum and other Cantonese delicacies. $$
Tien Tien Restaurant, 105 Soi Patpong. Tel: 234 8717, 234 6006. Located in the middle of busy, bustling Patpong. The decor takes second place to the food. $

Indian/Arabic/Muslim

Akbar Restaurant, 1/4 Soi 3 (Soi Nana Nua), Sukhumvit Road. Tel: 255 6935, 655 5097. Tasty northern Indian food. Try the prawn korma. $$
Bangkok Brindawan, 44/1 Soi 19, Silom Road. Tel: 233 4791. Simple decor and some excellent vegetarian dishes. Daily buffet lunch. $
Bukhara, Royal Orchid Sheraton Hotel, 2 Captain Bush Lane. Tel: 237 0022, 266 0123. Superb Indian cuisine with impeccable service. $$$
Cedar, 4/1 Soi 49/1, Sukhumvit Road. Tel: 391 4482. Excellent Lebanese and Greek cuisine. $$
Himali Cha Cha, 1229/11 Charoen Krung (New) Road. Tel: 235 1569. Northern cuisine created by a master chef. $$
Maharajah's, 19/1 Soi 8, Sukhumvit Road. Tel: 254 8876. Some tasty tandoori dishes. $
Moghul Room, 1/16 Soi 11, Sukhumvit Road. Tel: 253 4465. Popular, but more expensive than some. $$

Mrs. Balbir's, 155/18 Soi 11, Sukhumvit Road. Tel: 253 2281. Good north Indian cuisine, a favorite with Bangkok expats. $$
Rang Mahal, Rembrandt Hotel, 19 Soi 18, Sukhumvit Road. Tel: 261 7100. First-class cuisine and impeccable service in this rooftop restaurant. Excellent samosas. $$
Tandoor, Holiday Inn Crowne Plaza, 981 Silom Road. Tel: 238 4300. North Indian cuisine of exceptional quality. $$

Indonesian

Bali, 15/3 Soi Ruam Rudi, Ploenchit Road. Tel: 250 0711, 254 3581. The best of Javanese cuisine in a peaceful atmosphere. $

Japanese

Benihana, Marriott Royal Garden Riverside, 257/1-3 Charoen Nakhon Road. Tel: 476 0021/2. The preparation of the dishes is a combination of knife-wielding and juggling. The end result is always a superb meal. $$$
Benkay, Royal Orchid Sheraton Hotel, 2 Captain Bush Lane. Tel: 237 0022, 266 0123. The restaurant is noted for its exquisite Japanese cuisine served in an ambience of quiet elegance; a place for refined tastes. $$$
Endogin, Shangri-La Hotel, 89 Soi Wat Suan Plu. Tel: 236 7777. All that you would expect from one of Bangkok's top hotels. $$
Genji, Hilton International Hotel, 2 Witthayu Road. Tel: 253 0123, ext. 8141. Expensive. $$$
Hagi, Central Plaza Hotel, 1695 Phaholyothin Road. Tel: 541 1234. Popular, with reasonable prices. $$
Hanaya, 683 Si Phraya Road. Tel: 234 8095. Clean and unpretentious. $
Kagetsu, Asia Hotel, 296 Phaya Thai Road. Tel: 215 0808. Traditional cuisine and setting. Very popular. $$
Kiku-No-Hana, The Landmark Hotel, 138 Sukhumvit Rd. Tel: 254 0404. First-class Japanese cuisine. $$
Kobe Steak House, 460 Soi 7, Siam Square, Rama I Road. Tel: 251 1336. Excellent beef, good service. $

Mizu's, 32 Soi Patpong. Tel: 233 6447. One of the oldest Japanese restaurants in the city. The house specialty is sizzling steak. $
Nishimura, Siam City Hotel, 477 Sri Ayutthaya Road. Tel: 247 0120, 247 0130. First-class dining in style. $$$
Shogun, Dusit Thani Hotel, 946 Rama IV Road. Tel: 236 0450. Sashimi and other Japanese delicacies; elegant decor. $$$
Teio, Monarch Lee Gardens Hotel, 188 Silom Road. Tel: 238 1999. Sophisticated Japanese dining. Special family buffet lunches on Saturday and Sunday. $$
Tokugawa, Ambassador Hotel, 171 Soi 11-13, Sukhumvit Road. Tel: 254 0444, ext. 1569. The teppanyaki is delicious and fun to watch the chef preparing. $$

Kosher
Ohr Menachem Chabad House, 108/1 Rambutri Road, Khao San Road, Banglampoo. Tel: 282 6388, fax: 629 1153. Close to many guesthouses on Khao San Road, popular with young Jewish travelers. Open 12–9pm daily. $

Pacific
L'Orangery, 48/11 Soi Ruam Rudi, Witthayu Road. Tel: 253 6941. Interesting menu with Californian and Asian influences. $$–$$$
Trader Vic's, Marriott Royal Garden Riverside, 257/1-3 Charoen Nakhon Road. Tel: 476 0021/2. The unique style of oven gives a different flavour to the dishes. A delightfully different dining experience. $$$

Vegetarian
Ambassador Kitchen, Ambassador Hotel, Forum Bldg., 171 Soi 11-13, Sukhumvit Road. Tel: 254 0444. Excellent Chinese vegetarian cuisine. $$
May Kaidee, 117/1 Tanao Road, Banglampoo. Tel: (none). Near the Regal Fashion shop on a small soi opposite the eastern end of Khao San Road. Good service. Try the tofu curry. $
Veg House, 1/6 Soi 3 (Soi Nana Nua), Sukhumvit Road. Tel: 254

7357. Great selection of Indian and Thai dishes, emphasis on fresh ingredients. $
You Sue Vegetarian, 241 Rama IV Road, opposite Bangkok Centre Hotel. (Look for small sign in window which reads "health food.") Tel: 214 2801. Traditional Chinese menu, popular with locals. $
Whole Earth Café, 93/3 Soi Lang Suan. Tel: 252 5574. Branch at 71 Soi 26, Sukhumvit Road. Tel: 258 4900. Bangkok's best-known Thai vegetarian restaurant; comfortable and friendly. There is also a tasty menu of non-vegetarian fare with excellent Indian dishes. $$

Vietnamese/Burmese
Cherie Kitchen, 593/13 Soi 33/1, Sukhumvit Road. Tel: 258 5058. $
Le Dalat, 47/1 Soi 23 (Soi Prasanmit), Sukhumvit Road. Tel: 258 4192 and Patpong Bldg., 2nd Floor, Suriwongse Road. Tel: 234 0290. Two of the best in town in the moderate price range. $$
Le Danang, Central Plaza Hotel, 1695 Phaholyothin Road. Tel: 541 1234. A long-established Vietnamese restaurant renowned for its authentic cuisine. $$
Mandalay, 23/7 Soi Ruam Rudi, Witthayu Road. Tel: 255 2893. One of the only Burmese restaurants in Bangkok. Good food. $$
Saigon, Asia Hotel, 296 Phaya Thai Road. Tel: 215 0808. Luxury in an elegant setting under supervision of a Vietnamese chef. $$$
Saigon-Rimsai, 413/9 Soi 55 (Soi Thong Lo), Sukhumvit Road. Tel: 381 1797. Small, beautifully decorated and the Vietnamese chef produces a variety of dishes. $$
Vietnam, 82-4 Silom Road, (opp. Convent Road). Tel: 234 6174. Southern-style Viet cuisine. $

CHIANG MAI
Thai
Antique House, 71 Charoen Prathet Road, across from the Pornping Hotel, is situated in a wonderful old wooden house. $$
The Gallery, on Charoenrat Road, tel: 248 601, combines an art gallery with a Chinese garden and riverside terrace. $$

Kafe, 127-9 Mun Muang Road. Tel: 212 717. An old wooden building next to the moat. A fine selection of Thai and Western food. $
Krua Khun Phan, 80/1 Intrawarorot Road (near Suan Dok Gate), displays a variety of ready-made Thai dishes. $
Nang Nual, 27/2-5 Koh Klang Road. Tel: 281 961. A riverside restaurant, down river a few hundred meters off the Chiang Mai-Lamphun Road. $$$
Phuket Laikhram, 1/10 Suthep Road, an excellent southern Thai restaurant serving various curries and tom yam-style noodles. $
The Riverside Bar and Restaurant, 9/11 Charoenrat Road. Tel: 242 239. Excellent meals on the banks of the Ping River. Live music. $$
Tha Nam, 43/3 Mu 2, Chang Klan Road. Tel: 404 371. A large wooden building with a pleasant riverside terrace. $$
Whole Earth, 88 Sri Dornchai Road, tel: 232 463, serves vegetarian and non-vegetarian Thai dishes in a garden setting. $$

There are also Lanna *kantoke* dinners, where you can dine on northern Thai kantoke cuisine and then sit back to enjoy a program of northern dances and music. **The Diamond Hotel** on Charoen Prathet Road serves a nightly Lanna Kantoke dinner with classical Lanna and hill-tribe dancing. Tel: 234 155 for reservations. **Old Chiang Mai Cultural Centre** also presents a Kantoke dinner with a program of Northern and hill-tribe dances. Offered nightly from 7–10pm in a beautiful Northern Thai style house at 185/3 Wua Lai Road. Tel: 275 097 for reservations. Modest fee, begins at 7pm. Reserve ahead.

Asian
Akamon (Japanese), Chiang Mai Hills Hotel, 18 Huay Kaeo Road. Tel: 210 030. $$$
Ari-Rang (Korean), Star Inn Hotel, 36 Soi 4 Loi Kroh Road. Tel: 270 360. $$
Shere Shiraz (Indian/Muslim), 23-25 Charoen Prathet Road. Tel: 276 132. $$

European
Bier Stube (German), 33/6A Moonmauang Road (near Tapae Gate). Tel: 278 869. $
Café de Paris (French), 14-16 Kotchasan Road. Tel: 234 804. $$
Di-Dario's, off Sumonthewaraj Road, near hospital and airport. The only farang restaurant in town. Swiss-run. The Italian and Thai food gets rave reviews, but the restaurant is very difficult to find, especially at night. May be packed with locals. $
Haus Munchen (German), 115/3 Loi Kroh Road. Tel: 274 027. $$
Nan Phin Pub, 440 Sumonthewaraj Road, Amphur Muang. Tel: 772 640, 771 697. Ground floor of Nan Fa Hotel. Nightly folk music show, with traditional instruments. Arrive well before 9pm to avoid karaoke. $
Pensione La Villa (Italian), 145 Ratdamnern Road. Tel: 277 403. $
The Pub (English), Huay Kaeo Road, near the Rincome Hotel (Tel: 211 550), has English meals and a fireplace. $$

PATTAYA
Thai and Seafood
La Mer Grill, Montien Hotel, Pattaya 2 Road. Tel: 428 155/6. Maela Plaphao, Soi Siam Country Club. Tel: 716 181.
Thai House, 171/1 North Pattaya Road. Tel: 370 579/81.

Asian and Continental
Akamon (Japanese), 464/19 Pattaya 2 Road, North Pattaya. Tel: 423 727.
Chalet Swiss (Continental), 220 Beach Road. Tel: 429 255.
Diulio's (Italian), 192 Moo 9, Soi Foodland. Tel: 427 154.
Dolf Riks (Indonesian, Thai, Continental), 116/8 Pattaya-Naklua Road. Tel: 367 585.
Moon River Pub (Mexican), Thai Garden Resort, North Pattaya Road. Tel: 426 009.
Yamato (Japanese), Soi Yamato. Tel: 429 685.

PHUKET
Phuket Town
Ka Jok See, 26 Takua Pa Road. Tel: 217 903. Intimate dining in a delightful off-the-wall Thai restaurant. Newspaper table covers, household antiques and a porch with verdant potted plants create a raffish feel underscored by jazz music. $$
Mala, 5/72-73 Mae Luan Road. Tel: 214 201. Open-front restaurant decorated with vintage household artefacts. It also serves *kaow yam* mixed herbal dish good for your health. Tasty curries like masaman guay are made fresh each morning. $
Laem Thong, 31-39 Chana Charoen Road. Tel: 211 269. Large and urbane Chinese-Thai restaurant specializing in Thai seafood and Pekinese cuisine. Lobster, oyster, shark's fin and suckling pig draw dedicated gourmands. $$$
Le Café, Phuket Shopping Centre, Rasda Road. Tel: 215 563. French-style eatery in the town centre serving exotic coffees and teas by cup or pot. Reasonable selection of steaks, pizzas and ice creams. $$
Metropole Coffee Shop, Metropole Hotel, Montri Road. Tel: 215 050. Upmarket yet very good value lunch venue with a bountiful buffet spread of Thai cuisine from four regions of the country. Prompt table service. Thai classical music plays in the background. $$
Ocean Time Square, Tilok Uthit 1 Road. Tel: 213 213. Unremarkable modern shopping mall distinguished by very good Asian fast-food restaurants: the Noodle Garden and Joto Bar-B-Q (Chinese), Suan Mee Suki (Japanese), Uptown (Thai-Western). $$
The Rooftop, Pearl Hotel, Montri Road. Tel: 211 044. Exquisite Cantonese restaurant on the top floor of the hotel. Refurbished in classical Chinese style. Popular with local business community. Acclaimed by Gault Millault. $$$
Thai Naan, 16 Wichitsongkhram Road. Tel: 226 164/7. Mammoth teak-panelled Thai, Chinese and Japanese restaurant which claims to be the largest in South Thailand. Some small air-conditioned rooms. Live classical music. Good food and service despite size. Sumptuous Srivichai Room specializes in southern fare with show. $$$

Tung-ka Café, Top of Khao Rang Hill. Tel: 211 500. Romantic open-air Thai restaurant with sweeping views of Phuket town and the coast. Small selection of Japanese and Western dishes. Restaurant is at its best by night with views of the town lit up below. $$

Phuket Beaches
Bang Thao Ruen Thai, Dusit Laguna Resort. Tel: 324 320/9. Central Royal Thai cuisine served by waitresses in Thai classical costumes to the accompaniment of kim music. Romantic candlelit setting beside a lake. $$$
Tatonka, just outside Laguna Phuket. Tel: 324 349. Delicate and innovative fusion cuisine combining western, Thai, Mexican and Mediterranean influences in a café setting with wine bar. The kitchen is open for all to see. Surprisingly inexpensive. $$
Chalong Gan Eng 1, 9/3 Chaofa Road. Tel: 381 212, 381 323. Simple open-air restaurant on the waterfront. Popular with locals and tourists alike. Seafood dishes are a specialty. $$
Jimmy's Lighthouse, Moo 9 Chalong Bay. Tel: 381 709. Seafront maritime café popular with international yachtsmen. Ambitious menu successfully plunders the best of Europe and Asia. $$
Kamala Paul's Place, Kamala Beach Estate, Kamala Beach. Tel: 324 111. Trendy wooden Thai restaurant on stilts overlooking peaceful Kamala beach. Broad range of Thai dishes is served to the Chinese granite-top tables. Medium pricing. Good atmosphere from sunset onwards. Steak, pasta, schnitzel options too. $$
Karon Little Mermaid, 36/10 Patak Road. Tel: 396 628. Comfortable Scandinavian restaurant in the heart of Karon. The thoughtful menu allows diners to tick options like medium or rare for steaks, with fries or baked potato. $$
Old Siam, Thavorn Palm Beach Hotel. Tel: 396 116. A large restaurant with an emphasis on royal Thai traditions. Nightly kim classical music performances and

Thai dancing add ambience. Ask for one of the outdoor balcony tables with excellent views of Karon beach at sunset. $$

On the Rock, Marina Cottage Resort. Tel: 330 625. Very popular small restaurant on the rocks overlooking Karon Bay. Strong on Thai food, seafood and international items. Although a tad pricey, the superlative setting and taste compensate. Dinner bookings essential. $$$

The Terrace, Karon-Patong coast road. Tel: 286 030. Continental restaurant perched on a cliff overlooking Karon Bay. Specializes in dishes like tagliatelle alla vodka and Chateaubriand steaks. Thai menu too. $$$

Kata Boathouse Wine & Grill, The Boathouse, 2/2 Patak Road. Tel: 330 015/7. Refined Thai and European dining on a romantic terrace overlooking the sea. Large wine selection and set menus. $$$

Islanders, 6/3 Soi Tuey Ngam, Patak Road. Tel: 330 740. Busy open-air restaurant in south Kata. Diners are typically hotel residents going local. Seafood is the mainstay but Italian and Japanese fare also served. $$

Kampong Kata Hill, 112/2 Patak Road, opp. Kata Centre. Tel: 330 103. Steep flight of stairs leads to quaint Thai restaurant on a wooden balcony in what is effectively an Asian art gallery. Moderately priced food from all areas of Thailand and a few international dishes. $$

Nai Harn Regatta Bar & Grill, Royal Le Méridien Phuket Yacht Club. Tel: 381 156. Colonial feel to an opulent but understated Italian restaurant in one of Phuket's most exclusive hotels. Set menus or la carte. Eclectic wine list. $$$

Patong Ban Rim Pa, 100/7 Kalim Beach Road. Tel: 340 789, 341 768. Delightfully located romantic restaurant with views of Patong Bay. Refined central Thai dining by candlelight. Seafood, however, plays a minor role in the menu. Reservations are advisable. $$$

Bangla Seafood, 82/46 Soi Bangla, Patong Beach. Tel: 342 436. Place to go for excellent range of big lobsters, grilled crabs, juicy prawns and crispy-fried fish. Easy to run up a big bill if you choose lobsters. Fast business-like service in street-side open air café. Great location for watching assorted characters walk by. $$

Kubu Restaurant, Muen Ngoen Road, Patong. Tel: 292 191. Delightful hill setting at southern end of Patong Beach matched by high finesse of the Thai dishes. You order 24 hours in advance. Ingredients are bought in the market next morning. You taste the benefit in the evening. Romantic and surprisingly affordable. $$

Navrang Mahal, Soi Patong Resort, off Soi Bangla. Tel: 292 280. All corners of Indian cuisine touched here, from succulent northern tandoori dishes to spicy southern curries. A tad pricey. $$$

No. 4, 82 Moo 3, Soi Bangla, Patong. Tel: 342 319. No-frills, brightly lit seafood room at end of a shopping lane. Price advantage does not compromise taste. Extensive Thai and seafood choice. Afterwards you can write your name on the graffiti wall. $$

Pizzeria Napoli, Soi Patong Post Office. Tel: 340 674. Indoor dining on a wide range of pizzas, pastas and other Italian specialties. $$

KRABI

Krabi Town

Ruen Mai, Maharat Road, Krabi town. Tel: 631 797. Shade-dappled outdoor restaurant set among native trees, a kilometer out of town. Exclusively Thai menu at competitive prices reflects country cooking from south, central and northeastern Thailand. Open all day. $$

Barn Thai Issara, Ruen Rudee Road, Krabi town. Tel: 620 373. Family-run café which serves a limited range of high-quality pastas, salads, pizza breads, shakes and coffees. Superlative homemade bread. Open daytime only. $$

Ao Nang

Sala Thai, behind Beach Terrace hotel, Ao Nang. No phone. Atmospheric beachside seafood and Thai curry restaurant a little hard to find, but well worth seeking out. The unpretentious setting on bamboo tables beside lapping waves attracts hotel guests going local. Open all day. Moderately priced. $$

Gift's, Beach Road, Ao Nang. Tel: 637 193. Pleasant central rendezvous for all-day dining. Attentive informal service underpins consistently good Thai dishes. Pastas, cocktails and homemade bread are a bonus. $$

Drinking Notes

Many restaurants catering to western tastes whip up a delicious shake made of pureed fruit, crushed ice and a light syrup. Chilled young coconuts are delicious; drink the juice, then scrape out and eat the tender young flesh. Soft drinks are found everywhere. Try Vitamilk, a health drink made from soya bean milk. For a refreshing cooler, order a bottle of soda, a glass of ice and a sliced lime. Squeeze the lime into the glass, add the soda and enjoy. Sip the very strong Thai coffee flavored with chicory. The odd orange Thai tea is sticky sweet but delicious. On a hot day, Chinese prefer to drink a hot, very thin tea, believing that ice is bad for the stomach. Try all three over ice anyway.

Beers include Kloster, Carlsberg, Amarit, Singha and Singha Gold. Carlsberg and Heineken are now brewed in Thailand. Of the many Thai cane whiskeys, Mekhong is the most popular. It is drunk on the rocks, with soda and lime or with a bit of honey added to it.

Attractions

Leisure Pursuits

COURSES
Community Services of Bangkok, 15/1 Soi 33, Sukhumvit Road, tel: 258 4998, 258 5652, fax: 260 3563. This volunteer organization runs different courses each month on a variety of diverse subjects. More expensive for non-members, but still reasonable.
Oriental Hotel Cooking School, Soi Oriental, Charoen Krung (New) Road. Tel: 236 0400/39. Offers five-day classes in Thai cuisine and vegetable-carving.

Buddhist Meditation
Studying Buddhism is not an uncommon pursuit for foreign visitors to Thailand. There are many venues for such study throughout the country, including the following. Telephone or write first since schedules change frequently and accommodation is often limited.

Bangkok
House of Dhamma, 26/9 Soi 15 (Soi Chompon), Lard Prao Road. Tel: 511 3549, 511 0439.
International Buddhist Meditation Centre, Wat Mahathat, Maharat Road, Tha Phra Chan. Tel: 222 6011.
World Fellowship of Buddhists, 33 Sukhumvit Road (between Soi 1 and 3). Tel: 251 1188.

Provinces
Wat Khao Tham, Ko Pha Ngan, Surat Thani Province 84280.
Wat Pah Nanachat, Ban Bung Wai, Amphur Warin, Ubon Ratchathani 34310.
Wat Ram Poeng, Tambon Suthep, Amphur Muang, Chiang Mai 50000. Tel: (053) 278 620.

Wat Suan Mokkh, Amphur Chaiya, Surat Thani 84110.

HEALTH SPAS
The Banyan Tree, Westin Banyan Tree Hotel, Thai Wah II Tower, 51st Floor, Sathorn Tai Road. Tel: 679 1200. Hydrotherapy, seaweed masks, Swedish massage. Fabulous view from the tallest building in Thailand.
Grande Spa and Fitness Centre, Sheraton Grande Hotel, 250 Sukhumvit Road. Tel: 653 0334/8, fax: 653 0400. Swedish massage, hydrotherapy, algae and mud wraps.
JW's Health Club and Spa, JW Marriott Hotel, 4 Soi 2, Sukhumvit Road. Tel: 656 7700, fax 656 7711. Offers a flight reviver massage in addition to aromatherapy, Swedish massage, and body polishing.
The Oriental Spa, opposite the Oriental Hotel, 48 Oriental Avenue. Tel: 439 7613/4, fax: 439 7587. Seaweed treatments, foot massage, aromatherapy, papaya body polish. Special program to relieve jet lag. Advance booking recommended.

Sightseeing

BANGKOK
After touring the famous attractions like the Grand Palace, Wat Phra Kaeo, Wat Po, and Wat Arun, visit these lesser-known sites:

See Buddhist monks on their morning alms round by visiting **Wat Benchamabophit** at about 6.30am. Here, Buddhists take food to monks waiting silently outside the gates of the temple.

Tour **Vimarnmek**, the world's largest golden teak palace, and its superb collection of crystal, gold and silver art objects. Open daily, 9.30am–4pm. Admission is 50 baht or free with an entrance ticket to the Grand Palace.

Early in the morning, wander through Bangkok's largest wet market, **Pak Khlong Talat**, near the foot of the Memorial Bridge. Then visit the flower market on nearby Chakraphet Road.

Enjoy a traditional Thai massage

in the sala, or resting pavilion, near the eastern wall of the **Wat Po** compound and grounds.

Board the Chao Phraya river express from the Oriental Hotel or Tha Chang near the Grand Palace, and ride 45 minutes up river to Nonthaburi with its bustling market. Have a drink or a meal at the floating restaurant next to the beautiful old provincial office. Alternatively, take the boat downstream to the last stop near the Krung Thep Bridge.

Take a free guided tour of the **National Museum**, Wednesday–Sunday at 9.30am.

Enjoy the educational snake show (where cobras are milked) at the **Snake Farm** (formerly the Pasteur Institute) on Rama IV Road at 10.30am and 2pm on weekdays, 10.30am on weekends and holidays, admission 70 baht.

On Saturdays and Sundays, explore the **weekend market** at Chatuchak Park. Start early to avoid the midday heat.

Take the Chao Phraya river express to the **Tha Ratchawong** landing in Chinatown. Walk down Ratchawong Road and turn in either direction on Sampeng Lane for a staggering assortments of shops selling everything from gold jewelry to steel wool.

Stroll through a former century of gracious living at the **Jim Thompson House**, Soi Kasem San 2, Rama I Road, Monday to Saturday, 9am–5pm, admission 100 baht. Or visit the complex of old houses at **Suan Pakkad Palace**, Sri Ayutthaya Road (between Phaya Thai and Ratchaprarop Roads), Monday to Saturday, 9am–4pm, admission 150 baht.

Visit the **Ancient City** (Muang Boran in Thai) with its miniature replicas of the kingdom's chief architectural masterpieces.

Rent a private boat at the Oriental Hotel and cruise through Khlong Bangkok Noi, stopping at the **Royal Barge Museum**. Take the long route home, through the smaller canals to Khlong Bangkok Yai and back to the Oriental.

Attend a **Thai boxing** (*muay Thai*)

match at Ratchadamnern or Lumpini Stadium.

Watch a free *likay* performance at Lak Muang.

Make a wish and an offering at the **Erawan Shrine** at the corner of Ratchadamri and Ploenchit roads.

Take a stroll through **Bangrak Market** (on Charoen Krung (New) Road, behind the Shangri-La Hotel), to see the splendid and colourful array of cut flowers.

Get a traditional herbal cure from a pharmacy in **Chinatown**. Buy a love potion or a Buddhist amulet from the stalls in the covered lanes beside **Wat Ratchanadda**, off Ratchadamnern Road and across from the Golden Mount.

Try to locate the **gold leaf beater's shop** in a small soi behind Tanao Road in Banglampoo Market.

Visit the **monks' bowl neighbourhood** (Baan Baat), the only place in Bangkok where the bowls are still crafted by hand, in the small *soi* located behind the Golden Mount.

Stroll around the campus of **Chulalongkorn University**, between Henri Dunant and Phaya Thai Roads, which is surprisingly cool and peaceful in the midst of Bangkok. Ask someone where the bookstore is.

Go for a walk or jog in **Lumpini Park** at 6am. Watch the *taichi* exercises being performed.

Have cocktails in the rooftop bar at the **Dusit Thani**. Pay a visit to **Kamthieng House**, a folk art museum, at the Siam Society on Soi 21 (Soi Asoke), Sukhumvit Road. Open Tuesday to Saturday, 9am–5pm, admission 25 baht.

CENTRAL PLAINS

Take the train to the **Bridge on the River Kwai**. The State Railways of Thailand offers a day trip each Saturday. If you have several days, stay on one of the raft houses farther up the river.

Ride the *Oriental Queen* up the Chao Phraya River to Ayutthaya, visiting Bang Pa-In along the way.

Enjoy the water sports in **Jomtien** or the nightlife in **Pattaya**.

Take a bus to Phetchaburi to

explore **King Mongkut's palace and observatory** on top of the hill.

Drive to **Ratchaburi** to look at the beautiful ceramics crafted and sold there. Visit **King Narai's old palace** at Lopburi.

Take the train to Phitsanulok to see the Phra Buddha Chinaraj image in **Wat Mahathat**. Continue to Sukhothai to see Thailand's first capital city, then to Si Satchanalai for some quiet beauty. Complete the journey by dropping south to the walled city of Kamphaeng Phet before returning to Phitsanulok.

THE NORTH

Visit the hilltop temple of **Doi Suthep** at sunset for a panoramic view of Chiang Mai Valley.

Explore the **crafts studios** along the road to Borsang.

Drive the tree-lined road to Lamphun to visit **Wat Phra That Haripunchai** and **Wat Chamathewi**.

Take a trek to visit **hill tribes** outside of Chiang Mai or Chiang Rai. Attend the demonstration of elephant's skills in moving teak logs at the **Young Elephant's Training School** at Lampang or the **Chiang Dao Elephant Camp**.

Ride a longboat 3.5 hours down the **Kok River** from Tha Ton to Chiang Rai.

Visit Mae Sai on the Burmese border and then drive to the **Golden Triangle** where the borders of Laos, Thailand and Burma meet in the middle of the Mekong River.

THE NORTHEAST

Drive to the Northeast to see **Khmer temples** at Phimai, Phanom Wan, Phanom Rung and Muang Tham. Travel from Ubon along the **Mekong River** to Nong Khai. View Friendship Bridge at Nong Khai, linking Thailand and Laos.

THE SOUTH

Visit the islands of **Phang Nga Bay**.

Ride the train from Bangkok to **Penang** in Malaysia.

Roam the farm areas and coastal roads of **Phuket** in a rented jeep. Rent a motorcycle and visit all the beaches of **Ko Samui**. Cruise around Phuket on a **Chinese junk**.

Beaches

Beach facilities range from the rustic to the well-developed, each attracting a different clientele. On a rating of 1–3 (1=basic facilities only; 2=adequate but not luxurious facilities; 3=first-class hotels with restaurants, sports, shopping and sightseeing facilities).

PATTAYA AND JOMTIEN

Plenty of water sports and activities, but unfortunately the ocean is reputedly none too clean, so fewer people are swimming here. Best bets for water lovers are nearby islands or in hotel swimming pools. Pattaya has extensive services and facilities, excellent restaurants, golf courses, cultural shows, and, of course, the tatty nightlife. (2/3)

EAST COAST

The long stretch of sandy, tranquil, tree-lined coast running east of Ban Phe to Laem Mae Phim has numerous quiet resorts and good hotels set in leafy gardens. Water activities are generally confined to swimming and trips to nearby islands. An ideal area for families and those wanting a quiet, relaxing vacation. (2)

Ko Samet

This beautiful island is still a backpacker's retreat with rustic bungalows along lovely beaches. There are a few slightly more upmarket hotels, at cheaper prices than on the coast, but the lack of connection with the mainland, other than scheduled ferry boats, means that the island attracts a hardier crowd. Water sports facilities are increasing, along with the accompanying noise of jet-skis. Nighttime entertainment involves a few discos, video shows and beachside restaurants. (2)

Ko Chang

The size of Phuket, this quiet outpost, whose name means Elephant Island, is still a tranquil, forested oasis. Simple huts are slowly being joined by more upmarket resorts, but Ko Chang is too far from major centers to see huge changes soon. Diving here is very rewarding with wonderful coral and gorgeous fish. Lovely forest walks add to the island's quiet but potent charm. (2)

HUA HIN AND CHA-AM

In former times, royalty gathered here, and there is still an air of grandeur to its wide beaches. The area generally attracts families and older vacationers, but there are young couples as well. Excellent for quiet relaxation, strolling the fishing docks, a leisurely round of golf, riding ponies on the beach, or just sitting in a beach chair. Several international-class hotels and golf courses. (3)

PHUKET

Combining natural beauty with a complete range of resort facilities, Phuket has turned into a magnet for Asians and Europeans alike. Gone are most of the budget accommodations, but there are still low-priced as well as luxury hotels. It has land and water sports, a golf course, cultural shows, nightlife, drives around the island, in short, a full-fledged beach resort. (3)

PHI PHI

For years, its natural attractions were muted by its remoteness so that only budget travelers stayed in its thatched bungalows. It is still bungalow accommodation for the most part, but it has begun to move upmarket. Superb snorkeling, limited water sports, virtually no land sports, little nightlife, trips to nearby islands, restaurants and surpassing beauty is what it offers. Becoming overcrowded. (1.5)

KRABI

The newest of Thailand's beach resorts now offers some first-class hotels but smaller places and bungalows remain the main option. Snorkeling on offshore islands. (2)

KO SAMUI

Wide beaches and a laid-back lifestyle formerly drew only budget

travelers. An airstrip has made the island accessible and first-class hotels make it comfortable for better-heeled tourists. Some water sports and cultural activities. (2.5)

Trekking

It's called trekking, but a two- to seven-day hike in the northern Thai hills shouldn't conjure up daunting visions of the Nepali version. Thailand's tallest mountain, Doi Inthanon, is less than 2,600 meters (8,530 ft) in height. While you should be fit, you need not be excessively so. Retirees trek, and so do children as young as ten.

Seeing tribal people living and working in their natural settings is the primary reason most people take treks. For those who have been stuck in Bangkok, total immersion in clean air and green things may feel like a physical and mental necessity. Trekkers also tend to have interests in birdwatching, botany, agriculture, opium, herbal medicine or New Age ideas. For wildlife enthusiasts, there's a chance to spot small game, such as antelope, wild pigs, bats and, yes, large snakes.

Most of the walking is on level ground and well-worn paths. The going becomes tough only during the height of the hot season, from March to May. Even then, the nights are cool enough to require a blanket. The best season is from November to March. Second best may be in June and July, before the full onslaught of the rainy season.

No special equipment is required. You carry a change of clothing, toilet articles, a flashlight and mosquito repellent. The guide takes care of the rest, including food, water bottles and transportation. You pay for the optional toke of opium, which is, of course, illegal. Water purification tablets should be brought from home, but an adequate substitute, iodine, can be bought in Thailand (one drop to a liter). You can sleep on the hardwood floor of a villager's thatched house while pigs root in the open space below. It's spartan,

but no hardship for anyone who is accustomed to camping.

GUIDES and TOURS

The difference between a terrific and a disastrous experience depends greatly on your guide. It's therefore risky to book a tour from a large agency in Bangkok. Besides, whenever you arrive in Chiang Mai or Chiang Rai, it's always possible to join a trek leaving the following day. The choice of trekking tours in the two cities is so huge that it's discouraging. Every agency will promise "new" areas, unjaded villagers, multilingual guides and zero encounters with other groups.

You can narrow the choices by talking to tourists who have just returned from treks. In either city, or anywhere in northern Thailand, it's easy to meet such people, and they will eagerly pass on their recommendations and warnings. Keep in mind that they will recommend an individual guide, not the particular company he or she works for.

This emphasis also runs through the books of glowing handwritten customer comments that every self-respecting outfit displays.

You're more likely to hit an uncongested area if you bypass Chiang Mai and Chiang Rai altogether. Start with a small one- or two-person agency in a smaller town, such as Mae Hong Son, Pai, Mae Sai or Mae Sariang. Guesthouses can always direct you to someone. Guides in these places usually have completed a government training course and have previously been employed at low wages by slicker companies. More important, they are often tribesmen themselves or local Thais truly fluent in several tribal languages. Tribal guides usually speak English as well as, or better than, urban Thai guides.

SIGNING ON

Before you sign for any tour, determine how many hours you will walk, what you will eat and which tribes you will visit. As a rule of thumb, treks north of Chiang Mai offer more of the "colourful" tribes, the vividly adorned Akha and Hmong people. To the west, along the Pai river and close to Mae Hong Son, however, there's much less deforestation. Try to meet your companions the night before the trek. The optimum number is between six to ten. The trekking agency will store your luggage and valuables, but credit cards are safer on your person.

A portion, perhaps half, of the tour fee should be paid before setting out, but be skeptical of demands for full payment. If the agency doesn't deliver on the promises, there is no way you will get a refund. A basic three-day, two-night trek costs between 1,000 and 1,500 baht.

River rafting and an elephant ride can add an extra 500 baht. Elephant rides, it must be noted, become uncomfortable very quickly. And rafting means seeing fewer villages. But in the rainy season – from July to October – rafting is a welcome respite from midday heat and leeches.

GETTING ALONG

Many prospective trekkers worry that their presence will contribute to the disintegration of tribal cultures. There is merit in this view. The most zoo-like encounters take place at tribal villages close to major roads and at the chilling, artificial Ravan (Long Necks) villages outside Mae Hong Son. A tour bus will pull up on schedule. Exotically garbed tribal women will envelope the tourists, badgering them to buy clothing or trinkets. The tourists will snap photos for a price. When the bus departs, the women will replace their traditional dress with T-shirts and Thai sarongs.

With a good guide-cum-interpreter, trekkers can humanize interactions by asking villagers about their customs, history and legends. Show respect for their religious beliefs and ceremonies. Play with the children. Via sign language, ask people before taking their photos. Give only adults small gifts, such as soap, bandages and

sewing needles, which are the kinds of things for which they need money. It's certainly bad form to bargain for the clothing on a person's back, but it's hard to see why some tourists refuse to buy handwoven clothes or embroidered bags that have been made for sale. Such small sums may keep a village intact, and the purchase indicates a respect for the artisan's quality workmanship.

It also eliminates the much wealthier Thai middlemen who run the numerous tribal handicraft shops in Chiang Mai. Many tourists say they wouldn't mind overpaying for an item if the money reached the maker. You can maximize the amount that will reach the hill tribes by buying products marketed by charitable organizations, such as the Thai Hill-Crafts Foundation and Thai Tribal Crafts. Another way is to seek out the tribal vendors in Chiang Mai's night market. They are easily recognized by the colourful garments and jewelry they wear.

Nightlife

For years, Thailand has enjoyed a lusty reputation as a centre for sex of every persuasion and interest. While the reputation was not altogether undeserved, times and clienteles have changed. The American GIs of the 1960s and the German and Arab sex tourists of the 1970s have been replaced by upmarket tourists, usually traveling as couples. Also common are Japanese men on packaged sex tours, sex included. Western pedophiles are a continuing problem, especially in Pattaya.

While there has been no diminution in the number of massage parlors and bars, there has been an increase in other activities to meet the needs of the new breed of travelers, most of them in the 20–50 age range.

Jazz clubs, videotheques, discos and open-air restaurants are the most popular form of entertainment in towns.

A sign of the drastic changes is that the queen of nighttime

activities in Bangkok is shopping. Night markets have sprung up along Sukhumvit and Silom roads. Even that wrinkled old harlot of a street, Patpong, has not been immune to the breezes of change. Vendors' tables choke the street, drawing more patrons than the bars with a wealth of counterfeit Rolex watches, Benetton shirts and cassette tapes.

The change has rubbed off on the bars as well. Many of Patpong's bars have metamorphosed into discos, which begin to throb, so to speak, with life after 11pm.

Upcountry, the scene is essentially the same. Chiang Mai's night bazaar on Chang Klan Road attracts more tourists than the bars along Chaiyaphum Road.

In Phuket, "barbeers" (a bar which serves beer) line the streets of Patong beach's Soi Bangla and similar areas of Karon and Kata; but the hard sex of Bangkok's yesteryear has never established a foothold there.

MASSAGES

Massages fall into two categories: regular and "special". Establishments billing themselves as "Traditional Thai Massage" and "Ancient Thai Massage" offer therapeutic services according to age-old traditions, in other words, a legitimate massage. The best place for this, however, is at Wat Po.

The "special" type of massage is sexual. You pick a woman, or sometimes a girl, from behind a one-way mirror and then spend the next hour getting a bath and whatever else you arrange.

BANGKOK

Bars

There are three key areas in Bangkok where the types of entertainment for which the city has become famous can be found.

Patpong describes three streets: Soi Patpong itself and Soi Patpong 2, which is a welter of bars and bright lights, and Soi Patpong 3, which is almost exclusively gay. **Soi Cowboy** is a somewhat downmarket version of Patpong. Here, the entertainment is more basic. Midway between the two in geographic and entertainment terms, is the **Nana Entertainment Plaza** off Soi 4, Sukhumvit Road.

Gay and Lesbian Scene
Bank Studio, Soi 6, between Silom and Suriwongse. Tel: 236 6385. Daily 10pm–2am.
Dance club, popular with Thais, women welcome. DJ Station, 8/6 Soi 2, Silom Road. Tel: 266 4029. Daily 10pm–2am.
Gay disco, crowded. Henry Club, 8/10-11 Soi 2, Silom Road (opposite DJ Station). Tel: 632 7223. Daily 8pm–2am. Nightly show at 1am.
Sphinx, 98-104 Soi 4, Silom Road. Tel: 234 7249. Daily 7pm–1am. Elegant bar and restaurant. Good food.
Telephone, 114/11-13 Soi 4, Silom Road. Tel: 234 3279. Daily 8pm–2am. Bar/restaurant, good location for watching Soi 4 happenings. Telephones on each table enable patrons to dial other tables.
Utopia, 116/1 Soi 23 (Soi Prasanmit), Sukhumvit Road (opposite Tia Maria). Tel: 259 9619. Daily noon–2am. Shop, gay/lesbian social centre and café. Pub upstairs, Women's Night, Fridays; Drag Show, Saturdays.

Discos
Patpong also offers discos, many of which continue to throb long after the bars have closed down. Here, there are no sexual solicitations or other expectations.

Hotel discos worthy of consideration include: **Bubbles** at the Dusit Thani, **Cabaret Nightclub** at the Asia Hotel, and **Spasso's** at the Grand Hyatt Erawan.

Other discos include **Narcissus**, Soi 23 (Soi Prasanmit), Sukhumvit Road, tel: 258 2549; **Rome Club**, Soi 4, Silom Road, tel: 233 8836; and **Taurus**, Soi 26, Sukhumvit Road, tel: 261 3991/4. Generally, these venues appeal more to Thais than to foreigners, but there is room for both.

Music Clubs
This is not the kind of music you will find in New York, London or Tokyo, but it is very pleasant, and some of it is very innovative. Jazz clubs proliferate along Soi Sarasin, Soi Lang Suan, and elsewhere. They differ from their murky, hostess-filled counterparts in being open – usually glass-fronted and with sidewalk tables – with the emphasis on good live music and good conversation.

Music clubs appeal as much to professional Thais as they do to Westerners. Among the most popular with mixed nationality crowds are **Brown Sugar**, 231/19 Soi Sarasin, tel: 250 0103; **Round Midnight**, 106/2 Soi Lang Suan, Ploenchit Road, tel: 251 0652; and **Saxophone Pub Restaurant**, 3/8 Victory Monument, Phaya Thai Road, tel: 246 5472.

If you like Dixieland jazz and a lively atmosphere, head to **Bobby's Arms**, Car Park Building, First Floor, Soi Patpong 2 (behind Foodland), tel: 233 6828, on Sunday evenings. The band is comprised of local residents who play for the fun of it. Bobby's offers good British cuisine and lots of beer in a convivially British setting.

Most of the more sophisticated nightclubs are found in firs-class hotels. Classy and classic, the Oriental Hotel's famed **Bamboo Bar** nightclub is for dressier occasions. The scene is chic, normally with jazz singers from the United States playing long-term engagements. You can also find imported acts at the Dusit Thani Hotel's **Tiara Lounge**. Most hotels have lounge bars with good musical acts.

For other nighttime activities, check the daily newspapers for announcements of concerts, art shows, lectures and other offerings around the city. The Sunday morning *Bangkok Post* and *The Nation* carry listings for the following week.

Bars
Bull's Head, Soi 33, Sukhumvit Road (near Villa Supermarket). Tel: 259 4444. Pleasant pub

atmosphere. Popular with foreigners.
Delaney's Irish Pub, 1-4 Sivadon Bldg., Convent Road. Tel: 266 7160. The only place in Bangkok which serves Guinness on tap. Live music some nights.
Front Page, 14/10 Soi 1, Sala Daeng Road. Tel: 233 6315. Low-key neighborhood bar.
Hard Rock Café, Soi 11, Siam Square, Rama I Road. Tel: 251 0792/4, 254 0831. Live rock most evenings.
Jool's Bar and Restaurant, 21/3 Soi 4 (Soi Nana Tai), Sukhumvit Road. Tel: 252 6413. Understated British-style pub.
Witches Tavern, Soi 55 (Soi Thong Lo), Sukhumvit. Tel: 391 9791. Live music on weekends.

Cigar Lounges
Private Cellar, Pavilion Y, RCA, New Phetburi Road. Tel: 203 0926/30. Many fine cigars, impressive vintage wines, excellent port and malt whiskeys, bistro-style snacks. Dress Code. Expensive.
Regent Lobby, Regent Hotel, 155 Ratchadamri Road. Tel: 251 6127. Daily 6pm–1am. Excellent selection of imported cigars, staggering assortment of single malt whiskeys, great jazz band. Dress Code.

Microbreweries
The Paulaner Bruhaus, President Park, end of Soi 24, Sukhumvit Road. Tel: 661 1210, 661 1111/5. Good German food, including Sunday brunch.
Royal Hofbruhaus, 5 Soi Sala Daeng Place Bldg., Soi Sala Daeng, Silom Road. Tel: 636 0015/8. Comprehensive German menu, many fine German wines and spirits. There is also a branch conveniently located at Don Muang International Airport (Terminal 2) and pleasant for unexpected delays.
Taurus Brew House, Soi 26, Sukhumvit Road. Tel: 661 3535. Daily 5pm–2am. American style microbrewery offering four beers.

CHIANG MAI
Chiang Mai nightlife is subdued by comparison to that of Bangkok.

Perhaps it is the fatigue induced by trekking, the calmer nature of the town, or simply the calmer nature of the traveler. But in the evenings, Chiang Mai is very quiet.

Music Clubs and Bars
The normal evening entertainment is to sit in a restaurant or pub and listen to local musicians sing soft tunes. **Riverside Restaurant** on Charoenrat Road and **Chiang Mai Tea House** on the Chiang Mai-Lamphun Road are two examples of this kind of entertainment. Bars along Chaiyaphum Road in the vicinity of Tapae Gate offer live and recorded music. The latter also have bargirls but not in the numbers of Bangkok or Pattaya.

During the dry season, most of Chiang Mai's evenings are spent in outdoor restaurants like **Antique House** on Charoen Prathet Road, **The Brasserie** on Charoenrat Road, the sidewalk café in front of the **Suriwongse Hotel**, the **Smiling Monkey** on Bamrungburi Road, and **Daret's House**, located on Chaiyaphum Road.

Massages
Traditional massages are available at **Diamond Hotel**, Charoen Prathet Road, or at **Rin Kaeo Phovej**, 183/4 Wua Lai Road (beside the Old Chiang Mai Cultural Centre). Tel: 234 565, 235 969. Open from 8am–midnight.

PATTAYA
Pattaya's nightlife is still somewhat in the old mold, with bars proliferating in the South Pattaya area. Here, the emphasis is on picking up bargirls and drinking. There are one or two music clubs, where one can sip a beer and listen to 60s rock and roll.

Hotels have lobby bands and bars with lounge singers. The Beach Road and Pattaya 2 Road are lined with beer bars, which differ little from their cousins in South Pattaya.

PHUKET
As Phuket has become sophisticated, so has its nightlife. In Patong, **Simon Cabaret** (342

114) has evolved into a highly professional showpiece with elaborate stage sets and a few comic laughs. The cast is exclusively, and rather deceptively, it seems, feminine. Shows: 7.30 and 9.30pm.

The **Safari Pub**, a kilometer up the hill from Simon, heats up around 11pm with the live band luring an unlikely mix of cocktail-compromised Thais and tourists to the dance floor. In downtown Patong, the dance scene revolves around the evergreen **Banana disco** on Beach Road, the newly opened **Shark Club**, and the Thai-oriented **Tin Mine**. The **Sports Pub** at the Shark shows live sports events via satellite. Dozens of beer bars with hostesses still provide the backbone of Patong's nightlife in and around Soi Bangla. A-go-go thrives at **Extasy**, **Firehouse** and **Rock Hard**. Massage houses are many. **Christin Massage** is the glossiest. The traditional version is available at **Hutavat** in Phra Baramee Road.

In Karon there are beer bars opposite **Crystal Beach Hotel** and massage at the **Blue Moon**. In Kata there are a few beer bars south of the Siam Commercial Bank, but the upscale **Islander Bar** is a better bet.

The live music at Phuket town's **Timber Rock club** in Yaowarat Road is the best in town. Ten-pin bowling at **Pearl Bowl** on Montri Road is a tradition. The slick Thai-style coffee shop, **Bua Luang**, on Pattana Road, is a Phuket institution.

Culture

Culture
Modern pop culture seems to have gained ascendancy over traditional Thai arts, despite government support for Thai arts and performers. Foreign culture is promoted by the respective country cultural organizations, but little is done to attract foreign performers in the manner of, say, Hong Kong's Art Centre and the annual Hong Kong Arts Festival.

The many museums in Bangkok and in major towns around the country are devoted to preserving the past and contain some superb specimens.

Exhibitions of modern art are arranged by private gallery owners, foreign cultural centers, or by corporate patrons, usually banks.

Museums
BANGKOK
The **National Museum** on Na Phra That Road, tel: 215 8173, next to Sanam Luang in the heart of the old royal city, is a repository of archaeological finds, Buddha images, old royal regalia, ceramics and art objects (usually Buddhist) from neighboring countries. The walls of the Buddhaisawan Chapel in the museum grounds are covered in some of the finest Buddhist murals in Thailand. The museum is open from 9am–4pm, Wednesday to Sunday. Last ticket sold at 3.30pm. Admission is 20 baht.

The National Museum offers free guided tours of Buddhist and other art, and conducts them in a number of languages. The schedule is: **English:** Buddhism (Wednesday); Thai art and culture (Thursday). **French:** Thai art (Wednesday).

German: Thai art and culture (Thursday). **Spanish:** By special arrangement for groups.

Tours start at 9.30am and last about two hours. For information call the museum volunteers at 215 8173. Whatever tour you take, be sure to visit the Buddhaisawan Chapel and the Cremation Chariot Hall (Hall 17) afterwards.

Almost every urban centre in Thailand has a branch of the National Museum.

CHIANG MAI

The **National Museum**, near Wat Jet Yot on Highway 11. Open 9am–4pm Wednesday–Sunday. Collections of Sawankhalok china and Buddha images are highlights.

The **Folk Art Museum**, near the junction of Thiphanet and Wualai roads. Open 10am–4pm Friday–Wednesday. Collection of household items housed in a traditional-style house.

The **Tribal Research Centre**, on Chiang Mai University campus. A small ethnographical museum with costumes and implements of hill tribes on display.

Art Galleries

The **National Gallery**, to the north of the National Museum in Bangkok, across the approach to the Phra Pinklao Bridge at 4 Chao Fa Road, tel: 281 2224, displays works by Thai artists and offers frequent film shows. Open Wednesday to Sunday from 9am–4pm. Exhibitions of paintings, sculpture, ceramics, photographs and weaving are varied and numerous. Check the *Bangkok Post* for details.

Silpakorn University, opposite the Grand Palace on Na Phralan Road, is the country's premier fine arts college. It frequently stages exhibitions of students' work. Other promoters of Thai art and photography are the British Council, the Goethe Institut and Alliance Francaise, all of which sponsor various exhibitions.

Art galleries seem more interested in selling mass market

and "tourist" works than in promoting experimental art; but one, **Visual Dhamma**, takes an active role in ensuring that talented artists exhibit their works. As its name implies, it is interested primarily in a new school of Thai art which attempts to re-interpret Buddhist themes. It is located at 44/28 Soi 21 (Soi Asoke), Sukhumvit Road. Tel: 258 5879.

Concerts

The Fine Arts Department periodically offers concerts of Thai music and dance/drama at the **National Theatre**. On Saturday afternoons at 2pm, programs of Thai classical dance are presented at the auditorium of the **Public Relations Building** on Ratchadamnern Klang Avenue opposite the Royal Hotel. Each Friday, Bangkok Bank offers traditional Thai music on the top floor of its **Pan Fah** branch (Ratchadamnern Avenue at the intersection with Phra Sumen Road) at 5pm.

Concerts of European music and dance are now regular events. The Bangkok Symphony Orchestra gives frequent concerts, as do groups from western countries. See *Bangkok Post's* Sunday magazine for details.

Theaters

The **National Theatre** presents Thai works and, occasionally, big-name foreign ensembles like the New York Philharmonic. For more experimental works, Thai or foreign, look to the **Thailand Cultural Centre**. The Centre, which is a gift of the government of Japan, is located on Ratchadapisek Road north of Bangkok, tel: 247 0028. Its three stages present everything from pianists to puppets. See the newspapers for announcements of forthcoming performances.

It is also possible to find Chinese opera performed as part of funeral entertainment or during the Vegetarian Festival each September in Chinatown. These performances

are normally not announced, but are an unexpected surprise one stumbles across when wandering back alleys. It is hard to miss; the clash of cymbals and drums and the screech of violins identify it.

Likay, the village version of the great *lakhon* and *khon* dance/dramas of the palace, was once staple fare at temple fairs. Alas, most of the fairs have faded away in the city and are found only in rural areas. Even there, likay performances are often given second billing to popular movies shown in the open air on big screens. About the only place one can see truncated likay performances is at Lak Muang, where successful supplicants pay a troupe to perform for gods of the heavens and angels of the city.

Movies

Bangkok movie theaters present Thai, Chinese and subtitled Western films. The Western films are either megahits or are filled with violence – gore being substituted for dialogue. Thai films are either based on a set theme (good versus evil, with pathos, rowdy humor, ugly villains and plenty of fisticuffs) that appeal only to provincial audiences (and indeed are made primarily with them in mind), or are silly comedies on the theme of young love. Only rarely does a film of social significance appear.

Libraries

For reading or reference, stop in at one of these libraries. All carry books in English on Thailand. **American University Alumni** (AUA), 179 Ratchadamri Road. Tel: 252 8170/3. The library, which is sponsored by the U.S. Information Agency, is open to non-members. In Chiang Mai: 24 Ratchadamnern Road. Tel: 211 973, 278 407. **Neilson Hayes**, 195 Suriwongse Road. Tel: 233 1731. Open from 9.30am–4pm Monday to Saturday; and from 9.30am–12.30pm on Sunday. The oldest English language library in Thailand, with

over 20,000 volumes.
Siam Society, 131 Soi 21 (Soi Asoke), Sukhumvit Road. Tel: 258 3491. Open from 9am–5pm on Tuesday–Saturday.

Bookstores

Bangkok has perhaps the best bookstores in Southeast Asia, with a wide selection of books for information and for entertainment. If you want to read about something you have encountered in Bangkok or just want a good, light read for the beach, try one of these bookshops. Alternatively, your hotel bookstore may have something you are looking for.
Asia Books, with branches at 221 Sukhumvit Road (between Soi 15 and 17); Peninsula Plaza (153 Ratchadamri Road); Landmark Plaza (138 Sukhumvit Road); Thaniya Plaza (next to Soi Patpong 2); Times Square; World Trade Centre (4 Ratchadamri Road); Seacon Square (Si Nakharin Road) and Siam Discovery Centre.
Bookazine branches can be found on Ploenchit Road (Sogo Department Store, 3rd Floor); Silom Road (CP Tower, 313 Silom Road, near Convent Road); and Sukhumvit Road (Robinson Department Store).
D.K. Books, branches at Siam Square (Rama I Road); Mahboonkrong (opposite Siam Square); Sukhumvit Road (near Soi 12) and Seacon Square (Si Nakharin Road).
Chulalongkorn University (Phaya Thai Road, south of Siam Square) also has a good bookshop with some esoteric titles in English.

Festivals

Festivals and Fairs

Temple fairs upcountry are great fun to attend. They are usually held in the evenings during the cool season to raise money for repairs to temple buildings. There are carnival rides, freak shows, halls of horror, *rumwong* dances, food vendors and deafening noise – the one element without which a fair would not be a fair. If you see one in progress, stop, park and enjoy yourself.

The dates for these festivals and fairs change from year to year. Check the exact dates by calling the TAT in Bangkok.

JANUARY

New Year's Day is a day of relaxation after the festivities of the night before. It is a public holiday.

Phra Buddha Chinarat Fair is held in late January or early February. Enshrined in Phitsanulok's Wat Phra Si Ratana Mahathat, Phra Buddha Chinarat is one of Thailand's most sacred and delicately-cast Buddha images of the Sukhothai style. The fair includes a display of giant birds made from straw, folk performances and various forms of entertainment.

Don Chedi Memorial Fair in Suphanburi (late January) commemorates the decisive battle won by King Naresuan at Don Chedi. The fair features historical exhibitions, entertainment and local handicraft stalls.

Bo Sang Umbrella Fair, in Bo Sang near Chiang Mai, is held in the main street and celebrates the traditional skill of making gaily painted umbrellas and other handicrafts.

FEBRUARY

Flower Festival is held in Chiang Mai during early February. This annual event features flower displays, floral floats, beauty contests and coincides with the period when the province's temperate and tropical flowers are in full bloom.

Dragon and Lion Parade is held annually between January and February in the central Thailand town of Nakhon Sawan, by people of Chinese ancestry. The Dragon and Lion procession is a traditional homage-paying rite to the golden dragon deity in gratitude for his benevolence to human beings. The lively parade includes marching bands, golden dragon and lion dances, and processions of deities.

Chinese New Year is not celebrated with the boisterousness of other Asian countries. The temples are a bit busier with wishes made for good fortune in the coming year, but otherwise there is nothing to mark the period. Shops close and, behind the steel grilles, private family celebrations go on for three or four days.

Magha Puja, a public holiday in Bangkok and a Buddhist holiday on the full moon night of February, marks the spontaneous gathering of 1,200 disciples to hear the Lord Buddha preach. In the evening, Thais gather at temples to hear a sermon by the chief monk of the wat. Then, when the moon is rising, they place their hands in a praying position before their faces and clasping candles, incense and flowers, follow the chanting monks around the bot of the wat three times before placing their candles and incense in trays at the front of the bot. It is a most solemn and moving ceremony.

MARCH

Kite flying is not a festival but it would be difficult to convince kite enthusiasts otherwise. They gather at Sanam Luang, in Bangkok, in the afternoons as the brisk winds haul their large kites aloft, filling the sky with bright colours.

Barred Ground Dove Festival.
Dove lovers from all over Asia come
to Yala for this event. The highlight
is a dove-cooing contest involving
over 1,400 competitors.

APRIL

Chakri Day on 6 April celebrates
the founding in 1782 of the dynasty
that presently rules Thailand. It is
celebrated in the palace, but there
are no public ceremonies. An
official holiday, most Thais
celebrate it as a day off from work.

The **Phra Chedi Klang Nam Fair**
in April is one of the larger temple
fairs. It is celebrated at the wat on
the river's edge at Phrapadaeng, 15
km (9 mi) south of Bangkok, on the
Thonburi side of the river.

Songkran is a public holiday that,
in the past, was the traditional Thai
New Year – until royal decree
shifted the official new year's to
January 1. It most closely
resembles the Indian festival of Holi
which occurs at the same time.
Songkran is a time of wild revelry, a
chance for the normally placid Thais
to let off steam. The central event
is the sprinkling of water on one's
friends to bless them, but this
usually turns into a boisterous
throwing of buckets of water on
passers-by.

The celebration of Songkran in
Bangkok is a little more subdued
than in the north, and while it may
be safe for visitors to ride in an
open-windowed bus down the
street, they are advised to be
prepared when walking in the
street, riding a tuk-tuk or visiting
Bangkok's nightlife areas in
Patpong, Nana Entertainment Plaza
and Soi Cowboy.

To see Songkran at its most
riotous, travel down the western
bank of the Chao Phraya River to
the town of Phrapadaeng. There, no
one is safe, but in the April heat,
who cares? Songkran in the north
of Thailand, particularly in Chiang
Mai, is fervently celebrated over
several days and attracts many
visitors from Bangkok.

Turtle Releasing Fair. At Nai
Yang beach in Phuket, young turtles
are released for their journey to the

sea. The festival begins early in the
morning with alms offered to monks
and is accompanied by music,
dancing, sports and food.

MAY

Labor Day (May 1) is a public
holiday.

Coronation Day (May 5) is a
private royal affair and a public
holiday.

The **Rocket Festival** in Yasothon
in the northeast of Thailand is held
in early May. Well worth the trip to
witness the launching of the locally
made missiles of all shapes and
sizes, some as tall as a person.

The **Ploughing Ceremony** is a
colourful ancient tradition
celebrated only in Bangkok. Held at
Sanam Luang, it is presided over by
King Bhumibol and marks the
official start of the rice planting
season. Crimson-clad attendants
lead bullocks, drawing an old-
fashioned plough, around a
specially prepared ground. The lord
of ceremonies, usually the minister
of agriculture, follows behind,
scooping rice seed out of baskets
held by pretty maidens and sowing
it in the furrows left by the plough,
all to the accompaniment of blaring
conch shells and drums.

Visakha Puja is a public holiday
on the full moon night of May that
commemorates the birth,
enlightenment and death of
Buddha. The three things are all
said to have happened on the same
day. Visakha Puja is celebrated like
Magha Puja, with a triple
circumambulation around the
temple as the moon is rising.

Fruit Fairs. There are annual
fairs in Chiang Mai, Rayong,
Chanthaburi, Trat and several other
locations throughout Thailand to
celebrate the harvest of lychees,
durian, mangosteen, rambutan, jack
fruit and zalacca. Besides stalls
selling the produce of the
surrounding orchards, there are
beauty pageants, cultural shows
and local entertainment.

JUNE

Sunthorn Phu Day. This annual
celebration in late June

commemorates the birth of the Thai
poet Sunthorn Phu. The festivities
include dramatic performances and
puppet shows depicting his literary
works, poetry recitals and folk
entertainment.

JULY

Asalaha Puja on the full moon night
of July is the third most important
Buddhist holiday and marks the
occasion when Buddha preached to
his first five disciples. It is
celebrated on the full moon night in
similar manner to Magha Puja and
Visakha Puja. It also marks the
beginning of the three-month Lenten
season. Tradition says that Buddha
was approached by farmers who
asked that he bar monks from going
on their morning alms rounds for a
period of three months, because
they were trampling on the rice
shoots they had just planted. They
offered instead to take food to the
monks at the temple during this
period, a practice which has been
followed ever since.

Khao Phansa is celebrated
almost immediately following
Asalaha Puja and marks the
commencement of the annual three-
month Rains Retreat.

Candle Festival takes place
during Khao Phansa in the
northeast town of Ubon. It
celebrates the commencement of
Khao Phansa with a lovely
spectacle where some beautifully
embellished beeswax candles are
ceremoniously paraded before
being presented to temples.

AUGUST

Queen Sirikit marks her birthday
(August 12) by religious ceremonies
and private celebrations. It is a
public holiday.

SEPTEMBER

On the first day of the eighth lunar
month, Chinese celebrate the **Moon
Festival**. They place small shrines
laden with fruit, incense and
candles in front of their houses to
honor the moon goddess. It is a
lovely festival, the highlight of which
are the utterly scrumptious cakes
shaped like a full moon. They are

specially prepared, often by chefs flown in from Hong Kong, and found no other time of the year.

Phichit Boat Races. A regatta featuring long-boat races. Similar events are held in Phitsanulok and all over Thailand at this time of year. The low-slung, wooden boats are raced with great gusto.

Taan Khuay Salak. A series of races on the Nan River, northern Thailand, in long, narrow "dragon" boats propelled by 50 oarsmen. Mid-September to mid-October.

OCTOBER

The **Chinese Vegetarian Festival**, held in mid-October, is a subdued affair in Bangkok by comparison with the firewalkers of Phuket. Enormous amounts of vegetarian food, Chinese operatic performances and elaborate offerings are made at various Chinese temples around the city. A superb photographic opportunity. Only those wearing all-white attire are allowed in the area of the altar, so dress appropriately.

Ok Phansa marks the end of the three-month Lenten season, and the beginning of the Kathin season when Buddhists visit wats to present monks with new robes and other necessities. Groups will rent boats or buses and travel long distances to spend a day making gifts to monks of a particular wat. If you are invited, by all means go, because it is a day of feasting and fun as well.

Chulalongkorn Day (October 23) honors King Rama V (1868–1910), who led Thailand into the 20th century. On this public holiday, students lay wreaths before his statue in the plaza at the old National Assembly building during an afternoon ceremony.

Lanna Boat Races. If you miss the Phichit Boat Races, this regatta is just as exciting.

The **Buffalo Races** held in late October in Chonburi rival the excitement of the Kentucky Derby.

NOVEMBER

Golden Mount Fair, held the first week of November in Bangkok, is one of the noisiest of temple fairs. Carnival rides, food concessions, variety performances and product stalls are the main attractions.

The **Little Royal Barge Festival** at Wat Nang Chee in Phasi Charoen early in November is a smaller version of the grand Royal Barge procession, but it is marked by more gaiety in small towns.

Loy Krathong, one of the most beautiful festivals anywhere in Asia, is on the full moon night of November. It is said to have been started in Sukhothai in the 13th century. A young queen, Nang Nopamat, is said to have floated a small boat laden with candles and incense downstream past the pavilion where her husband was talking with his friends. Whatever the origins, it has grown to be one of the country's most enchanting festivals, a night when Thais everywhere launch small candle-laden boats into the rivers and canals to ask blessings. The tiny dots of light and shimmering water are mesmerizing.

Long-boat races have become increasingly popular in the past few years, and it is not unusual to open a newspaper during November and find that yet another race is being staged somewhere in Thailand. They are colourful and exciting and provide superb photo opportunities.

The **Elephant Round-Up** in Surin is held in mid-November and attracts visitors from all over Thailand and elsewhere.

The **Phra Pathom Chedi Fair** at the world's biggest chedi, in Nakhon Pathom, is another temple fair, and is regarded as one of the most exciting.

Khon Kaen Silk Fair. Silk weaving demonstrations and a chance to buy lustrous silk in a major centre of production.

River Kwai Bridge Week. A sound-and-light presentation recaptures this dark period of recent history when Asians and Europeans died in the thousands at the hands of the Japanese to build the infamous Death Railway during World War II.

Sunflower Fair. The photogenic sight of Mexican sunflowers in bloom is best seen in the hills of Doi Mae U-Khor, as Mae Hong Son holds a three-day festival of ox-carts decorated with the beautiful flowers. When the flowers finally fade, the seeds are used to make organic insecticides.

DECEMBER

Trooping of the Colours (December 3). The royal regiments dressed in brilliantly-coloured costumes pass in review before the king. Held on the plaza before the old National Assembly building, the Trooping of the Colours is the most impressive of martial ceremonies.

King Bhumibol celebrates his birthday (December 5) with a ceremony at Wat Phra Kaeo only for invited officials and guests and with a private party. It is a public holiday.

King's Cup Regatta. Long-distance yacht racing from Nai Harn Bay in Phuket with entries from around the world.

Constitution Day (December 10) is a public holiday in Thailand.

Christmas may soon be a Thai holiday if the merchants have any say in the matter. If endless repetitions of Christmas carols in department stores bludgeon everyone into acceptance, it may not be long before it becomes an official holiday.

But **New Year's Eve** on December 31 is indeed a public holiday.

Shopping

General

Whatever part of your budget you have allocated for shopping, double it or regret it. Keep a tight grip on your wallet or you will find yourself being seduced by the low prices and walking off with more than you can possibly carry home. If you cannot resist, see the "Export" section for an inexpensive way to get souvenirs home.

Over the years, there have been two major changes in the shopping picture. First, there have been subtle design alterations to make the items more appealing to foreign buyers. The purists may carp, but the changes and the wider range of products have found welcome reception by shoppers. At the same time, new products have been introduced which have found popular reception among visitors.

The other change is that while regional products were once found only in the towns that produced them, there has been a homogenization of distribution, so that it is now possible, for example, to buy Chiang Mai umbrellas in Phuket. The widest range of items are found in Bangkok and Chiang Mai, but if you never have a chance to leave Bangkok, do not despair; nearly everything you might want to buy in provincial towns can be found in the capital.

Export

SHIPPING
Most shops will handle documentation and shipping for your purchases. Alternatively, the General Post Office on Charoen Krung (New) Road, near the Oriental Hotel, offers boxes and a packing service for goods sent by sea mail. Packages can be shipped from most post offices. Post offices in most towns also sell cardboard boxes specially created for shipping packages and freight.

Thai Airways in Bangkok also offers a special service called THAIPAC that will air freight your purchases (regardless of the mode of transportation or the airline you are using) to the airline's destination closest to your home for 25 percent of the normal rate. Just take your goods to the airline's office at 485 Silom Road. They must fit into a special box and weigh no more than 33 kg (73 lbs) per box.

Thai Airways will also handle the documentation and customs clearance for a small charge.

EXPORT PERMITS
The Fine Arts Department prohibits the export of all Thai Buddha images, images of other religious deities and fragments (hands or heads) of images dating from before the 18th century.

All antiques and art objects, regardless of type or age, must be registered with the Fine Arts Department. The shop will usually do this for you. If you decide to handle it yourself, take the piece to the Fine Arts Department at the National Museum on Na Phra That Road, across from Sanam Luang, together with two postcard-sized photos of it. The export fee ranges from between 50 and 200 baht, depending on the antiquity – and authenticity – of the piece.

Fake antiques do not require export permits, but airport customs officials are not art experts and may mistake it for a genuine piece. If it looks authentic, clear it at the Fine Arts Department to avoid problems later.

Complaints

The customer is (nearly) always wrong might be the most candid way of putting it. Except for very large shops, expect that once you have paid for an item and left the store, or that unless the defect is very glaring and there is no possible way you could have caused it, the moment you walk out the door, that's it. You can report the shop to the Tourist Police, but they are not usually interested. Shop carefully. *Caveat emptor.*

Shopping Areas

BANGKOK
If you cannot find it in Bangkok, you will not be able to find it anywhere else in the country. Aside from the traffic problems, Bangkok is the most comfortable place to shop. Shopping venues range from huge air-conditioned malls to tiny hole-in-the-wall shops to crafts sections of large department stores.

Queen Sirikit's Chitralada stores sell the rare crafts she and her organization, SUPPORT, have worked so diligently to preserve by teaching the arts to village women. There are branches at the Grand Palace, in Oriental Plaza and the Hilton International Hotel, and at the airport, as well as in Pattaya.

Note that Nancy Chandler's Map of Bangkok, widely available in bookstores and hotels, is an invaluable reference for serious shoppers. It is not the best map for finding specific street addresses in Bangkok, but for pointing you in the direction of the top shopping areas, restaurants and sights, it is unparalleled. Also, the brightly coloured, hand-lettered map makes a wonderful souvenir to take home.

CENTRAL BANGKOK
World Trade Centre, 4 Ratchadamri Road. The flagships of this huge 8-floor shopping complex are Zen Central and Isetan, two well-regarded department stores. Other attractions include a **Duty Free Shop** on the seventh floor (passport and ticket must be presented), many fast-food outlets and bistro-type restaurants, and a wealth of small boutiques selling nearly everything imaginable.

Narayana Phand, the government handicraft centre, 127 Ratchadamri Road (across the street from the

World Trade Centre), is the very best place to go to see the whole range of Thai crafts, particularly if your time is limited. Wood carvings, bencharong, jewelry, pewter, ceramics, silk, handmade paper, textiles, and clothing can all be found at reasonable (and fixed) prices here. Pleasant restaurant on the second floor. The market in the basement beneath Narayana Phand is the best place in town for inexpensive blue jeans; leather goods, casual jewelry, videos and T-shirts are also available here.

Siam Square, Rama I Road (between Henri Dunant and Phaya Thai Roads), home to 7 movie theaters, several bookstores and innumerable Western and Asian fast-food outlets, also has many small shops selling clothing, electrical goods and gift items. Investigate the vendors along the central laneways. Popular, particularly with teenagers.

Across Phaya Thai Road, **Mahboonkrong** is a multi-level shopping complex offering a variety of items including leather goods, clothing, jewelry, audio tapes and CDs at mid-range prices.

Gaysorn Plaza, at the intersection of Ploenchit and Ratchadamri Roads, and Peninsula Plaza, 153 Ratchadamri Road, are two chic shopping malls with designer fashion outlets and a variety of small boutiques. **Amarin Plaza**, Ploenchit Road (near Erawan Shrine), is the place to go for up-market shoes and jewelry.

Pratunam Market, at the intersection of Phetburi and Ratchaprarop Roads, is a huge, bustling warren of stalls which caters less to tourists than to Thais. It is somewhat difficult to locate, but a good place to absorb lots of local colour. There are many street vendors along Ratchaprarop Road outside the market.

SUKHUMVIT ROAD

There are many craft shops in soi off the Sukhumvit corridor.

Among the best for a variety of items are these:

Gifted Hands, 172/18 Soi 23 (Soi Prasanmit), Sukhumvit Road. Tel: 258 4010. Handcrafted silver beads, necklaces, earrings.

Lao Song Handicrafts, 2/56 Soi 41, Sukhumvit Road. Tel: 261 6627. Village handicrafts, non-profit.

L'Arcadia, 12/2 Soi 23 (Soi Prasanmit), Sukhumvit Road. Tel: 259 9595. Thai and Burmese wood and lacquer items.

Nandakwang, 108/3 Soi 23 (Soi Prasanmit), Sukhumvit Road. Tel: 258 1962. Cotton table/bed linens and clothing.

Nature's Touch, 87 Soi 5, Sukhumvit Road. Tel: 251 6086/7. Khon masks, other papier masks items and pottery.

Rasi Sayam, 32 Soi 23 (Soi Prasanmit), Sukhumvit Road. Tel: 258 4195. High-quality handicrafts.

Siamraj Marketing, 160/4-6 Soi 55 (Soi Thong Lo), Sukhumvit Road. Tel: 391 8367, 392 4066. Silk flowers, bencharong and other ceramic items.

Vilai, 731/1, Soi 55 (Soi Thong Lo), Sukhumvit Road. Tel: 391 6106. Excellent fabrics.

Street vendors are common, particularly after dark, along both sides of Sukhumvit Road, between Soi 3 and 11. Perhaps the most useful items they sell are suitcases in a variety of sizes, handy to get all the extra shopping home.

CHAROEN KRUNG ROAD

River City, 23 Trok Rongnamkaeng, Yota Road (on the river, a little north of the Royal Orchid Sheraton). Tel: 237 0777/8, ext. 618. Daily 10am–8pm. Fashionable shopping arcade, the top two floors of which are devoted entirely to antiques. The merchants there are not fond of bargaining, but it can be done, particularly if you have some time to devote to the endeavor.

Oriental Plaza, Soi Oriental, Charoen Krung (New) Road, is another stylish shopping complex with a wide variety of top quality merchandise.

Bangrak Market, Charoen Krung (New) Road, between the Oriental and Shangri-La hotels, something of a contrast to the more

sophisticated shopping complexes in the area, sells Indian spices, fresh fruit and cut flowers, and a variety of household goods. **Street vendors** are common along Charoen Krung (New) Road between Silom and Suriwongse Roads.

SILOM ROAD

Soi Patpong hosts a bustling night market each evening from about 6pm. Provided you aren't bothered by the occasional flash of skin through the open club doors, or by the touts doing their best to lure you inside, it can be an enjoyable experience. Silver jewelry, audio and video tapes, T-shirts, dresses, ties, leather goods and watches are common here, and along Silom Road just outside Patpong. Bargain for everything.

Soi Lalai Sap, Soi 5, Silom Road (beside Bangkok Bank). Vendors offering a variety of inexpensive food, flowers, leather goods, watches and clothing line this small soi on weekdays only, until about 3pm. Interesting shops include: **Choisy**, 9/25 Suriwongse Road. Tel: 233 7794. Haute couture in Thai silk.

Jim Thompson's Thai Silk, 9 Suriwongse Road (near Rama IV Road). Tel: 234 4900. Daily 9am–9pm. Staggering array of silk items; expensive but top quality. **Motif**, 296/7 Silom Road. Tel: 233 1203. Export quality silk and cotton fabrics, handmade paper, paper flowers and a splendid range of cloth items.

Shinawatra Thai, at the intersection of Sathorn Tai Road and Soi Suan Plu. Tel: 286 9991/4. Large assortment of silk and cloth items, including table linen, cushion covers and lingerie.

Silom Village Trade Centre, 266 Silom Road (near Soi 24). An attractive complex of small shops offering a variety of leather goods, wood carvings, handmade paper products, Burmese lacquerware, jewelry and cloth goods. The coffee shop at the entrance is a good place to people watch.

Thaniya Plaza, Thaniya Road, off Silom Road. Small shopping complex with boutiques, book stores, a coffee shop, and one or two small gift shops. Legend on the 3rd floor has a good selection of handicrafts, including celadon, teak and baskets.

CHINATOWN

Even if you don't have any use for a dozen hand towels, six large rolls of gift wrap or entire bolts of cloth, a stroll down Sampeng Lane in the heart of **Chinatown** is a delightful, if somewhat sense-assaulting, way to pass several hours. There are many small soi leading off Sampeng which are jammed with shops selling fabrics, herbal remedies, toys, clothes, paper items and household goods.

Follow **Sampeng Lane** up to the canal and cross over into Pahurat, an adjoining market with a strong Indian flavour. This is the place to find batik and other textiles, sewing notions and a wide range of spices.

North of Pahurat you will find **Old Siam Plaza**, a market with an old world ambiance. The gun shops will likely be of little interest to the average tourist, but there are many handicrafts to be found here, as well as decent restaurants and coffee shops.

Beyond **Old Siam**, follow Charoen Krung (New) Road away from the river to reach **Thieves Market** (Nakhon Kasem in Thai). Brass, porcelain, antiques, musical instruments and amulets are among the items for sale in these narrow streets lined with old wooden houses.

Pak Khlong Talat is a huge, crowded riverside market at the northwestern edge of Chinatown. It is at its most atmospheric around 2 or 3 in the morning when large quantities of fresh flowers and vegetables are unloaded from the boats and made ready for sale the following morning.

BANGLAMPOO AREA

Banglampoo Market, a sprawling area beside the river northeast of Sanam Luang, caters more to the budget traveler than to the one with gold cards. This is a good market

for inexpensive clothing, audio tapes and second-hand books; there are a few craft shops along Khao San Road as well. Shops offering hair braiding and beading are a common sight in this area. Thai musical instruments can be purchased at **Duriyabanna**, 151 Tanao Road, and gold leaf beating takes place at 321 Phra Sumen Road (eastern edge of Banglampoo Market, before Prachatipatai Road) from 9am–3pm, Monday–Friday. There is also a bookstore with a good selection of Buddhist books next door.

On the other side of **Democracy Monument**, the markets at Tha Phra Chan and Wat Ratchanadda sell love potions and amulets to protect one from every conceivable misfortune. On Friday and Saturday, investigate the night market at Democracy Monument, mostly offering second-hand goods without a lot of the traditional tourist fare, but entertaining nevertheless.

CHATUCHAK MARKET

By far the most challenging (and often most rewarding) shopping experience is the huge weekend market at **Chatuchak Park** on Phaholyothin Road. Over 8,500 vendors ply their wares here on Saturday and Sunday; it's best to come early to avoid the heat. Antiques, clothing, jewelry, wood carvings, brassware, masks, baskets, handmade paper, and other crafts from around Southeast Asia can be found here, in addition to the usual fruit, vegetables, plants and animals.

Bargaining adds to the fun of a day at **Chatuchak**, and when energy levels start to flag, there are many food stalls, and even a coffee shop or two, to offer sustenance. If you're not content just to wander aimlessly through the many alleyways, the aforementioned Nancy Chandler map is essential to help you find your way to a particular area of the market.

Finally, no matter which area you find yourself in, most major department stores have special handicrafts sections carrying a wide selection of items. Try **Central** (branches at 1691 Phaholyothin Road; 306 Silom Road; and 191 Silom Road), **Robinson** (branches at 1 Phaholyothin Road; intersection of Silom and Rama IV Roads; and Soi 19, Sukhumvit Road), **Sogo** at Amarin Plaza, **Tokyu** at Mahboonkrong, and **Zen Central** at the World Trade Centre.

OUTSIDE BANGKOK

Chiang Mai also has air-conditioned department stores that sell household and personal products. Handicrafts can be found at studios along the 9-km (6-mi) road to Borsang and along Wua Lai Road. For fake antiques, you must travel farther, to Baan Tawai on the highway to Chom Thong. The famous Night Bazaar on Chang Klan Road and the vendors along Tapae Road are also places to pick up bargains.

Pattaya has malls like Mike's Shopping Mall, Big C, Royal Garden Shopping Plaza and Thai Pan, but most of the casual items are found on the Beach Road. Shops sell a good selection of casual wear.

Phuket offers fewer shopping areas, and most are concentrated on Highway 402 between the airport and Phuket town. Thai Village (km 2.5), Native Handicraft Centre (km 8.5), Shinawatra (km 9) and Cheewa (km 10.6) offer both local handicrafts and imported from other regions of Thailand. Thai Village has workshops where you can watch the artisans at work. For casual wear, check the shops and vendors along Patong's Beach Road and Soi Bangla, and in Kata and Karon. In Phuket town, browse vendors and shops along Ranong Road.

What to Buy

REAL/FAKE ANTIQUES

Wood, bronze, terra cotta and stone statues from all regions of Thailand and Burma can be found in Bangkok and Chiang Mai. There are religious figures and characters from classical literature, carved wooden angels, mythical animals, temple bargeboards and eave brackets. Note that most fake antiques passed off as real are crafted in Chiang Mai and surrounding villages.

Although the Thai government has banned the export of Buddha images, there are numerous deities and disciples which can be sent abroad. Bronze deer, angels and characters from the *Ramakien* cast in bronze do not fall under the export ban. It is also possible to buy and export Burmese Buddha images.

Chiang Mai produces beautiful wooden replicas modeled on antique sculptures. Sold as reproductions, with no attempt to pass them off as genuine antiques, they make lovely home decor items. Animals, Buddha's disciples and dozens of items range in size from small to life-sized.

Chiang Mai also produces a wide range of beautifully crafted wooden furniture. Cabinets, tables, dining room sets, elephant *howdah*, bedroom sets or simple items like wooden trays are crafted from teak or other woods and carved with intricate designs.

BASKETS

Thailand's abundant bamboo, wicker and grasses are transformed into lamps, storage boxes, tables, colourful mats, handbags, letter holders, tissue boxes and slippers. Wicker and bamboo are turned into storage lockers with brass fittings and furniture to fill the entire house. Shops can provide the cushions as well.

Yan lipao, a thin, sturdy grass, is woven into delicate patterns to create purses and bags for formal occasions. Although expensive, the bags are durable, retaining their beauty for years.

CERAMICS

Best known among the distinctive Thai ceramics is the jade green celadon, which is distinguished by its finely glazed surface. Statues, lamps, ashtrays and other items are also produced in dark green, brown and cobalt blue hues.

Modeled on its Chinese cousin, blue-and-white porcelain includes pots, lamp bases, household items and figurines. Quality varies according to the skill of the artist, and of the firing and glazing.

Bencharong (meaning five colours) describes a style of porcelain derived from 16th-century Chinese art. Normally reserved for bowls, containers and fine chinaware, its classic pattern features a small religious figure surrounded by intricate floral designs. The whole is rendered in five colours – usually green, blue, yellow, rose and black.

Earthenware includes a wide assortment of pots, planters and dinner sets in a rainbow of colours and designs. Also popular are the big, brown glazed Shanghai jars bearing yellow dragons, which the Thais use to hold bath water and which visitors use as planters. Antique stoneware includes the double-fish design plates and bowls originally produced at Sawankhalok, the kilns established near Sukhothai in the 13th century.

Some of the best ceramics come from Ratchaburi, southwest of Bangkok. The wide variety makes a special trip there worthwhile.

DECORATIVE ARTS

Lacquerware comes in two styles: the gleaming gold-and-black variety normally seen on temple shutters, and the matte red type with black and/or green details, which originated in northern Thailand and Burma. The lacquerware repertoire includes ornate containers and trays, wooden figurines, woven bamboo baskets and Burmese-inspired Buddhist manuscripts.

The pieces may also be bejeweled with tiny glass mosaics and gilded ornaments.

Black lacquer is also the base into which shaped bits of mother-of-pearl are pressed. Scenes from religious or classical literature are rendered on presentation trays, containers and plaques.

Beware of craftsmen who take shortcuts by using black paint rather than the traditional seven layers of lacquer. On these items, the surface cracks, often while the item is still on the shelf.

FABRICS AND CLOTHES

Thai silk is perhaps Thailand's best-known craft. Brought to world attention by American entrepreneur Jim Thompson, Thai silk has enjoyed enduring popularity. Sold in a wide variety of colours, it is characterized by the tiny nubs which, like embossings, rise from its surface. Unlike sheer Indian silks and shiny Chinese-patterned silks, Thai silk is a thick cloth that lends itself to clothes, curtains and upholstery. It is more popular as blouses, ties and scarves. It is also used to cover purses, tissue boxes and picture frames. Lengths printed with elephant, bamboo, floral and dozens of other motifs are turned into decorative pillowcases to accent rooms.

Mudmee is a northeastern silk whose colours are somber and muted. A form of tie-dyed cloth, it is sold both in lengths and as finished clothing or accessories.

Cotton is popular for shirts and dresses, since it breathes in Thailand's hot, humid air. Although available in lengths, it is generally sold already cut into frocks and shirts. Southern Thailand is a batik centre and offers ready-made clothes and batik paintings.

Burmese in origin and style, *kalaga* wall hangings depicting gods, kings and mythical animals have gained increasing popularity in the past few years. The figures are stuffed with *kapok* to make them stand out from the surface in relief.

GEMS AND JEWELRY

Thailand is one of the world's exporters of cut rubies and sapphires. The rough stones are mostly imported from Cambodia and Burma, as local mines are not able to meet the demand. Customers should patronize only those shops that display trade's official emblem: a gold ring mounted with a ruby, which guarantees the dealer's integrity.

Thailand is now regarded as the world's leading cutter of gemstones, the "Bangkok cut" rapidly becoming one of the most popular. Thai artisans set the stones in gold and silver to create jewelry and bejeweled containers. Artisans also craft jewelry that satisfies an international clientele. Light green Burmese jade (jadeite) is carved into jewelry and art objects. The island of Phuket produces international standard natural, cultured Mob (teardrop) and artificial pearls (made from pearl dust glued to form a globule). They are sold as individual items or are set into gold jewelry.

Costume jewelry is a major Thai business with numerous items available. A related craft which has grown rapidly in the past decade is that of gilding Thai orchids for use as brooches.

HILL-TRIBE CRAFTS

Northern hill tribes produce brightly coloured needlepoint work in a wide variety of geometric and floral patterns. These are sold either as produced, or else incorporated into shirts, coats, bags, pillowcases and other items.

Hill-tribe silver work is valued less for its silver content (which is low) than for the intricate work and imagination that goes into making it. The genre includes necklaces, headdresses, bracelets and rings the women wear on ceremonial occasions. Enhancing their value are the old British Indian rupee coins that decorate the women's elaborate headdresses.

Other hill-tribe items one might consider include knives, baskets, pipes and gourd flutes that look and sound like bagpipes.

METAL ART OBJECTS

Although Thai craftsmen have produced some of Asia's most beautiful Buddha images, modern bronze sculpture tends to be of less exalted subjects and execution. Minor deities, characters from classical literature, deer and abstract figures are cast up to 2 m (7 ft) tall and are normally clad with a brass skin to make them gleam. Bronze is also cast into handsome cutlery and coated in shiny brass.

Silver and gold are pounded into jewelry items, boxes and other decorative pieces; many are set with gems. To create nielloware boxes and receptacles, a design is incised in silver or gold. The background is cut away and filled with an amalgam of dark metals, leaving the figures to stand in high relief against the black background.

Tin, mined near Phuket, is the prime ingredient in pewterware, of which Thailand is a major producer. Items range from clocks and steins to egg cups and figurines.

PAINTINGS

Modern Thai artists paint everything from realistic to abstract art, the latter often a weak imitation of Western art. Two areas at which they excel are depictions of everyday village life and of new interpretations of classical Buddhist themes. Artists can also work from live sittings or photographs to create superb charcoal or oil portraits. A family photograph from home can be transformed into a painting. The price depends on size: a 40 cm x 60 cm (16" x 24") charcoal portrait costs around 1,000 baht. There are several street-side studios in Bangkok, Phuket and Pattaya that specialize in this art.

THEATRE ART OBJECTS

Papier mâché *khon* masks, like those used in palace dance/drama, are painted and accented with lacquer decorations and gilded to create superb works of art.

Shadow puppets cut from the hides of water buffaloes and displayed against backlit screens in open air theaters tell the Ramakien story. Check to be sure the figure is actually cut from hide and not from a sheet of black plastic.

Bright coloured shadow puppets cut from buffalo hide make excellent wall decorations.

Inspired by the *Ramakien*, craftsmen have fashioned miniature models of chariots and warriors in gilded wood or glass sculpture. These two materials are also employed to create reproductions of the famous Royal Barges.

UMBRELLAS

Chiang Mai produces lovely umbrellas and fans made from silk or *sa paper*, a fine parchment often confused for rice paper but made from pounded tree bark.

Sport

Participant Sports

Thailand has developed its outdoor sports facilities to a considerable degree and air-conditioned the ones played indoors. Nearly every major hotel has a swimming pool and a fitness centre; some have squash courts and jogging paths.

DEEP-SEA FISHING

For deep-sea fishing, go to Phuket or to Bang Saray south of Pattaya. At Bang Saray, marlin, king mackerel, cobia, yellow jack, barracuda, bonito, giant groupers, red snapper, rays and black tip sharks lurk among submerged rocks. Boats, tackle and guides are available for very reasonable fees. There are small hotels in Bang Saray, but most fishermen spend the night in Pattaya and head out early in the morning. Fishing trips can be arranged by calling Bang Saray Fishing Lodge at its Bangkok office. Tel: 233 7719, 234 3094.

The waters off Phuket offer numerous challenges to deep-sea fishermen. Sailfish, barracuda, albacore, marlin, wahoo, tuna and king mackerel are just a few of the varieties awaiting a baited hook near Raja islands, east of Phuket.

The **Travel Company** on Patong Beach near Soi Patong Post Office, tel: (032) 321 292, offers daily cruises aboard converted Thai fishing trawlers equipped with fixed sockets to hold the rods. The price for one day is around 6,000 baht for charter, usually with food and drink. No minimum number of persons is required and the cruise is offered year-round. Travel Company also offers night fishing tours that leave Patong at 4pm and return at 9am the following day.

FITNESS CENTERS

In Bangkok, the Asia-wide **Clark Hatch** has a branch in the Thaniya Plaza, off Silom Road. Tel: 231 2250. **Fitness International** is located in the Dusit Thani Hotel. Part-time membership is available. All the top hotels in Bangkok have well-equipped fitness centers.

In Phuket, there is a **Clark Hatch Fitness Centre** in Le Méridien Hotel, tel: 321 480/1, ext. 1428, that is open from 7am–8.30pm. The **Holiday Inn** in Patong also has a fitness centre. The **Pattaya Fitness Centre**, with weights, gym and a sauna, is near the Regent Marina Complex.

FITNESS PARKS

One corner of Bangkok's **Lumpini Park** boasts a fitness park. In Chiang Mai, there is a free fitness park on **Nimmanhaemin Road** that is open from 5am–10pm. In Pattaya, the fitness park is located on the slopes of **Pattaya Hill**; in Phuket, it sits atop **Rang Hill** in the middle of Phuket town.

GOLF

Thais are great golfing buffs, going so far as to employ some of world golfing's stellar architects to design international-class courses. The best courses are in Bangkok, Phuket and Pattaya, with other courses in Chiang Mai, Khao Yai and Hua Hin. Greens fees range from 500–1,000 baht per round on weekends, and it is generally not difficult to reserve a time.

Among Bangkok's courses is the **Navathanee Golf Course** (22 M.1, Sukhapiban 2 Road. Tel: 376 1020) designed by Robert Trent Jones Jr. It is open from 6am–6pm. The **Army Golf Course** at 459 Ram Intra Road, tel: 521 1530, is open from 5am–9.30pm. The **Railway Training Centre Golf Course**, on Phaholyothin Road, tel: 271 0130, west of the Hyatt Central Plaza Hotel, opens at 6am, closes at 8pm. The **Krungthep Sports Golf Course**, 522 Hua Mark Road, tel: 379 3732, opens at 5am, closes at 5pm.

In Chiang Mai, the **Lanna Golf Course** on Chotana Road, tel: 221 911, is open 6am–6pm.

In Pattaya, try the **Siam Country Club Golf Course** 10 km (6 mi) east of town in rolling hills.

Phuket has excellent, if pricey, golf courses at the **Banyan Tree** (324 350), **Blue Canyon** (327 440), the **Phuket Country Club** (321 365, 321 038) and **The Century** (321 329).

HORSE RIDING

There are no public horse-riding facilities in Bangkok, but in Chiang Mai there is a stable on Chotana Road near the new provincial hall. It is open on Saturday and Sunday from 6am–noon and the cost is 200 baht per hour. Telephone 247 478 for more information.

In Phuket, ride at **Crazy Horse Club** at 17 Moo 2, 1 km (0.6 mi) down the back road connecting Kakata Inn with H 4028. Instructors accompany riders through rice fields and down the beach. Morning rides into the jungle are also offered. During the dry season, owners take riders on 2-hour trips into the hills.

ICE SKATING

Undoubtedly one of the more unusual tropical pursuits, ice skating has a certain popularity in Bangkok. Try it at the **World Ice Skating Centre**, World Trade Centre, 8th Floor, 4 Ratchadamri Road. Tel: 255 9500. Monday–Friday and Sundays: 10am–2.45pm and 4–9pm, Saturdays: 8.30am–4pm and 5–9pm.

JOGGING

Two jogging sites for those wise enough not to challenge Bangkok's traffic for right-of-way are in **Lumpini Park** and **Chatuchak Park**. The Siam-Intercontinental, Hilton and Ambassador hotels, among others, have jogging paths.

In Chiang Mai, joggers run up the hill to **Doi Suthep** and catch a mini-bus back. In Pattaya, jog up **Pattaya Hill**. In Phuket, try **Rang Hill**, a 1.3 km (0.8 mi) jaunt. There is a fitness park at the top.

SNOOKER

Thailand has produced some excellent snooker players who are nipping at the heels of world champions in international competitions. As a result, parlors have sprung up everywhere in Thailand as budding aspirants focus their eyes on complex shots and potential riches. In Bangkok, there are numerous snooker parlors around the city. The "Rooks" chain is the most popular and dozens of its snooker parlors can be found.

SCUBA DIVING

Shops in Pattaya and Phuket's Patong beach provide comprehensive courses leading to internationally-recognized PADI or NAUI certification. In Pattaya, try **Seafari** and **Dave's Divers Den**, both on the Beach Road.

Ko Tao is popular with experienced and first-time divers alike; the many placid bays and leeward shores are perfect for the beginner. The visibility is generally exceptional in the pristine waters off this tiny island, and sightings of spotted rays, trigger fish, whale sharks and even giant clams are not uncommon.

There are upwards of 20 diving schools on Ko Tao with 100 or more professional instructors, including **Buddha View Dive Resort**, tel: (01) 229 3948, (01) 229 4466; **Gecko Divers**, tel: (01) 229 5515, (01) 725 0711; **Samui International Diving School/Planet Scuba**, tel: (077) 231 242, in Bangkok, tel: (02) 253 8043.

In Pattaya, **Seafari Sports Centre** on the Beach Road. (Tel: 419 060), and **Dave's Divers Den** at Soi 6 on the Beach Road offer PADI and NAUI courses and diving trips to the outer islands. The water in the bay is murky and visibility is limited.

In Phuket, **Fantasea** (340 088), **South East Asia Liveaboards** (340 406), **Santana** (340 360), **Sea Bees** (381 765) and **Marina Divers** (330 272), among others, have a good reputation. Shop around and you can find scuba trips aimed at German, Scandinavian, French, Thai

and Japanese customers. For beginners, the four-day **PADI Open Water course** costs around 8,500 baht, including classroom theory, shallow water introduction, and four dives, usually in Phi Phi, Shark Point or Raja Island.

Day trips for divers with an Open Water card typically visit **Phi Phi**, **Shark Point** or the two **Raja islands**. Day trips average 1,500 baht, plus 500 baht for full equipment rental.

There is a trend towards live-aboard trips to the high visibility dive sites at the **Similan** and **Surin islands**, and even into Burma. These places offer a better chance of seeing large turtles, whale sharks, manta rays and the like. Depending on the vessel, which can be basic or luxurious, trips run 2,500–6,000 baht per person per day. Trips last 2 to 7 days.

Spectator Sports

Despite the hot climate, Thai men and women are avid sports enthusiasts, actively playing both their own sports and those adopted from the West according to international rules.

The king of foreign sports is soccer and is played by both sexes. Following a close second is badminton, with basketball, rugby, track and field, swimming, marksmanship, boxing, tennis and golf trailing only a short way behind. Check the English-language newspapers for schedules.

The principal sports venues in Bangkok are the National Stadium, on Rama I Road just west of Mahboonkrong Shopping Centre; the Hua Mark Stadium, east of the city next to Ramkhamhaeng University; and the Thai-Japanese Sports Centre, at Din Daeng near the northern entrance to the expressway.

In Chiang Mai, games are played at the Chiang Mai Stadium and at Chiang Mai University; in Phuket, at the Phuket Stadium on Vichaisongkhram Road.

Thailand has also created a number of unique sports and these

are well worth watching as much for the grace and agility displayed as for the element of fun that pervades every competition.

KITE FIGHTING

The heat of March and April is relieved somewhat by breezes that the Thais use to send kites aloft. **Sanam Luang** in Bangkok and open spaces everywhere across the country are filled with young and old boys clinging to kite strings.

The Thais have also turned it into a competitive sport, forming teams sponsored by major companies. Two teams vie for trophies. One flies a giant star-shaped male *chula* kite nearly 2 m (6.5 ft) high. The opposing teams (there may be more than one) fly the diminutive diamond-shaped female *pakpao* kites. One team tries to snare the other's kite and drag it across a dividing line. Surprisingly, the odds are even and a tiny female pakpao stands a good chance of pulling down a big chula male. Teamwork and fast action make for exciting viewing. Competitions at Bangkok's Sanam Luang start at 2pm.

TAKRAW

With close relatives in the Philippines, Malaysia and Indonesia, *takraw* employs all the limbs except the hands to propel a woven rattan ball (or a more modern plastic ball) over a net or into a hoop. In the net version, two three-player teams face each other across a head-high net, like that used in badminton. As the match heats up, it is not unusual for a player to turn a complete somersault to spike a ball across the net.

In the second type, six players form a wide circle around a basket-like net suspended high in the air. Using heads, feet, knees and elbows to keep the ball airborne, they score points by putting it into the net. A team has a set time period in which to score as many points as it can, after which it is the opposing team's turn.

Tournaments are held at the **Thai-Japanese Sports Centre** (Tel:

465 5325 for dates and times) four times a year; admission is free. Competitions are also held in the northwest corner of Bangkok's **Sanam Luang** during the March–April kite contests. Free admission. During the non-monsoon months, wander into a park or a temple courtyard anywhere in the country late in the afternoon.

THAI BOXING (MUAY THAI)

One of the most exciting and popular Thai sports is Thai boxing. In Bangkok, **Ratchadamnern Stadium** on Ratchadamnern Nok Avenue offers bouts on Monday, Wednesday, and Thursday at 6pm and on Sunday at 4.30 and 8.30pm. The Sunday matinee at 4.30pm is recommended, as it has the cheapest seats. Ticket prices run between 500 and 1,000 baht for ringside seats (depending on the quality of the card), running downwards to 100 baht.

Lumpini Boxing Stadium, on Rama IV Road, stages bouts on Tuesday and Friday at 6.30pm and on Saturday at 1 and 6.30pm. Ticket prices are the same as at Ratchadamnern. As above, weekend afternoon matinees are the cheapest.

There are also televised bouts on Saturday and Sunday, and at 10.30pm on some week nights. For many visitors this will be sufficient introduction to the sport. The **Rose Garden** and Phuket's **Thai Village** offer short demonstrations of Thai boxing, but these are played more for laughs than for authenticity.

Thai boxing bouts in Chiang Mai can be seen at the Dechanukrau boxing ring, on Bumrungrat Road, on the weekends. Bouts are staged each Friday at 8pm at the **Phuket Boxing Stadium** at Saphan Hin (to the right of the tin dredge memorial where Phuket Road meets the sea). Most large rural towns have their own boxing gyms and stage weekly bouts by young hopefuls.

Language

Origins and Intonation

For centuries, the Thai language, rather than tripping from foreigners' tongues, has been tripping them up. Its roots go back to the place Thais originated from, in the hills of southern Asia but overlaid by Indian influences. From the original settlers come the five tones which seem designed to frustrate visitors, one sound with five different tones to mean five different things.

When you mispronounce, not only are you saying the word incorrectly, chances are you're saying another word entirely.

It is not unusual to see a semi-fluent foreigner standing before a Thai running through the scale of tones until suddenly a light of recognition dawns on his companion's face. There are misinformed visitors who will tell you that tones are not important. These people do not communicate with Thais, they communicate at them in a one-sided exchange that frustrates both parties.

Thai Names

From the languages of India have come polysyllabic names and words, the lexicon of literature. Thai names are among the longest in the world. Every Thai first name and surname has a meaning. Thus by learning the meaning of the name of everyone you meet, you would acquire a formal, but quite extensive vocabulary.

There is no universal transliteration system from Thai into English, which is why names and street names can be spelled three different ways. For example, the surname Chumsai is written Chumsai, Jumsai and Xoomsai depending on the family. This confuses even the Thais. If you ask a Thai how you spell something, he may well reply "how do you want to spell it?" Likewise, Bangkok's thoroughfare of Ratchadamnern is also spelled Rajdamnern and Ratchadamnoen. Ko Samui can be spelled Koh Samui. The spellings will differ from map to map, and book to book.

Phonology

The way Thai consonants are written in English often confuses foreigners. An "h" following a letter like "p", and "t" gives the letter a soft sound; without the "h" the sound is more explosive. Thus, "ph" is not pronounced "f" but as a soft "p". Without the "h", the "p" has the sound of a very hard "b". The word Thanon (street) is pronounced "tanon" in the same way as "Thailand" is not meant to sound like "Thighland". Similarly, final letters are often not pronounced as they look. A "j" on the end of a word is pronounced "t"; "l" is pronounced as an "n". To complicate matters further, many words end with "se" or "r" which are not pronounced; for instance Suriwongse, one of Bangkok's main thoroughfares, is simply pronounced "Suriwong."

Vowels are pronounced like this: **i** as in *sip*, **ii** as in *seep*, **e** as in *bet*, **a** as in *pun*, **aa** as in *pal*, **u** as in *pool*, **o** as in *so*, **ai** as in *pie*, **ow** as in *cow*, **aw** as in *paw*, **iw** as in *you*, **oy** as in *toy*.

In Thai, the pronoun "I" and "me" use the same word but it is different for males and females. Men use the word *phom* when referring to themselves; women say *chan* or *diichan*. Men use *khrap* at the end of a sentence when addressing either a male or a female i.e. *pai* (f) *nai, khrap* (h) (where are you going? sir). Women add the word *kha* to their statements as in *pai* (f) *nai, kha* (h).

To ask a question, add a high

tone *mai* to the end of the phrase i.e. *rao pai* (we go) or *rao pai mai* (h) (shall we go?). To negate a statement, insert a falling tone *mai* between the subject and the verb i.e. *rao pai* (we go), *rao mai pai* (we don't go). "Very" or "much" are indicated by adding *maak* to the end of a phrase i.e. *ron* (hot), *ron maak* (very hot).

Listed below is a small vocabulary intended to get you on your way. The five tones have been indicated by appending letters after them viz. high (h), low (l), middle (m), rising (like asking a question) (r), and falling (like suddenly understanding something as in "ohh, I see") (f).

Useful Phrases

NUMBERS

1/*Nung* (l)
2/*Song* (r)
3/*Sam* (r)
4/*Sii* (l)
5/*Haa* (f)
6/*Hok* (l)
7/*Jet* (l)
8/*Pat* (l)
9/*Kow* (f)
10/*Sip* (l)
11/*Sip* (l) *Et* (l)
12/*Sip* (l) *Song* (r)
13/*Sip* (l) *Sam* (r) and so on
20/*Yii* (f) *Sip* (l)
30/*Sam* (r) *Sip* (l) and so on
100/*Nung* (l) *Roi* (h)
1,000/*Nung* (l) *Phan* (m)

DAYS OF THE WEEK

Monday/*Wan* (m) *Jan* (m)
Tuesday/*Wan* (m) *Angkan* (m, m)
Wednesday/*Wan* (m) *Phoot* (h)
Thursday/*Wan* (m) *Pharuhat* (m, h, l)
Friday/*Wan* (m) *Sook* (l)
Saturday/*Wan* (m) *Sao* (r)
Sunday/*Wan* (m) *Athit* (m, h)
Today/*Wan* (m) *nii* (h)
Yesterday/*Mua* (f) *wan* (m) *nii* (h)
Tomorrow/*Prung* (f) *nii* (h)
When/*Mua* (f) *rai* (m)

GREETINGS AND OTHERS

Hello, goodbye/*Sawasdee* (a man then says "*khrap*"; a woman says "*kha*"; thus, *sawasdee khrap* or *sawasdee kha*)

How are you?/*Khun sabai dii, mai* (h)
Well, thank you/*Sabai dii, Khapkhun*
Thank you very much/*Khapkhun Maak*
May I take a photo?/*Thai roop* (f) *noi, dai* (f) *mai* (h)
Never mind/*Mai* (f) *pen rai*
I cannot speak Thai/*Phuut Thai mai* (f) *dai* (f)
I can speak a little Thai/*Phuut Thai dai* (f) *nit* (h) *diew*
Where do you live?/*Khun yoo thii* (f) *nai* (r)
What is this called in Thai?/*An nii* (h), *kaw riak aray phasa Thai*
How much?/*Thao* (f) *rai*

DIRECTIONS AND TRAVEL

Go/*Pai*
Come/*Maa*
Where/*Thii* (f) *nai* (r)
Right/*Khwaa* (r)
Left/*Sai* (h)
Turn/*Leo*
Straight ahead/*Trong pai*
Please slow down/*Cha cha noi*
Stop here/*Yood thii* (f) *nii* (f)
Fast/*Raew*
Hotel/*Rong raam*
Street/*Thanon*
Lane/*Soi*
Bridge/*Saphan*
Police Station/*Sathanii Dtam Ruat*

OTHER HANDY PHRASES

Yes/*Chai* (f)
No/*Mai* (f) *chai* (f)
Do you have...?/*Mii ... mai* (h)
Expensive/*Phaeng* (m)
Do you have something cheaper?/*Mii arai thii thook* (l) *kwa, mai* (h)
Can you lower the price a bit?/*Kaw lot noi dai* (f) *mai* (h)
Do you have another colour?/*Mii sii uhn mai* (h)
Too big/*Yai kern pai*
Too small/*Lek kern pai*
Do you have bigger?/*Mii arai thii yai kwa mai* (h)
Do you have smaller?/*Mii arai thii lek kwa mai* (h)
Hot (heat)/*Ron* (h)
Hot (spicy)/*Phet*
Cold/*Yen*
Sweet/*Waan* (r)
Sour/*Prio* (f)
I do not feel well/*Mai* (f) *sabai*

Further Reading

General

Amranand, Pimsai. **Gardening in Bangkok**. Bangkok: Siam Society. Good work on plants though could do with more photos.
Cooper, Robert and Nanthapa. **Culture Shock: Thailand**. Singapore: Times Books, 1990. Very useful look at Thai customs and how to avoid faux pas. Written and illustrated in highly amusing manner.
Gray, Denis, et al., **National Parks of Thailand**. Bangkok: Industrial Finance Corporation of Thailand, 1994.
Hollinger, Carol. **Mai Pen Rai**. Boston: Houghton Mifflin. Expatriate life in the 1950s.
Ingram, J.C. **Economic Change in Thailand 1830–1970**. Palo Alto, California: Stanford University Press, 1971.
Segaller, Denis. **Thai Ways**. Bangkok: Thai Wattana Panich, 1979. Collection of columns on Thai customs by a longtime resident.
Siam Society, Culture and Environment in Thailand. Siam Society: Bangkok, 1989.
Sternstein, Larry. **Thailand: The Environment of Modernisation**. Sydney: McGraw-Hill, 1976. Excellent geography text.
Stockmann, Hardy. **Thai Boxing**. Bangkok: D.K. Books, 1979. Excellent, well illustrated book on the basics of Thai boxing.
Warren, William. **The Legendary American**. Boston: Houghton Mifflin. The intriguing story of American Thai silk king Jim Thompson.

History

Chakrabongse, Prince Chula. **Lords of Life**. London: Alvin Redman, 1960. A history of the Chakri kings.

Kasetsiri, Charnvit. *The Rise of Ayudhya*. London: East Asian Historical Monographs, 1976. A narration of the history of early Ayutthaya.

Coedes, George. *The Indianized States of Southeast Asia*. Trans. Susan Brown Cousing. Ed. Walter F. Vella. Honolulu: East-West Centre Press, 1968. Well written scholarly work.

Hall, D.G.E. *A History of South-east Asia*. 3rd ed. London: Macmillan, 1968. The classic text.

Hutchinson, E.W. *1688: Revolution in Siam*. Hong Kong University Press. The events leading to the expulsion of the foreigners from Ayutthaya.

McCoy, Alfred W. *The Politics of Heroin in Southeast Asia*. New York: Harper & Row, 1973. The pioneering work. Readily found in Bangkok.

Moffat, Abbot Low. *Mongkut, the King of Siam*. Ithaca, New York: Cornell University Press, 1961. Superb history of one of Asia's most interesting 19th century men.

Phongpaichit, Pasuk and Chris Baker. **Thailand's Boom!** Chiang Mai: Silkworm, 1997. Two academics give a lively, popular account of the forces that fueled a decade of rapid economic growth. Some portents of the collapse.

Van Beek, Steve. *Bangkok Only Yesterday*. Hong Kong: Hong Kong Publishing, 1982. Anecdotal history of Bangkok illustrated with old photos.

Vella, Walter F. *Chaiyo!* Honolulu: University of Hawaii Press, 1979. The life and times of King Vajiravudh (1910–1925).

Wright, Joseph. *The Balancing Act: A History of Modern Thailand*. Oakland: Pacific Rim Press, 1991. Accessible and detailed history of modern Thailand.

Wyatt, David K. *Thailand: A Short History*. Bangkok/London: ThaiWattana Panich/Yale University Press, 1984. Concise and well-written.

People

Aylwen, Axel. *The Falcon of Siam*. London: Methuen, 1988. A fictionalized story of Constant Phaulkon, Greek adventurer in Siam in the late 1600s.

Collis, Maurice. *Siamese White*. London: Faber, 1965. Fictionalized account of a contemporary of Constant Phaulkon in 1600s Siam.

Ekachai, Sanitsuda. *Behind the Smile, Voices of Thailand*. Thailand. Thai Development Support Committee, 1990. Well-written and informative portraits of Thai life by local journalist.

Lewis, Paul and Elaine. *Peoples of the Golden Triangle*. London: Thames and Hudson, 1984. Excellent text and photos on the hill tribes.

Seidenfaden, Erik. *The Thai Peoples*. Bangkok: Siam Society, 1967. Solid work by long-time resident.

Skinner, G. William. *Chinese Society in Thailand*. Ithaca, New York: Cornell University Press, 1957. Gives an insight into an important segment of Bangkok's history.

Religion

Bunnag, Jane. *Buddhist Monk, Buddhist Layman*. Cambridge: Cambridge University Press, 1973. Gives an insight into the monastic experience.

Nivat, Prince Dhani. *A History of Buddhism in Siam*. Bangkok: Siam Society, 1965. One of Thailand's most respected scholars.

Rahula, Walpola. *What the Buddha Taught*. New York: Grove Press, 1974. Comprehensive account of Buddhist doctrine; other editions available.

Art and Culture

Diskul, M.C. Subhadradis. *Art in Thailand: A Brief History*. Bangkok: Silpakorn University, 1970. Dean of the Fine Arts University.

Klausner, William J. *Reflections on Thai Culture*. The Siam Society: Bangkok, 1987. Observations of a longtime resident anthropologist.

Rajadhon, Phya Anuman. *Essays on Thai Folklore*. Bangkok: D.K. Books. A description of Thai ceremonies, festivals and rites of passage.

Van Beek, Steve & Tettoni L.I. *The Arts of Thailand*. London, Thames & Hudson, 1991. Lavishly illustrated, includes the minor arts.

Warren, William. *The House on the Klong*. Tokyo: Weatherhill. The story of the Jim Thompson House.

Wray, Joe, Elizabeth Wray, Clare Rosenfeld and Dorothy Bailey. *Ten Lives of the Buddha; Siamese Temple Paintings and Jataka Tales*. Tokyo: Weatherhill, 1974. Well illustrated, valuable for understanding Thai painting and the Tosachat (Jataka Tales).

Natural History

Gray, Dennis, Collin Piprell and Mark Graham. **National Parks of Thailand**. Bangkok: Industrial Finance Corp. of Thailand, 1991. Accommodation information is very unreliable. Otherwise, this is a useful survey of the natural assets of many national parks.

Lekagul, Boonsung and Philip D. Round. **A Guide to the Birds of Thailand**. Bangkok: Saha Karn Bhaer, 1991. The standard handbook.

Rabinowitz, Alan. **Chasing the Dragon's Tail: The Struggle to Save Thailand's Wildcats**. New York: Doubleday, 1991. Well-told tales from a zoologist.

Stewart-Cox, Belinda and Gerald Cubitt. **Wild Thailand**. Bangkok: Asia Books, 1995. A coffee-table book with a solid text and a sobering tone.

ART & PHOTO CREDITS

INSIGHT GUIDE
THAILAND

Maps **Polyglott Kartographie**
Berndtson & Berndtson Publications
Cartographic Editor **Zoë Goodwin**
Production **Caroline Low**
Design Consultants
Klaus Geisler, Graham Mitchener
Picture Research **Hilary Genin**

Index

a

Akha 80
alms bowls 150
Amarin Vinitchai Throne Hall 142
amulets 90, 147
Anand Panyacharun 56
Ananda Mahidol (Rama VIII) 53, 59
Ananta Samakom 162
Ancient City (Muang Boran) 111, 179
Ang Sila 275
Angkor 35
Ao Khai 282
Ao Nang Bay 321
Ao Po 317
Aranyaprathet 286
architecture 109–11, 112–13
art thieves 259
Asian elephant 64
Ayutthaya 34–41, 157, 195–200, 226

b

Baan Hin Taek 234
baht 58
Bamrung Muang 150
Ban Bangkao 307
Ban Bangrok 325
Ban Bat 150
Ban Chiang 25–26, 263
Ban Houei Sai 238
Ban Hua Thanon 307
Ban Kao 186
Ban Mae Hat 311
Ban Pa Klang 246
Ban Pha Phrae National Park 281
Ban Phe 281
Ban Renu 265
Ban Tak 220
Ban Taling Ngam 308
Ban Tha Rua 313
Bang Pa-In 200
Bang Saen 276
  bird refuge 276
Bang Saphan 297
Bang Sare 278
Bang Tao 317
Bangkok 137–172
Bangkok Bank of Commerce 58
Bangkrak 165

Bangrak (Big Buddha Beach) 308
Banharn Silpa-archa 58
Bhumibol Adulyadej (Rama IX) 55, 59, 88
Bhumibol Dam 220, 241
birds 64
Bloody May 57
Bo Phut 308
Boon Bang Fai (skyrocket festival) 205
Boworn Bazaar 327
Brahman influences 26, 91, 150, 205
Bridge on the River Kwai 184
Buddhaisawan Chapel 148
Buddhism 29, 71, 87–91, 92–93, 181, 207, 257
bull fighting 329
Bung Boraphet 203
Burmese empires 36, 40, 44, 195, 221, 226

c

Cathedral of St Joseph 196
ceramics 103
Cha Loak Lam 309
Cha-am 295
Chaiya 27, 302
Chakri Maha Prasad 143
Chan and Muk 313
Chan Kasem Palace 197
Chanthaburi 283
chao lay (sea gypsy) 315
Chao Phraya 25, 141, 154
Chao Phya Chakri 41
Chao Phya Sarasih 41
Chao Sam Phraya National Museum 198
Chao U-Thong 34
Charoen Krung (New Road) 163
Chattuchak weekend market 172
Chavalit Yongchaiyudh 58
Chaweng 307
Chedi Luang Phaw Utama 188
Chiang Dao 231
Chiang Dao Elephant Camp 230
Chiang Khan 266
Chiang Khong 237
Chiang Mai 27, 30, 225–29
Chiang Rai 236
Chiang Saen 237
China 29
Chinatown 162–65
Chinese 75–76

Chitralada Palace 59, 161
Chom Thong 240
Chonburi 275
Chuan Leekpai 57–58
Chulalongkorn (Rama V) 46–47, 161, 204
Chulalongkorn University 48, 169
Chumphon 298
Church of the Immaculate Conception 285
Communists 55, 266
Conrad, Joseph 155
coral reefs 65
coup d'etat 49
Crocodile Farm 179
curry 117
cuisine 117–21

d

Damnoen Saduak 184
dance-dramas 97
Deerhunter, The 187
Democracy Monument 54, 56, 152
Devaraja (god-king) 35
Discovery Centre 172
Doi Chiang Dao 231
Doi Inthanon 240
Doi Inthanon National Park 240
Doi Kong Mu 243
Doi Phu Kha 246
Doi Phu Kha National Park 246
Doi Pui 229
Doi Suthep 229
dolphins 286
Don Muang Airport 49
Dusit 161
Dusit Maha Prasad 143
Dusit Maha Prasat 201
Dusit Zoo 162
Dutch 38

e

economy 58
Ekatat 40
Ekatotsarot 38
elephant kraal 199
elephants 64, 199, 231, 235, 245, 259
Emerald Buddha 41, 44, 59, 141
England 46
Erawan National Park 187
Erawan Shrine 91, 170

f

Fang 233
festivals 82–83
films (shot in Thailand)
 Deerhunter 187
 Killing Fields 296
 King and I 45
 Man with the Golden Gun 320
fish sauce (*nam plaa*) 117, 281
floating market 184
flora and fauna 63–65
forests 63
Fort Carnot 238
Friendship Bridge 263
Friendship Highway 255

g

garuda 109
gemstones 102, 284, 286
Germany 204
Giant Swing 150
gold standard 49
Golden Mount 151
Golden Triangle 237
government 72
Grand Palace 141–44
green lanterns (*khom khiew*)
 163
Guomintang (Nationalist) army
 233

h

Had Yaow 322
handicrafts 102
Hat Khuat 310
Hat Rin 310
Hat Supin 299
Hat Tien 310
Hat Yai 329
Hellfire Pass 187
hill tribes 75, 78–81, 242, 229,
 248–49
Hin Dat 187
Hmong 79, 229
hoon krabok puppets 98
Hot 241
Hua Hin Railway Hotel (Hotel
 Sofitel Central) 296
Hua Hin 295–96
Huai Yang 297

i

Indian influence 26
International Monetary Fund
 (IMF) 58

islands (*ko*)
 Chang 286
 Kha 221
 Khao Ping Gun 319
 Kut 286
 Lanta 322
 Larn 278
 Mak 286
 Pak Nam 299
 Pha Ngan 309–11
 Phi Phi 322
 Samet 281
 Samui 307–09
 Si Chang 277
 Talu 319
 Tao 311
 Tarutao 325
 Yor 331

j

ja-kae 99
jai yen 69
Japanese 38, 54
Jataka Tales 246
JEATH Museum 184
jewellery 102, 284
Jim Thompson House 172
Jomtien 277
Jui Tui 314

k

Kaeng Krachan Dam 295
Kaeng Tanna National Park 260
Kamala Bay 317
Kamphaeng Phet 203
Kamthieng House 170
Kanchanaburi 184–85
Karen 78, 242
Karon Beach 316
Kata 315
Kata Noi 315
Kayan (Padaung) 80, 81
Khai Nern Wong 285
Khao Chamao National Park
 282
Khao Chong Center of Wildlife
 and Nature Study 328
Khao Khieo Open Zoo 276
Khao Kien 319
Khao Lak 300
Khao Luang 295
Khao Noi 330
Khao Phlu 308
Khao Phra Taeo National Park
 317
Khao Phra Viharn 259
Khao Ploi Waen 286

Khao Rub Chang 178
Khao Sam Roi Yot National
 Park 297
Khao Seng 331
Khao Sok National Park 301
Khao Wang 295
Khao Wong caves 282
Khao Yai National Park
 177–78, 255
Khlong Yai 286
khlong 109, 157
Khlong Bangkok Noi 156
Khlong Thom 321
Khmers 26, 186, 207, 256,
 258, 260, 264
khom khiew (green lanterns)
 163
Khon Kaen 257
Khorat Plateau 63
Khorat (Nakhon Ratchasima)
 255
khun 77
Khun Chang, Khun Phaen 100
Khun Sa 234
Khunying Mo (Tao Suranari)
 255
Killing Fields, The 296
King and I, The 45
kings *See* monarchs
Klaeng 282
Klai Klangwan 295
klawng yao 100
Ko Ang Thong National Marine
 Park 308
Ko (Island)
 Chang 286
 Kha 221
 Khao Ping Gun 319
 Kut 286
 Lanta 322
 Larn 278
 Mak 286
 Pak Nam 299
 Pha Ngan 309–11
 Phi Phi 322
 Samet 281
 Samui 307–09
 Si Chang 277
 Talu 319
 Tao 311
 Tarutao 325
 Yor 331
Ko Tarutao Marine National
 Park 325
Krabi 321
Kraburi 298

l

Laem Mae Phim 281
Laem Ngop 286
Laem Prom Thep 315
Laem Sing 285
Lahu 80
Lak Muang 145
lakhon 97
Lam Takhong 255
Lamai 307
Lampang 222
Lanka Chio 298
laquerware 103
Leonowens, Anna 46
likay 98
Lisu 80
literature 100
Loei 265
Loha Prasad 152
Lopburi 200
Luang Larn National Park 219
Luang Pibulsongram 49
Lumpini Park (Suan Lumpini)
168

m

Mae Chan 236
Mae Hong Son 243
Mae Klang Falls 240
Mae Sa Valley 230
Mae Salong 233
Mae Sariang 243
Mae Sot 219
Maenam 308
Maha Uma Devi 167
Maha Uparaja (second/deputy
king) 44
Mahachakrapat 36
Mahakan Fort 152
Mahboonkrong (MBK Centre)
172
Mai Khao 317
mammals 64
Man with the Golden Gun, The
320
Manangasila 208
Mangrai 30, 225, 228, 236
mangroves 321
Maugham, Somerset 110
Maya Bay 322
mekhong 120
Mekong River 237, 266
Memorial Bridge 156
merit 89
Mien (Yao) 79, 233
military 71
missionaries 39

monarchs
Ananda Mahidol (Rama VIII)
53, 59
Bhumibol Adulyadej (Rama IX)
55, 59, 88
Boromakot 40
Chakri, Gen. (Rama I) 44,
237
Chulalongkorn (Rama V)
46–47, 161, 204
Ekatat 40
Ekatotsarot 38
Intradit 207
Li Thai 30, 203–204
Lo Thai 30, 208
Lu Thai 209, 211
Mangrai 30, 225, 228, 236
Mongkut (Rama IV) 45–46,
90, 156, 201, 208, 297
Narai 38, 200
Naresuen 37
Prajadhipok (Rama VII) 49
Rama II 44, 150
Rama III 44
Ramathibodi I 34
Ramathibodi II 36
Ramesuen 35
Ramkamhaeng 28, 29, 87,
148, 207
Taksin (Phya Tak Sin) 41,
285, 327
Trailok 35–36
Vajiravudh (Rama VI) 48, 161
Mongkut (Rama IV) 45–46, 90,
156, 201, 208, 297
monks 88
Mons 26
mother-of-pearl 103
Muaklek 255
Muang Boran (Ancient City)
179
Mukdahan 265
music 99
Muslims 331

n

Na Muang 307
Na Thon 307
naga 109
Nai Harn 315
Nai Yang 317
Nakhon Kasem 164
Nakhon Nayok 177
Nakhon Pathom 181
Nakhon Phanom 264
Nakhon Ratchasima (Khorat)
255
Nakhon Sawan 202

Nakhon Si Thammarat 325
nam plaa (fish sauce) 117, 281
Nam Tok Krating 286
Nan 244–46
nang thalung (shadow-puppet)
326
nang yai (shadow-puppet) 97
national parks
Ban Pha Phrae 281
Doi Inthanon 240
Doi Phu Kha 246
Erawan 187
Kaeng Tanna 260
Khao Chamao 282
Khao Phra Taeo 317
Khao Sam Roi Yot 297
Khao Sok 301
Khao Yai 177–78, 255
Ko Ang Thong 308
Ko Tarutao 325
Luang Larn 219
Phu Kradung 266
Phu Rua 266
Sai Yok 187
Tanboke Koranee 320
Wang Takrai 177
Narai 38, 200
Narathiwat 332
Narayana Phand 171
National Assembly (Parliament)
162
National Gallery 148
National Library 49
National Museum 49, 147–48,
237, 244, 260, 326
National Peacekeeping Council
56
National Stadium 172
neck rings 81
New Road (Charoen Krung)
163
Ngam Muang 236
Ngao 236
ngiew (Chinese opera) 98
Nong Khai 263
Nong Nooch Village 278
noodle dishes 118

o

Oasis Sea World 286
Ob Luang Gorge 242
Old Customs House 156
opium 230, 233, 237
Oriental Hotel 155, 165

p

Pak Thong Chai 256
Paknam Chumphon 298
Pansea Bay 317
Pasang 222
Patong 316
Patpong 167
Pattani 331
Pattaya 277
People's Party 49
Phang Nga 318
Phatthalung 327
Phaulkon, Constantine 39, 201
Phayao 236
Phetchburi 295
phi (spirits) 91
phi nai 99
Phi Phi Don 322
Phi Phi Ley 322
Phiman Mongkut Pavilion 201
Phipat 99
Phitsanulok 212
Phom Phet 196
Phom Seti 203
Phra Aphaimani 100
Phra Buddha Chinaraj 212
Phra Buddha Sihing 148
Phra Mondop 142
Phra Ngam 255
Phra Pathom Chedi 181
Phra Pok Klao Bridge 156
Phra Ruang 28
Phra Si Ratana Chedi 142
Phra Thep Bidom 142
Phra Yantra Bhikku 188
Phrae 246
Phu Kradung National Park 266
Phu Rua National Park 266
Phuket 313–17
Phuping Palace 229
Phya U-Thong 34
Pibul 54
Pig Memorial 149
Ploughing Ceremony 91, 205
poachers 65
pohng kham stones 221
Pongsawadan (Annals of Ayutthaya) 35
porcelain 295
Portuguese 36
Prachuap Khiri Khan 297
Pranburi 296
Prasat Hin Phimai 256
Prasat Muang Singh 186
Prasat Muang Tham 259
Prasat Phanom Rung 259
Prasat Phanom Wan 256
Pratunam 171

Pridi 53
Pridi Panomyong 49
Pridi Phanaomyong 147
Prince Boworadet 53
prostitution 166

q

Queen Saowapha 149
Queen Sirikit 59
Queen Suriyothai Chedi 196

r

Rafflesia 301
rain forest 64
Ramakien 45, 97–98, 100-101
Ramkamhaeng 28, 29, 87, 148, 207
Ramkamhaeng Nat'l Museum 207
Ranong 299
Ratchaburi 295
Rattanakosin 141
Rawai 314
Rayong 278, 281
Reclining Buddha 144
rice 117, 205
River City Shopping Complex 156
Rose Garden (Suan Sam Phran) 180
Royal Bangkok Sports Club 169
Royal Barge Museum 156
Rua Sam Pao 275
rubber trees 329

s

Sa Kaeo 286
sabai 69
Sai Ngam 257
Sai Yok National Park 187
Sakon Nakhon 264
Sampeng Lane 162
Samut Prakam 179
Samut Sakhon 183
Samut Songkhram 183
Sanam Chand Palace 182
Sanam Luang 146
Sangkhlaburi 188
sanuk 69
Sao Din 246
Saowapha Institute (Snake Farm) 168
Saphan Pla 299
Saraburi 255
Saranrom Palace 146

Sarika Falls 177
Sattahip 278
sea gypsy (*chao lay*) 315
second/deputy king (Maha Uparaja) 44
Seni Pramoj 54
Seri Thai 54
Seven Storey Mansion 164
sex, attitudes 73
sex industry 166, 168
shadow-puppet
nang thalung 326
nang yai 97
Shan 80
Si Racha 276
Si Saket 259
Si Satchanalai 211
Siam Centre 172
Siam Square 172
Sichon 327
silk 102, 256
Silom 167
Silpa Bhirasi 152
Silpa caves 332
Silpakorn University 147
skyrocket festival (Boon Bang Fai) 205
Smithsonian Institution 264
Snake Farm (Saowapha Institute) 168
snakebite 168
Songkhla 329
University 329
National Museum 330
spirit houses 91
spirits (*phi*) 91
Srivijaya empire 27, 302, 326
Suan Amporn 161
Suan Lumpini (Lumpini Park) 168
Suan Mok 302
Suan Pakkad 171
Suan Sam Phran (Rose Garden) 180
Subanahongsa (Royal Barge) 156
Suchart House 326
Suchinda Krapayoon 57
Sukhothai 27–28, 207–11
Sukhumvit 170
Sunthorn Phu 100, 152
Sunyataram Forest Monastery 188
Surat Thani 302
Surin 259, 325
Surin Beach 317
Suttha Sawan Pavilion 201

t

Tak 219
Takua Pa 300
Tanboke Koranee National Park 320
Tao Suranari (Khunying Mo) 255
teak 104, 219
temples *See* wat
Thai Noi (Little Thais) 27
Thale Noi 327
Thale Sap 331
Tham Erawan 266
Tham Lod 319
Tham Malai 328
Tham Nak 319
Tham Pha Thai 235
Tham Prakayang 298
Thammasat University 56, 147
Thanin Kraivichien 56
That Phanom 265
Thaton 233
Thoen 221
Thompson, Jim 102
    house 172
Thonburi 44
Thong Pha Thum 188
Thong Sala 309
Three Pagodas Pass 188
Trang 325
transvestites 73
Trat 286
Tripitaka 89

u

Ubon Ratchathani 260
Udon Thani 263
United States 55

v

Vietnam War 55, 255, 264
Viharn Phra Mongkol Bophit 197
Viking Cave 322
Vimarnmek 111, 162

w

wan phra 90
Wang Luang 197, 241
Wang Na (Palace at the Back) 44, 111
Wang Takrai National Park 177
wat 88
    Arun 44, 156
    Bang Korn 286

Benchamabophit 161
Bowon Niwet 152
Buddhabat Sam Yot 275
Buddhaisawan 196
Chai Wattanaram 196
Chaichumpol 185
Chakrawat 163
Chalong 314
Chana Songkhram 209
Chang Kham 245
Chang Lom 211
Chang Rob 204
Chedi Chet Thaew 212
Chedi Klang Tung 203
Chedi Luang 228, 237
Chedi Sao Phra 222
Chiang Man 226
Chom Chang 237
Chom Kiri Nak Phrot 203
Chong Kram 235
Chong Kum 243
Dhamma Nimitr 275
Doi Suthep 229
Hat Supin 299
Hua Khuang 245
Intharam 275
Jet Yod 228
Kamphaeng Laeng 295
Khao Sukim 282
Khao Tham 311
Kho Tham 331
Konthi Thong 198
Kukut 222
Lampang Luang 221
Li 236
Mae Chi 331
Mahathat 147, 208
Mangkon 164
Na Phra Meru 197
Nang Phya 212
Pa Mamuang 211
Pa Sak 237
Pan Tao 228
Pathum Wanaram 171
Pathuma Kongkha 164
Phanan Choeng 196
Chedi Klang Nam 180
Kaeo (Emerald Buddha) 44, 141, 236
Keo Don Tao 222
Mahathat 198, 326
Phai Luang 209
Ram 198
Si Iriyabot 204
Si Ratana Mahathat 212
Singh 227, 236
Sri Ratana Mahathat 212
Sri Sanphet 197
Cha Haeng 246

Si Chom Thong 240
Phu Khao Thong 199
Phumin 245
Po 144
Chom Kitti 237
Haripunchai 222
Rakang 156
Ratchabophit 149
Ratchaburana 198
Ratchanadda 152
Saket 151
Sala Loi 256
Saphan Hin 211
Si Chum 210
Si Khom Kham 236
Sra Sri 209
Sri Sawai 209
Suan Dok 229
Suthat 44, 149
Suwan Dararam 199
Suwannaram 156
Teppitakpunnaram 255
Thamwaran 301
Thung Si Muang 260
Traimit 165
Trakuan 209
U Mong 229
Wangwiwe Karam 188
Yai Chai Mongkol 199
Yai Suwannaram 295
white elephants 37
women 73
woodcarving 104
World Trade Centre 171
World War I 48
World War II 54

y

Yala 331
Yaleh the Insufferable 183
Yaowarat 163
Young Elephants Training Center 235

The Insight Approach

The book you are holding is part of the world's largest range of guidebooks. Its purpose is to help you have the most valuable travel experience possible, and we try to achieve this by providing not only information about countries, regions and cities but also genuine insight into their history, culture, institutions and people.

Since the first Insight Guide – to Bali – was published in 1970, the series has been dedicated to the proposition that, with insight into a country's people and culture, visitors can both enhance their own experience and be accepted more easily by their hosts. Now, in a world where ethnic hostilities and nationalist conflicts are all too common, such attempts to increase understanding between peoples are more important than ever.

Insight Guides:
Essentials for understanding
Because a nation's past holds the key to its present, each Insight Guide kicks off with lively history chapters. These are followed by magazine-style essays on culture and daily life. This essential background information gives readers the necessary context for using the main Places section, with its comprehensive run-down on things worth seeing and doing.

Finally, a listings section contains all the information you'll need on travel, hotels, restaurants and opening times.

As far as possible, we rely on local writers and specialists to ensure that information is authoritative. The pictures, for which Insight Guides have become so celebrated, are just as important. Our photojournalistic approach aims not only to illustrate a destination but also to communicate visually and directly to readers life as it is lived by the locals. The series has grown to almost 200 titles.

Compact Guides:
The "great little guides"
As invaluable as such background information is, it isn't always fun to carry an Insight Guide through a crowded souk or up a church tower. Could we, readers asked, distil the key reference material into a slim volume for on-the-spot use?

Our response was to design Compact Guides as an entirely new series, with original text carefully cross-referenced to detailed maps and more than 200 photographs. In essence, they're miniature encyclopedias, concise and comprehensive, displaying reliable and up-to-date information in an accessible way. There are almost 100 titles.

Pocket Guides:
A local host in book form
However wide-ranging the information in a book, human beings still value the personal touch. Our editors are often asked the same questions. Where do *you* go to eat? What do *you* think is the best beach? What would *you* recommend if I have only three days? We invited our local correspondents to act as "substitute hosts" by revealing their preferred walks and trips, listing the restaurants they go to and structuring a visit into a series of timed itineraries.

The result: our Pocket Guides, complete with full-size fold-out maps. These 100-plus titles help readers plan a trip precisely, particularly if their time is short.

Exploring with Insight:
A valuable travel experience
In conjunction with co-publishers all over the world, we print in up to 10 languages, from German to Chinese, from Danish to Russian. But our aim remains simple: to enhance your travel experience by combining our expertise in guidebook publishing with the on-the-spot knowledge of our correspondents.

> 66 I was first drawn to the Insight Guides by the excellent "Nepal" volume. I can think of no book which so effectively captures the essence of a country. Out of these pages leaped the Nepal I know – the captivating charm of a people and their culture. I've since discovered and enjoyed the entire Insight Guide series. Each volume deals with a country in the same sensitive depth, which is nowhere more evident than in the superb photography. 99

Sir Edmund Hillary

The World of Insight Guides

400 books in three complementary series cover every major destination in every continent.

Insight Guides

Alaska
Alsace
Amazon Wildlife
American Southwest
Amsterdam
Argentina
Atlanta
Athens
Australia
Austria
Bahamas
Bali
Baltic States
Bangkok
Barbados
Barcelona
Bay of Naples
Beijing
Belgium
Belize
Berlin
Bermuda
Boston
Brazil
Brittany
Brussels
Budapest
Buenos Aires
Burgundy
Burma (Myanmar)
Cairo
Calcutta
California
Canada
Caribbean
Catalonia
Channel Islands
Chicago
Chile
China
Cologne
Continental Europe
Corsica
Costa Rica
Crete
Crossing America
Cuba
Cyprus
Czech & Slovak Republics
Delhi, Jaipur, Agra
Denmark
Dresden
Dublin
Düsseldorf
East African Wildlife
East Asia
Eastern Europe
Ecuador
Edinburgh
Egypt
Finland
Florence
Florida
France
Frankfurt
French Riviera
Gambia & Senegal
Germany
Glasgow

Gran Canaria
Great Barrier Reef
Great Britain
Greece
Greek Islands
Hamburg
Hawaii
Hong Kong
Hungary
Iceland
India
India's Western Himalaya
Indian Wildlife
Indonesia
Ireland
Israel
Istanbul
Italy
Jamaica
Japan
Java
Jerusalem
Jordan
Kathmandu
Kenya
Korea
Lisbon
Loire Valley
London
Los Angeles
Madeira
Madrid
Malaysia
Mallorca & Ibiza
Malta
Marine Life in the South
  China Sea
Melbourne
Mexico
Mexico City
Miami
Montreal
Morocco
Moscow
Munich
Namibia
Native America
Nepal
Netherlands
New England
New Orleans
New York City
New York State
New Zealand
Nile
Normandy
Northern California
Northern Spain
Norway
Oman & the UAE
Oxford
Old South
Pacific Northwest
Pakistan
Paris
Peru
Philadelphia
Philippines
Poland
Portugal
Prague

Provence
Puerto Rico
Rajasthan
Rhine
Rio de Janeiro
Rockies
Rome
Russia
St Petersburg
San Francisco
Sardinia
Scotland
Seattle
Sicily
Singapore
South Africa
South America
South Asia
South India
South Tyrol
Southeast Asia
Southeast Asia Wildlife
Southern California
Southern Spain
Spain
Sri Lanka
Sweden
Switzerland
Sydney
Taiwan
Tenerife
Texas
Thailand
Tokyo
Trinidad & Tobago
Tunisia
Turkey
Turkish Coast
Tuscany
Umbria
US National Parks East
US National Parks West
Vancouver
Venezuela
Venice
Vienna
Vietnam
Wales
Washington DC
Waterways of Europe
Wild West
Yemen

Insight Pocket Guides

Aegean Islands★
Algarve★
Alsace
Amsterdam★
Athens★
Atlanta★
Bahamas★
Baja Peninsula★
Bali★
Bali Bird Walks
Bangkok★
Barbados★
Barcelona★
Bavaria★
Beijing★
Berlin★

Bermuda★
Bhutan★
Boston★
British Columbia★
Brittany★
Brussels★
Budapest &
  Surroundings★
Canton★
Chiang Mai★
Chicago★
Corsica★
Costa Blanca★
Costa Brava★
Costa del Sol/Marbella★
Costa Rica★
Crete★
Denmark★
Fiji★
Florence★
Florida★
Florida Keys★
French Riviera★
Gran Canaria★
Hawaii★
Hong Kong★
Hungary
Ibiza★
Ireland★
Ireland's Southwest★
Israel★
Istanbul★
Jakarta★
Jamaica★
Kathmandu Bikes &
  Hikes★
Kenya★
Kuala Lumpur★
Lisbon★
Loire Valley★
London★
Macau
Madrid★
Malacca
Maldives
Mallorca★
Malta★
Mexico City★
Miami★
Milan★
Montreal★
Morocco★
Moscow
Munich★
Nepal★
New Delhi
New Orleans★
New York City★
New Zealand★
Northern California★
Oslo/Bergen★
Paris★
Penang★
Phuket★
Prague★
Provence★
Puerto Rico★
Quebec★
Rhodes★
Rome★
Sabah★

St Petersburg★
San Francisco★
Sardinia
Scotland★
Seville★
Seychelles★
Sicily★
Sikkim
Singapore★
Southeast England
Southern California
Southern Spain★
Sri Lanka★
Sydney★
Tenerife★
Thailand★
Tibet★
Toronto★
Tunisia★
Turkish Coast★
Tuscany★
Venice★
Vienna★
Vietnam★
Yogyakarta
Yucatan Peninsula★

**★ = Insight Pocket Guides
with Pull out Maps**

Insight Compact Guides

Algarve
Amsterdam
Bahamas
Bali
Bangkok
Barbados
Barcelona
Beijing
Belgium
Berlin
Brittany
Brussels
Budapest
Burgundy
Copenhagen
Costa Brava
Costa Rica
Crete
Cyprus
Czech Republic
Denmark
Dominican Republic
Dublin
Egypt
Finland
Florence
Gran Canaria
Greece
Holland
Hong Kong
Ireland
Israel
Italian Lakes
Italian Riviera
Jamaica
Jerusalem
Lisbon
Madeira
Mallorca
Malta

Milan
Moscow
Munich
Normandy
Norway
Paris
Poland
Portugal
Prague
Provence
Rhodes
Rome
St Petersburg
Salzburg
Singapore
Switzerland
Sydney
Tenerife
Thailand
Turkey
Turkish Coast
Tuscany
UK regional titles:
  Bath & Surroundings
  Cambridge & East
    Anglia
  Cornwall
  Cotswolds
  Devon & Exmoor
  Edinburgh
  Lake District
  London
  New Forest
  North York Moors
  Northumbria
  Oxford
  Peak District
  Scotland
  Scottish Highlands
  Shakespeare Country
  Snowdonia
  South Downs
  York
  Yorkshire Dales
USA regional titles:
  Boston
  Cape Cod
  Chicago
  Florida
  Florida Keys
  Hawaii: Maui
  Hawaii: Oahu
  Las Vegas
  Los Angeles
  Martha's Vineyard &
    Nantucket
  New York
  San Francisco
  Washington D.C.
  Venice
  Vienna
  West of Ireland

Louise Penny is the Number One *New York Times* bestselling author of the Inspector Gamache series, including *Still Life*, which won the CWA John Creasey Dagger in 2006. Recipient of virtually every existing award for crime fiction, Louise was also granted the Order of Canada in 2014 and received an honorary doctorate of literature from Carleton University and the Ordre Nationale du Québec in 2017. She lives in a small village south of Montreal.

Praise for Louise Penny and the series:

'Louise Penny is one of the greatest crime writers of our times' Denise Mina

'She makes most of her competitors seem like wannabes' *The Times*

'A cracking storyteller, who can create fascinating characters, a twisty plot and wonderful surprise endings' Ann Cleeves

'Outstanding . . . a constantly surprising series that deepens and darkens as it evolves' *The New York Times*

'No one does atmospheric quite like Louise Penny . . . a fantastic series' Elly Griffiths

'Louise Penny's writing is intricate, beautiful and compelling. She is an original voice, a distillation of both PD James and Barbara Vine at their peaks and a worthy successor to both' Peter James

'[An] atmospheric, distinctive series' Kate Mosse

'Penny is an absolute joy' *Irish Times*

'The series is deep and grand and altogether extraordinary . . . Miraculous' *Washington Post*

The Gamache series

The Madness of Crowds
All the Devils Are Here
A Better Man
Kingdom of the Blind
Glass Houses
A Great Reckoning
The Nature of the Beast
The Long Way Home
How the Light Gets In
The Beautiful Mystery
A Trick of the Light
Bury Your Dead
The Brutal Telling
A Rule Against Murder
The Cruellest Month
A Fatal Grace
Still Life

LOUISE PENNY

A Better Man

HODDER

First published in the United States in 2019 by Minotaur
A division of St Martin's Press
First published in 2019 by Sphere
This edition published in 2021 by Hodder & Stoughton
An Hachette UK company

1

Map by Rhys Davies

A CIP catalogue record for this title is available from the British Library

B format ISBN 978 1 529 38666 0
eBook ISBN 978 1 529 38667 7

Printed and bound in Great Britain by Clays Ltd, Elcograf S.p.A.

Hodder & Stoughton policy is to use papers that are natural, renewable
and recyclable products and made from wood grown in sustainable
forests. The logging and manufacturing processes are expected to
conform to the environmental regulations of the country of origin.

Hodder & Stoughton Ltd
Carmelite House
50 Victoria Embankment
London EC4Y 0DZ

www.hodder.co.uk

A LETTER FROM LOUISE

When I was thirty-five, I thought the best was behind me.

I was lonely, and tired, and empty. Plodding through life.

At thirty-five.

By the time I was forty-five, I was married to the love of my life, and my first book was about to be published.

And now I'm sixty. Living in a beautiful Québec village, surrounded by friends, with thirteen books to my name. And counting.

This milestone birthday gives me a chance to look back in wonderment. And gratitude. And amazement. That I should be here, happy, joyous, and free.

No one quite appreciates, and recognises, the light like those who've lived in darkness. That awareness is what I try to bring to the books. The duality of our lives. The power of perception. The staggering weight of despair, and the amazement when it is lifted.

The gap between how we appear and how we really feel.

Those are foundations of the Gamache books.

Initially they were called the Three Pines books, which, of course, they are. Three Pines is the tiny hidden village in Québec. Not on any map, it is only ever found by those who are lost.

But, once found, never forgotten.

At their core, though, these books are about the profound decency of Armand Gamache, and the struggles he has to remain a good person. When 'good' is subjective, and 'decent' is a matter of judgement.

These books might appear, superficially, as traditional crime novels. But they are, I believe, more about life than death. About choices. About the price of freedom. About the struggle for peace.

Armand Gamache, of the Sûreté du Québec, is inspired by my husband, Michael Whitehead. A doctor who treated children with cancer. Who spent his life searching for cures. Who saved countless young lives, boys and girls who now have children of their own.

Despite the dreadful deaths and broken hearts all around him, Michael was the happiest man alive. Because he understood the great gift that life is.

Michael gave that perception to Armand.

Michael died of dementia. And it broke my heart. But I still have Armand. And Clara, and Jean-Guy. Myrna and Gabri and Olivier. And crazy old Ruth.

At thirty-five, I thought the best was behind me.

As I celebrate my sixtieth birthday, I can hardly wait to see what happens next.

Ring the bells that still can ring
Forget your perfect offering
There's a crack in everything.
That's how the light gets in.

Welcome to the very cracked world of Armand Gamache and Three Pines. I am overjoyed to be able to share it with you. Meet you in the bistro …

Louise Penny
March 2018

This book is dedicated to Bishop, our golden.
No better dog, no more loving companion.

The World of Three Pines

Rivière Bella Bella

Du Moulin

Old Stage Road

Du Moulin

CHAPTER 1

⌒

'**M** *erde.*'
'*Merde?*' Myrna Landers looked over her bowl of café au lait at her friend.

'I'm sorry,' said Clara Morrow. 'I meant to say fuck. Fuckity fuck fuck.'

'That's my girl. But why?'

'Can't you guess?'

'Is Ruth coming?' Myrna looked around the bistro in mock panic. Or maybe not-so-mock.

'Worse.'

'That's not possible.'

Clara gave Myrna her phone, though the bookstore owner already knew what she'd find.

Before meeting Clara for breakfast, she'd checked her

1

Twitter feed. On the screen, for the world to see, was the quickly cooling body of Clara's artistic career.

As Myrna read, Clara wrapped her large, paint-stained hands around her mug of hot chocolate, a *specialité de la maison*, and shifted her eyes from her friend to the mullioned window and the tiny Québec village beyond.

If the phone was an assault, the window was the balm. While perhaps not totally healing, it was at least comforting in its familiarity.

The sky was gray and threatened rain. Or sleet. Ice pellets or snow. The dirt road was covered in slush and mud. There were patches of snow on the sodden grass. Villagers out walking their dogs were clumping around in rubber boots and wrapped in layers of clothing, hoping to keep April away from their skin and out of their bones.

It was not possible. Somehow, having survived another bitterly cold Canadian winter, early spring always got them. It was the damp. And the temperature swings. And the illusion and delusion that it must be milder out, surely, by now.

The forest beyond stood like an army of winter wraiths, skeleton arms dangling, limbs clacking together in the breeze.

Woodsmoke drifted from the old fieldstone, brick, clapboard homes. A signal to some higher power. Send help. Send heat. Send a real spring and not this crapfest of slush and freezing, teasing days. Days of snow and warmth.

April in Québec was a month of cruel contrasts. Of sublime afternoons spent sitting outside in the bright sunshine with a glass of wine, then waking to another foot of snow. A month of muttered curses and mud-caked boots and splattered cars and dogs rolling, then shaking. So that every front entrance was polka-dotted with muck. On the walls. On the ceilings. On the floors. And people.

April in Québec was a climatological shitstorm. A mind-fuck of epic proportions.

But what was happening outside the large windows was comforting compared to what was happening on the small screen of Clara's phone.

Clara's and Myrna's armchairs were pulled close to the hearth, where logs popped and sent embers fluttering up the fieldstone chimney. The village bistro smelled of woodsmoke and maple syrup and strong fresh coffee.

Clara Morrow is going through her brown period, Myrna read. *To say her latest offerings are shit is to be unfair to effluent. Let's hope it is just a period, and not the end.*

'Oh,' said Myrna. Putting down the phone, she reached for her friend's hand. '*Merde.*'

'*Tabernac.* Someone from Serious Crimes just sent a link. Listen to this.'

The other agents in the conference room looked over as he read off his cell phone, '*This is Armand Gamache's first day back at the Sûreté du Québec after a suspension of nine months following a series of ill-advised and disastrous decisions.*'

'Disastrous? That's bullshit,' said one of the officers.

'Well, it's bullshit retweeted by hundreds.'

Other agents and inspectors scrambled for their phones, tapping away while glancing out the open door. To make sure ...

It was eleven minutes to eight, and members of the homicide department were gathering for the regular Monday-morning meeting to discuss ongoing investigations.

Though there was very little 'regular' about this meeting. About this morning. The room was electric with anticipation.

3

Now heightened even further by what was blowing up on their phones.

'*Merde*,' muttered an agent. '*Having achieved the pinnacle of power as Chief Superintendent of the Sûreté*,' she read, '*Gamache promptly abused it. Deliberately allowing catastrophic amounts of opioids onto the streets. After an investigation, he was demoted.*'

'They have no idea what they're talking about. Still, that's not too bad.'

'It goes on. *He should have been fired, at the very least. Probably put on trial and thrown in prison.*'

'Oh.'

'That's insane,' said one of the senior officers, grabbing the phone and reading it for herself. 'Who's writing this crap? They don't even mention he got the stuff back.'

'Of course they don't.'

'I hope he doesn't see it.'

'Are you kidding? He'll see it.'

The room fell silent, except for the soft clicking from each device. Like the sound of near-dead tree limbs in the breeze.

Words were muttered under their breaths as they read. Words their grandparents had considered sacred but were now profane. *Tabernac. Calice. Hostie.*

One senior officer put his head in his hands and massaged his temples. Then, dropping them, he reached for his phone. 'I'm going to write a rebuttal.'

'Don't. Better if it comes from the leadership. Chief Superintendent Toussaint will set them straight.'

'She hasn't yet.'

'She will. She trained under Gamache. She'll defend him.'

Off in the far corner, one agent was staring at her phone, a deep line forming between her brows.

While the others were pale, she was flushed as she read not a text or tweet but an email.

Though in her mid-forties, Lysette Cloutier was one of the newer recruits to homicide, having been transferred from the Sûreté's accounting department. She'd spent years quietly keeping track of the budget, now surpassing a billion dollars, until Chief Superintendent Gamache had noticed her work and thought she'd be helpful tracking down killers.

While she couldn't follow a DNA trail or a suspect to save her life, she could follow the money. And that often led to the same place.

Everyone else in that conference room had worked hard to get into the most prestigious department in the Sûreté du Québec.

Agent Lysette Cloutier was doing her best to get out. And get back to nice, safe, predictable, understandable numbers. And away from the daily horrors, the physical violence, the emotional chaos of murder.

Cloutier always chose the same seat at these meetings. Making sure her back was to the long whiteboard, on which were tacked photographs.

She considered the email she'd just received, then typed a response and hit send before she had time to reconsider.

'What do you wanna bet some of these tweets are from Beauvoir?' said one of the younger agents.

'You mean Chief Inspector Beauvoir?'

All heads turned to the doorway. And then there was a scramble and a scraping of chairs as everyone got to their feet.

Isabelle Lacoste stood, cane in hand, staring at the young agent. Then her expression softened to a smile as she looked around at the familiar faces.

The last time she'd been in the Monday-morning meeting, she'd chaired it, as head of homicide. Now she entered limping.

Her injuries, though almost healed, were not completely gone. And never would be.

Officers and agents crowded around, welcoming her back, while she tried to explain she wasn't really back. Promoted to Superintendent, she was in the building for meetings to discuss the timing and conditions of her return to active duty.

But it was no coincidence, everyone in that room knew, that she was there this Monday. Not just any old day. Not just any old meeting.

She took a chair by the head of the table and nodded to the others to retake their seats. Then she looked at the young agent who'd made the comment about Chief Inspector Beauvoir.

'What did you mean by that?'

Her voice was calm, but she sat unnaturally still. Veteran homicide agents who'd served under Chief Inspector Lacoste recognized the look. And almost pitied the foolish young agent who found himself in her crosshairs.

'I mean that we all know Chief Inspector Beauvoir is leaving the Sûreté,' he said. 'Moving to Paris. But not for another couple of weeks. What happens before then? With Gamache coming back. I'd rather be in a firefight than be Chief Inspector Beauvoir walking into this meeting today. I bet he feels the same way.'

'You'd lose,' said Lacoste.

The room grew quiet.

He's young and foolish, Lacoste thought. Probably longing for some desperate glory.

She knew this agent had never been in a so-called firefight. Even using the ridiculous phrase gave him away. Anyone

6

who'd actually raised a weapon, sighted another human, and shot. Again, and again. And been shot at. Would never consider that glory, nor call it a firefight.

And would never, ever wish to be there again.

Those in the room who'd been on that last raid were looking at the agent. Some with outrage. But some almost wistfully. Remembering when they'd been that young. That naïve. That immortal.

Nine months ago.

They thought back to the summer afternoon. In the pretty forest by the Vermont border. How the sun broke through the trees and they could feel the warmth on their faces.

That moment that seemed to hang in midair before all hell broke loose.

As weapons were raised and fired. And fired. Cutting down the saplings. Cutting down the people.

The screams. The chocking, acrid stench of smoke from the weapons. Of wood and flesh burned by bullets.

Chief Inspector Lacoste was one of the first to fall. Her actions giving Chief Superintendent Gamache that one moment he needed to act. And act he had.

Isabelle Lacoste hadn't seen what Chief Superintendent Gamache had done. By then she was unconscious. But she'd heard about it. She'd read the transcripts of the investigation, after he'd been suspended.

Gamache had survived the events that day.

Only to be cut down by his own people.

And the attacks were continuing, even as he returned to work.

Isabelle Lacoste, and every veteran officer in that room, knew that the decisions Chief Superintendent Gamache had made were audacious. Daring. Unconventional. And, unlike what the tweets claimed, hugely effective.

But it could very well have gone the other way.

It had been a coup de grâce. The last desperate act of the most senior officer in Québec, who felt there was no other option.

Had Gamache failed, and for a while it appeared he would, the Sûreté would have been crippled, leaving Québec defenseless against an onslaught of gang violence, trafficking, organized crime.

Gamache had prevailed. But just barely, and at a cost.

Any reasonable person making those decisions would expect a consequence, no matter the outcome. The Chief Superintendent was reasonable. He must've expected to be suspended. Investigated.

But had he expected to be humiliated?

In their own coup de grâce, the political leadership had decided to save their own skins by putting Gamache's career out of its misery. Though vindicated in the investigation, he would be offered a job he could not possibly accept. Chief Inspector of homicide. A position he'd held for many years. One he'd handed over to Lacoste when he'd been promoted to head of the Sûreté. After she'd been wounded, it was a job now filled by Jean-Guy Beauvoir.

It was a demotion, the leadership knew, that Armand Gamache could not agree to. The humiliation would be too great. The cut too deep. He would resign. Retire. Disappear.

But Armand Gamache refused to go. To their astonishment, he'd accepted their offer.

His fall from grace would be completed here. In this room. Today.

And it appeared he'd land, with a thump, right on top of Jean-Guy Beauvoir.

It was seven minutes to eight. The two men would soon walk through the door. Both holding the rank of head of homicide.

And then what would happen?

Even Isabelle Lacoste found herself glancing at the door. Wondering. She didn't expect trouble but couldn't help thinking about what George Will called the 'Ohio Event'.

In 1895 there were only two automobiles in the whole state. And they'd collided.

No one knew better than Lacoste that the unexpected happened. And now she found herself bracing for the collision.

'It's your own fault,' said Ruth Zardo. 'You should never have agreed to it, if you ask me.'

No one had.

'Listen to this one,' the elderly poet continued, reading off the phone. '*Clara Morrow's contribution is trite, derivative, and banal.* They left out clichéd and pedestrian. Or maybe someone says that further down the thread.'

'I think that's enough, Ruth,' said Reine-Marie Gamache.

She glanced at her watch. Nearly eight. She wondered how her husband was getting on. It did not take a savant to know how Clara was doing.

Her friend had dark circles under her eyes and looked drawn. And slightly painted. There were dabs of cadmium red and burnt umber on her face and in her hair.

Clara was wearing her usual jeans and a sweater. Success as an artist had not changed her fashion sense. Such as it was. Perhaps because recognition had come later in Clara's life. In her late forties now, she'd been working in her studio for decades, creating works that went unnoticed. Her greatest success had been her Warrior Uterus series. She'd sold one.

To herself. And given it to her mother-in-law. Thereby weaponizing her art. And her uterus.

Then, after an evening in the bistro with women friends from the village, Clara had gone back to her studio and started something different. Portraits. Oil paintings. Of those women.

She'd painted them as they really were, their lines and lumps and wrinkles. But what she'd really captured, in her bold strokes, were their feelings.

The portraits burst onto the art scene, lauded as revolutionary. Bringing back a traditional form but revitalizing it. Her portraits were luminous. Joyous. Vibrant. Unsettling at times, as the loneliness and brute sorrow in some faces became apparent.

Her portraits of the women were challenging and bold and audacious.

And now, this April morning, many of those same women had joined Clara in the bistro. They'd celebrated her successes here. Today they came to comfort.

'They don't know what they're talking about,' said Myrna. 'It's just mean, malicious.'

'But if I believed them when they loved the works, shouldn't I believe them now?' asked Clara. 'Why were they right then but wrong now?'

'But these aren't art critics,' said Reine-Marie. 'I bet most of them haven't even seen the exhibition.'

'The art critic for the *New York Times* just posted,' reported Ruth. 'He says in light of this disaster, he's going to go back to your earlier works, the portraits, to see if he'd been wrong about them. Shit. He can't mean the portrait you did of me, can he?'

'Fuck, fuck, fuck,' muttered Rosa. The duck was sitting on Ruth's lap and looked irritated. But then, ducks often did.

'It'll be fine,' said Myrna.

'That I believe,' said Clara, running her hands through her thick hair so that it stood out from her head. Making her look like a mad madwoman.

Perversely, Ruth, who almost certainly really was mad, looked perfectly composed.

'The good thing is, nobody will see your crap,' said Ruth. 'Who goes to an exhibition of miniatures? Why in the world would you agree to contribute to a group show of tiny oil paintings? It's what bored society women in the 1700s painted.'

'And many were far better than their male counterparts,' said Myrna.

'Right,' said Ruth. 'Like that can be true.'

Rosa rolled her duck eyes.

'You paint portraits on large canvases,' Ruth persisted. 'Why do tiny landscapes?'

'I wanted to stretch myself,' said Clara.

'By doing miniatures?' asked Ruth. 'Bit ironic.'

'Did you see Clara's works?' Reine-Marie asked.

'Don't have to. I can smell them. They smell like—'

'You might want to take a look before you comment.'

'Why? Apparently they're trite and banal.'

'Do you write the same poem over and over?' asked Myrna.

'No, of course not,' said Ruth. 'But neither do I try to write a novel. It's all words, but I know what I'm good at. Great at.'

Myrna Landers heaved a sigh and shifted her considerable weight in her armchair. As much as she longed to contradict Ruth, she couldn't. The fact was, their drunk and disorderly old neighbor in Three Pines was a brilliant poet. Though not much of a human being.

Ruth made a noise that could have been a laugh. Or indigestion.

'I'll tell you what is funny. You crash and burn trying to do something different while Armand destroys his career by agreeing to go back and do the same old thing.'

'No one's crashing and burning,' said Reine-Marie, glancing at her watch again.

The atmosphere in the conference room was crackling.

'So how's this going to work?' asked one of the agents. 'Are we going to have two Chief Inspectors?'

They looked at the visiting Superintendent. '*Non*. Chief Inspector Beauvoir will be in charge until he leaves for Paris.'

'And Gamache will be . . . ?' asked another agent.

'Chief Inspector Gamache. This's a transition for a few weeks, that's all,' said Lacoste, trying to sound more confident than she actually was. 'This is a good thing. There'll be two experienced leaders.'

But the men and women in the room weren't idiots. One strong leader was great. Two led to power struggles. Conflicting orders. Chaos.

'They've worked together for years,' said Lacoste. 'They'll have no trouble working together now.'

'Would you be okay taking orders from someone who'd been your subordinate?'

'Of course I would.'

But despite her annoyance, Lacoste knew it was a legitimate question.

Could Beauvoir bring himself to give orders to his former boss and mentor?

And, more to the point, could the former Chief Superintendent take them? Gamache, as respectful as

12

he might be, was used to being in charge. And in charge of Beauvoir.

'But it's not just that, is it?' said a senior officer.

'There's more?' asked an agent.

'You don't know?' The officer looked around, intentionally, it seemed, avoiding the warning in Lacoste's eyes. 'Gamache wasn't just Beauvoir's boss. He's his father-in-law.'

'You're kidding,' said the agent, knowing that the officer was not.

'*Non*. He's married to Gamache's daughter, Annie. They have a kid.'

While the personal connection between Gamache and Beauvoir wasn't exactly a secret, neither did the two men go out of their way to advertise it.

There was a snort from down the table, and an agent looked up from his cell phone. 'They're really going after the man. Listen to this—'

'*Non*,' said Lacoste. 'I don't want to hear it.'

There was movement by the door.

They looked over, then jumped to their feet.

The senior officers saluted. The younger ones looked momentarily taken aback.

Some in the room had never seen Armand Gamache in person. Others had not seen him in months. Not since that steamy hot July afternoon in the forest. The air filled with the stench of gun smoke and the cries of the wounded. When it had cleared, they'd seen the head of the Sûreté, weapon in hand. Hauling a body through the pretty woods.

Had Gamache known when he'd dressed that summer morning, putting on the clean white shirt and the suit and tie, that that was how the day would end? With blood on his clothing. And on his hands.

He'd risen that sultry day the Chief Superintendent of the Sûreté du Québec. A confident leader. Unhappy about, but committed to, a dangerous course of action.

He left the woods, late that afternoon, shattered.

And now he was back.

A better man? A bitter man?

They were about to find out.

CHAPTER 2

The man they saw at the door was in his late fifties. Tall, not heavy but sturdy. Clean-shaven. And while not classically handsome, he was more attractive, certainly more distinguished, than the pictures on social media that morning had led the younger agents to believe.

Armand Gamache's hair, once dark, was mostly gray and slightly wavy. His complexion was that of someone who'd spent hours in open fields, in damp forests, in knee-deep snow, staring at bodies. And tracking down those who'd made them.

He had the appearance of someone who'd spent years shouldering heavy responsibility. Weighing dreadful choices.

The lines down his face spoke of determination. Of concentration. Of worry spread over years. And sorrow. Spread over decades.

But as the agents watched, Gamache smiled, and they saw that the deepest of those lines ran from the corners of his eyes.

Laugh lines. Far more pronounced than those caused by worry and pain. Though they did meet, mix, intersect.

And then there was the unmistakable, unmissable scar at his temple. Like a calling card. A mark that distinguished him. It cut across the worry lines and laugh lines. And told a story all its own.

That's what the newer agents saw.

For the veterans it was different. They didn't so much see as feel.

There was silence, stillness, as Armand Gamache stood on the threshold, looking at them, meeting eyes that were suddenly moist.

The agents in the room never thought he'd return. Not to the Sûreté and certainly not to homicide. This senior officer they'd worked alongside for years. Who'd mentored most. Who'd taught them how to catch killers. And not lose themselves in the process. How to be great officers and even better men and women.

He'd taken each for a leisurely walk, early in their placement in homicide, and told them the four statements that led to wisdom.

Never repeating them.

I was wrong. I'm sorry. I don't know. I need help.

They'd watched, impotent, as Gamache had been brought down. Then thrown aside.

But today he'd come back. To them.

He always wore a suit and tie, a crisp white shirt, as he did today. Even in the field. As a sign of respect for victim and family. And as a symbol of order in the face of the chaos that threatened.

He looked unchanged. But that, they knew, was superficial. Who knew what was going on underneath?

Gamache stepped into the conference room. *'Bonjour.'*

'Bonjour, patron,' came the response.

He nodded, subtly acknowledging the salutes, while also indicating they weren't necessary.

'Superintendent, I didn't expect to see you here.' He put out his hand, and Isabelle Lacoste took it. A far more formal greeting than the one they'd exchanged when she and her family visited the Gamaches in Three Pines.

'I was in the neighborhood,' she said.

'I see.' He glanced at the wall clock. 'Your first appointment is in half an hour, I believe.'

Isabelle Lacoste smiled. He knew. Of course he'd know. That she was there that morning for a round of interviews, speaking to various departments. To see which one she'd head up once her leave was over in a few weeks.

Though it wasn't a complete coincidence she'd scheduled the appointment on Chief Inspector Gamache's first morning back.

'It is. I'm starting at the top.'

'The janitorial service?'

'Of course. A girl can dream.'

'All your years cleaning up my messes—'

'Finally paying off, *oui*.'

He laughed.

Gamache knew that Isabelle was actually starting with the Serious Crimes division. Which would make her, in effect, his boss.

'You have your pick of positions, Superintendent. Any one of them would be lucky to have you.'

'*Merci*.' She was genuinely moved by what he said.

He turned then and offered his hand to the young agent closest to him. 'We haven't met. I'm Armand Gamache.'

The agent froze, staring at the hand, then into the smiling face. Into his eyes.

Not the eyes of the moron some were claiming in the tweets. Not the eyes of the cold-blooded killer others were depicting.

As the agent introduced himself, he caught a very slight scent of sandalwood and rose.

'Ah, *oui*,' said Gamache. 'You were with the security detail at the National Assembly in Québec City.'

'*Oui, patron.*'

'Settling into Montréal all right?'

'Yes, sir.'

Leaving the agent slightly stunned, and more than a little ashamed of what he'd said earlier, Gamache circled the table. Introducing himself to those he hadn't met. Chatting briefly with the officers who'd worked under him in the past.

Then he looked around.

The chair at the head of the table was empty, and Gamache walked toward it, all eyes on him. Then, pulling out the seat to the right of it, he sat and nodded to the others to also take their places.

He'd arrived a few minutes early for the meeting, knowing it might be necessary to clear the air. And answer some questions. Get it out of the way before Jean-Guy Beauvoir arrived.

Truth be told, he had not expected that the air would be so foul.

'You were talking about a blog post, I believe,' he said.

He'd brought out a handkerchief and was wiping his eyes.

'A tweet, actually,' said the agent, and got a filthy look from the others. 'Not important, sir.'

He put the phone down on the table.

'We're not going to start out by hiding the truth from each other, are we? It was important enough to mention before I arrived. I'd rather colleagues didn't talk behind my back.'

18

He met their eyes, then smiled. 'I know this's awkward. I've read some of the posts. I know what they're saying. That I should've been fired. That I should've been put in jail. That I'm incompetent, perhaps even criminally so. Is that right?'

He was no longer smiling, but neither was he angry. Armand Gamache was simply stating facts. Clearing the air by exposing the crap.

He leaned forward. 'You can't possibly think I have a thin skin, do you?'

Heads shook.

'Good. I doubt you're going to read anything I haven't heard before. Let's get it out in the open. I'll answer your questions, once, and then we can put it behind us. *D'accord?*'

The unhappy young man was again clutching his phone and willing the building to collapse.

No one reached the top rank of a police force as large and powerful as the Sûreté without being ambitious. And ruthless. And the agent knew what Gamache had had to do to get to the top. He also knew what they were saying about Gamache on social media. That he was no better than a sociopath.

And now that man was staring at him. Inviting him to walk into what was almost certainly a trap.

'I'd rather not, *patron.*'

'I see.' Gamache lowered his voice, though all could still hear the words. 'When I was Chief Superintendent, I had a framed poster in my office. On it were the last words of a favorite poet, Seamus Heaney. *Noli timere.* It's Latin. Do you know what it means?'

He looked around the room.

'Neither did I,' he admitted when no one spoke. 'I had to look it up. It means "Be Not Afraid".' His eyes returned to

19

the unhappy young agent. 'In this job you'll have to do things that scare you. You might be afraid, but you must be brave. When I ask you to do something, you must trust there's a good reason. And I need to trust that you will do it. *D'accord?*'

The agent looked down at his phone, clicked it on, and began reading.

'*Gamache is a madman. A coward,*' he read. His voice was strong and steady, but his face was a bright red. '*He should be locked up, not sent back to duty. Québec isn't safe as long as he's there.*'

The agent looked up, his eyes pleading to be allowed to stop. 'They're just comments, sir. Responding to some article. These aren't real people.'

Gamache raised his brows. 'Unless you're suggesting they're bots—'

The agent shook his head.

' – then they are real people. I'm just hoping they're not Québécois.'

'That one's from Trois-Rivières.'

Gamache grimaced. 'Go on. Anyone else have one?'

They went around the table, reading wildly insulting posts.

'*Gamache doesn't even want to be back,*' one agent read. '*I heard he turned the job down. He doesn't care about the people of Québec. He only cares about himself.*' The agent looked up and saw a slight wince.

'Others are saying the same thing. That you didn't want to come back to homicide. To work with us. Is that true?'

'Partly, yes.'

No one in the room expected that answer. All phones were lowered to the table as they stared.

'I did turn down the offer to return to homicide as Chief Inspector,' said Gamache. 'But not because I didn't want it.'

'Then why?'

'Because you have an exceptional leader in Chief Inspector Beauvoir. I would never displace him. I wouldn't do that to him, or to you.'

There was silence as the officers took that in.

'You're wondering if I really want to be here or if I took the job to spite those who only offered it to humiliate me?'

Now they stared at him, clearly surprised by his candor. At least the younger ones were. Isabelle Lacoste and other veterans looked on with amusement at their amazement.

'Did you?' asked an agent.

'No. I turned the offer down when I thought Chief Inspector Beauvoir was staying. But when he told me he was taking up a job in private industry, in Paris, he and I talked. I spoke to my wife and decided to accept the position.' He looked around the room. 'I understand your concern, but I wouldn't be here unless I wanted to be. Working in the Sûreté, in any capacity, is a privilege. It's been the greatest honor of my life. I can think of no better way to be useful, or better people to serve with.'

He said it with such conviction, such unabashed sincerity, that the motto on their warrant cards, their vehicles, their badges, suddenly had real meaning.

Service, Intégrité, Justice.

Gamache turned his attention to the long whiteboard covering a wall. He'd come in over the weekend, when it was quiet, and sat in this conference room studying the files. The photographs. Going over the cases, the faces on the wall.

He knew where the investigations stood and what each lead investigator had done – or not done.

Just then all eyes shifted to behind Gamache.

*

When Jean-Guy Beauvoir had arrived twenty minutes earlier, he'd gone directly to his office and closed the door. It wasn't something he normally did. Normally his door was wide open. Normally he went straight to the conference room. Normally he was the only Chief Inspector of homicide there.

But this was not a normal day. How the next half hour or so went would set the tone going forward.

He needed to gather himself.

How would his agents and inspectors react to having not just their former Chief Inspector back but one so storied? A private man who'd become a public figure.

But, even more complex for Beauvoir, he wasn't really sure how he himself would react. He and Armand had discussed it, of course, at length, but theory and reality were often very different.

In theory, this would go smoothly. He would not be intimidated, prickly, which he knew he tended to be when feeling insecure. He would not be defensive or resort to sarcasm.

Chief Inspector Beauvoir would be confident. Calm. In control of the meeting and, even more vitally, of himself.

That was the plan. The theory.

But the reality was that the vast majority of his career had been spent working alongside, and slightly behind, Gamache. It was natural for him, at this point almost instinctive, to give Gamache the final word. The authority.

Jean-Guy took a deep breath in. Deep breath out. And wondered if he should call his sponsor but decided to just repeat the Serenity Prayer a few times.

He opened his eyes when a familiar ding sounded on his phone. An email from Annie.

Are you with Dad? You need to see this.

Clicking on the link, he read. Following the thread. Tweet

after tweet. Comment, reply. Like some demented call and response. A liturgy gone wrong.

'Christ,' he muttered, and closed the link.

He was glad his wife had sent it. She was a lawyer and understood the importance of preparation and information. Even things, especially things, we didn't really want to know.

The clock in front of him said one minute to eight. He rubbed his sweaty hands on his slacks and looked at the photo on his desk. Of Annie and Honoré. Taken at the Gamache home in Three Pines. In the background, unnoticed except by someone who knew it was there, was a framed picture on the bookcase. A smiling family shot of Annie, Honoré, Jean-Guy, Reine-Marie, and Armand.

Armand. Always there. Both a comfort and an undeniable presence.

Taking a deep breath, Jean-Guy placed both hands on the desk and thrust himself out of the chair. Then he opened his door and walked, strode, across the huge open space, past near-empty desks piled with reports and photographs and laptops.

He walked into the conference room. '*Salut tout le monde.*'

Everyone got to their feet, including Gamache.

Without hesitation, Jean-Guy put out his hand, and Armand took it.

'Welcome back.'

'*Merci.*' Gamache nodded. '*Patron.*'

CHAPTER 3

⁓

They looked to Chief Inspector Gamache first, of course. Speaking to him. Reporting to him. Looking for his comments, his approval, as they went through their cases.

Gamache, for his part, listened closely but did not speak. Instead he looked to his left. To Chief Inspector Beauvoir.

For direction.

And Chief Inspector Beauvoir gave it. Calmly, thoughtfully. He asked clear questions when needed. Guiding, at times prodding. But otherwise he just listened.

He did not become defensive, or prickly.

Though, to be fair, he did feel no small annoyance, but not at Gamache. Not even at his investigators. Just at the situation. And the higher-ups he suspected had done this on purpose. Pitting two senior officers against each other. For the sake of the force? *Non.* For fun. To see if they could drive a wedge between them. Create enemies from friends in a kind of malevolent alchemy.

And perhaps, a slight warning voice suggested, for more than fun.

To his left, Superintendent Lacoste watched all this. Aware of the forces at work. Hoping for the best but half bracing for the collision.

Yet as the meeting went on, Jean-Guy Beauvoir was showing a side to himself she hadn't seen before.

She'd seen him display incredible bravery. Fierce loyalty. Dogged, often brilliant commitment to finding killers.

What she'd never seen before, in this kinetic man, was restraint.

Until today.

Somewhere along the line, probably in that sunny Québec forest, Beauvoir had learned which battles needed to be fought. And which did not. What mattered and what did not. Who were true allies and who were not.

He'd entered the woods a second-in-command. He'd left it a leader.

It was a shame, Lacoste thought, that it should happen just as he was about to leave the Sûreté.

They went through the cases, one by one, each lead investigator speaking succinctly about the homicide they were heading up. Giving updates on forensics, interrogations. Motives. Suspects.

As always, cell phones had been turned off and put away, banned for the life of the meeting.

As the gathering went on, the investigators slowly stopped looking to Gamache. Stopped glancing toward Superintendent Lacoste. And turned their full attention to Chief Inspector Beauvoir. Who gave them his.

Where arrests had been made and they were going to court, Beauvoir wanted to know what the Crown Prosecutor thought of the case. Though the fact was, he already knew. No homicide went to trial without Chief Inspector Beauvoir's

being completely aware of the strengths and weaknesses of the case.

His questions were for the benefit of the team.

Beauvoir sat now with his elbows on the shiny table, hands clasped, leaning forward. Intent, focused. He hoped he gave off an aura of calm and steady leadership. The truth was, he gave off a sense of energy. Vitality. Extreme alertness.

As he glanced at his investigators, Jean-Guy Beauvoir's eyes were bright and encouraging. His glasses gave the impression he was older than he actually was. In his late thirties, he was younger than many of the senior investigators in the room.

Twenty years younger than the man to his right.

Slender and well-groomed, Beauvoir had dark hair that was just beginning to show some gray. And his once-lithe frame was filling out slightly.

As he'd approached the conference room, he'd heard some of the comments. And knew who they came from. It was no surprise. These were the agents most likely to question.

When Gamache was the Chief Superintendent, Lacoste and Beauvoir had gone to him asking that these same troublesome agents be removed.

'Remember what happened before,' said Beauvoir.

There was, within the Sûreté du Québec, a before and after. A line drawn in their collective and institutional memory.

'Before' was a time of fear. Of distrust. Of enemies disguised as allies. It was a time of vast and rampant brutality. Of senior officers sanctioning beatings and even murders.

Gamache had led the resistance, at huge personal risk, and had eventually agreed to become Chief Superintendent himself.

No one left standing in the Sûreté who'd been through that could ever forget what had gone 'before.'

'We have to get rid of these agents,' Lacoste had said.

'They were transferred into homicide when things were out of control, just to cause trouble.'

Gamache nodded. He knew that was true.

But he also knew that few were more loyal than those who'd been given a chance.

'Keep them on,' Gamache had said. 'And train them properly.'

They had. And now, under Chief Inspector Beauvoir, those agents had become leaders themselves. Battle-hardened and trusted.

Which wasn't to say they didn't have their own opinions, opinions they were keen to voice.

Those had been the very homicide agents Beauvoir had heard questioning Gamache, just before he had arrived in the conference room.

With the Monday-morning meeting about to wrap up, something caught Beauvoir's attention, and he looked down the long conference table.

'Are we boring you?'

Agent Lysette Cloutier looked up, and her eyes grew round.

'*Désolée*,' she said, fumbling with her phone.

Chief Inspector Beauvoir continued to stare at her until she put it down.

The meeting continued, but only for another minute, before Beauvoir stopped it again.

'Agent Cloutier, what're you doing?'

Though it was clear what she was doing. She was typing on her phone. Again.

She looked up, flustered.

'I'm sorry. So sorry, but—'

'Is it a personal emergency?' Beauvoir asked.

'No, not really. I don't think—'

27

'Then put it away.'

She lowered the phone to the table, then picked it up again. 'I'm sorry, sir, but there is something.'

'For us?'

'I don't know. Maybe.'

The final report was wrapping up, and the others in the meeting wanted to finish and get out of there. Which meant they wanted her to put down the damned phone and shut up.

Feeling all eyes on her. Feeling her heart pounding in her chest. In her neck. In the vein at her temple. Agent Cloutier clutched the phone and spoke up.

'A friend has emailed me. His daughter is missing. Been gone since Saturday night.'

'Where?' asked Beauvoir, pulling a pad of paper toward him.

'In the Eastern Townships.'

'How old is she?'

'Twenty-five.'

His pen stopped. He was expecting a child. He was relieved, but also slightly annoyed. Agent Cloutier could see this and tried to get him onside.

'She was on her way to visit him up north but never arrived.'

'Is she married?'

'Yes.'

'What does her husband say?'

'Nothing. Homer, her father, has called him over and over, but Carl just says there's nothing wrong and to stop calling.'

'But she isn't at home?'

'Apparently not. Carl won't say where she is. He just hangs up on Homer. Now he isn't answering at all.' She was talking rapidly, trying to get it all in. Searching the Chief Inspector's

face for some sign of concern. Some sign she was getting through to him.

'Where does the father live?'

'North of Montréal. In the Laurentians. Ste.-Agathe.'

'Has he gone down?'

'No. He wanted to give it until today.'

Beauvoir considered the woman at the far end of the table. This was, as far as he could remember, the first time Agent Cloutier had spoken in a meeting.

'I can see why you'd be concerned, but this is a local issue. Let the local detachment handle it.'

Beauvoir returned his attention to the inspector who was just wrapping up her report.

'Homer called the local Sûreté. They sent a car but didn't find anything. That was yesterday. She's still missing. He's getting really worried.'

'Then he needs to file a missing-persons report. You can help him with that.'

He didn't mean to sound callous, but there were clear delineations of duties, and best not to step into someone else's lane.

'Please, *patron*,' said Cloutier. 'Can I go down? Take a look around?' She could see that Chief Inspector Beauvoir was undecided. Teetering. 'She's pregnant.'

Cloutier felt everyone turn to her. Flushing wildly, she kept her eyes on the Chief Inspector.

Beauvoir considered her again and weighed his options.

The fact this woman was pregnant shouldn't change anything. And yet, for Beauvoir, it did.

Missing. Pregnant. Unhelpful husband.

These were worrying signs. Warning signs.

Lysette Cloutier was not an experienced or, let's face it,

effective criminal investigator. If he freed her up to look into it, just for the day, she'd come back with nothing. Probably because there was nothing to find.

The missing woman had probably just gone away for the weekend. Told her husband she was visiting her family but was really with girlfriends. Or a lover.

Far from the first person to do that.

'What do I tell her father?' Cloutier pressed. 'He's really worried. It's not like her.'

'He might not know her as well as he thinks he does.'

'But he knows his son-in-law.'

'What does that mean?'

'He's never said it outright, but I know he doesn't like him.'

'That's not a reason to engage the resources of the homicide department, Agent Cloutier.'

'He thinks something bad's happened.' She could see she was losing him. She racked her brains for something else to say. 'How would you feel, sir? If your child didn't come home?'

She could see that the words had hit home, but not in the way she'd hoped.

Chief Inspector Beauvoir now looked angry.

Beside him, Superintendent Lacoste watched and braced. There'd be a collision after all, but not with Gamache. Chief Inspector Beauvoir was about to run over Agent Cloutier.

'My son is an infant,' Beauvoir said, his voice cold. 'There's a difference.'

'But if you love them, age doesn't matter, does it? Really?' she persisted, barely believing she was doing this. 'They're still our children.'

Beauvoir stared at her, the whole room holding its breath while the Chief Inspector weighed the options.

'What's the name?'

'Vivienne. Vivienne Godin.'

Beauvoir wrote that down. 'And husband?'

'Carl Tracey.'

If this Vivienne Godin really was missing, then something bad had happened, and time counted.

Unfortunately, Cloutier was pretty much their Clouseau. She would not find the woman, even if standing next to her in line for a Double Double at Tim Hortons.

It wasn't that Cloutier was an idiot, just that this was not her strength. It wasn't why she was brought into homicide.

In a swift glance, Beauvoir took in the officers around the table. All had their hands full with active murder investigations. Where murders had indeed been committed and killers needed to be found. Urgently.

His eyes came to rest on the one officer as yet unassigned.

Jeez, thought Beauvoir, *am I really going to do this to him?*

'Would you work with Agent Cloutier and see if there's anything there? Just for the day?'

'With pleasure,' said Chief Inspector Gamache.

CHAPTER 4

—

'I'm sorry,' Beauvoir said under his breath as they left the meeting.

'Why?' asked Gamache.

'You know why.' Beauvoir cocked his head toward Cloutier, who was at her desk. 'She stapled her transfer papers to her thigh the first day here.'

'She isn't armed, is she?' asked Gamache.

'Are you kidding?'

'Is she working out?' Gamache asked. After all, it had been his decision to transfer this desk agent into homicide.

'Actually, if kept off the streets and away from any citizens or anything sharp, yes.'

'Good to know.'

Gamache watched Agent Cloutier sitting at her desk, staring into space. He tried to believe she was thinking, but the look on her face said that she was paralyzed by indecision.

'*Noli timere*,' said Beauvoir with a grin.

'Huh. Well, maybe just a little *timere*,' admitted Gamache. As he considered Agent Cloutier, he thought about her question.

How would you feel . . . ?

How would he feel if his daughter, a grown woman, a married woman, had been missing for a day and a half?

He'd be frantic. He'd hope and pray that someone would pay attention. Someone would help.

Agent Cloutier's persistence had shown courage. Her question had shown empathy.

Both were extremely valuable, he told himself, even as he watched her knock her phone off the desk. Into the garbage.

She was nervous, that much was obvious. About the missing young woman? About working with him? About failing? Or was there something else?

'I've arranged for another desk to be put into the office,' said Beauvoir. He'd almost said 'my office' but had stopped himself.

'*Merci.* I appreciate the thought, but I'd like to sit out here.'

'Really?' Beauvoir looked around.

Desks were placed together, facing each other, two by two. Some neat, some with documents piled high. Some personalized, with family photos and memorabilia. Others antiseptic.

Gamache followed Beauvoir's gaze. It had been years, decades, since he'd sat in an open bullpen. At a desk like any other.

An investigator like any other.

Far from the humiliation it was meant to be, this actually felt comfortable. Comforting, even. Someone else was in charge, and he could just concentrate on the job at hand.

'If it's all right with you, I'll take that desk.' He pointed to the empty one across from Cloutier.

'It's all yours.' Putting his hand on Gamache's back, Beauvoir said, 'If you need anything, or just want to talk, my door's always open.'

Gamache recognized it as something he said to raw recruits. 'When's your last day again?'

Beauvoir laughed. 'It's good to have you back. Sir.'

Gamache took a deep breath. The place smelled of sweat. Of coffee burned to the bottom of the glass pot. Every day. For years.

For intelligent people, no one in homicide, it seemed, ever learned to turn the thing off. Or make a fresh pot.

It smelled of paper and files, and feet.

It smelled familiar.

When a nervous Agent Gamache had walked in, his first day at homicide, the place had been a riot of noise. Of agents yelling to each other. Phones ringing. Typewriters clacking.

Now there was a murmur of voices, the soft buzz of cell phones, and the tippity-tap of laptops.

Plus ça change, plus c'est la même chose.

The more things change, the more they stay the same.

While the technology had changed, the job had not.

Killers were still killing, and Sûreté agents were still hunting them down.

Only then did Gamache realize how much, deep in his core, he'd missed this.

They left the island of Montréal, driving over the Champlain Bridge to the south shore.

He was in the passenger seat while Cloutier drove. Below them, the St. Lawrence River was packed with broken ice, as the spring melt took hold. Rivers across Québec were freezing and thawing, then freezing again. Creating massive ice jams. The rivers, swollen with melting snow and April showers, had nowhere to go. Except to burst their banks.

It happened every spring, the flooding. But this, he could see, was different.

Gamache hated heights, preferring to look straight ahead whenever he drove across the impressive bridge. But now he forced himself to look down. Feeling light-headed and slightly dizzy, he gripped the door handle and stared over the edge, at the huge, jagged columns of ice thrusting toward him out of the river.

As far down the St. Lawrence as he could see, there was ice. Cracked and heaved. And heading their way.

Turning to the front, he began breathing again, and with each breath he prayed to God the warm weather would take hold and melt the jams. Melt the dams. Relieve the rivers before they burst free.

But it didn't look promising, he thought as the wipers of their vehicle swept wet snow off the windshield. And the sky ahead was choked with cloud.

'Tell me what you know,' he said to Agent Cloutier.

'Vivienne Godin and Carl Tracey live on a farm in the countryside not far from Cowansville. Before we left, I did a bit of digging. The local Sûreté detachment sent someone to her place yesterday, after Homer called them. They searched but found nothing. No evidence of violence.'

'And no Madame Godin.'

'*Non.* They'd been called to the home three times in the past, all for domestic violence. But each time they arrived, Madame Godin withdrew the complaint and refused to let them in.'

So her father had been right, thought Gamache. Something bad was happening.

'Officers no longer need a formal complaint,' he said. 'They can make an arrest if they themselves see evidence of abuse.'

'Yes, but I guess there wasn't enough evidence.'

'So no arrests?'

'*Non.*'

They rode in silence, each looking out at the gray, damp day. Thinking.

Gamache about this young woman, Vivienne Godin.

Cloutier about Vivienne's father, Homer.

When she went to turn off the highway, Gamache instructed her to continue on.

'We need to get as much information as possible before visiting her home and speaking to her husband. We'll get one shot at that before he kicks us off the property. We have to make each question count. Take the next turnoff, please, and head for the local detachment. They're the ones who took the calls, right?'

'Yes, but I've already spoken to them.'

'Speaking on the phone and doing it in person are two different things. There's also the issue of respect. This's their territory. We shouldn't just barge in and start questioning people. Besides, we'll probably need their help.'

A few minutes later they turned in to the town.

'Down here, please,' said Gamache, pointing to a side street and then at a low building with the Sûreté emblem out front.

CHAPTER 5

～

'Bonjour. I'm Chief Inspector Gamache, this is Agent Cloutier.' He slipped his Sûreté ID under the glass partition, and the receptionist took it. 'We'd like to see Commander Flaubert, *s'il vous plaît.*'

The man behind the glass, a civilian, glanced at the ID, then at them, and pointed to a hard bench where a drunk was slumped.

'Wait over there.'

'*Merci,*' Gamache said, and took a seat under a photo of the Premier Ministre du Québec, the man responsible for his demotion.

Crossing his legs, he leaned back on the bench and waited. Apparently just staring into space.

Cloutier paced, checking her phone for messages, gazing at posters, photographs, warnings, commendations on the walls. Photos of the Sûreté hockey team. She checked her phone for messages. Again.

Finally an officer came out and hurried across the entrance hall. Her hand extended. 'Chief Superintendent—'

'Inspector,' Gamache corrected, and wondered how

many times he'd have to do that. 'Chief Inspector.' He was on his feet.

'Brigitte Flaubert,' she said, shaking his hand.

'Yes, I remember,' said Gamache.

As Chief Superintendent, he'd made it a point to visit each detachment in the province. To sit down with the commander, and especially the agents. To get their take on what needed improving.

'Sorry to keep you waiting.' Commander Flaubert looked at Gamache with an increasingly familiar searching gaze. He suspected he'd have to get used to it.

Different from the curious looks he normally got on the street, as passersby tried to place this familiar face. The looks today were not so much to place him as to judge him.

Flaubert shot a displeased glance at the receptionist, who did not seem to care, then she turned to Agent Cloutier, as Gamache introduced her.

'If you'll come with me,' said Flaubert.

They followed her into the back of the station and to her office, walking past desks occupied by busy Sûreté officers, who glanced up as they passed, then back down.

Then up again. Realizing that the large man in the parka wasn't a stranger at all but the former head of the whole damn force.

For his part, Gamache scanned the room, meeting eyes that quickly dropped.

But one officer caught his attention. He was hefty though not fat. Solidly built, he sat at his desk, and when the others dropped their gaze, he did not.

Gamache moved on, but not before thinking he knew the man. Recognized him from somewhere.

He'd be about thirty. Short, dark hair. Built like a truck.

Six feet tall, maybe six-one, Gamache guessed, though it was hard to tell with him sitting down.

Where had he met this officer? The academy? Had he taught him? Had he presented him with a medal? Service? Bravery? Distinction?

Gamache didn't think so. He'd remember. And yet he knew this man.

There was also the issue of his eyes. Where the other officers in the room seemed curious, this one seemed wary.

The commander waved them to chairs on the other side of her desk and closed the door.

'How can I help you?' Flaubert asked.

Gamache took off his coat and nodded to Agent Cloutier to start.

'Ummm. Well.' She tried to gather herself. 'We're interested in a local woman. Vivienne Godin. We understand she's missing.'

She placed a photo of Vivienne on the commander's desk.

Flaubert saw a young woman. Straight brown hair pulled back in a ponytail. Her eyes were a clear, almost piercing blue. She didn't look particularly happy, but neither did she look angry or upset. Vivienne Godin looked almost blank.

While she might have been attractive in real life, this picture drained all the life from her, leaving her pretty features dulled.

Commander Flaubert looked up from it, then from one to the other, eyes resting back on Agent Cloutier.

'I'm sorry, I'm not familiar with her. She's local, you say?'

'Yes. Married to Carl Tracey.'

'Ahh. Tracey I know.' Flaubert went to the door and called another officer over. The one who'd caught Gamache's attention when they'd arrived.

'This's Agent Cameron.'

Gamache rose and saw immediately that he'd been wrong. This man wasn't six feet tall or even six-one. He'd be at least six-three. And formidably built.

His face from a distance was unremarkable.

But that changed once up close. What was remarkable about it was the scarring. There was a permanent cut through his lip and another through his left brow. His left cheekbone was slightly flattened, as was his nose.

Gamache also noticed, though it was admittedly hard to miss, the ring on Cameron's finger.

That's where he knew him from.

'*Patron*,' said Cameron.

Gamache pointed to the ring. 'A great game. I was there. Alouettes came from behind. You had some very impressive blocks. One at the end of the third quarter, right? Allowed the quarterback to run for a touchdown.'

'Right.' Cameron smiled as his beefy hand released Gamache's grip. He remained standing, squeezed into the small room. 'That was a long time ago.'

'Not so long. It's Robert Cameron, *n'est-ce pas?*'

'Bob. Yes.'

This man had been a tackle with the Montréal Alouettes. Helped them win the Canadian Football League's Grey Cup a few years back.

And now he was with the Sûreté.

His brown hair was cut short, and his eyes had a sharp focus. An athlete's eyes. Always aware of his surroundings. Prepared to act and react.

Also a useful quality in a Sûreté agent, thought Gamache. As long as react didn't become overreact. In a man this size, it could be brutal. Even fatal.

But when Cameron spoke, it was almost in a whisper. His voice was deep, audible, more gentle than soft. Many large men enjoyed lording over, looming over, lesser beings. Intimidating with their height and girth. But Bob Cameron seemed anxious to put people at ease. To try to fit into a world not made for him.

It was both endearing and perplexing. Because Gamache had seen this man play football.

Had seen what Cameron was capable of. What he was good at. What he clearly enjoyed. And that was not just blocking and tackling. It was doing damage, to flesh and bone.

Gamache was pleased to see that off the field, and in a Sûreté uniform, Bob Cameron was not a natural brute. In fact, he reminded Gamache of his own son, Daniel. Taller than his father. Heftier. But gentle and thoughtful. Though there was that other side to him.

Gamache knew it was folly to assume Agent Cameron had the same qualities as his son, but still, he found himself warming to the man. While keeping an image in his mind of the left tackle in action. Grabbing hold of opponents. Slamming them to the ground.

'Bob, are you aware of a missing woman?' the commander asked. 'Vivienne—'

'Godin,' said Cameron. '*Oui*. Her father called yesterday, and I spoke to an agent from Montréal this morning.' He turned to Cloutier. 'You?'

'*Oui*.'

'Has something else happened? She's not—'

He knew that Gamache had been returned to homicide. And like everyone else in the station, in the Sûreté, probably in the province, he'd also seen the posts on social media that morning.

But he hadn't heard that a body had been found, never mind this body.

'No,' said Gamache. 'But we thought we'd look around, if it's all right with you.'

'Fine with me, but like I told her father, we don't consider her missing.'

'Why not?'

'After his call, agents went to the place. Spoke to Tracey. When told his wife never arrived at her father's home, he apparently laughed. Said he wasn't surprised. He said she was probably off with some lover.'

'That's not—' Cloutier began before Gamache signaled her to be quiet.

'And they believed him?' he asked.

'Not completely, of course. They looked in the house and the outbuildings. There was no sign of her. Her car was gone, and they also didn't see any sign of violence. They had to leave it at that.'

'You say "they,"' said Gamache. 'You weren't with them?'

'No. I had other assignments.'

'I see,' said Gamache. 'We hear there were complaints of domestic abuse.'

'Yes. I answered those calls, but Madame Godin would never press charges.'

'You don't need her to,' Gamache pointed out.

'I know, but she didn't want us to do anything. Asked us to leave.'

'Madame Godin isn't at home and isn't with her father,' said Gamache. 'So where do you think she went?'

'Honestly?'

'Yes, please.'

'She was obviously being abused. I tried to help. First time she called, I gave her the number for the local shelter.'

'You think she might be there?' Cloutier asked.

'I called and asked. She isn't. I think she just took off. She's holed up in some motel, trying to get as far from Tracey as possible.'

'Then why didn't she go to her father?' asked Cloutier.

'Maybe she just needed time to herself.'

It seemed a strangely unsatisfactory answer.

Gamache thought for a moment. 'Does she have a cell phone?'

'No. There's no reception up there in the mountains.'

'You don't seem particularly worried, Agent Cameron,' said Gamache. 'An abused woman disappears and you just go about your day?'

'I'm worried,' snapped Cameron, then pulled back. '*Désolé.*'

Not so slow to anger after all, thought Gamache.

'Yes, I'm worried,' said Cameron. 'I know what a piece of work Tracey is. But she'd been gone only a few hours at the time. I was going to give it until noon today, then alert missing persons.'

They looked at the clock. It was ten thirty in the morning.

'Do you mind my asking why you're here?' he asked. 'How did you even hear about this?'

'Her father emailed me this morning,' said Cloutier. 'We're old friends.'

'So this's unofficial?' asked Cameron.

'Oh, no,' said Gamache. 'This's official. You might be right and she's safe in a motel. But let's be certain.' He turned to the commander. 'Can you send out an alert, please? And make sure the information gets to all the shelters in the province.'

'*Oui, absolument.*'

'What did her friends tell you?'

'I didn't ask,' said Cameron.

'Why not?'

'Because it wasn't an active investigation,' said Cameron. 'Look, if Vivienne needs time away, I for one can't blame her. I'm not going to track her down for her husband.'

'But it's not for him,' said Cloutier. 'It's for her father. He was expecting her Saturday night. It's now Monday. You don't think she'd have called him by now, if she was safe?'

'Maybe she's afraid of him, too,' said Cameron. 'Maybe they didn't get along.'

'Then why would she say she was going to him? She must've been in trouble. Where else would she turn? Where else would she feel safe?'

Gamache suspected that was true. But he also knew, from experience, people escaping abusive situations often made a fatal, though understandable, error.

They went to where they felt safe. Their families, their best friends.

Obvious places for support. But also obvious places to be found.

Where would the abuser look first, except family and friends?

If Vivienne Godin was leaving her abusive husband, Gamache hoped she'd changed her mind and instead of going to her father, she'd gone to some motel. Or shelter.

'Is that the woman you met?' He pointed to the photo on the desk.

'That's her,' Cameron said in his gentle voice.

But Gamache wasn't fooled. He'd seen the man play. Had watched, cheered, as the Alouettes won the Grey Cup on that snowy day. Had seen how ferociously, certainly gleefully, this man had plowed into oncoming defensive tackles. Protecting his quarterback with all his might. And he was certainly mighty, even now.

Though something perplexed Gamache. That scarring. Football players wore helmets with grilles to protect their faces. While they could get concussions and twisted arms and legs, it would be almost impossible to get injuries like that to his face.

Those came, Gamache knew, from other types of blows.

'When was the first time she called for help?'

'Last summer sometime. I answered the call.'

'You obviously remember it,' said Gamache. He saw Cameron flush and tucked that away.

'And she called you more than once?' said Cloutier.

'Not me, 911. But yes, mostly when welfare checks came out.'

'They're unemployed?' asked Gamache.

'Yeah, but Tracey does pottery.'

'Pottery?' said Gamache, far from sure he'd heard right. 'Like clay?'

'Yes. He makes things that people can't use. Useless. Like the man.'

Carl Tracey was an artist, thought Gamache. But then, why not? Having known many artists in his life, especially through Clara, he'd grown to realize they were often not the most stable, or house-trained, individuals.

'When was the last time you were called to the home?' Gamache asked.

'Two weeks ago. Again she refused help.'

'Why would she call, then refuse help?' asked Cloutier. 'It doesn't make sense.'

'She just wanted the beating to stop,' said Cameron. 'But she didn't want him arrested. I think she knew he'd be out in hours and then things would get really bad.'

Gamache nodded. It was the terrible flaw in the system.

It appeared to help the abused while actually just piling on more abuse. Worse abuse.

'There was nothing more we could do, really,' said Cameron.

'Really?'

'Sir?' asked Cameron.

'You said there was nothing you could do ... really.' Gamache let that sit for a moment. 'But was there something you did do?'

Cameron hesitated before finally answering. 'I took Carl aside when I saw him in town last week. I warned him.'

'What did you say?' asked Gamache.

'I told him I knew what he was doing to his wife and if there was one more complaint, I'd beat the shit out of him.'

'You did what?' asked Gamache while beside him Cloutier muttered, 'Good.'

Gamache stood up and faced the mammoth man.

The small room grew even smaller. Suffocating.

'That was the wrong thing to do,' said Commander Flaubert, recognizing that something needed to be said, though her tone was without real reproach.

'Why was it wrong?' asked Cameron, addressing Gamache. 'He needed to know.'

'Know what?' asked Gamache. 'That cops with an ID card and a gun will be judge and jury and carry out the sentence? Did you want him to know that punishing one beating with another is the way we do things in the Sûreté? Did you want to cede all moral high ground?'

Gamache spoke clearly. And slowly. Choosing his words carefully and swallowing the ones that were screaming to get out. Though his outrage was evident. In his extreme stillness. And in each tightly. Controlled. Word.

'Threats of violence will not be tolerated. You're an officer

in the Sûreté du Québec, not a thug. You set the tone, the atmosphere. You act as a role model, either consciously or unconsciously.'

'My concern was for a vulnerable woman, a pregnant woman and her unborn child. Not for the entire population of Québec.'

'The two are the same. No citizen is safe in a state where police feel free to beat those they don't like. Who take the law into their own hands.'

'And you didn't?' asked Cameron.

'Agent Cameron!' snapped Commander Flaubert.

It was too late. The words were out, the line had been crossed.

Cloutier's mouth dropped open, but she said nothing. Just stared at the two men, staring at each other.

'I did,' said Gamache. 'And paid the price. Knew I would. Knew I should. You seem to think you're perfectly within your rights to threaten assault. To maybe even do it. Without censure.'

Cameron couldn't deny that.

'At what stage did you think a threat of violence was appropriate?'

'At the stage, sir, when I realized the law could not protect Vivienne Godin.'

'So you would? By piling violence on violence?'

'If you'd seen her—'

'I've seen worse.'

The truth of that, the horror of that, pressed up against them in the tiny room.

'I'm not saying what was happening to Vivienne Godin was all right,' Gamache went on. More gently. 'Of course it wasn't. Of course it's tempting to do something, anything, to stop

it. It's horrific when, as people sworn to protect, we cannot. When someone we know to be guilty is beyond our reach. When they can keep doing it and we can't stop it. But it's even worse if the cops become criminals, too. Do you understand?'

'Yessir.'

'Do you really?' asked Gamache.

There was a pause as Agent Cameron considered, then finally nodded.

'There's one other thing,' said Gamache, his voice now back to normal. 'Did you consider what a threat like that would do to a man like Carl Tracey? Did you really think it would stop him from abusing his wife? Or would it, could it, enrage him even more? And who would he take it out on? You – or her?'

There was silence as Cameron considered a question he hadn't thought of before.

'Consequences,' said Gamache. 'We must always consider the consequences of our actions. Or inaction. It won't necessarily change what we do, but we need to be aware of the effect. That's the contract we have with the people of Québec. That those who have an ID card and a gun also have self-control.'

'Yessir.'

'*Bon.*'

He at least now understood why Cameron hadn't gone to the farmhouse himself yesterday.

Gamache sat down again. 'Go on, Agent Cloutier.'

The room, still tingling, settled back to near normal.

'Do you know if Vivienne has any friends we can contact?' Cloutier asked. 'Anyone she might be with?'

Cameron shook his head. 'Tracey didn't provide any names, and no one's come forward or shown concern.'

They were getting a picture of Vivienne Godin's life, and what they saw was not good.

A woman isolated in a remote farmhouse. It was, they knew, one of the warning signs of extreme abuse. Control.

'Any gossip?' Cloutier asked.

'You mean an affair?' asked Cameron. 'Again, if there was, I never heard it.'

'And Tracey, does he have any friends?'

'Drinking buddies,' said Cameron. 'But even they seem to have disappeared. Last time I saw him in town, he was drinking alone at the joint on the edge of town.'

'Name?' asked Cloutier. She was getting the hang of this.

'Le Lapin Grossier.'

'The Dirty Rabbit?' she asked as she wrote.

'More like filthy,' said Cameron.

'The Obscene Rabbit,' said Flaubert. 'It's a strip joint.'

The interview was winding down.

'Thank you for your help,' said Gamache as he stood and took his coat off the back of the chair.

'What're you going to do now, if you don't mind my asking?' said Cameron.

'We're going to visit Monsieur Tracey,' said Gamache.

'Would you like me there?'

Gamache paused. He'd been about to decline, given Cameron's last encounter with Carl Tracey, but now wondered if it mightn't work in their favor. While Cameron's threat to beat Tracey was wrong, it was done. Gamache, the realist, knew that showing up with this agent might just shake some truth loose.

'If you don't mind,' he asked the commander, who nodded, 'that would be helpful. You can show us the way.'

'I'll get my coat,' said Cameron.

After he left, the commander said, 'I'm sorry he threatened Tracey. I didn't know about that.'

'Are you? Sorry?'

Commander Flaubert reddened. 'I understand why he did it.'

Gamache thought for a moment, looking at the closed door through which the large man had disappeared.

'The scars on his face?' he said. 'Not from football.'

'*Non*. Those are thanks to his father.'

Gamache took a deep breath and shook his head. Had Bob Cameron turned that hurt, that pain, that betrayal, into something useful? Into sport? And now into protecting others?

Or had he learned something else from his father?

That day in the bitterly cold stands in Montréal again came to mind. Wrapped in blankets with Reine-Marie and their son, Daniel, watching the Grey Cup final. Hearing the crashes and grunts and shouts from the field.

The brutality. As the massive left tackle found his quarry. And decked him. Standing over the body and opening his arms in a primal display of domination.

To wild applause. To approval.

Was he still doing it, only now in a Sûreté uniform?

Once in the car, following Agent Cameron's vehicle, Gamache asked Agent Cloutier, 'What do you think of him?'

'Cameron? I don't know.'

'Think about it.'

She thought. 'He called her Madame Godin, but when he got angry, he called her Vivienne.'

'*Oui*. When you spoke with him this morning, did you mention she was pregnant?'

50

Cloutier went back over the conversation. 'No.'

'I see.'

And yet, thought Gamache, Agent Cameron knew that Vivienne was going to have a baby.

Now, how was that?

As they got closer to the farmhouse, the wipers pushing the wet flakes off the windshield, Agent Cloutier did what she always did in times of extreme stress.

Two times four is eight.

Three times five is fifteen.

Her times tables. Laid out neatly, in rows and columns.

Five times four is . . .

Her meditation. Her happy place. No chaos could survive in the tightly packed numbers. Everything in its place. In its home. Safe. Predictable. Known. Every question had an answer.

Twenty.

Terrible things did not happen to the pregnant daughter of an old friend, in the times table.

Six times six is . . .

Only, Cloutier knew, something had happened. And it was up to them to find the answer.

. . . thirty-six.

Thirty-six hours Vivienne was now missing.

CHAPTER 6

❦

'What do you think?' Gabri asked Clara as they stood on the stone bridge and looked into the Rivière Bella Bella below.

He had to speak up, over the roar.

The water rushing beneath them, so clear and gentle in summer, was seething. Frothing with brown foam and great chunks of ice and tree limbs swept into it in the spring runoff.

All very natural. All very predictable.

But there was a problem.

There was too much of it. Too much water. Too much ice. Far too much forest swirling in the waters.

Gabri and Clara turned around and looked downriver.

'Damn,' muttered Clara, and then, raising her voice, she turned to Gabri. 'A dam is forming. I think it's time to start sandbagging.'

'Did someone say sandbagging?' asked Ruth as she joined them on the bridge.

She'd put a moth-eaten woolen scarf over her short white hair and tied it at her chin, so that she looked like an elderly Victorian gentleman with a toothache. And a duck.

'Now, Ruth.' Gabri spoke with exaggerated patience. 'We've been through this before. When we call for volunteers to sandbag, we don't mean to hit each other over the head with sand-filled socks.'

'Shit,' said Ruth.

'No,' said Gabri. 'Not shit either, as we learned last spring.'

Clara had returned to the other side of the bridge and looked at her garden, which backed onto the Rivière Bella Bella. The river had risen rapidly in the last hour and was now just inches from the top.

'I've never seen it so high so early,' said Gabri, joining her.

'Are you talking about the river or Ruth?' asked Clara.

Gabri laughed, then regarded their neighbor more closely. Ruth looked fairly sober, somber even. Though the duck looked bleary. But then, ducks often did.

'What do you think, Ruth?' Gabri asked, raising his voice so she could hear over the rushing waters and her natural inclination to not listen.

She was the oldest resident of Three Pines. But how old was a matter of some debate.

'We found her under a rock,' Gabri's partner, Olivier, was fond of explaining. And she did appear more than a little fossilized.

She also happened to be the chief of the volunteer fire department. Not because she was a natural leader but because most villagers would rather run into a burning building or a river in full flood than face Ruth Zardo's sharp tongue.

She tipped her head back and looked into the sky. It had stopped snowing but was still threatening moisture of some sort. Exactly what they did not need.

'I think we should order more sand,' she said, dropping her eyes to consider the river below. 'I checked yesterday, and we

have enough in the pile behind the old railway station for a normal flood, but this doesn't look normal to me.'

If anyone had a knowledge of abnormal, it was Ruth.

'I've only seen it this high once before,' she said. 'Yes, I guess it's time.'

'For what?' asked Clara.

'Another hundred-year flood.'

'Oh, shit,' said Gabri. 'Fuckity fuck fuck. *Merde.*' Then he paused. 'What's a hundred-year flood?'

'Surely the name is a giveaway,' said Clara.

They followed Ruth as she turned toward the bistro.

'A hundred-year flood happens every hundred years, right?' Gabri whispered to Clara.

'I'd have to say yes.'

'Then how could Ruth have seen one before?' He dropped his voice still further. 'How old is she?'

'Not a clue. I'm still trying to figure out how old the duck is,' said Clara.

Just then Rosa, in Ruth's arms a few paces ahead, turned her head 180 degrees. And glared at them.

'The Devil Duck,' whispered Gabri. 'If her head spins all the way around, I'm running for the hills.'

But Rosa just turned back and nestled into the crook of Ruth's arm. And went to sleep.

Unaware of, or unconcerned about, the rising waters.

But then, thought Clara, as they entered the bistro, ducks could fly. And people could not.

Their tires spun in the thick mud, and the car slewed sideways on the hill.

The spring thaw had once again brought hope and muck. It was a beautiful filthy season.

'Stop, stop,' said Gamache. '*Arrêt*,' he commanded when Cloutier gunned it one more time. And the car slipped a few more feet sideways, toward the gully.

Up ahead, Cameron's patrol car was sliding backward. Toward them.

'Back up,' said Gamache. 'Slowly.'

He kept his voice calm and level, even as he watched Cameron's vehicle gather speed on the steep slope.

'What you want to do,' he said, 'is—'

'I know, I know.'

As he watched, she put the car in reverse and touched the gas. Nursing it backward. Gamache braced, watching Cameron's car coming at them even as Cloutier applied gas and theirs sped up.

There was a small thud as the Sûreté vehicles met. Cloutier expertly nursed the brakes as both slowed down and came to a halt on the shoulder.

She'd executed the maneuver perfectly. Gamache doubted he could have done nearly as well.

'*Formidable*,' he said, and saw her smile.

'Please don't ask me to do that again.'

He laughed. 'Believe me, Agent Cloutier, if that ever needs to be done again, you're the one I'll call.'

Cameron had gotten out and was sliding toward them, gripping the cars as he went. Finally stopping at Gamache's window.

'That was impressive. *Merci*.' Bending in, he looked at Gamache. 'What now?'

'Now' – Gamache grabbed his hat and gloves – 'we walk.'

Cloutier looked up the hill. 'It's at least half a kilometer to their place.'

'Then we'd better get going,' said Gamache, already out of the car and looking around.

The plump April snowflakes had stopped, and the air was cool and fresh. He took a deep breath and smelled sweet pine needles and musky leaves and mud.

And heard –

'What's that?' asked Cloutier, cocking her head.

'A river,' said Cameron. 'It must've broken up. The spring runoff's started.'

Gamache turned toward the sound coming from deep in the woods.

While the river could not be seen, it could be heard. The waters rushing down the side of the mountain. It was a sound as familiar to those in the Québec countryside as sirens were in the city.

When he'd left Three Pines early that morning to get into Montréal, all had been silent. Except for the gentle tap-tap-tapping as the huge flakes landed on the trees and homes and vehicles.

But something had broken, something had woken, in the meantime. Something not at all gentle.

He took another deep breath, but with less pleasure.

All sorts of things woke up in the spring. With the warmer weather. Bears. Chipmunks. Skunks and racoons. And rivers.

They came to life.

There were few things more powerful, or destructive, or terrifying, than a hungry bear or a river in full flood.

Gamache knew exactly where the river was heading. While he'd never been along this road before, he knew the area. They weren't all that far from his own village.

Which meant the roar they heard was the Rivière Bella Bella, heading straight into Three Pines.

He took out his phone to call Reine-Marie, to warn her

and find out how things were, but Cameron was right. There was no signal.

He clicked the phone off, put it back in his pocket, and turned to look up the muddy road.

'Come on,' he said, and started the climb.

'The lottery ticket,' said Isabelle Lacoste, looking over the file at Jean-Guy Beauvoir.

'What?'

Lacoste was between meetings. She'd dropped by to chat, and instead he'd put her to work, tossing her files and saying, 'Take a look at these and tell me what you think.'

The two sat in companionable silence, reading about sometimes gruesome, sometimes straightforward, always tragic murders. Every now and then, Superintendent Lacoste had asked a question. Or made a note. Or a comment.

'In the Anderson case,' she said. 'The victim was found with a lottery ticket in her pocket.'

'*Oui*. A group of co-workers were in a pool.'

'Which she organized.'

'Yes.' He leaned over so he could read the file she was holding. 'But it was a losing ticket.'

'Doesn't matter.'

'Then what does?'

'Everyone in her section was in the lottery pool, right? Ten people?'

'Yes.'

'But it says here there're eleven in that division. One was left out. Which one?'

Beauvoir sat back and thought. It seemed a tiny detail, but that was the thing about murders. And murderers. They hid in the details. The small things easily overlooked.

'You think whoever was left out killed her for the lottery ticket? But why not take it?'

'*Non.*' Isabelle was shaking her head. Then she suddenly looked at her watch. 'I'm going to be late for the next meeting.'

'But wait, why leave the ticket behind if that was the motive?' asked Beauvoir, calling after Lacoste as she made for the door.

'Because the ticket wasn't the motive. Being left out was. And it probably wasn't the first time. What happens when someone is shunned, over and over?'

He grabbed the dossier and scanned it, muttering, '*Merde*. She might be right.'

Chief Inspector Beauvoir called the lead investigator and suggested he find out all he could about the co-worker who had not been included.

Then he sat back down and continued to go over the files.

He was damned if he was going to leave a mess for his replacement. Especially since he'd be spending holidays with that replacement for years to come.

In ten days' time, he and Annie would get on a flight to Paris with Honoré, to start their new lives. And he to start a new job in private industry.

It was almost impossible to believe.

April in Paris. The trees would be in leaf. The gardens, laid out so formally, would be in bloom. Parisians would be sitting at sidewalk cafés enjoying the warmth and their aperitifs.

The City of Light at its most luminous.

He looked out his large window at Montréal. He couldn't see the top of Mont Royal for the low-hanging clouds.

While the snow had stopped, the gloom had not.

Late spring in Québec was beautiful.

Early spring, on the other hand, was a pile of shit. Literally, in some cases. Some places.

He could almost smell it now. In the city it was not really noticeable. But in the countryside?

After years visiting the Gamaches at their home in the tiny village of Three Pines, Jean-Guy had gotten much closer to nature. To the rhythms. The surprises. The miracles.

Close enough to confirm that he hated the countryside. It was dirty and unpredictable. And it smelled.

Beauvoir still harbored the suspicion that those who could live in Montréal or Québec City but chose the countryside had at least one screw loose. This was confirmed when he'd first met the residents of Three Pines, and especially the old poet. Who seemed to have lost all her screws and, as a result, spent her time screwing with others. Or at least with Jean-Guy.

It didn't help that many of the villagers were Anglophones. And Jean-Guy was an Anglophobe.

They scared him. Partly because while his English was good, he rarely caught the nuances. Or the cultural references. Who was Captain Crunch? Captain Kangaroo? Why so many captains? Why not generals? And why did they eat frites with ketchup and not mayonnaise? And how do you begin to explain plum pudding? It looked, and smelled, like early spring.

And they ate it.

Over time, he'd grown to not just like the village but love the villagers. To accept their foibles. As they accepted his.

But still, plum pudding? It sounded so good and tasted so bad.

Anglos.

His cell phone rang, and he answered immediately.

'*Salut*,' came the cheerful voice. 'Am I calling at a bad time?'

'If it was, I wouldn't answer.'

Though they both knew that wasn't true. Short of being in the middle of a shoot-out, when Annie called, he answered.

A successful lawyer, Annie had arranged a transfer to the Paris office and was now studying to get her license to become an *avocat* in France.

'Do you think you can go to Three Pines tonight?' she asked.

'I wasn't planning to. Why?'

'I just called Mom, and she told me the Bella Bella's going to flood.'

'It does every spring.'

'This seems different. She tried to sound casual, but I could hear that she's worried. She wanted to make sure Honoré and I weren't going down.'

'That bad?'

It would have to be near catastrophic for his mother-in-law to give up precious time with them.

Jean-Guy dropped his feet off the desk and leaned forward.

'They'll need help sandbagging,' said Annie. 'Still, how bad can it be? It's the Bella Bella, not the St. Lawrence or the Mighty Mississippi. The worst that can happen is water in the basements, right? It's never completely flooded before.'

Beauvoir walked to the window.

Lots of things never happened before, he knew. Then suddenly did. It only took once. Murder, for instance. A person was only killed once. And that was enough.

Yes, just because something had never happened, that didn't mean it couldn't. Or wouldn't.

And Annie was worried. Otherwise she'd never have called and asked him to go down.

After he hung up, he continued to look out the window. She'd mentioned the St. Lawrence. If the Bella Bella was flooding, what was the huge river that encircled the island of Montréal doing?

Through the skyscrapers, he could see the river was still frozen. He sighed with some relief. Now, that would be a problem. . . .

But then he looked more closely, and as his eyes adjusted, he could see fissures. And long shadows. That meant columns of ice had pushed their way up and out. Great chunks were piling up, and unless something happened soon, the St. Lawrence would also flood. And worse. The force of it could crush the pylons holding the bridges in place.

He picked up the phone. As he waited for Chief Superintendent Toussaint to answer, he thought again about Paris. Where the flowers were in bloom.

Where his little, growing family would live. In peace.

CHAPTER 7

⌒

Awful! Arrogant poseur #MorrowSucks

Overrated. No talent. #MorrowSucks

Just plain shit. #MorrowSucks

Lock him up #GamacheSux

The donkeys noticed first.

They turned in the field and started forward. Toward the fence. One or two were braying.

Carl Tracey came out and stood in the doorway of the barn and watched as three figures, covered in mud, trudged down the drive.

They looked like something out of a horror film. Golems, heading his way.

Tracey reached over and took hold of the pitchfork.

Gamache raised his hand in a fist, to signal them to stop.

Cameron, familiar with the silent combat gesture, did.

62

Cloutier did not.

'Agent Cloutier.'

When she turned, Gamache nodded forward, and she saw it then.

Framed in the open barn door was a man straight out of some horror film.

He was disheveled. Filthy. With a pitchfork.

———

Tracey watched them closely. The two men were large. Disheveled. Filthy. The woman was small and filthy.

He tightened his grip on the pitchfork.

'Monsieur Tracey?'

'What do you want?' he shouted. In English.

Gamache lifted his hands, to show they held no weapon, and stepped forward. Cameron instinctively went to join him, to protect his quarterback, but once again Gamache gave him a signal.

To stand down. But remain alert.

The Chief Inspector took a few steps toward Tracey. There were at least fifteen paces to go before they'd be face-to-face, but already he could smell the booze.

'We're with the Sûreté du Québec—' Gamache began, in English.

'Get off my land.'

'My name is Chief Inspector Armand Gamache. This is Agent Cloutier. And this—'

'I know who that is.' Now that they were closer, Tracey recognized the man who'd threatened him with a beating not long ago. 'Get him the fuck off my land.'

He lifted the pitchfork and pointed it toward Cameron. Making a small jabbing movement. It was a futile, almost comic gesture.

But Gamache wasn't smiling. Instead he put his arms out at his sides and took a few steps closer.

Carl Tracey was in his mid-thirties. Slightly shorter, slightly lighter than Gamache. But where Gamache was solid, this man was not. As he jabbed, he jiggled.

Still, Gamache knew it was never wise to underestimate anyone. Especially someone with a pitchfork.

He stopped.

'We'd like to speak with your wife, please. Vivienne Godin. Is she here?'

'No. I already told the cops that she's gone away.'

'And you haven't heard from her? She hasn't called?'

'No.'

The only one who'd called him was her crazy father. Every hour, on the hour. Even through the night. Threatening him. But he wouldn't tell them that.

He noticed Cameron had opened his jacket. To reveal a gun on his belt.

Shit.

But the man standing just a few feet away, the guy in charge, displayed no weapon. In fact, he seemed to be trying to lull Tracey into some sort of trance. So deep and calm was his voice.

When Gamache took another step toward him, Tracey also stepped forward and thrust the pitchfork at the cop. 'Stop right there.'

The sharp tines stopped within a foot of Gamache's face. But he didn't flinch. Instead he looked right past the points. Straight into Tracey's eyes.

His gaze, Tracey saw with some alarm, wasn't angry. Wasn't threatening. Certainly wasn't frightened. It was thoughtful.

Anger, rage, violence Tracey could handle. But this was just confusing. And off-putting. And a little frightening.

Gamache, a pitchfork away from Tracey, could see the bloodshot eyes. And sense the havoc.

'I'm going to reach into my pocket and bring out my Sûreté ID.' As he spoke, he did just that, watching the man closely. Tracey's nostrils flared with each breath. Longing to attack. And he probably would have, Gamache knew, if it weren't for Cameron. And his earlier threat to beat Tracey. This man obviously knew it was not an empty threat.

While Gamache did not have a loaded gun, he did have Cameron. A biological weapon.

Bringing out the card, he offered it to Tracey, who pushed his head forward and read.

'It says here you're Chief Superintendent.'

'My new card hasn't arrived.'

'So you were the big boss, but not anymore?'

Tracey was more with-it than Gamache had given him credit for. Replacing the card, Gamache shrugged and smiled.

'I messed up. It happens.'

He looked at Tracey now with a slightly conspiratorial gaze. Wanting Tracey to try to guess what he could possibly have done to warrant such a demotion.

Gamache knew what a man like Tracey would naturally assume.

It would have to be something illegal. Almost certainly brutal. If Tracey thought Cameron was threatening, just wait for it . . .

So now Tracey was well and truly confused.

Gamache's manner was courteous, calm. But he intimated he was capable of something else.

'What do you want?' demanded Tracey.

'Do you know what I'd really like?'

'What?'

'Water. And to use your phone.'

'What?'

'Do you mind?' asked Gamache.

It appeared such a reasonable, though random, request that Tracey was struck dumb for a moment.

'There's a hose over there.' He gestured to the side of the barn. 'I'll bring the phone out. Make your call, then leave.'

'*Merci*. I'm most grateful.'

Everyone in the farmyard was now staring at Gamache with open astonishment, including the donkeys. But human behavior often astonished them.

'Are you okay, *patron*?' asked Cameron when Tracey left.

He'd walked over to the Chief and scanned him for blood, concerned he might have hit his head on a rock in one of the many falls as they'd made their way, slipping and sliding, up the hill.

'How would you have had me handle this?' Gamache asked as they walked over to the hose. 'Grab the pitchfork and beat him with it?'

Cameron flushed. It was, actually, exactly what he'd expected. And would have done.

Gamache gestured to the others to take the water first.

'You could've demanded to see Vivienne,' said Cloutier, reaching for the hose.

'I did ask.'

'Ask, yes, but couldn't you have pushed harder?'

'To what end? Do you know what he'd have done? Run us

off his property, and he'd have had every right. We have no warrant.' Gamache glanced behind him to make sure Tracey wasn't approaching. Then he lowered his voice.

'We have to assume we're dealing with a person capable of murdering his pregnant wife. And everything we've heard about him confirms he's abusive. Violent.'

Gamache reached over and patted a donkey, taking in the barnyard as he did. He also assumed Tracey was watching them from the house.

There were a lot of places to bury a body here. Though he doubted that Carl Tracey would be stupid enough to put her on their own property.

But then, people did stupid things. Like kill each other. And Carl Tracey did not strike him as the brightest of people.

Besides, he held out some hope that Vivienne Godin was indeed alive and had fled this terrible place.

'Violence, threats, he understands,' said Gamache quietly, as though speaking to the donkey, who was now nuzzling him. Leaving a slimy trail of drool and grass on his already filthy coat. 'The best way to keep Carl Tracey off balance is to be courteous. Didn't you notice how confused he became?'

'So you want us to be nice to him?' asked Cameron.

'Exactly. We can always ratchet it up later. Steps. Degrees. And always keep something in reserve. And,' said Gamache as he took the hose once Cameron had finished. 'We have to keep something else in mind.'

'That he's a killer,' said Cloutier.

Gamache bent over and drank. He was parched, and as he gulped, it struck him as ironic, and so like nature, to provide Tracey, a rancid man, with such sweet water.

'That he might be innocent,' said Gamache, lowering the hose, washing off his muddy hands, and turning off the tap.

'Of murder, let's hope,' said Cloutier. 'But not of beating his wife. His pregnant wife.'

'True,' said Gamache. 'But we're here to investigate, not convict. Try to keep your emotions in check. A clear head, right, Agent Cloutier?'

'*Oui, patron.*'

'You want the phone or not,' shouted Tracey, stepping off the porch and holding the handset out. 'Make the call and get off my fucking land.'

Gamache clicked it on and heard a dial tone. Finally, a phone that worked. In the background, almost unnoticed by now, was the sound of the Rivière Bella Bella, rushing toward Three Pines.

As Gamache dialed the number from memory, he watched Carl Tracey walk over to the donkeys, who nuzzled him, pushing him playfully. Tracey produced huge carrots and gave one to each.

The phone rang a few times before being answered.

'*Oui, allô,*' Gamache said, clearly relieved. 'Yes, everything's fine. No cell-phone coverage here, so I've had to borrow a phone. How are things with you? . . . I see. . . . Yes. Sandbagging. Good idea. . . . I will.' He looked at Tracey, who'd, at the mention of sandbagging, turned from the donkeys with a look of some alarm.

'But I do need a favor,' said Gamache. 'I'm at the farm where Vivienne Godin and her husband live. Carl Tracey refuses to answer questions or let us into the house or barn. I need a search warrant immediately. T-R-A-C-E-Y. . . . *Oui.*'

Tracey's face went slack. As though he'd been sandbagged.

'You can call back at this number,' continued Gamache. 'If you don't get an answer, send patrol cars up. They know the place. In fact, when the search warrant comes through,

send them up to help search. But tell them the road is pretty much impassable . . . No, everything's fine. I'll let you know when we have more news about Madame Godin. *Au revoir.*'

At Sûreté headquarters, Jean-Guy Beauvoir hung up and quickly made out a warrant request, then put in a call to a judge.

'Yes, Your Honor, we need it immediately. Chief Inspector Gamache is on-site and waiting. A woman is missing and perhaps murdered by her husband. I'm sending the request now.'

He hit the send key. 'Please let me know.'

Then he hung up and looked out the window.

The rain had begun. It was pissing April showers.

CHAPTER 8

———

Gamache handed the phone back to Tracey, with a smile. '*Merci.* Most helpful.'

'What the fuck was that?'

'You heard, Mr Tracey. In a few minutes, that phone will ring again. It'll be about a warrant to search your property. Best to answer it. Let's go into your house, and while we wait for the call confirming the search warrant, you can answer some questions.'

Tracey's face hardened. He looked like an obstinate child.

'Or not,' said Gamache pleasantly. 'But we're cold and wet and would appreciate your cooperation.'

He could almost hear Cameron and Cloutier gagging at his courteous tone.

Tracey, it seemed, had gotten the point. He gestured for them to follow.

The mud had hardened onto their coats and pant legs and boots. They looked and felt like Québec's version of the Terra-Cotta Warriors. The Sûreté officers took off their coats and boots, leaving them on the porch. But they couldn't very well remove their wet and filthy slacks.

Tracey had no such hesitation about trailing muck through his house and had kept his rubber boots on.

It was hot in the home, almost stifling. An elderly mutt lay by the woodstove in the kitchen.

'Beer walk soon,' said Tracey, gesturing toward the dog.

Gamache knew what that meant, though the others did not. He looked past the gray muzzle into the tired old eyes and thought of the walk into the woods, with the rifle.

And wondered if the same fate had befallen the dog's mistress.

Dishes, pots, and pans were piled into and out of the sink. The place stank of grease and rotting food. Booze and old dog and cigarettes. The smell was almost overpowering.

Gamache took a deep breath through his nose. Wondering if, in the sweltering heat, he could pick up another scent.

Something familiar. Something unmistakable. Something far worse.

But he could not. It was, perhaps, masked by the other rotting odors. But he doubted it. There was really no masking that one putrid stench.

The three Sûreté officers had joined Tracey at the Formica kitchen table. Tracey lit a cigarette while Cloutier and Cameron waited for Gamache to do something.

But he was doing something. Armand Gamache was listening.

For a sound, however remote, telling him that there was someone else in the home. A tapping. A muffled call.

Anything.

But there was only silence.

Finally he said, 'Monsieur Tracey, you say your wife isn't here. Do you know where she is?'

Cloutier had brought out her iPhone and was recording everything.

'I already told you cops. All I know is when I woke up yesterday morning, she was gone. No note, no nothin'.'

'Any ideas?'

Tracey laughed. 'She could be anywhere. On a bender. Shacked up with some guy. I'll tell you, when she comes back—'

He remembered, too late, who he was talking to.

'Yes?' said Gamache. 'Go on.'

'Nothin'.'

Armand Gamache had looked across lots of tables, at lots of murderers. He didn't kid himself that he had, even after all these years, some sort of special talent. To spot a killer.

He didn't really know if he was looking at one now. But he found himself increasingly repulsed by Carl Tracey.

'We understand from Vivienne's father that she's pregnant.'

'Yeah. Who knows who knocked her up? Doubt it's mine. And if she thinks I'm going to raise the bastard, she has another thing coming.'

'And what would she have coming?' asked Gamache.

Tracey smirked. 'How would you feel if your wife screwed another man and got pregnant?'

Gamache raised his chin and stared at Tracey.

And Carl Tracey stared back across the table into those calm, focused eyes and knew that while that shot had missed, this Sûreté officer was human. And therefore vulnerable. And he'd find that chink eventually.

'Aren't you worried at all about her?' asked Agent Cloutier.

Tracey took his eyes from Gamache and shifted to the woman cop. 'Why should I be? Look, like I said, she's probably just taken off, and when that guy gets tired of her, she'll come back. I don't even know why it's any of your business.'

Just then the phone rang.

'You might as well answer it,' said Tracey. 'It's for you.'

Gamache clicked it on, but before he could say anything,

he was met with a torrent of abuse. Culminating in the man shouting, 'Where's my daughter? If you don't tell me, I'm coming down, and I'm going to beat it out of you. You understand?'

Everyone in the room heard the voice, and Gamache could see Tracey looking triumphant.

See what I have to put up with? his expression said.

'Monsieur Godin?' Gamache began.

'Who is this?'

'My name is Gamache, I'm with the Sûreté—'

'Oh, God, has something happened? Have you found her? Oh, God—'

'*Non, monsieur.* We have no news of your daughter. I'm here with Lysette Cloutier. She's a friend of yours, I understand. Agent Cloutier asked us to investigate.'

There was heavy breathing on the other end as Godin composed himself.

'We're interviewing Monsieur Tracey right now.'

'Monsieur Tracey? Monsieur? The man's a monster and you call him "monsieur"? He might've . . . he could've . . . Do you know she's pregnant?'

'Yes. Please, calm yourself. We're doing all we can. I promise you, we'll find her.'

'You will. Alive?'

It was said so pathetically. Not just a word but a world. Alive. Alive. And all that meant. For him. For her. For the child. A life spread out before them. With birthdays and holidays. Celebrations.

Alive.

'We'll find her,' Gamache repeated, and wondered if Monsieur Godin noticed he hadn't said 'alive'. 'Do you have someone with you?'

'*Non, non.* Vivienne's my only child. My wife died a few years ago. I was expecting her here, you know. She was going to leave him. I'd begged her for years to leave that son of a bitch.'

There was a pause. Gamache heard heavy breathing, almost sobs, before Monsieur Godin was able to speak again.

'What has he done with her? Ask him. He knows. Make him tell you. If you don't, I will.'

'Stay at home, Monsieur Godin. In case she calls.'

Even as he said it, Gamache recognized it as cheap, potentially cruel manipulation. But he had to keep Godin away from Tracey. And there was still a chance his daughter was alive and would call her father.

'I'll be in touch with you when we're finished here. *D'accord?*'

There was a deep, deep breath on the other end of the line. And finally, *'D'accord.'*

'Can I speak to him?' whispered Cloutier, her hand out for the phone. 'Homer, it's Lysette. ... *Oui. Oui.* ... I promise. ... *Oui.'*

She'd dropped her eyes to the table and was listening intently. Homer Godin's voice was now quieter, so the others couldn't hear what he was saying.

'Chief Inspector Gamache will call you as soon as possible,' said Cloutier once Vivienne's father had stopped talking. '*Oui.* I promise.'

Her voice, gentle, calming, seemed to be having an effect. After saying goodbye, she placed the phone on the table.

'The man's a shithead,' said Tracey, speaking to the phone as though it were his father-in-law. 'You heard him threaten me. He's the dangerous one.'

'Enough,' said Cameron, hitting the table with such force

that the ceramic roosters took flight and spilled salt and pepper over the table.

'Agent Cameron,' said Gamache sharply.

'Sorry,' he muttered, bringing himself under control.

Gamache shifted his attention back to where it belonged. 'How long have you and Madame Godin been together?'

'I dunno. Four, five years.'

'How did you meet?'

'It was in a bar. Where did you think? Church? The gym? Look, I have things to do around the farm. Those animals need to be fed, and this one needs to be taken into the woods.'

He gestured toward the old dog, who looked up and gave a single, tired flop of his tail.

'Like you took Vivienne?' asked Cloutier.

'What? Kill her?' He made a dismissive noise. 'Why would I? Believe me, she's alive.'

Try as he might, Gamache couldn't get Monsieur Godin's voice out of his head. The deep breaths, the attempt to control the terror that seeped out anyway. The desperation of a father.

How would he feel if . . .

'You said she had lovers.' He was careful to keep his tone neutral. 'Can you give us names?'

'Of course not. She didn't exactly list them.'

'And women friends?' Gamache asked.

'Women? No. Why would she?'

It was as Cameron had said. Tracey had isolated his wife here, and since there was no one to contradict him, he was free to say anything he wanted about her.

'We're going to need the make, model, and license-plate number of her car,' said Cameron.

Tracey gave them the information.

'Where were you on Saturday?' Gamache asked.

'I was here, working on my pots. Where else?'

'Anybody see you?'

'Vivienne did. You can ask her when she gets back.'

'Anyone besides your wife.'

'No. Who'd come here?'

Who indeed? thought Gamache.

'So you never left the property on Saturday?'

'No. Wait a minute, I did go into town to buy supplies. Needed to get them before the road turned shitty. Can't drive on it now.' He eyed them closely. 'But that's probably not news to you.'

'And yet,' said Cloutier, 'you say your wife managed to drive out later in the day.'

There was silence, and they could see Tracey's brain skidding in the muck.

'She could, but you couldn't?' Cloutier pressed.

'She left at night, when the roads had frozen again.'

He'd hit on an explanation bordering on reasonable. After Tracey had given them the names of the stores he'd visited, Gamache asked, 'When was the last time you saw your wife?'

'Saturday night, like I said. We'd been drinking. Vivienne got pissed and started yelling abuse. Told me the kid wasn't mine. I went into my studio to do some work and get away from her. When I got up next morning, she was gone.'

The phone rang.

'You take it,' said Tracey.

Gamache picked it up and listened. *'Bon. Merci.'* He hung up. 'We have the warrant.'

CHAPTER 9

L ike the rest of the house, the bedroom was a shambles. Bed unmade, bedding dirty. A partly drunk bottle of beer was on the floor next to the bed. An ashtray was overflowing with butts.

In the bedside table, there was a small stash of pot. And rolling papers.

'Yours?' Gamache asked Tracey.

'Hers.'

Gamache nodded, taking that in but not necessarily believing it.

The clock radio blinked 12:00.

Gamache stood in the middle of the room and turned full circle. Clothing was left on the floor where it fell. Socks, underwear, sweaters, jeans. Not just one day's worth but days. And days.

An agent was going through the closet and the dresser drawers, photographing and cataloging what was there.

It was very difficult to tell if anything had been taken.

Gamache asked Tracey about the clothes. Were they all his? Were some Vivienne's?

'All mine.'

In Vivienne's closet clothing was hung up. Her drawers were a bit haphazard, with underwear and turtlenecks and jeans shoved in. But at least clean and off the floor.

Looking at the top of the dresser, he noticed jewelry. Inexpensive. Bright. Bulbous. No photographs, though.

She might've taken those with her.

Gamache hoped that was true.

'Is there a suitcase missing?' Gamache asked.

'Suitcase? We don't have any of those. Why would we?'

Gamache nodded. That alone was pretty telling. And slightly chilling.

In the bathroom, Gamache pointed to a toothbrush. 'Is this hers?'

'No. That's mine. This's hers.' Tracey pointed to the other one in the holder. The bristles were worn almost flat.

Maybe she'd left this one and bought a new one, Gamache thought.

He hoped that was true.

The forensics officer bagged both brushes. For DNA testing.

Gamache opened the medicine cabinet. Nothing extraordinary there. No prescriptions, just cold meds and ointments. There were no gaps on the narrow shelves. Nothing obviously missing.

Then he left and walked from room to room, with Tracey following him. A shadow.

Other officers arrived and were searching the outbuildings.

'There's no sign of her, *patron*,' reported Agent Cloutier. She found him in the living room, kneeling by the sofa. 'But they have found something, just off the kitchen.'

'I'll be right along, *merci*.' He brought out a pen and moved a potato-chip wrapper aside. Then, standing up, he called to the forensics officer in the room. 'Can you check this, please?'

He stepped away and turned to Tracey. 'I think it's blood. Is it?'

'Could be. Might be hers. Might be mine. Who knows?'

'We will, soon. What happened here?'

'I told you. We got into a fight.'

'You hit her?'

'And she hit me. Gave as good as she got. Look, I know you think I've done something, but I didn't. I left her here.' He pointed to the sofa. 'Alive.'

'Check the rest of the room carefully,' Gamache advised the officer.

Brushing past Tracey without a word, Gamache followed Agent Cloutier into the kitchen and through a door he'd assumed was a pantry. But instead it led into what had once maybe been an outhouse. Or a pigsty or chicken coop. It had been knocked through to connect to the main house.

He stood at the door and prepared himself. Clearly there was no body inside. He'd have been told right away. Nor was this an obvious crime scene. Again, he'd have been told.

But it did strike him as a place where unpleasant things might have happened. To animals. Or people.

He went in.

What struck him first was the extraordinary heat.

The agents working in there were perspiring and trying not to drip sweat and contaminate the room. On seeing him they stood up and started to salute. But with a gesture he stopped them and indicated they should continue working.

Then he looked around.

Not a slaughterhouse at all. Not an old outhouse. It was much larger than that. An old garage. Converted into a workshop.

No, not a workshop. A studio.

He saw a potter's wheel. He saw plastic bags filled with clay, their tags still on. The walls were lined with shelves holding unglazed pieces. He saw what Cameron had meant. No one could possibly use Tracey's works for anything practical. They wouldn't hold food or drink or flowers.

But they did hold the attention. Not unlike the man himself.

Carl Tracey seemed an unfinished, partially formed man. Soft. Useless. And yet there was also something about the man. Not attractive. In fact, Gamache felt repulsed by him. But he also felt his eyes returning to him. Carl Tracey was a presence. There was no denying that. A statement piece. Like his works.

But while his pottery looked, to Gamache's eye, good, Tracey did not.

Gamache turned and saw, in the corner, the source of the extraordinary heat.

A kiln.

It had obviously been fired up in the last day or so.

Kneeling down, he looked into the opening in the bottom of the kiln. It was filled with ash.

'Make sure you collect this,' he said, straightening up. 'Have you found anything?'

'Not yet,' said the agent in charge. 'If there's any blood here, it'd be impossible to hide or clean. The bricks and clay are porous. If it's here, we'll find it.'

'*Bon. Merci.*'

He turned and saw Carl Tracey looking in.

'The kiln's been used recently,' said Gamache.

'Yes. I was firing some works.'

'When?'

'Saturday night.'

'It's still hot.'

'Takes a long time to cool down. Needs to be really hot to bake the clay.' He examined Gamache, then laughed. 'You don't think ...' He looked astonished. 'You actually think I stuck Vivienne in there? Piece by piece? Are you crazy? Do you know how much work that would be? And imagine the mess.'

Gamache knew Tracey was trying to get under his skin. Denying the murder and cremation of a woman and her unborn child not because it was abhorrent but because it was too much work.

'Look,' Tracey said as he followed Gamache into the kitchen, 'it wasn't much of a marriage, but she did her thing, I did mine. Why would I kill her?'

'Why would you kill him?' Gamache pointed to the old dog, still lying by the warm stove.

'Because he's no use anymore. He can't hunt and isn't gonna guard the place. He just eats and shits. Gonna get a new dog. A better dog.'

'Maybe that's why you'd kill your wife,' said Gamache. 'So that you could get a new one.'

'Why kill her? I'd just chuck her out.'

'Because she'd take you to court and get half the property,' said Gamache.

'Yes,' said Tracey, nodding. 'That would be a good reason.'

It was as close to a confession, without actually being one, that the head of homicide had heard.

Tracey looked down at the dog. 'He's not mine. He's hers. Came with her, and he can leave with her. The sooner the better.'

He made a shooting gesture with his hand. The dog struggled up, took a step closer to Tracey, and licked the trigger finger.

*

They found nothing. After conferring with the local agents, it was decided they'd done all they could. It was time to leave.

'What do we do now?' asked Agent Cameron as they put on their coats and boots.

They stepped onto the porch and looked around, at the acres and acres. Miles and miles. Of forest. At the donkeys in the field. Patiently watching them.

And they heard, again, the growl of the Bella Bella, from deep in the woods.

It seemed louder. Closer.

'First step is to declare Vivienne Godin missing,' said Gamache. 'And then to visit her father.'

A large drop landed with a plop at the foot of the steps. Then another.

He looked up. It was early afternoon, but the clouds were so thick, and the sun so obscured, that it felt like dusk. Or an eclipse.

Gamache put his hand in his pocket but remembered that there was no cell-phone coverage.

'Can you give us a lift back to our cars?' Gamache asked one of the agents.

'Absolutely, sir. I saw them when we arrived. Just down the hill.'

'Right. How'd you manage to get up the hill?'

'We didn't. We came around and down from the other side.'

She glanced again at the Chief Inspector's clothing. He and the others looked like they'd crawled up the muddy slope on their hands and knees to this terrible place.

Which they practically had.

'Do you have a radio in your car?' asked Gamache.

'Yessir. We're all equipped with them, in case our phones don't work.'

'Good.' Gamache turned to Carl Tracey, who'd just stepped onto the porch. The old dog at his side. 'We'll be in touch with more questions, I'm sure.'

'He's done it, hasn't he?' said Agent Cloutier as they walked to the Sûreté vehicle. 'Killed her.'

Gamache said nothing but looked grim.

Once at the car, he leaned in and, taking the handset off its hook, identified himself and asked to be put through to Chief Inspector Beauvoir of homicide.

As he waited, more rain fell. Tracey disappeared off the porch and reappeared with a .22 rifle.

'How does he have that?' asked Gamache. 'Does he have a permit?'

'Unfortunately, yes,' said Cameron. 'He's never been convicted of an offense, so there was no way to take it from him. We didn't find any others.'

Gamache shook his head. As strict as the laws were governing firearms in Canada, they could be tighter. Here was a man known to abuse his wife, and he's allowed to have a gun?

'Did you test it? Has it been fired recently?'

'We tested, and no, it hasn't been fired in a while.'

Gamache looked into the dog's eyes and knew that was about to change.

'There you are, finally,' Beauvoir's voice came out the tinny speaker. 'Did you get my messages?'

'No, we're out of cell-phone coverage. About what?'

'A state of emergency's been declared. Leaves have been canceled. There's flooding across the province. Looks bad.'

'The dams?'

'Hydro's sending engineers up there now to assess the situation.'

If they burst . . .

But Gamache didn't say it. They all knew what would happen if the massive hydroelectric dams in James Bay were breached.

But that wasn't the only potential disaster.

'Where's the worst flooding?'

Beauvoir detailed it. As he spoke, Gamache visualized the map of Québec and saw the danger points. Where rivers met larger rivers. Inevitably that was also where towns and cities had been built. At the junctions of the great waterways.

'The St. Lawrence?' he asked. And held his breath. Though in his heart he knew the answer already. He'd seen the ice buildup just a few hours earlier and had called it in.

Beauvoir quickly and succinctly described the affected areas. Ending with the worst-hit.

'Montréal.'

'Montréal,' repeated Gamache.

'I've been trying to reach you. There's a meeting here they want you at. Starting in half an hour. How soon can you get back?'

Gamache looked at his watch. 'I can be there in forty minutes.'

'Hurry.'

'Jean-Guy?'

'*Oui?*'

'The Bella Bella?'

'Still rising.'

Gamache looked south. Toward his village. He could be there in minutes. Then he looked north. To Montréal.

'*Merci,*' said Gamache. 'I'll be there as soon as possible.'

He gave the handset back to the agent and started to walk around to the passenger side. But paused.

'Sir?' asked the agent. The car was running. Waiting.

'*Un moment,*' said Gamache.

As the others watched, the Chief Inspector walked back to the porch, took out his wallet, placed bills at Tracey's feet. Then walked back to the car. The old dog in his arms.

As he got in, he said, 'His name's Fred.'

CHAPTER 10

⌒

The patrol car slid down the road, but the agent managed to guide it to where they'd left their vehicles. She dropped them off and continued down the hill. Opening the windows to air out her once-pristine vehicle. That now smelled of old wet dog, and mud, and donkeys.

'What do we do now, *patron*?' asked Cameron as they stood in the rain outside their cars.

'You return to your station. You'll be needed for flood control or evacuations. We're heading back to Montréal.'

Once in the car, Agent Cloutier asked, 'What about Vivienne? What do I tell Homer?'

'I'll call him once we're out of the mountains and have communications.'

Rain was hitting the windshield. The clouds were low, mingling with the mist clinging to the forest.

'Can I stay on it, though? Keep looking for her?'

'You'll do as you're ordered, Agent Cloutier,' said Gamache. 'As will I.'

He turned toward the woods, where the Bella Bella, invisible, was rushing toward the valley. And the village.

*

Ruth stood at the top of the fieldstone bridge and watched the activity around her.

The whole village was out, filling sandbags. It was something they did most springs, but until now it had been a precaution, that had morphed into a tradition, that had become a party. A celebration. To mark the end of a long winter.

The spring runoff often coincided with the running of the maple sap.

They'd fill sandbags and hold a sugaring-off party, with baked beans and crêpes and cauldrons boiling down the sap into syrup. A fiddler played as children, and Gabri, stood around the pots waiting to pour the sweet liquid onto snow, where it turned into a sort of soft caramel called *tire d'érable*.

While mothers and fathers, friends and neighbors filled sandbags to build walls along the Bella Bella, children, and Gabri, used twigs to roll the *tire*, then ate the maple candy and watched horses return from the forest bearing buckets brimming with more sap.

It was a festive end to winter. After all, the river had never broken her banks. There'd never been reason to worry.

But today was different. The fiddler was holding a shovel. The kids were safely in St. Thomas's Church, their evacuation center. There was no *tire*. Only tired and sodden villagers.

Ruth stood in the rain, almost sleet, and watched as they bowed, then straightened, then bowed again, filling the sandbags in what looked like a pagan ritual.

But if this was a ritual, it was to an angry, vindictive deity.

I just sit where I'm put, composed / of stone and wishful thinking. Ruth muttered one of her own poems as she watched her neighbors and friends bow and lift. Bend and shovel. *That the deity who kills for pleasure / will also heal.*

Villagers, under Ruth's direction, had formed two lines

and were passing the bags along, then piling them one on top of the other. Building a wall on either side of the Bella Bella.

The old poet turned from surveying her dripping and dirty neighbors and looked upstream.

She tried not to let her face reflect her feelings. Gnawing her cheek to stop the fear from showing, she looked at the Bella Bella. Until recently it had been beige with froth, but now it was almost black. As the churning became more and more violent. Dredging up muck and sediment and God knew what else from the river bottom. Things left undisturbed for decades, centuries perhaps, were now roiling to the surface. Rotten. Decayed.

Ruth watched as the bloated river swept great chunks of ice and tree limbs down the mountain. Crashing toward them. Jamming, then breaking apart.

But eventually, she knew, the jam would be too dense. The debris too solid. It would hold. And then . . . ?

Until this day, the villagers had considered the Bella Bella a friendly, gentle presence. It would never hurt them.

Now it was as though someone they thought they knew well, someone they loved and trusted, had turned on them. The only thing more shocking would be if the three huge pine trees in the center of the village broke free and began to attack them.

Gabri and Olivier were handing out hot drinks. Tea, coffee, hot chocolate, and soup. Monsieur Béliveau, the grocer, and Sarah the baker, were taking around trays of sandwiches. Brie and thick slices of maple-cured ham, and arugula on baguettes and croissants, and *pain ménage*.

Though the most popular proved to be the ones Reine-Marie had made before she took a place in the line, filling sandbags.

'God,' said Clara, taking a huge bite. 'These are delicious.'

Her gloves were wet through, and her large hands trembled in the cold.

'What do you have?' asked Myrna as she swallowed a huge bite of baguette.

'Peanut butter and honey on Wonder Bread,' said Clara, barely intelligible through the thick peanut butter.

'Oh, jeez,' said Myrna, breaking from the line and turning to look for Sarah the baker. 'I'm going to get one of those.'

'Here,' said Billy Williams. 'Take mine.'

Though he was famished, he offered her half his sandwich.

Myrna smiled and shook her head. 'It's okay. I'll get my own. But thanks.'

Billy looked after her, then down at his damp sandwich. And understood that he had nothing that Myrna wanted.

She was unattainable, and he worried he'd love her for the rest of his life.

Gabri walked over to the bridge and offered Ruth a coffee. 'I put a shot of brandy in it.'

'That's okay,' shouted the old poet over the sound of the river. She reached for a steaming mug. 'I'll take the soup.'

Gabri paled. It was, he knew, a sign of the End of Days. Ruth refusing booze.

He looked down and saw that the river was not just angry, there was a madness about it. As though all the indignities visited on all the waterways in the New World, by generations of settlers, were coming to the surface.

The waters were rising up, not in protest but in revenge.

He could barely hear himself think for the howling.

It was, he thought as he walked off the bridge, the sound a soul might make as it approached hell.

*

Gamache's mind was racing. Had they thought to open the spillways for the dams across the province?

Hospitals needed to be put on alert. Other provinces contacted and asked for possible assistance. The water-filtration plants needed to be protected. Hydro crews needed to be ready to restore power. Military reserves and first responders called out. Emergency measures put in place.

A sudden catastrophic event, natural or otherwise, brought with it turmoil. Places so pastoral and pretty one minute became war zones the next.

A populace unused to these sudden emergencies needed to be rallied and directed. And kept calm.

It was vital to take control.

Gamache tried to stop his mind from going there. And his hand from reaching for his phone to call Emergency Management. Call his successor at the Sûreté. Call the Premier Ministre. And tell them what to do.

Instead he took a deep breath and forced himself to sit back in the passenger seat.

This was no longer his job. No longer his responsibility. They knew what they were doing. They did not need him.

Still, he felt like a swimmer treading water offshore. Watching some terrible event unfold on the mainland and being unable to stop it. Or even help.

Once out of the mountains, his phone had gone wild with emails. Texts. Phone messages.

He tried Reine-Marie first and finally got through to Olivier in the bistro, who called Reine-Marie in.

'We're all right, Armand. Sandbagging, of course. But there's no panic.'

'Ruth didn't—'

'Put valium in the hot chocolate again?' asked Reine-Marie. '*Non*. But I am feeling very, very calm.'

Actually, she sounded tired.

'How is it really?' he asked.

'We're getting the barriers built. The Bella Bella's higher than anyone's ever seen it. A few inches from the top. But even if it floods, it won't be too bad.'

Reine-Marie had never been in a flood. He had. It wasn't just a few inches of water in basements. A wave of water, even a small one, that had traveled that distance contained almost unimaginable energy. The force of even a minor breach could knock down walls. Buildings. Wells would be contaminated. Power lines knocked over. People, animals swept away.

It didn't take as much water as people thought.

'I'll get there as soon as I can.'

'Where are you?'

'There's a state of emergency. I'm on my way into Montréal.'

There was the briefest of pauses. 'Of course.'

She'd tried to sound upbeat, but the disappointment in her voice took his breath away. He was heading away from her, not to her.

'I'm sorry.'

'Don't you dare be sorry. We're fine. We really are. Be careful. You have your water wings?'

'The blow-up swan? Always.'

'Good. Make sure you wear it.'

He laughed. 'Now, that would be a photo for social media.'

Hearing her laughter as she imagined her husband in suit, tie, and pink swan around his waist, directing emergency operations, went some way to healing his heart. They talked another minute or so before hanging up.

Then he phoned Monsieur Godin. It was a difficult call. He had to tell Vivienne's father that the search for his daughter was temporarily on hold, during the emergency. But would be resumed as soon as possible.

'You can't stop,' said Homer. 'You have to find her. You promised.'

'I'm sorry,' said Gamache. 'There's nothing we can do right now, but believe me—'

'I'm coming down.'

'No, don't.' Gamache's voice was sharp. 'The roads will wash out soon. Bridges will be closed. You'll be trapped away from home. Stay where you are. In case she calls.'

There it was again. Giving Vivienne's father what Gamache suspected was false hope. For a call he was more and more convinced would never come.

But he had to keep the man away. For any number of reasons, not just the flooding.

As soon as he hung up, Agent Cloutier put the siren on. They were on the autoroute now, racing toward the city. As they headed over the Champlain Bridge, he asked her to pull over and put the flashers on.

'But there's no emergency lane, sir. We'll block traffic.'

'This won't take long.'

Once the car stopped, he got out quickly, before he could change his mind.

Hardly believing he was doing this, he made for the side of the bridge.

It was only a few steps away, but he had to fight for every inch.

Terrified of heights and suffering from vertigo, he felt himself grow instantly light-headed. And wondered if he'd pass out.

But he had to look. Had to see.

He battled his way forward, just a few feet that felt like miles. Reaching out, he gripped the concrete wall that separated him from the void. The wind and rain hit his face. Closing his eyes, he took a deep breath. Then, opening them, he leaned out.

And gasped. His eyes wide, his knuckles white.

The world seemed to spin, and he realized, with horror, that he was in danger not of falling but of throwing himself off the bridge. The vertigo was dragging him over the edge. And there was nothing to stop his fall. Nothing between the bridge and the water.

He could hear, as though from very, very far away, cars honking. He thought he heard his own name called and had the peculiar feeling it was coming from the void below.

But still he stared, willing his eyes to focus.

And when they did, he saw. It was worse than that morning. Much worse. Ice was heaving, pushing against the pylons of the bridge. Halfway up already, and climbing.

He looked out at the wide, wide expanse of river. Some open water was visible, dark jagged lines between the fissures. The ice floes, many feet thick, were crashing together. Mounting each other. Forcing huge shards of ice to jut out.

Then he heard the rumble and forced himself to look farther out, farther upriver. The sound grew louder and louder, moving quickly now. A frost quake was tearing toward the bridge.

Gamache took a couple of deep breaths. And tightened his grip on the low concrete wall.

Trying not to close his eyes. Trying not to flinch.

He stood up slightly straighter as the rumble turned into a roar.

And then the boom. Like cannon fire, as the ice ruptured under the pressure. About fifty meters away.

He exhaled.

If it was this bad here, it must be just as bad, if not worse, all around the island of Montréal. Never mind all the other rivers. All the other bridges, across Québec.

He needed to leave. To make it to that meeting at headquarters. But first he had to get back to the car. Across the vast few feet of asphalt. He found that his grip was so tight he couldn't let go.

He ripped his hands off the concrete and, turning, took a few shaky steps, then practically threw himself the last three feet.

'*Patron?*' asked Agent Cloutier on seeing his face.

'It's all right,' Gamache said, his hands in tight fists so that the trembling wouldn't show. 'But we need to hurry.'

Sûreté headquarters was buzzing. Officers rushing along the hallways.

Bullpens on each floor were all but empty, only skeleton crews remaining to answer calls and continue the most urgent of investigations.

Everyone else had been reassigned to the flooding.

Gamache went directly to homicide and met briefly with Jean-Guy.

On entering the office, he saw Beauvoir on the phone, looking energized, in his element. Though the younger man would no doubt fiercely deny it, Jean-Guy Beauvoir liked nothing better than an emergency.

He hung up and raised his brows. 'Been to a spa?'

'Spa?'

'Mud bath.'

'Oh, that.' Gamache looked down at his caked coat and slacks. He'd forgotten that he was covered in muck. 'More like mud wrestling.'

'Who won?'

'Not me.' He took off his heavy coat and hung it on the hook at the back of the door. 'I'll tell you about it later. Oh, there is one thing I'd like to leave here with you. Do you mind?'

'Not at all.'

'His name's Fred. He might like some water.'

He left the bedraggled dog and the befuddled man staring at each other and hurried upstairs.

The meeting in Chief Superintendent Toussaint's office was well under way by the time Gamache arrived.

He'd made a quick trip to the bathroom and tried to clean up, but the facilities and time didn't allow for much more than a good scrub of his hands and face.

He looked in the mirror and ran his hands through his hair.

Then shook his head and gave up. There were far more important things to focus on.

'Chief Inspector.'

Chief Superintendent Madeleine Toussaint greeted her predecessor. If she noticed his unusually disheveled appearance, she didn't show it. 'You know everyone here.'

She was confident enough to invite her predecessor to the meeting and savvy enough about the realpolitik of power to highlight Gamache's diminished status by emphasizing his new rank.

There were senior representatives from the Corps of Military Engineers, from the RCMP, from Hydro-Québec. Environment Canada's chief meteorologist was there, as was the Deputy Premier of Québec.

All men and women Gamache knew well.

'I see some of the crap thrown at you today on Twitter has stuck,' said the senior officer from the RCMP, gesturing at Gamache's clothing.

Gamache smiled. 'Fortunately, it won't stain.'

'But it does smell,' said the Mountie, with a wry smile. 'Helluva first day back on the job, Armand.'

'It is that.'

'We were going over the situation,' said Toussaint, bristling slightly at the obvious familiarity and warmth between Gamache and the RCMP officer.

She waved him to the huge ordnance map of the province, where the others had gathered.

It didn't just show where the problems were now, but also the knock-on effects farther downriver. And Québec had a lot of rivers, a lot of water.

Gamache had bent over many such maps, from his time occupying this very office. Ones that showed criminal activity and natural disasters.

But he'd never seen anything quite like this.

There were so many markings the map was almost unrecognizable.

'I was just about to show this,' said the chief meteorologist. She nodded to a colleague who was sitting at a laptop. After a few taps, another map of Québec appeared, projected on the wall. 'These are our predictions of what we think could happen in the next twenty-four hours.'

An animation began playing, but nothing Disney would recognize.

It showed a natural disaster of epic scope. As rivers flowed into each other. As ice jams piled up. As tributaries broke their banks.

Whole islands disappeared.

Populated islands, Gamache knew.

His eyes widened, and his stomach twisted. Cities and towns that had stood for centuries, along the St. Lawrence in particular, were engulfed.

And then it stopped. And the water receded. Leaving mud and rubble.

Below the animation was a timeline. All this took just a day.

There was silence in the room. And finally the chief meteorologist spoke.

'Would you like to see it again?'

'*Non*,' they said in unison.

Non. It wasn't necessary. Everyone in that room would go to their graves with those images playing.

'That's the worst-case scenario,' said the meteorologist. 'If the dams burst. Unlikely, but possible.'

Gamache wanted to ask the Hydro rep the only question that mattered at the moment.

Will they hold?

But he refrained, knowing this was Toussaint's meeting. Not wanting to undermine her.

While the others looked to him, he turned to her. And slowly they all looked at the new Chief Superintendent.

'Will they hold?' the Mountie finally asked.

The Hydro-Québec rep gave a curt nod. Her face grim. 'They're holding for now. The thaw hasn't reached that far north yet. And when it does, we can open the floodgates and relieve the pressure.'

Gamache turned to Toussaint, who was clearly thinking.

Ask, he thought. *Ask*.

'Will it work?' she asked.

'If the gates don't jam, and if the ice pressure on the structure isn't too great, yes.'

If, if, if . . .

There was silence in the room while they replayed the animation in their heads, if the ifs didn't happen.

'But even if they hold,' the meteorologist added, 'what we're looking at is a catastrophic combination of record snowfall through the winter, record cold creating thick ice, a flash thaw and freeze-up, and now heavy rains. So that the melt is pouring into the rivers before the ground has thawed and the ice has left. Backing everything up.'

'Right,' said the Deputy Premier. 'We can see that. The question is, what do we do about it?'

'There're emergency measures—'

'Yes, yes,' he said. 'I know that. That's how we're responding. I want to know how to stop this. Or at least lessen the impact. What can we do?'

His voice wasn't just urgent, it was tinged with panic and some petulance. A child who suspects he won't be getting what he wants.

Silence met his pleas.

Gamache had put on his reading glasses and now glanced over at the chief meteorologist. He'd had many meetings with her, in this very room. Leaning over ordnance maps.

But never had he heard the dry, precise, careful scientist use that word.

Catastrophic.

'What do you think?' he asked.

'It's our worst fear realized,' said the meteorologist, her voice weak with exhaustion. Her shoulders sagged. 'What wakes any forecaster in the small hours. *All that most maddens and torments.*'

'What're you talking about?' demanded the politician. 'Was that some quote? Have you lost your mind?'

Gamache recognized the quote, though he couldn't quite place where it was from.

'Maybe,' said the meteorologist, rubbing her face. 'I've been up for two days solid running simulations. I do feel as though my brain is caked.'

'You wanted to say something, Chief Inspector?' Once again Toussaint emphasized his rank.

He'd removed his glasses and was looking at her intently.

But she'd also been watching him. From the moment he arrived, she'd been waiting for Gamache to take over.

But instead he'd held off. Deferring to her.

It appeared respectful, but now she wondered if he had another reason. Did he see, even before she did, that whoever was in charge would be blamed?

Madeleine Toussaint was beginning to appreciate her mistake. And the near-impossible position she found herself in. If she took charge, she'd be blamed if her ideas failed. If she let Gamache take over, all her authority would disappear.

She'd invited him to the meeting partly for his expertise, but she'd also seen her chance to make a point in front of the other senior officials.

There was a new sheriff in town. The old one was weakened, diminished. Demoted.

She hadn't counted on the fact that the others in the room would naturally turn to him. Out of habit, perhaps. Or because he still commanded their respect.

Except for the Deputy Premier, of course. Who despised the man.

Nor had she counted on the fact Gamache would voluntarily hand the lead to her. In an act of apparent humility.

Toussaint hadn't seen her former boss in months, but now, seeing him again, she felt some shame at doing this to him.

But mostly she felt annoyance. That he didn't seem to notice he'd been diminished.

Gamache tapped the map with his glasses, then looked at her. 'We might have less time than you think.'

He told them about the ice and the Champlain Bridge.

'How do you know about it?' Toussaint asked.

'Because I looked.'

'How?'

'I got out of the car just now and looked.'

'Over the edge?' she asked. 'You stood on the bridge and looked over?'

While Gamache's fear of heights was not generally known, those who had served with him longest knew, or at least suspected, he had that phobia.

'I did.'

'That means the bridges will have to be closed soon,' she said to him. 'And roads, I expect.'

Gamache gave the tiniest of nods. Of agreement. And Toussaint felt both gratified and annoyed at herself, for wanting, needing, his approval.

'Demolition teams are on their way to the major trouble spots,' said the head of the Corps of Engineers for the Armed Forces. 'Including the Hydro dams, of course. We'll blow the ice jams, if necessary.'

'Good. Thank you, Colonel,' said Toussaint, regaining control.

'Wait a minute,' said the Deputy Premier. 'You're suggesting setting off explosions all over the province? Can you imagine the panic?'

'I'd rather be panicked than drowned,' said the military officer.

'But can't we do anything else?' asked the politician.

'Like stop the rain, sir?' asked the chief meteorologist. 'I've tried. Doesn't work.'

'I have a thought.' Gamache turned to the Hydro rep. 'You talked about the floodgates. Can we do the same thing farther south?'

'There are no dams farther south. No gates to open.'

'I know, but we can dig runoffs, can't we? It comes to the same thing.'

He looked around for support.

'I can't see that working,' said Toussaint.

'Why not?' Gamache asked, apparently genuinely interested. 'What're you thinking?'

'I think it would take far too much equipment to do anything effective,' she said. 'We'd have to divert some from the dams, and that's just too dangerous. It would leave them vulnerable.'

'That's a good point,' said Gamache, returning to stare at the map.

'Still,' said the RCMP officer. 'If we could, it would relieve some of the smaller rivers. We could divert the water before it gets to the big rivers.'

'Chief Superintendent Toussaint is right,' said the head of the Corps of Engineers. 'It would take a huge amount of equipment and personnel, and we just don't have the resources for that. The crisis is moving quickly and is widespread. Emergencies have just been declared in Ontario and the Maritime provinces. We're deploying across the east.'

'Wait a minute,' said the politician. 'Are you saying that not only are you not giving us more people and equipment, you're actually taking some away?'

'I was going to tell you,' said the colonel.

'When? When we're treading water?'

'The Van Doos will be assigned to help, but that's all,' said the colonel, refusing to be provoked. 'We need the other regiments for other areas.'

Gamache straightened up. The Royal 22e Régiment of the Canadian Armed Forces was based just outside Québec City. A storied regiment, affectionately nicknamed the Van Doos, they'd be, Gamache knew, a formidable help in any emergency and had already been deployed.

But they would not be enough. Not nearly.

He, along with everyone else in the room, looked with some dismay at the senior armed forces engineer, who dropped her eyes before meeting their stares again.

'Désolée.'

As were they.

'But if you redirect most of the resources we do have, it could be done,' pressed the RCMP officer.

'I don't like the sound of that,' said the Deputy Premier.

'You don't like the idea of setting off explosions, you don't like redirecting resources,' said the Mountie. 'You demand action, then refuse to actually act.'

Toussaint turned to Gamache, seeing her chance. 'What do you suggest?'

Two people could play at humility, and this would put him not in the driver's seat but in the hot seat.

'It's a risk,' agreed Gamache. 'But one I think we need to take.'

'Just to be clear,' said the Hydro rep. 'Are you suggesting removing the equipment and teams from the dams?'

'Yes,' said Gamache, nodding slowly. He turned to the chief meteorologist. 'You said it yourself. The thaw hasn't hit there yet. Might not. Why keep precious resources there when they're needed down south, where the crisis isn't just imminent, it's upon us.'

'Because if the dams go, we're blown back into the Stone Age,' said Toussaint. 'If there's a flash thaw, like there has been down south, we're screwed. We won't be able to get the workers and equipment back up there fast enough. If even one of those dams breaks . . .'

She didn't need to say more. They all finished her thought.

Hundreds of millions of tons of water would be released, shooting straight down the province. Gathering ice and debris. Trees. Houses, cars, bridges. Animals. People.

Until much of Québec was smeared across Vermont.

'So we have a choice,' said the colonel. 'Keep the dams safe and guarantee terrible flooding down south. Or risk the dams.'

'Like you say,' said the RCMP officer. 'One's a risk, the other's a certainty.'

'To put it another way,' said the colonel. 'One's catastrophic, the other's Armageddon.'

It sounded melodramatic, but anyone who'd witnessed a tidal wave, a tsunami, would know it was no exaggeration.

The Deputy Premier moaned.

'Bet you're glad you're not sitting in my seat now,' Toussaint said to Gamache.

He smiled. 'I'm glad you're in this office, yes. We all are.'

She doubted that was true. 'Any more advice, Armand?'

He thought, looking at the map. 'I think you should open the sluice gates at the dams now. As a precaution—'

'But we'd lose power,' said the Hydro rep, and the politician moaned again.

'*Non*. You'd lose money. But we both know you have plenty of power in reserve you could use.' Gamache stared at the executive. 'We won't be shivering in the cold and dark just yet.'

That had been a threat, by Hydro, by politicians, for decades, justifying all sorts of draconian measures by the massive utility.

There was a long silence before the Hydro exec gave a curt nod. The politician just glared at Gamache. The old lie exposed.

'You keep one team at the most vulnerable dam,' said Gamache. 'In case opening the gates isn't enough. Then redirect all possible resources to digging those runoffs, the spillways along the tributaries.'

'*Merci*,' Toussaint said, in an attempt to interrupt. To stop this torrent of advice.

'There're clearly key spots,' the colonel from the Corps of Engineers said, taking up the suggestion and pointing to several rivers. 'We can choose a dozen of the most significant tributaries. Maybe here . . . and here.'

'*Oui*,' said Gamache, familiar with the terrain. 'We don't have to divert all of them.' He looked up from the map and held Toussaint's eyes. 'And we could get local farmers to help. Use their equipment to dig—'

'We?' she asked, and once again the room grew still. Except for the smile that was spreading across the politician's face.

'You,' said Armand, straightening up and removing his reading glasses. 'This's your operation, Chief Superintendent. You asked for my help and advice. I'm simply giving it.'

'Thank you.'

'A battle might be won on a single front,' he pressed on. 'But a war is won on many. You're concentrating your forces on the most urgent need. Which makes sense. But you can also get out in front of the crisis. Though it is a risk.'

'Not just a risk, Gamache,' said the Deputy Premier. 'It's reckless.'

While the others watched, Gamache raised his head and turned to the politician.

'This would be a calculated risk, *monsieur*.' His voice formal, freezing. Those listening were surprised the words didn't come out in an icy vapor. 'There's more risk in paralysis. In reckless indecision.'

'You think so? Maybe we should ask those under your command who were wounded and killed because of your so-called calculated risks. You shouldn't even be here. You should be at home, or guarding some Walmart. Or in prison.'

No one spoke, no one breathed. Eyes opened wide. Even Madeleine Toussaint was shocked by the vitriol.

'Chief Superintendent Gamache did—' she began, but a look from the politician silenced her.

'When your committee offered me the chance to return as head of homicide, sir,' said Gamache, glaring at the Deputy Premier, 'you must've known there was a risk that I'd take it.'

At least two in the room snorted in amusement. Or it might have been amazement.

'We never thought you'd be that desperate. Or that stupid,' said the politician.

'Well, you took your best shot,' said Gamache, with a thin smile. 'And yet here I am. Still standing. Right in front of you.'

'You think that was our best shot, Armand?'

There was shocked silence then, until Chief Superintendent Toussaint jumped in.

'I think we hold the course. Keep the equipment at the Hydro dams to prevent a catastrophe and dynamite as it's necessary down south.'

The Deputy Premier, ignoring her, leaned over the map. 'I see in your scenario, Gamache, one of the villages spared

would be your own. Don't you live in some tiny backwater in the townships? I can smell it on you. Smells like shit.'

'Actually, it's donkey.' He stared at the politician. 'What's your point, Pierre?'

'Oh, Armand, I think you know my point. Once again you would misuse power for your own gain. And ...' The Deputy Premier paused and inhaled. 'I think what I smell isn't a donkey. It's an ass.'

The room bristled.

'You're right,' said Gamache. 'One of the places in the path of the flooding is mine. A small village, insignificant by your standards, called Three Pines. No one's ever heard of it, and if it disappeared in the deluge, I suspect it wouldn't be missed. But it would still be a tragedy. As it would for all the other towns and villages you're ignoring.'

'Thank you for coming, Chief Inspector.' Toussaint put out her hand. 'We'll take it from here. I'll let you get back to your own work now.'

They stared at each other. The former occupant and the current occupant of the highest office in the Sûreté.

He was dismissed.

He found himself unceremoniously on the other side of the door as it closed.

Armand Gamache had been put in his place.

When he walked into Beauvoir's office to get his coat and boots and dog, Jean-Guy stood up at the desk. Isabelle Lacoste was also there.

'Interviews over?' Gamache asked.

'Interviews canceled,' she said. 'Because of the emergency.'

'Meeting over?' asked Beauvoir.

'Not yet. I gave my opinion, and we'll see. There're smart people in there.'

'So why're you out here?' asked Beauvoir.

'I guess I'm not so smart,' said Gamache with a smile.

'I'm sorry,' said Lacoste. 'They shouldn't—'

'It's all right,' Gamache assured her. Then noticed that Jean-Guy's suit, his papers, his chair, and the ceiling had little brown dots all over them.

'Your dog shook,' explained Beauvoir.

'Oh, dear.'

'Yes. That's pretty much what I said as I washed myself off and scraped down my desk. Gosh, I said. Bit of a mess.' His eyes widened in a crazed look, and Lacoste laughed.

'By the way, do you mind my asking why you have a dog?'

'He belongs to the missing woman.'

'I see.' Beauvoir looked down at the smelly old thing, lying contentedly on the now-filthy rug. 'I'm sorry we have to put that search on hold.'

'Actually, we don't. Or at least I don't. If it's all right with you, I'd like to speak to her father in Ste.-Agathe, before the roads are closed. Do you mind if I take Agent Cloutier with me?'

'No, of course not. You don't need to ask, *patron*,' said Beauvoir.

'But I do.' Gamache smiled.

'Mind if I come, too?' asked Lacoste. 'Seems I'm free for the afternoon.'

'That would be great,' said Gamache. Not only did he value her judgment and company, but he knew that she was a mentor to Agent Cloutier.

Isabelle Lacoste had been a young woman when, to everyone's surprise, he'd chosen her for homicide. That hadn't been all that many years ago.

Now her hair was prematurely graying and there were lines

at her forehead and from her mouth. Caused by stress. And pain. She walked with a limp and a cane, still recovering from near-fatal injuries almost a year earlier.

He'd often wondered if he'd really done her, done Jean-Guy, done any of them such a favor by recruiting them into homicide. But they were adults, he told himself, and could make their own decisions.

And now one had decided to leave and one had decided to return.

As he waited for the elevator, with Isabelle and Fred, he looked out at Montréal. So much rain was sliding down the window, it looked as though the city was underwater.

Gamache put his hands behind his back, one gripping the other, and felt his core grow cold. And saw again the animation. Of much of Québec sliding into Vermont. Sent there by a flood of water and a fear of making the wrong decision.

'*All that most maddens and torments*,' he said.

'*Moby-Dick*,' said Lacoste. 'Studied it at university.'

'Right,' said Gamache, turning to her. 'I couldn't remember where it's from.'

'But why remember it at all?'

'Just something someone in the meeting said.'

'Well, that can't be good,' said Isabelle Lacoste as they stepped into the elevator. 'Hardly reassuring.'

'*Non.*'

CHAPTER 11

⁓

They pulled in to the driveway of the neat bungalow in the center of Ste.-Agathe forty minutes later.

As they stood on the driveway, they could see that ice still covered the lake. But it was heaved up here and there. Ice-fishing cabins had been abandoned, and there was a huge fissure through the middle of the hockey rink twenty feet off shore.

Lac des Sables was breaking up. It had obviously hit swiftly. Taking the villagers by surprise.

Even from there they could hear the bangs. Booms. As new cracks formed in the thick ice.

The thaw was moving north. More swiftly than imagined. More swiftly, certainly, than hoped.

Gamache put his hands in his pockets and brought his shoulders up against the wind.

They were in the Laurentian Mountains, and it was considerably colder. What had been coming down as rain farther south was turning to ice pellets here. And soon, he thought, freezing rain.

They'd have to be quick about this if they hoped to make it back home.

Chief Inspector Gamache brought out his phone and

called in the report of the ice breakup. He rang off just as a man appeared at the door.

Homer Godin had clearly been waiting for them. He came out of his house, but he stopped short and brought his hand to his face.

'Fred,' he said.

On seeing Monsieur Godin, Fred slithered out of the car. The man dropped to his knees to embrace the old dog.

Then Godin got up and wiped his face as he turned to Gamache and put out his hand.

'Thank you, thank you for coming. I'm Vivienne's father.'

Not, Gamache noticed, Monsieur Godin. Not Homer. But Vivienne's father. That was his identity now. And, perhaps, had been since his only child's birth.

'Armand Gamache. We spoke on the phone.'

'Yes. I stayed here, as you suggested. But she hasn't called.' Monsieur Godin searched Gamache's face for reassurance. That she would.

But Armand Gamache was silent.

Homer looked down. At the dog. His shoulders rose and fell. And there was a gasp. A sob. His hands covered his face, and through the fingers came the muffled words.

'This's all my fault.'

'No, no, that's not true, Homer,' said Lysette Cloutier, reaching out to touch his arm.

But he didn't seem to notice. Then he finally dropped his hands, and wiped his face with his sleeve.

'I'm sorry. I'm better now.' He pulled himself up, rigid. Then noticed the third person.

Gamache introduced Superintendent Lacoste.

'Thank you for coming. Thank you, thank you,' said Godin, composed. Of stone and wishful thinking.

He was in his late fifties, maybe early sixties. Gray stubble was beginning to form a beard. There were dark circles under his eyes, which were weary and bloodshot. And moist.

Homer Godin was tall, solidly built. A man clearly used to physical labor. He spoke with the broad country accent of someone who'd left school early to work on the land.

Lacoste knew this man. Not personally, but her own grandfather was just such a Québécois. Still vigorous at ninety-one, he liked nothing better than getting into the forest, even in winter, and chopping wood.

'I thought you couldn't come,' Godin said, turning to Gamache. 'That there were more important things—'

He stopped here. Unable to go on.

'There's nothing more important to us, Monsieur Godin,' said Gamache, 'than finding your daughter. There is, though, that state of emergency I mentioned. We are, for now, the only ones assigned to the search.'

Godin looked at the three of them, with new eyes. An accountant. A woman with a cane. A man covered in mud and smelling like – 'You're not needed?'

'Non.'

With some surprise Gamache realized he had become part of the refuse he'd spent his career salvaging.

But that didn't mean he was useless. Just, maybe, repurposed.

'Come inside, out of the weather,' said Godin. 'I'm sure this's nothing. I'm sure Vivienne's off with girlfriends, having fun, and I'm worrying for nothing. She'll call soon.'

He searched their faces. Trying to find some reason to hope that what he'd just said could possibly be true. A patient in a doctor's office, self-diagnosing the lump as a cyst. The confusion as exhaustion. The numbness as a pinched nerve.

111

The missing daughter on holiday. Soon to call. Full of apologies.

Gamache recognized the natural, and probably necessary, delusion. That allowed parents, children, spouses, to go on. At least temporarily.

'I'm sure that's true,' said Cloutier, as they followed Homer through the neat house and into the kitchen.

But Vivienne's father was watching Gamache.

'What do you think has happened to her?' Homer asked, sitting at the kitchen table.

Gamache, taking a seat across from Homer, could hear the fear creeping back into his voice. The dread. A frost quake, approaching.

'We don't know. We've just come from her home—'

'That was never her home. This's her home.'

And it felt like a home. Smelled like a home. It was modest in size, comfortable and welcoming, with slightly worn furniture. A La-Z-Boy was close to the woodstove, positioned perfectly to see the television.

One chair. This was a man who not only lived alone but didn't often have company.

Fred lay on the floor, his head on Monsieur Godin's feet.

'Has he done something to her?'

Again the eyes were pleading with Gamache for reassurance. But there was, in them, more desperation than conviction.

'We don't know,' said Cloutier. 'We—'

'That bastard's done something, hasn't he.'

It was a statement now, not a question.

'Why do you say that, sir?' asked Gamache.

'Because she'd have called me. I know my Vivienne. She'd know I was worried. She'd never—'

He stopped and looked down. Breathing heavily from the strain of carrying such terror.

Gamache watched as Vivienne's father groped his way forward. Into a terrible new world. Stumbling over shards of words he dared not say. Falling into emotions he dared not admit. Picking himself up. Moving forward.

Walking that tightrope of needing to push for action while not yet admitting the reason.

'Is there someplace you think she could have gone?' asked Gamache.

'I've called all her old friends. No one's seen her. They haven't even heard from her in a long time.'

'How about friends she made since moving away?'

'If she had any, she never mentioned them. But I haven't seen her for a while myself.'

'Why not?'

'He wouldn't let her come here, and I knew I wasn't welcome there. I tried a few times, but he wouldn't even let me on the porch. Said some terrible things.'

'Like what?'

Homer paused, clearly unhappy with the question – and the answer. 'That Vivienne didn't want to see me. That she hated me. That I was a terrible father.'

He hung his head, his mouth falling open. After an excruciating few seconds, a thin line of spittle dropped from his parted lips.

His huge hands were trembling in his lap, and his breath came in short, sharp inhales and exhales. Panting. Like a wild animal in pain.

Lysette Cloutier reached out toward him, but Gamache put his hand on her arm and stopped her.

The man needed his space. His illusion of privacy.

Having seen more than his share of grief, Gamache knew that Vivienne's father must be allowed to cry, without well-meaning people trying to stop it. An act that looked like mercy but was more about their own extreme discomfort than any comfort they could offer him.

'He wasn't wrong,' said Godin at last, his voice squeezing through his throat. 'I wasn't a good father.'

'What do you mean?' Gamache asked. 'You said something similar when we arrived. You said it was all your fault.'

'Did I? I meant that I should've said something. Done something. Way back even when they got engaged. I knew he was trouble. But I didn't want her to think, after her mother died, that I was jealous or anything. And I wasn't even sure if that's why I hated Tracey so much. It was confusing. But I could see, I could just see, that he wasn't good for her. But I never thought' – he paused to take some more breaths – 'he'd hurt her. Not at first, anyway. Not like this.'

'Hurt her in what way?' asked Gamache.

Though they knew, they needed to hear what Vivienne's father also knew.

Homer's mouth moved, trying to form the words. But no sound would come out. Finally he just stared at Gamache. Begging him not to make him say it.

Cloutier went to speak, but Lacoste stopped her.

And still they waited.

'He beat her.'

The words came from Vivienne's father like blood from an open vein. Quiet. Almost belying the cost of it.

He continued to stare at Gamache. Pleading now. Not for understanding, because it seemed Godin himself didn't understand. How he could have suspected his precious child was being beaten and not stopped it.

He was pleading for help. To say what needed to be said. To admit the inexcusable. The inconceivable.

That he suspected his little girl was being hurt but had failed to stop it. Failed her.

'Do you have children?' he asked Gamache.

'Two. A son and a daughter.'

'I'm guessing she'd be about Vivienne's age.'

'*Oui*. Her name's Annie.'

'You?' Homer asked Lacoste.

'Two as well. Son and daughter.'

Homer nodded.

Lacoste watched this man. Was it possible to really put herself in his place? Inside the nightmare?

'He kept her away from me,' said Homer, speaking now to Lacoste. 'The few times I was able to see her in the past year, she was thin. There were bruises.' He held his arms. 'I begged her to leave him. To come to me, but she wouldn't.'

'Why not?' asked Isabelle Lacoste.

'I don't know.' He looked down at Fred, dropping his hand to stroke the sleeping dog.

'You tried,' said Lysette. 'There's nothing more you could've done.'

'Oh, there was something I could've done.' He looked at Gamache. 'What would you have done? If your Annie . . .'

'When was the last time you saw Vivienne?' he asked, deflecting the question.

Godin smiled a little. 'Not going to answer that, are you? Probably smart. But sometimes ya just gotta be stupid, you know? If I'd killed the shit, she'd be here today instead of you.'

'But you would not be,' said Gamache.

'Do you think I care?' said Godin. 'I'd trade my life for hers like that.' He snapped his fingers.

'When, Monsieur Godin?' Gamache repeated.

'I saw her just before Christmas. I went down to drop off presents. I'd even bought one for him. Oh, God.' He stared at Gamache in disbelief. 'I was so afraid of losing her I was willing to' – he fought to control himself again – 'suck up to him. What was I thinking? Oh, God. She didn't invite me in. I think he was there. So I just left. That was the last time—'

Lysette Cloutier reached out, and this time Gamache didn't stop her. She put her hand on Homer's forearm and left it there.

'But you did hear from her again,' said Gamache.

'Yes. She called on Saturday morning.'

Godin seemed confused now. Could it have been so recently? Just two days ago? Time made no sense anymore. Days, dates, they were meaningless and would be for the rest of his life. There would only be before Vivienne disappeared and after.

A firm line drawn against which all else would be measured. Until the day he died.

'What did she say?'

'She told me she was pregnant and was finally going to leave him. I was so happy I could barely speak. I said I'd come and get her, but she told me not to. She needed to pick the time. When it was safe. When he was gone or passed out. She told me she'd be here sometime that night or maybe Sunday morning. She made me promise not to come. So I just waited.' There was a long, long exhale. 'I should've gone to get her. Why didn't I?'

But there was no answer, and Gamache was not going to give this dignified man some drivel.

They sat silently, staring at each other. Vivienne's father and Annie's father.

116

'It's my fault,' Homer whispered.

'*Non, monsieur.* This isn't your doing.'

But Gamache knew that no matter what he said, Godin would spend the rest of his life in an endless loop. Skidding along the same ground. Going back over and over and over the last conversation. And what he did or did not do. What he could have done, what he should have done.

As I would, thought Gamache.

'You said you called all her old friends,' Gamache continued, 'but do you know if she had a more recent friend? Someone special?'

If Godin caught his meaning, he chose to ignore it.

'No. No one.'

And Gamache was forced to be more blunt.

'Carl Tracey says she had a—'

'I know what Tracey says,' the man erupted. 'He's trying to make her sound like some sort of . . . some sort of . . .' He couldn't bring himself to utter the word. 'Vivienne wasn't like that. She never would, would she?'

He appealed to Cloutier, who managed not to respond.

Godin looked down at his hands, gripped so tightly on the edge of the table that the entire thing rattled. Like a visitation from the other side.

He brought himself under control, though his knuckles remained white.

'Besides,' he said, his voice strained, 'how would she meet anyone? He barely let her off the property.'

'We have to ask,' said Gamache. 'If she did have a lover, she might've gone to him. Or he might be the one who—'

'She didn't.'

'Though you say you hadn't seen her in a while. She might have—'

'She didn't,' he all but shouted. 'I know her. Look, why're you wasting time? If something's happened to Vivienne, we all know who did it. If you won't make him tell, I will.'

'That wouldn't be wise, Monsieur Godin,' said Gamache, getting to his feet.

'Really? Really?' demanded Godin, also getting up and turning to face Gamache. 'And what would you call "wise"? Was what I did on Saturday wise? Doing nothing? Maybe it's time to do something stupid.'

There was silence.

'Imagine your Annie was pregnant. I want you to imagine that.'

'Monsieur Godin—'

'Now imagine her missing. Them missing.'

Despite himself, Gamache felt tugged into that world. Just for an instant, he crossed the line. To where the unimaginable happened. Where monsters lived. Where Vivienne's father now lived.

'You're right, *monsieur*. You have to act now. But confronting Carl Tracey won't get you anywhere. He won't tell you anything, and he'll just have you arrested. It would only make it worse.'

Now Godin almost laughed. Almost.

'It can't get worse. And to be clear, Chief Inspector, I don't plan on confronting him. I plan on beating him until he tells me where Vivienne is. And then I'll beat him to death.'

Gamache regarded Godin and knew he was serious. He made a decision.

'Come with us now. I live in the area. You can stay with my wife and me. We'll organize a search for Vivienne. You can help us. Will you do that?'

'Stay with you?' Homer asked. 'Are you serious?'

It was, not surprisingly, exactly the same question Lacoste wanted to ask. Was he serious?

'Yes.'

'Give me two minutes. I'll pack a bag.'

Homer ran from the kitchen and along the corridor, the small home practically shaking with the force of his feet.

'Was that wise?' asked Lacoste, looking down the now-empty hallway. 'You're taking him to within a few kilometers of the man he wants to kill.'

'He'd have gone there himself, probably as soon as we left. This way we have some control. I can watch over him.'

'I know him,' said Cloutier. 'If he says he'll kill Tracey, he means it. You can't watch him twenty-four hours a day.'

'And what would you have us do, Agent Cloutier? Leave him?'

She thought and finally shook her head.

'*Non*,' said Gamache. 'This isn't the best solution, I agree, but it's the only one I can think of right now. And we're running out of time.' He looked out the window, where ice pellets were slapping against the panes. 'Maybe Monsieur Godin's right. Sometimes we have to do something stupid.'

It did not seem to Isabelle Lacoste a great addition to the Sûreté motto.

Service, integrity, justice, and, occasionally, stupidity.

CHAPTER 12

——

Clara Morrow stood in her studio, her dog, Leo, at her side. Her shoulders were drooping from exhaustion as she wondered which, if any, paintings she'd rescue, should the evacuation order come.

Would she take the miniatures? Were they worth saving? Had they earned their place on the ark? Two days ago she thought so. Now she wasn't so sure.

And with the water rising, decisions had to be made.

They'd run out of sandbags two hours earlier. Then villagers had begun bringing pillowcases and feed bags, garbage bags. Anything that could hold sand.

And then they'd run out of sand.

And then they'd run out of light.

And then they'd run out of steam.

And still the rain kept coming. Changing to ice pellets, then freezing rain, then back to rain.

It had stopped for half an hour, giving them hope that maybe . . .

And then it started to snow.

But still the villagers were reluctant to leave the wall they'd built. Four bags high. Two bags thick. Running a hundred

meters on either shore of the Bella Bella. From Jane Neal's back garden, along Clara's garden, to the bridge. Then it continued behind Monsieur Béliveau's general store, Sarah's Boulangerie, the bistro, and Myrna's bookstore.

And ten meters beyond that, to the bend in the river.

It had been a herculean task. But as they finally dragged themselves back to their homes, for hot showers and dry clothes, each villager suspected that it was not enough. That the Bella Bella would rise up in the night and overwhelm Three Pines.

And there was nothing more they could do to stop it.

Ruth had stayed on the stone bridge, with Rosa. Like a droopy sentinel. Unwilling to leave her post. Staring at the river that had been her friend.

Until Clara and Myrna, Reine-Marie and Sarah the baker had coaxed her off. It wasn't fine words that did it, or fine food, or even the bottle of fine scotch that Myrna had brought with her.

It was Reine-Marie pointing out that Rosa was getting cold. It was finally love that drew Ruth away from the river.

As the women accompanied the old poet back to her home, a car had appeared on the hill.

'Armand,' said Reine-Marie.

'He's not alone,' said Clara.

'Is it numbnuts?' asked Ruth.

'No, Jean-Guy's staying in Montréal,' said Reine-Marie.

She'd long since given up trying to stop Ruth from calling her son-in-law 'numbnuts.' And even he'd begun answering to it.

The car stopped in front of the Gamache home, and two men and a dog got out.

*

Homer Godin looked around.

All he could see through the sleet and darkness was a ring of lights that seemed to hang in midair. He knew they came from homes, but those were invisible.

They'd stopped in Montréal and dropped Lysette and that superintendent woman at Sûreté headquarters.

Homer had sat in the outer office, listening, while Gamache met with a fellow named Jean-Guy something.

The young fellow was obviously another cop. Senior, it seemed. Gamache's equal? At times it seemed so. His superior? At times it seemed so. His subordinate? At times it seemed so.

They'd discussed the flooding. It was far worse than Homer had realized.

'Have they dynamited the jams on the St. Lawrence?' Gamache asked.

'Not yet.'

'What're they waiting for?' asked Gamache.

'A decision, I guess. The Corps of Military Engineers is pushing for it, but the Deputy Premier seems afraid it'll set off a panic.'

Gamache took a deep breath and let out a long exhale. '*Bon*. I'm almost afraid to ask, but ... the dams?'

The dams? thought Homer. *What dams?*

And then he realized what dams they were talking about. The huge hydroelectric dams in James Bay. He leaned his head around the doorway and asked, 'Are they in trouble?'

And for one brief moment, his personal catastrophe was replaced by the collective disaster that was threatening.

'*Non*,' said the younger man. But Homer Godin recognized a lie when he heard it.

It was said in the same grim tone Vivienne used every time he'd asked if Tracey was hurting her.

Non.

The two continued to talk, but now in tones that suggested much more than just colleagues. These men were friends.

'Keep in touch,' said Gamache, at the door.

'You too. Good luck, *patron*.' Then this Jean-Guy Someone turned to Homer. 'I promise, once the crisis is past, we'll do everything we can to find your daughter. In the meantime Chief Inspector Gamache will help. He's the best.'

Godin looked at Gamache and couldn't help but think if he was the best, why weren't they using him in this emergency? Why send him away?

Homer couldn't help himself. He grabbed the younger man's arm. 'I need more. Help me, please. Help.'

'We're doing all we can. I'm sorry.'

And now Homer Godin stood in the bleak village. In the mud. In the half rain, half snow, and while he couldn't see much, he could hear a great deal.

He looked toward the sound. The river. That was in full flood. And he thought of his daughter. Disappearing into the night. Disappearing into the flood.

Then he looked past the lights. Somewhere in the darkness, not all that far away, was Carl Tracey.

Homer wasn't sure how, but he'd get to him.

Lysette Cloutier poured herself another glass of wine and returned to the sofa.

She was at home now, having volunteered to help with the emergency measures but told she wasn't needed.

She was both very annoyed and very relieved. Mostly she was very worried.

Lysette hadn't been completely honest with Chief Inspector Gamache and Superintendent Lacoste about her

relationship with Homer, such as it was. But also her relationship with Vivienne. Such as it was.

She wasn't sure why, but it had seemed important not to tell them that she was Vivienne's godmother. Perhaps because she was a god-awful godmother. Not having had one herself, Lysette had no idea what was expected. Except for her to take Vivienne, should anything happen to her parents, Kathy and Homer.

But beyond that?

The only other thing she could remember from the baptism was being told she needed to act as Viv's guardian. To guard her. To keep the child safe.

'Well,' she mumbled. 'Fucked that one up.'

After taking a long gulp, perhaps even a guzzle, of wine, she pulled her laptop onto her lap and logged in. Agent Cloutier had been told to find out everything she could about Carl Tracey. Might as well start.

She was prepared to have to do a fairly deep dive into government records but had decided, as a lark, to just put his name into a Google search.

She sat there, openmouthed, when up came a website.

'Can't be.'

Clicking on it, she looked at the photo of the man. Definitely Tracey. Surrounded by his pottery.

'Shit,' she said, and clicked on more links. To exhibitions he'd had. To a buying link. To a brief bio that mentioned his wife, Vivienne, and their dog, Fred.

Like most of the stuff on the Web, it was bullshit. The life people wanted people to see. The neat front yard, not the squalor behind the front door.

She snapped the laptop closed in disgust and, putting it on the floor, she lay back and grabbed the TV remote. But then

she looked down at the slender rectangle sitting on the floor below her. And she got to wondering.

How did a man without internet have a website?

Isabelle Lacoste ignored the phone call from Lysette Cloutier.

It was her strict policy to leave work behind, at least until the kids were fed and in bed. Unless the call was from Monsieur Gamache or Jean-Guy.

Besides, she was on leave.

It was only after the third attempt that Isabelle picked up.

'*Oui, allô?*'

'I'm so sorry to disturb you, *patron*.' The voice was just the tiniest bit off. Not slurred. If anything, the words were too well enunciated. Too precise.

'What can I do for you?'

'Carl Tracey has a web page.' And then came a sound between a laugh and a snort.

'Yes.'

'But he doesn't have internet. He also has an Instagram account. That's active. So how does he do it?'

Now Lacoste's mind was engaged. How did he do it? There was only one answer –

'He has a webmaster,' said Cloutier. 'Some woman named Pauline. She must manage it all for him. Post for him.'

'Okay,' said Lacoste, sitting at her own laptop and putting in Carl Tracey's name.

'Dinner,' her husband called.

'Be right there.'

'You're coming here?' asked Cloutier with alarm, looking at the almost empty wine bottle and empty bag of chips.

'No, I was speaking to my husband.' Putting her hand over the receiver, she called, 'Start without me.' Then she

returned to Cloutier. 'Is there anything incriminating on the sites?'

'Not that I can see, but there might be a private Instagram account that they use, just the two of them.'

'That no one else can see? That's possible?'

'Yup.'

'How would we know?'

'We wouldn't, unless we asked and she told us.'

'And to get access to the private account?' asked Lacoste. By now she'd found the public Instagram account. It was pretty standard, clearly meant for marketing his pottery.

'Need to be invited.'

'Why would they have a private account?' Lacoste asked.

'Dunno.' Then Cloutier thought. 'Private messages. That's why.'

She sounded both triumphant and a little surprised she'd managed that answer.

'Things they don't want public,' said Lacoste.

Cloutier sang, 'Someone's trying to hide their privates.' Then she definitely snorted.

Lacoste looked at the phone. She'd mentored the older woman since she'd been transferred, kicking and screaming, from accounting into homicide. Never once had the account-ant snorted. Or even made a joke. She'd barely smiled.

She's drunk, Lacoste knew. Now, why would Lysette Cloutier get drunk?

'Are you all right?'

'Just fine.' Now Cloutier sounded insulted. 'I thought you'd be pleased about this.'

Now she sounded hurt and a little irritated.

'I am. Look, it's been a long, difficult day. You've done well. Leave it and start fresh in the morning. And for God's sake,

don't contact this woman, right? We don't want Tracey to know we're interested in his private Instagram. Right?'

'Right.'

Lysette Cloutier hung up but did not take that advice.

She should have.

Clara put on the outdoor lights at the back of her home.

On warm summer evenings, she and her friends would sit in the garden having drinks and dinner. The lights were placed to illuminate the perennial beds of delphiniums and phlox and old garden roses.

Beds that had been first planted more than a century ago.

But on this cold April evening, Clara had climbed the ladder and repositioned the lights so that they pointed into the night, to where her garden met the river.

Now the lights illuminated an expanse of mud and the wall of sandbags.

'Floodlights,' said Gabri, standing beside Myrna in the kitchen and staring out the window.

They'd gathered in Clara's home, partly out of habit, partly out of a need to be together, partly because it was the best vantage point to monitor the Bella Bella and still be protected.

And privately out of fear that this would be the last time.

The neighbors put the food they'd brought onto the kitchen island, buffet style. And now they gathered around the window, to see if they could see anything.

But Clara herself had left them and gone back to the doorway into her studio, where Reine-Marie joined her.

'You okay?'

'I'm well in body,' said Clara. 'But considerably rumpled up in spirit.'

Reine-Marie laughed. Easily recognizing the lines from the Anne of Green Gables books she, her daughter, and now her granddaughters loved so much.

She put her arm through Clara's. 'Fortunately, you're among kindred spirits.'

Clara squeezed her hand and continued to stare into the studio.

'What're you thinking?' Reine-Marie asked.

'I'm thinking that if we need to leave, I can't take all my paintings. So which do I choose, if any?'

'If any?'

Clara turned to look at her. 'Are they crap?'

'Why would you say that?'

'You know why.'

'You haven't let those comments get into your head, have you? Those people are ignorant—'

'It was the *New York Times*. And *Art World*. Thank God the *Oddly Report* hasn't said anything.'

'The what?' asked Ruth, who'd sensed pain and had gone over to bask in and, with luck, magnify it. 'The *Oddly Report*? What's that?'

'The one major art journal that's never reviewed my work. Wouldn't you know it? It's the biggest, the most prestigious. Most people just call it *Odd*.'

'And obviously the smartest,' said Ruth.

'Now I'm glad they've ignored me,' said Clara, snapping off the lights.

But, having reexamined the miniatures, she was both heartened and confused. They were, she felt, actually very good. Exceptional, even. Why couldn't others see what she saw?

She joined her friends, crowded around the kitchen

window, while Ruth limped into the living room and stood behind the one person not watching the Bella Bella.

Homer Godin was staring out a window in the other direction. Into the forest.

Ruth's reflection, like an apparition, hovered in the window just over his shoulder. The rain coursed down both their faces.

'She's out there somewhere.' Homer's words fogged the windowpane. He didn't turn around, but his eyes in the reflection met Ruth's. 'Please. Can you help me?'

In the background, the CBC was broadcasting continuous updates on the flooding.

Reports were coming in from all over Ontario, Québec, the Maritimes, while Vivienne's father stared at Rosa's mother.

She reached out and touched his arm.

Homer closed his eyes tight. 'Oh, please. Help.'

Armand checked the wall of sandbags.

Floodlights had been set up on either side of the river. One pointing upriver, the other pointing down. So that the villagers could see what was happening. From where he stood, he could also see the lights in Clara's back garden.

The rain mixed with snow was teeming down, and he hunched deeper into his coat as a gust of wind lashed water into his face.

Every half hour since getting back, he went out to check the height of the river. It was, Ruth had made clear, his assignment. The least he could do.

'You don't think you can just swan in here and relax by the fire after we spent all day building the goddamned wall?' said Ruth.

Rosa, in her arms, bristled. She didn't like swans.

'Clearly the Sûreté doesn't think you're much use, or you wouldn't be back here. And don't get me started on what they're saying on Twitter, the dumb-asses. Not that I disagree.'

'Ruth!' said Reine-Marie.

'What? It's the truth.'

'*All truth with malice in it*,' said Armand.

'But still the truth,' said Ruth.

Reine-Marie walked Armand to the door. 'That was from *Moby-Dick*, wasn't it?'

Rosa turned and looked at Ruth, who whispered reassuringly, 'Dick. Not duck.'

'Yes,' said Armand. 'Someone quoted from the book today. Now it's lodged in my mind.'

'Well, there's a coincidence,' Ruth said to Clara. 'You were talking about it, too.'

'What were you hearing? I was talking about my art, not a book.'

'You were talking about your critics, and the big one that got away,' said Ruth. 'Your white whale.'

Armand went to put on his heavy rubber boots, then realized he'd grabbed the wrong pair. Looking around, he noticed they all had much the same boots, all bought at Monsieur Béliveau's general store.

'Don't let Homer out of your sight,' he said to Reine-Marie as he did up his coat. 'And whatever happens, make sure he doesn't get any car keys.'

'You don't want him bolting,' said Reine-Marie.

He nodded. 'Bolting' was one way of putting it.

As he trudged through the mud, head bent into the sleet, Armand heard splashing behind him and turned to see Olivier running toward him.

The slender man was bundled up so that he would be unrecognizable, except to someone who knew him well.

'Thought you could use some help,' said Olivier, above the roar of the water.

'To look at a river?'

'Okay, some company.' On seeing the expression on Armand's face, Olivier amended that. 'Okay, it was time to do dishes.'

Armand laughed. Knowing that in fact Olivier had come out into the frigid night to offer help. In case.

'*Merci.*'

At the wall, Armand put his arm out to Olivier. 'Hold my hand.'

'This is so sudden,' said Olivier. 'But not unexpected.'

'Silly man,' said Armand with a grunt of laughter. 'Just hold on so I don't fall in.'

With Olivier gripping his hand and sleeve, Gamache climbed over the wall and leaned out. Clicking on his flashlight as he did.

He saw that while there was certainly ice and debris in the swiftly moving river, it was at least moving.

They checked several other spots downriver.

At the last stop, Armand took longer. And leaned farther.

'Okay, that's enough,' yelled Olivier. 'I'm losing my grip.'

'Another moment.' The floodlights didn't reach this far, so Armand shone his flashlight on the frothing water.

'What?' asked Olivier, the strain of holding on apparent in his voice.

'There's some buildup beginning. In the bend in the river. I can see ice and some tree limbs.'

He stayed there another few seconds. Trying to see more clearly. Though the sleet was hitting his face and he had to blink away the moisture.

'Better come back. Now.' The strain in Olivier's voice was apparent, and Armand could feel his grip slipping.

He climbed back over the sturdy wall of sandbags. His brow furrowed in thought.

Wiping the rain from his eyes, he looked upriver. Past the stone bridge. Past Clara's home. Past St. Thomas's Church, lit so that even through the rain he could see the three stained-glass boys, trudging forever through the mud of some far-off foreign field.

'We need Billy Williams,' he yelled above the river.

'Why?'

'The Bella Bella's about to break her banks. The sandbags will hold for a little while, but there's too much water coming down, and ice is backing up at the bend.'

'What can Billy do? Break it up?'

Gamache looked upriver again, remembering the donkeys in the field and the sound of the Bella Bella behind them.

'He can dig a trench.'

It was an oddity of Armand's relationship with Billy that they had a strangely close connection and yet Armand could not understand a word the man said. Granted, Billy Williams had a thick backcountry English accent, though Gamache managed to understand everyone else.

Despite this, Billy remained for Armand both a cipher and a confidant.

Olivier had run back to Clara's home and brought Billy out with him. Now the three stood next to the Bella Bella.

'How can I help?' Billy asked.

All Armand heard was a series of guttural sounds ending in an upward inflection. He looked at Olivier, who translated.

Armand told him what he wanted. Billy considered.

'For God's sake, hurry up and tell us,' said Olivier, his teeth chattering in the cold.

'I'll need my backhoe,' said Billy, pointing to the piece of machinery he'd used earlier in the day to move the piles of sand. 'But it's heavy. It won't make it up the hills in this mud. The place you're suggesting is kilometers away.'

Olivier translated again.

'I was afraid of that,' said Armand. After all, he'd had an experience with a hill earlier in the day.

Billy made some more noises and gestures.

'When?' asked Olivier.

More sounds from Billy.

'Will it work?' asked Olivier.

Billy thought, then nodded. 'Yurz.'

That Armand got. 'It's possible, then?'

'But you'll have to wait until the temperature drops and the ground hardens,' said Olivier. 'He figures it'll be sometime after midnight.'

Armand looked over to the river. Then at his watch. It was almost 10:00 p.m.

'Do we have that long?' Olivier asked.

'I don't know,' said Armand.

They went back inside and reported what they'd found as they toweled off their faces and hair, then stuck their hands out to the fire.

The others listened in silence. There was nothing to say and nothing to do, except wait.

Jean-Guy called from Montréal and reported that they'd decided to blow the ice dams on the St. Lawrence. 'They'll issue a public warning and close the bridges while it's being done.'

'Good. Let me know if it works.'

'I will.'

Armand lowered his voice. 'And the dams?'

'No word. No mention of them now, even on the secure channels.'

Gamache took a deep breath and said a silent prayer.

'How's it going there?' Jean-Guy asked.

'We've designated St. Thomas's as an evacuation center. Most of the residents have been moved up there, but some are staying behind.'

'You speaking to numbnuts?' came a familiar voice in the background.

'Do witches float?' asked Jean-Guy.

'I believe they do,' said Armand.

'Shame.'

'I see he's staying where it's safe and warm,' said Ruth. 'I'd expect nothing less. Or more.'

'Bitch,' muttered Jean-Guy.

'Bastard,' said Ruth. 'Oh, and tell him to give my love to my godson. And tell Honoré I have a few more words for him to learn, and a special hand signal.'

When Ruth moved on, Armand told Jean-Guy their plans for the Bella Bella.

There was a pause. 'That's still two hours away, at best. Will the sandbags hold?'

'Hard to tell.'

Armand exhaled, and Jean-Guy could hear the strain.

'Annie and Honoré are safe here, and I'm just sitting at HQ with my thumb up my—'

'Got it.'

'I'm coming down to help' – he glanced at the clock – 'if I can get off-island before they close the bridges. See you soon.'

'But—'

But the line was dead.

'Jean-Guy's coming down to help,' he reported to the others.

'Dumb-ass,' said Ruth.

But Armand could see relief in the ancient face, illuminated by the flames from the log fire.

'I'm sorry sir, you'll have to go back. We've closed the bridge.'

Beauvoir flashed his credentials, and the officer stepped aside and waved him through, alerting agents along the span to let this vehicle pass.

Just as he made it over, Beauvoir heard a huge explosion. He winced and instinctively ducked, even though he knew what it was. In the rearview mirror, he saw a plume of snow and ice shoot into the air.

A few minutes later, some distance down the autoroute, he heard another, more muffled explosion.

The ice was packed in tight, the St. Lawrence beginning to flood. If this didn't work . . .

As he drove, he monitored the secure Sûreté channels, while dynamite went off in a ring around the island and across Québec.

At least Annie and Honoré were safe on high ground. And he'd return to them by dawn. Even if he had to swim across the St. Lawrence to get there.

CHAPTER 13

It had been decided by Ruth, apparently in consultation with a duck and a bottle of scotch, that sentries would be placed on the bridge to sound the alarm should the Rivière Bella Bella break through the sandbags.

Reine-Marie and Armand chose to take the first shift.

At the door Ruth made sure their heavy raincoats were well fastened. 'You have your whistle, in case something happens?'

'I do,' said Reine-Marie.

'And your *Boys' Big Book of Flooding*?'

'Always,' said Armand.

'Then we'll be fine,' said the old poet.

'Fucked up,' said Gabri.

'Insecure,' said Olivier.

'Neurotic,' said Clara.

'And egotistical, yeah, yeah,' said Ruth. 'Now, no necking, you two, and be home by midnight.'

'Yes, Mom.'

As the rain and ice pellets hit her face, Reine-Marie called to Armand, 'Heck of a date.'

*

Inside, a discussion had begun around the fireplace. What to take, if an evacuation order was given.

'I'd take Gabri,' said Olivier.

'I'd take the espresso machine,' said Gabri. 'And some croissants.'

At the bridge they stood, backs to the wind, shoulders hunched, hoods raised. Reine-Marie put on her flashlight and pointed it into the Bella Bella.

'It's rising,' she shouted.

'*Oui.*'

'I'd take my Jehane Benoît cookbook,' said Myrna. 'The photo album. The Lalique vase. That hand-knotted Indian rug—'

'Hold on,' said Gabri. 'Do you have a moving van? Can we use some of it? I'd take my grandfather's Victorian sofa.'

'Oh, no you don't,' said Olivier. 'The only good thing about a flood wiping out our entire lives is that it'd take that monstrosity with it.'

Armand and Reine-Marie walked over the stone bridge. And back again. Over and back. Pausing every couple of minutes to switch on the powerful flashlight and check the level of the Rivière Bella Bella.

Then continue on.

Like guards on a lonely frontier.

Back and forth. Back and forth.

Armand could barely hear his own thoughts for the sound of the water rushing below and the ice pellets hitting his coat.

What he thought about, as he walked back and forth, back and forth, was Vivienne. Out there somewhere. And Vivienne's father. And Annie.

He tried to keep their daughter out of it, knowing how dangerous it was to personalize investigations. But perhaps his resistance was lowered by the cold, by the competing stresses, by incipient exhaustion, but he couldn't seem to stop putting himself in Monsieur Godin's place.

Suppose Annie were missing? And everyone he turned to for help, while nice, didn't actually help? If he pleaded with them, begged them, and all they did was smile and offer soup?

It would be a nightmare. He'd be mad with worry.

Pausing again at the top of the bridge, he took Reine-Marie's hand. Suddenly feeling the need for comfort.

The water in the beams of light was frothing, foaming. Like something rabid. It scudded along the lip of the shore-line. Rising faster than they'd expected. The jam, just a little way downriver, out of Three Pines, must be getting worse.

And then.

Armand heard a low hum, almost a moan, from Reine-Marie. As they watched, the Bella Bella broke up and over her banks.

It was now racing along the bottom of the sandbags.

'They'll hold,' she said. 'There's a long way to go before the river reaches us.'

'*Oui*.'

Though they both knew that the problem wasn't necessarily the height of the river but the force of it. The danger wasn't that the water would cascade over the wall but that it would knock it down.

They'd built it two bags thick. So it shouldn't.

But then, the Bella Bella should never have gotten this high.

A lot of things were happening that shouldn't.

Just ask Homer Godin, who was living the great 'should not be happening.'

Reine-Marie lifted her eyes and through the sleet saw the lights of St. Thomas's Church on the hill. Where volunteers were making sure the children were sleeping soundly and not afraid. They were setting up more cots and organizing food, fresh water, generators, and composting toilets. Should the worst happen.

Then she shifted her gaze to the woods.

'Where is she, Armand?'

'I don't know.'

'Is she—'

'I don't know.'

'But you suspect. Have you spoken to the husband?'

'This afternoon. He's a piece of work. Sûreté's been called to their home more than once. Alcoholic. Maybe drugs.'

'Abusive?'

'*Oui.*'

A buildup of trouble that had broken its banks, thought Reine-Marie. And the young woman was taken at the flood.

'She's pregnant?'

'*Oui.*'

'How could someone—'

But there was no use finishing the question. And there was no answer.

They continued to pace. Back and forth. Back and forth.

Still the question rankled.

How could someone . . . ?

'Can you make him tell you?' Reine-Marie shouted above the torrent.

'Short of putting a gun to his head or beating it out of him, no.'

In her silence, he knew what she was feeling, if not thinking.

Maybe, just this once . . .

Maybe in some cases it was justified. Maybe torture. Maybe beatings. Maybe even murder was justified. Sometimes.

'Situational ethics?' he asked.

'Don't be smug,' Reine-Marie said. 'We all have them. Even me. Even you.'

She was right, of course.

It was the asp at the breast of any decent cop. Any military leader. Any politician.

Any mother or father.

Any human.

Maybe. Just this once . . .

'I'd take Ruth,' said Olivier.

'Thank you,' said the old poet.

'Because she's a witch and would float?' asked Clara.

'Of course,' said Olivier. 'We could cling to her.'

'I'd rather drown,' said Gabri.

They turned to Billy.

'I think you'd know what I'd take,' he said.

'Your tractor?' asked Myrna.

'So that's how you're doing it,' Lysette Cloutier muttered as she stared at the IP address. 'You shit.'

Over the fifteen years she'd worked in accounting for the Sûreté, Lysette had rarely used foul language. And rarely had she heard it.

But in homicide she'd heard, and discovered within herself, a whole new vocabulary. It was, she thought, a form of verbal violence to counter the horrific things they saw every day.

Instead of lashing out physically, they lashed out verbally.

And yet, she thought as she put more commands into her

laptop, she'd rarely heard Chief Inspector Gamache swear. She tried to think if she'd ever heard him.

Maybe that's why he was in charge. What was it he'd said to that Cameron? The population had a right to expect that people with a gun and a badge would also have self-control.

Maybe he had greater control over himself than most.

But what was he controlling? And what would happen if it ever broke free?

Bob Cameron sat in his car. The sleet had stopped. The skies were clearing. The temperature dropping.

His windshield was frosting over, but he could still see stars, the Milky Way. And that single light in the house.

In the bedroom.

Was Tracey lying on the bed, on top of that comforter with its bright pink and green flowers that Vivienne's mother had left her in her will?

Was he drinking himself stupid?

Stupider.

Was that even a word?

Or was he packing? Planning to run away.

Cameron hoped so. That's what he'd been waiting for. Hoping for.

Expecting.

Come on. Come on, you shit. Get in that truck of yours and just try it.

Cameron had been reassigned from the effort to find Vivienne Godin to setting up emergency shelters. Sent home to rest, he'd come here instead.

Tracey was a weak man, Cameron knew. The sort who'd try to run.

And then what would I do?

But he knew the answer to that. He'd pull Tracey over. Tell him to get out of the vehicle.

And he'd do what he should have done weeks ago.

He looked at his watch. It was almost 1:00 a.m. He should go home. His wife might be wondering. But he couldn't. Not quite yet.

Come on, you dumb-ass. Come on out. Come to me.

Billy Williams stood on the road out of town. He held a long, gnarled stick, and as Reine-Marie and Armand watched, he drove it into the mud. As he'd done every twenty minutes for the past couple of hours.

He was testing to see how far the stick would sink in, but also, it seemed by his cocked head, listening for some sound from the earth. Some permission.

The sleet had stopped an hour earlier, and the temperature had plummeted. Exactly what they needed.

Maybe now . . .

'Well?' asked Reine-Marie, just as Armand noticed a glow on the hill above them.

Headlights. That could be only one person. Jean-Guy had arrived.

Billy spoke.

'Thank the Lord,' said Reine-Marie, turning to Armand. 'Billy says it's frozen.'

CHAPTER 14

⁓

They stood on the frozen field, a few kilometers upriver of Three Pines, and watched as Billy's backhoe dug into the banks of the Bella Bella.

The strong beam from the light on the front of his cab illuminated the ice and muck and stones as the shovel dug in.

Reine-Marie held her phone in her mittened hand. They had, away from the forests and on the clear, crisp night, a fragile signal. That came and went. But was at least there. For now.

Jean-Guy was beside the river, and Armand stood on the running board, guiding the digging of the trench. While Reine-Marie listened for reports back from Three Pines.

They'd left Clara and Myrna on the bridge. The river was now up to the second sandbag.

Ruth was in Clara's cottage with her landline. Reporting back.

'River's still rising,' Ruth shouted into the phone. Partly to be heard over the roar of the river and partly because she always shouted into a phone.

'Did you see that?' Myrna shouted into Clara's ear.

Damn her, thought Clara, who was busy trying to pretend she hadn't seen anything.

But Myrna rarely looked away from some awful truth. Preferring to know rather than to live in blissful, if dangerous ignorance. It was one of her worst qualities.

'They've shifted.' Myrna turned and yelled across to Ruth. 'Tell them to hurry. They've shifted.'

'What's that?'

'They've shifted!'

'Well, you're pretty shitty, too!'

Gabri, standing beside Ruth in the kitchen, grabbed the phone. 'Here, give me that. Reine-Marie? The sandbags are beginning to shift.'

'*Merde.*'

'Hey! Hey!'

They turned and saw a flashlight approaching.

'Keep digging,' Armand yelled into Billy's ear, then jumped off the backhoe.

'What're you doing? This's my land,' came a man's voice.

Armand gestured to Reine-Marie to stay where she was and walked toward the light and the shout. 'Sûreté. Who are you?'

But he knew the answer to that. Because he knew whose land they were on.

Jean-Guy left the river and joined Armand. The man was still twenty paces away. And held a flashlight in one hand and something else in the other.

'He's got a gun,' said Jean-Guy, his sharp eyes not leaving the man slipping and stumbling toward them.

'*Oui,*' said Armand, and took a step in front of Reine-Marie. 'A .22. Hunting rifle. Saw it earlier, in the search. He has a permit.'

'Fuck,' muttered Jean-Guy, shaking his head.

A .22. Small-gauge. But it could still do damage. To a gopher. A fox. A human.

'This's private property,' Tracey shouted. 'Get off.'

They were downwind of him and could smell the whiskey. The donkeys had been put in the barn overnight, so it was just humans now, in the field.

'Monsieur Tracey, it's Armand Gamache. We met earlier today.'

'I don't care who you are. You're on my land.' Tracey stopped ten paces away and raised his rifle. 'Get off.'

'Armand?' said Reine-Marie, stepping forward.

'It's all right,' he said, and put his arm out to gently move her behind him.

Obviously, she thought, his idea of 'all right' and hers were very different.

'What's happening?' came Gabri's tinny voice down the phone. 'Reine-Marie?'

'Drop the gun,' commanded Beauvoir.

'Gun?' came the tinny voice. 'Hello?'

'Get off my goddamned land,' yelled Tracey. The rifle still raised.

Billy had stopped digging. Armand turned to him and shouted, 'Whatever happens, keep digging.'

'Yurz.'

The machine began again, and Tracey stepped forward, slipping slightly on the snow and mud.

The danger, Gamache could now see, wasn't just that he'd fire the rifle on purpose but that he'd slip and it would go off accidentally.

'I said stop,' yelled Tracey.

'And I said drop the gun,' said Beauvoir, stepping directly in front of Armand. Directly in front of the gun.

'Oh, my God,' shouted Armand, and waved toward the river.

Reine-Marie, alarmed, turned.

As did Tracey.

The only one who didn't was Beauvoir, who was expecting Gamache to do something like this. Divert, just for a moment, Tracey's attention.

Jean-Guy's hand shot out and wrenched the rifle from his grip.

When Tracey lunged for it, Beauvoir pivoted and knocked him to the ground.

Gamache bent down and lifted the drunken man to his feet.

'We're diverting the river,' he explained. 'To stop the—'

'You have no right. This's private land,' Tracey shouted. With a yank, he twisted away from Gamache and ran toward the backhoe, waving and shouting, '*Arrêt! Arrêt!* Stop.'

But, of course, Billy did not.

He hadn't seen that Beauvoir had disarmed him. As far as Billy knew, a man with a rifle was running toward him. And might very well shoot.

But Billy didn't care. Myrna was down there. The bags were shifting. And only he could stop it.

He pushed the shovel in deeper and dragged it forward into the field just as Gamache caught up with Tracey and, grabbing him around the waist, hauled the man around and away.

With a gush, the Bella Bella began pouring into the field.

'Hello?' came a tinny voice.

There was no deluding herself any longer.

The wall was coming down.

It was time to leave, Clara knew. Not just the bridge but her home. The village. Time to abandon Three Pines to fate.

Myrna and Clara quickly made their way off the bridge, half walking, half running.

The last of the villagers had to get out of Clara's home, out of Three Pines, and up to the church.

From there they would witness the destruction.

'Wait,' said Clara, grabbing Myrna's arm.

Every particle of Myrna's being was straining forward. Telling her to flee. Now.

But she stopped. And waited, for a moment. Because Clara had.

Too afraid to even speak, she stared at the circle from Clara's flashlight. It rested, trembling, on the now-askew sandbags. Some had fallen, some were preparing to slide away, pushed by the force of the water.

She had to make sure.

'Oh, shit,' she heard herself whisper.

Armand was physically holding Carl Tracey around the abdomen, while the man kicked and squirmed.

Jean-Guy hurried over to help contain him, but just as he arrived, Tracey slowly stopped thrashing, and a moment later he was standing still, clasped against Gamache's body.

Both men were staring.

'Stop!' This time it was Gamache who was shouting at Billy.

The floodlight on the top of the backhoe was pointing at the bucket of debris Billy had just dropped onto the field, next to the water rushing out of the Bella Bella.

'What's that?' asked Reine-Marie, taking a step closer.

Beauvoir saw then why Gamache had stopped the digging. Why Tracey had stopped fighting. And why he'd been so hysterical to stop the digging.

'What's that?' Gabri shouted at Clara and Myrna. He tried to keep the panic out of his voice. 'What're you saying?'

The two women were waving their arms and yelling something about the river. If he had to guess, and it seemed he might have to, whatever they were shouting was not good news.

Billy went to dismount his machine, but Armand waved him to stay where he was. And told Reine-Marie the same thing.

Then he and Jean-Guy slowly approached the trench.

'Armand, Gabri's saying something. Something's happened.'

'What?' yelled Billy from the cab of the machine.

'What?' yelled Gabri again, completely forgetting he had Reine-Marie on the line.

'What?' came the tinny voice.

'The water level's going down!'

Gabri and Reine-Marie heard it at the same moment. Clara's shout. And then Reine-Marie heard shouts of joy. Even Ruth was cheering. At least she thought that cackling was a cheer.

'The water level's dropping!' Reine-Marie reported. 'It's worked. It's dropping.'

Billy gave a whoop. But while both Armand and Jean-Guy looked over, Armand smiling with relief and Jean-Guy nodding, they quickly looked away.

In the harsh beam from Billy's backhoe, something pink was lying in the muck.

Armand knelt and reached out.

It was a bright pink duffel bag. With a name tag. A single embossed letter.

V.

CHAPTER 15

'What've you done with her?' Gamache demanded.

'Nothing. I've done nothing. Maybe it isn't hers.'

'It's hers,' said Gamache. 'It's Vivienne's, and you know it.'

Tracey recognized it. But Gamache also recognized something. The look on Carl Tracey's face. He'd seen it before, when a piece of damning evidence, thought hidden, was found.

It was the unmistakable look of dread.

While he stayed with Tracey and the duffel bag, Beauvoir went to the river and was walking the banks. Shining his flashlight, to see if he could see something else. Someone else.

As he walked, Beauvoir's heart thudded in his chest, in his wrists, at his temples, and in his throat. His skin tingled. His face, in the cold, was flushed.

He'd spent much of his adult life looking for bodies, at bodies. What was out there didn't scare him.

What frightened him was what was in there. Inside himself. What dark thing had been aroused, awoken, when he realized he was in the presence of someone who'd almost certainly thrown his wife and unborn child into a freezing river. To die.

It was all Jean-Guy Beauvoir could do not to turn around. March back to Tracey. Tell Armand and Reine-Marie and Billy to look away while he forced Tracey to a kneeling position, took out his gun. Placed it at the base of the monster's skull. And fired.

Jean-Guy paced. Pointing the flashlight this way and that. Trying to settle his mind and focus on the job at hand.

What he saw were shards of ice, rocks, roots uprooted. Debris. Rushing water. But no Vivienne.

At Beauvoir's request, Billy had turned his backhoe so that its light faced the river.

From the cab, Billy Williams watched Jean-Guy pace. He knew torment when he saw it.

Then he looked over at Armand. Standing right up against Carl Tracey. Not side by side but facing him, in an act of extreme and ghastly intimacy.

Billy Williams knew that what he was witnessing was also an act of love. Not for Tracey, of course, but for Jean-Guy.

Armand had sent the younger man away to, on the surface, do the worst job. To look for the body of a young woman and her unborn child. But in reality, Armand was saving Jean-Guy. From himself.

Gamache was standing that close to Carl Tracey so that Beauvoir didn't have to.

When Tracey backed up, Gamache moved forward. Not letting the weaselly man step away. Get away. Gamache was at least two inches taller, twenty pounds heavier, and twenty-five years older than Tracey.

He had the advantage of height, weight, control, and sobriety.

But Tracey had the greater advantage of knowledge. He knew where Vivienne was.

Gamache's boots thucked in the mud as he stepped even closer to Tracey.

'Tell us,' Gamache repeated, his eyes not leaving Tracey's. 'Where's Vivienne?'

'I don't know. She went away,' said Tracey. 'Ran away with some guy she was—'

'Enough,' said Gamache. 'What did you do with her?' Then he modulated his tone. Corralling, with difficulty, his anger. His voice, when he spoke again, was unnaturally reasonable. Coaxing a brute to do one decent thing. 'Tell us, Carl. Let us give her some rest.'

Behind them, the Bella Bella ran off into the mucky field. The night air was crackling with cold and outrage.

'I have no idea where she is. Maybe she got drunk and fell into the river. Or maybe whoever got her pregnant tossed her in.'

Out of the corner of his eye, Armand saw Reine-Marie take a step closer. Her hand gripped the phone, as though it were a baseball bat.

Somehow this vile man had managed to stir up in Reine-Marie an outrage that bordered on violence.

Gamache's own breath, through his nostrils, came out in long, warm puffs. Like a bull longing to charge.

He barely registered that behind him, Billy Williams was speaking.

'There's no sign of her,' called Beauvoir. 'Billy says he thinks the duffel bag came from farther upriver.'

'There's an old logging road about a kilometer from here.' Billy waved behind him. 'A bridge goes over the Bella Bella. It's been closed for a while now, but hunters sometimes use it in the fall.'

Jean-Guy translated what was said.

Gamache turned and looked at the .22 leaning against the backhoe. A hunting rifle.

'Can you show us?' he asked.

'Yurz.'

'What about the bag?' Reine-Marie asked.

'We'll take it with us,' said Gamache.

'You can't,' said Tracey.

'Then we'll open it here,' said Beauvoir.

Gamache asked Reine-Marie to use her phone to record the search of Vivienne's bag while Billy took his place beside Tracey.

'No,' said Tracey. 'Stop. It doesn't belong to you. It's on my property. It belongs to me.'

'It belongs to your wife,' said Beauvoir, unzipping it.

The duffel bag contained all the things you'd expect someone to pack who was going away for a few days. T-shirts, a pair of jeans. Some shorts. Pajamas. Underwear. Toiletries.

'What are these?' Gamache held up a bottle of pills and read off the label, 'Mifegymiso.'

When the others shook their heads, Gamache held them out for Tracey to see.

'How should I know? Probably some street drug she picked up, the—'

'Enough.' Beauvoir got to his feet and took a step toward Tracey.

'Jean-Guy,' snapped Gamache.

The cold, the exhaustion, the find, the growing certainty of what had happened to this young woman and who'd made it happen, were all fraying their nerves.

Beauvoir glared at Tracey but managed to contain himself.

'We're done,' said Gamache, zipping the duffel bag shut. 'We'll take this with us and give you a receipt.'

'I don't want a receipt. I want the bag.'

'You're coming with us,' said Beauvoir, and shoved him toward the car as they all trudged across the field. Leaving the backhoe to sink further into the mire.

When they reached the car, Beauvoir placed the duffel bag in the trunk, and Gamache, having removed the bullets, put the .22 back there, too.

Tracey stood beside the car.

'Get in,' said Gamache.

When Beauvoir went to get in beside him, Gamache held out the keys.

'Why don't you drive? Can you get in the front seat?' he asked Reine-Marie, who'd stopped recording and slipped the phone into her pocket.

Gamache and Billy got into the backseat, with Tracey between them.

'She isn't dead, you know. She's messing with you all. Trying to get me into trouble. I bet she threw that fucking bag into the river herself. You wait. When she shows up, after a bender with some guy, I'll be suing your ass.'

'Let's hope,' said Gamache.

Beauvoir drove while Billy pointed the way to the old logging road.

They came to little more than a break in the trees. Turning in, Beauvoir felt the tires begin to sink. 'We have to walk from here.'

The five of them followed the flashlight beams down the narrow lane through the trees.

The limbs of the trees loomed overhead, a tunnel of dead branches. Their flashlights created shadows so macabre that even Beauvoir, not given to fantasy, felt his skin crawl. This was how horror films began. Or ended.

And then it got worse.

Beauvoir's stronger beam landed on something up ahead. Blocking the way. A car.

'Stay here,' Gamache said to the others while he and Jean-Guy approached.

It was Vivienne's.

Gamache nodded to Beauvoir, who carefully walked around to the other side and shone his light through the rear window while Gamache looked in the front.

Nothing.

Opening the driver's door, careful not to touch too much, Gamache played his light over the seat. The wheel. The footwells. There were assorted wrappers, some change. It smelled of stale cigarette smoke. He checked the ashtray and found stubs.

The same brand Tracey smoked.

There was a smear of blood on the steering wheel and another in the shift. The hair on the back of Gamache's neck was standing on end. Something awful had happened here.

He pulled a lever and popped the trunk.

'Nothing,' Beauvoir reported.

Gamache closed the car door, and both investigators made for the wooden bridge.

'Don't worry,' shouted Tracey. 'It's safe.'

'No it's not,' called Billy. 'It's probably rotten.'

Beauvoir reached out and stopped Gamache, who was just about to step on the wooden boards. Armand had heard Billy but hadn't understood.

Beauvoir turned and glared at Tracey, who was smiling.

'Worth a try,' Tracey said, his eyes cold. Calculating.

Reine-Marie took a step away from this creature while

Beauvoir wondered if all five of them would make it out of the woods.

From the safety of solid ground, Gamache and Beauvoir shone their beams along the old logging bridge. Then stopped. The two circles of light converged on a single spot.

A section of wooden handrail was missing. The side opened up to thin air.

Gamache pointed his beam down. Into the drop-off. Twenty feet below, maybe more, was the churning river. Grabbing, dragging, swallowing all that it could.

They played their lights over both shores, but there was nothing. Then Beauvoir's beam stopped.

'Wait, I think I see something.'

Gamache swung his flashlight over to the far shore.

'What is it?' called Reine-Marie. 'Have you found something?'

'No, it's nothing,' said Beauvoir, relieved. 'Just branches. They looked like a body for a moment.'

He moved his flashlight away. 'We can't search the bridge or shoreline right now. Too dangerous. It'll have to wait 'til morning.'

But Gamache's light hadn't moved. In the beam, he saw what Beauvoir had seen. Tree branches, bobbing slightly in the current. Nothing more.

He could see why Beauvoir would mistake –

Opening his mouth, Gamache took a sharp breath, almost a gasp.

'What is it?' asked Beauvoir. 'Do you see something?'

Once more he swung his light over, to join Gamache's, until the two became one bright spot.

Beauvoir looked more closely at the clump of debris on the opposite bank. But still saw nothing. Certainly not

anything that would explain the expression on his father-in-law's face.

It was one of surprise. Shock, even.

'Vivienne's not here,' Gamache said, then looked at Beauvoir. 'But I think I know where she is.'

CHAPTER 16

⁓

The two men ran along the path, the river on one side, the forest on the other.

Jean-Guy skidded once and went down on one knee in the mud. Armand grabbed his jacket and hauled him to his feet.

And then they continued on. Their flashlights bobbing wildly ahead of them, illuminating trees, path, rocks, river.

They didn't have far to go. Just to the bend in the river.

When they'd arrived back in Three Pines, they'd taken Carl Tracey to the bistro, where they found Olivier and Gabri, now that the danger of flooding had passed.

'Keep him here,' Gamache had instructed them. 'Billy will stay with you. Homer?'

'At your place,' Olivier said. 'Clara and Myrna took him there hoping he'd get some sleep. They're staying with him.'

'What time is it?' asked Reine-Marie.

'Two thirty,' said Gabri.

'That late?'

'That early,' he said. 'The wee hours, as Ruth calls it.'

'Where is she, by the way?'

'She went home. Had to wee.'

Reine-Marie glanced at Tracey. He was in the far corner,

where he'd been placed by Jean-Guy. Far away from the warmth and soft light of the fireplace.

Then she turned to Armand. 'I'll make sure Homer doesn't come over here. You go.'

And Armand and Jean-Guy did.

Even though both men knew there was no need to rush, still they ran. Down the path. Beside the wall of sandbags. They ran behind the general store, the boulangerie, past the back of the bistro and the bookstore. The Bella Bella on one side, forest on the other.

And then they were there.

Gamache was panting and holding his flashlight out in front of him with both hands, like a gun. Aiming the beam, steadying it as he stood beside Beauvoir.

Their lights, pointed in the same direction, merged.

And then they saw it. Her.

Gamache had been there earlier, when he and Olivier had checked the river levels.

They hadn't come quite this far, but still, he'd seen it then as he'd leaned out. Olivier holding on to him.

The growing dam.

He'd noted the pale tree limbs and leaves bobbing up and down in the current. Trapped in the broken ice and debris that was forming.

He'd hesitated, trying to get a closer look. But Olivier's grip had been slipping, and he was pulled away.

Now he was back. And he saw, in the bright circle of light, his mistake.

At the logging bridge, Beauvoir had momentarily taken trees for a body. And in that moment, Armand Gamache realized he'd done the same thing, only in reverse.

He'd mistaken a body for trees.

Now he looked once again at the tangle of ice and tree limbs. Debris and detritus picked up by the Rivière Bella Bella as it rushed down from the mountains.

Here was Vivienne Godin.

This is where she'd come to rest.

Her dark hair, like leaves, floated on the surface, moving with the current. Her pale arms and legs. Limbs. Now so clearly human.

Armand Gamache crossed himself, just as Beauvoir shoved his flashlight into Gamache's hands.

'What're you doing?'

'What does it look like?' Beauvoir stripped off his coat. 'I'm going to get her.'

'You can't.' Gamache placed himself between Beauvoir and the Bella Bella and reached out. 'Stop.'

But Beauvoir wasn't listening to reason. He looked at the bobbing head. At the arms.

And he saw Annie.

'Step aside,' he said to Gamache.

'*Non.*'

'Step aside. That's an order.'

'*Non.*'

Jean-Guy then did something he'd not have thought possible twenty-four hours earlier. An hour earlier. A moment earlier.

He shoved his father-in-law. Who dropped the flashlights and took a step back, partly from the force of it, partly from the shock of it.

'Get out of my way,' Jean-Guy yelled, desperate to get to the young woman. As he hoped someone would try to save Annie, if . . .

This time Gamache saw him coming and wrapped his

160

arms around Jean-Guy. Gripping him in a bear hug so tight that Jean-Guy could smell the slight scent of sandalwood and feel Armand's heart thudding against his own.

'It's too late,' Armand said, directly into Jean-Guy's ear.

But still he struggled. Finally the fight went out of him. And he sagged in Gamache's arms.

'She's gone,' Armand whispered, his own eyes screwed shut.

'She's pregnant,' sobbed Jean-Guy.

'Yes. I know.'

'Annie. Annie's pregnant. Almost three months.'

Armand's eyes opened. And he heard a sob.

One. Single. Burst of emotion. Which might have been Jean-Guy's. Or his own. Or maybe it came from the Bella Bella as the river cried out.

And then he realized where it had come from.

Releasing Jean-Guy, he turned and looked up the path. In the darkness there was a greater darkness. A large figure, a father figure, outlined against the trees, standing silent. Rigid.

Then Vivienne's father started forward. One. Step. At a time. Picking up speed. Until he was running down the path.

'Homer, stop!' shouted Gamache.

But Vivienne's father didn't. Couldn't.

He made not a sound but ran straight for the river.

Gamache and Beauvoir just had time to step between Homer Godin and the water. But they might as well have been made of paper. Homer plowed right through them, running straight into the Bella Bella. Wading in. Breaking through the thin ice at the shore, he fought his way forward. To get to his little girl.

Gamache and Beauvoir plunged in after him.

The water was so cold their eyes watered, and their breath

came in gasps. But on they lurched, toward the man thrashing through the current ahead of them.

The water churned and frothed as Godin, his arms flailing wildly, knocked them off.

He fought ferociously. Screaming now. Wailing. Baying. Sobbing.

Gamache got an elbow in the head and was knocked backward, submerged. So cold was the water that his chest locked and he couldn't breathe, even when arms pulled him to the surface.

It was Jean-Guy. Armand stared at him for a moment, then managed, with a great whoop, to get air back into his lungs.

Then it was back to Godin. Who, after what seemed like hours, finally tired of dragging them with him. Like some great whale, harpooned, he slowed. Slowed. Sobbing.

Then stopped. It took both of them to drag Vivienne's father back to shore.

But Homer Godin wasn't finished yet. Once again he tried to break free, but this time they were ready for him. And he had little fight left in him.

'Stop,' said Beauvoir softly.

And he did.

'Vivienne?'

'I'm sorry,' Armand said.

Homer looked out into the river. 'Please,' he whispered. 'I need to get her.'

'We will,' said Beauvoir. His teeth were chattering, and he was finding it difficult to form words.

He looked over at Gamache, whose lips were purple and trembling in the cold.

They were all on the verge of exposure. With Homer

Godin also suffering from shock, it was a potentially fatal combination.

'Not you,' said Homer, his voice shaky. 'Me. I have to help her. I can get to her. Let me try.'

'The water's too cold. You'll drown,' said Gamache through chattering teeth.

'Does it matter?'

'It matters.'

But Armand understood. He'd try, too. He'd fight, too. He'd run back into that freezing water, too. If . . .

Homer turned away from him, to once again face the river. And his daughter in the middle of it. Bobbing gently up and down in the current. Her body knocking against the ice.

A small sound escaped the large man.

Only then did Armand notice a figure standing farther down the path, toward the village. Even at a distance. Even in the dark. He knew who it was.

He walked toward her.

'I'm sorry,' said Reine-Marie. 'I tried to stop him, but he ran out of the house so fast. He must've been watching from the bedroom window and seen you come here.'

Armand bent his face close to hers. 'Your face. It's bruised.'

'Is it?'

'Did he hit you?'

'Not on purpose. He didn't know what he was doing. I reached for his arm to try to stop him—'

Armand brought one shaking finger to within a millimeter of the bruise on Reine-Marie's cheekbone, below her eye. It was swollen, and swelling further.

Gamache could feel himself begin to tremble uncontrollably. It came in waves, sending shudders through his body.

It was, he recognized, the beginning of hypothermia. And outrage.

'My God, Armand, you're soaked. You need to get warm.' She looked down the path and only then noticed that Jean-Guy and Homer were also dripping wet. Homer was standing on the shore of the Bella Bella, staring. She followed his eyes. 'Is that ...?'

'*Oui.*'

CHAPTER 17

The water cascaded over Armand's body as he showered. Over his head, over his upturned face. He opened his mouth and shut his eyes. And felt his body finally getting warm.

But then, unbidden, a sudden panic took him.

He was back in the water. Submerged. But this time Jean-Guy wasn't there. No one was there, to reach down and save him.

His eyes flew open, and he dropped his head, away from the water. Reaching out, he leaned against the wet tiles of the shower.

As he breathed, he knew his momentary terror was just a tiny part of what Vivienne must have gone through.

The horror of those final moments. Breaking through the railing. Hanging in midair. Nothing between the bridge and the water to stop her fall.

And then she fell.

Hitting the freezing-cold water. The breath knocked out of her. The shock. The bitter Bella Bella closing over her. And then she breached. Breaking the surface. Mouth open, fighting for air.

The struggle to keep head, mouth, nose above the water. To take a breath. Turning, tumbling, thrashing in the current. Hitting rocks and branches.

The terror. The tumult. The desperate struggle. Growing less and less desperate as the cold and the battering began to win.

And finally the knowing.

Both hands on the tiles, his head hanging down, warm water hitting his back, Armand gasped for breath. And watched the water swirl around the drain.

Annie's pregnant. Annie's pregnant, he repeated, following the words to the surface. And trying not to allow the rest of that thought to seep in. But still, it was there.

And so was Vivienne.

He opened his eyes and finished his shower.

Then went downstairs, to face Vivienne's father.

Homer and Jean-Guy were in the kitchen, in front of the woodstove, wrapped in Hudson's Bay blankets. Mugs of strong tea in their hands.

Armand kissed Reine-Marie, softly, on her bruised cheek. 'You okay?' he whispered.

The bruise wasn't as bad as he feared, more a glancing blow. But a blow nonetheless.

'I am.'

Armand looked at her, closely, to make sure she was telling the truth. Then he turned his attention to the others.

Jean-Guy had stopped trembling.

Homer had not.

As soon as they'd returned to the house, they'd called the Sûreté divers and a Scene of Crime squad from homicide. But with the state of emergency across the province,

166

they were told it could take some hours. Not before morning, for sure.

After letting Isabelle Lacoste and Agent Cloutier know what had happened and asking them to come down, they'd split up.

Jean-Guy had grabbed a shower first, while Armand helped Homer to strip off his wet clothing and get into his own shower. He stayed with the man, who'd sunk into silence, until the shower was over and Homer was in warm, dry clothes.

Armand stayed with him in the kitchen until Jean-Guy returned.

While he knew it wasn't Homer's fault, and it would almost certainly never happen again, he was damned if he'd leave Reine-Marie alone with Homer. Mad with grief, Vivienne's father was capable of almost anything.

Certainly, Armand knew, capable of murder. Though that was aimed at only one person.

After his own shower, Armand returned to the kitchen and caught Jean-Guy's eye. Both men turned to Reine-Marie.

'What?' she asked.

'Jean-Guy has something that might make you feel better,' said Armand quietly.

'Can you come with me?' Jean-Guy stood up.

After a brief, baffled, glance at Armand, Reine-Marie followed her son-in-law out of the kitchen.

Fred had put his large head on Homer's slippered feet, and Henri did the same with Armand. Little Gracie was curled up on a blanket close to the fire.

The only sound was the slight rattle of the old windows as the night tried to get in. Not, perhaps, realizing it was already dark in there.

A few minutes later, Reine-Marie and Jean-Guy returned.

She was flushed, and her eyes were moist. And when she met Armand's, his, too, began to burn. She brought her hands to her mouth, and he embraced her.

'I just spoke to Annie. A baby,' she whispered, words meant only for Armand.

Homer did not need to know that they were living his dream, while he lived their nightmare.

Excusing himself now, Armand went into his study and, picking up his phone, tapped in a familiar number.

'I'm sorry,' he heard the polite young receptionist say, 'but Chief Superintendent Toussaint can't take your call right now.'

'Tell her it's Armand Gamache.'

There was a pause. 'She knows.'

Now it was his turn to pause. *'Merci.'*

Then he called the senior RCMP commissioner who'd been in the meeting the day before.

'Armand, what is it?' He sounded weary.

'I wanted an update on the flooding.'

'Did you call Toussaint?'

'I tried.'

Again there was a pause. Gamache could feel the embarrassment down the line.

'It's a hectic time,' the officer said.

'Oui. Can you tell me what's happening?'

'The dynamiting on the St. Lawrence worked, but it looks like a temporary reprieve. The thaw's moving north.'

'The dams?'

'Holding. Barely. The pressure's building. And they still can't decide whether or not to open the floodgates.'

'Go on.' Gamache, who knew the man well, could hear the hesitation.

'I've consulted with the armed forces engineer and Hydro-Québec. We're not waiting for approval. Hydro's going to open the gates.'

Gamache took a deep breath. 'You know that what you're doing could be considered insubordination.'

'You think? Well, you're the expert, I guess,' the Mountie said with a laugh. He sounded drained. 'Once the floodgates are open, we'll pull the machinery from all but the most vulnerable dams and move it south. The corps of engineers will then begin digging trenches along rivers that're threatening communities. More insubordination. I don't think they're going to let us play together anymore, Armand. You're a bad influence.'

Gamache gave a small sound of amusement. It was all he could muster.

'Armand?'

'*Oui?*'

'Be careful of Toussaint.'

'She's doing well,' Gamache said. 'These are difficult decisions. She'll grow into the job.'

'But what job? She has political aspirations.'

'Nothing wrong with that.'

'Except she's using her position in the Sûreté not as a responsibility but as a tool, a springboard. Surely that was obvious in the meeting. She needs to distance herself from you. Distinguish herself from you.'

'Your point being?'

'With this flood, with our decision to follow your suggestion and not waiting for her approval, she'll be gunning for you.'

'Not literally, I hope.'

But there was silence down the line. Both remembering

when that was exactly what senior officers had done to each other, literally. In the time 'before.'

'*Non*. But she's no friend of yours. You have the support and loyalty of the rank and file, Armand. She doesn't.'

'Give her time.'

'Have you been following the social-media posts? About you?'

'A bit.'

'Where do you think some of that information's coming from?'

'Are you kidding?' said Gamache. 'You think Madeleine Toussaint is leaking it?'

There was silence.

'You're wrong,' said Gamache.

'How can you be loyal to her, Armand, when it's so clearly not mutual?'

'Does it have to be mutual? She's a decent person, who stepped up. She's earned my loyalty. And she'll grow into a great leader. I know that. Otherwise I'd never have suggested her for Chief Superintendent.'

'There was no one left,' said the Mountie, his exasperation growing. 'Everyone else was either wounded or tainted by your actions. Even if you hadn't recommended her, Toussaint was the only one standing. Look' – there was a heaved sigh down the line – 'I hope I'm wrong. Just be careful. You've gotta know, once she gets wind of what we're doing, she'll blame you, even if we're successful.'

'God willing we are. That's all that matters.'

'*Inshallah*.'

'*B'ezrat HaShem*,' said Gamache. 'We'll worry about the rest later. Good luck. Let me know.'

'I will, my friend. Anything I can do?'

Armand looked toward the kitchen. 'Do you have any divers you can spare?'

'Huh?'

———

As the RCMP divers reached the body, Beauvoir heard a sharp intake of breath and prepared to grab hold of Vivienne's father, if necessary.

But it wasn't.

Homer Godin stood on the shore. Face rigid. Body at attention.

Only when the team turned Vivienne over did he move. But not forward, as they expected and were prepared for.

Vivienne's father sank, slowly, slowly to his knees. Then slowly, slowly he folded over. His head in the muck. His hands clutching the ground. The big man curled himself around his heart.

As Vivienne Godin approached the shore, her father lifted his head, sensing more than seeing her close by. Then he raised his body. Sitting back on his heels. And, with the help of Gamache and Beauvoir, he struggled to his feet.

They kept their hands under Homer's arms. Supporting him. Holding him upright.

Homer was swaying, openmouthed. Eyes glazed. As Vivienne was lifted onto a stretcher.

Dr Harris bent over the body. Glancing at Gamache and Beauvoir, she shook her head. Confirming what was painfully obvious.

'I need to see her,' said her father.

Dr Harris whispered to Gamache. 'It isn't good. She's been in the water at least two days.'

'We need an identification,' said Beauvoir.

Lysette Cloutier, who'd just arrived, said, 'I'll do it.'

'Me,' said Vivienne's father. 'Me.'

'I'll take you over,' said Armand quietly. 'But you must promise not to touch her. If we're going to get enough evidence to convict, no one but the investigators must touch Vivienne. Do you understand?'

Homer's heavy head bobbed up and down.

'Are you ready?' Armand asked.

He nodded again.

They escorted Vivienne's father to Vivienne's body.

He stared down at her. With the eyes of a man who'd reached the end of a long tunnel and realized there was no light there.

He gave one curt nod. And mouthed, 'That's Vivienne.' Then, with more effort, he said it out loud. 'That's Vivienne.'

He brought his hand up to his face, covering his mouth, in a grotesque imitation of Reine-Marie's joy just hours earlier.

Gamache looked down at the body.

Her blue eyes were open, not in fear but in that surprise they often saw in those suddenly, prematurely meeting Death. He wondered if Death had been just as surprised.

Gamache swiftly, expertly took in the condition of her body before meeting Beauvoir's eyes. And nodding.

'Come away.' He spoke softly to Homer. 'We'll let the officers do their job.'

'No,' said Homer. 'I need to stay. With her. Until ... Please. I won't make trouble. I promise.'

He motioned toward a tree stump, and Gamache nodded. 'Of course.' Then turned to Cloutier. 'Stay with him, please.'

Gamache noticed then a uniformed agent walking down the path toward them.

'What're you doing here?' Gamache asked. 'You're supposed to be guarding Carl Tracey.'

'I was relieved.'

'By whom?'

'Agent Cameron.'

'He's there with Tracey? Alone?'

'Well, there're others. The owners of the bistro—'

'Come with me.'

Through the windows of the bistro, Gamache could see Bob Cameron. He was standing within feet of Carl Tracey, who was crammed into a corner. His chair overturned at his feet.

Cameron held something in his right hand. Something black. His gun?

No, Gamache took in quickly as he made for the door. Not a gun. Too big. It was a fireplace poker. As lethal as a gun, if swung at a person's head.

And it looked, by his stance, that that was exactly what Cameron was preparing to do.

Tracey was raising his arms to protect himself.

Gamache opened the bistro door with a bang, and Cameron turned around.

'He's going to kill me,' shouted Tracey. 'Stop him.'

'Shut up, you stupid shit.'

'Cameron,' snapped Gamache. 'Step away. Now.'

After a slight pause, Cameron threw the poker onto the floor in disgust. And stepped back.

'I wasn't going to hit him,' he said. 'I just wanted to scare him.'

'Get over there,' said Gamache, pointing to the far corner.

The former left tackle jerked toward Tracey, who squeezed tighter into the corner. Then Cameron marched away, shoving a table as he passed Gamache.

'What's happening?' asked Gabri, coming cautiously out of the swinging door between the bistro and the kitchen, followed by Olivier, who was holding up a frying pan.

'Nothing,' said Cameron.

'Nothing?' demanded Tracey. 'He was going to hit me with that.' He pointed to the poker.

'Did you see anything?' Gamache asked Gabri and Olivier.

Both men shook their heads.

'He told us to go into the kitchen and stay there,' said Olivier.

'He'd picked up the poker,' said Gabri. 'We didn't need to be told twice. I tried to call you, but of course your phone didn't work.'

He held up the receiver, still clutched in his hand.

Gamache turned to the agent who'd accompanied him and gestured toward Tracey. 'Watch him.'

Then he led Cameron farther away from the others.

'What were you thinking?' he demanded.

'What're you saying?' demanded Tracey. 'I have a right to know. He was going to kill me.'

'Be quiet, please,' said Gamache, and while his tone was polite, anyone who saw the man would not be fooled by the courtesy.

Even as he turned back to Cameron, Gamache admitted that what Tracey said might very well be true. It certainly looked like that.

But how things looked and how they really were, were often two very different things in a murder investigation.

He waited for an answer.

'I wanted to get a confession out of him,' said Cameron. 'I wanted to scare him, not beat him. I had my phone on, recording. I can show you.'

'You recorded yourself threatening a suspect with a fireplace poker?' asked Gamache, incredulous. 'You know that any confession you might've gotten would've been inadmissible, and the whole case thrown out.'

'I would've erased the beginning,' said Cameron.

Now Gamache stared, clearly dumbfounded. 'You say that as though you expect me to go along with you. I warned you about this just hours ago, and now you do exactly the same thing?'

'Not the same. You warned me about hitting a suspect. I never laid a hand on him.'

'Threatening a beating is still brutality,' said Gamache. 'If you were under my command, Agent Cameron, I'd relieve you of duty right now.'

'I'm happy to leave.' He took a step away.

'You'll leave when I tell you to. What're you even doing here? This isn't your assignment.'

'You think my responsibility stops at the end of my shift? Does yours?'

'Don't question me, young man. This isn't about me, it's about your behavior—'

'Yeah, well, you're quite a role model. Sir.' Cameron glared. 'I've been following the Twitter feed about you. Have you?'

'I asked you a question. What're you doing here?'

'How can you lead, sir, if you don't have the support of the population? Wasn't that the whole point of your lecture to me? Trust? Looks like you've lost it. Have you lost it?'

And the inflection made it clear that Cameron was talking about more than trust.

'Answer my question now, Agent Cameron, or I'll charge you with interfering in a murder investigation.'

Gamache knew exactly what Cameron was doing. He was trying to throw him off balance. Put him on the defensive. Get control of the narrative and take focus away from the real question.

Why was Agent Cameron there? Why was he threatening Tracey for a confession?

This spoke of more than a cop going off the rails. Emotionally het up about the horrific crime. It spoke, and smelled, of personal involvement.

'Tell me,' said Gamache. 'You know I'll find out.'

And Cameron could see that was true. Here was a man determined to, trained to, born to find things out.

Chief Inspector Gamache, sharp intent in his eyes, did not seem like the slightly pathetic, definitely incompetent, occasionally dangerous man described in the tweets.

'I came because I care about Vivienne,' said Cameron.

And there it was. Confirmation of something that had become obvious to Gamache.

But Bob Cameron didn't just care, he cared so deeply he no longer had control of his actions. Or judgment.

'I see.' Gamache paused. Studying the man. 'Were you having an affair?'

'No.'

'The truth.'

'No. I wanted to help her. I asked her to call me, to have a coffee together. To just talk. But she never did.'

'Did you go to the house?'

Cameron lowered his head, no longer looking Gamache in the eye. 'A few times. When I knew he wasn't there. When he was in the bar or in jail to sober up.'

'You detained the husband, then went up and propositioned the wife?'

Cameron's face flushed, the scars turning white against the red. 'It wasn't like that.'

'I think it was,' said Gamache. 'And you just don't want to admit it. She wasn't interested, but you continued to harass her.'

'I wasn't harassing her. She was afraid.' Cameron shot a filthy look at the man across the bistro. 'She wanted to leave him, I could tell. I was just trying to help her break away.'

He lifted his head and met Gamache's eyes. 'I love my wife. I have two children. But there was something about Vivienne. Something . . .' He stopped and thought. 'Not innocent. Not even fragile. She seemed strong, but confused. Beaten down. I just wanted to help her.'

Gamache looked at Cameron's face. Disfigured. And knew how deep the blows went. How deep the disfigurement went. And knew how much this man, while a boy, would have wanted someone to help him.

Motivations were rarely straightforward, as he knew all too well. And Gamache wondered how confused Cameron was, between helping Vivienne and helping himself.

Gamache considered the man, then nodded. 'Stay where you are,' he said, and walked across the bistro.

He had a duty to perform. No matter how ludicrous it seemed.

'Monsieur Tracey,' said Gamache, squaring himself in front of the man.

'What?'

'I'm sorry to have to inform you—'

'So she is dead,' said Tracey.

'Yes. I'm afraid so. Her body was found in the river, just outside the village. She was thrown off that bridge.'

'Thrown? You make it sound like it was done on purpose.'

'We think it was.'

'Prove it.'

'Pardon?'

'How do you know she was thrown? I think she jumped. Killed herself.' His voice changed. 'She was very depressed, you know. It sometimes happens to pregnant women. Hormones. She talked about killing herself for weeks. I did my best. Tried to comfort her. Begged her to get help.' Tracey's voice had become wheedling. Rehearsing lines for a judge. 'But she wouldn't. She was drinking too much. Then she just disappeared. I was distraught.'

A long, long silence greeted that. While Tracey smiled, the others in the bistro stared.

Gamache tilted his head slightly. Then he nodded. Slightly.

Tracey, with the instincts of a rodent, stopped smiling. Had he had hackles, they would have gone up. And for good reason.

He'd goaded the wrong person.

'Your wife was pregnant,' said Gamache. His voice quiet. Unnaturally calm. 'The night she disappeared, she told you the child wasn't yours. You have a history of drunk and disorderly. Police have been called to your place more than once for domestic violence. Judges are smart. Juries are smart. What do you think they'll make of that?'

'I'll tell you what they'd make of it.' His voice rose. 'That I'm a shit husband, but not a killer. She was drunk and knocked up, and she left me. Try to prove otherwise.'

'And you never asked who the father was?' demanded Gamache. 'I didn't care.'

'You cared. You cared about how it looked to others. You cared about being made a fool of. We found blood in your living room and in her car. What did you do to her?'

Tracey was silent.

'What did you do, Carl?'

The others in the room stayed absolutely still. Frozen.

'I have a right to know who my wife was screwing, okay. I didn't do anything you wouldn't do. Anything any normal guy wouldn't do.'

He looked around but met only disgust.

'So what did you do? Come on, Carl. Tell me.'

'I gave her what for.'

'You beat her.'

'My drunk and knocked-up wife? She was leaving me to go to the father. What did she think was going to happen? It was her fault.'

But something, besides the grotesque description, struck Gamache.

'Her father or "the" father?' he asked. 'What did she say? Who was she going to?'

'The father. Her father. What difference does it make? I took a bottle and went to my studio. Passed out. When I woke up next morning, she was gone. But she was alive when I left her.'

Tracey's gaze shifted to something over Gamache's shoulder. Gamache turned.

Homer Godin was standing at the door.

Staring.

'I'm sorry, *patron*,' said Agent Cloutier, coming through behind Godin. She was out of breath from running. 'I was watching the coroner, and when I turned around, he was gone.'

'Don't let him close to me,' said Tracey, backing away. 'He's crazy.'

'Homer.' Gamache held his hands out in front of him, as though approaching a wounded wild animal. Or an explosive.

It wasn't that Gamache was afraid of him. Or afraid if Godin burst forward, they wouldn't be able to stop him before he killed Tracey. They could and would. But . . .

But would that really matter? Maybe, if I step aside . . . If I was a little slow to react . . .

Gamache knew then what he was really afraid of. Himself. *How would I feel . . . ?*

With effort, he shoved those thoughts away. To be replaced by a certainty.

They might stop him now, but they couldn't keep Homer Godin from Carl Tracey forever.

'You have your car here?' he asked Cameron while not taking his eyes off Godin, who wouldn't take his eyes off Tracey.

'*Oui.*'

'Good. I'm placing him under arrest. I want you to take him in.'

'Yessir,' said Cameron with enthusiasm, and turned toward Tracey, who backed up further.

'*Non,*' said Chief Inspector Gamache. 'Not him. Him.'

Even Tracey turned to Gamache with surprise.

The Chief Inspector was pointing at Homer.

'You mean Carl Tracey, sir,' said Cameron.

'No. I mean him.' He took a step closer to Vivienne's father and said, 'Homer Godin, I'm placing you under arrest.'

Godin's eyes remained on Tracey, then slowly refocused on Gamache.

'What did you say?'

'I'm arresting you.'

'What for?' asked Agent Cloutier, going to stand beside Homer.

'For assault.'

'I haven't done it yet. Give me a moment.' Godin's voice was flat, his cold stare returning to Tracey. 'And you can make it murder.'

'I mean the assault on Madame Gamache. You punched her in the face.'

'I did?'

'He what?' said Gabri.

'Take him in,' said Gamache. Then, in front of everyone, Gamache did something he'd never done before. He apologized, even as he made the arrest. *'Désolé.'*

'I hit your wife?' asked Homer, more stunned by that than the arrest. 'Is she all right?'

'She will be.'

'Oh, God,' sighed Homer. 'What's happening?'

They walked out of the bistro. Homer Godin in custody. And Carl Tracey a free man.

CHAPTER 18

The morning sun was just slanting over the trees as Clara and Myrna stood on the edge of the village green and watched.

Ruth joined them, limping out of her home, clutching Rosa to her chest.

'What's going on?'

'I think they found Vivienne,' said Clara, pointing to the coroner's car and then down the path along the river.

Ruth and Rosa shook their heads. 'It's tragic. So young.' Then Ruth's eyes and voice sharpened. 'What's he doing?'

'Looks like he's arresting Homer,' said Myrna as they watched Armand walk with Homer to the Sûreté car.

'He can't think—' Clara began.

'Jesus, even Clouseau can't be that stupid,' said Ruth.

'Fuck, fuck, fuck,' muttered the duck.

Just then Homer stopped and turned. As did Gamache. As did everyone else on the village green.

Vivienne Godin was being brought out of the woods. In a body bag.

The bistro door opened, and Carl Tracey stepped out. Into the fresh air. And sunshine.

He saw the stretcher, took a deep breath, and said, 'I wonder.'

'What?' demanded Olivier, coming out behind him.

'I wonder if she was insured.'

Staring silently at the long black bag as it was slid into the coroner's vehicle, Homer Godin crossed himself. As did Gabri and Olivier. Even Ruth, unseen by the others, made the familiar gesture.

After the coroner's vehicle drove away, Vivienne's father closed his eyes and tilted his head as far back as it would go. Exposing his throat to the Universe.

'Chief Inspector?' said Beauvoir as he came around the corner from the path along the river.

He indicated Homer, clearly in custody, by the car.

'I'll explain,' said Gamache, then instructed Cameron to take Godin into the local detachment. 'Don't book him. I'll be in to do the paperwork later. Make him comfortable, but don't let him out of your sight.'

Cameron turned to Homer. 'I'm sorry, sir. Would you mind?'

Homer got into the backseat without complaint.

As Cameron went to walk to the driver's side, Gamache stopped him.

'One moment, please. I have a question for you.' He led Cameron a few feet from the car. 'Was the child yours?'

Cameron's eyes widened. 'No, of course not. I told you, nothing happened between Vivienne and me.'

'You knew she was pregnant before we said anything. She told you. Is the child yours? Tell me the truth.'

'I am. It's not mine. Couldn't be.'

'I think you're lying. I think there's a lot you aren't telling us. I understand you're worried about your family.

Your job. But you know it'll come out. Best if you tell us yourself.'

'There's nothing to tell.'

Gamache pressed his lips together and gave a single curt nod. 'You're helping a murderer.'

'How?'

'By muddying the waters. By leaving questions unanswered. Questions we have to now take precious time investigating.'

'I have answered them.'

'But not truthfully.'

Gamache made a mental note to call the Alouettes organization and ask why they'd let Bob Cameron go. And why no other football team picked him up.

———

'May I go with him, sir?' Lysette Cloutier asked Chief Inspector Beauvoir.

He looked at her a moment. 'Why?'

'Why? Because he's my friend. He's just lost his daughter.'

Beauvoir nodded. 'Is it possible, Agent Cloutier, that you're more than friends?'

'More . . . ? *Non.* I care about him, but his wife was the one who was my friend. My best friend. I was maid of honor at their wedding.'

'When did she die?'

'Five years ago. Ovarian cancer.'

'I'm sorry.' He paused. 'You've kept up a relationship with Monsieur Godin?'

'There is no relationship. Not in the way I think you mean. We're old friends, that's all.' On seeing Beauvoir's skepticism, she pressed her lips together before nodding. 'All right,

you're right. But my relationship isn't with Homer, it's with Vivienne. She was my goddaughter.'

She dropped her gaze and studied her muddy boots before lifting her head and looking him straight in the eyes. Perhaps, he thought, a little too straight.

'I should've told you sooner, but I was afraid.'

'Of what?'

'That you'd think I was too close. That you'd take me off the case.'

'You're right. I probably would've.'

Cloutier shook her head. 'I've screwed up everything. I promised Katherine I'd look after her daughter. Keep her safe. I made that promise at the baptism, and I made it again at her deathbed. I didn't do a good job of it, did I? But what I can do now is help catch her killer. That's all I want.'

'And Homer Godin?'

'What about him?'

'More than professional interest?'

'Of course not.'

'You took his hand.'

'I was trying to comfort him. Haven't you ever held the hand of the mother, or father, of a murder victim? To console them?'

Beauvoir had to admit he never had.

He'd seen Chief Inspector Gamache do it.

And he himself had reached out, come within inches of that brute sorrow, but something stopped him every time.

They were different men, with different strengths. And maybe, he thought, that was one of the many reasons he was leaving the Sûreté. Heading to Paris. He knew, deep down, that there was a level, deep down, he could never reach as an investigator.

While Jean-Guy Beauvoir explored the tangible, what could be touched, Armand Gamache explored what was felt. He went into that chaotic territory. Hunting. Searching. Tracking. Immersing himself in emotions until he found one so rancid it led to a killer.

Beauvoir stopped at the door. Gamache went through it.

Which wasn't to say Beauvoir was insensitive to feelings. Watching Agent Cloutier, he'd picked up on hers.

There was something between her and Homer Godin, he was sure of it. Though he doubted Godin knew that. He wondered if Cloutier had even admitted it to herself.

'May I go with them, sir?' she asked again.

Beauvoir looked over at Homer. As though the day wasn't bad enough, now he found himself alone in the back of a police car. While the man who killed his daughter was standing in the sunshine.

'Go.'

He might not be able to hold Homer's hand, but he could offer comfort in other ways.

Clara, Myrna, and Ruth stepped back as the cop car passed them.

Ruth shook her head and looked over at Gamache and Beauvoir, conferring on the village green.

'Shouldn't there be a third Stooge?' Just then another car arrived. 'Never mind. Spoke too soon.'

Isabelle Lacoste got out and walked, limping slightly, over to her two colleagues.

⌣

'Was that Monsieur Godin in the back of the patrol car?' Lacoste asked. 'Is he under arrest?'

Gamache explained to both of them what he'd done, and why.

'I know Reine-Marie won't press charges. It was an accident. But maybe we can hold him long enough to collect evidence.'

'Against Tracey, *oui*,' said Beauvoir, glancing over his shoulder at the man lounging, like a reptile, in the early April sun.

He turned to Lacoste and Gamache. 'Walk with me, please.'

Isabelle raised her brows in amusement and wondered if Gamache recognized those words. It was something he'd often said to them during murder investigations.

Now they fell into step and waited for Beauvoir to speak.

'What do you think?' he said.

'This one might be difficult,' said Lacoste. 'Proving she was murdered.'

'Is it possible she wasn't?' asked Gamache.

Beauvoir considered, glancing over at Tracey, then back to his two colleagues. 'Possible, I suppose, but I don't believe it was an accident, or suicide. Do you?'

'Not for a moment,' said Lacoste.

Gamache nodded. It was murder. He knew that. What he didn't know was whether they could prove it.

'Did you know that Agent Cloutier was Vivienne Godin's godmother?' Beauvoir asked.

'Huh,' said Gamache. 'Why didn't she tell us that before?'

'Says she was afraid of being taken off the case. But I'm not convinced. Why keep that a secret unless there's more there?'

Gamache then told them about Bob Cameron.

'*Merde*,' said Beauvoir. 'He was having an affair with her?'

'Denies it,' said Gamache.

'You don't believe him?' asked Lacoste.

'I don't.'

'You think he might've killed Vivienne?' Beauvoir couldn't keep the skepticism out of his voice.

'I think he and Vivienne were much more involved than he admits. And where there're secrets—'

'There's fire. What do you think happened?'

'I think one possible scenario is that they arranged to meet on that side road by the bridge. Where they wouldn't be seen. If she told him then that the child was his and that she'd left Tracey to be with him—'

'Is he married?' Lacoste asked.

'*Oui*. With two children.'

'You think in a moment of madness he pushed her off the bridge,' she said.

'Or just pushed her away and she fell against the railing. I've seen him play. He's strong. And it's the sort of instinctive move a left tackle makes.' Gamache mimicked the pushing motion. 'It wouldn't take much for Vivienne to break through the railing and fall.'

'And he just left?' asked Lacoste.

'Once she was in the water, he couldn't save her even if he wanted to.' Once again, and just for an instant, Gamache felt himself submerged in the bitterly cold water. Unable to breathe.

'And now he's too afraid to admit anything,' said Beauvoir. 'Still, do you think that's what happened?'

It didn't take Gamache long to answer that. '*Non*.'

'We all know who did this,' said Lacoste.

'*Bon*,' said Gamache, and turned to continue walking, but

188

when he realized Beauvoir had not joined him, he stopped and returned.

'There's something I'd like to ask you,' said Jean-Guy.

'*Oui?*'

Reine-Marie had walked around the village green and joined Olivier and Gabri outside the bistro.

'Jesus, he did hit you, didn't he?' said Gabri, looking at the bruise on her face. 'You okay?'

'Nothing Honoré hasn't done, also by accident.' She touched her bruised cheekbone lightly. 'I put frozen peas on it.'

They brought her up to speed on what had happened, and as they talked, she took another few steps away from Carl Tracey, who was sitting at a table on the *terrasse*. Drinking a beer. At eight in the morning.

'Does that remind you of anything?' Olivier asked.

'A clown in a sewer?' Gabri suggested.

'No, not him. Them.' Olivier gestured toward the three Sûreté officers on the village green.

Reine-Marie cocked her head, staring. And then she gave a short puff of amusement and recognition.

Isabelle. Jean-Guy. Armand.

Three colleagues.

Three friends. A trinity. Sturdy. Eternal. Together.

'Three Pines,' she said.

'Three Stooges,' said Ruth as she walked by and entered the bistro.

'I know I assigned this to you, that you're the lead investigator, but do you mind if I take over?' Before Gamache could answer, Beauvoir held up his hand. 'I know it's a lot to ask.'

'You have a perfect right to assume command of any investigation. May I ask why?'

'This will probably be my last case with the Sûreté. With any police force. This's the one I want to go out on.'

When Gamache didn't answer, Beauvoir asked, 'What is it?'

'Have you thought that maybe this isn't the one you want as your final case?'

'What do you mean?'

'We're pretty sure we know who did it.'

'More than "pretty sure," I'd say. Tracey all but admits it.'

'He admits he beat Vivienne, not that he threw her off the bridge. He keeps insisting it was suicide, and we're going to have a helluva problem proving it wasn't at least an accident. And, as you said, even if we can prove it's murder, it might be extremely difficult to convict the man.'

'We've had more difficult cases,' said Lacoste.

'True.'

'Are you reluctant to give it up? Because of Annie? I've seen how much you sympathize with Godin. More than usual.'

Armand smiled and nodded. 'It's true. This one's gotten under my skin. And yes, because of Annie. I'm trying not to, but the truth is, I find myself asking how I'd feel, if . . . And even more since you told us Annie's pregnant.'

'Pregnant?' asked Lacoste. When Jean-Guy nodded, she gave him a quick embrace. 'Félicitations.'

'Merci.'

'I think you feel the same way,' said Gamache. 'About Vivienne and Annie.'

'Not really.'

Gamache stared at his son-in-law, frankly and openly amazed. 'I beg your pardon?'

'This is a terrible case, absolutely. But I haven't personalized it.'

There was silence as Gamache watched him. And then spoke.

'You almost killed yourself trying to get to her body,' he pointed out. 'I've seen you desperate to stop a murderer, but I've never seen you take it so personally.'

'I'm not.' Then he relented. 'Okay, maybe a little. It's hard not to. But I have my feelings well under control. Don't worry.'

Isabelle Lacoste looked from one to the other. Both, she knew, were personalizing this. Far more than she'd ever seen. Far more than was healthy.

If they weren't worried, she was.

'*Bon*,' said Gamache. 'I'm happy to hand over the case. May I act as your second-in-command, *patron*?'

'For the first time?'

'And, with luck, the last.'

Beauvoir gave a small laugh and put out his hand. 'Welcome aboard. I'll try to go easy on you, son. Just don't screw up.'

'You inspire me already, Chief Inspector.'

'Now, isn't it your nap time?'

'You might want to consider grabbing some sleep yourself,' said Gamache. 'Long day behind us and long day ahead.'

'Work still to be done. I need to set up an incident room.'

'I'm sure your second-in-command can do that.'

'You're my second-in-command.'

Gamache gave a short grunt of laughter and clapped Beauvoir on the arm. 'Well, good luck.'

But as he walked away, Armand's smile faded. Replaced by a slight frown.

He called his RCMP colleague as soon as he got back home.

It rang. And rang. Finally clicking over to voice mail.

Gamache looked at his watch. The sun had been up for slightly over an hour.

The floodgates at the mighty dams had been open for slightly under an hour.

What was happening up there?

He left a message, then went upstairs, suspecting he wouldn't be able to sleep. But the moment his head hit the cool, fresh pillow, he was out.

Reine-Marie, also exhausted, had joined him, and in their sleep they moved to the middle until their warm bodies touched.

Beauvoir and Lacoste walked past the thick wall of sandbags, pausing to consider them.

'Came close,' she said, pointing to the ones that had been pushed over by the force of the river.

Beauvoir grunted.

How close they all were, without knowing it, to disaster. All the time.

They walked over the stone bridge to the old brick train station. It had seen its share of reunions. And partings. Its share of tears. And shouts of joy.

Even he, fairly immune to fantasy, could feel that every time he entered the familiar building.

It had also seen its share of murder investigations, having been used in the past by Chief Inspector Gamache as temporary headquarters for the homicide unit.

Now Chief Inspector Beauvoir directed his team to set up shop.

Abandoned decades earlier by the railway, the building was now home to the Three Pines Volunteer Fire Department, overseen by its chief, Ruth Zardo, who glared down at them

from the official photo, taken when she'd been given the Governor General's Award for poetry.

'*I didn't feel the aimed word hit,*' Beauvoir said, looking up at the embittered old poet. '*And go in like a soft bullet.*'

> *I didn't feel the smashed flesh*
> *closing over it like water*
> *over a thrown stone.*

'What was that, *patron*?' asked one of the agents.

'Nothing.'

'Sounded like poetry,' she said with some alarm.

'Keep working.' Beauvoir caught Isabelle Lacoste's eye and saw amusement there. And recognition.

My God, he thought. *I'm turning into Gamache.*

But while he feigned alarm, what he actually felt was a sort of contentment. That on his last case he should finally turn into his mentor.

He stood still amid the activity and let the evidence come to him. But what came to him was an image. Clear as day. Young and pregnant Vivienne Godin, breaking through the railing. Arms out. The duffel bag, her worldly possessions, falling with her.

Her blue eyes wide, as realization hit.

And then the water. Cold as ice. Closing over her.

. . . like water over a thrown stone.

How would I feel if it was Annie . . .

Armand was right, of course. He was struggling to separate the two women.

> *Does my twisting body spell out Grace?*
> *I hurt, therefore I am.*

Faith, Charity, and Hope
are three dead angels
falling like meteors –

'Always cheerful, eh, you old witch,' muttered Jean-Guy as he gave one last glance up at Ruth before turning to examine the sodden items at his feet.

They'd found Vivienne's purse in the tangle of the dam. Its contents were spread out on the sanitized plastic sheet on the floor, alongside the things from the duffel bag.

An agent described each item for the recording as it was removed. Tagged. Cataloged. Photographed. Swabbed. Examined.

Private items transformed, like black magic, into public property.

Finally the entire contents were spread out.

From the purse they'd taken a wallet, with a hundred and ten dollars and change. Driver's license. A bank card but no credit card. Some paper, too wet to read, the water having turned it into pulp. Some mints. A Bic lighter but no cigarettes. What looked like house keys and car keys.

'Nothing unusual,' said Lacoste. But something had caught her eye. Taken from the duffel bag.

Wearing gloves, she picked up the pill bottle and sounded out the label. 'Mifegymiso. I don't know it.'

'I do,' said one of the agents, looking over. 'It's an abortion pill.'

'You mean the morning-after pill?' asked Beauvoir.

'No, that's different. That's for the day after sex, to stop insemination from going further. This's for pregnancies in the first few months. To terminate them.'

'I didn't know there was such a thing,' said Beauvoir. 'Legal?'

'Yessir.'

'What do you think?' he asked Lacoste as they stared down at the collection of items.

'I think it's strange that Vivienne Godin was beyond three months pregnant and she takes abortion pills with her. I'm assuming they won't work this far into a pregnancy. If she had the pills, why not use them earlier?'

'Maybe she thought they would work,' said Beauvoir. 'Maybe she was waiting to see how the father would react, and if it went badly, she'd take them.'

'This isn't prescription,' said Lacoste. 'There's no doctor or pharmacy on the label. Not even her name.'

'Black market,' said Beauvoir.

'Seems so. If they're legal, why go onto the black market?'

'And why would she tell her husband that the baby wasn't his, even if it was true? She must've known how he'd react. Why not just get out while she could?' said Beauvoir.

Tracey, goddamn him, had said the same thing. That Vivienne knew what he'd do. That he'd hit her. Beat her. Though surely she never thought he'd kill her.

'Maybe she didn't tell him,' said Lacoste. 'We only have Tracey's word for that.'

Beauvoir was considering. 'Then why would he say it? He gave us a motive. He's clever enough to know that.'

'He told the Chief that they were drunk,' said Lacoste. 'Maybe she didn't mean to tell him but it just came out. Maybe it wasn't even true.'

Beauvoir nodded. He, more than most, understood the corrosive effect of booze. How it stole judgment and inhibitions until things were said and done that could never be unsaid. Undone. Alcohol stole dignity and friends and family and livelihoods before finally taking the life.

Alcohol was a thief. And often a murderer.

'She wanted to hurt him before she left,' said Lacoste. 'She couldn't match him physically, but she could hurt him with words.'

The aimed word . . . like a soft bullet, thought Beauvoir, glancing up at the photo of Ruth scrutinizing them.

'Sober Vivienne probably knew better, but drunk . . . ?' he said. 'The toxicology report will tell us more.'

'There's something else,' said Lacoste. 'The clothes she packed don't make sense.'

'Why not?'

'Where're the sweaters? The heavy shirts? The socks?'

'There're shirts and jeans.'

'Summer weight. It's freezing out. Why take those?'

'Maybe she planned to go south. Florida.'

'Maybe,' said Lacoste.

'Or . . . ?'

'Or maybe she packed in a hurry. Just grabbing things. Or—'

'Maybe she didn't pack the bag,' said Beauvoir. 'Maybe he did.'

Lacoste nodded. 'To make it look like she'd gone away. No woman in her right mind would take those clothes in early April.'

'The problem we're going to have,' he said, 'is proving that Tracey packed the bag. Even if we find his DNA and fingerprints on the items, his defense would argue they were there because they lived together.'

'*Oui*,' said Lacoste. 'But if his prints are on that' – she pointed to the pill bottle – 'we might have something. I think he tossed it in not knowing what it was.'

'Not exactly a smoking gun,' said Beauvoir, but he could

feel hope rising, if not faith and charity. This might be the first nail.

Lysette Cloutier sat in the Sûreté detachment. She'd chosen a desk with direct line of sight into the cells. Where she could watch Homer.

The sandwiches and coffee she'd taken in were untouched.

Lysette had stayed with him for a while, but he seemed lost in his own world. Oblivious to her presence. Even, she felt, a little annoyed by it.

He clearly wanted just to be left alone.

If she couldn't comfort him, there was one thing she could do.

Glancing around, making sure she wasn't being watched, she went online. Found Carl Tracey's Instagram feed. And typed.

Reviewing it, going over each word. Changing one, adjusting another. Until it was just right.

Then she hit send and tapped the pen on the desk, waiting for a reply.

CHAPTER 19

—

@NouveauGalerie: Hello @CarlTracey Love your ceramic
pieces. Am a gallery owner looking for exciting new talent.
Can we meet?

The phone woke Armand with a start. He was
instantly alert and grabbed it before it could wake up
Reine-Marie.

'*Oui, allô?*'

'Sorry to disturb you,' said Beauvoir.

'Not at all,' said Armand, rubbing his hand across his face
and feeling the stubble. 'You have news?'

'The search warrant has come through.'

'Excellent. I'll meet you at the car in . . .' He checked the
bedside clock. It was 9:40 in the morning. He'd been asleep
for just over an hour, but felt refreshed. 'Twenty minutes.'

Armand quickly and quietly showered and shaved, not
wanting to wake up Reine-Marie, though he did check and
make sure she was okay.

The bruise now spread across the left side of her face, but
there was little swelling. Still, it hurt him to see it.

She roused and opened her eyes, giving a start on seeing his face so close to hers.

'Everything all right?' she mumbled, still half asleep.

'I'm just going out. You okay? That must hurt.'

He reached out but didn't touch it. Not wanting to add to the pain he knew she must be feeling.

'Well, I now have a much better idea, *mon coeur*, what you've gone through.'

'Me? Oh, no,' he said with a smile. 'Anytime a fist comes even close, I drop to the ground and play dead. Let Jean-Guy sort it out.'

'Belly up, feet and hands to the ceiling, like a bug. Yes, I've seen that. You also do it when Ruth enters a room.'

'I'll get you a Tylenol,' he said, smiling, and returned a minute later with a couple of pills and a glass of water. She was sitting up in bed now, and he sat beside her.

They talked about Annie and Jean-Guy's news. A brother or sister for Honoré. Another grandchild for them. Yet one, neither said but both knew, who would grow up a continent away.

'There's something I need to tell you.' He did up his tie as he spoke. 'I arrested Homer Godin.'

'Yes, I know. You think he killed his daughter?'

'No, but I need to keep him from Tracey. I charged him with assault. For that.'

He pointed to her face.

'But—' she began, bringing her own hand to her face.

'I know. I won't follow through. I just needed to get him off the streets, so he won't go after Tracey.'

'So this might've been a good thing.' She touched the bruise.

'*Non.*' He kissed her before getting up. 'Jean-Guy's waiting for me.'

'What will you do without him, Armand?'

He opened his mouth, but there was no answer.

'I'm sorry,' she said. 'I shouldn't have asked.'

'No. It's good to talk about it. Jean-Guy reminded me it's less than two weeks away.'

It wasn't, of course, just losing Beauvoir as a colleague and friend, it was losing Annie and Honoré. And now the new baby. With their son, Daniel, and his wife and two daughters already in Paris, it meant they had no children or grandchildren close by.

But, for Reine-Marie, the dread went deeper. Something she'd never admitted to Armand. For many years she'd felt that as long as Jean-Guy was close by, he'd protect Armand.

They were meant to be together. Had been, in her opinion, for many lifetimes. As colleagues, as father and son. As brothers. As long as they were together, both would be safe.

Once downstairs, Armand flicked on the television to cable news and placed a call.

As Radio Canada interviewed an increasingly agitated Deputy Premier about the terrible flooding, Armand waited for the phone to be answered.

The phone rang, as the politician tried to explain that it could have been worse.

The phone rang, as the journalist tried to explain that it was pretty damn catastrophic for those towns that were underwater.

Both, Gamache knew, were right.

The graphic on the screen showed where work was under way to divert floodwaters upriver.

The phone rang. And rang. Then clicked over to voice mail.

The RCMP commissioner wasn't answering. Or couldn't answer.

Armand hung up. And decided that no news was good news. There was nothing he could do about it now, anyway.

He grabbed his coat and joined Beauvoir and Lacoste.

'Knock, knock,' said Myrna.

'Who's there?' asked Clara, not looking up.

'Me.'

'Me who?'

'No, this isn't a knock-knock joke,' Myrna said, entering the studio. 'I just didn't want to startle you. We were supposed to meet at the bistro for breakfast, weren't we?'

'Sorry. I lost track of time.'

Myrna sat on the low sofa, her considerable derriere hitting the concrete floor, as it always did. She groaned, more in annoyance than pain. Would she never learn?

From her vantage point, essentially on the floor, Myrna could see that Clara was staring at a series of miniatures on her easel.

'I've been sitting here trying to decide if the tweeters are right,' Clara explained. 'If these're shit.'

'I believe we call those people twats, and no, they're not right. And you think that's bad, you should see what they're saying about Armand's return to the Sûreté. Madman with a gun. At least you only have a paintbrush. How much damage can you do?'

'You'd be surprised, apparently.'

Myrna brought out her phone. 'Listen to this.'

'I don't want to hear it.'

'*Strange, intense, feverish,*' Myrna read.

'Is that about me or Armand?'

'It's about van Gogh. Here's another. *The museum could have saved a good chunk by getting the plan and having the thing run off by the janitors with rollers.* That was a review of an early Barnett Newman. I looked it up. One of his paintings just sold for eighty-four million.'

'Dollars?'

'Dog biscuits.'

At that, Leo got to his feet, tail wagging. Myrna dug into her pocket and brought one out before returning to her phone. *'He's a madman, desperate for conquest.'*

'Picasso?'

'Gamache.'

Clara made a retching sound. 'Just shit. Lies.'

'So if you know the tweets are wrong about Armand, why don't you know they're wrong about you and your art?'

'Because one's objective and one's subjective,' said Clara. 'The record proves that Armand didn't do any of what he's accused of. And what he did do was to save greater pain. He's been investigated, exhaustively, and cleared. But what I do' – Clara returned her gaze to the easel – 'is open to interpretation. I had an email from my gallery in Montréal. A few collectors are asking about returning the paintings they bought, some from years ago. They're concerned that the value has fallen through. That I'm not a real artist at all but ... what did one tweet call me? A poseur.'

Actually, thought Myrna, that was one of the more polite descriptions she'd seen.

'Those are just mean people.'

'Just because it's mean doesn't make it wrong,' said Clara, tilting her head this way and that. Examining her works on the easel.

'All truth with malice in it,' said Myrna.

'What did you say?'

'Just a quote, from *Moby-Dick*,' said Myrna. 'Something Armand said yesterday.'

'You think there's truth in those tweets?'

'No, no, I didn't mean that.' Myrna's arms were pinwheeling as she tried to back up the conversation. 'There's no truth in them. Believe me. Just malice.'

But Clara was shaking her head. Her confidence shaken.

'Come on over for lunch later,' said Myrna, lugging herself off the sofa with a groan. 'You need to get out of the studio. And out of your own head.'

'Or someplace lower?' asked Clara.

'All truth . . .' said Myrna, and heard her friend laugh. 'You know, *Moby-Dick* was also savaged when it first came out. Now it's considered one of the great novels of all time.'

Clara didn't answer. She'd gone back to staring at the miniatures on her easel.

Myrna almost pointed out that what had happened to Vivienne Godin, what her father was living, was a tragedy. What Clara was going through was a setback. Nothing more.

But she didn't. Myrna understood how damaging it was to compare pain. To dismiss hurt just because it wasn't the worst.

As she walked back across the bright village green, her feet squelching in the soft turf, Myrna thought about those miniatures Clara had painted.

Perhaps, she admitted to herself privately as she walked past the wall of sandbags, not Clara's best work.

CHAPTER 20

—

@CarlTracey: Cannot meet you now @NouveauGalerie.
What exactly do you want?

Agent Cloutier smiled. Had she been an angler, she'd have recognized a nibble on the bait.

She was also amused, and reassured, by the cautious, even terse, response.

But mostly it was the speed of the response that grabbed her attention.

This was Carl Tracey's Instagram account, but it was not Carl Tracey she was communicating with. He had no cell phone. And no cell phone coverage.

'Best not to discuss business publicly,' she typed, having already composed this response in her head. 'Do you have a private account?'

Her phone was ringing the *Bonanza* theme, and she answered it but continued to stare at the screen. Trying not to see the amused looks of the other Sûreté agents in the open room.

'Cloutier,' she said.

'It's Beauvoir. The search warrant's come through. Meet us at the Tracey place.'

'On my way, *patron*.'

But still she stared at the screen, and then, just as she was about to shut it down, a single word appeared.

'*No*.'

Far from being disappointed, Cloutier smiled. It was the response she'd expected. Hoped for.

A normal potter, approached by a gallery about representing them, would be falling all over themselves to invite them into the private address. To talk business. But Carl Tracey or Pauline Vachon or whoever Cloutier was communicating with, was not.

Now, why was that?

Only one answer. They didn't want anyone else to see what was on the private account. Posts. Photographs.

She had them in her sights now. It would just take a little time. A little teasing. A tastier bait. But she'd get there. She'd get them.

With effort, she didn't type the response she'd already formulated.

Let them stew.

Before leaving, she checked on Homer.

'Do you need anything?'

There was no answer. He was staring straight ahead.

She wondered what he was seeing, though she could guess. The image he would see for the rest of his life.

'We're searching the home. I'm heading there now. We'll get him.'

That penetrated, at least a little. Homer turned to her and smiled weakly.

'*Merci*, Lysette.'

Her fingers were around the bars, and he reached out and touched her hand.

It took most of the day to go over the Tracey property.

Where the earlier search was for Vivienne, today they were looking for her killer. And the evidence to convict him.

It had been decided that Lacoste would stay behind in the incident room, to coordinate the information as it came in and assign agents as necessary.

Beauvoir dropped Gamache off at the Tracey house, while he himself continued to the dirt road and the car. And the bridge.

His team had been there for hours, calling in engineers to first secure the bridge so they could walk on it safely.

While one crew did that, another went over the car.

'Tell me what you know.'

'There're smears of blood on the outer and inner door handles, the steering wheel, the gearshift, a small smear on the trunk handle, and a drop on the backseat.'

'A drop, not a smear?'

'Exactly.' The agent showed Beauvoir. It had the telltale splatter of blood that had formed a drop, then hit. Maybe from a bleeding nose or lip.

'Prints?' Beauvoir asked.

'From at least three different people. There're butts in the cigarette holder. We've bagged them, and we've taken dirt samples from the tires, of course. To see if we can work out where she's been recently.'

'Tire tracks?'

'None. The rain washed everything away, including boot prints.'

'Damn,' said Beauvoir, looking around.

'Chief,' said an agent standing by the bridge. 'We're ready.'

'Chief?'

'*Oui?*' Gamache turned to see Agent Cloutier at the door to the living room.

'There's something curious in the bedroom,' she said. 'Something different from when we were here yesterday.'

He followed her through the rambling old farmhouse to the bedroom and saw immediately what Agent Cloutier meant.

When he was last there, the room was a mess. Now it was tidy. Not, perhaps, ready for a photo shoot in *Country Living*, but far neater than it had been.

He brought out his phone.

'There's no reception, sir,' said the inspector in charge.

'*Merci,*' he said, and continued to scroll until he found what he was looking for. The photographs he'd downloaded the day before, from the first search of the Tracey home.

'Here's what this room looked like yesterday when we came looking for Vivienne Godin.'

He turned the phone so that the inspector could see. The photo was taken from exactly the place where they now stood.

It showed a room in disarray. Clothing scattered on the floor and draped on a chair. Bed unmade and sheets dirty. Though not bloody. Which wasn't to say traces of blood weren't there. Just unnoticeable except by people trained to find them.

'Get Monsieur Tracey up here, please,' said Gamache, and Cloutier hurried away.

'We've looked, *patron*, and we can't find any clothes that obviously belonged to Madame Godin.'

They heard footsteps on the stairs, and Tracey appeared.

'What do you want?'

'What did you do with your wife's belongings?' asked Gamache.

'Well, she didn't need them anymore.'

'How did you know? You haven't been back here since her body was found. Which means you got rid of her things before you knew she was dead. Unless you did know.'

'All I knew is that she'd left me and I was pissed off. Before I went to bed last night, I took all her shit and burned it in the kiln.'

'I'll get Scene of Crime to check the kiln,' said Cloutier, and left.

'You cleaned the place with bleach?' The inspector held up a swab.

'What can I say? Place was a shithole.' He turned to Gamache. 'You saw it. What did you think?'

When Gamache didn't answer, Tracey sneered. 'I live in a pigsty and you judge. I clean it up and you judge. Well, fuck you. I'm finally free to live the way I want.'

They were, Gamache recognized, the words of either an extremely well-balanced person who didn't care what others thought. Or a psychopath. Who didn't care what others thought.

'Why in the world do you care what others think?' demanded Ruth as they sat in the bistro, in front of the warm fire.

'Because I'm human and live in the world,' said Clara. 'With other humans.'

Part of her felt that Ruth was probably right. She shouldn't care. But she also felt there was a criticism there, that Ruth was implying she was weak or needy. For caring.

'People are canceling their orders for my works,' said Clara.

'So?'

'So this's my life, my career. My livelihood.'

'What do you need money for, anyway?' asked Ruth. 'We live in a tiny village. We buy clothes from the general store, barter turnips for milk, and the booze is free.'

'Not free,' said Olivier, pouring her another shot of what looked like scotch but was actually cold tea.

There was a suspicion Ruth knew about the substitution but played along. Because, as with so much else in her life, she didn't really care.

As she watched Ruth, Clara remembered that in the past few hours someone had gone onto Twitter and defended her.

You ignorant turd. Clara's works are genius. #MorrowGenius

If it wasn't Ruth, it was someone doing a damn fine imitation of the foulmouthed poet.

Those tweets were trending. Not because, Clara realized, they were insightful defenses of her creations but because the tweets were in themselves a form of genius.

There was now a Twitter account from someone calling themselves @ignorantturd.

'You're far too needy,' said Ruth, watching as Rosa dipped her beak into the glass of cold tea.

The duck raised her head and muttered, 'Fuck, fuck, fuck.' Apparently realizing it wasn't really scotch.

'And you,' said Clara, 'are an ignorant turd.'

There was a hush as everyone else around the fireplace braced for impact. But Ruth, after a moment, just chuckled.

'I'll do it,' said Beauvoir, putting out his hand.

'I think I should, sir,' said the young agent. 'I'm trained.'

And once again Chief Inspector Beauvoir found himself facing what had become a familiar decision tree.

In fact, since becoming head of homicide, he'd faced a veritable forest of comments like that. Testing his authority and certainly questioning his competence.

Once again, he stood at the verbal crossroads.

Should he reply, 'Give me the testing kit, you stupid shit. How do you think I got to be Chief Inspector? By sitting on my thumbs?'

Or should he say, with a patient smile, 'That's all right, I do know what I'm doing. But I appreciate your concern.'

As Gamache might have answered. Had indeed answered many times, sometimes in response to Agent Beauvoir's own somewhat insulting comments.

When asked about it one night, years into their relationship, Armand had explained, with a laugh.

'After I'd said something especially patronizing to my first chief, he just looked at me and said, "Before speaking, Agent Gamache, you might want to ask yourself three questions."'

'Not the ones that lead to wisdom,' said Beauvoir, who'd heard them before.

'*Non.* Those are statements, these are questions. Are you paying attention?'

'What?'

They'd been sitting on the front porch of the Gamaches' home, in the height of summer. An iced tea beside Beauvoir, a beer beside Gamache.

As he spoke, the Chief Inspector raised a finger, counting the questions.

'Is it true? Is it kind? Does it need to be said?'

'You're kidding, right?' said Jean-Guy, shifting in his seat to look at Armand. 'That might work in our private lives, but with other cops? You'd be laughed out of the room.'

'You don't necessarily say them out loud,' explained the Chief.

Which was true. Beauvoir had never heard Gamache run through those questions, but he had heard, more often than not, a patient and constructive reply.

'Civility,' Armand had said. 'How can we expect it if we don't give it? Besides, when we do get angry, people pay more attention. Otherwise it's just white noise.'

Is it true? Is it kind? Does it need to be said?

Beauvoir, with effort, ran through the questions as he stood on the bridge, looking at the young agent.

Then he heard himself say, 'That's all right. I do know what I'm doing. But thank you.'

You stupid little shit.

Yes, it did need to be said, but maybe not out loud.

Though he did now wonder what Gamache had chosen not to say out loud.

Beauvoir took the harness from the agent and attached it, expertly, to himself, then put his hand out for the evidence kit.

'I'll go out first. If it's safe, you can join me. One at a time. *D'accord?*'

'*Oui, patron,*' said the agents.

Turning around to face the rickety old bridge, Beauvoir took a breath and whispered to himself, *Don't pee, don't pee, don't pee.*

CHAPTER 21

How can they let that murderer back in the Sûreté?
#losingallrespect

@dumbass: Do you mean self-respect?

They dropped Agent Cloutier at the local detachment and headed through the bright spring day, into the morgue.

Gamache had insisted on driving when he saw how exhausted Jean-Guy was.

Beside him, Jean-Guy's lids were heavy, and he fought to keep his eyes open in the warm car as it moved smoothly along the autoroute.

'I couldn't be happier for Annie and you,' said Armand. 'Your family is growing.'

'As is yours.'

As an only child, growing up without parents, Armand had always yearned for a large family. For brothers and sisters. For aunts and uncles. It was an abstract, though potent, wish.

And now, in his late fifties, he had it. Children. Grandchildren. Sons and daughters. Of the flesh and of the

heart. Those he'd held in his arms and those comrades-in-arms whose lives he held in his hands.

His family.

'When's the baby due?'

'October.'

'Boy or girl? Do you know?'

'We do.' Jean-Guy smiled at his father-in-law. 'But you're not going to get it out of me. Annie and I want to keep that to ourselves.'

'Fair enough. Have you chosen a name?'

Jean-Guy laughed. 'You're not really very good at this interrogation thing, are you?'

'I'm hoping to learn from you, *patron*.'

Beauvoir smiled, and Gamache fell silent. Knowing if he did, Jean-Guy would lose the battle and let himself drift off to sleep.

He'd told Beauvoir about the search of the Tracey home. Then Beauvoir had reported on their preliminary findings at the bridge.

Now Gamache, in the silence as Jean-Guy slept, went back over that conversation.

'We lifted three sets of fresh prints off the interior of the car,' Beauvoir had said. 'Probably Vivienne's and Tracey's. But the third?'

'Can we prove that she wasn't alone? That someone was on the bridge with her?'

'No. That's a problem. The heavy rain washed away all foot and tire prints.'

'Shame.' Gamache thought for a moment. 'But we still think she either met someone there. Something happened, and she went off the bridge. Or—'

'Or Tracey followed her there and killed her.'

'But if he wanted her dead, why wait until she left?' mused Gamache, keeping his eyes on the highway. 'He struck me as someone who doesn't plan ahead. I can imagine him lashing out and killing her that night, in their home, either on purpose or in a fit of rage, but to follow her?'

'He told you he left her in the living room and went into his studio and drank, right?'

'*Oui.*'

'Maybe he worked himself into a rage. Getting angrier and angrier the more he thought about Vivienne and another man. He sees her leave and decides to follow her, thinking she's meeting her lover.'

Gamache nodded. That, he could see.

'He'd confront them. Do you think there really was a lover?' Beauvoir asked, then yawned.

'Must have been,' said Gamache. 'At least in your scenario. Otherwise why would she drive to the bridge?'

'Okay, she goes to meet a lover, but then wouldn't Tracey kill him, too?'

'Maybe he did. But I doubt it,' Gamache said. 'Like all abusers and bullies, Tracey's a coward. He wouldn't attack someone who could fight back.'

'So if he did follow Vivienne, he found her alone on the bridge. Waiting. And threw her in.'

'What did you find there?'

'I discovered I don't like rotten bridges over rivers in flood.'

'Ahhh,' said Gamache. 'Most helpful. Anything else?'

'Wouldn't take much to break through the railing. It was broken from the inside out and looks recent. I think there's little doubt that's where Vivienne fell.'

'Any actual proof?'

'Not yet. We're testing the wood for fibers and blood.

We've removed the section where she broke through so technicians can take a closer look in the lab. Then there's the duffel bag,' said Beauvoir. 'Lacoste pointed out that most of the clothes are for summer.'

'Huh,' said Gamache. 'That's strange.'

'Not the only strange thing. You know those pills in the bag?'

'Yes.'

'They're abortion pills.'

'They're what?' Gamache glanced over quickly before returning his eyes to the road.

'Medication to end an early pregnancy. Looks like she got them on the black market.'

'I wonder how far along she was,' said Gamache.

It had looked to both of them as though she was beyond what could be called an early pregnancy. But the coroner would tell them.

'Isabelle doesn't think she packed the bag, and neither do I,' said Jean-Guy, yawning again. Between the heat of the car and the gentle hum of the engine, Jean-Guy could feel himself losing the fight to stay alert. To even stay awake.

'You think Tracey packed the bag,' said Gamache.

'Yes. I think it was a simple mess of a murder. You found blood in the living room. And we found blood in the car. Tracey admits beating her. I think either he killed her in the home, beat her to death, drove her to the bridge, and threw her over, wanting to make it look like suicide or an accident, or he took her there while she was still alive and threw her off.'

'I don't think he beat her to death in the house. There wasn't enough blood. And if she was still alive, why would she get into the car with him?'

'Yes, that's a problem. She wouldn't. Not voluntarily, anyway.'

'So the most likely explanation is that he knocked her unconscious, drove her there, and threw her off the bridge,' said Gamache. 'Hoping, like you said, it would look like an accident or suicide. He packed the duffel bag, grabbing things at random, and threw it in after her. But people don't pack for suicide. If that's what he wanted us to believe, he made a mistake.'

'There's another problem,' said Beauvoir. 'The blood smears are on the driver's side. It looks like she was hurt, but conscious enough to drive.'

'So she took herself there,' said Gamache, considering. 'And there's no physical evidence of anyone else on that bridge with her.'

'Not yet. You think he didn't do it?'

'Tracey? Oh, he did it. It's just a matter of understanding the evidence. And getting enough to convict.'

He glanced over at his companion. Jean-Guy's eyes were just about closed.

Within a minute of Gamache's falling silent, Jean-Guy had fallen asleep.

By the time they pulled in to the morgue, Gamache had been over that conversation a few times but was no closer to a solution.

When Agent Cloutier returned to the local detachment, she found a very different Homer Godin from the man she'd left.

'How come I'm in here and he's free?' he demanded. 'Let me out.'

'I can't.'

'Of course you can. You're a goddamned cop.'

Lysette paled. Not used to being spoken to that way. And

certainly not by Homer. She stared into those angry eyes and knew in her rational mind that it wasn't Homer speaking. It was grief.

But though her brain told her that, her heart still recoiled.

She saw Homer now in a different light. Not as a man but as a father. Not having children herself, she hadn't quite appreciated the depth of his feeling for his daughter. Now she knew what her friend Kathy had been talking about. That bond between father and daughter. It was almost cliché and, in some cases, mythic.

Kathy had long complained, but Lysette, as much as she loved her friend, could understand why Vivienne would be drawn to her father and not her mother.

Kathy was not demonstrative. She was efficient. Kept a clean and tidy and orderly home. But Homer brought the joy into it. As Vivienne brought joy into his life.

It was a perfect little ecosystem. But it left Kathy on the outside looking in.

As soon as Vivienne had been born, her father had become simply skin stretched over his love for his daughter.

But now she was gone. And there was nothing holding him together.

Except hatred.

Chief Inspector Gamache had seen that before anyone else. He knew, perhaps because of his love for his own daughter, what a person in that position could do. Would do.

Unless they were locked up.

Though Agent Lysette Cloutier did just wonder if it would really be such a bad thing, if she opened the cell door.

Homer would murder Carl Tracey, of course. But he'd almost certainly be given as light a sentence as the justice system allowed.

He would not be held criminally responsible. And he would clearly not be a menace to society. Just to one man.

She would also be arrested and tried, for letting him out. But at least Homer would know what she was willing to do for him.

The other agents in the room, including Agent Cameron, looked at her as she returned to her desk and brought up the Instagram account.

Do they suspect what I'm considering doing?

Did it matter?

Lysette Cloutier looked down at her computer and saw, again, the curt *No* on the screen. Now a few hours old. She typed in her own reply.

@NouveauGalerie: Sorry. Busy with buyers. No worries. Lots of other promising ceramicists. I'm sure you have other options. Good luck to you.

Within two minutes there was a reply. Again, terse. But enough. It contained an invitation to join Carl Tracey's private Instagram account.

CHAPTER 22

—

@NouveauGalerie: Thanks for the access. Looked at your
work. Ceramic pieces promising, but not right for the
gallery. Good luck @CarlTracey.

@SeriousCollector: Rethinking the Morrow portrait I
bought. Three old women laughing. Weaker than I first
thought. Sorta superficial.

Holy shit. Check out this video. #GamacheSux

There was, Gamache knew, an unmistakable smell
about a morgue.

Not the sickly aroma of rot. He could pick that up from a
distance after years of approaching corpses. And killers.

No. The morgue smelled of extreme, almost severe
cleanliness.

It turned his stomach.

As the door swung open, sterile air met him, and he
braced himself.

But Armand Gamache knew the slight sick feeling in the
pit of his stomach this time went beyond the smell. Went

beyond, even, the gnawing thought that this could be Annie on the metal slab.

Only once before in his career had he felt this particular sensation.

It was doubt. Not that they could find the killer. He was pretty sure they'd already done that. But that they could convict him.

That other time, his first year as head of homicide, he had indeed failed. And a killer had gone free.

And now he looked down at the body of Vivienne Godin. Saw her bruises. Saw the incision on her belly.

And felt that wave of nausea. That fear that whoever did this would walk free.

'What do you have?' Jean-Guy Beauvoir asked Dr Harris.

'As you can see, the body is badly damaged. Some trauma clearly postmortem, but some done while she was alive.'

'She was beaten,' said Beauvoir.

'Well—'

'Well, what?' he snapped, then put up his hands in apology. '*Désolé.*'

'It's okay. I feel it, too. This's a particularly nasty case. The problem is, I can't say for sure which injuries, if any, were done in a beating just before she died and which ones were caused by being battered in the river while still alive. There're some obviously older bruises.' Dr Harris pointed to some yellow and greenish blotches on Vivienne's arms and legs. 'But these' – the coroner pointed to other marks on Vivienne's body – 'are harder to explain.'

'They're fresh,' said Gamache.

'*Oui.* But what made them? A person? Or rocks and tree limbs? She'd have been tossed around in the floodwaters. That could've done a lot, even all of the damage we see.'

They looked down at Vivienne's naked, battered body.

'The fetus?' asked Gamache. 'How far along?'

'I'd say she'd be about twenty weeks.'

'She?' said Beauvoir. 'A baby girl?'

Jean-Guy paled and looked across the body. To his father-in-law. And Armand knew then.

Annie and Jean-Guy were having a daughter. A baby girl.

'Yes.'

If Dr Harris noticed this moment between the two men, she chose not to say anything.

'What I can say for sure is that she was alive when she went into the river. There's water in her lungs.'

'If questioned on the stand,' said Gamache, giving Jean-Guy a moment to compose himself, 'what would you say about the bruising?'

She considered the body again. 'Some of her wounds could have happened before she went into the water, but most have signs of battering consistent with being hit by rocks. It's a sort of tumbling action as a body's swept along.'

'You say most of the wounds are consistent with battering in the water,' said Beauvoir, recovered. 'But not all?'

'There are two bruises that're harder to explain.' She pointed to Vivienne's upper chest, just below the collarbone.

Beauvoir and Gamache leaned closer.

At first it looked like one large blue mark spreading across her chest. But, looking closer, they could see other marks. Like something trapped below the surface. One on either side.

Armand put on his glasses and leaned closer still. 'What do you think made them?'

'At a guess?' Dr Harris raised her hands, palms toward them. Then thrust forward.

'She was shoved,' said Beauvoir. He looked at Gamache, who nodded.

'*Oui*.' She put her hands over the bruises. 'You can see that the hands are quite big.'

'Could you say for sure those marks were made by a person and not by debris?' Gamache asked.

Dr Harris sighed. 'I've been struggling with that. I'm not sure I could swear to it. What I can say is that the chances of two identical bruises happening while she was being tossed about in the river are astronomically small. These' – she looked back down at Vivienne – 'were done at the same time, by the same thing. The only explanation I have is that she was pushed, violently.'

'Intentionally.'

'Maybe in a fit of rage, but yes, whoever did this wanted to shove her back. Hard.'

'Can you measure those bruises?' Gamache asked.

'To give you the size of the hand? I could, but it wouldn't be very accurate. There's weeping of the blood around the edges. Again, any defense will argue, quite rightly, that the hand could've been smaller. Besides, a lot of people have hands that big.'

Tracey's hands, Gamache knew, were not large. But as the hands of a potter, they'd be powerful.

And he could think of one person related to the case whose hands were very big.

Bob Cameron.

Left tackle's hands. And what did a left tackle do? He pushed and shoved. Violently. Perhaps, at this stage, instinctively. When threatened.

'Any idea how long she's been dead?' asked Beauvoir.

'Two, maybe three days. The water was cold, so that has

to be taken into account. This is Tuesday? I'd say she went into the river on Saturday night, maybe at a stretch early Sunday morning.'

Gamache was nodding. Thinking. And finally asked the question Jean-Guy Beauvoir did not seem willing to ask.

'Is there any evidence, any proof, that she was murdered?'

Sharon Harris paused before answering. 'I'm sorry. I looked. Hard. But I can't find anything. It could've been suicide. It could've been an accident. I think she was murdered. I think that she was hit so hard in the chest she fell off the bridge. But as for absolute proof?'

She raised her hands. No.

'And the blood work?' Beauvoir asked.

'Very preliminary. None of the more detailed results yet, but I can tell you that she'd been drinking.'

'She was drunk?' asked Beauvoir.

'No, but she'd had a few ounces of alcohol shortly before her death. No sign of drugs. But if there're just traces, that won't show up until I get the detailed report. I've put a rush on it, and we should have something by later this afternoon.'

'Can you ask them to check for this?' Beauvoir brought out the pill bottle in its sterile baggie.

Dr Harris examined it while Gamache walked back to Vivienne's body.

He looked down at her, at the wounds caused by the river. By the fall. By her husband. And by the coroner. Who'd cut into this young woman in an effort to find out who'd caused the other wounds.

He picked up her hand, to tuck it next to her body and draw the sheet over her.

The hand was, as he expected, cold. It would have shocked him to the core had Vivienne's hand been warm.

He held it for a moment and realized he was, unconsciously, trying to comfort her. He noticed then that there was a gash on her palm.

'Doctor, what's this? It looks like a defensive wound.'

'Not from a knife,' she said, joining him. 'Too jagged.'

'Could it have been caused by reaching out for the railing,' Gamache asked. 'And having it break?'

Dr Harris lifted up Vivienne's hand to take a closer look.

Then, stepping away from the body, Dr Harris stood straight and lifted both hands in front of her.

Anyone would have thought she was being threatened by the two Sûreté officers.

Her face was intent. Her body rigid in feigned alarm. Then she leaned away from them and reached behind her. With her right hand.

'What height is the railing?'

'Ninety-eight centimeters,' said Beauvoir.

Dr Harris adjusted her hand to just over three feet off the floor. Then she nodded and walked over to her desk.

Doing quick calculations of Vivienne Godin's height. The height of the railing. The angle of the cut on her hand and the likely trajectory of her body. The coroner then returned to the metal slab.

'What's the thickness of the handrail?'

Beauvoir needed to consult his notes for that and gave the dimension to her.

Harris measured the wound and reexamined it closely.

'Still no splinters, but I'll do a microscopic examination. There might be something wedged into the flesh. It looks likely that it was caused when she fell and not when she was in the water.'

'How can you tell that?' asked Beauvoir, stepping closer.

'Because the cut starts here' – Harris pointed to just above Vivienne's wrist, where the palm began – 'and tears up to her middle finger. It would be unlikely a cut like this would be made when a person was going headfirst down the river. Her hands would be out in front of her, if possible, and a cut would go from fingers down, not wrist up.'

'You think it was made when she was going backward, not forward,' said Gamache, also moving closer. He put his glasses back on.

'I do.'

'So Vivienne was pushed backward while on the bridge,' said Beauvoir, and when Dr Harris didn't contradict him, he went on. 'She reached for the railing' – he also mimicked the action – 'to stop herself, and it broke.'

There was what felt like an eternal silence while the two Sûreté officers stared at the coroner. And the careful coroner considered.

'Probably.'

'Yes.' Beauvoir clenched both fists in excitement, knowing what that would mean to their investigation.

'Probably,' said Gamache, more cautious. 'But not definitive?'

'No. It's likely that's what happened. I could testify to it. But the defense could argue that it was caused in the water. That her body was twisting around so it was at times going backward down the river, and that's when the cut was made. It would be difficult, but just possible. I'd have to testify to that, too.'

'What do you need to be sure?' asked Gamache.

'What we don't have. A splinter that matches the wood from the railing.' Then she paused. 'You say it was rotten?'

'*Oui*,' said Beauvoir. Perking up. Noticing the slight shift in her tone. 'Very.'

'Do you have a sample?'

'We've removed that whole section. It's in the lab.'

'Good. Have them test for spores. For algae. For microscopic traces of organisms. Lots of things make their home in rotting wood. And flesh. I'll take samples from the cut and test as well. It's possible not everything was flushed out. We'll see if what's found on the wood matches what's in the cut.'

'And if it does, that would place her on that bridge,' said Gamache. 'Going backward through the railing. It would prove the wound wasn't made after she went into the water.'

'Yes. Absolutely.'

'But,' said Gamache.

'But,' said Beauvoir, looking at him. Knowing what he was thinking and coming to the same conclusion.

'But what?' asked Dr Harris.

Gamache nodded to Beauvoir, inviting the lead investigator to explain.

'A clever defense would still argue that she might've tripped. She was drinking, after all. She might've just lost her balance and fallen backward. Or she might've been leaning against the rail and it broke.'

'That I can refute,' said the coroner. 'By the angle of the cut, she was at least two feet from it when she reached back and fell—'

'Or was pushed,' said Beauvoir.

' – against it. And yes, she was trying to save herself. So you can rule out suicide at least.'

Gamache exhaled.

It was far from the first time he'd stood over the corpse of a woman who'd been punched and kicked, belittled and shamed and pushed to the end of her rope. And beyond.

Vivienne Godin, it seemed, had reached the end and had

226

made a choice that cold and dark April night. She'd chosen life. For herself and her baby girl.

Le beau risque. The great risk. The beautiful risk. To climb out of the hole and start again.

Like Annie and Jean-Guy, heading to Paris with their young and growing family. Away from the dangers here. To start fresh.

But while they could escape, Vivienne could not.

Once again, Gamache felt the tightening in his stomach.

Isabelle Lacoste stood in the doorway of the Cowansville detachment, leaning on her cane. And looked around the open room.

'She's over there,' said the receptionist, waving toward Agent Cloutier, working at her laptop.

'*Merci.*'

But the receptionist had already left.

Heads turned as she limped through the room. There was about her an air of ease and confidence. This stranger who belonged.

Then, one by one, they realized this was no stranger. Though most had never met Superintendent Lacoste, they knew her by reputation. Knew what she'd done. And what had, as a result, been done to her. The cane being only the most visible sign.

'Superintendent,' said one young agent, getting up to stand at his desk.

'*Bonjour,*' said Lacoste, not bothering to correct him and explain she was on leave. Though the rank still held.

'Agent Cloutier,' said Lacoste as she approached the desk.

Lysette Cloutier gave a start and looked up into the familiar face. Then she quickly stood up, smiling.

'*Patron*. I didn't expect to see you. I thought you'd be with the Chief Inspector. Sssss.'

Lacoste laughed. With more than one, the grammar became problematic.

'I've struck out on my own,' she said. 'Are you free?'

'For sure. Do you need my help?'

'You seem to be working on something.'

'I traced the IP address for Carl Tracey's website. It's through a local server, and the billing address is a home here in Cowansville, registered in the tax rolls to the same woman I told you about last night. Pauline Vachon.'

Lacoste was slightly surprised Lysette Cloutier could remember anything from their call the night before.

'So that confirms it,' she said, taking a seat. 'And we have an address. Well done.'

The website was on Cloutier's laptop, and Lacoste scrolled through. It showed a man bending over a wheel, intent on the lump of clay he was forming. Down the sides of the page, there were photographs of different works.

'Huh,' said Lacoste. 'Quite nice.'

'Yes. He's talented.' Cloutier would give him that. 'Then I went onto the Instagram account and looked around. Not particularly interesting. Just what they want us to see.'

'Yes,' said Lacoste, cautious now. 'We talked about this, too, last night. I told you not to do anything else. We don't want to alert them that the police are interested in any possible private account.'

'Right, well, we're in.'

'In where? In what?'

'Their private Instagram account.' Cloutier was beaming. Lacoste was not.

'What've you done?'

228

'I asked if we could communicate privately, and she gave me access.'

'To a cop?'

'Well, not exactly. Like you said, we didn't want her erasing anything that could be evidence, so I pretended I was someone else.'

'Who?'

Now Lysette Cloutier clicked again, and another website came up. An art gallery in Old Montréal called NouveauGalerie. Specializing in modern Québécois art.

It was a slick, minimalist site. Very cool.

'Who're they?' Lacoste asked.

'They're me. I created it.'

'Wait a minute,' said Lacoste, trying to keep up. 'You're pretending to be this NouveauGalerie?'

'*Oui*. I showed interest in his work, asked to speak privately. After refusing a few times, this Pauline finally give me access to their private Instagram account.'

'Why would she do that?'

'So we can discuss business,' said Cloutier. Her tone said that must be obvious.

'Why wouldn't she just pick up the phone?'

'Phone? Young people don't talk on phones. Everything's done through texts and social media. And with the private Instagram account, she can show galleries – me—' said Cloutier with a smile, 'works in progress. Things they might not want public yet. Besides, she's trying to pretend she's Carl Tracey. God knows, you don't want that asshole talking to galleries.'

'Got it,' said Lacoste. 'So private Instagram it is.'

Where anyone could take on a false identity. And often did.

Lacoste didn't know whether to be pleased with

the brilliance of this or angry that Cloutier had disobeyed orders.

Before she made up her mind, Cloutier said, 'Look at this.' She clicked again. 'Voilà.'

Up came photographs and posts. Private messages between Carl Tracey and Pauline Vachon. Just the two. No one else, it seemed, had access to the private account.

Except, now, NouveauGalerie.

And one thing was immediately obvious.

'They're lovers,' said Lacoste.

'Oui.'

'Can you zoom in on this picture, please,' said Lacoste, leaning closer.

It was a selfie Pauline Vachon had taken. She was lying on a sofa in a very suggestive pose.

'There. And there,' said Lacoste, reaching out and moving the image until it showed a close-up of the woman's bare arm.

Bruises.

'Goddamn,' said Cloutier, with disgust and, Lacoste thought, a touch of triumph.

'What're they saying to each other?' Lacoste asked.

'I've just gotten in. Haven't gotten to their messages yet.'

Just then Lacoste's phone vibrated, and she read the email.

It was from an agent back at headquarters, reporting on the phone messages into and out of the Tracey home for the past few weeks. There weren't many. They'd all be checked, but what Lacoste scanned down to were the ones for that Saturday.

None had come in, and just two numbers were called from the house that day. One of them repeatedly.

'Is either of these Pauline Vachon's number?'

'Non. But it is a Cowansville exchange,' said Cloutier.

'I can look it up. That other one is to her father. That's Homer's number.'

Lacoste nodded. And realized Cloutier must know it well.

While Cloutier looked up the second number, Lacoste called Beauvoir.

'*Oui, allô.*'

'The phone records from the Tracey place have come in,' she said, without preamble. 'It shows the call to Vivienne's father, like he said, on Saturday morning. But someone in that house called another number, repeatedly, early Saturday evening. Most of the calls lasted only seconds.'

'Where to?'

'A local number. Agent Cloutier's checking now.'

Beauvoir stayed on the line and could hear the clicking of computer keys. Then silence. Before he heard Agent Cloutier's voice.

'The number belongs to a Gerald Bertrand.'

Jean-Guy put his hand over the phone and relayed the information to Gamache.

'The lover?' Beauvoir said.

'Could be,' said Gamache.

'We'll find out,' said Lacoste, rising with the help of her cane.

After hanging up, Beauvoir returned to the coroner.

'Have you done a DNA test on the fetus?'

'I have. The results will be in with the rest of the tests, later today.'

'About the medication that was found in her duffel bag—'

'Mifegymiso. Yes.'

'It's an abortion pill, right?'

'Yes.'

'Does that mean she was trying to end her pregnancy?'

'It's unclear. It's only legal in Canada up to ten weeks, and she was further along than that. I'll test for both in her blood, but I can tell you there were no signs of an imminent miscarriage.'

'Meaning what?'

'Meaning I doubt she took the pill. And you know that this bottle' – she held it up – 'wasn't from a prescription, right? It's almost certainly black-market.'

'Yes.'

'I have a question for you,' said Gamache.

'*Oui*,' said Dr Harris.

'Is Mifegymiso free?'

'If prescribed by a doctor, yes.'

'So if it's both legal and free, why would anyone pay for it on the black market?'

'Well, I guess if she was twenty weeks along, no doctor would prescribe it,' said the coroner.

'Possible,' said Gamache.

'But you don't think so,' said Beauvoir.

'I'm wondering if Vivienne got those pills,' said Gamache. 'Or if Tracey did.'

'Why would he do that?' asked Dr Harris.

'He would,' said Beauvoir, 'if he knew the baby wasn't his and wanted her to abort. Probably without her knowing.'

'Which would mean he knew all that long before Saturday,' said Gamache. 'But if he knew what the drug was for and he packed her duffel bag, why put them in?'

'Maybe to confuse us,' said Beauvoir.

'Well,' said Gamache, and raised his brows. It was working . . .

'Or maybe—'

Dr Harris watched as the two investigators discussed possibilities and probabilities.

She'd worked with them for years. Seen their relationship blossom and wither. Seen it through all its spasms, incarnations, hoops, and dips. The ruptures and the mendings.

Things are strongest where they're broken.

Gamache had said that, quietly, once. Years ago. In the cathedral in Québec City, at the funerals for four of his agents, killed in a raid. He'd whispered it to himself as he knelt, head bowed, during one of the silent prayers. Not realizing, perhaps, that anyone other than God was listening.

And God knew, as did Sharon Harris, that the relationship between Gamache and Beauvoir had been shattered, more than once. But it had survived to this day, stronger than ever.

She listened, and marveled, and envied this bond.

She also noticed that in each scenario they knew exactly who the murderer was. Which was a good start.

'Or,' said Gamache, 'Vivienne did pack the bag, intending to leave her husband. She put the pills in because she was still undecided about the baby.'

'At more than three months out? Why would she decide to end the pregnancy now? I think protecting the baby was the reason she left him. Vivienne wanted to start a new life, with the child.'

'The problem is, we can't always get clean away,' said Dr Harris. 'Not when we're running from our demons.'

She knew. She was surrounded by their work every day.

Gamache nodded and caught Beauvoir's eye.

They'd spent decades tracking the creatures. Into dark alleys. Into homes. Deep into lives. Often in the guise of friends, lovers, caring colleagues. Sometimes complete strangers. Sometimes they were of people's own making.

Vivienne's demon had found her on that bridge.

Though Gamache had never really doubted it, now, thanks to that long, jagged cut on her hand and the ghostly bruises, he was sure. Vivienne had been murdered.

And, what was more, he could put a face and a name to this particular demon.

Now they had to prove it.

CHAPTER 23

⁓

@CarlTracey: @NouveauGalerie, We have other more
recent work. Would that help?

@NouveauGalerie: No. @CarlTracey, Moving on. But
thank you.

In the car on the way over to Gerald Bertrand's place,
Isabelle Lacoste read the Instagram exchange between
Pauline Vachon, pretending to be the artist, and Agent
Cloutier, pretending to be the gallery owner.

It was true, she thought. Nothing, and no one, on social
media was as they seemed.

Still, it looked as though Cloutier had been masterful in
her manipulation. Turning Tracey down. Forcing Vachon to
almost beg NouveauGalerie for attention.

Stringing Vachon along. Until she got exactly what
she wanted.

When they pulled in to Gerald Bertrand's driveway,
Lacoste put away her phone and rang the bell.

'Gerald Bertrand?'

'Oui?'

'My name is Isabelle Lacoste. I'm with the Sûreté du Québec. This is Agent Cloutier. May we come in?'

The man was young, perhaps early twenties. With the burly arms and torso of a fellow who did manual labor. There was about him a sort of cologne of testosterone.

His dark beard was bushy but groomed and his hair styled shorter to his head. His brown eyes were clear and bright, and he held, in his sturdy arms, an infant.

For an instant, Isabelle Lacoste forgot she was married. With two children. She hoped her mouth hadn't dropped open, but she was pretty sure her eyes had widened.

Beside her, Lysette Cloutier was smiling. Grinning, really. Having lost both her heart and apparently her mind.

'The Sûreté? What's this about?' he asked.

'We need to speak with you about a homicide.'

'A murder? Here?'

He looked out the door and held his baby closer to his body, instinctively protecting her.

Cloutier swallowed whatever drool had pooled in her mouth.

'No, not right here,' said Lacoste, who'd recovered most of her wits. 'May we come in?'

'Yes, sorry.'

He stepped back, and after removing their dirty boots, they followed him into the kitchen of the modest home.

He lived in a subdivision of Cowansville, in a cluster of bungalows exactly the same.

'Can you tell us about your relationship with Vivienne Godin?' Lacoste asked as she took the chair he'd indicated, the best one in the room, and leaned her cane against the arm.

Monsieur Bertrand had taken them to the back of the

house, past the small front room normally used as a formal living room, but in this home it held workout equipment.

The kitchen opened to a sitting area with a sofa, two chairs, and a huge television on which cartoons were playing. A card table doubled as a dining table, though Lacoste doubted there'd been many, if any, dinner parties there.

Dishes were piled in the sink, and a near-empty baby bottle was on the counter.

The place was messy, but not, Lacoste could see, dirty.

'Don't tell my sister,' he said as he muted the sound.

'I'm afraid I can't promise that,' said Lacoste. 'It's very serious. We might have to talk with her, too.'

'Really? Well, I can tell you now that she doesn't approve.'

'Few would.'

'It's not really that bad, is it?'

It was about here that Isabelle Lacoste began to suspect they were discussing two different things.

'What isn't?' she asked.

'Television. Vendredi likes Babar, so I put it on when Pam isn't around.'

'Vendredi?' asked Cloutier.

'She was born on a Friday.'

'Pam's your sister?' asked Cloutier.

'*Oui.*'

'So this isn't your child?' asked Agent Cloutier.

'No.' He smiled. 'I look after her whenever I can. I'm off work right now. Construction season'll start again in a couple of weeks.' He looked at the little girl and grinned at her, and she grinned back. 'Gotta spend as much time with Dee as I can.'

The agents exchanged looks. Both thinking much the same thing.

237

That he was adorable. And maybe a murderer.

But would a mother, a sister, trust her baby to a man, a brother, capable of murder? A sibling would probably know, would have seen some of that darkness, that menace, as they grew up.

But maybe he hadn't intended to kill his lover. Maybe it was a terrible accident and he was afraid to come forward. If he was afraid to tell his sister about an animated elephant, how would he feel about admitting to murder?

Superintendent Lacoste repositioned herself so she was facing him directly.

'Your relationship, sir. With Vivienne Godin.'

His brow dropped in concentration as he bobbed his niece, gently, on his knee.

'I'm sorry, I don't think I know her. Is she the one who was killed?'

They watched him closely, but neither agent could see any distress, beyond a normal human reaction when hearing that a stranger was dead.

'Please just answer the question,' said Lacoste.

Despite the fact Agent Cloutier was clearly the elder of the two and should have been the more senior, Gerald Bertrand understood innately that the young woman with the old eyes and cane was in charge.

'I have. I don't know her. Why do you think I do?'

'Think a little harder,' said Lacoste.

'I don't know what to tell you,' said Bertrand, looking from one to the other.

Then another thought occurred to Lacoste. Maybe it wasn't Vivienne who called.

'How about Carl Tracey?'

'What about him?'

'Do you know him?'

'No. Never heard of him either. What's this about? Why do you think I know these people?'

'Because either Vivienne or Carl called you on Saturday. Repeatedly.'

'Oh, *merde*. That was her? Some woman kept calling. The first time I tried to tell her she had the wrong number, but she seemed really upset. I'm not sure she was listening. She called back, and I tried again, but after that I just ignored the calls. She left a couple of messages—'

'Can we listen to them?' asked Cloutier.

'I erased them.'

Of course you did, thought Cloutier. What else would a guilty person do?

But then she rethought that.

What else would an innocent person do? She did the same thing with messages from wrong numbers.

She was beginning to see how quickly something completely normal could suddenly seem sinister, if you chose to see it that way.

'May we have a look around?' Lacoste asked.

Gerald Bertrand looked surprised but nodded.

'Do you have a girlfriend?' she asked as they surveyed the small home. It was very messy and very masculine. A man-child lived here, alone. It was furnished with pieces that looked like they'd come from friends or family or a dumpster. Some hockey trophies. A pile of skis and skates and hunting gear was in the basement.

There were a few photos, of Gerald with mates, with teams, with his family. But none of him with Vivienne.

'Who's this?' Lacoste looked at a photo among many on the fridge.

'Old girlfriend. We broke up a couple of months ago.'

'You keep her picture up?'

He shrugged. 'I forgot it was there.'

It showed the two young people in bathing suits at the lake, faces smashed together for a selfie. Beaming.

'Do you own a gun?'

'A hunting rifle, yes. I have a license.'

He showed them the weapon, safely locked up, with ammunition locked in a separate room. He produced from his wallet the license.

Lacoste inspected the rifle. Clean. Well maintained.

'Where do you hunt?'

'Wherever my buddies want to go, but mostly up north. The Abitibi. But haven't been for a while. Not since Vendredi was born.'

'Why not?'

'Lost my taste for killing things, I guess.'

'Where were you on Saturday afternoon and evening?' asked Lacoste.

'You're kidding, right?'

But it was clear by her expression that she was not.

Bertrand thought for a moment. 'I was looking after Dee until about six, when my sister finished work and came over to get her, and then some buddies dropped by and we watched the game.'

'Which game?'

'The hockey game.' He seemed shocked she needed to ask. 'Canadiens and Leafs. Terrible game.'

He was right. Lacoste had watched it with her husband and kids. The Leafs won.

'May I have their names, please. Your friends,' said Cloutier, bringing out her notebook.

'You're going to talk to them?' he asked.

'Yes.'

'But they'll think I had something to do with this.'

'Names, please.'

Gerald Bertrand hesitated and, in doing so, moved up the suspect list. Carl Tracey still held the top spot and would be hard to tumble, but this anxious man was closing in.

He gave them some names and phone numbers.

'Please don't get in touch with them, Monsieur Bertrand,' said Cloutier. 'We can easily check up on your calls.'

By now Bertrand was sheet-white. He hugged the baby to him as though she were the one threatened.

Superintendent Lacoste considered the child.

No bruising. No sign at all of anything other than comfort and happiness.

This man might have been a threat to Vivienne Godin, but Lacoste was assured he was no threat to the baby.

'*Merci, monsieur*,' said Lacoste, giving him her card as they walked to the door. 'We're probably going to ask you for fingerprints and a blood sample—'

'Come on,' he said, clearly upset now. 'Why? I had nothing to do with whatever happened. I don't even know these people.'

'Then your prints and DNA will clear you,' said Lacoste.

Cloutier opened the door, and they stepped out.

'Did you know she was pregnant?' asked Lacoste.

'I didn't know her,' he said, his voice plaintive. Then he paused, and his muscular shoulders sagged a bit. 'She was pregnant?'

'Yes.'

'And someone killed her?'

'Yes.'

'The baby . . . ?'

'Died, too.'

He covered Vendredi's ears and said, 'Goddamned fucking shit of a fucking horrible world.'

Then he uncovered his niece's ears and kissed her. Gently.

'That's either a really great guy,' said Cloutier, putting the car in gear, 'or a monster.'

Lysette Cloutier never dreamed, while working in accounting, that it could be so difficult to tell the two apart. But it was.

As Beauvoir and Gamache slid into the booth at the café in Cowansville, Gamache's phone rang. It was from the RCMP.

'Excuse me.' He slid back out and went outside to take the call.

'Armand?' came the familiar voice, shouting over a familiar noise. 'Sorry, meant to get to you sooner, but I wanted to see it for myself.'

'Are you in a helicopter?'

'*Oui*. Over the La Grande-3 dam.'

One of the oldest, Gamache knew. If any dam was going to –

'We've opened the spillways,' the RCMP officer shouted above the rotors.

'And?' Gamache shouted back.

Inside the café, Beauvoir could hear Gamache's voice through the window and saw him hunkered over, a hand covering his other ear, straining to hear whoever was on the other end.

'It seems to be working. Will let you know about the others.' Gamache heard him give muffled instructions to the pilot. 'Call you back.'

'And the diversions farther south? Are they being dug?'

Gamache shouted into the phone, but the connection had been broken.

Gamache hung up and exhaled. Closing his eyes for a moment. It just might work.

'What was that about?' Jean-Guy asked when he returned, but there was no chance for an answer.

Someone was walking toward them.

'Thank you for coming, Simone,' said Gamache, as the elegant woman in her early forties approached their booth. 'I'm not sure you've met Chief Inspector Beauvoir. He's the head of homicide for the Sûreté. Jean-Guy, this's Simone Fleury. She's on the board of the Réseau de Violence Conjugale du Québec and runs the local women's shelters. We've sat on several committees together.'

'Committees.' Madame Fleury made a dismissive, almost rude noise.

She looked at Beauvoir's outstretched hand, ignored it, and sat down.

'Nothing's changed. Women are beaten, women are killed. That's why we're here, isn't it?'

'*Oui*,' said Beauvoir, dropping his hand and sitting down next to Gamache.

'I see you're back at work, Armand.' Her voice was abrupt. There was a tone of displeasure and impatience. 'Not everyone seems pleased.'

'I'm sure the vast majority are thrilled I'm back,' he said with a smile.

'They're just too busy to mention it on Twitter, I suppose,' she said. 'Though you do have one defender. A dumb-ass.'

Beauvoir looked at her with surprise. But Gamache just gave a small grunt of laughter. What Madame Fleury said next confirmed Beauvoir's suspicions about her.

'Let's get on with it.' She looked at her watch. 'I have a hair appointment, then a luncheon.'

Rich. Bored. The kids gone, husband busy making more money. A do-gooder.

Simone Fleury regarded Beauvoir.

A bundle of coiled energy she found repulsive. Here was a young guy promoted beyond his competence. Just beginning to develop a paunch. Probably going to seed, she thought.

He was good-looking, clean, well groomed, but Madame Fleury had trained herself to look beyond what could be seen.

Probably went home and whaled on his wife when the Habs lost. Or after he'd had a few. Or just because.

Simone Fleury did not like cops. She tolerated Gamache. Barely.

'What can you tell us about Vivienne Godin?' Beauvoir asked, placing the photo of her on the table so that the blank-faced young woman was looking up at them.

'Tea, please,' said Madame Fleury to the waitress.

Beauvoir ordered one as well, while Gamache took a coffee.

The waitress had looked Madame Fleury in the eye as she ordered. Brief enough, meaningless enough. Except she hadn't made eye contact with either Beauvoir or Gamache.

'I've seen that,' said Madame Fleury, pushing the photograph back across the table to Beauvoir. 'You sent it to me, Armand. I asked around. She didn't show up at any of the shelters, and if she called, she didn't use her own name. Most don't.'

'So she could've called but didn't give her name.'

'Isn't that what I just said? We get twenty-six thousand calls a year.' She let that sink in and was gratified to see the look of surprise on Beauvoir's handsome face. 'Most never give their name. Most never show up.'

'Why not?'

'Most women, when they call for help, don't want to leave the relationship. They just want the beating, that beating, to end.'

It was, Gamache knew, exactly what Cameron described with Vivienne.

'But they must know there'll be another,' said Beauvoir. 'Why—'

'Don't,' Madame Fleury snapped. 'Don't you dare ask why they don't leave. Don't you dare judge these women for staying.'

'But it's a legitimate question, isn't it?' He looked from Madame Fleury to Gamache.

'There's an implied criticism,' said Madame Fleury. 'That these women are weak or stupid.'

'I never said that.'

'No, but you think that. Why don't they leave? Because they've been conditioned to believe it's their fault. Because they've been isolated. They have no money and no support. Because they have a shred of hope or delusion. Because they actually love the guy. Because they're stuck. Because they're terrified. And for good reason. Because it's all they know and all they think they deserve. Because they believe there's nothing better out there. You can see it in her face. That dazed look. As telling as bruises.'

She jutted her slender hand toward the photo on the table. The picture had been taken before Vivienne was married, but Gamache didn't bother to correct her.

'That's why the law was changed,' he said instead. 'With Madame Fleury's help. So that when police show up, they can use their discretion and arrest the abuser. The woman doesn't have to be the one to lay charges.'

'Yeah, right,' said Madame Fleury. 'But how often does that actually happen? Goddamned cops. You need "sufficient information." I think that's the phrase, right?'

'You know it is,' said Gamache.

'Did she call the cops?' asked Madame Fleury, looking from one to the other.

'She did,' said Beauvoir. 'Charges were never laid.'

'Insufficient information,' said Madame Fleury. 'How long before she was killed was that?'

'First time? Thirteen months. There were other calls after that, but no arrest.'

'And then he kills her.'

She looked from Beauvoir to Gamache. Neither of whom disagreed.

'*Alors*,' said Madame Fleury, raising her manicured hands. 'All we can do is provide a safe place for those who do break free.'

'Would they know where to go, though?' asked Beauvoir.

The location of shelters was closely guarded. For good reason.

'We don't advertise the location of shelters, if that's what you mean.'

It clearly was not what Beauvoir meant. He was coming to deeply dislike this woman, who had a knack for taking what he said and exaggerating it, twisting it, into something ridiculous.

'If they want help, we arrange to meet them,' she continued. 'And bring them to a shelter.'

'But still,' said Beauvoir, 'must be hard in a small community to keep that secret. Neighbors and all.'

'It is. How did she die?'

'Pushed off a bridge into a river in flood. She either

drowned or was battered against the rocks. She was pregnant.'

Simone Fleury raised her head so that she was looking down her long nose at Beauvoir.

He realized he was being brutal. Stating the facts as though they were just words. Matching her own matter-of-fact tone. Beside him, he heard Gamache take a deep breath of disapproval.

He pulled himself back in. 'It's a terrible thing.'

There was a pause, until through those thin lips came one word: 'Yes.'

She turned to Gamache. 'Her husband, of course, otherwise I wouldn't be here.'

'He's a suspect, *oui*.'

'If you have any trouble convicting him, just send him over to the shelter. We'll take care of him.'

'*Merci*,' said Gamache. 'We might have trouble.'

Barely under her breath, as she squeezed her tea bag, Madame Fleury muttered, 'Cops.'

'If an abuser does show up at a shelter,' said Beauvoir, 'what do you do?'

'Invite him in for tea and petits fours. What do you think we do?'

Is it true, is it kind, does it need to be said? Beauvoir held his tongue. Barely.

'You call the cops,' he finally said, through his own thin lips.

'Yeah, right. And wait the twenty minutes until they move their fat asses?'

'That's not true,' said Gamache.

'Okay, that might be true, but not fast enough. Never fast enough when the guy's pounding on the door.'

'So what do you do?' Beauvoir persisted.

'We take care of it.'

'How? Do you have a gun?'

'Are you kidding? Do I look crazy?'

Gamache cleared his throat in a warning to Beauvoir not to answer that.

'Believe me,' Madame Fleury continued, 'those of us who managed to escape won't put up with that bullshit ever again. No one gets through the front door. No one touches any of those women. Never. Ever.'

'Us?' asked Beauvoir. 'You?'

'You don't think I do this out of the goodness of my heart?'

Beauvoir did not think that.

'Listen, Chief.' She almost spat the word out. 'Doctors go home and beat their wives. Lawyers. Cops. There's a huge instance of abuse from cops.' She glared at him in what he realized, with some shock, was a warning. Maybe even an accusation.

'My father was a judge,' she continued, 'and inside our big old house in our respectable neighborhood, he beat us kids. And worse. I married a banker at eighteen, to get away, and guess what? He beat me, too. Then he'd bring me flowers and jewelry and he'd cry. He'd sob and say how sorry he was. And that he'd be a better husband. He'd never do it again. And you know what?' Her eyes opened wide as she stared at Beauvoir. 'I believed him. Because I wanted to. Because I had to. I put on the beautiful silk scarf he brought me, to hide the bruises, and went to the country club for lunch.'

She let that sink in.

'Without realizing it, we go to what's familiar. When I finally told my best friend, she didn't believe me. No one did. They didn't want to know. There was only one shelter here

at the time. Overflowing. But they took me in and gave me a mattress on the floor. I slept on it for three months. First time in my life I felt safe. You know why it's safe? Not because the cops protect us but because we look after ourselves. We make sure it is.'

'"We" the workers?'

'"We" every woman there. You asked if we have a weapon? We do. And you gave it to us, with every blow. Every bruise. Every broken bone. It's the toy at the bottom of the cereal box.' She clunked her mug down on the table so hard that tea shot out the top and other patrons looked over.

'Rage,' said Beauvoir.

'Baseball bats,' said Madame Fleury. 'Next time you see a group of women in a park practicing their swings, you think about that.'

She wiped up the spilled tea with a thin paper napkin, then pointed to the words Gamache had just written in his notebook. 'What you just wrote is true, but no excuse. Cycle of abuse. My husband was beaten by his father. He saw his mother hit. But he was an adult when he hit me, and responsible for his own actions. They all are. After a beating they feel horrible and buy presents and promise to be better men, but they don't change. They don't grow up. They remain out-of-control children in a man's body.'

'Simone,' said Gamache, 'a bag was found on the side of the river with some of her belongings in it, but it was a strange assortment. Summer clothing. Medication she probably didn't need anymore.'

'So?'

'We're wondering if she packed it herself.'

Madame Fleury considered. 'Might've, in a panic. Some women leave suddenly, just take off. But most have thought

about it for a while. They have a bag packed and hidden, ready to grab. I had one packed for almost a year before I got up the courage to leave.'

Beauvoir tried to imagine Simone Fleury as a frightened young woman. But then, he knew that few people would look at him and imagine the wreckage he'd crawled out of, not all that long ago.

Madame Fleury glanced at her watch. 'I'm leaving. My hairdresser doesn't like it when I'm late. If you need anything else, you know how to reach me.'

And leave she did. Armand did not offer her his hand, and she did not offer him hers.

But Beauvoir did. As a sort of peace offering.

Simone Fleury looked at it and walked away.

'She thinks every man's an abuser,' said Beauvoir, dropping his hand to his side. 'That's unfair.'

'She was beaten by two men she trusted. That's unfair. She works with abused women every day. She's surrounded by it. It's incredible she can even bring herself to look at us, never mind talk to us in anything close to a civil manner.' Gamache nodded toward Beauvoir's hand, which was at his side, his fingers relaxed into a loose fist. 'What would you do if a weapon were thrust at you?'

Beauvoir looked down. He saw a hand. One that wrote notes, and chopped vegetables, and bathed his son. But Madame Fleury saw something else.

Twenty-six thousand calls a year, he thought.

As they stepped into the sunshine and the unseasonably warm April day, Beauvoir instinctively scanned the faces and realized with some amazement why he always did that.

He was unconsciously looking for danger. Always. He saw potential threats everywhere. In everyone. In the elderly

man across the way, with that bag. In the kids laughing and shoving each other. In the SUV heading a little too quickly down the main street.

Suppose . . .

It had become second nature. Hardwired into him.

Jean-Guy Beauvoir knew that every person had a killer inside them.

And Madame Fleury knew that every man had an abuser inside of him.

Both were unfair. But such was their experience. And conditioning.

That was one of the many reasons he had to leave. Had to escape the Sûreté and get far, far away. From a world filled with threats. He longed to see a kinder world.

He realized it might be too late. Too much damage might've already been done. But Jean-Guy Beauvoir had to try to break free.

As they walked by the window of the café, he glanced in and saw the young waitress clearing their mugs and picking up the money they'd left.

She looked at him and quickly dropped her eyes.

Jean-Guy Beauvoir returned his gaze to the road ahead. Scanning it.

CHAPTER 24

—

@MyrnaLanders: I love @ClaraMorrow works. They're genius.

@ClaraMorrow: Thanks @MyrnaLanders, but you sent this to me privately. Did you mean to? I'm sitting with you in the bistro. Oh, oh. Here comes Ruth. Look busy!

@MyrnaLanders: #ClaraSucks *Merde.*

@ClaraMorrow: @MyrnaLanders That one you put out on the public twitter feed. You just agreed with everyone who says my art is shit.

@MyrnaLanders: #ClaraSucks Did I? Fuck

@ClaraMorrow: @MyrnaLanders Please stop.

The incident room in Three Pines was filled with the aroma of wet socks, sweat, cilantro, and lime.

Olivier and Gabri moved aside the firefighting equipment and set out the ginger-garlic chicken soup, sandwiches, and drinks.

Along with the senior officers, there were the more junior agents. Cloutier and the big guy. Cameron. They suspected he'd eat lots.

'Any news on the flooding?' Isabelle Lacoste asked.

'Here?' asked Olivier. 'The Bella Bella's gone down. Thank God.'

'Across the province,' said Isabelle.

'Only what we see on the news,' said Gabri. 'You probably know more than we do.'

'Maybe not,' she said. 'We've been busy.'

'Well, according to CBC, they're digging huge trenches to divert some rivers,' said Gabri. 'That must've been where you got the idea from, Armand.'

'Good,' said Gamache, and exhaled. 'Good news.'

'Did you see the Deputy Premier in the scrum when that reporter asked about it?' said Olivier.

Gabri and Olivier reenacted, with some exaggeration, Gamache suspected, the Deputy Premier's face as it went from bafflement to anger to confidence when he was told it seemed to be working.

'And then, just as he'd said he was in the meeting where it'd been decided to dig, another journalist asked about the angry farmers whose fields were now flooded,' said Gabri.

His face fell into an expression somehow combining annoyance and obsequiousness.

'Poor man,' said Olivier, putting linen napkins on the table. Beauvoir watched all this and wondered if they'd pull a candelabra out of the hamper next. 'Can't win.'

While food was being organized, Gamache picked up a landline and went into the storage room. No need for the others to hear this call.

'Alouette Organization,' came the cheery voice.

'The general manager, please.'

'I'm afraid he's in a meeting. Can I take a message?'

'If you could ask him to step out for a moment, this won't take long.'

Gamache explained who he was, and a minute or so later the phone was picked up.

They talked for less than a minute. When Gamache hung up, he thought for a moment, then returned to the table.

Olivier and Gabri had left, and now, as they ate, the Sûreté officers compared notes.

'So this Gerald Bertrand denies knowing Vivienne Godin,' said Beauvoir.

'*Oui.*' Lacoste picked up an egg salad sandwich on a fresh baguette, spiked with just a little curry, poached raisins, and arugula. 'He says it was a wrong number. Says she was slurring her words and upset. Probably drunk.'

Beauvoir casually reached out and took the peanut butter, honey, and banana sandwich on crusty white bread after noticing Cloutier also eyeing it.

'Not drunk,' said Gamache. 'Beaten. The coroner's report says she'd had a few ounces, but not intoxication level.' He passed around hard copies of the preliminary report. 'The slurring was probably from being hit.'

He put down his sandwich.

'Nothing more from Dr Harris?' asked Lacoste after quickly scanning the coroner's report.

Beauvoir checked the emails again and shook his head. 'Nothing. What else did you find?'

'Gerald Bertrand's alibi checks out,' said Agent Cloutier. 'His friends confirm they were over at his place watching the hockey game on Saturday night. They arrived just before seven. None of them knew anything about Bertrand

having an affair with Vivienne Godin. In fact, none had even heard of her.'

'The other thing is the baby,' said Lacoste. 'He was looking after his niece until six on Saturday night. Not much time to meet Vivienne on the bridge and get home before his friends arrived.'

'You don't think it was him, do you?' said Beauvoir, sitting back in his chair and taking a large bite of the sandwich.

'No,' admitted Lacoste. 'I think logistically it would've been tough, but I also believe he's telling the truth. I saw him with his niece. He likes kids. I think if his lover had told him she was pregnant, he might not have been thrilled, but he wouldn't have killed her and the baby.'

Gamache looked at Beauvoir to continue the questioning but saw he was struggling to chew the sandwich, his mouth apparently glued almost shut.

'So the other possibility is that he was telling the truth,' said Gamache, picking up the mantle. 'He didn't know her. Which means Vivienne was calling the wrong number. But over and over?'

'Looks like it.'

'I wonder who she was trying to call?' he said. 'They were made in a cluster, right? At six fifteen.'

'Starting then. There were four calls over ten minutes. All to Bertrand's number.'

'Strange to have called the same wrong number over and over,' said Gamache. 'Once, maybe, if you hit the wrong button. We've all done it. But to make the same mistake over and over? Even if disoriented you'd think she'd hit different numbers.'

'What do you think it means?' asked Lacoste.

Once again Gamache looked at Beauvoir, who was now

regretting not the sandwich itself but taking such a huge bite. Jean-Guy chewed more vigorously and gestured to Gamache to continue.

'I think,' he said, 'that Vivienne was given a number to call but had written it down wrong. So while she was dialing correctly, she didn't realize she was calling the wrong number. Was there a piece of paper found on her body, with a number?'

'No,' said Lacoste. 'In her wallet we found paper, but it was wet through. Disintegrated.'

'Nothing legible?'

'No.'

'But that explains why she kept making the same mistake,' said Cloutier, nodding. 'She wrote it down wrong and didn't realize that. So who did she think she was calling?'

'I'm not willing to give up on Bertrand yet,' said Beauvoir, finally swallowing. 'What you say is true. She can't have made exactly the same mistake over and over. So maybe it wasn't a mistake at all. She meant to call Bertrand and did. We have no idea what she actually said to him. Someone met her on that bridge, and she'd have had to arrange it. I think he's lying. I'll put an agent on his place.'

'There is something else,' said Lacoste. 'Something Agent Cloutier here discovered.'

She turned, like a proud parent, to the older woman.

This was the accountant's moment to shine. Lysette Cloutier gathered her notes.

'Vivienne Godin might have been having an affair, but her husband certainly was.'

'How do you know?' asked Beauvoir.

'The internet,' said Cloutier.

'Wikipedia?' asked Beauvoir, half joking, half dreading the answer.

'*Non,*' laughed Cloutier. 'Google.'

Beauvoir opened his mouth, but Lacoste jumped in. 'Let her explain.'

'Since Tracey doesn't have internet at home,' said Cloutier, 'but does have a website and a social-media presence, it seemed pretty obvious someone was doing it for him, so I tracked down the IP address and found her. I then went onto his public Instagram account and convinced her to give me access to their private account.'

'How did you do that?' asked Beauvoir.

'I set up a dummy website and Instagram account. NouveauGalerie. Said I was a gallery owner looking for new artists. I needed to communicate in private and to see more of Carl Tracey's work.'

'So she gave you access to their private account, not knowing who you were?' said Gamache.

'Smart,' said Beauvoir.

'*Merci.*' She smiled and looked at Isabelle Lacoste, who nodded encouragement. 'This's what I found.'

She turned her laptop around for Beauvoir and Gamache to see the photos of Tracey and Vachon together. It was obvious they were lovers.

They scrolled through the pictures and read the private messages between Carl Tracey and Pauline Vachon.

'Look at this one,' said Cloutier. '*She's a drunken slut. You deserve better.* That's from Pauline. Pretty clear.'

'Of an affair,' said Gamache. 'Maybe. But murder?'

'Look here, *patron,*' said Lacoste. 'On the day of the murder.'

Both Beauvoir and Gamache leaned closer to the laptop as she found the posts sent Saturday around midday.

Stuff's in the bag. Everything's ready. Will be done tonight. I promise. That from Carl Tracey.

And Pauline Vachon's reply: *Finally. Good luck. Don't mess it up.*

Beauvoir sat back and exhaled. '*I promise.* Jesus. So this Vachon was in on it.'

'More than that,' said Lacoste. 'I think it was her idea.'

'Well, her encouragement anyway,' said Gamache.

'Enough to charge her with being an accomplice,' said Beauvoir.

'Is it enough to arrest him for murder?' asked Cloutier.

'I doubt it,' said Lacoste, and she turned to Beauvoir. 'What do you think?'

'I think it's turning into a very strong circumstantial case. And that might be the best we can do. Any jury would be able to follow this evidence directly to Tracey. The admitted abuse, these photos and posts clearly showing he was having an affair, the fact, admitted here, that he packed her bag.' He stopped to think. 'That might explain the summer clothes. He just took things at random or maybe took things he knew Vivienne wouldn't miss.'

'To make it look like she'd decided to leave on her own,' said Cloutier.

'Tracey even told this Pauline that it was happening that night,' said Beauvoir. 'Doesn't get more incriminating than that, the dumb shit. Well done, Cloutier.'

'*Merci.*'

'Have you spoken to this Pauline Vachon?' asked Beauvoir.

'*Non,*' said Lacoste. 'I wanted to see if there was more that Agent Cloutier could get out of her, posing as the gallery owner.'

Beauvoir was nodding. Considering.

He used to kid Gamache when he'd find him at his desk, staring into space. The Chief would patiently explain that being still and doing nothing were two different things.

Now Beauvoir stared into space while his mind worked.

This was no time for a misstep. It seemed Pauline Vachon was key. If they could get her to turn on Tracey, testify against him, in exchange for a deal, they had their case.

'Is he okay?' Cloutier whispered to Lacoste, who couldn't suppress a smile.

'He's thinking.'

'Looks like he has a headache.'

'Let me tell you,' said Beauvoir, slightly annoyed, 'what I think might've happened that night.'

As he spoke, the others saw clearly what he was describing.

'Suppose Tracey beat Vivienne, maybe into unconsciousness, then went to get piss drunk before finishing her off. He might've even thought she was already dead. While he was gone, she came to and made those calls to Bertrand. Pleading for help. Maybe telling him to meet her on the bridge. Tracey hears and sees an opportunity. Much better than putting her body in the woods. He decides to follow her, with the duffel bag he'd packed. Once there, he pushes her off. Vivienne reaches out to stop herself, making that deep cut in her palm from the rotten wood. Then Tracey tosses the bag in after her and leaves. The heavy rain washes away all the footprints and tire marks.'

Done.

That was the scenario he'd take to the Crown Prosecutor when the time came. Unless something showed up to contradict it. Which he doubted.

'And Bertrand?' asked Lacoste.

'Doesn't show up.' He nodded. It fit. 'But let's keep digging. I want to go for premeditation. Those posts prove first-degree, but I want more.'

He looked around the table.

Gamache nodded. He also wanted first-degree but felt somewhat comforted knowing if all else failed, they probably had enough circumstantial evidence right now to convict Tracey of manslaughter.

But still, a few things perplexed him.

'It's strange that Madame Vachon would let you see those private messages,' he said, returning to the laptop. 'Even if she didn't know you're with the Sûreté.'

'She might've forgotten they were there,' said Lacoste. 'And unless you knew they were planning a murder, you wouldn't guess from those posts. On the surface, they could be about anything.'

'*Oui*,' said Gamache. 'And that could be a problem.'

'One thing I don't understand,' said Beauvoir, leaning forward and putting his elbows on the table, 'is how Tracey managed to send those messages if he doesn't have internet at home.'

'You can log into an account from anywhere,' said Cloutier. 'He must've been in town and used someone else's device or an internet café. I'll see if I can track down where they originated.'

Beauvoir paused to study the posts again.

Stuff's in the bag. Everything's ready. Will be done tonight. I promise.

'I don't want to blow this,' said Beauvoir. 'It needs to stick.'

Lacoste was nodding. 'It will.'

'On another issue, I'd like to release Monsieur Godin,' said Gamache.

'But,' said Cloutier, 'won't he—'

'Try to kill Tracey?' said Gamache. 'Maybe. But I'm hoping we can convince him that an arrest is imminent. That putting Tracey through a trial and then in prison is far worse than killing him.'

'Would you?' Cloutier asked. 'Be convinced?'

Gamache stared at her. She turned beet red and stammered an apology.

'I'm sorry, sir, it's just that I know you have a daughter about Vivienne's age, and I thought—'

'Don't presume, Agent Cloutier,' he said, his voice uncharacteristically hard. Showing Lacoste and Beauvoir, who knew him well, that while Cloutier's comment was inappropriate, she had indeed hit a nerve.

While they studied him, Gamache studied Agent Cloutier.

He realized that something about her made him wary. And he knew Jean-Guy felt the same way.

While it was obvious that his love for his own daughter had created an emotional frisson about this case, it was equally obvious that Lysette Cloutier cared very deeply for Homer Godin. Perhaps too deeply.

But did that matter?

And was it even true? Could her protectiveness toward him not be the natural instincts of a close friend?

That was one of the problems with being a homicide cop. Interpreting innocent, even admirable, acts as somehow suspicious. Once that started happening, it was hard to change the perception.

'I'd like you to come with me,' he said to Cloutier. 'You might be able to help calm Monsieur Godin. Talk sense into him.'

'I'll try,' she said. '*Merci.*'

She seemed to think it was a peace offering, never dreaming this courteous senior officer might have other motives for asking her along.

'Is this all right with you?' Gamache asked Beauvoir.

'Can we talk?' Beauvoir jerked his head toward the window at the far end of the room, away from the others.

Gamache followed him, and despite himself he felt, if not annoyed, then perplexed, and he realized with some amusement that he'd asked Beauvoir out of consideration, not expecting he might actually disagree.

As they walked to the window, Beauvoir heard the Chief's footsteps. Familiar yet foreign. He was used to hearing them in front of him. Leading. Not behind, following.

This was not getting any easier, he realized. He'd certainly disagreed with Gamache in the past, sometimes arguing quite forcefully. But he'd always understood that the final word would be Gamache's. As would the responsibility.

But now it was his. He was in charge. The decisions, and responsibility, were his.

He turned and faced his mentor and father-in-law.

'Cloutier's right. Homer Godin's gonna try to kill Tracey. You know that. I think you're making a mistake.'

He watched Gamache closely. And saw him nod.

'Would you rather we didn't release Monsieur Godin?'

Jean-Guy relaxed and realized Armand Gamache would not make this difficult. 'I'd like to understand your reasoning.'

Gamache considered Beauvoir for a moment. His protégé, now his boss.

He remembered the first time he'd seen the younger man. They met at the outpost where Agent Beauvoir had been assigned straight out of the academy. He'd been placed, by the station commander, in the basement evidence locker because none of the other agents liked working with the arrogant, cocky, disgruntled new guy.

Agent Beauvoir was composing his letter of resignation, in which he'd tell them, yet again, what he really thought of them, when the famed head of homicide for the Sûreté showed up to investigate a murder.

The station commander had assigned this difficult young agent to help the Chief Inspector, in hopes that he'd run afoul of either Gamache or the killer, and one or the other would rid them of the problem that was Jean-Guy Beauvoir.

Gamache had stared through the bars at the caged young man. Beauvoir had stared back.

And they'd recognized each other.

From lifetimes past. From battlegrounds past.

And on the spot, to the shock of everyone except himself, Chief Inspector Gamache had hired the unruly young agent. The human refuse no one else wanted. Eventually promoting him, several years later, to be his second-in-command.

And now this would be their final investigation together. As Jean-Guy broke free and Armand let him go.

It would be, if Gamache had anything to do with it, a successful end to a courageous career.

But they weren't over the finish line yet.

'Why would you even consider letting Monsieur Godin go,' Beauvoir was saying, 'before we've arrested Tracey? Knowing what he planned to do. Unless—'

Beauvoir stopped. Almost in time.

'Unless?' asked Gamache, and once again Jean-Guy could feel the natural authority of the man. It radiated off him. 'You think I want him to kill Tracey?'

'*Non*, not at all. It's just ... honestly?' said Jean-Guy. 'Between us? I can understand how Homer feels. And obviously you do, too. If we couldn't convict Tracey, if he walked free, I'd be tempted to just step aside and let him do it.'

Gamache tilted his head and stared at his son-in-law.

'Don't tell me that you wouldn't be tempted, too,' said Beauvoir.

'Tempted, maybe. I honestly don't know what I'd do, Jean-Guy. But I hope to God not that.'

'So why do you want to let him go now?'

'I'm worried that holding him any longer will just make things worse. My reason for detaining him was to give him a cooling-off period. When he couldn't do anything. But if it lasts much longer, instead of cooling off, his anger will heat up. I agree that letting him go is a risk, but so's keeping him in jail. Besides, it's just not right.'

Beauvoir thought about it, glancing out the window at the Bella Bella and the sandbags lining the river. At the ones still standing and the ones fallen down.

So close to tragedy. It didn't really take much to tip the balance.

'Okay. Let him out. I'll have an agent watch his place and follow him if he leaves.'

'You won't have to. I was thinking of inviting Monsieur Godin to stay with us. His things are already here. And that way I can keep an eye on him. Besides, he shouldn't be alone.'

'Is that smart?'

'Probably not,' said Gamache with a small laugh. 'Is it my first choice? *Non.* But sometimes you have to do something stupid.'

Beauvoir laughed. 'I never thought I'd hear you say that. Sounds more like something I'd say.'

'Guess you're rubbing off on me, *patron.*' Gamache smiled, then it faded. 'Am I my brother's keeper?'

'He's not your brother,' said Jean-Guy.

'*Non,* that's true. And Vivienne isn't Annie. But still, I'd want someone to do this for me, to watch over me, if . . .'

If Annie . . . If Reine-Marie . . .

Beauvoir considered and realized that if anything happened to Annie. . . . To Honoré . . .

Someone would have to do the same for him.

'Agreed, *patron*,' he said. 'By the way, who were you talking to in the store room?'

'The Montreal Alouettes.'

'What did they say about Cameron? Why'd they let him go?'

'Too many penalties. He was a good player but was costing them yards.'

'Roughing?' asked Beauvoir.

'I'd have thought so, but no. Holding. Apparently it was almost a reflex of his, to grab hold of something and not let go. They couldn't break him of it.'

As Gamache walked to the car, listening to Agent Cloutier go on excitedly about continuing to string Pauline Vachon along in hopes of getting more evidence, he felt some anxiety stir.

It wasn't the slight sour feeling he'd had in his gut earlier. The worry they wouldn't be able to nail Tracey. That was still there, but less and less as the evidence mounted and now threatened to bury Carl Tracey.

This was something else. A prickling at the back of his neck.

Something was wrong. A mistake had been made, or was about to be made.

'Who's that?' asked Myrna, nodding toward a car just arriving in Three Pines as Armand's vehicle left.

'Probably more Sûreté,' said Clara. 'They've set up in the old railway station again.'

'Huh,' said Myrna. 'It's stopped in front of your house.'

'Really?' said Clara, turning to take a closer look.

'Is that who you've been looking for?' Reine-Marie asked Ruth. The elderly poet had been glancing out the bistro window all morning.

Now Ruth was smiling as she, too, watched the car arrive.

'What've you done?' asked Myrna.

'You'll see.' Ruth turned to Clara. 'You might want to go say hello.'

A young woman was just getting out of the car.

'Why?' asked Clara, not at all liking the satisfied expression on the old woman's face.

'*All that most maddens and torments,*' said Ruth. '*All that stirs up the lees of things. Moby-Dick.*'

'Have you stirred up the lees of things?' Myrna asked.

Ruth was so pleased with herself she was almost exploding with pleasure. It was not an attractive sight.

As they watched, the stranger knocked on Clara's door and, getting no answer, turned to look around.

And Clara recognized her. 'Oh, God, Ruth. What've you done?'

'Your white whale,' said Ruth, triumphant. 'Thar she blows.'

CHAPTER 25

~

@CarlTracey: I've put up more pictures of Carl's work for
you to see.

@NouveauGalerie: Who's this? I thought I was
communicating with Tracey.

@CarlTracey: Pauline Vachon. Carl's partner.

@NouveauGalerie: Business or life partner?

@CarlTracey: Does it matter?

@CarlTracey: Hello?

@CarlTracey: Hello?

@CarlTracey: Both.

Gamache sat on the cot across from Homer Godin
while Lysette Cloutier stood by the open door to the
holding cell.

Homer looked sick. Gaunt. His eyes were bloodshot and puffy, his face blotched. Bright red in places, white, almost green, in others.

'We've come to release you,' said Gamache. 'If you promise not to do anything to Carl Tracey.'

'Or yourself,' said Cloutier.

Homer continued to stare at his large hands, hanging limp between his knees.

When he finally spoke, his voice was remote. 'I can't promise.'

'Then I can't release you,' said Gamache. He leaned forward and dropped his voice even further, so that Homer had to also lean forward. Had to make some small effort.

Which he did.

'You can do this,' Armand said softly.

'There's only one thing I want to do.'

That sat between them. The silence stretching on. Until Homer finally broke it himself, lifting his eyes to Armand's.

'How'm I gonna go on?'

Armand placed his hand on Homer's. 'You'll come stay with us. We'll keep you safe.'

'Really?'

And for a moment, a split second, Armand saw a glimmer amid the gloom. And then it was gone.

'I can't come to your house.'

'Why not?'

The two men were quiet for a moment before Homer spoke again.

'You've been kind. Your wife—' Homer lifted his hand to his own face. 'I'm sorry. I didn't mean to ...'

'I know. She knows. Are you worried about doing it again?'

Homer shook his head. 'No. Never. But if I stay with

you, I'll hurt you in other ways. When I kill Tracey, they'll blame you.'

'And what's this?'

Dominica Oddly went to lift the corner of the canvas, but Clara stopped her.

'Something I'm working on.'

'A portrait?'

'Sort of.'

Clara's uninvited guest raised her brows in a way that would be comical, cartoonish, if it weren't so terrifying.

Ruth Zardo had somehow managed to convince the art critic for the online journal *Odd* to come from Brooklyn to Québec. To come into the countryside, to Three Pines. To come into Clara's home. Where Clara, against every instinct, had invited her into her studio.

Seemed courtesy beat good sense. Almost to death.

'Come,' Dominica Oddly said after an all-too-cursory glance around.

She indicated the shabby sofa against the wall of Clara's studio. They sat side by side, the young woman turning her lithe body to Clara.

She was dressed in sort of harem pants, with combat boots and a T-shirt that read YES, HE'S A RACIST.

Clara doubted she'd passed thirty. Her hair was in long dreadlocks. Her face was unlined and unblemished. No piercings and, from what Clara could see, no tattoos. She didn't need those to prove she was cool. She just was. So cool that Clara felt goose bumps rise on her forearms.

To say Dominica Oddly was a rainmaker was to vastly underestimate her power. Clara knew that the woman sitting next to her didn't just make rain, she made the whole

goddamned environment. She could cause the sun to shine on your career. Or a tsunami to sweep your life's work away.

She had an eye for the avant-garde, an ear for undercurrents, and, perhaps above all else, a savant's gift for social media.

Oddly had understood early that those platforms were the new 'high ground.' The place from which attacks could be launched. Territory could be captured. Where hearts were influenced and opinions made.

Her online journal, *Odd*, had millions of subscribers while still managing to position itself as underground, even subversive. Dominica Oddly was like some hipster oligarch.

Clara subscribed to *Odd*, and every morning over coffee she read Dominica's daily column.

Oddly's pithy, articulate, often cruel, always elegant prose both amused and appalled Clara, as the critic stripped away the artifice in the art world. Ruthlessly.

All truth with malice in it.

But, despite Clara's rise, Dominica Oddly had never reviewed her works. As far as Clara knew, Oddly had no idea she existed. She'd never met the woman and certainly had never seen her at one of her shows.

Every artist, every gallery owner, every agent, every collector scanned the horizon for Dominica Oddly.

And here she was. In Clara's studio. Amid half-finished canvases, empty yogurt containers. A banana peel lay flopped on the arm of the sofa. Clara shoved it off with her elbow, but not fast enough for the keen, and disconcertingly amused, eyes of the critic.

Ruth was right when she'd described this young woman as her white whale. The one she sought. The one she dreamed of landing.

But where Ahab was obsessed with vengeance, Clara was

not. There was nothing to avenge. Clara really just wanted Oddly to notice her. To acknowledge her. Okay, and to love and laud her art.

Now that she had the critic's attention, Clara began to see something else. The size of the creature, and what would happen if it turned on her.

But it was too late. The white whale was in her home. In her studio. On the sofa kneading Leo's ears.

With her latest show taking so many hits, one from this woman would be enough to sink Clara Morrow.

'Cake?' she asked, and saw Dominica Oddly smile. It was a nice smile. A nice face.

It was the sort of look that happened just before you're eaten, Clara thought.

'I don't think you can stop me.'

Annie's father had no doubt that Vivienne's father was right. He probably couldn't stop him.

Homer Godin would leave this jail cell and spend the rest of his life trying to kill the man he could not name.

And, once done, Homer would almost certainly then kill himself.

'Suppose you didn't.'

'*Pardon?*'

'Suppose you didn't kill Tracey,' Gamache repeated. 'What would your life look like?'

The question, so simple, seemed to stump Godin. It was like asking him, Suppose you could fly. Suppose you became invisible. Suppose you didn't kill the man who just murdered your daughter.

He was asking Vivienne's father to consider the inconceivable.

'Think about it while I do the paperwork.'

Chief Inspector Gamache got up and left, taking Cloutier with him and leaving Godin alone with thoughts that inevitably circled back to his daughter. He saw her face as she fell, backward. Off the bridge. Arms pinwheeling.

And then the splash.

He rammed shut his eyes until all he saw was darkness. Then Vivienne's face floated up, to hover just below the surface.

Accusing.

'It's in,' said Isabelle Lacoste, grabbing a chair across from Beauvoir in the incident room.

No need to say what 'it' was.

Beauvoir quickly clicked over to his email and opened the document from the coroner, with the attachment.

Both scanned it, then went back to the top and read more closely. Their faces, their expressions, almost exactly the same.

At first triumphant. And then perplexed.

'I do this because I love art. I love the whole world of art. Being around people who are creative and daring.'

As she spoke, Dominica's face became almost luminous. Her voice, while deep, was also light, bright.

'I search the world for people who have a true muse and not just some insatiable hole in their soul they need to fill with fame and money. And when I find the real thing . . .'

Her entire face opened, in unguarded delight. An awe rarely seen in the cluttered world of ego and fear and greed that was the international art scene.

'I take aim at the poseurs and try to lift up those who create

from their very being.' Dominica's hand, clenched into a fist, thumped her breastbone and stayed there. 'Those who are daring and brave and willing to be vulnerable. Like you.'

'Me?' said Clara.

'Yes, you.' Dominica laughed, and Clara almost tumbled forward into her arms, so magnetic was the woman. And so welcome the words.

'If you feel like that,' said Clara, 'why haven't you reviewed any of my shows?'

'Did you hear what he said? And you're still going to let him out?' asked Cloutier, following Gamache across the open room to Cameron's desk.

It didn't warrant a reply, so Gamache did not offer one.

Agent Cameron saw them coming and rose. 'Sir.'

'I'd like to start the paperwork to release Homer Godin.'

'Yessir. I was expecting that, so I've filled it in.'

Gamache scanned the page. No charges filed. As far as the law was concerned, Homer Godin was never in a jail cell. It had never happened.

As the officer who'd brought Godin in, Cameron would have to countersign the release.

'Can you redo this, please, but remove your name.'

'But I was the—'

'I know.' Gamache held his eyes. Unwavering. 'Just do it.'

Though confused, Cameron sat back down and redid the paperwork while Chief Inspector Gamache tore up the evidence that Agent Cameron had anything to do with releasing a man who'd vowed murder.

He then signed the new form so that his name, and his name alone, would be seen.

'Now,' said Gamache, dropping the pen, 'we'll let Monsieur

Godin out in a few minutes. First, tell us what you've found out about Tracey's movements on Saturday.'

'Turned out to be quite easy,' said Cameron. 'He was in Sherbrooke at an art-supply shop. Apparently that's where he gets most of his clay and other things he needs. His bank card shows a purchase there at eleven forty.'

'Roughly the same time as the posts,' said Cloutier.

'What did he buy?'

'A bag of clay, some glazes,' said Cameron.

Gamache nodded. They'd found unopened clay wrapped in plastic and new pots of glaze in Tracey's studio.

'I've also been to the local pharmacist about the abortion drug. She has no account for Vivienne Godin or Carl Tracey and confirms that bottle is black-market.'

'Why would Vivienne need to get it on the black market?' asked Cloutier. 'She could get it for free, right?'

'With a prescription, *oui*,' said Cameron. 'If you don't have one—'

'Or you want to terminate a pregnancy too far along,' said Gamache.

' – then you go on the black market to get the drug.'

'Mail order?' asked Gamache, and said a quiet prayer.

'Many are, but the pharmacist didn't think so in this case. Buyers are beginning to realize that while pushers might not be the most reliable people, mail order is even worse. I know a few dealers. People we've dealt with in the past. Want to come?'

Gamache looked in the direction of the holding cell where Godin waited. The abortion drug could be one of the keys to the case against Tracey. If it turned out he was the one who'd bought it. It could strengthen their argument that he wanted to end the pregnancy, one way or the other.

'*Non*. There're other things I need to do. But let me know as soon as you have any information.'

'*Oui, patron*,' said Cameron, pushing back from his desk.

'Good.' Gamache brought out his iPhone. 'Give me your cell number.'

Cameron did.

As Gamache was putting it in, his own phone vibrated with a call.

'*Excusez-moi*.' He took a few steps away.

'Coroner's report is in,' said Beauvoir. 'They found spores in her hand. An exact match for the ones on the rotten wood.'

Gamache exhaled. They'd just taken a big step closer to making an arrest.

'This proves she was on the bridge,' said Beauvoir. 'And she died trying to save herself.'

'*Oui*. But we still need to place Tracey there. And prove it wasn't an accident.'

'We're going over Tracey's clothes to see if we can find any of the microorganisms. The forensics team found something else, *patron*. When they moved her car, they found boot prints. They'd been protected from the rain by the car.'

'Are they a match for Tracey's boots?' asked Gamache.

'They're looking now.'

'Good, good,' said Gamache, his thoughts moving quickly ahead. Is it enough? Is it enough?

He made up his mind.

'I'm going to hold Godin for another couple of hours until you find out more. By then—'

·'We might have enough to nail Tracey. I think it's time we brought Pauline Vachon in.'

'Agreed.'

'I've applied for a warrant to search her place while she's being questioned,' said Beauvoir. 'As soon as it comes through, I'll have her picked up. Isabelle will interview her at the station. She'd like Cloutier there. Any news from your end?'

'Agent Cameron has a lead on the abortion drug found in Vivienne's bag. Definitely black-market. I'm hoping we can get proof that Tracey bought it.'

'About that,' said Beauvoir. 'We have news on the fetus.'

Gamache listened, his eyes narrowing as he absorbed the information. When Beauvoir finished, Gamache simply said, *'Merci.'*

'What is it, *patron*?' asked Cloutier, seeing his expression after he'd hung up.

Gamache paused for a moment, staring at the blank wall in front of him. His lips were pressed together in concentration. Then he clicked his device off and slipped it into his pocket.

'Superintendent Lacoste will be by in a few minutes,' he said, striding back to the desk. 'We're bringing in Pauline Vachon.'

'But there's more I can get from her private Instagram account,' said Cloutier. 'I'm sure of it.'

When he turned to her, she was surprised to see that the anxiety that had flitted across his face a few moments ago was gone, replaced by a smile.

'You've done a good job. It's only because of you we've found Madame Vachon and the pictures. And the damning messages. Chief Inspector Beauvoir feels we have enough, and I agree with him. Now the job will be to turn her. Pay attention to Superintendent Lacoste. Learn from her. She'll lead the interrogation. You'll be there to support.'

It wasn't lost on either Cloutier or Cameron that he'd said 'interrogation.' Not 'interview.'

They were almost there. They could see the finish line. It was just a matter now of dashing across it. Without falling.

'And Homer?'

'Let Monsieur Godin know he'll be released soon. Agent Cameron, I'll come with you after all. Chief Inspector Beauvoir will meet us there.'

'*Oui, patron.*'

As they made for the door, Cameron reached behind him, to double-check that he had his gun. He knew he did, but best to be certain. Besides, touching it was a comfort.

But he noticed, as he followed Gamache, that the Chief Inspector was not carrying a weapon.

He wondered if he should say something. Remind him that drug dealers were dangerous. But then he remembered who this man was and what he'd seen. And what he'd done.

Chief Inspector Gamache did not need to be schooled. He was the principal.

Beauvoir stood at his desk in the incident room in Three Pines and checked his belt.

The gun, as always, was there.

He wondered if he'd feel naked going into work every day as a senior executive at the engineering firm in Paris without this accessory.

Jean-Guy Beauvoir quite liked the feel of it. The heft. The ability to just pull back his jacket and expose it. To see people's eyes widen.

The gun on his belt meant not simply safety but power. Though just lately, something odd had begun to happen.

It had felt heavier. More awkward. Less natural. The gun had begun to feel foreign.

Was this how it had started with Gamache? Surely as a young agent, as an inspector, even, he'd worn a gun? At what stage had he taken it off?

When does a cucumber become a pickle? It was the question Gamache sometimes asked when contemplating human behavior. And now Jean-Guy asked himself that.

When does change occur? Change that is irreversible.

At some point guns had become, for Armand Gamache, a necessary evil. But still, and undoubtedly, evil.

Gamache had knelt beside too many corpses. Had made too many.

Had reached behind him and pulled the weapon from its holster. Had swung it up, steadied his hand. Pointed. And Armand Gamache had fired. Into another human being.

Felt the recoil. Smelled the discharge. Seen the body drop. The person drop.

Someone's son, daughter, husband, father.

It was a terrible, terrible thing to have to do.

Seeing the bullet strike was almost as bad as feeling it hit, as Jean-Guy knew too well. Being lifted into the air by the impact. The shock. The pain. The terror.

That was almost as bad as seeing colleagues go down. Gunned down.

Seeing Gamache himself hit. Lifted off the ground. And collapse.

Jean-Guy Beauvoir pushed that image, that memory, away. Unable still to really face it. Face the fact he himself had done it once. Had seen Gamache through his sights and fired. Felt the report. Smelled the discharge.

Seen him rise and watched him fall.

It was the worst moment of Jean-Guy Beauvoir's life. And it had changed his life.

His hand now closed briefly over the holster, but instead of feeling the usual reassurance, he felt a wave of revulsion.

And he knew, in his gut, it was time to leave. He'd done his bit, done his best.

Time to take a job where the only weapon was his mind. Where there were no victims, only clients. And no suspects, only competitors. Where everyone who started the day with a heartbeat ended the day with one.

Or, if not, it wasn't his doing.

But he wasn't there yet. Soon. Just this one, last case. Jean-Guy Beauvoir just had to get across the finish line.

Instead of answering Clara's question, why she'd never reviewed her shows, Dominica Oddly had hauled herself out of the sofa and was wandering around the studio. Nodding as she took in the collection of stuff.

A jumble of old works. Failed and abandoned pieces sat beside finished and lauded portraits. There were stones and twisted tree roots. Feathers and sticks and assorted broken eggs, fallen from nests. It was as though Clara had left the door to her studio wide open and the wilderness had blown in.

Oddly took a deep breath and closed her eyes. The studio smelled of oil paint and turpentine and wet dog. And something else.

Clara had given up trying to look sophisticated and had rolled off the low sofa onto her hands and knees, and now she got to her feet with a grunt.

To Clara's horror, Oddly had stopped in front of a collection of dusty ceramic pieces. And was taking photographs.

'What do you call these?' she asked.

'Warrior Uteruses.'

Oddly laughed. A deep, rich rumbling sound that filled the space with genuine amusement.

'Perfect. Have you shown them?'

'They're old. I did them maybe ten years ago,' Clara explained. 'Showed them once.'

'And?'

'Not a success.'

Oddly nodded, clearly not surprised. Then she turned back to Clara. 'I've been to all your shows, you know. Privately.'

She walked over to the small portrait lounging against the wall. The one of Ruth. The old woman glared back at the young woman, her whole being filled with rage and pain, with bitterness and disappointment. Ruth gripped her worn blue shawl at her scrawny throat and looked out at a world that had left her behind.

'I didn't get it at first,' Dominica admitted, as though talking directly to the old woman. 'Didn't see what others saw. All I saw were portraits done in a predictable, conventional style. Granted, the subjects were interesting, but that struck me as a sort of cheat. A shorthand to cover up for a lack of technique. A lack of depth.'

Dominica Oddly turned away for a moment, to look at Clara, and then returned her gaze to the portrait.

'I had my review all written. Scathing. I especially hated her.'

She lifted her chin toward Ruth. Who clearly hated her right back.

'But something stopped me from publishing it. I decided to reserve judgment. I went to all your other shows and slowly, slowly began to see.'

'See what?'

'That I was wrong. But more than that. I saw why. When

I looked at your portraits, I saw the work of a middle-class, middle-aged white woman, living in middle-of-nowhere Canada. Working in a traditional, conventional medium. I was prejudiced. I couldn't believe that you, Clara Morrow, could come out of nowhere and possibly rock the art establishment. But you have.'

She turned back to Ruth.

'This's the woman who contacted me about your work, right? Who convinced me to come here, isn't it? This's the poet, Ruth Zardo?'

'Yes.'

She nodded, her dreadlocks bouncing on her shoulders.

'*Who hurt you once, so far beyond repair?*' She muttered the words of Ruth's most famous poem, then looked at Clara. 'You painted her as the Virgin Mary. The mother of God. Forgotten, bitter, filled with despair. Which would have been amazing enough. Without—' She reached up her hand and pointed. At a small white dot in the rheumy eye. 'That.'

It was the smallest hint of light. In a soul that had known much too much darkness.

'No fraud could do that. Once I saw that, I revisited all your other paintings and saw what you were really doing. You're subversive, my friend. A sort of artistic agent provocateur. Appearing to be one thing while actually being something else. Something quite extraordinary. Undermining all conventions. You don't just paint people, you capture them. Make them give you their emotions. Not just despair and hope but joy. Hatred. Jealousy. Love. Contentment. Rage. How you managed to capture belonging is beyond me, but you did. The Three Graces? I actually wept. I stood in front of it, all alone in the gallery, crying. I still don't know why it made me cry.' She turned to Clara. 'Do you?'

'I don't know,' she said quietly. 'But I think you do.'

Dominica smiled and gave a single grunt of either laughter or recognition.

'I saw your latest exhibition,' said Dominica. 'In the cooperative collection of miniatures at the Brooklyn Art Space. Very generous of you, by the way, to agree to show with unknowns.'

Clara closed her eyes briefly. This was it. Finally. She had what she wanted. Needed. Dominica Oddly would tell the art world, all the naysayers and trolls and shits who'd turned on her, that they were wrong. Clara Morrow was a force within the art community.

Clara Morrow would get her revenge.

'Thank you,' she said. 'You must know how important this is to me. You've seen all the horrible things people have said on social media. My own home gallery is threatening to drop me. People are saying I'm a ... what did you just call it ... ?'

'A poseur. A fraud.'

'Yes. A fake. But a good review from you would change all that. Would stop all the attacks.'

'I've seen what they're writing, yes.'

Then a thought occurred to Clara. Dominica was, for all her confidence, still young. Maybe she's afraid that if she voices a dissenting opinion, she'll lose credibility.

'I have no problem telling it like it is,' Oddly said, as though reading her thoughts. 'Going against popular opinion. It's one of my favorite things to do.'

'Then why haven't you posted? Why wait to defend me? Damage is being done.'

'Because I don't disagree.'

'Pardon?'

'Your miniatures are appalling, Clara. Trite. Predictable. A

blunder.' She turned back to the Warrior Uteruses. 'I admire an artist for trying something different,' and then she looked at Clara again. 'But your miniatures show not just a shocking lack of technique but an almost insulting lack of depth, of effort. They're cowardly.'

Clara stood stock-still in her studio.

'I was about to publish the review when Ruth Zardo's invitation arrived. I decided to wait until I saw you. Until I had a chance to look you in the eye. And thank you personally for your previous work, and tell you how I feel about your latest. I think all those people posting are right. You're insulting those who once loved your work, who once supported you. You're insulting the art world. And, worst of all, you've squandered, cheapened your talent. Betrayed the gift you were given. And that's a travesty. No real artist would do that, could do that.'

She brought a piece of paper out of her pocket. 'Here.'

As she held it out to Clara, she caught, again, that elusive scent. Below the oils, below the turpentine, the wet dog, the old bananas.

It was lemon. Not the sour smell but the fresh, sweet scent of lemon meringue pie.

Clara reached for the paper, even as she felt the thrashing and heard the crunch of bones.

CHAPTER 26

‎—

Catch this video. Sick. #GamacheSux

Heard Odd about to post review of Morrow stinkers. Finally. #ClaraMorrowSucks

@CarlTracey: Carl, trying to reach you. What's happening? Call me.

Information was coming in quickly now.

Sitting in his car on rue Principale in Cowansville, Jean-Guy Beauvoir scanned the messages from his agents.

Smiling, he clicked the phone closed and got out to join Gamache, who'd sent him the address and had just arrived himself outside the pizza joint.

'The boot prints match Tracey's,' said Beauvoir without preamble.

'*Bon*,' said Gamache. 'It's all coming together.'

'They're in there,' said Cameron, coming around the corner to join them.

He pointed to an old low-rise apartment building.

'Used to be a crack house, run by the mother of one of the kids. We busted her, but the kid now runs his own operation out of there. Not crack but black-market shit.'

'Kid?' asked Gamache.

'Minor. Fifteen. Name's Toby.'

There was a character in a book Beauvoir read to his son every night named Toby. A mischievous boy with a pet balloon.

Honoré found the adventures of Toby and his balloon hilarious. Jean-Guy found them strangely moving, as the boy struggled mightily to protect his vulnerable friend. And no matter what happened, to never let go.

'He runs a gang of kids dealing mostly prescription meds, painkillers. But other stuff, too. We catch them, but they're on the street again in no time. Don't be fooled by their age.'

'We aren't,' said Beauvoir.

They followed Cameron into the building.

The place reeked of damp and mold and rot. The chipped concrete stairs were sticky.

They climbed up one flight, but just as Cameron stepped onto the landing, there was a sharp whistle and the sound of footsteps racing on the floor above.

'Shit,' said Cameron, and ran up the stairs, taking them two at a time, followed by Gamache.

Beauvoir, though, seeing where this was going, ran downstairs, out the front door, and into the side alley, scanning for the back door.

There was a loud bang as a door flew open, and kids piled out of the basement.

Gamache and Cameron split up, chasing different kids down the hallways. Cameron cornered one in the stairwell leading to the roof.

'Where's Toby?'

'Dunno.'

He frisked her and came away with packets of foil and a switchblade.

He cuffed her to the railing and moved on.

Gamache chased another kid into an apartment, where he tackled him, both of them falling onto one of the stained mattresses pushed together on the floor. Getting quickly to his feet, Gamache put the kid in a hold, patting him for weapons and scanning the room for other occupants. It was then he noticed pill bottles neatly arranged on shelves lining all four walls.

'Are you Toby?'

The boy was silent.

Gamache pulled a knife, a bottle of pills, and an ID from his pockets.

Not Toby.

'Where is he?'

Beauvoir grabbed hold of the collar of the largest kid as he tried to escape down the alley and swung him around. Not a he. A she. A girl about fifteen.

'Let her go,' came a voice from above.

Beauvoir turned, still holding the girl, and saw a skinny kid on the fire escape. Pointing a gun.

'You a cop?' the kid asked. 'Of course you are.'

The girl yanked her jacket out of Beauvoir's grip and stepped away.

'Toby?' Beauvoir asked the kid holding the gun.

'Get his gun,' said Toby.

The girl reached out, but Beauvoir backed away. 'You don't want to do that.'

'Give her your gun, old man,' said Toby.

'Or what? You'll kill a cop?'

Beauvoir looked at the large girl standing in front of him. Her eyes were wide, round. She was stoned and afraid.

Then he looked at the kid on the fire escape and felt his heart leap in his chest.

He was not afraid. Not stoned.

His gray eyes were empty. Not cold. But not hot. Not glaring, not even threatening.

Chief Inspector Beauvoir had seen eyes like that, often. But only in the recently dead.

'I'm a minor,' said Toby. 'What're they gonna do to me?'

'You know what they'll do to you?' came a voice down the alley.

Toby immediately turned his gun on the older man walking toward them. His hands were out by his sides, his jacket was open to show he wasn't armed.

'If you kill a cop, if you even hurt one, they'll try you as an adult. You're close enough, right? What're you?' Gamache turned his attention to the girl beside Beauvoir. 'Fourteen. Fifteen.'

'Almost fifteen,' she said.

'Shut up, Daph,' said Toby, not moving the gun from the newcomer.

'There's a third cop, you know, Daphne,' said Gamache. 'Is that your name?'

She gave a small nod.

'If your friend shoots Chief Inspector Beauvoir—' He saw the girl's eyes widen even further, though Toby did not react.

Gamache stopped where he was and addressed himself now to Toby. 'That's right. Not just a cop, but Monsieur Beauvoir here is head of homicide for the Sûreté. If you shoot him,

287

you'll have to shoot me, too. And our colleague will almost certainly then have to shoot you. Both.'

He let that sit there before speaking again, this time to Daphne. 'Do you want to see fifteen?'

'I'm fifteen,' said Toby. 'It's not so great.'

'No,' said Gamache. He'd also noticed the look, or lack of it, in the boy's eyes. 'I don't suppose it is. And I'm sorry about that. But it can get better.'

Just then Cameron rounded the corner, skidding in the slush as he tried to stop himself. Regaining his balance, he pulled out his gun. Pointing it at first one, then the other kid, finally settling on Toby on the fire escape.

'Put down your weapon, please,' said Gamache. And to everyone's astonishment, it was clear he was talking to Cameron. 'You might keep it at the ready. But just lower it.'

'But—'

'Do it,' said Beauvoir.

The girl Daphne had backed up and, quite sensibly, was now standing a few paces away from Chief Inspector Beauvoir.

But Daphne was not the problem. Nor was she the solution.

'We've come to ask you about a bottle of pills we found in a murder investigation,' said Beauvoir. 'Mifegymiso. It's an abortion drug.'

'I know what it is. I know all the shit I sell.'

'So you do sell it?' said Gamache. 'But probably not a lot.'

As he spoke, he moved a step closer to the fire escape but away from Beauvoir. Dragging Toby's attention, and his gun, toward him. Forcing Toby to choose between them. Making it more difficult for the boy to shoot both before Cameron could get off a shot.

'Stop,' snapped Toby before glancing at Daphne. 'I said get his gun.'

To Beauvoir's dismay, he felt his gun removed from its holster. This was, he knew, another reason Gamache never wore one.

Because it could be taken. Used against him. Them. Anyone and everyone. Most guns used in crime were stolen from people who had them legally.

And here was one more on the street.

Gamache looked over his shoulder at Cameron, warning him not to react. Not to overreact.

Nothing had happened yet. Not really. Nothing that could not be undone. But once a trigger was pulled, there was no going back.

'We need to know who bought the drug from you,' said Beauvoir. 'That's all.'

His own voice was steady, matter-of-fact. Trying not to betray the fear he felt. Trying not to flash back to what it was like. To feel the bullet strike. To be lifted – He stopped there and fought to harness his thoughts. 'Then we'll leave.'

Toby did what Beauvoir hoped he'd do. He turned his attention, and his gun, away from Gamache. And onto him.

What Toby could not see, what no one could see, was that Beauvoir's knees had begun to tremble. But his face remained placid. As though this were an everyday occurrence and nothing to worry about.

Cameron, watching this, his weapon lowered but ready to raise and shoot, felt he was looking into some parallel universe. Where people held reasonable conversations while pointing guns at each other. And were not terrified.

Because he was very afraid. And Cameron knew one thing, from his time on the gridiron and his time as a cop. People who were afraid often did very stupid things.

Don't be the one. Don't be the one. Don't be the one to do something stupid. And please, please, don't let me be the one shot.

289

Gamache was very still. Alert to any movement. Anything that could trigger the boy with the empty eyes. The only comfort, if it could be called that, was that Toby would almost certainly get off only one shot before Cameron took him down.

Still, by Gamache's calculations there seemed a better-than-average chance at least one of them would die in that alleyway.

He took another step away from Jean-Guy, forcing Toby's attention, and weapon, back onto him.

'Stop,' said the boy. 'Not another step. You think I won't shoot, you dumb fuck, but I will.'

'I know you will, Toby,' said Gamache. 'But I hope you don't.'

'We just want one thing,' said Beauvoir. 'The name of the person who bought the pills from you.'

'You think I asked for his name? You're a fucking idiot.'

His, thought both cops. *His* name.

So Vivienne hadn't bought the drug. A man had. Almost certainly Carl Tracey.

'Can you describe him?' Beauvoir asked. They had to be sure.

'Are you kidding? Look, the guys I sell to don't like it when I tell the cops on them.'

'I can appreciate that,' said Gamache. 'My friends don't like it when I pass their address on to burglars.'

Daphne laughed, but Toby did not. Though he did cock his head with interest at the old cop, with the gray hair and thoughtful eyes.

He held those eyes for a moment, sensing something else in them. There was menace, for sure. Here was a man who might be old but wasn't weak. And with a start, Toby recognized him.

He wasn't just a cop. The fucker had failed to say he'd been the head of the whole Sûreté. Toby knew that because he'd seen the video that morning, posted on Twitter and going viral.

Gamache noticed the change in the boy. Saw a look come into those eyes. It was venal. Feral. Triumphant.

My God, thought Gamache. *He's going to shoot me.*

He stared into the boy's eyes and thought of Reine-Marie. And silently apologized for what was about to happen.

But what did happen was unexpected. Toby relaxed. Just a little. But enough to get Gamache's heart going again.

'Okay, old man. He was Anglo. Not fat, but soft. I didn't like him. Didn't trust him.'

'How many people do you trust?'

Toby gave one gruff laugh. But didn't answer.

'I think we have enough,' said Beauvoir. 'We're going to leave you now.'

He slowly lowered his arms and held out his hand toward Daphne.

This was the moment.

'My gun, please.'

Daphne looked up at Toby, who raised his gun slightly.

Seeing this, Cameron raised his slightly, before Gamache could signal him to stop.

Toby, alarmed, raised his gun more, until it was pointing at Beauvoir's head.

Jean-Guy was staring straight down the barrel.

Everyone froze.

This was, Jean-Guy knew, a bullet he would not feel.

'It's all right,' said Gamache softly. 'No one needs to get hurt. We're almost done.'

He stopped talking. Allowing the tension to ease.

He saw Toby's gun lowered. Slightly.

It was a millimeter in the right direction. But they weren't out of it yet.

Please, Gamache begged. *Please don't let anyone come into the alley now. Please.*

The moments stretched on. Elongating.

Gamache wanted desperately to say more, to try to reason with the boy. But he knew it would be a mistake. If they were to avoid a bloodbath, the next move had to come from Toby.

'Go,' said Toby.

'My gun,' said Beauvoir. 'You know I can't leave it behind.'

'Do you want to die, man?' shouted Toby. 'Get out, before I change my mind.'

Oh, for God's sake, what're you doing? Cameron's mind screamed. *Let's go. Oh, please, let's go.*

And Jean-Guy Beauvoir wanted to. With every part of his being, he wanted to turn and walk away. Run away. Go back to Annie. Hold her tight. Smell the sweet, fresh scent of her. Hold Honoré in his arms. Get on a plane to Paris and never look back.

But he couldn't go. Couldn't let go. Not yet.

Instead he stood there, staring. Willing the boy to see what he saw. They held each other's eyes.

Finally Toby spoke. 'I'm fucked, aren't I? If I shoot, he'll kill me. If you leave without the gun, you'll be back to get it. You have to. You'll find us and arrest us. Daph and me.'

'That's true,' said Beauvoir.

He gave Toby a small nod. Of admiration. Acknowledging the boy's logic. And clarity.

'So either I kill you all now. Or I give up.'

Oh, God, thought Cameron. *Oh, God, here it comes.*

'*Oui*,' said Beauvoir. 'That's about it. One you live. One you die.'

Toby seemed to make up his mind. He braced.

It was slight and too subtle for Cameron to see. But Gamache could, and he knew what it meant. Every muscle tightened, even as he realized there was nothing he could do.

Toby was about to shoot. Jean-Guy.

'You know,' said Beauvoir, his voice remaining conversational even as his knees threatened to give way. 'I once faced exactly the same situation.'

'Shut the fuck up.'

'I'd reached the end. Couldn't go on. I didn't care anymore.'

'Shut up.'

'I thought about killing myself. But when it came down to it, I realized that what I really wanted was for the pain to stop. I didn't really want to die, but I didn't know how to live. How to go on.'

There was silence then. Utter, almost suffocating silence. As the air was sucked out of the alley.

'What did you do?'

'I let go.' Beauvoir closed his eyes. 'I let go.' Then he opened them again and met Toby's. 'Sometimes we just have to let go. And trust. There is a way back. Believe me.' He smiled and opened his arms wide. 'And look at the great place it brought me.'

The words hung in the air of the void before the boy laughed.

Jean-Guy cocked his head. 'Toby, I don't want to die. And I don't think you do either.'

Toby closed his eyes, and while they could have moved, no one did.

Then, eyes still shut, Toby let go of his gun.

CHAPTER 27

@SûretéCrooked: I knew it! Cops killing kids.

@dumbass: You morons. That tape's doctored. Here's
the real one.

@CommonGround: @SûretéCrooked Can't we all just
get along?

@SûretéCrooked: @CommonGround Go fuck yourself.

'Your name?' asked Superintendent Lacoste.
'Pauline Vachon.'
'Your profession?'
'Web designer and manager.'
'Do you know this man?' Isabelle Lacoste placed a photograph on the metal table in the interview room.

Lysette Cloutier sat off to the side. Watching closely.

Pauline Vachon was younger than she appeared in the Instagram pictures.

Her hair was clean and nicely done. Makeup carefully applied. She was pretty.

Her clothes were simple, almost elegant, thought Cloutier. Black slacks and a white blouse, with a bright red silk scarf.

Lacoste was also taking in Vachon's appearance. The makeup was cheap, clumping, and too heavily applied. The slacks were from a discount store, and the red scarf was rayon. Masquerading as silk. And hiding, Lacoste could see, a coffee stain on the white blouse.

Lysette Cloutier saw what she was meant to see. Isabelle Lacoste saw the truth.

Still, Lacoste knew that making the most of herself, on very little money, while holding together her own company at the age of twenty-one, was far from criminal. In fact, it was remarkable.

Pauline Vachon was a remarkable young woman. But she was also a nervous young woman. She clearly had not expected them to connect her to Tracey. And certainly not this quickly. And certainly not in any way that would lead her to be sitting in a Sûreté interview room.

Beneath Pauline's calm, helpful veneer, Lacoste could sense alarm. Barely suppressed. But suppressed. This was indeed a self-possessed young woman.

So why had she hooked up with the mess that was Carl Tracey? That was just one of many questions that came to mind.

Pauline sat upright in the interview room. Almost prim. And looked down at the photo on the metal table.

'Yes. He's one of my clients. Carl Tracey.'

'And what do you do for him?'

'I set up his website and manage his social media.'

'Which platforms?'

'Instagram mostly.'

'Can you give us the address of his website and social-media accounts?'

Cloutier wrote it down, though, of course, she already knew it. Vachon did not volunteer the private account.

'Many followers?' Lacoste asked.

'Not really. I tried to tell him that you need to post a lot to get interest, but honestly, what can a potter post that could go viral? More pictures of a lump of clay on a wheel?'

Lacoste smiled. 'I sympathize. Unreasonable clients. The worst.'

Pauline relaxed a little. 'He's not really that bad. He just doesn't understand.'

'You post for him?'

She nodded.

'Why doesn't he do it himself?' asked Lacoste.

These were softball questions. Every interrogator had a particular technique. Hers was to set people at their ease. Have them lower their defenses.

'He's an artist. Not great at technical things. Besides, there's no internet at his place. Can you tell me what this's about?'

It interested Lacoste that it had taken this long for Pauline Vachon to ask. It was normally the first question out of anyone's mouth. But then, this young woman already knew the answer.

'Has something happened to Monsieur Tracey?'

She looked directly into Lacoste's eyes. Not blinking. Brown eyes all innocent with just the right touch of curiosity. Without, it would appear, guilt or guile.

'I'm afraid his wife has drowned, and we just have some questions.'

'Oh, that's terrible.' Pauline looked from Lacoste to Cloutier and back again.

'Yes,' said Lacoste. 'Did Monsieur Tracey ever talk about his wife?'

Vachon paused to gather her thoughts. To sort through the truth and lies and decide which to choose.

'A bit. He didn't seem happy. He said she drank. Was depressed. I felt sorry for him.'

'Pauline,' said Lacoste, leaning forward a little and dropping her voice so that it sounded as though she were about to confide in the young woman. 'I really hope you don't mind, but I'm going to ask you some questions that might seem odd. Is that all right?'

'Sure. Of course.' She looked at her watch. 'I have an appointment in an hour—'

'Oh, this won't take that long. Don't worry,' said Lacoste with a motherly smile, despite the fact there weren't that many years between them. It wasn't years but choices that separated these two women.

'How old was your mother when she had you?'

Both Vachon and Cloutier looked at her with surprise.

'You weren't kidding about the strange questions,' said Pauline with a laugh. Though she was slightly guarded now. 'She was sixteen.'

'Young. Must've been difficult. And your grandmother? How old was she when she had your mother?'

'Do you really need to know this? What does this have to do with Carl's wife?'

Cloutier had the same question and just barely stopped herself from nodding agreement.

'I'm sorry,' said Lacoste, and looked it. 'I just need your help understanding some things about this community. How judgmental it can be of young women.'

It was a vague answer but seemed to satisfy, mollify, Pauline.

'My grandmother was fifteen.'

'And you're twenty-one?'

'Yes.'

'How old were you when you first got pregnant?'

That hovered between the two women.

'Why—'

'Please, Pauline. It would help a lot.'

Cloutier could see that Vachon realized she'd created a problem for herself. She'd offered to help, needed to appear willing to help. And these questions were not, on the surface, threatening or even, it must be admitted, pertinent.

But they were deeply invasive.

'I was sixteen.'

'And what happened?'

'I had an abortion.'

'The next time?'

Now Pauline shifted in her seat. 'Why are you asking this? It's not illegal. It was all done by a doctor in a hospital.'

'Yes, I know. But I also know that small towns can be supportive, but they can also be pretty awful. You get a reputation. ... Nasty rumors spread. Rumors with just enough truth in them to do damage. People don't always like it when you're a success, do they?'

'Not always,' Pauline said, lifting her chin slightly.

Isabelle Lacoste found herself admiring this young woman. Who refused to give in. She had guts. But did she have a conscience?

'Non,' said Lacoste quietly. 'They're not always as kind as we'd like. Especially painful when friends aren't happy for you. You're trying hard to get out, to make a career for yourself. To make a success of your business. Get a little money.

And people are all, "Oh, she's too good for us now," just because you dress nicely and take some care. Right?'

Pauline nodded but was guarded. Though not as guarded as she should have been.

'Can I tell you something?' Lacoste lowered her voice. 'Something no one else outside the police knows.'

Pauline nodded, leaning forward.

'Vivienne was pregnant. That's why I'm asking. But we don't really know who the father was.'

'Really? Got it,' whispered Pauline. 'Poor Carl.'

'Yes. Poor Carl. Who can blame him for wanting out of that marriage?' Lacoste leaned back in her chair, her voice once again businesslike. 'Now, the second time you were pregnant, another hospital procedure?'

'D and C, yes.'

'And the third time?'

There was now, in Lacoste's tone, a slight edge. Not of judgment but of warning. Tell the truth.

'How did you end that pregnancy, Pauline?'

'I know who you are,' said Toby, sitting at a desk in the station, not all that far from where Lacoste was interviewing Pauline.

'You're the cop everyone hates,' said Daphne.

She was at the next desk over, also being booked.

Gamache smiled. 'Not everyone, I hope.'

'Everyone I know.'

Gamache was not particularly surprised to hear that teens running a criminal operation might not be fans.

'I saw the video of you killing those kids,' said Toby. 'Brutal.'

Cameron, the arresting officer, stopped typing on his computer. Jean-Guy Beauvoir, sitting nearby and going over messages, looked up.

And Armand Gamache tilted his head slightly, the smile fading. 'What video?'

Toby laughed. 'You haven't seen it? Posted about an hour ago. Gone viral. Funny that I watched it, then there you were.'

Gamache drew his brows together. There was a video out there of him gunning down children? How could that be?

He turned to Jean-Guy, who still looked pale, after that confrontation in the alley. As they'd driven back, Gamache had noticed Beauvoir trembling, and quietly asked if he was okay.

'I didn't think I'd get out of there alive,' Jean-Guy said, under his breath.

Gamache had thought the same thing, but didn't say it. He still felt the acid burning his stomach.

'You'll be on the Champs-Élysées soon,' he'd said. 'In the sunshine.'

'Not soon enough.'

While Jean-Guy knew Paris wasn't immune to danger, it would at least be unlikely. There was a far better chance of returning home each day.

Now, on hearing what Toby said, Jean-Guy swung around to his laptop, hitting the keys.

Sûreté, video, kids.

Gamache, video, shooting.

'I coulda shot you, you know,' said Toby. 'Payback. For what you did.'

'Why didn't you?'

Toby sat back and crossed his arms. 'You weren't worth the bullet. And you sure aren't worth dying for. He'da killed me.'

He nodded to Cameron, who was staring at the boy.

'You got that right,' said Cameron.

Toby turned back to the older man. With the gray hair. And that nasty scar by his temple. That made him so recognizable.

The cop's face wasn't so much wrinkled as lined. From a great distance, from half a century away, he looked to the boy like a man broken and pieced back together.

Humpty Dumpty. Who'd had a great fall.

'*Patron,*' said Beauvoir from the other desk, breaking into Toby's thoughts.

His voice was hushed. Almost a whisper.

Annie was working from home in Montréal. Studying for the French law admission exams.

A friend from her firm in Montréal had sent a link. And a warning. But, of course, she had to look.

Clicking on it, she watched. Blood draining from her face.

Honoré, on her knee, was also watching. But she quickly took him away, placing him in his playpen. Then she returned to her laptop, approaching it warily.

The screen was paused on an image of her father.

Her eyes were wide. Her breathing shallow. She muted the sound and hit play.

Reine-Marie covered her mouth with her hand and closed her eyes. The bruise on her face forgotten, she now felt as though she'd been hit, hard, in the gut.

Then, opening them again, she asked Myrna to go back to the beginning.

'Are you sure?' Myrna asked.

They'd gone up to Myrna's loft over the bookstore, where the internet was most stable. Annie had sent the link. She

knew that her mother would want to know. To be warned about what was out there.

In the few minutes it had taken the women to get upstairs, more and more messages had come in from friends who were alarmed and upset. Who wanted to warn both her and Armand.

Myrna and Clara were in the loft with her. As were Olivier and Gabri. Ruth was sitting beside her in front of the computer, her veined hand holding Reine-Marie's.

'Please,' said Reine-Marie.

Myrna clicked, and the short video played again.

'Do you mind if we use your meeting room?' Beauvoir asked the station commander, who, on seeing him at her door, clicked her computer closed. And reddened. But not before Beauvoir had heard the telltale sound of muffled gunfire coming from her laptop.

'Not at all.'

Beauvoir closed the door to the private office and placed his laptop on the table. Gamache stood beside him, staring at the frozen image on the screen. It was of himself, in flak jacket. Weapon out. And raised. Eyes sharp. Preparing to shoot.

'It's bad,' said Beauvoir.

Gamache nodded. 'Go on.'

He stood straight and faced the screen. Much as he'd faced the boy on the fire escape earlier that day.

Beauvoir hit play.

The images were jerky but still fairly clear. It had been pieced together from old video, taken from the raid on the factory. They were images both Gamache and Beauvoir had seen before. Many taken from the cameras they themselves had worn.

But there were other images. Ones neither had ever seen. Video culled from God-knew-where on the internet. Of kids being gunned down. Many of them black kids. Clearly unarmed.

As Armand Gamache watched the screen, Beauvoir watched him.

Saw the narrowing of the eyes, the wincing at the terrible images.

The video had been edited to make it appear that Gamache was responsible for all of it.

The editing was rough. Not really designed to fool anyone. Except those who wanted to be fooled.

As Jean-Guy Beauvoir watched Gamache, he realized he'd never seen anyone actually gutted before. Until now.

Madeleine Toussaint sat at her desk with her second-in-command and watched the video.

Her email, her phone lines, had lit up. All guiding her to this travesty.

She watched it three or four times.

'What're you going to do?' her second-in-command asked. 'There has to be a response. The Sûreté has to condemn—'

'I know what has to be done. Leave me.' After a moment she added, 'Please.'

When alone, Chief Superintendent Toussaint got up and walked over to the wall map. It showed the current flooding. Of which there was a lot, and more to come.

But her eyes rested on the massive hydroelectric dams. Without her consent, without her knowledge, the floodgates had been opened.

And, more, the resources had been diverted south.

Runoffs had been dug, were still being dug. River levels lowering. There was collateral damage, to farms and fields, but most farmers not only understood but had helped.

Toussaint accepted the congratulations from the Prime Minister for her handling of the situation. Smart enough not to acknowledge it hadn't been her doing.

She herself had still been considering the options when she'd been told there were no more options. The decision had been made. An irreversible action had been taken.

And she suspected by whom.

She looked across her vast office, at the image on the screen. Of the former occupant. Gunning down black teens. Some, she realized with horror, not even that old. She felt sick. Physically ill.

They could be her own son.

Yes, something had to be done about Gamache. Something more than what she'd already done.

Madeleine Toussaint sat back down and composed her response. Then, before she could regret it, she hit send.

Reine-Marie was sitting in Myrna's kitchen with a shot of scotch. Talking with Annie on the phone while the others huddled together. Conferring.

All except Ruth. Who'd returned to the computer. Drawn back, like a compass to magnetic north, to the unimaginable violence. Done to those children.

Done to Armand.

Reine-Marie, phone to her ear and listening to Annie vent, watched as Ruth clicked away on the keyboard. Her bony fingers thudding the keys as though punishing the computer for its complicity.

Then, with a final flourish, the old woman hit one last key and sat back. Smiling.

'Annie, I have to go,' said Reine-Marie.

'I need to call Reine-Marie,' said Armand, reaching for the phone.

'I'll call Annie.'

Jean-Guy got through, but Armand did not. After trying home, then the bistro, he finally reached her at Myrna's.

'I saw it,' said Reine-Marie before he'd even spoken. 'Don't worry. No one believes it. It's crude.'

'It's cruel,' came a voice shouted in the background. 'But I fixed it.'

Ruth, Armand recognized. 'How did she fix it?'

'Armand?'

It was Jean-Guy's voice. He had Annie on the line and was sitting once again at his laptop.

'Hold on,' said Armand, and he turned to his son-in-law. 'What is it?'

'Annie sent me a link. Just posted.'

'The same one . . . ?' Armand began to ask as he walked around to the laptop.

But he stopped walking. Talking. Breathing.

The image frozen on the screen was clearly from the same raid on the factory. But this was a different video. It was, he could see immediately, from the original recording. The true record of what had happened that day.

It was never meant to be made public. Never meant to be seen outside the Sûreté and the official inquiry. But the video had been leaked and posted years ago, in a violation so profound it had taken Gamache, Beauvoir, the families, years to get over.

Scenes had obviously been taken from it to create the bastardized video that had gone up that morning.

Armand now knew how Ruth had 'fixed' it.

Thinking she was helping a friend, she'd reposted the original. In hopes of showing the truth.

What the old poet didn't realize, or had forgotten, was that social media was less about truth than perception. People believed what they chose to believe.

Neither did she appear to understand the damage she'd just done.

'I have to let you go,' Armand said into the phone.

When he hung up, he looked briefly at the clear image on the screen, taking one deep breath after another. Trying to control his outrage.

Then, reaching for the phone, he said to Jean-Guy, 'Can you give me a few minutes?'

Jean-Guy stepped toward the door, paused, then turned around. He knew what Armand was about to do. '*Non.*'

'*Non?*'

'I'm staying with you.' He sat down. There would be no argument.

Jean-Guy did not leave his side as Armand called the families of the officers who'd been slain that day. Whose deaths, like some horrific snuff film, were once again played out in public.

Armand placed call after call.

They were numbers he knew by heart, since he spoke to the mothers, fathers, husbands, and wives every week and visited the families whenever he was invited.

Now he called to warn them. To listen to their rage. To absorb, again, their agony.

When he'd finished, he asked Jean-Guy to leave him. Just for a couple of minutes.

And this time, Jean-Guy did.

When he was alone, Armand sat quietly, then dropped his face into his trembling hands.

Things are strongest where they're broken, the young voice reassured him. And Armand gasped with pain as he held the agent, no more than a boy, in his arms.

CHAPTER 28

———

'Some abortion drug.'

Those were Pauline Vachon's words. Too ashamed to go back to her doctor, she'd gone where desperate women had for centuries. Into a back alley.

But this time it wasn't some sadist with a coat hanger. It was a kid with a pharmacy.

'Mifegymiso?' Lacoste asked.

'Maybe. I dunno. I just took it, and it worked.'

'Is that how Carl Tracey knew about it?'

There was silence. Except for the ticking of the old clock on the wall. As the reality of what they were really talking about hit Pauline.

'I was just trying to help a client. Nothing wrong with that.'

Lacoste remained silent.

'His wife was pregnant,' Vachon went on. 'He said it probably wasn't his, that they hadn't had sex in months. So I told him about the drug.'

'And where to get it.'

'Yes.'

'You knew he was going to give it to her, probably without her knowledge, and that was fine with you?'

'What he did with it was his business.'

Lacoste struggled not to show her disgust. At Tracey. But also at this alarming young woman who didn't seem to see anything wrong with this.

'It didn't work,' said Lacoste. 'Vivienne was still pregnant when she died.'

'She couldn't have been. This was last summer,' said Vachon.

Isabelle Lacoste's mind raced.

It seemed they were talking about two different pregnancies. Carl Tracey had ended one with the abortion drug last summer. But now Vivienne was pregnant again.

Had she suspected what he'd done? Was that one of the reasons, perhaps the main reason, she'd decided to finally get out now? So the same thing didn't happen to this child?

'Well, she was,' said Lacoste. 'Pregnant. You didn't know?'

'I didn't know him all that well. He didn't tell me everything.'

'You knew him well enough to set up an illegal drug buy. Well enough to help him abort the baby, without his wife's knowledge. Well enough to sleep with him.'

Lacoste opened the file in front of her and removed the photographs, taken off the private feed. She placed them, one at a time, on the table.

Pauline was momentarily taken by surprise but then recovered herself. With speed rarely seen by Lacoste, she grasped the situation. And made a decision.

'I'm not exactly picky, am I?' said Pauline, smiling.

Lacoste realized she'd underestimated this young woman and how remarkable she really was.

This was strategic. Mix truth in with lies, so it became more and more difficult to tell them apart.

'It meant nothing,' Pauline explained. 'Might not've been the smartest thing I've done, having sex with a client, but hey, people've done worse.'

'Like murder,' said Lacoste.

There could be no more doubt about the relationship between Tracey and Vachon, and neither was there any doubt about the relationship between interviewer and interviewee. One was in charge, the other in trouble.

Pauline Vachon looked down at the photographs, her lips compressing. 'How did you get these?'

'You've been corresponding with NouveauGalerie, I believe,' said Lacoste.

'You?' said Vachon, looking first at Lacoste, then at Cloutier, who gave a curt nod.

The clotted makeup could not conceal the panic in her face.

Lacoste opened the file again and read, '*Stuff's in the bag. Everything's ready. Will be done tonight. I promise.* That was a message from Carl Tracey to you, around noon on the day Vivienne disappeared. And your reply?'

'Look, I had nothing to do with it.'

'*Finally. Good luck. Don't mess it up.*' She looked up from the file. 'But he did, didn't he? He messed it up royally. That's why you're here, Pauline.'

The younger woman was flushed. But she tried one more twist to get off the hook.

'Those were about the clay Tracey was buying. He was going to do more pieces that night. I told him not to mess it up. He'd been promising some for weeks.'

Lacoste got up. 'I'll let you think about what you just said. Unless something happens in the next few minutes,

310

like a meteor strikes, you'll be charged with the murder of Vivienne Godin.'

She and Cloutier left the room. Leaving the file behind.

'We have her,' said Lacoste, walking up to Beauvoir, who was standing outside the meeting room. 'Pauline Vachon doesn't admit to being part of the murder – yet – but she will. I'm letting her stew for a few minutes. She was clearly shaken when she realized we'd seen the private account.'

'You should've seen her face,' said Cloutier.

Lacoste nodded. 'She admits she used the abortion drug herself and was the one who told Carl Tracey how to get it on the black market.'

How Lacoste got the young woman to admit to a third abortion, never mind buying the black-market drug, still amazed Cloutier. It had been a masterful combination of guile, of guesswork, of knowing when to push and when to make nice. Until Vachon had nowhere to go but the truth.

Cloutier was looking at Lacoste with something close to awe. But there was caution there as well. She did not want to make the same mistake as Vachon.

Whether by natural instinct or honed skills, Isabelle Lacoste had the power to see things people wanted to hide.

And they all had them, as Lysette Cloutier knew only too well.

But while Cloutier was focused on Lacoste, Lacoste was focused on Beauvoir.

'What is it?'

He told them about the video.

Before Lacoste could react, the door opened and Gamache stepped out. He was pale but composed.

Every agent in the open room looked over at him.

They'd all read the Twitter feed and seen the doctored video that was blowing up online. They had yet to see the real video that had just been posted.

'What can we do, *patron*?' Lacoste asked, going to him and touching his hand.

'There's nothing to be done. *Mais merci*, Isabelle. I've spoken to the families.' His smile was tight and his voice brisk. 'How did the interview go with Pauline Vachon?'

As they returned to the meeting room to talk privately, both Lacoste and Beauvoir noticed that Gamache's right hand was closed into a tight fist. But still it trembled.

They watched on the monitor as Pauline Vachon turned the folder around and went through the photographs and printouts.

Then she sat back in her chair. And stared at the far wall.

Seeing, Lacoste knew, all her work, all her dreams, dissolving.

Then Beauvoir closed the feed on his laptop and turned to Lacoste.

'Tell us what happened.'

When Lacoste finished, Beauvoir thought for a moment. 'She'll crack.'

'I'm not so sure,' said Lacoste. 'She's clever and she's tough. Makes me so angry. She really could've made something of her life. I still don't know why she'd hook up with Carl Tracey.'

'She saw a shortcut,' said Beauvoir.

'To what? An abusive relationship in a remote farmhouse? Not exactly Cinderella.'

'She probably thought she was smarter, tougher than Vivienne Godin,' said Beauvoir. 'That she could control Tracey.'

'We saw the bruises on her arms,' said Cloutier. 'She must know.'

'Maybe she does. Maybe it's the cycle of abuse, right, *patron?*' said Beauvoir, and Gamache nodded.

Beauvoir and Lacoste exchanged glances but said nothing. They'd give him time, and space, to return to them.

Beauvoir sat forward, his voice all business. 'The coroner's report came in. The fetus, a baby girl, was his.'

'His who?' asked Lacoste, needing to be absolutely clear.

'Carl Tracey. The baby was his.'

'You're kidding.' It was, of course, rhetorical. Isabelle Lacoste sat back in her chair. What did this mean?

'Do you think Vivienne knew this and was messing with Carl when she told him it wasn't his?' she asked. 'Or did Vivienne really believe the baby was someone else's?'

'We only have Tracey's word on it that she said anything,' Beauvoir pointed out. 'I think that's bullshit. Her father said she was desperate to get out as soon as she could, that day. Why would she provoke Tracey by saying anything?'

'What did Pauline Vachon say about the messages on the private Instagram?' Gamache asked, speaking for the first time in the meeting. 'How did she explain them?'

'Said they were about clay he was buying.'

Gamache frowned. 'Smart. She's quick on her feet.'

'She is that,' agreed Lacoste. 'This might not be as easy as we'd hoped.'

'But she must know no one in their right mind would believe that,' said Beauvoir. 'Not after what happened.'

'Do you get the impression she cares for Tracey?' Gamache asked.

'Not especially,' said Lacoste. 'I think she has sex with him

313

for the same reason she has sex with so many other men. It's a form of self-loathing.'

'What role do you think she has in all this?' Gamache asked.

'I don't know, but I can tell you she's involved. And she knows we know.'

'What do you think would happen if you told her the baby was Tracey's?' Beauvoir asked.

Lacoste considered that.

'It'd be a surprise. A shock. Not because she loves Tracey, but it would prove to her that he lied about that. He can't be trusted.'

'Exactly,' said Beauvoir, sitting forward. 'She's smart. She must realize that he'd blame the killing on her in a second if he was cornered.'

'So we need to press that home,' said Lacoste. 'She must be thinking about it even now. This information about the fetus might be just that last shove we need.'

'Give it another go, Isabelle,' said Beauvoir. 'Try to turn her. We have enough now to arrest him, but her testimony would secure a conviction.'

Lacoste gave one curt nod. 'Leave it to me.'

'I'll apply for an arrest warrant for Tracey, but we'll wait to hear from you. Even if you can't turn her, we'll bring him in. He'll crack, even if she won't.'

'She will,' said Lacoste. 'I'll make sure of it.'

Clara Morrow dropped the printout onto the bistro table and sat down across from Dominica Oddly.

'Do you really think this?'

'I do.'

'You say here' – she tapped the paper – 'that I was once promising. Exceptional, even. But then I got lazy.'

'Yes.'

'But it's not true.'

'No?' asked Oddly. 'Are you sure?'

The critic had left Clara in her studio to read in private the review that had just gone public. She'd strolled across the village green, and, brushing slush off the bench, she sat, looking at the three pine trees that clearly gave the place its name. It seemed a little 'on the nose' for Oddly. Too obvious. Three pines in Three Pines.

She'd have preferred if there were two pines. It would make the place more interesting. Give it a story. What happened to that third tree? Granted, not much of a story, but better than none.

As it was, this hidden little hamlet was pretty but banal. She could almost see the stone and brick and clapboard homes, the church on the hill and the forest behind, turning into a watercolor before her eyes. Something not quite real. Not quite of this world. Certainly not of the gritty, noisy, aggressive world she'd just left.

This was like a pretty painting by some elderly, marginally gifted artist.

Nice. Sweet. Predictable. Safe.

Oddly smiled as she thought of the residents peering through their curtains at the wild black woman in dreadlocks and combat boots sitting in the middle of their peaceful village. She must, she thought, scare them to death.

She'd spotted the bistro when she'd arrived, and now she made for it. Her boots, veterans of sidewalk garbage and dog shit, squelched on grass and mud.

She opened the door and was prepared to enter a space decorated with Grand-mère in mind. All lace and gingham. Stuffed with old snowshoes and spinning wheels and

dusty twig baskets filled with dried flowers hanging from the rafters. Furnished with cheap imitation pine tables and uncomfortable chairs.

If Oddly knew one thing about Québec, it was that it was a cheap imitation of the real thing. France.

Instead what she found was a place both contemporary and somehow ageless. It seemed to straddle the centuries. Comfortable armchairs upholstered in fresh linens sat around an assortment of rugged old tables. Dark oak. Maple. Pine. Tables made from the forests that surrounded the village. They were scratched and dented and worn by a century or more of meals. Of drinks. Of companionship. And hardship.

The place settings, displayed in an old Welsh dresser, were white china with clean modern lines.

Oriental rugs, hand-tied, were scattered on the wide-plank floors. The walls were freshly plastered and painted a shade that contrasted nicely with the warm wood and stone.

She looked up.

Nothing hung from the sturdy beams.

The bistro smelled of rich coffee and subtle maple smoke from the fieldstone fireplaces at either end of the room.

It was a place of confidences. Of companionship. Where secrets were exchanged and yearnings admitted. Where children grew into adults, into seniors. Where homecomings were celebrated and lives celebrated by those left behind.

It was a place where both grandmother and granddaughter would feel at home.

'*Bonjour*,' said a young woman coming from behind the long bar to greet her. '*Une table? C'est votre choix.*'

She smiled at Dominica, as though dreadlocked New York critics were their regular customers, and pointed to the near-empty room. It was midafternoon, between rushes.

The few other customers had glanced at her, then gone back to their conversations. Showing little interest and no fear.

'Ummm,' said Oddly, not at all sure what the young woman had said.

'Oh, sorry. English. Sit anywhere you like. The fireplace has just come open. I'll clean the table for you.'

The young woman spoke in slightly accented English. As Oddly followed her to the large armchair by the fire, she thought she might have to do something rare for her.

Reconsider her opinion.

This was no France wannabe. This was genuine Québec. With its own history, etched into flesh and bone, into stone and wood. Into the cushions of the armchairs and sofas, retaining the impressions of warm bodies who'd sat there before her. Eating, talking, commiserating, laughing. For generations.

This was no imitation, but the real thing.

By the time Clara found her, Dominica had enjoyed a glass of red wine and a delicious buttery Riopelle de l'Isle. A cheese made on a tiny Québec island, and named after one of her favorite artists. Jean-Paul Riopelle. Dominica hadn't realized that the abstract expressionist painter came from Québec. And lived, worked, and died on a small island.

She smeared the cheese on a baguette fresh from the bakery next door, and looked at the village, framed by the mullioned windows.

She was wondering how much homes around the village green cost, and if any of her subscribers would notice, or care, if she decamped to Canada.

Though, looking at Clara Morrow's face, she knew one person who might not be pleased.

*

Vivienne's father closed his eyes and, bringing his hand to his heart, made a sound.

Gamache, sitting across from him, watched closely. It wasn't clear if Homer was sighing or moaning. Whether he was relieved or having a heart attack.

Armand noticed that the hand over his heart was crunched into a fist. But not tight. Not in pain. At least not physical pain. His heart, under attack for days, might just, with the news of the imminent arrest of Carl Tracey, finally be fighting back.

'I know you're not messing with me, Armand, but I need to hear it again. You're arresting him. For what he did.'

'Yes. I'll be going with Chief Inspector Beauvoir. We'll be bringing him in probably within the hour. You're free to go, but, Homer' – it was the first time he'd used the man's first name to his face – 'I'd like Agent Cloutier to drive you back to Three Pines.'

'To get my things.'

'No. To stay with us. Just for a few days. You shouldn't be alone.'

'No. I want to go home. I need to be with ...' He made a vague gesture. 'Alone.'

Armand knew he'd feel the same way, if Annie ... If Reine-Marie ... If Daniel ...

It was instinctive. A badly wounded animal, crawling off alone. To lick wounds. Or, if they proved too deep, to die.

Gamache had seen it more than once. People died from grief.

Carl Tracey had killed the daughter. Gamache was damned if he'd let him kill the father, too.

'You don't have to be social, but you shouldn't be alone.' Armand leaned forward and touched Homer's hand, lightly, and whispered, 'Please.'

He saw Agent Cloutier bristle a bit. Perhaps annoyed that it was not she who was comforting Homer.

But that's why Gamache had asked her to drive Homer down to Three Pines, so that Homer would have the company of someone he knew and trusted. Someone he felt comfortable with. It might even be the bonding experience they both needed.

'I can leave your place whenever I want?' Homer asked. 'And go home?'

'Yes, of course,' said Armand. 'Lysette will stay with you until I get there.'

That served several purposes. It kept Homer company, kept him there, and kept Reine-Marie safe. Armand doubted Homer would lash out again, but he wasn't going to take that chance.

'You're going to arrest him?'

It was the third time Homer had asked and the third time Armand had said yes. And he was happy to say it all day and into the night.

Yes. Yes. Carl Tracey would face a judge and jury for what he did to Vivienne. Carl Tracey would spend the rest of his life in prison.

'And he'll be convicted. You promise?'

Gamache hesitated for a moment. 'There's one more piece of evidence that will seal it. Someone's testimony.'

Godin's eyes widened in surprise. 'Someone was there? They saw what happened?'

'No. There're no actual witnesses. Though there rarely are. A case is built from evidence. And we have plenty. But this last piece would guarantee a conviction.'

'You promise?'

Annie's father stood up and put out his hand to Vivienne's father. 'I promise.'

Homer took it, then leaned forward very slowly. As did Armand. Until their foreheads touched.

They stayed there for the briefest of moments, eyes closed.

Then Homer pulled back and caught his breath, wiping his face with his sleeve.

'Sorry. Out of Kleenex.'

'Here,' said Lysette, offering a box she'd plucked from a nearby desk.

Homer took it without really noticing who was attached to the offering. *'Merci.'*

'Ready?' asked Armand.

Homer blew his nose, then stooped to pick up all the balled-up tissues he'd dropped on the floor.

'Leave them,' said Armand.

But the large man would not, could not, leave a mess for someone else to clean up.

CHAPTER 29

⌒

Jean-Guy Beauvoir sat behind the wheel of the unmarked car. By tradition, the senior officer rode in the passenger seat. But Beauvoir could not bring himself to do that while Gamache was in the vehicle. Except that once, when he was too exhausted to drive.

Now they sat side by side. As they had for years. Watching the home of a murder suspect. Waiting for word from Lacoste. Waiting to give the word to go.

'What do you mean you're staying the night?' demanded Clara.

'Sorry, but my flight from Burlington to New York was canceled,' Dominica Oddly said.

What she didn't say was that she herself had canceled it. And spoken to the big gay guy about a room at their bed-and-breakfast. Or, as he insisted on calling it, bed-and-brunch.

If their B&B looked like their bistro and tasted like the bakery, she really might never leave. She did not tell Clara that. The woman already looked like her hair was on fire.

'Can't you stay over in Burlington?' asked Clara, her voice rising. 'Close to the airport?'

'Too late,' said Gabri, dropping a key into Dominica's hand. 'She's booked in. The Basquiat Suite.'

'Since when do you name your rooms?' Clara all but hissed at him.

'Since she showed up,' said Gabri, unapologetically. 'And if you're not careful, we'll call the public bathroom the Toilette Clara Morrow.'

'You know what she's just posted online about my works,' said Clara, watching as Ruth and Myrna joined the critic at the bistro fireplace.

Reine-Marie had gone home, feeling the need for a long shower after watching those vile videos.

Gabri turned to face Clara, his expression no longer a little goofy. 'I do. And now you have twenty-four hours you didn't have before to change her mind.'

'She won't change her mind.'

They walked over to the bar, and while Clara helped herself to a licorice pipe from the jar, Gabri poured her a red wine.

'You don't know that.' He smiled and touched her hand. 'People do change. Minds change. I know you know that.'

Clara turned and glared at Dominica Oddly, now laughing and chatting with her best friend and her mentor. In her seat. By the fireplace.

She felt the bile grow. Felt the subtle demonisms of thought take hold.

Lysette had tried to engage Homer in casual conversation. But, understandably, the only thing he was interested in hearing about was their investigation.

Lysette wasn't really sure how much to tell him but suspected he would not pass any of it along. And it would be public knowledge anyway, as soon as Tracey was arraigned.

Besides, she was desperate to connect with him. To let him know the important role she'd played in having Tracey arrested.

To let him know she wasn't just on his side but by his side.

In the twenty-minute drive from Cowansville to Three Pines, she'd been debating how much to reveal. Not just about the case against Tracey but about herself.

About her feelings.

It was just dumb luck that Chief Inspector Gamache had given her this time alone with Homer. He couldn't possibly know what it meant to her. But now she needed to actually use it.

They were getting closer and closer to Three Pines.

Now was the time.

But what should she say? She couldn't just blurt out, 'I love you.'

Or could she? Maybe he needed to hear it. Especially now. To know someone loved him. Deeply.

Just before cresting the hill that would take them down into Three Pines, she reached over and placed her hand on top of his.

He didn't pull away.

As they arrived at the Gamache home, just before putting the car in park, she squeezed.

And he, she was pretty sure, squeezed back.

Jean-Guy checked his phone again. It was instinctive.

There were, as he already knew from the last time he checked, no bars. No reception. Which was why he'd chosen a car with a radio connecting them to the station.

Now he stared at the handset. While beside him, Gamache stared out the window. Into the twilight. Through the trees to the lonely home and the single light at a single window.

Jean-Guy checked his phone again.

*

'That's not true.'

'It is. The coroner just confirmed it. That baby was Carl's.' Lacoste leaned forward. 'A little girl. His daughter. Kinda makes you wonder, doesn't it, Pauline?'

Pauline was silent, but Lacoste could see her mind whirring.

Superintendent Lacoste had another question for Pauline Vachon.

'Where were you on Saturday afternoon and evening?'

Homer knelt and put his face against the smelly old dog, rubbing him, mumbling to him, before standing back up.

'Armand called to say you were coming,' said Reine-Marie, standing at the door as Henri and Gracie ran out to greet the new arrivals. 'I'm glad.'

She was freshly showered and had put on slacks and a soft sweater. She turned to Agent Cloutier. 'I have soup and sandwiches in the kitchen. You must be hungry.'

She was. 'Yes, please. *Merci.*'

As they entered the home, Homer stepped closer to Reine-Marie, looking at her face. Then he shook his head.

'I did that,' he said, pointing to the bruise. 'I can't believe it. I'm so sorry. I don't know what came over me.'

'I do,' she said. 'And I think you showed amazing restraint. I shouldn't have tried to stop you. I'd have ripped the head off anyone who tried to stop me.'

If it had been Annie dragged from the river. Or Daniel. Or Armand. She'd have done far worse to anyone standing between her and them.

'Your room is waiting for you. Would you like to freshen up, then meet us in the kitchen?'

He nodded, and the two women watched as he slowly climbed the stairs. Followed, slowly, by Fred.

'Homer?' said Lysette, not sure what to do.

'I'll be fine, Lysette.'

Even something as small as hearing him say her name thrilled her.

'Chief Inspector, this is Cameron.'

Beauvoir snatched the mouthpiece off its cradle and pressed the button. *'Oui.'*

Gamache turned to watch, holding Beauvoir's eyes.

'We have the warrant for Tracey's arrest.'

Beauvoir exhaled. They had it.

But he wanted more.

'Is Superintendent Lacoste still in the interview room?'

'Yes.'

'Tell her to call as soon as she comes out.' He went to replace the handset, but Gamache stopped him.

'I have an idea.'

'Hold on, Cameron,' said Beauvoir, and clicked the handset off while Gamache explained.

Beauvoir nodded approval, then clicked the handset back on. 'Still there, Cameron?'

'Oui, patron.'

'This is what I want you to do.'

Agent Cameron knocked on the door, then entered.

Lacoste glanced at him with some annoyance. It was unusual to be interrupted in the middle of what was proving a difficult interrogation.

Pauline Vachon was holding unexpectedly firm.

She would not admit that Tracey planned to kill his wife and that that's what the posts were about.

Cameron bent down and whispered in her ear, then left.

Lacoste smiled and turned back to Vachon, who was watching her with feigned boredom. But after a few seconds of silence, Vachon's brows lowered.

'What?' she demanded.

'I probably shouldn't tell you this, but an arrest warrant has just been issued for Carl Tracey. For the murder of Vivienne Godin. Chief Inspector Beauvoir is bringing him in. He'll be here in half an hour.'

Lacoste got up and, collecting the papers, closed the file.

'Can I go now?'

'Not quite yet. I want to hear what Monsieur Tracey has to say. Then you can go.'

She walked to the door. And stopped when she heard that one word. That beautiful word.

'Wait.'

The radio crackled, and Jean-Guy reached for it so quickly it bobbled out of his hand.

He juggled it for a moment before finally grasping it.

'Beauvoir.'

'We have him,' said Isabelle Lacoste. 'Pauline Vachon just admitted they'd discussed killing Vivienne. That Tracey planned to do it.'

'She'll sign the statement? Testify against him?'

'Yes.'

They knocked on the door.

By now it was dark. Not even the porch light was on. Though there was still the one light on. Upstairs.

They knocked again. Still no answer.

Beauvoir turned to the two uniformed Sûreté agents and

signaled them to go around back. Then he and Gamache exchanged glances.

Beauvoir turned the handle of the front door. It was unlocked. He swung it open.

'Tracey? Carl Tracey?' Beauvoir called. 'Sûreté. We have a warrant for your arrest.'

He walked in, slowly, carefully, with Gamache right beside him. Both seasoned officers scanned the room. Looking for a killer.

They found him passed out, drunk, on the bed. In a puddle of his own vomit.

CHAPTER 30

The arraignment was held the next morning, in Superior Court at the Palais de justice in Montréal.

Once he'd sobered up, Carl Tracey had been given a shower and a change of clothes. He spent the night at the Cowansville detachment, where he'd been booked for murder.

From there, early in the morning, he'd been driven to a cell in the Montréal courthouse.

Chief Inspectors Beauvoir and Gamache met there first thing and interviewed him, with his court-appointed lawyer present. Predictably, his lawyer told him not to say anything. Equally predictably, Tracey couldn't help but talk.

After Tracey claimed he had nothing to do with Vivienne's death, Beauvoir presented him with Pauline Vachon's statement.

'She says you talked about killing your wife—'

Tracey snorted. 'Who doesn't say that every now and then?'

'I don't,' said Chief Inspector Beauvoir.

'You will.'

Beauvoir knew he shouldn't let this man get up his nose, but Tracey was firmly lodged there. That smug, weaselly look. From a man who'd just killed his wife and unborn child.

'You know nothing—' Beauvoir began.

'Chief Inspector,' said Gamache, a warning in his voice.

Carl Tracey turned to Gamache. 'I wouldn't kill my own wife. Too obvious. But someone else's . . . That was your wife in that village, right? Looks like you and I have something in common. That bruise on her face?'

Gamache grew very still, very quiet. Then he turned back to Beauvoir, who was staring, dumbfounded by what Tracey just said.

The lawyer ended the session there.

Beauvoir and Gamache walked down the hallway. Finally Gamache spoke.

'He'll confess.'

'You think?'

'*Oui*. He's a foolish, weak man. If he doesn't actually mean to confess, he'll incriminate himself with his bravado. He'll hang himself.'

'If only.'

Gamache glanced at Beauvoir but said nothing.

They stood as the judge took her seat.

The prosecutor, with Chief Inspector Beauvoir beside him, was on one side of the courtroom. Tracey and his lawyer on the other.

Gamache and Agent Cloutier sat immediately behind the prosecution desk, with Homer Godin between them. Behind them sat Simone Fleury with at least twenty other women.

Young. Middle-aged. Elderly. Stony-faced.

Valkyries. Warrior Fates. Magnificent and terrifying.

Gamache caught Madame Fleury's eye. She nodded.

The seats behind Tracey were empty.

Barry Zalmanowitz, a prosecutor they knew well, had

been given the case. He was feeling confident enough to kid Gamache when the Sûreté officers showed up at his office.

'I see you're trending, Armand. Of course, I knew the video was faked. You're not that good a shot.'

He smiled. Obviously trying, with a spectacular lack of success, to lighten the mood.

Seeing the grim look on Chief Inspector Gamache's face and the anger on Beauvoir's, the prosecutor dropped his voice and added, 'I also saw the real thing. I can't believe it was posted again. I'm sorry. I hope they find out who did that. Someone calling themselves "dumbass."'

'We have an idea,' said Beauvoir.

He'd stayed away from Three Pines, not wanting to see Ruth. Not wanting to say things that could never be taken back. He knew that the elderly woman actually meant well. But in true Ruth fashion, she'd managed to inflict a wound.

And this one went deep.

Before the proceedings started, Beauvoir had pulled Vivienne's father aside and said, 'This won't take long. The judge will ask Tracey how he pleads—'

'What will he say?'

'We think his plea will be not guilty.'

Beauvoir waited for the outburst, but there was none. Monsieur Godin, in the past twelve hours, had managed to harness his emotions. Though Beauvoir could see it was a struggle.

Gamache had prepared the man the night before, as much as possible, for what would happen.

Carl Tracey would be led in. He'd sit at a distance from them, but Godin would certainly see him.

'Will you be able to control yourself?' Gamache had asked.

'I think so.'

Gamache had paused before speaking again. 'If you don't think you can, then you shouldn't go. If there's an outburst, you'll be thrown out, or even arrested. You'll do yourself and the case no favors.'

Homer had glanced into the fire, mesmerized by the liquid flames. It was just the two of them now, and Fred the dog.

They'd had dinner in the kitchen with Reine-Marie and Lysette Cloutier. It was a simple meal of lentil soup and thick-cut fresh bread, warm from the oven, and cheese.

Homer managed a few spoonsful and finished off one piece of bread, with melted butter.

Now they sat alone in the restful room, with coffee and a plate of untouched chocolate chip cookies. Reine-Marie had gone to bed. Henri and Gracie trailing along behind her. Agent Cloutier had driven back to Montréal.

'I'll control myself,' said Homer.

Gamache studied the man. And nodded. He wasn't completely convinced Godin would do it, or that it was even possible. But he also knew there was no way to prevent Vivienne's father from being there when Carl Tracey was arraigned for Vivienne's murder.

Homer had to face his daughter's killer.

They talked into the night. About Vivienne. About her mother. About everything except what had happened.

Finally, at just after two in the morning, Godin fell silent. After a few minutes, he got up.

'I think I'm ready for bed.' He looked at Armand. 'I've never had a brother. Not even a close man friend. Know a lotta guys, but we never really talk. Now I wonder why not.' He paused and gathered himself before speaking again. 'This has helped.'

'I'm glad.'

Gamache slept lightly, listening for the sound of restless footsteps. But finally Homer had to be woken from a deep sleep at six thirty.

'There's coffee and breakfast, if you'd like,' Armand had said after poking his head in the door and seeing a groggy Homer. 'Then we need to drive in.'

And now they sat in the courtroom. The early April, late-morning sun struggling through the grimy windows.

Homer ran his hands, shaking a little, through his short gray hair and then jerked when there was a sound off to their left. A door opening.

He reached out and grabbed Armand's arm as a passenger on a suddenly doomed aircraft would reach for the person in the next seat.

Gamache turned with him, as did everyone else, and watched as Carl Tracey, in handcuffs, was led in.

Homer rose to his feet and stood stock-still, face immobile, hands clenched at his sides. Eyes fastened on his former son-in-law. Willing Tracey, daring him, to look in his direction.

But Tracey did not.

Homer stared, in a pose so contained, so dignified, so stoic it both amazed Gamache and bruised his heart.

Armand had also gotten to his feet, to stand with Homer. And now the others joined them, as the bailiff announced, 'Silence. All rise, please. The Superior Court is now in session, the Honorable Caroline Pelletier presiding.'

The judge, in long black robes, entered. With a signal, everyone in the courtroom sat back down. Except Godin.

'Homer,' whispered Gamache, getting back up and touching, slightly tugging, his arm. The man, roused from a sort of trance, sat.

But continued to glare at Tracey.

The rustling stopped as Judge Pelletier got herself organized. And then there was silence. One that went on. And on.

Gamache's face revealed nothing, but he grew wary. Alert. This protracted pause was unusual.

He knew the judge. She was strict. No-nonsense. Not chummy or clubby. She brooked no informality and no bending of the rules or the interpretation of the law.

She was, in his opinion, a great jurist.

But now she was looking down at her papers, shuffling them a bit, instead of doing what she should have been doing, which was to have the charges read and ask the defendant how he pleads.

It was rote. Routine. Something they went through all the time. Clear, simple.

Tracey would be remanded for trial. Led away. And that would be it.

Except . . .

Out of the corner of his eye, Gamache could see Beauvoir stirring. The prosecuting attorney was staring intently at the judge.

Beauvoir turned in his seat and mouthed, 'What's up?'

Something was up. Something was wrong.

Judge Caroline Pelletier looked out at the courtroom.

Her heart sank when she saw the women ranged behind Chief Inspector Gamache.

She knew who they were and why they were there.

She intentionally skimmed past the man beside Monsieur Gamache. She assumed it was the victim's father.

Judge Pelletier did not want to catch his eye.

Instead her gaze moved to the defense table and rested on the man sitting next to his lawyer.

The defendant, Carl Tracey.

Judge Pelletier had been up most of the night, going over and over the file. The evidence.

She knew it was folly, and ethically wrong, to prejudge. But judges were, after all, human. And some cases were just obvious.

There was very little doubt in her mind who had killed Vivienne Godin. Nor was there much doubt about the outcome of the day.

Still, to be sure, she'd called up colleagues and asked opinions.

Then asked more colleagues, judges across the country, and collected more opinions.

She'd even phoned her old, now retired, law prof and gone through the case against Carl Tracey.

All, save one, said the same thing.

And now it was her turn to say it.

'There is, I'm afraid, a poisonous tree in this case.'

Jean-Guy Beauvoir stared at the judge in amazement, then turned to the prosecutor. Zalmanowitz's mouth had fallen open. Beauvoir swiveled to look at Gamache, whose eyes were wide, his mouth also slightly open.

'It goes back to the very beginning,' said Judge Pelletier, her voice almost a monotone. 'Even before Vivienne Godin's body was found.'

'What's she saying?' asked Homer, his voice below normal conversation, but above a whisper. 'What does this mean?' He could tell, a child could tell, that something unexpected had just happened. Something bad. 'What's a poisonous tree?'

'In a minute,' whispered Gamache, glancing briefly at Homer before returning his attention to the judge.

'When Vivienne Godin's overnight bag was found on the shores of the river—' Judge Pelletier turned to Beauvoir. 'You did not have a warrant, I believe, to go onto that private property.'

Beauvoir shot to his feet. 'No, Your Honor, we didn't. But it was an emergency. The river was in flood, and it needed to be diverted. The law allows us to enter private property in an emergency. We don't need a warrant to rescue people from a fire, for example.'

'True, but in going onto private property you didn't just create a runoff for the flood. You discovered the victim's duffel bag. Did you open it?'

'We did.'

Judge Pelletier nodded. '*Oui.* That's what it says here.' She placed her hand on the papers in front of her. 'There's video evidence of that, too, which has been submitted. Your written statement says that upon opening it and examining the contents, you realized it belonged to the missing woman, which led you to the bridge, which led you to her body—'

'What's happening?' Godin whispered, more urgently.

'Just listen,' said Gamache, keeping his voice low, calm, reasonable. He reached over and touched the man's arm, feeling it so tense it might snap.

His own body was taut. He could see where this was going, though he barely believed it.

A poisonous tree? Surely not.

He'd become hyperaware of his surroundings. The world was bright and in sharp focus. Sounds were magnified. The smallest movement noted. Every word, every inflection absorbed.

It was the way he became when under attack. For this felt

like an attack. Like someone had just tossed a grenade into the courtroom.

And there was nothing he could do to stop it from going off.

Off to the side, at the defense desk, he could see the court-appointed lawyer equally surprised. But unlike the prosecution, who was looking at the judge as though he'd been hit in the face, the defense was smiling.

Zalmanowitz, the prosecuting attorney, got to his feet. 'If it pleases the court, there's case law covering this. Where officers go onto private property to stop a crime being committed and in the course of that come across another crime—'

'True.' The judge stopped him there with an upraised hand. Predicting just this objection. 'But no crime was being committed. A river was flooding. It was an act of nature. A violent one, potentially dangerous, granted. I have no doubt that the actions of the officers saved property if not lives. It was the right thing to do. Except when they found the duffel bag, they should have immediately applied for a warrant, before removing it. And certainly before opening it.'

Beauvoir, in near panic, looked once again at Gamache.

Gamache himself was shocked. Never had he heard such a severe, such a narrow interpretation of the law. He immediately scribbled on a piece of paper and handed it to the prosecution, who read it and said, 'Your Honor, a life was at stake. As you said, Madame Godin had not yet been found. She could have been hurt, or kidnapped. They needed to search the overnight bag, to determine if it was hers and if it could lead them to her. Which it did.'

'And that might have been justified,' said the judge. 'Had they not been on the defendant's private property. Let me ask

you this: did the officers get Mr Tracey's permission before opening the bag?'

The prosecution turned to Beauvoir, who had gone so pale his lips were almost white. He thought and thought, glancing at Gamache once.

Beauvoir was not pausing to remember, Gamache knew. He remembered perfectly well, as did Gamache. Carl Tracey shouting at them not to open the duffel bag. That it was none of their business.

No. Jean-Guy Beauvoir was pausing to decide whether or not to tell the truth.

Judge Pelletier was giving them a potential out. A way to cut down the poisonous tree. Whose roots and branches and fruit looked to infect so much of their case against Tracey.

'While not formally sworn in, Chief Inspector,' the judge said, 'you are presumed under oath.'

She could see his thoughts, his struggle. And it seemed clear to Gamache that she sympathized. This was not giving Judge Pelletier any pleasure. But it was, according to her lights, the law.

Before Beauvoir could answer, the defense got to his feet. 'Your Honor, my client tells me he told them—' Tracey grabbed his arm, and the lawyer bent down to listen to his client, then straightened up. 'He begged them not to open the bag. But they did, anyway.'

'I see,' said the judge. 'Just out of interest's sake, why didn't he want the police to open the bag? If it could have helped them find his wife, which, presumably, he wanted.'

That was met with silence. It was a very good question.

Both Gamache and Beauvoir would have been amused by Tracey's bringing this scrutiny on himself had they themselves not been so appalled by what was happening.

The lawyer consulted his client, then turned to the judge. 'He says he believed his wife was alive and that the bag contained things she wouldn't want strangers to see. Like underwear.'

'Oh, for Christ's sake,' burst out of Homer. 'You're not ... You can't ... This's ...'

'Homer,' said Gamache, turning to him, but Godin was already on his feet.

Gamache also rose and faced Homer, who was glaring at Tracey with all the violence a look could contain. Then Gamache turned to the judge.

'Please, Your Honor,' he said.

'For you, Monsieur Gamache, I will give you a moment to settle him. I'm assuming that is the young woman's father?'

'He is, and thank you.' Gamache turned back to Homer. 'Do you need to leave? Look at me.' He stood between Homer and Tracey, breaking Homer's line of sight. Forcing Homer to focus on him. 'You need to hold it together.' Gamache was speaking so quietly that no one else could hear. And so forcefully that Godin would not just hear but listen. 'Or you need to leave. Do you understand?'

Godin nodded.

'Do you want to stay?'

Godin nodded.

'And you'll control yourself, no matter what happens?'

'What is happening, Armand?' The man's voice now sounded almost like that of a child.

'I don't know, but losing control will only make it worse. You understand?'

'You promised. You promised it would be okay.'

'Please,' said Gamache. 'Just sit down.'

Homer sat, and Gamache turned to the judge and gave a nod that was almost a small bow. *Merci.*

The judge looked tired, strained. Even, Gamache thought, a little sad. Which did not bode well.

She turned back to Beauvoir. 'You still haven't answered my question, Chief Inspector.'

Beauvoir got back to his feet. 'No, Your Honor, we didn't ask, and the defendant did not give us permission to open the bag.'

'I see.' She gestured to him to sit back down.

As he did, he glanced at Gamache, who nodded approval. A lie would make this even worse. Besides, there was the video Reine-Marie had taken at his request.

'The opening of the bag is, in my opinion, a poisonous tree,' said Judge Pelletier, 'and everything that stems from that act is its fruit and therefore tainted and inadmissible.'

The prosecutor leaped up. 'I object!' Speaking more forcefully than was perhaps wise.

'Noted,' said Judge Pelletier.

'Are we in trouble?' Agent Cloutier leaned across Homer to whisper to Gamache.

'We're all right. We have Pauline Vachon's signed statement. That didn't stem from the discovery of the duffel bag.'

'Right. Good.'

'Now,' said Judge Pelletier, no longer looking up at them. 'On to the other issue.'

The world seemed to stop for Gamache.

Other issue?

He could feel, almost hear, his heart throbbing. Everything, everyone else seemed to recede, except the judge. He was completely, totally, focused, and when she next spoke, it was as though her words were deposited directly, and uniquely, into his head.

'The statement by Madame Vachon. I've considered this

and consulted colleagues across the country, many of whom are beginning to form judgments on the issue of social media and boundaries.'

'What's she saying?' hissed Beauvoir. 'My God, she's not . . .'

But he couldn't continue. Couldn't conceive that –

'The boundaries of a person's house are clear,' said the judge. 'The property line. The front door. A warrant is needed to cross. A warrant is needed to tap into a phone and listen to private conversations, to read private emails. But the very notion, even the name, of social media confuses issues of trespass. How can something social, public, be trespassed? There are limits, of course. Laws against hate speech. Pornography. But even those are unclear, blurry. When is social media private and when is it public? Pauline Vachon and her relationship to Carl Tracey were discovered after a Sûreté officer tricked Madame Vachon into giving her access to her private Instagram account.'

Agent Cloutier's eyes opened wide. 'What . . . ?'

'Oh, my God,' whispered Beauvoir.

'Armand?' said Homer. 'What's this?'

The judge had not raised her head. Would not look their way. And appeared to be reading now from notes.

'There's not much jurisprudence on this as yet, but the vast majority of jurists I consulted agreed that in posing as NouveauGalerie, it was the equivalent of a robber posing as an electrician to gain access to a private residence. Under false pretenses. With the intent to compromise the occupant.'

The prosecution shot to his feet. 'I object. That isn't the correct analogy.'

'And what is?'

'Undercover operations,' snapped Zalmanowitz. 'A police

officer posing as someone they are not in order to gain evidence in a criminal case.'

'Yes, I did consider that,' said Judge Pelletier. 'Except there was as yet no reason to suspect Madame Vachon of anything criminal. Monsieur Tracey, perhaps, but as soon as Agent Cloutier realized she was corresponding with this Pauline Vachon, she should have disengaged. Instead she tricked Madame Vachon into giving her access to an account that led to not just evidence of an affair but to those incriminating posts.'

Judge Pelletier turned to Carl Tracey. With her voice flat, she began to speak.

Armand Gamache held his breath.

Don't do it. Don't do it.

'Monsieur Tracey, I am having the charges against you dropped. You're free to go.'

'No!'

Godin shot to his feet, as did Gamache.

He reached for Homer and braced himself but was still propelled backward as Vivienne's father exploded forward. Toward Tracey.

There was sudden mayhem as chairs and benches were knocked over. Guards ran to yank the judge off the dais and into the back room.

People fell over, and others joined the fight to stop an inconsolable, uncontainable father.

Gamache felt his feet go out from under him and fell backward, dragging Homer down with him. They landed in a pile on the marble floor.

There was an eerie silence. Then the squealing of overturned chairs being shoved aside as arms and legs reassembled themselves into individual people.

There were moans and groans. Orders issued by guards and cops.

Beauvoir, who'd leaped over the railing to try to stop Homer, now rolled off the man's back. And tried to get air back into his own lungs.

'Armand?' he gasped.

'Okay. You?'

'*Oui.*'

Gamache freed his legs and, scrambling to his knees, bent over Homer's inert body. So still was the man that Gamache felt for a pulse, then lay down, his cheek on the cold marble floor. Face-to-face. Their noses almost touching.

'Homer?'

His eyes were closed, and Armand noticed blood on the floor. 'Get an ambulance.'

A court officer ran to make the call.

Beauvoir was keeping the guards away, explaining the man wasn't armed. Wasn't a danger.

Homer's eyes fluttered, then opened. And focused on Armand.

'You promised,' he whispered.

CHAPTER 31

~

Vivienne's father was taken by ambulance to the Hôtel-Dieu hospital.

Gamache had wanted to go with him but sent Cloutier and Cameron instead.

It had been Bob Cameron who'd finally brought Godin down. He'd come into the courtroom late, standing unnoticed at the back, as the judge had given her reasoning and conclusion.

And when Homer had burst forward, Cameron had instantly seen what was happening. And what needed to be done.

The left tackle did what he'd been trained to do.

He'd run into the fray, diving at the last minute, using his body to sweep Godin's legs out from under him. And, in so doing, also tackling Gamache. And Beauvoir. And Cloutier. And anyone else hanging on to Vivienne's father.

'Give me a few minutes,' Zalmanowitz, the prosecutor, said to the Sûreté officers once the ambulance had left and order had been restored. 'I'll speak to the judge. Then we can talk.'

Judge Pelletier had decided not to charge Monsieur Godin. Clearly sympathizing with the man. The father.

'*Merde, merde, merde,*' muttered Beauvoir.

'*Merde,*' added Lacoste.

She'd been in another interview, to possibly take over command of Public Security, when word had reached her about what had happened in the courthouse.

She'd hurried over, and now the three of them walked along the slushy cobblestoned streets outside the courthouse. In need of fresh air and to try to clear their heads.

'A shitshow. What the fuck was that?' Beauvoir stopped, took a deep breath, closed his eyes, then opened them again. 'Sorry. But really. What the fuck was that?'

They circled the building in Old Montréal. Feeling the sun on their hot faces. And the fresh air in their lungs.

They spoke a little, mostly curses from Beauvoir. Gamache, who had said almost nothing since the judge's pronouncement, let them vent. While he walked and considered.

Then they all fell silent, lost in their own thoughts. The same thoughts.

Partly about what had gone wrong, mostly how to fix it.

Beauvoir's phone buzzed. A text from Zalmanowitz. As terse as the man.

Meet me in my office.

The three Sûreté officers were around the back of the building, but Gamache knew the way in, past the trash and recycling bins. After he'd pressed the button and stared into the camera, the door was unlocked. It helped that Gamache knew the guards by name and they knew him. After decades of trials. And tribulations.

Beauvoir and Lacoste followed Gamache along grimy, ill-lit corridors. Taking the service elevator, they finally emerged into the gleaming marble hallway. The public face, hiding the smelly, dark underbelly of justice.

'Well, that was a clusterfuck of a decision,' said Zalmanowitz, not bothering to get up or even look up from his laptop, as they entered. 'I spoke to Judge Pelletier, who walked me through it.'

'And?' asked Beauvoir.

'And we'll appeal, of course,' said the prosecutor.

'Will we win?'

'Hard to say.'

'Try.'

Now Zalmanowitz gave them his complete attention, turning from his screen. 'Honestly? I doubt it. As much as we hate the decision, Judge Pelletier did her due diligence, even canvassing jurists across the country—'

'But a poisonous tree?' interrupted Beauvoir. 'Come on.'

'I know. I can't explain her interpretation. Well, I can. But it's an incredibly narrow view of the law.'

He rubbed his eyes and sighed. Then, looking up, he smiled weakly. 'You know what they say about lawyers—'

Gamache gave Beauvoir a warning glance.

' – that we're like children in the dark, imagining all the monsters.'

It was, Gamache knew, a pretty apt description of his job, too.

'Seems I missed one,' said the lawyer. 'Two, really.'

'We all did,' said Beauvoir.

Zalmanowitz nodded his thanks for sharing the blame. 'Judge Pelletier had latitude. It could have gone the other way, and I think she genuinely struggled with it. Especially since, as she privately told me, our case was a lock—'

Beauvoir's hands slammed down on the wooden arms of his chair, and he growled, 'Jesus.'

Getting up, he paced the room, trying to blow off the

pent-up frustration. The others let him pace until he'd regained control of himself.

Sitting back down, he didn't apologize. But he did look directly at Zalmanowitz and say, 'Someone needs to make sure Tracey gets what's coming to him.'

'We're trying.'

'Try harder.'

'Look, you're the ones who opened that duffel bag,' he said, his voice rising, his frustration getting away from him with every word. 'Who let an inexperienced agent loose to goose-step around in that Instagram account—'

Zalmanowitz stopped himself, with effort. Putting his hands out in front of him as though to protect them from his wrath.

He sat back in his chair. Which bounced with the force of his body.

Staring at Gamache, he saw that while the Chief Inspector's tone had been civil so far, and his face calm, his jaw muscles were clamped tight.

This was not a relaxed man. This was a man who was simply better at containing his emotions.

'I'm sorry.' Zalmanowitz took a deep breath and looked at the three investigators. 'This isn't your fault.'

'Of course it is,' snapped Beauvoir. 'I fucked up.'

'So did I,' said Gamache. 'I'm the one who actually opened the duffel bag.'

'And I let Agent Cloutier pursue the Instagram account. Even encouraged her,' said Lacoste, shaking her head.

'None of us looks good in this,' Zalmanowitz admitted. 'I'm the lawyer, the prosecutor. I should've seen that there might be a problem. But I didn't.'

Now he rubbed his face with his hands. Trying to erase his expression of defeat.

'That is true. This's mostly your fault,' said Beauvoir, and when the prosecutor looked at him, Beauvoir smiled. And Zalmanowitz gave one gruff laugh.

Truce.

'As I said, I'll file an appeal,' said the prosecutor. 'But that'll take months to be heard. The poisonous tree is the most damaging ruling. It's just unfortunate that so much stems from something so early on. It affects almost every bit of evidence.'

'"Unfortunate" isn't the word,' said Lacoste.

Zalmanowitz nodded. 'Her decision on the poisonous tree sits right on the boundary, which is why no other judge will overturn her ruling. And you'd better note it, because it'll become case law from now on. And affect all other searches. But' – now he leaned forward, arms on his desk – 'the more gnarly decision, by her own private admission, concerns the social-media issue.'

'The Instagram account,' said Lacoste, pulling her chair closer to the desk.

'Exactly. Judge Pelletier's right, of course, that courts are struggling to figure out the laws around social media. The government's working on legislation, but it's controversial and sensitive, and you know how politicians love those two things.'

He waited for their laugh of appreciation. Instead all he got were three glum stares.

'If this judgment stands,' he went on, 'it'll redefine boundaries.'

'But it's not right,' said Beauvoir. 'It ties our hands when it comes to social-media accounts. It pretty much locks us out and lets people do anything they want.'

'As they can in the privacy of their own homes,' said Zalmanowitz. 'That's the analogy she's using. As Pierre

Elliott Trudeau said when he was Prime Minister, the government has no place in the bedrooms of the nation.'

'But there are limits,' said Gamache. 'Assault, child pornography, murder. Just because people do it in the privacy of their homes doesn't mean they're beyond the reach of law. But I also know we aren't solving anything by going over and over this. A decision was reached. You'll appeal. In the meantime, Carl Tracey is free. Do we have other evidence, untainted, that can be used?'

'Vivienne called her father that day, to say she was finally leaving Tracey,' said Beauvoir. 'That sure suggests she was afraid.'

'There's the evidence of Agent Cameron, who responded to Vivienne's 911 calls,' said Lacoste. 'It was clear there was abuse.'

'But not clear enough for him to actually bring Tracey in. He didn't feel it met the "reasonable suspicion" test. Besides, abuse isn't murder. What else do we have?'

'There's that young man, what's his name,' said Beauvoir. 'The one she called over and over the day she was killed.'

'Gerald Bertrand,' said Lacoste. 'He claims it was a wrong number.'

'And you believe him?' asked Zalmanowitz.

'Yes, I think I do. We checked him out, and there's absolutely nothing connecting him to Vivienne or Tracey. I think she wrote the number down wrong.'

'What number was she calling again?' asked Gamache.

Lacoste gave it to him.

'I don't understand why, if she was so afraid, she didn't ask her father to come get her,' said Zalmanowitz.

'He offered,' said Gamache. 'But she said it was too dangerous, that she had to choose her time carefully.'

'So she feared for her life?' said Zalmanowitz. 'She told her father that?'

Gamache considered, remembering that first conversation with Godin, in his home in Ste.-Agathe. 'Not specifically. I think she was afraid and let him know that, but not for her life. I think if she'd told him that, Monsieur Godin would have definitely gone to get her. He didn't want to make it worse or trigger any violence. So he stayed home.'

'That poor man,' said Zalmanowitz. 'How do you live with yourself?'

There was no answering that.

'So,' said Zalmanowitz after a pause. 'Vivienne was obviously afraid of her husband.'

'*Oui*. Afraid of what he'd do if he knew she was leaving—'

'But wait a minute.' Zalmanowitz raised his hand to stop Gamache. 'According to the girlfriend, Pauline Vachon, Tracey wanted to get rid of her. Wouldn't her leaving solve the problem, and then they wouldn't have to kill her? Why not just let her go? He didn't really have to kill her.'

'He might not have realized she planned to leave,' said Beauvoir. 'He says she told him, but does that really seem likely?'

It did not.

'So you think he killed her without knowing she was leaving anyway?' asked Zalmanowitz.

'Even if he knew, Tracey still had a motive,' said Gamache. 'He admitted to me he had no intention of giving half the home to her. Or to support the child.'

He told them about his exchange in the kitchen when Tracey admitted that Vivienne's leaving and taking half the farm with her was a pretty good motive.

'So there's your answer,' said Beauvoir. 'Tracey's violent.

Drunk. He planned to kill her, and he did. The fact she was going to leave anyway only drove him more crazy.'

'And the bag?' asked Zalmanowitz. 'How did it get into the river? Who packed it?'

'We think Tracey did,' said Beauvoir. 'Based on strange things in the bag and the private message to Vachon.'

'*Stuff's in the bag,*' Lacoste read from her notes. '*Everything's ready. Will be done tonight. I promise.*'

Zalmanowitz sighed. 'Damning. And completely inadmissible. But what I don't get is if she did plan to leave, like she told her father, why didn't she pack the bag? Oh, never mind.' He flung himself back in the chair again and threw up his hands. 'It's all academic. The duffel bag is out of bounds. It's as though the bag never existed.'

'*Non,*' said Beauvoir. 'It's as though we didn't find it. But it happened. And now we need to find another way to get him.'

They looked at him. Beauvoir had climbed out of his outrage, more determined than ever. Far from defeated.

They'd get Carl Tracey. Somehow.

The prosecutor leaned forward again, drew his notepad toward him, and picked up a pen.

'Right. What we can use is Carl Tracey's first statement to you,' the prosecutor said to Gamache. 'That was before the bag or the body was found.'

'And we have the first interview with Homer Godin, when Vivienne was still missing,' said Beauvoir. 'And we have the phone records that led us to Gerald Bertrand.'

They went back over and over those conversations.

Tracey saying Vivienne was drunk and abusive.

Tracey claiming she was having affairs.

That she told him the baby wasn't his and that she was leaving him. That she'd gone off with some lover.

Tracey admitting to hitting her that Saturday night. And then going into his studio with a bottle, getting wasted, and passing out. When he woke up, she was gone.

'Okay,' said Zalmanowitz. 'That's his version of what happened. We know it's all bullshit. How did he seem to you, Armand, when you first spoke to him?'

Gamache thought back. It seemed months ago now, not mere days. 'Belligerent. Violent.'

He described the pitchfork and the shouts to get off the property.

'Not very cooperative,' said Zalmanowitz. 'The one good moment from a shitty day was the judge asking Tracey why he didn't want you to open the duffel bag, if he was so worried about his wife. It's a good question. A telling question. It must eat her up to have to release him. But you know, something's bothering me. After meeting Tracey and hearing more about him, I can understand him killing someone. What I don't understand is the method.'

'How so?' asked Gamache.

'Wouldn't you expect this fellow to do something stupid and brutal?'

'Throwing his pregnant wife off a bridge to be battered and drowned in a freezing river isn't brutal enough for you?' asked Lacoste.

Zalmanowitz regarded her. 'No. It's not. Given his history, I'd have expected something simpler. More hands-on. Beating her to death. Shooting her. Hitting her with a shovel and burying her. Why throw her off a bridge half a kilometer away?'

'Maybe it was Pauline Vachon's idea,' said Lacoste. 'She seems smart.'

'No messages to support that it was her idea?'

'Where she suggests throwing Vivienne off the bridge?' asked Lacoste. 'Yes, but we decided not to show you.'

For one brief moment, Zalmanowitz believed her, then lowered his brows.

'Of course there weren't,' said Lacoste. 'They must've come up with the plan when they were together. We've canvassed the neighbors. A few saw him entering her place last week. She says that was for business.'

'Right,' said the prosecutor. 'And even if there were explicit posts, describing it in detail, we couldn't use them, thanks to NouveauGalerie and that agent.'

'It wasn't her fault,' Lacoste repeated. 'Like I said, she ran it by me and I approved. Encouraged her, even. So lay off her.'

'Okay, sorry, you're right,' said Zalmanowitz. 'Back to the bridge. How did Tracey even get Vivienne there?'

'The coroner thinks the most likely explanation is that he beat her senseless at home, put her in the car, and drove her to the bridge,' said Beauvoir. 'Her blood on the car handle and steering wheel might've come from her blood on his hands.'

'But that doesn't explain his boot prints,' said the prosecutor. 'How would they get under the car if he drove her there?'

'Made when he was scouting the place, maybe,' said Beauvoir. 'We don't really know the details. And probably never will. Another possibility is that part of what Tracey said is true. Vivienne arranged to meet her lover on the bridge. Tracey overheard and got there first.'

'Okay,' said Lacoste. 'But then, what happened to the lover? And when did she call him? There were only five calls out of the house that day. Four to what we think is a wrong number and one to her father.'

'You said you believed Bertrand when he said he didn't know her,' said Gamache. 'Is it possible you were wrong?'

Lacoste considered. 'It's always possible.'

Gamache nodded, even as he recognized it for what it was. Desperation. But sometimes that uncovered something useful.

And they had precious little left to them except desperation.

'All right, let's walk through it,' said the prosecutor. 'Vivienne is afraid. She calls her father, telling him she's leaving her husband but has to choose her time. That evening Tracey beats her senseless, and then, either thinking she's dead or trying to work up the courage to finally kill her, he goes into his studio and gets drunk.'

'Then Vivienne regains consciousness and calls Bertrand, her lover,' said Beauvoir. 'Begging for help. Telling him to meet her on the bridge. But this Bertrand fellow doesn't show up. She was a fling to him, nothing more. He sure didn't want to get involved with a pregnant woman running from a dangerous husband.'

'Vivienne gets in the car and drives herself there,' said the prosecutor. 'Bertrand doesn't show, but Tracey does. He's waiting for her. He throws her off the bridge and tosses the bag in. The one he'd already packed, according to the posts.'

'There is another possibility,' said Gamache. They turned to him, and he sat forward. 'That Bertrand did show up.'

'Go on,' said Zalmanowitz.

'Suppose Tracey didn't pack the bag, but Vivienne did. Suppose she called Bertrand, telling him to meet her on the bridge.'

'Why there?' asked the prosecutor.

'Maybe that's where they always met,' said Gamache. 'She shows up and waits for him.'

As he spoke, the cold, dark April evening appeared before them. Vivienne Godin, bruised from Tracey's latest and last

beating, stands on the bridge. Bertrand's headlights appear down the disused dirt road. Little more than a path.

He gets out, and she tells him she's pregnant. Maybe even that the baby is his. She might have even believed it.

Tells him she's leaving her abusive husband and needs his help.

And then Bertrand snaps. Sees his frat-boy life changing completely. In panic, he pushes her backward. Into the railing. It breaks, and, to his horror, she falls.

Beauvoir, Lacoste, Zalmanowitz sat in silence, once again imagining Vivienne's face as she hung in the air between the bridge and the water. Then disappeared.

'To cover his tracks, he throws her bag in after her,' said Beauvoir.

'Or maybe she had it in her hand or over her shoulder,' said Lacoste. 'And it went in with her.'

'But what about Tracey's boot prints under Vivienne's car?' asked Zalmanowitz.

'Maybe they weren't Tracey's,' said Gamache. 'It's a pretty common boot. Monsieur Béliveau even sells it in his general store in Three Pines. And it's a standard size for a man. Ten.'

'Are you seriously suggesting that Carl Tracey did not kill his wife?' asked Zalmanowitz. 'But that this Gerald Bertrand did?'

'*Non*,' admitted Gamache. 'I'm just following possibilities. Things any defense would throw out there. I have no doubt that Tracey is the murderer, but there are questions.'

Zalmanowitz was quiet, lost in thought, then looked at Gamache again. 'Was he afraid?'

'I'm sorry?'

'Tracey. When you first went there to interview him about

his missing wife. You said he was belligerent. But did he seem nervous? Afraid?'

Gamache thought, then shook his head. 'No. Nor did he seem concerned that his wife was missing, as any normal husband would be.'

'Or any husband smart enough to pretend,' said Lacoste.

'We're just running in place,' said Zalmanowitz. 'Going back over crumbs and trying to assemble a banquet. The only thing we know for sure, besides that Vivienne was killed, is that she called her father that morning, then made four calls to what might, or might not, be a wrong number. Shit.'

He threw down his pen. 'All of this could've been avoided if she'd just asked her father to come get her. He's clearly the sort who could hold his own in a fight and would move heaven and earth to rescue her. And he sure wouldn't shy away from beating the shit out of her abusive husband. We saw that today.'

As Zalmanowitz spoke, he continued to look at Gamache.

'He reminds me a bit of you, Armand. You have a daughter about Vivienne's age, don't you?'

'Annie, *oui*.'

'What would you do if you knew her husband was abusing her?'

Armand raised his brows at Jean-Guy. Barry Zalmanowitz had obviously forgotten, or didn't know, that they were married.

'I think it's best if I didn't answer that.' Then he grew serious. 'What I can tell you is that Homer Godin confronted Tracey several times, but when it came down to it, Vivienne always intervened and denied abuse. It's not clear if she was trying to protect her husband or her father. Or, most likely, was afraid of another beating. Eventually Tracey isolated

her, as abusers often do, refusing to allow Homer to visit. Refusing to allow Vivienne to visit him.'

'In his statement, Tracey says it was Vivienne who didn't want to see her father,' said Zalmanowitz.

'That's clearly a lie,' said Beauvoir.

'Obviously, but there's no one except Homer to contradict him,' said Zalmanowitz. 'And unfortunately, any statement by him could be seen as colored by animus.'

'There is Lysette Cloutier,' said Lacoste.

'Who?' asked Zalmanowitz. 'Her name sounds familiar.'

'It would. She's the Sûreté agent who posed as NouveauGalerie,' said Lacoste. 'She's an old friend of the Godin family. It's because of her that we got onto Vivienne being missing. Homer had asked for her help.'

'They're friends?' asked Zalmanowitz.

'She was best friends with Homer's late wife,' Lacoste explained. 'They stayed in touch.'

'And she's Vivienne's godmother,' said Gamache. 'There seem to be feelings there, between Agent Cloutier and Monsieur Godin. At least on Cloutier's part. It's unclear how Homer feels.'

'Hmmm,' said Zalmanowitz. 'Might be worth seeing if she can add anything.'

'I think if she could've added something, she would've,' said Lacoste. 'But I'll ask.'

Again they all recognized it for what it was. Desperation.

'Any word from the hospital on Godin's condition?' Zalmanowitz asked.

'There's no concussion,' said Gamache. 'They're releasing him soon.'

'Good about the concussion thing, but now what? You know he'll try to—'

'Yes, we know,' said Beauvoir with a sigh. That seemed to be the only thing they did know. 'I've put an agent on Tracey. To protect him.'

He actually felt his stomach sour as he said it. But he also remembered what Tracey had said in the interview room while looking directly at Gamache.

'There's a restraining order on Godin, is that right?' asked Beauvoir. 'Keeping him away from Tracey.'

'Yes,' said Zalmanowitz. 'It was issued after that fracas in the courtroom.'

'I'd like one put on Carl Tracey as well,' said Beauvoir. 'Keeping him a distance from Godin and from Three Pines.'

'Three Pines? Your village, Armand?' Zalmanowitz had been taking notes. Now he looked up at the man.

'*Oui*,' said Gamache. 'I doubt he was serious, but he threatened my wife.'

'Really? Jesus, he is stupid. Is it enough to arrest him?'

'*Non*. It was vague,' said Gamache.

'He said he wouldn't kill his own wife, but someone else's …' said Beauvoir, using the same upward inflection Tracey had used. 'He was looking at Monsieur Gamache as he spoke.'

'I see. I'll apply for a restraining order against Tracey.' Zalmanowitz made a note. 'But we all know if someone really wants to do harm, a piece of paper won't stop them.'

But a baseball bat … thought Gamache.

'I take it Godin will be returning home?' said Zalmanowitz.

'I've asked the agents to bring him back to Three Pines,' said Gamache. 'He can stay with us.'

'And if he doesn't want to? You can't force him, Armand,' said Zalmanowitz.

'Since when was it against the law to imprison another

human being?' asked Armand. 'Oh, wait. I do remember something from my training.'

Lacoste laughed, and Zalmanowitz smiled.

'Okay, I get it. You know what you're doing. But you can't keep him there, even with his consent, forever. He'll want to leave eventually. And I doubt time will blunt his desire to kill the man who killed his daughter.'

'I doubt it, too,' said Gamache. He took a deep breath, then sighed. 'I'd hate to have to arrest him for that.'

'And I'd hate to have to prosecute him,' said Zalmanowitz.

'What would he get?' asked Beauvoir. 'Out of interest's sake.'

The prosecutor thought about that. 'He'd be charged with murder. His defense would probably say that he was not criminally responsible. Diminished capacity, brought on by extreme grief. If they're smart, his lawyers will try the case in front of a jury. He'd be convicted, probably of manslaughter, but wouldn't serve much time. A year, probably less. Maybe time served.'

'That's not so bad,' said Beauvoir.

Gamache was staring at him. He wasn't considering taking the protection away from Tracey? Leaving the path clear for Godin to kill the man.

Surely Jean-Guy's last act as head of homicide would not be as an accessory to a homicide.

They'd have to talk.

Chief Inspector Beauvoir looked at Lacoste, then over to Gamache. And finally back to the prosecutor.

'We don't have enough evidence, untainted by the poisonous tree or the social-media fiasco, to convict Tracey. Do we.'

'No,' said Zalmanowitz. 'Not even close. Unless you can find something else, we're screwed.'

'And Carl Tracey gets away with murder,' said Lacoste.

Beauvoir got up, and the others rose. '*Merci*. I'm sorry about this.'

'So'm I. I'll put in the appeals. Even Judge Pelletier asked me to. She feels awful about it. I think she's more than half hoping she'll be overturned.'

He walked them to the door and shook their hands. When it came to Gamache, he leaned in and whispered, 'I'm sorry about the videos. Shitty day. I don't know if dumbass has done you a favor or not. Releasing the real video.'

'I know the answer to that,' said Gamache.

Zalmanowitz nodded. 'There is one more thing, Armand.'

'*Oui?*'

'Did you steal Tracey's dog?'

Now both Beauvoir and Lacoste turned and stared, first at the prosecutor, then at Gamache.

'I took Fred, yes. But I paid Tracey for him.'

'Apparently not enough. He wants the dog back. He's filed a complaint.'

'You stole the dog?' Beauvoir asked. 'I thought he came with Homer.'

'No. He was Vivienne's dog. Tracey was going to shoot him, so I took him. And I'm not giving him back.'

On this day of blurred boundaries, one clear line had to be drawn, and it seemed to have been drawn at the dog. They couldn't save Vivienne, they might not even be able to save Homer. But they could save Fred.

Barry Zalmanowitz stared at Gamache, then nodded. 'I'll take care of it. Don't worry.'

'*Merci.*'

Now the prosecutor watched as the three of them, Gamache flanked by the two younger officers, walked down the corridor.

And he remembered the images on the real video. Gamache, amid ferocious gunfire, dragging a critically wounded Beauvoir to safety. Stanching the wound. Then having to leave him there and head back into the battle.

Then, later in the tape, Isabelle Lacoste was seen kneeling beside Gamache, holding his bloody hand as he lay, apparently dying, on the factory floor. Shot in the head and chest.

Now the three of them walked down the corridor, their feet echoing along a bright marble hall that hid so much stench below.

And while the prosecutor didn't envy Armand Gamache anything about what was happening, with the case and with the social-media attacks, he did envy him this.

He watched until the three of them walked out the huge double doors and disappeared into the crisp April day.

Once hit by the cold air, Beauvoir, as though slapped awake from a reverie, began to talk.

'I'm not going out like this.'

'What do you suggest we do?' asked Lacoste.

'We head back to the incident room in Three Pines and go over the evidence we can use. Again and again. Until we find something we missed. There has to be something else there. Isabelle, I know you're still officially on leave, but—

'I have an overnight bag in the car, all ready to go,' she said with a grin. 'Old habits, right, *patron*?'

Gamache smiled. Old habits. Always being prepared to head out at a moment's notice.

'I have to get back to headquarters,' she said. 'I'll meet you down in Three Pines when I've finished.'

Gamache and Beauvoir paused by their cars.

'How're you going to keep Homer at your place?'

'Helps that he won't have his own car, and I'll ask the others to stay with him.'

'He'll walk there if he has to, Armand.'

'*Oui*,' said Gamache. 'But he needs help, and I don't know what else to do, Jean-Guy. Do you?'

He was genuinely asking. But Jean-Guy Beauvoir had no answer.

As he drove down the familiar highway, Chief Inspector Beauvoir hoped and prayed they'd find something they'd overlooked.

Something.

Anything.

CHAPTER 32

—

Gamache was in his car, following Beauvoir and talking with Reine-Marie on the phone, explaining, or trying to explain, what had happened in court.

'Homer?' she asked. 'How is he?'

Armand paused, unsure how to answer that.

Out of his mind with grief and pain and rage?

Incensed that a system that called itself 'just' would allow his daughter's murderer to go free? On a technicality. Or two.

Inconsolable? Working out how to punish Carl Tracey himself?

Instead Armand gave the only answer he knew for sure. 'There's no concussion. He can go home. But do you mind—'

'If he stays with us? Of course not. But—'

'Will we be able to keep him from Tracey?' said Armand. 'I don't know. Can you hold on for a moment?'

Agent Cloutier was calling.

'Chief Inspector? We have a problem.' She was whispering, urgency in her voice.

'What is it?'

'We're still at the hospital. They're just releasing him, but he won't come back to your place.'

'He wants to go home?'

'Yes, but mostly he says ...' Her voice faltered.

'Go on.' Though Gamache suspected he knew what she was about to say.

'He says he never wants to lay eyes on you again.'

'I see.' Gamache took a breath.

He did see. It wasn't just that Tracey had walked free. That somehow the investigators had screwed up. It was that he'd broken his promise to Homer.

'Give him the phone, please.'

There was a pause. 'He won't take it.'

'Then hold it up to his ear.'

He knew he had seconds to get through to the man. Only one word, two at most, before Homer would pull away. He had one shot. And he took it.

'Fred.'

Pause. Pause.

There was a rustling of the phone, some muffled conversation, then Cloutier's voice. 'He'll come. But just to get the dog. He won't stay.'

'Tell him I'm asking for one night. Just one. Then he can take Fred and go.'

There was more muffled conversation.

Come on. Come on.

Finally, Cloutier's voice. 'One night, *patron.*'

'*Bon.*'

It was something. Twenty-four hours he didn't have before.

'I'll be in the incident room,' said Gamache. 'Let me know when you get to Three Pines.'

'*D'accord, patron.*'

He hung up and went back to Reine-Marie. And explained what had just happened.

'And you? Are you all right?' she asked.

How could he answer that?

'Never mind,' she said. 'I know. Come home soon.'

'We're not far. Should be there in—'

'What is it, Armand?'

In the car ahead of him, Jean-Guy had put on the brakes and swerved, taking a dirt road off to the right.

They were almost at Three Pines. But now Jean-Guy was heading away from the village. At speed. Recklessly bumping along the washboard road.

The agent guarding Tracey had just reported that instead of going straight home, as he'd been advised to do after being discharged, Tracey had headed to his local bar.

To celebrate.

'What do you want me to do, *patron*?' the agent asked. 'Should I go in?'

'No, stay where you are. I'm coming to you.'

Jean-Guy knew he shouldn't, but still he did. He turned the car and now was gunning it toward Carl Tracey.

Beauvoir pulled in to the parking lot of the dive bar and parked beside the very well-marked Sûreté vehicle.

Normally, when doing surveillance, they wanted to be discreet.

But Beauvoir had specifically asked for a vehicle with 'Sûreté du Québec' clearly marked. 'In neon if possible,' he'd said. 'And I want the agent in uniform.'

Tracey needed to be in no doubt that he was being not just guarded but watched.

As Beauvoir walked toward the bar, his hands flexed into tight fists, then opened. Then closed again. Into weapons.

Jean-Guy knew this was a mistake. The issue wasn't whether he was about to step into a pile of something soft

and smelly. That much was obvious. The only question was, how big would it be? How deep would he go?

And could he stop himself before . . . ?

Chief Inspector Beauvoir walked right past the agent sitting in the car and said only two words.

'Stay here.'

He heard a car pull in to the parking lot. As he reached the door to the bar, his hand on the knob, he heard the familiar voice behind him.

'Jean-Guy.'

But for one of the few times in his life, Beauvoir chose to ignore Gamache.

'Stay here,' said Chief Inspector Gamache as he strode by the agent who was beginning to get out of the car.

She stayed.

Beauvoir stepped into the bar.

It was dark. Smelled of stale cigarettes and fresh urine and flat beer.

A television was on, showing an *Andy Griffith* rerun. Opie had questions for his father. Again. But the answers were drowned out by the burst of laughter from a group of grubby men at the bar.

Four of them, Beauvoir saw immediately. No, five.

Two bottles of rye on the bar. Beer bottles clasped in hands, the men turned and squinted into the unexpected and unwanted light through the open door before it swung shut.

'Who the fuck are you?' one of them demanded.

Beauvoir didn't answer. He just stood there. Staring.

At Carl Tracey.

'Wait a minute,' said Tracey. 'A little respect, please. This's

Chief Inspector Beauvoir. The guy who arrested me. Come to apologize?'

That brought more laughter.

Beauvoir did not react. Did not speak. Did not move.

Tracey lifted his beer. 'Come on in. Jean-Guy, isn't it? Now that it's over, we can be friends. No hard feelings. Beer?'

He held the drink out toward Beauvoir, who could smell the musky, familiar aroma.

Gamache had stopped at the door. Through the dirt-smeared window, he was just able to make out the occupants of the bar.

Every cell in his body was straining forward. Demanding that he go in. To rescue Jean-Guy, from himself.

He was pretty sure, judging by the look on Beauvoir's face, that the head of homicide for the Sûreté du Québec was about to beat the crap out of Carl Tracey.

Maybe worse. Maybe he wouldn't stop at the crap.

But still, Gamache stopped himself. And he wondered why.

Then the thought appeared. Was it possible he wanted Beauvoir to do it?

Jean-Guy Beauvoir stood ten paces from Carl Tracey.

He stared but didn't move. Didn't speak. Didn't react at all.

Even when Tracey stepped toward him, goaded on by his drinking buddies, Jean-Guy's face remained completely impassive. A mask.

Gamache's expression changed. He was still watchful, vigilant. Prepared. His hand on the door. But now there was a very small smile. Of surprise and recognition.

Still, he remained prepared to act.

*

Watching Tracey laughing, Beauvoir felt himself almost overcome with rage.

But still he stood. Still.

'Come on,' Tracey shouted, holding his beer by the neck and swaying slightly. 'You're not joining in the celebrations.'

But the men behind Tracey were growing uneasy in the face of this relentlessly still man at the door.

A couple continued to shout encouragement, but their voices were thinning. Their enthusiasm waning.

Carl Tracey was right up against Beauvoir now. But Beauvoir didn't react.

'Why're you here?' shouted Tracey. 'I'm going to file a complaint. This's harassment.'

Beauvoir's silence. His blank stare. Were driving Carl Tracey mad. And his friends away.

⸺

Gamache's smile had disappeared, and he prepared to enter the bar. Enough was enough.

Tracey staggered back.

His drinking buddies moved away and watched as he tripped and fell to the floor. Spilling his beer.

As silently as he'd entered, Chief Inspector Beauvoir left. Leaving behind four drunks staring down at the man wallowing on the floor. Tracey's eyes lifted, and for a split second as he turned, Beauvoir thought he saw sadness there. Sorrow.

And then Carl Tracey threw up.

Once outside, Jean-Guy closed his eyes and, turning his face to the sky, took a long, long breath of the fresh, pine-scented air.

When he opened them, he saw Armand Gamache standing right in front of him. Staring.

Then Gamache's eyes crinkled at the corners. Wordlessly, because there was nothing to say, Gamache walked him back to his car, pausing for Beauvoir to speak to the agent.

'I'm going to get another officer here. I want one of you to stay in the vehicle and the other to stand outside the bar. Look through the window at Carl Tracey. So that he can see you. Whatever happens, don't engage him. If he comes to you, don't react. Only if he physically attacks you.'

'So you want me to just stare at him, *patron*?'

'Yes. And when he leaves, follow him. Always keeping a distance. But I want him to see you. Understand? If he goes into a shop, stand outside and stare. If he meets someone, stop and—'

'Continue to stare?'

'*Oui.*'

'Why?'

Beauvoir bristled slightly. Not liking being questioned. But he knew his orders were unconventional in the extreme.

'This's a man who understand threats and violence. But this?'

'But what is "this"?' the young agent persisted.

'A conscience.'

'Huh?'

Chief Inspector Beauvoir recognized the expression on the agent's face. It was exactly the same look he'd given Gamache. For years. When the Chief Inspector had said, or ordered, something unconventional. Or downright odd.

That blank stare, colored slightly by concern that the senior officer had lost his mind.

Beauvoir now smiled. In the same way Gamache had smiled at him. For years.

While he could have simply left it at that, he wanted the agent to understand. And to never be afraid to question the orders of a superior.

As Gamache had patiently explained things to Beauvoir. For years.

'Your job is to protect the man, but you will also act as a sort of external conscience for a man who obviously doesn't have one.'

He could see it dawning on her. And she, too, smiled. 'Got it. I'll be the ghost of his dead wife.'

'*Oui*. That's a good way of looking at it.'

For a brief moment the agent considered asking if she could take a selfie with Chief Inspector Beauvoir and Chief Inspector Gamache.

But wisely decided against it.

As they walked to their cars, Armand Gamache placed a hand on Jean-Guy's back.

'Well done.'

'It was close,' said Jean-Guy, leaning toward him and lowering his voice. 'You have no idea how much I wanted to—'

'I know.'

Jean-Guy grunted. 'Yes. You do.' He looked behind him. 'It won't change anything. This …' He waved toward the agent now standing outside the bar. Staring. '… won't make him confess. Not to murder.'

'No. But it might make that young agent realize there're other weapons at our disposal besides our guns.'

Gamache tapped his temple.

'Honestly? I suspect she thinks it's more …' Beauvoir raised his finger to his own temple and twirled it in a circle. 'Thank God I told her I'm Chief Inspector Gamache.'

Now Armand did laugh. 'I am going to miss you, old son.'

'And I'm going to miss you, too, sir. But I won't miss this.'

He gazed at the fresh young agent standing straight and tall, twenty feet away from the cruddy bar.

Staring.

At a man Chief Inspector Beauvoir, as lead investigator, had let get away with murder.

Jean-Guy did not need anyone staring at him to know that it would be a long time, if ever, before his own conscience was clear.

CHAPTER 33

⌒

They spent the balance of the day in the incident room going back over all the evidence. Over and over.

Starting with what little was still admissible, then moving on to what they knew to be true but couldn't use.

Homer Godin returned to Three Pines, and according to Reine-Marie, after quietly walking Fred around the village green and being offered and declining food, he went into his room and closed the door.

Agent Cloutier stayed in the house, checking on him every now and then, to make sure. . . .

As Armand talked to Reine-Marie on the phone, he looked through what had once been the ticket window. He could see the bridge over the Rivière Bella Bella, the sandbags still in place. And beyond that, his home on the far side of the village green.

Between him and his home was a stranger, sitting on the bench.

'Who's that?' he asked Reine-Marie.

'Dominica Oddly.'

Reine-Marie explained who she was and why she was there.

Gamache grimaced. Seemed Clara was having a day to rival his own. Both thanks, in no small part, to Ruth.

He turned and looked up at the photo of the old poet, glaring down at him.

When he hung up, Armand rubbed his eyes. Then, putting his reading glasses back on, he returned to the statements. Trying to find something.

Anything.

Isabelle Lacoste arrived. She barely had her coat off when Jean-Guy handed her a bunch of files.

'Here. You take these.'

They divvied up the evidence, the interviews. Going over one another's work. Fresh eyes on old evidence. Looking for something overlooked.

'I'd like to speak to Monsieur Bertrand,' said Gamache, getting up.

It still struck Gamache as unlikely that Vivienne would call this man again and again on the day she died, and its being a wrong number.

Surely she knew him. Surely he's lying.

'So would I,' said Beauvoir, putting on his coat.

Gerald Bertrand was cordial. Young. Attractive. Holding his baby niece in his arms. He was apparently eager to help, but with nothing helpful to add.

Gamache tried. This way. That. He prodded, looking for holes. For chinks. For hairline fractures in Bertrand's story. In his demeanor. But found nothing.

They came away just as convinced as Lacoste. Bertrand was telling the truth. He did not know Vivienne. Or Tracey.

'Tracey lied, of course,' said Beauvoir. 'Vivienne didn't have a lover.'

'At least,' said Gamache, 'not this lover.'

Still, Vivienne Godin had spent the last few minutes of her life doing one thing.

Reaching out to one person.

But who was it? Who did a desperate, terrified woman call for help?

Not her father – he was too far away, thought Gamache. Was she trying Cameron?

But there was someone else in the picture. Someone who'd been in Vivienne's life, all her life. Her godmother. Who was, after all, a woman and a cop.

On the way back, they stopped at Pauline Vachon's place. Her signed statement had implicated Carl Tracey, but not herself. Now the investigators wanted the whole truth.

'Did I want her gone?' Pauline said. 'Yes, for sure.'

'Why?'

'So I could have Carl.'

'You don't seem to even like him,' said Beauvoir.

'I did at first. I like older men.' She leered at Gamache.

'And after that?'

'Well, there'd be money, right? If she divorced him, he'd lose money, probably lose the house. But if she died . . .'

'Yes?'

'Well, there'd be an inheritance. There's always money when someone dies.'

'Not always,' said Beauvoir.

Jesus, he thought. Vivienne was killed for money she didn't have?

'Why didn't you tell the other investigators this?' he asked.

'What? That there might be a reason I'd want her dead? Let's guess. . . .'

'Then why tell us now?' asked Beauvoir.

'Well, it doesn't matter now. My lawyer says you can't touch me. Besides, Carl did it, not me.'

Gamache considered her so closely she began to fidget.

'I'm not going to confess, you know,' she said. 'So you might as well leave.'

She got up, and they followed her to the front door. As she held it open, Gamache tried one more time.

'Tell us what happened that day, Pauline. For her father's sake. For yours. Get it off your chest.'

'Oh, you're interested in my chest, are you?' she said, in a way that was so artless it made her seem very young. 'And as for her father . . .' She made a rude, dismissive noise. 'Have you asked yourself why she'd marry a shithead like Carl Tracey?'

'You were going to marry him.'

'I was going to live with him.'

'Until the money ran out?' asked Beauvoir.

'Fuck you. This's none of your business. Now, get out.'

'He lied to you. And he killed his wife,' said Gamache. 'We saw the photos. Those bruises on your arms.'

'I like it rough.' Again she leered at Gamache, who just stared back. In a way that made her uncomfortable. Not because it was sexual but because it was a look she couldn't remember ever seeing before. It took her a moment to put a word to it.

Concerned. This man was concerned for her.

But she knew it was a lie. An act. No one had cared before. Why would this stranger?

'No happy person,' he said quietly, 'no healthy person, seeks out pain. Be careful.'

'Yeah, well, what the fuck do you care?'

And the door slammed shut in his face.

'Well, that was a waste of time,' said Beauvoir. 'But had to be done.'

As they walked to the car, Gamache thought about the look on Pauline Vachon's face. That leer. Meant to be seductive, but there was, at its core, something cruel. Definitely something calculating. Though, just for a moment ... And then it was gone.

'Homer?'

The voice of the elderly woman penetrated the closed door as Homer lay on the bed, staring at the ceiling. Working out how ... Fortunately, there was no thought of trying to get away with it. No need.

He didn't answer.

'It's Ruth Zardo. We met at Clara's home the other night. I know you're there and can hear me. There's something I want to say to you.'

What he heard then was a very soft murmur. It sounded like *fuck*, *fuck*.

He sat up in bed but didn't open the door. He had no desire for company.

Undaunted, Ruth said her piece, then left.

'There,' said Isabelle Lacoste, dropping a pair of boots at Beauvoir's feet with a thud.

'Been shoe shopping?' he asked, picking them up.

He'd left Gamache at his home and returned to the incident room. Now he held the boots at arm's length, examining them.

They were olive green. Rubber. Lined with felt. And came up to the knees.

'A going-away gift for Paris?' he asked. 'Too kind, my little cabbage.'

'More of that and you'll find them up your ass.'

'Should the new head of organized crime be talking like that?' He smiled at her. 'Congratulations. I've heard from other senior officers that you accepted the job.'

'Not quite yet,' she said. 'Have to talk to my family. And you do know I won't actually be heading up a crime family, right?'

'*Merde*, I thought we'd be getting free appliances for life.'

'Silly man. Free cheese, maybe.' She took a seat at her desk. 'About the boots, I got them from Monsieur Béliveau's general store. The Chief was right. According to Monsieur Béliveau, those're the most common boot he sells. Everyone has a pair.'

'And why wouldn't they? Very stylish.' Beauvoir dropped them to the floor. 'Same ones as Tracey has, right?'

'Right. Same boots that made the print under Vivienne's car. Same size. Ten. Even Chief Inspector Gamache has a pair.'

'Are you suggesting he's a suspect?'

'Yes, yes I am,' she said with a patient smile. 'You know what I'm saying.'

Jean-Guy did know. He picked up the boots again and examined them.

She was right, of course.

They were exactly like the ones that had made the boot prints under Vivienne's car. Like the ones they'd found in Tracey's home and used for evidence. Evidence now deemed poisonous fruit.

And, apparently, like the footwear everyone in rural Québec owned.

'I put them on,' Lacoste said, 'and walked around in the snow and mud. Took pictures of the prints I made. The strange thing is, while those're size-ten men's, my feet are size seven.'

'Women's.'

'Thank you. Yes. But because the rubber sole is so thick and the treads so deeply stamped, my boot prints look exactly like the ones under the car.'

'Exactly?' He turned the boots over. The treads were made from tough rubber, designed to insulate and grip. And not to wear down. So that the tread of a five-year-old boot would not be much different, if at all, from that of a brand-new one.

'I sent the pictures to the lab, and they'll analyze them, but I couldn't see a difference.'

'So—'

'So anyone could've made those boot prints under her car. A man, a woman – a child, even, I suppose.'

'This isn't getting us closer to Tracey,' he said. 'In fact, you're making the defense's case, if a case was still needed.'

'I know,' she said.

It didn't have to have been a large man on that bridge. It could have been a smaller woman. And now that Beauvoir thought about it, the coroner had said that those handprints on Vivienne's chest, bruises made in a shove, probably were made by a large man.

But –

The coroner also pointed out that bruises bleed. Spread internally. Dr Harris had left the possibility open that they, too, could have been made by a smaller woman.

'Pauline Vachon?' he asked.

Lacoste nodded.

Lysette Cloutier got to her feet when Chief Inspector Gamache entered the kitchen.

Homer and Reine-Marie sat in front of the woodstove,

a pot of tea and some shortbread cookies on a tray on the hassock between them.

Fred lay on the rug at Homer's feet, barely raising his head to look at the man who'd just come in.

Henri and Gracie had run to the door to greet him and now chased each other into the kitchen, getting between Armand's legs, almost tripping him up. But he was used to it.

Homer stared down at his large hands, which gripped each other tightly.

Then he got up slowly and turned to Armand. There was a bandage on the left side of his head, above his temple, where he'd hit the floor of the courtroom, knocking himself out. He had a black eye and bruising into his hairline.

His face, as he faced Armand, was impassive. A mask.

He just stood. And stared. And stared.

And then, silently, he moved. Brushing past Armand.

'Homer?' said Armand.

But the man had left the warm kitchen. There was a whistle from the living room. Fred lifted his head, struggled to his feet, and followed the sound.

'Please stay here,' said Armand to the others.

Homer was on the front porch with the old dog.

It was five in the afternoon, and the shadows were long. The temperature was dropping with the sun.

Woodsmoke rose from the homes, slightly scenting the chilly early-evening air.

Armand held the door open, and, at a nod, out shot Henri, followed by Gracie, who was looking, and behaving, more and more like a chipmunk every day.

They caught up with Homer and Fred, who were walking with a measured pace along the edge of the village green. Neither in nor out of the circle.

Lights were on in homes around Three Pines, and Armand could see the glow from the old railway station across the still-swollen river and knew that Jean-Guy and Isabelle were in there, working to solve a crime that seemed to be getting away from them.

Then he turned to the grizzled man, walking through the twilight.

'I'm sorry,' he said as he fell in beside Homer, keeping slow pace with him.

But Homer didn't reply. Just stared ahead, at the hills and forests growing darker and darker around them.

At the path into the woods, which followed the Rivière Bella Bella and went to the place where Vivienne was found, Homer stopped. It was now little more than a slightly darker opening in a dark forest.

Then he turned and looked in the opposite direction. Upriver. Where Vivienne had first gone into the water. Where she'd last been alive.

His breath came out in warm, soft puffs. Joining, mingling with Armand's.

'What do you want from me, Armand?'

'Nothing.'

'That's not true. I can see it in your eyes.' He turned to face him. 'What is it? Forgiveness? You want me to say it's okay that you messed up? That I now have to do what you couldn't? Get justice for my little girl.'

Armand was quiet. And he thought maybe Homer was right.

He wanted to be absolved of his guilt.

Vivienne's father was quiet for a long time, his eyes returning to the river. Before he finally spoke.

'Is it possible some things can't be forgiven? They're

just too terrible? Abuse? Murder?' He looked at Armand. 'Could you?'

'Forgive murder?' asked Armand. He thought about it. He was being asked to consider the murder not of a stranger but of his wife. His child. His grandchild. Could he forgive? Sincerely. 'It would take years and a huge amount of work. And help. And still . . .'

'Yes?'

'I hope I'd get there—'

'But?'

'But I think it would take a better person than I am,' admitted Armand.

Homer deserved the truth. And there it was. Could he forgive? In his heart, in his soul? Armand was far from sure.

'Would it help if whoever did it was genuinely sorry?' asked Homer. He searched Armand's eyes.

'Yeeesss, I think it would.'

Homer nodded. 'I wonder if Vivienne believed it.'

'You think Tracey said he was sorry?'

Armand doubted that Tracey would ever have apologized, but maybe he had. Abusers often did. They begged forgiveness. Declared their love. They brought flowers and gifts, and through a flood of tears they promised to never, ever do it again.

And maybe they were even sincere. Until the next time.

'You don't have to forgive him,' said Armand. 'You don't have to forgive me. But for your own sake, for your own sanity, you do need to give up this obsession with revenge.'

'Have you given up?'

'Trying to get Tracey? *Non*.'

'Then why should I? Does your badge give you more of a duty to Vivienne than I have, as her father?' He let that sit

there for a moment before going on. 'That old woman came to your house to see me this afternoon. I didn't let her into my room. Didn't want to see anyone. But she said something anyway, through the door.'

'What old lady?'

'I think she's a poet.'

Armand tensed. Had Ruth done to Homer what she'd done to Clara? To himself? In trying to help, had she made things worse?

'What did she say?' Armand braced.

'Something from St. Francis. Something he said to a woman who'd lost her child in a river.' Homer closed his eyes. *'Clare, Clare, do not despair. Between the bridge and the water, I was there.'*

CHAPTER 34

'N*on*, nothing new,' Jean-Guy reported over the phone to Gamache, who was calling from his study at home. 'The warrant we applied for a couple days ago to look into Vivienne's bank accounts should come through soon. We'll see if Pauline Vachon was dreaming or if there really is something there.'

'That number Vivienne was calling is still bothering me,' said Gamache. 'If it wasn't Bertrand's, then whose? Is there anyone related to the case with a number close to it?'

'I've checked that,' said Beauvoir. 'Nothing.'

Gamache smiled. He should have known Beauvoir would be on top of that.

'You must be hungry,' he said. 'Clara's invited us over for an easy dinner. Let's take a break.'

Beauvoir sighed and looked over at Lacoste.

She'd taken her regular room at the B&B but hadn't yet dropped her bag there.

'Dinner at Clara's?' he called across the room.

'Sounds great.' But she didn't look up.

They were chasing their tails, and they knew it. A break would do them good.

'We'll meet you there,' he said into the phone. 'Another half hour.'

Jean-Guy picked up the statements again. And started reading. Again.

———

Gamache hung up and turned to Agent Cloutier.

They were alone in his study.

Homer was in the kitchen with Fred, as Reine-Marie prepared a squash, pear, and blue cheese soup to take to Clara's. Homer seemed to find her company restful.

Cloutier, on the other hand, clearly did not feel the same way about Monsieur Gamache's company.

'Tell me about Vivienne.'

'Vivienne?'

'Yes. You must've known her well.'

'I suppose so. To be honest, I wasn't the best godmother. I never had one, so I had no idea what was expected, except that if anything happened to Kathy and Homer, I was to take her.'

'What was she like?'

Lysette thought about it. 'Shy. A little hard to get to know. Bit of a homebody. She was a beautiful girl. You can see that in the pictures.'

Gamache nodded. 'Was she nice?'

'I suppose.'

But there was reservation there.

'Go on.'

'No, it's just that Kath found her difficult at times. I guess most mothers and daughters fight sometimes.'

'Do you mean fight? Or argue?' Gamache asked.

'Argue,' said Cloutier. 'You don't think Kathy actually hit her?'

Gamache raised his hands. 'I have no idea what happened in that home. That's why I'm asking you.'

'They argued. Quite a lot. But just words, nothing more. Like I said, that's natural, isn't it? Between mother and daughter. I sure did with my mother.'

Gamache nodded, remembering the foot stomping and dramatics from Annie and Reine-Marie's narrowed eyes and tightly clamped jaw. Trying not to say something mean that she didn't really mean.

Though Annie had no such qualms or restraint.

But now Annie and her mother were very close. Annie was a mother herself. He suspected that helped. With another child on the way. A girl.

Like Vivienne –

He brought his mind back to the job at hand.

'In what way did she find Vivienne difficult?'

'I actually don't think it was Vivienne's fault.' Lysette dropped her voice. 'I think Kath was a little jealous of her.'

'Why?'

'Vivienne and her father were always close. From the moment she was born. Homer adored both his girls, as he called them. But there was a bond between him and Viv. Fathers and daughters, I suppose.'

'Yes,' said Gamache. Annie. Annie. Healthy and happy. And alive. And leaving . . .

'It was hard on Kathy. She didn't help herself, though. The more jealous she got, the angrier and more demanding she got. It just pushed Vivienne even further away.'

'And toward her father.'

'*Oui.*'

A self-fulfilling prophecy, thought Gamache. How often we made our worst fears come true, by behaving as though they already were.

'He took her to soccer practice,' said Cloutier. 'Coached her hockey team. When she was a child, he'd read to her at bedtime. Babar. Tintin. I've never seen a daughter more loved by a father, or a father more adored. I felt bad for Kathy. To be honest, I was never sure if she was jealous of Vivienne or Homer. But I do know that Vivienne left home as soon as she could.'

'Pushed out by her mother?'

Lysette nodded. 'And then Kathy died. It makes this even worse for Homer. Not having Kathy here to turn to.'

'Was it a happy marriage?'

Lysette thought. Finally nodding. 'It got better once Vivienne was out of the house.'

'When we visited Pauline Vachon this afternoon, she said if Vivienne died, Carl would come into money. We're checking out accounts and insurance, of course, but do you know if Vivienne had any money of her own?'

'Vivienne? I don't think so.'

'Did her mother leave her anything in her will?'

'No. She left some jewelry and a comforter that came from her grandmother, but no money. I was a liquidator. She didn't have much, and what she had, she left to Homer. Do you mind my asking why you want to know all this? We know who killed her – we just have to get him.'

'We have to regroup,' Gamache explained. 'And part of that is getting to know Vivienne better. Is it likely she was having an affair?'

'I know what Tracey said, but I can't see that happening. She always seemed more a loner, really.'

'Did you like her?'

Cloutier frowned. 'What little I saw, yes. I guess.'

It was not exactly a ringing endorsement. But then, Gamache suspected that Cloutier's opinions were affected, perhaps even infected, by what her friend Kathy had said. It was all too easy, Gamache knew, to believe the worst of others.

He thought for a moment. 'Why do you think she married Carl Tracey?'

Cloutier considered. 'Small community. Not much choice. She probably thought he was the best she could do. Maybe he wasn't so bad at first. I don't really know.'

Gamache nodded.

Could there have been love there once? Or was Vivienne punishing her parents? Look what you made me do. Or was it a childish attempt to make her father jealous?

Everyone made mistakes. Gamache had made his fair share, especially when young. Annie had married and divorced before finding Jean-Guy. As had Jean-Guy, before finding Annie.

Vivienne's mistake just happened to be far worse than she could have planned or imagined.

They'd come to the end of what Agent Cloutier could tell him about Vivienne. Though there was one more thing.

'Did she like dogs?'

'*Pardon?*'

'Dogs. Did she like them?'

'Well, yeah. Loved them. Look at Fred. She rescued him as a puppy. Found him hurt on the road. He's been with her a lot longer than Carl.'

'*Merci,*' he said.

CHAPTER 36

'Chief Inspector and Madame Gamache, this,' said Clara, with a slightly manic flourish, as though producing the dinner guest out of thin air, 'is the famous art critic Dominica Oddly.'

Ta-da.

Then poof, Clara disappeared.

'Madame Oddly,' said Armand, shaking her hand.

'Chief Inspector?' said the critic.

'Armand.'

'Of the Sûreté? Sounds like some old Nelson Eddy/Jeanette MacDonald movie. *Gamache of the Sûreté.*'

Armand smiled. 'That was the Mounties. No horse, I'm afraid.'

'And yet quite a lot of horseshit,' said Ruth, joining them.

Dominica's eyes flickered to the duck in Ruth's arms, then back up to the elderly woman's face. Choosing to ignore the fowl, she said, 'I didn't mention before that I like your poetry.'

'Thank you. Her name's Rosa.'

'Fuck, fuck, fuck,' said Rosa.

'Poetry,' Reine-Marie whispered in Ruth's ear. 'Not poultry.'

'Oh.' She turned back to Dominica, looking her up and down. 'Are you related to the maid?'

Reine-Marie dropped her eyes, and Armand gazed around as though he'd never met the old woman before.

'Maid?' asked Dominica.

When Ruth began to point toward Myrna, who was talking with Clara by the fireplace, Reine-Marie jumped in. 'How could you possibly know about Nelson Eddy?'

'I love classic cinema,' explained Dominica. 'When the art form was just beginning.'

'And you'd consider *Rose-Marie* a classic?' asked Ruth. 'I suspected you had no taste. That's why I thought you'd like Clara's art.'

Dominica laughed. 'But I like your poetry. And your poultry.'

'An aberration. The exception that proves the rule.'

'Not a rule,' the critic pointed out. 'An opinion.'

Dominica Oddly hadn't yet decided if the people who chose to live in this small Canadian hamlet were wonderful and creative or simply inbred.

'Beer?' asked Gabri, bringing a bottle over to Dominica. She'd left the group and was looking around.

'Thank you. Is the duck okay? She looks strange.'

'Oh, the duck's okay. It's the fuck who's strange.'

Dominica laughed. 'But a great poet.'

'And Clara's a great artist.'

To that, Dominica just raised her bottle. 'Thanks for the beer.'

Across the room, Clara was trying to keep the smile on her face and the bile down as she watched the young woman, who'd just destroyed her career and was now drinking her

beer and eating her food. She wouldn't be surprised if she found this young woman sleeping in her bed.

The wolf, not at her door but in her home. In her life. And tearing it apart. With a smile.

Jean-Guy and Isabelle joined them in time for dinner.

Jean-Guy had spied Ruth and begun walking toward her when Armand headed him off.

'Don't.'

'But she needs to be told,' said Jean-Guy, watching the old poet swig scotch and talk with the critic, who seemed fascinated by her.

'Told what?'

'That the video she posted has hurt people. You. The families.' He paused. 'Me. That she had no business doing that.'

'She did it out of kindness. She thought she was protecting me.'

'That doesn't change anything. She should never have done it.'

'I agree. But it's done now. Let it go, Jean-Guy.'

Still, as Jean-Guy passed Ruth, he whispered, 'Dumb-ass.'

'Numbnuts,' she replied with a laugh. Clearly not understanding his message.

Armand was tired and wouldn't normally have accepted Clara's invitation. But he knew that Homer didn't want to see him. Didn't even want to know he was in the same house. And he'd promised the man time alone. This was one promise he could keep.

So they'd come here and left Homer and Lysette to have dinner by themselves.

Everyone at Clara's had heard what had happened in court

that day, though only Ruth had asked about it. If asking how they'd managed to make a clown-car disaster out of a sure thing was a sincere query.

Beauvoir seethed. Gamache remained quiet. Only Isabelle responded. She reached out and held the old woman's veined hand and whispered, 'Shut the fuck up.'

It delighted Ruth, who laughed. And, for once, did as she was told.

After dinner, while Armand and Reine-Marie cleared the table and Gabri made coffee, Jean-Guy took Dominica aside for a quiet word.

'Pottery?' Dominica asked when she and Beauvoir were far enough away from the others. She was clearly surprised this cop wanted to talk about ceramics of all things.

She launched into a discourse on the history of ceramic artworks, some of which survived beyond the peoples and cultures that made them. Some of which he even found interesting.

'What about in modern art?' asked Jean-Guy.

'What about it?'

'Can a person make a living from doing pottery stuff?'

She studied the man in front of her. Having grown up in the Bronx to an activist mother, Dominica found that she was wary, even privately afraid, of cops. She'd seen her brothers, her friends, her lovers harassed too often to see cops as anything other than threats.

She'd had very little respect for them and almost no contact with them socially. They lived on different continents and came from different tribes.

Gabri had told her about the murder of the young woman and what had happened in court that morning.

This officer had been involved. In charge. And now they were making small talk about pottery, over after-dinner drinks.

Though watching this cop, his intensity, Dominica Oddly began to suspect this was not actually small talk.

'Are you thinking of making a career change?' she asked, and was relieved to see him smile.

'Not to the art world. Way too dangerous.'

'Yes. I've heard the critics can be brutal.'

'It's the artists who scare me.' Then his smile faded. 'Ceramics,' he reminded her. 'Pottery. Much of a market?'

'For art pottery? Not the kind we eat off of?'

'*Oui.*'

She considered. 'There's always a market at the high end. But you have to be very, very good. And very, very lucky. Lucie Rie, for instance. Highly collectible. Modern, but inspired by ancient Roman pottery. Grayson Perry in the UK is huge. Won the Turner Prize for his ceramics. Elisabeth Kley is a New York artist. Festive yet—'

'How about this?'

He brought out his phone and clicked on Photos.

Dominica Oddly felt a spike of annoyance. She wasn't used to being interrupted. Most people were in awe of her and hung on every word.

But she realized they were not, in all probability, actually talking about pottery. They were discussing murder.

She leaned in.

Up came a picture of a vase. Then a bowl. Then another piece. One after another appeared. She asked him to stop scrolling as she examined a few. Enlarging them.

'Huh,' she finally said, looking up. 'Whose is it?'

'A fellow named Carl Tracey. Ever heard of him?'

'No.' She stepped back and examined his face. 'Is he the one who killed the girl?'

'We think so, yes. What do you think?'

'What do you think?' Clara asked.

She'd taken some of her friends into her studio, to show them copies of the miniatures that had been savaged by the critics. Including, and especially, the critic in her living room.

'Not bad at all,' said Gabri.

Clara felt her heart squeeze and a sort of panic wash over her. She was expecting an immediate and passionate, 'They're brilliant! She's wrong!'

Not this muted reply.

She looked over at Reine-Marie, whose head was tilted, as though maybe that would help. There was a strained look on her face, like a child with the beginnings of indigestion.

'These are the ones that didn't make the cut, right? The ones you were less happy with?' Reine-Marie asked, barely meeting Clara's eyes.

'Yes,' she said. She lied.

The tiny oils on the easel in her studio were almost exact replicas of the series she'd sent to the collective show in New York.

The critics, the other artists, even the gallery owners could all be dismissed. The crap on social media certainly could be. Or if not outright dismissed, at least explained.

Jealousy. Nothing more.

But now her own friends, her cheering section, were tilting their heads, squinting their eyes, and offering faint praise.

Damn, thought Clara. *Damn*.

That Oddly woman had poisoned the well. Turned even her most ardent supporters against her. Or, at least, against

her art. Which was almost the same thing, so deeply intertwined were the woman and her creations. An attack on one
felt like an attack on the other.

She felt her world sinking, and Clara Morrow was far from
certain she could keep her head above the swiftly rising tide
of opinion.

Ruth put a thin, veined hand on Armand's. 'You did your
best, you know.'

He looked down at her hand, then into her rheumy eyes.

'But he got away. Thanks in large part to me.'

'Not on purpose.'

'Does it matter?'

'You're a cop, doesn't intent always matter? If you didn't
intend to hurt ...'

He wondered if this was Ruth's way of apologizing for
posting that video. Knowing now the pain she'd caused.

'That could be true,' he said. 'But Vivienne is dead, and
her killer is free.'

'Not for long. Homer's going to kill the man who killed
his daughter, isn't he?'

'He's going to try.'

'Will you stop him?'

'I'll try.'

'In a halfhearted way?'

Armand turned to her in surprise. 'No. With all
my heart.'

'Why?'

She looked at him with genuine curiosity. As did the duck.
But then, ducks were often curious.

Why would he stop Homer?

'Because it's not for us to be judge, jury, and executioner.'

'Yeah, yeah, yeah. Cliché. And in the real world, when the system fails?'

'Then we have to look somewhere else for a solution.'

'You mean revenge.'

'For some, yes.'

'And others?'

'You know the answer to that.'

'You mean giving up? Just' – she waved her hand – 'letting it go and getting on with life?'

'I mean grabbing hold of something other than rage and revenge. You came over to the house this afternoon.'

'Yes,' said Ruth. 'What of it?'

'You said something to Homer.'

'So?'

'I think that's why you visited him. To offer Homer that option, a way out. If not to forgiveness, perhaps to peace. It was a quote from St. Francis, to a woman who'd lost her child in a river. The thing is, I looked it up, or tried, and couldn't find it anywhere.'

'Meaning?'

'Meaning, does it exist?'

'Does it matter? Isn't the power in the belief and not the proof?' She looked at him, hard. 'Wouldn't you want to believe, Armand? If it had been Annie?'

In the silence that followed, he met her eyes.

'*Clare, Clare*,' she said, her voice shaky and her eyes steady, '*do not despair. Between the bridge and the water, I was there.*'

'Does she always carry the duck around?' Dominica Oddly asked Reine-Marie as they left to walk home.

The cold April night air seeped past Dominica's light coat and into her bones. She wrapped her arms around herself.

'Always,' said Reine-Marie. 'Would you leave your child behind?'

'Child . . . ?' Dominica began to dismiss the statement but then heard Rosa muttering and saw the resemblance between mother and duck.

They took a few steps in silence before Reine-Marie spoke again.

'You do know how much your review hurt Clara, don't you?'

'It was brutal,' said Olivier.

'I was just telling the truth.'

'All truth with malice in it,' said Ruth.

'But it's still the truth.'

'Maybe,' said Reine-Marie. 'But you need to also own the malice.'

Jean-Guy dropped back to where Armand and Isabelle were walking, a few paces behind the others.

Isabelle was tired, and her limp was more pronounced.

'I asked her' – Jean-Guy indicated Dominica Oddly – 'about Tracey's pottery. She said it was quite good. Showed actual promise.'

'Jesus,' said Isabelle, 'don't tell Clara that. Her head'll explode.'

'I was thinking that might be another motive,' said Jean-Guy. 'To kill Vivienne.'

'How?' asked Isabelle.

'If Tracey knew he was about to be a success?' said Jean-Guy. 'He sure wouldn't want to share it with Vivienne.'

'But isn't "success" relative? Even successful ceramicists couldn't make much money, could they?' asked Isabelle.

'They can make hundreds of thousands, even millions, if they become collectible,' said Jean-Guy, as though he knew that from experience.

'Does she think Tracey's likely to be that successful?' asked Armand.

'Not sure. She said it's possible. Takes a lot of luck, of course.'

'I wonder,' said Isabelle, then lapsed into silence.

'Wonder what?'

'If a scandal could be considered luck.'

'A scandal like being a murder suspect. Shit.' Beauvoir broke away and jogged up to Dominica Oddly. 'I have a question for you.'

'Yes?'

'If an up-and-coming artist is accused of murder, then let go on a technicality, what would that do to his career?'

'Are you kidding?' she asked. Staring at him. 'You're not seriously thinking—'

'The question. Please answer it.'

They'd stopped, and now Armand and Isabelle joined them. Dominica Oddly thought about it, but not for long. 'He wouldn't be the first artist to benefit from something like that. The cult of celebrity can be pretty perverse. Just look at—'

'Tracey,' Jean-Guy reminded her, before the lecture began. 'Would getting away with murder help him?'

She nodded. 'Probably. But how would he know he'd get away with it?'

'Maybe it didn't matter,' said Isabelle.

'Would matter to him,' said Oddly. 'His art might start selling for tens of thousands, or more, but what good would it do him if he's executed?'

'We don't actually kill prisoners in Canada,' said Lacoste.

'Are you sure?' asked Oddly.

'What're you thinking?' Gamache asked Lacoste.

'Who would benefit,' she whispered to Gamache and Beauvoir, 'if Vivienne was murdered and her suddenly famous artist husband was convicted?'

'Pauline Vachon,' said Beauvoir. 'You think she's that clever?'

'You met her, what do you think?'

Myrna and Billy helped Clara clean up, though most of it had already been done by the others.

'You okay?' Myrna asked her friend.

'Just fine.'

'Pour yourself a vat of wine, cut a huge slice of chocolate cake, sit by the fire, and know you're loved. You and your art. Okay?'

'Okay.'

'I'll walk you home,' said Billy as they put on their coats to leave.

'That's all right. It's not far.'

'I know. I'd like to.' He put on his gloves and hat and was glad Myrna couldn't see his face.

'Billy—' Myrna began as they walked along the road.

'Don't say it. Please.'

If only he hadn't allowed himself to imagine their lives together. What might have been. The quiet nights. Reading. Cooking. Having friends over. Meals in the bistro. Together.

Growing old. Together.

He left her at her door, then got in his truck and drove home. Alone.

Clara took Myrna's advice, as she almost always did.

It helps, she thought, as she cut herself a huge wedge of cake and carried it into the living room, *to have a wise friend. Who can bake.*

As she sat in front of the fireplace with Leo, Clara tried to clear her mind. But found it cluttered with Dominica Oddly. And that review.

Leo placed his magnificent head on her lap, and they both stared into the roiling fire.

'I've been thinking about Tracey and his pottery,' said Isabelle.

'Yes?' said Beauvoir.

They'd walked over to Gabri and Olivier's bed-and-breakfast, where Isabelle had 'her' room. With its familiar four-poster bed and eiderdown comforter, the fireplace laid and ready to be lit. The armchair in front of it. With a carafe of tawny port, a glass, and a small box of her favorite chocolates.

While Dominica Oddly had gone upstairs to work, Isabelle had deposited her bag in her room and returned to the living room of the B&B to join the others.

And work.

'Isn't that just a little bit of a stretch?' asked Isabelle. 'To think Tracey killed his wife so that his art would be noticed? Besides, he's not smart enough to think that far ahead. I doubt he even knows what he's having for lunch most days.'

'Tracey couldn't plan it,' Jean-Guy agreed as he poked the fire, then grabbed a chocolate chip cookie off the tray on the sideboard and joined the others. 'But like we said, Pauline Vachon might.'

Isabelle nodded. 'I can see her planning it. But really, would she kill Vivienne on the off chance it would give

Tracey's career a boost? Seems a pretty drastic marketing tool. I don't believe it.'

'It obviously wouldn't be the only motive,' said Beauvoir. 'There're lots of reasons she'd want Vivienne dead. She'd get Tracey, for one. And any inheritance, real or imagined, coming his way as Vivienne's husband. And if his pottery did hit, she'd be right there to collect. If there's a scandal, like a murdered wife, to help it along, so much the better.'

Up until now, Gamache had preferred to listen as the two investigators tossed around ideas. Taking in what they were saying. Letting his mind both focus and be free. Now he got up from the comfortable armchair.

'Excuse me,' he said, bringing out his phone. 'I just need to check something.'

He stepped over to the window, where the wavering signal was strongest, and returned a couple of minutes later. His face grim.

Dominica checked her site. The review of Clara's art was up and getting good notice. Lots of hits. Lots of shares. The new item she'd just posted was also beginning to trend.

Not yet tired, she Googled around, and then, bored, she typed in 'Jean-Guy Beauvoir.'

A few items came up, including a commendation. There was a photo of this Chief Inspector Gamache, giving him a medal. But the line under the photo identified him as Chief Superintendent Gamache. The head of the Sûreté du Québec.

Curious, she put in 'Armand Gamache. Sûreté.'

Lifting her brows at the number of stories, she scrolled down. The photographs, clearly taken over the course of a long career, showed a man aging. From dark, wavy hair to

gray. From smooth-faced to lines, growing deeper and deeper with each passing story.

And then that scar appeared. At his temple. The first time was in a photo of him in dress uniform. Grim-faced, with a cane. In a funeral procession.

But there was one constant. His eyes. Intelligent and thoughtful. And even kindly.

It was disconcerting. In a cop.

There was a link to a recently posted video, with half a million views already.

Dominica Oddly sat in her quiet room, in the quiet village, and watched, horrified, as the quiet man with the kindly eyes shot a succession of young, mostly black, kids.

She recognized that the video had been hacked together. And knew it was probably bullshit, but she found herself sucked in. Probably because she was predisposed to believe that's what cops did.

Did that explain his demotion? Is this how the good folk of Canada react to mass murder? A wrist slap?

Then another video came up. Also newly posted. With almost the same number of hits.

Her eye, trained to see the manipulation of images, realized this was the real thing. Uncut. Unedited. Raw. The parent of the previous, perverse video. The place from which those images had been culled, to create a false, but compelling, narrative. Of a man, a cop, out of control.

But this second video showed something very different. A commander in complete control. Leading a raid on a factory. Against what were clearly heavily armed gunmen.

In shaky but clear images, she watched Sûreté agents, including the three people she'd just met over a civilized dinner, advance through the gunfire.

Jean-Guy. Isabelle. Armand.

'Christ,' she whispered as she watched last rites hurriedly given by one agent to another.

As hoarse last words were placed by one dying officer into another.

She watched as Jean-Guy fell, hit in the abdomen, and Armand dragged him to safety, kneeling over him to stanch his wound. Then he headed back into the battle. But before he did, Chief Inspector Gamache bent down and, for all the world to see, kissed the frightened young man on the forehead and whispered, 'I love you.'

Words they both must have believed would be the last Jean-Guy Beauvoir would ever hear.

Minutes later, Isabelle was holding Armand's hand as blood ran from the wounds at his temple and chest, and he whispered to her, barely audible, words he must've thought would be his last.

'Reine-Marie.'

Dominica Oddly was shocked by the violence, and even more shocked by the tenderness.

She snapped her laptop shut. And for the first time felt real revulsion for social media.

That would cut, twist, put a lie to the truth.

That would nail decent people to posts.

And then she remembered what she'd just done.

'What is it?' asked Jean-Guy.

Armand turned his phone around for them to see.

There, beneath the title 'All Truth with Malice in It', was the story of a man in the remote Québec countryside. An undiscovered but important ceramic artist. Who also happened to be, allegedly, a murderer.

'*Merde*,' said Jean-Guy as he read.

'How'd you know?' Isabelle asked Gamache.

'If you're given a lead, don't you follow it? She's a critic, but she's also a journalist and an entrepreneur. And a good one. We handed her a great story. What else was she going to do with it?'

'Be a decent human being?' suggested Isabelle. 'Respect Homer Godin's pain and not promote a murderer.'

'I handed it to her,' said Jean-Guy.

'We all did,' said Armand.

'It's disgusting, but it won't harm the case,' said Isabelle.

'What case?' demanded Jean-Guy. 'And what'll Homer make of this? It's not enough that that asshole Tracey killed his daughter, now he's profiting from it. Thanks to us.'

'He might not see it,' said Isabelle. 'Why would he?'

'Why would we see the video?' said Jean-Guy. 'Because people sent us the link.'

'There's something else,' said Gamache, looking at the two of them. 'Something I should have thought about earlier. Vivienne's dog.'

'Fred?' asked Jean-Guy. 'That's what you're thinking about?'

'Exactly,' said Armand. 'Ruth told Dominica that she never leaves Rosa behind. And we'd never move and leave Henri and Gracie. So why didn't Vivienne take Fred with her to the bridge? Agent Cloutier told me Vivienne rescued him as a puppy and adored him.'

'Maybe she couldn't take him with her,' said Isabelle. 'Maybe she was going someplace where a dog wasn't allowed.'

Armand was shaking his head. 'She'd never leave him with Carl. She must've known what he'd do to Fred.'

'So what're you saying?' asked Jean-Guy.

'I don't know,' said Armand slowly.

As they walked back to the Gamache house, Armand and Jean-Guy noticed that the light was out in Homer's room. But Reine-Marie was still awake.

Reading in bed and waiting for him, Armand knew.

'Long day,' said Reine-Marie when he finally got into bed. 'Bad day.'

'*Oui.*' No use denying it.

Though the walls of the old home were thick, Armand could still hear Jean-Guy's voice. He couldn't make out the exact words, nor did he try. But he knew that he was speaking to Annie. Telling her about the long, bad day. Not hiding anything.

After a few minutes, there was silence, except for Reine-Marie's steady, deep breathing.

The minutes ticked by. Armand found he couldn't settle. It was midnight. Then 1:10 a.m. Then 1:35.

Tick, tock. Tick, tock.

At 2:07 he heard a sound. Movement. Footsteps in the hall outside their room. Then down the stairs.

Armand got up. The room was chilly as the fresh spring air drifted through the open window. The curtains billowing slightly.

Slipping his phone into the pocket of his dressing gown, he stepped out into the hallway. Going carefully, slowly, to the stairs, he looked down and saw Homer by the front door. His coat and boots on.

Homer knelt and said something to Fred, who'd followed him there. Then, kissing the dog on the forehead, he left. Leaving Fred to stare at a closed door.

Armand raced down the stairs, taking them two at a time. Throwing on his outdoor clothes and grabbing the flashlight, he, too, slipped out.

It was a clear, cold night. Below freezing. The moon was full, and he didn't need to turn on his flashlight.

Still, it took him a moment to make out Homer, up ahead. Walking up the hill out of Three Pines. His feet crunching on the frozen ground.

Armand followed. This was it, he knew. And he also knew he'd almost missed it. Had he been asleep, Homer would have left unnoticed. And walked those kilometers to Tracey's home unhindered.

At the top of the hill, Homer stopped. Getting his bearings, Armand suspected. He, too, stopped.

He wanted to give Homer a chance to change his mind. He felt he owed it to the man.

Homer took a few steps forward, then hesitated again. And finally made up his mind.

Turning left, he climbed the steps to the front door of St. Thomas's Church. And entered.

Armand sat at the back, in the very last pew. While Homer sat at the front.

If he knew Armand was there, he didn't show it.

Homer didn't kneel. Didn't cross himself. He just sat there, staring at the stained glass.

Armand wondered if Homer was thinking of St. Francis. Thinking that there was another way forward.

As the minutes ticked by, into an hour, Armand's mind wandered. Not to a prayer but to Dominica Oddly's piece on Carl Tracey.

And the now familiar refrain.

He sat there, and in the quietude he turned the case around. In the calm, he saw what had eluded him before.

Armand rose to his feet, then slowly sat back down as the import of it struck him.

Until all he knew to be fact was revealed as fiction.

Until the givens were gone and another story emerged from the cold, dark depths of this murder.

All truth with malice in it.

CHAPTER 36

'I saw a light down here,' said a groggy Jean-Guy. 'How long have you been up?'

'A little while,' said Armand, gazing over his reading glasses.

He'd left the church an hour earlier, with Homer, who'd finally turned around and, looking at Armand without surprise, said that he was ready to go home. To bed.

The two men had walked in silence back to the Gamaches' place, and from there Armand had gone to the old railway station. He picked up files and laptops and, returning home, settled into the living room.

Where he could see if Homer tried to leave again.

When Jean-Guy came down, he found Armand in front of the lit fireplace with a mug of coffee, reading.

Armand was unshaven. His hair messed. But his eyes were bright and alert. No sign of fatigue.

Outside, clouds had once again rolled in and brought with them snow. Again. Huge soft flakes, as though the clouds themselves were breaking up and drifting down in pieces.

'Can you call Isabelle?'

'It's five twenty. In the morning. It's still dark out.'

But Armand just looked at him as though none of that mattered.

And it didn't, Jean-Guy realized.

'What's up?' he asked as he walked into the study and dialed the familiar number.

'I'll tell you when Isabelle gets here.'

As he waited for the line to engage, Jean-Guy looked across the village green, past the three tall trees. And noticed that theirs wasn't the only light in Three Pines.

'*Oui, allô,*' said Isabelle, instantly awake.

Clara sat on the stool in her studio. Stale chocolate crumbs and icing in her hair. Leo at her feet.

The miniatures on the easel in front of her.

Suppose, her drunken mind had allowed the traitor thought in. Suppose ...

'Suppose,' Gamache began as they sat with their coffees around the warm wood fire, 'we were wrong.'

Isabelle had arrived, looking more than a little scruffy herself, but at least fully dressed.

Jean-Guy had also showered and dressed while they waited for Isabelle. Armand stayed in the living room, not wanting to risk Homer sneaking out.

'What do you mean?' she asked, putting her mug of coffee down and leaning closer. 'Wrong about what?'

'Just suppose,' Gamache said, 'Carl Tracey was telling the truth.'

Jean-Guy's eyes narrowed. 'How much wine did you have last night?'

Gamache ran his hand through his hair, but instead of smoothing it down, he just managed to make it stand

up even more. Far from looking comical, he looked deadly serious.

Armand Gamache might hold a rank equal to or even below their own, for now. But both knew he was in fact their superior. Always would be. And had earned the right to be heard. If not agreed with.

So now, they supposed . . .

Gamache remained quiet, watching their faces. Seeing the concentration and the skepticism. Seeing them try to imagine the inconceivable. What it might look like if Carl Tracey had been telling the truth.

Isabelle was the first to put into words what Jean-Guy could not. 'But that would mean Tracey didn't kill his wife?'

'Perhaps. I don't know. What I do know is that we're stuck. There seems no way to convict him.'

'So we try to convict someone else?' asked Jean-Guy. At the look of surprise on Gamache's face, he backtracked. '*Désolé*. I didn't mean you were suggesting we arrest an innocent person, just . . . I can't quite get my head around what you're saying. And why.'

'There're enough things in this case that we can't explain,' said Gamache. 'Why Vivienne left her dog behind. Why was she on that bridge at all? Why would Carl Tracey kill her there and not at home? Who was she calling in the last hour of her life?'

'Why she didn't want her father to come get her when he offered earlier in the day,' said Isabelle.

'All last night a phrase kept repeating itself. Dominica Oddly even used it as the title of her piece on Tracey.'

'*All truth with malice in it*,' said Beauvoir. 'It's a quote, right? Where's it from? Not "The Wreck of the Hesperus," I hope.'

'As a matter of fact,' said Gamache, clearing his throat in advance of a recitation.

He smiled slightly as Jean-Guy's eyes widened and he recoiled from what promised to be an onslaught of poetry. It was a familiar bit of mutual self-mockery.

Dear God, thought Isabelle. How're they going to live without each other?

'*Non*,' she said, smiling at this set piece. 'It's from *Moby-Dick*.'

'You were thinking about a fish?' asked Jean-Guy.

'About human nature,' said Armand. 'About obsession. About allowing rancor to cloud judgment. About what happens when we see the malice but fail to see the truth. We were all appalled by what happened to Vivienne. Even before she was found, we more than suspected that her drunken, abusive husband had done something to her. I thought that myself. I had absolutely no doubt that if something had happened to Vivienne, her husband did it.'

'It wasn't a wild guess,' said Isabelle. 'Experience points to him. The statements of others, including a local Sûreté cop, point to him. Her father. Even Agent Cloutier.'

'Yes, that's true,' said Gamache.

He leaned forward. Trying to get them to see what he saw.

'And that's the point. It was all so obvious, we never even considered anything, anyone else. Not seriously, anyway. I'm not saying Tracey didn't murder Vivienne. I am saying we owe it to her to look at all possibilities. Including that he was telling the truth.'

'That's what you've been doing all night?' asked Beauvoir, looking at the papers scattered on the coffee table and sofa.

'Yes.' Gamache sorted through them until he found Tracey's statements.

'I'll call in Cloutier and Cameron,' said Beauvoir. 'We'll need their help to go back over all this. Again.'

It was impossible to miss the exasperation in his voice. This was, Beauvoir knew, a waste of time. They should be concentrating on nailing Tracey, not looking elsewhere.

But then he wondered if that wasn't exactly what Chief Inspector Gamache was doing. Trying to get Tracey. Sometimes, sometimes, if you didn't look directly at a thing, something caught your attention. Out of the corner of your eye.

When Beauvoir looked at Gamache, as he did now, he saw a man who would easily, even in a bathrobe, perhaps especially in a bathrobe, pass as a college professor. A decent and thoughtful man. Who loved sitting by the fire, or in his garden, or in the bistro with a book. He loved good food and poetry and friends. He loved his wife and children and grandchildren. And Armand Gamache loathed violence.

But out of the corner of his eye, Jean-Guy Beauvoir saw cunning. A man who was calculating. Shrewd. Ruthless at times.

And determined. He would stop at nothing to catch a murderer. To catch Tracey.

'Why don't you look over these.' Gamache handed over Tracey's statements. 'I'll call Cameron and Cloutier.'

'But before you do . . .' Beauvoir looked him up and down, and Gamache smiled.

'Good point.'

He left Beauvoir and Lacoste by the fireplace. With their coffees. Reading.

As he mounted the stairs, Gamache looked back at Jean-Guy. He saw a man carefully held together. Taut. Intense. Nervous energy simmering close to the surface. Curt at times. Fierce in a fight. A man who blew off tension by happily smashing opponents into the boards in his hockey games.

But out of the corner of his eye, Armand Gamache saw kindness. Loyalty. A deep, almost inconceivable capacity for love.

Jean-Guy Beauvoir would stop at nothing to catch a killer. This killer.

'Oh, shit,' said Clara.

She was sober now. She felt she'd never been more sober.

Getting up from the easel, she had a shower, put on clean clothes, made a pot of strong coffee, and took a mug over to her kitchen window.

It was dawn. But barely light. Huge flakes only April could produce were falling. Plump with moisture, they hit the ground and melted. But not all. Some stayed behind.

A thin layer of white covered the grass, the road. It clung to the three huge pines. The cars and bench.

It should have been beautiful, except that by April most yearned to look out and see green. Not winter, clinging on.

Clara returned to her studio, but instead of going in, she snapped off the light and closed the door.

Then, needing fresh air, she took Leo for a walk. Their feet making dark tracks in the bright snow.

While Isabelle and Jean-Guy read over the files, Armand showered, shaved, and changed into slacks and shirt and tie. Quietly. So as not to awaken Reine-Marie.

Gray light and a cool breeze were now coming through the windows.

Before going downstairs, he looked in on Homer, to make sure he was all right and to see if Fred was hungry and eager to go out. Homer was asleep, and Fred just lifted his head, then lowered his gray muzzle to his paws.

Armand returned with food and water bowls, which he placed on the floor, then softly closed the door.

When he returned to the living room, he looked up the numbers for Agents Cameron and Cloutier in the Sûreté files. He reached for the phone, but that was as far as he got.

'When you're ready, *patron*.'

Jean-Guy's voice broke into Armand's thoughts. Broke his concentration. His hand still resting on the phone, Armand looked over and saw Jean-Guy and Isabelle staring at him. Waiting for him.

'*Alors*,' said Jean-Guy, adjusting his glasses. 'We went through Carl Tracey's statements and cross-checked with those of others, including Pauline Vachon and Homer Godin.'

'And made a list of what it might mean if he was telling the truth,' said Isabelle.

Gamache nodded. Listening. He had his own notes beside him on the sofa.

'He said she was alive when he left her,' said Jean-Guy. 'If that's true, then someone else murdered her. If that's the case, my money's on Pauline Vachon. With or without Tracey's knowledge.'

'But probably with,' said Isabelle.

By habit, they glanced at Gamache to gauge his reaction, but the Chief was noncommittal. Simply listening. Though it seemed to Jean-Guy that Gamache was struggling to remain focused.

'Is something wrong?'

'*Non, non*, go on. Pauline Vachon. I'm following.'

Jean-Guy glanced quickly at Isabelle, who'd also noticed the uncharacteristic distraction.

'I'll get to that later,' said Jean-Guy, 'but for now let's go back to what Carl Tracey told you when you first visited his

412

home. Before Vivienne was found. He said they'd both been drinking. That was later confirmed by the autopsy report on Vivienne's blood-alcohol level.'

'*Oui*,' said Isabelle. 'So that much was true. He said she was drunk. That was an exaggeration. They had an argument. She told him the baby wasn't his.'

'This's directly contradicted by Monsieur Godin,' Jean-Guy pointed out. 'In his statement, he said Vivienne wanted to sneak away. That she was afraid of her husband. She'd never have provoked him like that.'

'So does that mean Homer was lying?' asked Isabelle.

'It could mean that Vivienne meant to sneak away,' said Jean-Guy, 'as she told her father, but then had a drink. Maybe for courage. But it backfired. She had too many, and things got out of control.'

'So let's say Vivienne had just enough alcohol to lower her defenses,' said Lacoste. 'She said things she hadn't planned to. What does Tracey do? He hits her. Then he said he left her, alive, and went into his studio to start a new piece but passed out instead. When he woke up, Vivienne was gone.'

It was the picture of a catastrophically unhappy home. Of a sick relationship. That could not possibly continue. And into which a baby was going to be born.

Unless something changed.

'Can that be true?' asked Jean-Guy. 'Are we supposed to believe that Tracey left her alive?'

'For now,' said Gamache. 'For argument's sake. Yes.'

They sat quietly, trying to argue.

'So,' Jean-Guy finally said. 'Who killed her if not Tracey?'

They looked at Gamache.

He had no definite answers, though he had spent the better part of the night looking into the dark corners of the case.

Beyond the malice, to where some fact, some feral truth, might be waiting to be found.

'Pauline Vachon,' said Isabelle. 'She had motive. She wants desperately to get out, to have a better life. And she's brighter than Tracey.'

'That's not saying much. Henri here is brighter than Tracey,' said Jean-Guy.

The shepherd raised his head and swiveled his mighty ears toward Jean-Guy. He was not, they all knew, a dog of great intellect. The main purpose of his head seemed to be to support his formidable ears, which were tuned to key words. Treat, dinner, walk, Henri.

Henri kept all he needed to know, all that really mattered, safe in his heart. Where there was no need of words. Except, maybe, good boy.

Armand lowered his hand and stroked Henri until the shepherd dropped his head to his paws.

'Pauline Vachon could plan it and pull it off,' Isabelle was saying. 'Shoving a woman who'd had a few drinks, who wasn't expecting to be attacked, from a bridge wouldn't take much. Those bruises could've been made by anyone.'

'And the boot prints,' said Jean-Guy. 'She could've been wearing Tracey's. Trying to implicate him.'

'But how did she arrange to meet Vivienne on the bridge?' asked Isabelle. 'There were no calls into the house that day and only those two numbers dialed out.'

'Tracey told Vivienne to go to the bridge,' said Jean-Guy.

Isabelle stared at him in disbelief. 'Now, that's really stretching it. You actually believe she'd go? To meet her husband's lover? All Vivienne wanted was to get as far away, as fast as possible. There's no way she'd agree to meet Pauline Vachon on a lonely bridge at night. Why would she?'

'To confront Pauline,' said Jean-Guy. 'To give her hell. Suppose Tracey tells Vivienne he's meeting his lover on the bridge, knowing she'll go there.'

'Come on. Maybe on paper that works, but in reality?' said Isabelle. 'Everyone who talks about Vivienne describes a woman frightened out of her wits.'

She looked over at Gamache, who was considering it.

The scenario Jean-Guy described was possible. Just. In normal circumstances a wife might go to confront her husband's lover. Except these were not normal circumstances.

'Why the bridge?' he asked. 'If they wanted her dead, there're easier ways. Why go through all that rigmarole?'

'Rigmarole?' asked Jean-Guy, always amused when Gamache used odd Anglo words.

'Yes,' said Gamache. 'It means either taking or luring a young woman to a bridge and throwing her off.'

'Really?' asked Jean-Guy.

'*Non.* But it does mean making something complicated that could be simple. There's something else that argues against Vachon,' said Gamache.

'What?' asked Jean-Guy, not liking the sound of that.

Gamache picked up the notes at his side and, putting on his reading glasses again, scanned them until he found what he was looking for.

'*Stuff's in the bag,*' he read. '*Everything's ready. Will be done tonight. I promise.*' Gamache looked up at them. 'The messages between Carl Tracey and Pauline Vachon on the day of the murder. And her reply: *Finally. Good luck. Don't mess it up.*'

'Pretty damning,' said Isabelle.

'But the person it damns isn't Pauline Vachon,' said Gamache, removing his glasses. 'It shows that while Pauline

Vachon knew about the murder plans, she wasn't actually there. So suppose there's another interpretation?'

'What?' asked Jean-Guy, not liking the sound of that either.

'Suppose Carl Tracey and Pauline Vachon were telling the truth.'

'Oh, come on,' said Jean-Guy. 'You're kidding.'

'You think I'm joking?' Gamache stared hard at Jean-Guy. 'Just suppose that this exchange' – Gamache held up the page and shook it – 'is about Tracey's pottery. He was out of clay and went to the art-supply store. The Instagram post originated from there. We know that. And we found a new bag of clay, unopened, in his studio. *Stuff's in the bag. Everything's ready. Will be done tonight.* He might've been referring to new works.'

They stared at him in disbelief. Did Gamache really think that was possible?

'So you're saying Tracey didn't pack Vivienne's bag?' asked Jean-Guy. 'That Vivienne did, and she tossed in those abortion pills even though she was well along in her pregnancy? The clothes she packed were for summer, even though it was minus five degrees that night. Why'd she do that?'

Gamache turned to Isabelle. 'You answered that yesterday.'

'I did?'

'*Oui.* And so did Madame Fleury, when we talked with her about the shelters.'

Gamache looked at Jean-Guy, though try as he might, Jean-Guy couldn't come up with anything.

But Isabelle did. 'You mean my overnight bag. I keep it in the car, in case.'

'*Exactement,*' said Gamache. 'In case. Simone Fleury said many abused women pack a bag and keep it hidden. Sometimes for months – years, even. Ready to grab when the moment is right.'

A knot was forming between Jean-Guy's brows.

Was it possible?

And suddenly Vivienne came into stark relief. A shattered, frightened young woman. Her bag packed. Waiting for her chance. Waiting. Enduring the loneliness, the humiliations. The beatings.

And when she was pregnant, deciding she really did need to leave. For her baby.

This one she'd save. This one she'd protect from Carl Tracey.

It would explain the timing. And it would explain the clothing.

'She packed in the summer,' he said. 'And the bag sat in her car since then.'

'Until Saturday,' said Isabelle.

'I think so, but there's a problem with that, too,' said Gamache. 'How did it get into the river? Would Carl Tracey or whoever killed her know it was in her car? Presumably he didn't realize before, so why would he look for a bag after he killed her?'

'She must've taken it out of the car with her,' said Isabelle.

'But why?' asked Jean-Guy, imagining that cold night. On the bridge.

'Maybe she was getting into another car,' said Isabelle. 'Her lover's?'

'But wasn't she going to drive to her father?' asked Jean-Guy.

'She might've changed her mind,' said Isabelle. 'Tracey also said she told him she was going to "the" father, not "her" father.'

'But how would the lover know she'd be there?' asked Jean-Guy. 'Vivienne only called those two numbers. And one of them was a wrong number.'

'It might've been prearranged,' said Isabelle. 'Every Saturday night. Tracey would either be in the local bar or passed out drunk at home. They'd meet on the bridge. Maybe that's why she told her father not to meet her. Her plan was to talk to her lover, tell him about the baby, and with luck he'd take her away. She'd call her father later and change the plans.'

'So she goes there,' said Jean-Guy, 'meets her lover at their normal place, takes the bag from her car to put in his, and he kills her. Why?'

'The baby,' said Isabelle. 'Vivienne might've really believed it was his. He didn't want the complication in his life, the burden. He might've pushed her away, too hard, and she fell through the railing.'

It fit. Some loose ends still. Like Fred. But the rest fit.

'Shouldn't Cloutier and Cameron be here by now?' asked Beauvoir, looking at the clock. 'You called them nearly an hour ago. Cameron for sure should've arrived.'

'I didn't call them,' said Gamache.

'Why not?'

Gamache paused to corral his thoughts. This was delicate but needed to be said.

'We talked about jealousy. Agent Cloutier said it turned Vivienne's mother against her own daughter. That bond between Homer and Vivienne was so strong, no one else could get in. The only way to break it was to get rid of Vivienne.'

'But Mom's dead,' said Jean-Guy. 'She didn't kill her daughter out of jealousy.'

'*Non*, I don't mean her. I mean someone else who wanted a relationship with Homer. But who might've also run up against that unbreakable bond. Someone who might also need to get rid of Vivienne.'

'Lysette Cloutier?' asked Isabelle. 'You think she killed Vivienne?'

Clearly, Isabelle did not.

'I don't know,' said Gamache. 'I doubt it, but since we're looking at other possibilities, that one comes to mind. How many murders have we investigated where a relationship was at the center? Where jealousy had turned to hatred. To murder.'

'We need to speak with her,' said Jean-Guy.

'Let me do it,' said Isabelle.

'There's something else.' Gamache handed Jean-Guy his notebook.

As Jean-Guy read, his eyes opened and his brows shot up. Then he handed it over to Isabelle, who looked at it, then over to Gamache.

They knew then why Chief Inspector Gamache had seemed distracted. And why he'd been so insistent they consider other options.

'I think we should call them now,' said Jean-Guy. 'Don't you?'

CHAPTER 37

While they waited for the two Sûreté agents to arrive, Lacoste went back over the forensic evidence. Beauvoir read the reports on Vivienne's finances.

And Gamache went for a walk. To think.

He strolled once around the village green. His hands clasped behind his back, he watched Henri and Gracie playing in the mud.

Reine-Marie might not thank him for this, he thought.

'Come along,' he called to them, and together they walked up the road out of town. Stopping on the crest of the hill, he turned to admire the view, which stretched past Québec and well into the Green Mountains of Vermont.

The snow was heading off somewhere else but had left a centimeter behind. It was, he knew, almost certainly the last snowfall. The end of a season. And the beginning of another.

He brushed off the bench that he and Reine-Marie had placed there for all to rest on.

As he did, familiar words were uncovered, etched deep into the wood.

Surprised by Joy

And below that:

A Brave Man in a Brave Country

Marilynne Robinson's words always made him think of his father and mother.

'*I'll pray that you grow up a brave man in a brave country,*' he whispered. '*I will pray you find a way to be useful.*'

Would their prayers for him have been answered?

But mostly he thought of his grandchildren. Florence, Zora, Honoré.

And soon, a new granddaughter.

He closed his eyes. Briefly. And tried not to think that the country they'd grow up in wouldn't be his own.

Then, opening his eyes, he looked at the white world and thought of the white whale. That devoured reason.

All that most maddens and torments; all that stirs up the lees of things; all truth with malice in it.

That was where the quote ended, for him. He didn't know the rest. But in the small hours, in front of the fireplace, while Reine-Marie and Homer slept, while Henri snored at his feet and Gracie ran free in her dreams, he'd looked up that quote and read the rest.

All that cracks the sinews and cakes the brain; all the subtle demonisms of life and thought; all evil . . .

It was difficult, in this peaceful place, looking out over the quiet little village just waking up, to imagine the torment that cracks the sinews and cakes the brain.

But it existed. He met it every day. The subtle demons of life and thought.

That turned something horrific into something acceptable. That turned a crime into a punishment. That somehow made it okay to push a young, pregnant woman off a bridge to her death.

That twisted reality, until malice and truth were intertwined and indistinguishable.

Had the demons caught up with Lysette Cloutier, in love with Homer? Had they caught up with Cameron? With Pauline Vachon? Carl Tracey?

He was honest enough to recognize that it wasn't just murderers who harbored those demons. Cops did, too. He did, too.

His prejudices. And preconceptions. His blinders. And blunders. And outright mistakes.

He heard a car approach. Then slow down. And stop. He heard Henri's and Gracie's collars clink as they raised their heads and looked.

The car idled by the side of the road.

Then silence.

Gamache did not look behind him but continued to stare off into the distance, into the wilderness.

He felt the presence first, then saw it out of the corner of his eye.

'*Clare, Clare, do not despair.*' Gamache spoke the words slowly, deliberately, sending them out over the peaceful village below. '*Between the bridge and the water, I was there.*'

Then he turned and faced the person standing beside the bench.

'And so were you.'

Clara stared at the closed door to her studio. Then went in.

Turning on the lights, she stood directly in front of her easel. Arms at her sides. Shoulders back. Almost at attention. A coward caught. Called out. And facing what was coming.

She lifted her chin in defiance and stared at her works. Daring them to do their worst.

And they did.

As she watched with growing dismay, the tiny paintings shifted before her eyes and went from something brilliant to something less than brilliant. And another shift.

My God, Clara thought. *They were right*.

The critics.

The gallery owners.

Dominica Oddly.

The assholes on social media. So filled with bile they were easily dismissed. One described her as a painter whose art began with an *f*. That juvenile comment got hundreds of retweets. Someone else said she was an artist who painted only in brown.

And she saw now that it was true.

The miniatures were shit.

It wasn't that she'd tried to be bold and failed, it was that she hadn't tried. Exactly as Oddly had said. She'd whipped them off without thought. Without feeling. Without caring. Fooling herself into believing that because it was a new medium, new territory for her, it was a brave experiment.

It was not.

She had betrayed the gift. Cheapened it.

Sitting down on the stool, she felt the lump forming in her throat.

When she was able to move, she took the miniatures off the easel, got out a hammer. And went to work.

Then she placed a clean canvas in front of her. And stared at it. White. White. It grew larger and larger. Huge. It was taunting her, daring her to approach.

'You'd better sit down,' said Gamache.

And Bob Cameron did.

He felt the holster on his belt push into him. As though reminding him it was there.

There'd been something in Chief Inspector Beauvoir's tone when he'd called and invited him to the Gamache home. Not the incident room, as he'd expected. And it was put in the form of an invitation. As though he weren't an agent to be ordered but a civilian to be invited.

He'd suspected then, but now, looking at Chief Inspector Gamache, Cameron knew. That they knew.

'Does your wife know?' Gamache asked.

'*Non*. How did you . . . ?'

'The phone number. Your personal cell phone. Not your home number, not your work number. But you have another cell phone. When I looked up your file this morning, to call you, there it was. It's a single number off the one Vivienne was calling over and over on the day she died. She was calling you. You must've known we'd find out.'

'Why would you? You were so focused on Carl Tracey, I thought you wouldn't get there.'

What Cameron said was true. With, Gamache recognized, a touch of malice.

'Yes,' said Gamache. 'That was a mistake. Being corrected now.' He put out his hand. 'Your weapon, please.'

'You know I didn't kill Vivienne, don't you?'

'I know you lied. I know you were her lover. I know you were on that bridge.'

'But not that night.'

Still, Gamache's gloved hand was held out. Steady. It would not move until Cameron's weapon was placed in it.

'Are you afraid I'll use it, *patron*?' asked Cameron.

'Give it to me,' said Gamache.

'I didn't kill her.'

'Give it to me.'

And finally Cameron reached behind him and brought out the gun. And placed it in the Chief Inspector's hand.

'*Merci.*' Gamache put it in his coat pocket. 'Before we get to how it ended, tell me how it began.'

Superintendent Lacoste pointed to a chair at the kitchen table.

They'd moved from the living room into the kitchen, where Homer, still in his bedroom, couldn't hear what they were saying.

'Sit down, please.'

Agent Cloutier raised her brows but did as she was told.

Her mentor stared at her for what seemed an eternity. Chief Inspector Beauvoir was also there. Looking at her. His face stern. His eyes watchful.

She knew that look.

It was the one he gave suspects. She didn't have to wait long to have it confirmed.

'As you know, Agent Cloutier, when we investigate a murder, we look for motive. You have a motive.'

'*Pardon?*'

'Homer Godin.'

'I don't understand.'

'Of course you do. You understand too well. I can see it in your eyes.'

Agent Cloutier was silent.

'Tell me about your relationship with Homer Godin,' said Lacoste.

'There is no—'

'Enough. It's time for the truth. You clearly care for him. His wife's been gone for five years now. He's free. You're

425

free. Have you told him how you feel? Or is something, or someone, stopping you?'

But still Cloutier remained mute. Partly out of fear of saying too much. But also, now, she found herself incapable of describing feelings that had run so deep, for so long. That had been the undercurrent of her life, for so long. And with each passing day, week, year, getting stronger.

She could feel herself growing fonder and fonder of her best friend's husband. Even while Kathy was alive. And yes, part of it was the tenderness Homer showed his infant daughter. His patience. His gentleness with her, so in contrast to Kathy's abruptness. Her efficient care. Her rules and rigid structure for the day.

Kathy couldn't help it. It was who she was. And Homer was who he was. And Lysette was who she was.

She never acted on her feelings, but she did visit when she could. To see Kathy. To see her goddaughter. To see him.

And then, after Kathy died, that heady mixture of guilt and excitement. Of hope and longing.

Allowing herself to imagine what life might be like. If –

And then, that first time she'd caught him looking at her with tenderness. That first small smile.

'What happened, Lysette?' Lacoste asked.

Even though she knew it was a trap, Lysette was too tired to avoid it. And she realized she wanted to talk. About Homer. About Vivienne. About what happened.

'You know how it started,' said Cameron.

'And you know you need to tell me yourself,' said Gamache.

Cameron, more used to action than talk, put up his hands in an instinctive defensive maneuver, then lowered them. He searched his vocabulary for unaccustomed

426

words. Some way to describe feelings. Overwhelming. Unexpected. Unwanted.

From the moment she'd opened the door and he'd looked into Vivienne's eyes, he'd been branded. The emotions painful and permanent.

Gamache looked into that broken face and felt his pain. It was, Gamache knew, a hurt that went far back. Deep into Bob Cameron's earliest memories.

Here was a man born into chaos. Into abuse. Forged by it. Molded and shaped, literally, by it.

Some with similar upbringings grew up to be abusive themselves.

But some found the space between the bridge and the water.

Gamache had seen this man play football. Had seen his almost maniacal need to protect his quarterback. Even taking penalty after penalty to hold off those who'd hurt his teammate.

It had cost him his job.

But Bob Cameron couldn't help it, Gamache suspected. It was ingrained, as surely as those scars and smashed bones.

The need to protect. First his mother and siblings. Then his teammates.

And now he was a Sûreté officer. Protecting the population.

And Vivienne Godin?

'How did it start?' Gamache asked again.

'The moment she opened the door that first time,' said Cameron. 'She was polite. Dignified, even. She thanked me for coming but asked me not to arrest her husband. That it would only make things worse.'

He paused, to remember. It seemed so long ago. And he was getting confused now, with images of his sister's face. His mother's. His own, in the mirror. Damage that could never, ever be repaired.

Gamache waited, giving the man the space he needed.

'She smiled then. And her lip split open, where he'd hit her.' Cameron raised his finger to his own lip and touched it. 'It bled. It caused her pain, but she still smiled. At me. I knew then.'

'What did you know?'

'That I loved her.'

'But you didn't know her.'

'I knew enough.'

Gamache paused. And believed him. 'What did you do?'

'Nothing, not then. I gave her my card and asked her to call.'

'Did she?'

'Not me. But she did call 911 again. I went out, and again she refused to let me into the house. I could see him. I could smell the booze. But there was nothing I could do. I asked her to meet me that night, after he went to bed. At the bridge.'

'You knew it?'

'From hunting. Yes. It was close to her home and private.'

Gamache said nothing. They were almost there. Almost.

'It was summer. Dark. Hot. She was there when I arrived.'

'You had sex?'

'We made love.'

But that wasn't the end. Not yet. Not even close.

'You confronted Tracey outside the bar in town,' said Gamache. 'More than once.'

'Yes.' Cameron was defiant, still far from willing to admit it was wrong.

'You told him to stop hurting his wife.'

'Yes.'

'It didn't work, of course. As she predicted, it only made it worse,' said Gamache.

'Yes.'

'When did your affair start?'

'Last July.'

'How often did you meet?'

'Every Saturday night. At midnight. By then Tracey was drunk and passed out.'

'And your wife? Didn't she suspect?'

'I always took the Saturday-night shift at work. No one else wanted it. It was quiet, so I could get away.'

'Last Saturday night?'

'No, no, you don't understand. I broke it off. In the fall.'

'Why?'

'I didn't want to lose my family. My job.' He paused. 'Have I lost them?'

'Why didn't you tell us this?'

'I knew you suspected—'

'You knew because I came right out and asked, and you denied it.'

'Because I knew how it would look. And I knew I hadn't killed her. Vivienne was gone. Carl Tracey killed her. Admitting the affair would just muddy things. Hurt the investigation.'

'You mean hurt you.'

'No.'

'She was calling you.' Gamache pushed. 'You'd given her your private cell-phone number. You told her only to call in an emergency. And she hadn't called. Hadn't needed to, until that night. She told her husband she was going to meet her lover—'

'Not me.'

'The father of her child—'

'Not me.'

Hearing the anger in Cameron's voice, Henri got to his feet and turned to face him. A low, low growl in his chest. Little

Gracie stood beside him, all eyes. Barely larger than Cameron's boot, she tried to stare down the man who loomed over them.

'Stop lying.' Gamache dropped his hand to Henri's head. To reassure him. 'It was your number she was trying to call. The affair wasn't over, was it?'

'It was.'

'She wanted to meet you earlier. That's why she called.' Something about that statement gave Gamache a moment's pause. But he had to press on. 'She didn't get through to you, because she'd written your number down wrong. One digit was off. So she showed up at the prearranged time. Midnight. And there you were. For the regular assignation.'

'No.'

'Expecting sex. Instead she told you she was pregnant and the child was yours. She might even have believed it. She told you she was leaving her husband, for you. She had her duffel bag over her shoulder. All packed. Had been for months, waiting for the right time. And this was it.'

'No!' Cameron shot to his feet.

Gamache could see the veins throbbing on Cameron's forehead as the big man tried to control his anger.

'It was over. I wasn't there.'

Gamache also got up. And got right into Cameron's space. Into his face. 'What did she do? Threaten to go to your wife? Your work? And when she refused to just go away, you pushed her.'

'No.'

'You pushed a pregnant woman to her death.'

'No, never!'

Cameron heaved off and gave Gamache a mighty shove. Propelling him backward.

Henri barked and crouched, prepared to lunge.

'Henri, stay!' Gamache commanded as he regained his balance.

And Henri did. As did Gracie. Just. It clearly went against their every instinct.

Because he was prepared for it, had intentionally provoked it, Gamache had staggered but managed to keep to his feet, despite the force of the blow.

Which was far more than a young woman taken by surprise could possibly have done.

'Vivienne happened,' said Lysette Cloutier.

Lacoste recognized the look in Cloutier's eyes. It was the expression of someone who'd made up her mind to walk off a cliff. And was just about to do it.

Still, Isabelle coaxed her forward. 'Go on.'

'Homer and I hadn't been intimate yet, but it was close. We finally admitted our feelings. I wonder if you know what that's like? To be in love with someone for years, maybe decades, and then, in your forties, to have those feelings returned. It felt like a miracle. It was a miracle. But Homer said he owed it to Vivienne to tell her, before we took it further.'

Lysette lowered her head and narrowed her eyes. Then she raised her head. High. And looked directly at Superintendent Lacoste.

'I didn't kill her.'

'What happened?' Lacoste asked.

She noticed that Beauvoir had turned back to his laptop and was reading something. A message. But she kept her focus on the middle-aged accountant–cum–homicide agent. Cum suspect. In front of her.

'Vivienne told him to break it off.'

And there it was.

'Why?'

'Why did she do anything?' Long trapped deep inside, Cloutier's demons finally split the sinews and came tumbling out. 'Because she was weak and afraid and needy and manipulative.'

'What was she afraid of?'

'Of not being the center of Homer's life. She'd managed to come between Homer and Kathy, and now she came between us. I should've seen it coming, but I thought it was specific to her mother. A teenage thing. She was all grown up now. Married. It never occurred to me she'd tell him it was her or me.'

'Is that what she said?'

'Yes.'

'And what did Homer do?'

'You know what he did. He broke it off.'

'He chose his grown married daughter over a woman he loved?'

'Yes.'

'Why?'

'Obviously he didn't love me enough. Didn't love me as much.'

'As much as Vivienne?'

'As much as I loved him.'

'What did he do?'

'Nothing. He just said we couldn't see each other anymore.'

'And you accepted that?'

'What could I do?'

Lacoste looked at her. They both knew what she could've done. Might've done.

'How long ago was that?'

432

'Almost a year ago. We haven't seen each other since then. Until he emailed and told me Vivienne was missing.'

'Where were you on Saturday?'

'It was my day off. I was at home doing laundry. Chores.'

'Alone?'

Lysette nodded. Always alone.

'Did you go down to see Vivienne? To confront her?'

'Of course not. It was over and done with almost a year ago. Why would I do it now? What're you saying?'

'I'm saying things grow. Fester. Time doesn't always heal. Sometimes it makes things worse. Is that what happened to you, Lysette?'

'Of course not.'

'Did you think about it, about him, every day?'

'No.'

'Did you think about what might've been, if Vivienne hadn't done that? How your life would be so different?'

'No.'

'Did you arrange to meet her? Offer her something she wanted?'

'No.'

'Money, maybe?'

'No.'

'Did she suggest the bridge?'

'No.'

'Did you push her off?'

'No!'

'Did you want her dead?'

Pause.

'Yes.'

CHAPTER 38

◯

As soon as Reine-Marie walked into the kitchen, she could see she was interrupting.

'I'm sorry,' she said, stopping at the door. 'Is something wrong?'

'*Non*,' said Isabelle. 'We were just chatting.'

Though that was clearly not true.

'I was going to make breakfast,' said Reine-Marie, going to the fridge. 'Why don't you continue your chat in the study?'

Isabelle Lacoste smiled and nodded. '*Merci*. I think we will.'

'Where's Armand?'

'Out for a walk. He took the dogs. Is Monsieur Godin still asleep?'

'Yes,' said Reine-Marie. 'I looked in but didn't want to disturb him. Is Jean-Guy with Armand?'

'*Non*,' came the familiar voice.

Jean-Guy had gone to the study to print something and now returned to the kitchen holding the papers. 'But I do need to find him. Be back soon. Don't let Isabelle eat everything. You know what she's like.'

Reine-Marie smiled and watched him go.

The home settled. The bacon sizzled and popped. The

coffee perked. The fire in the woodstove roiled as the women went into the study to continue whatever they were talking about, and Jean-Guy left to find Armand.

A mist was rising from the thinning layer of snow. The air warmer now than the ground. Giving the pretty village an otherworldly feel. Except for the mud.

Beauvoir's boots made a thucking sound as he walked quickly toward the bridge and the sandbags still in place against a threat no longer there.

The three huge pines, around which all life in the village revolved, stood in front of him now. Partly obscured by the mist. As though they existed in both this world and the other.

Whenever he and Annie visited with Honoré, Jean-Guy would bring him to the green to play. Sometimes, as he sat on the bench and watched his son, Jean-Guy had the oddest feeling that the little boy was playing not among the trees but with them.

He was almost at the bridge on his way to the incident room, where he expected Gamache had gone, when he noticed movement up on the ridge of the hill out of town.

Gamache and Cameron were standing, facing each other. It looked natural enough. But it was the posture of the dogs that alerted Beauvoir that this was not a pleasant discussion. For any of them.

And he knew what they must be talking about.

Picking up his pace, *thuck, thuck, thuck,* he headed up there. As he approached, he heard Cameron shout, 'No!'

He saw Gamache get right up into Cameron's face.

While he couldn't hear what the Chief Inspector said, he could hear Cameron's reply. Another 'No' blasted.

Cameron raised his hands.

Henri crouched.

Gracie barked.

And Armand braced.

When the blow landed, he staggered back.

Beauvoir shouted.

But neither heard.

They continued to stare. Cameron at the man accusing him of murder. Gamache at a man who could so easily be provoked into an act which, under different circumstances, would prove fatal.

———

'Are you going to lay charges?' Beauvoir asked as he and Gamache walked a dozen paces away from Agent Cameron.

Gamache looked behind him.

Cameron wasn't watching them. Instead, he gazed, dazed, out over the village.

Gamache wondered what he saw. The forests and mountains, the shifting reds and purples of the sunrise, with the mist rising pink-tinged below?

Did he see Vivienne? As she hung between the bridge and the water.

Cameron's huge hands were grasping the back of the bench. So that the words etched there now read '*Surprised by—*'

The joy had disappeared.

'For assault? *Non*,' said Gamache. 'We're after bigger fish.'

'A whale, even?' asked Beauvoir. 'Look at this.'

Gamache took the paper, then reached into the breast

pocket of his coat and brought out his reading glasses. But they were broken.

Wordlessly, he replaced them and squinted to read the printout.

He made a guttural noise that sounded like 'Huh.' Then his eyes focused on the man in front of him. 'What do you think it means?'

'I have an idea, but I think we need to ask him.'

Homer Godin looked down at the printout.

He'd stared at it for a while, clearly trying to focus his mind.

They'd left Cloutier and Cameron in the kitchen while the senior officers met with Homer in Gamache's study.

'Viv's bank statements,' he finally said, raising his eyes to Lacoste, then over to Beauvoir.

'Yes. They show that every month since last July you transferred two thousand dollars into her account.'

'True.'

'Why?'

'She asked for it. Said they needed it to pay their mortgage. I didn't want her to be homeless.'

'And yet, it just sat there, accumulating,' said Beauvoir. 'There's eighteen thousand dollars in that account.'

Homer shook his head. 'Maybe she didn't need it after all.'

'Then why did she keep taking it?' asked Beauvoir. When Homer didn't answer, Jean-Guy went on. 'I think she was saving up. To leave Tracey. I think that was her plan for a long time.'

'Could be,' said Homer.

'I think with a baby on the way, she decided now was the time to get out and start a new life, with the money you'd given her.'

'I hope so.' Homer seemed confused now. As though what Beauvoir described were still possible.

Beauvoir looked over at Gamache, then to Lacoste, all thinking the same thing.

Homer Godin was not a rich man. He'd labored all his life. Had a modest home he'd paid off. Lived a modest life in a small Québec town.

These sorts of sums would almost certainly clean him out. And then some.

He seemed to follow their thoughts. 'She said she'd pay me back. She'd get a job when she could. What would you do?'

And there was that question again. Variations on the theme that had haunted them since this case had begun. How would they feel, if ...?

What would they do, if ...?

If Honoré came to his parents, in distress, and needed more money than they had?

If Annie went to her parents ...?

If money would solve the problem?

They'd pay it. And more. To save their child? They'd give all they had. And more.

As Homer had.

'She called you on Saturday morning, telling you she was finally going to leave Tracey, is that right?' said Lacoste.

'Yes.'

'Think carefully, Monsieur Godin,' said Lacoste. 'Did she say she was coming to you or going to someone else?'

'Me. Who else was there?'

'Tell us about your relationship with Lysette Cloutier,' said Lacoste.

Homer was shaking his head. 'Vivienne wouldn't go to Lysette. They barely knew each other.'

'No, I don't mean that,' said Lacoste. 'Your relationship with her.'

'How'd you know about that?'

'She told us.'

'She shouldn't have. It was private.'

'She didn't want to,' said Gamache. 'She had to be pushed, hard. But she finally told us.'

'What did she say?'

'I think you need to tell us what happened,' said Beauvoir.

Homer raised his head and looked stubborn. Then relented. 'Doesn't much matter. We tried, and it didn't work.'

'Why didn't it work?' asked Gamache.

'It just didn't. I thought of her as a friend. She wanted more, but I didn't. Couldn't.'

'Did you talk to Vivienne about it?' asked Lacoste.

Homer looked surprised. 'About Lysette? No, why would I? There was nothing to talk about.'

Beauvoir looked at Gamache, then to Lacoste.

'So who's telling the truth?' asked Lacoste. 'Lysette or Homer?'

The senior officers had walked to the incident room, where they could talk without fear of being overheard.

'Maybe Homer gave Lysette the impression that Vivienne wouldn't approve,' said Beauvoir. 'Without actually saying it.'

'You mean he blamed his daughter?' asked Lacoste. 'Is he that much of a coward?'

Beauvoir remained silent, not bothering to tell her how often he'd made up all sorts of far-fetched stories to get out of relationships. Granted, that was when he was younger.

'Could happen' was all he said.

'Or maybe Homer didn't outright blame his daughter,' said Gamache, 'but Cloutier did. Maybe it was easier on her feelings to think Vivienne forced it, rather than that the man she loved rejected her.'

'Easier to blame someone she already didn't like,' said Lacoste. 'And she might've even believed it.'

'If she really got it into her head that Vivienne stood between her and Homer,' said Beauvoir, 'that sort of thing can eat away at a person. You said it yourself, *patron*. It's a simple, clean motive. Most are.'

It was true. When the mist and smoke and fireworks dissipated, what was left in a murder investigation could be rendered down to a few words. Greed. Hate. Jealousy.

But really, it was even simpler than that. Even those words had a common parent.

Fear.

Cameron was afraid of losing his family.

Cloutier was afraid of losing Homer.

Pauline Vachon was afraid of losing her ticket out.

Carl Tracey was afraid of losing his home, his studio, his pottery.

If Vivienne lived.

'But how would they set up the meeting?' said Beauvoir. 'There's no record of a call between Cloutier and Vivienne.'

'True,' said Lacoste.

They'd checked all the calls into and out of the farmhouse, going back months. It was not as arduous as it sounded. There were hardly any, and those there were, were easily traced.

'One of the things I don't understand,' said Gamache, 'is why Vivienne didn't leave earlier.'

'She had to get up courage,' said Lacoste, a little surprised

by the question. 'We've talked about this. Lots of abused women never leave—' Her phone buzzed. 'Sorry. *Allô?*'

'A message just came in,' said Agent Cloutier. 'I'd asked the forensic accountants to look into the bank accounts of all the people involved.'

'Yes? And?' asked Lacoste.

'I've forwarded it to you.'

Lacoste went to her emails. 'Got it.' She clicked on it. 'What'm I looking at?'

She waved the others over to her laptop.

Gamache and Beauvoir bent and stared at the screen while Lacoste put Cloutier on speaker.

'Scroll down,' said Cloutier. 'To the bottom link.'

Lacoste did, and clicked. 'But this's Monsieur Godin's bank account.'

'I didn't ask for it to be part of the search,' explained Cloutier. 'But his name must've been on the list of people involved in the case. So the forensic accountant included him, I guess.'

They looked at the numbers. Twenty thousand dollars had been transferred into Homer Godin's bank account on Friday. And taken out in cash that afternoon.

'It's a mortgage loan,' said Cloutier. 'You can tell by the code attached to the transfer. He must've taken it out against his house.'

'Why?' asked Beauvoir.

'I don't know,' said Cloutier. 'But I thought you should see it.'

'Anything in the other accounts?' asked Lacoste.

'Tracey's massively overdrawn, and Pauline's credit cards are maxed out.'

'And Vivienne was sitting with eighteen thousand dollars in her account,' said Beauvoir.

'And twenty thousand in cash with Homer,' said Lacoste. '*Merci.*'

Lacoste hung up, and Beauvoir looked at Gamache, who'd cocked his head to one side. Considering.

'Must've been for Vivienne,' said Lacoste. 'Don't you think? She knew she was leaving Carl and asked her father for more money.'

'When? And wasn't the eighteen thousand enough?' asked Beauvoir. 'This would give her almost forty thousand. Why would she need that much? And in cash? And why didn't he tell us about it?'

'He had other things on his mind,' said Lacoste.

'And he just forgot about the twenty thousand?'

'Maybe he did tell us,' said Gamache. 'Well, not us exactly, but Lysette Cloutier. She says they hadn't kept in touch since he broke it off, but that might not be true. Homer didn't say they'd lost touch. Maybe he asked her advice on how to raise the money.'

'Yes, she's a trained accountant, after all,' said Lacoste. 'So he asked her, and she told him about the home loan. Maybe that was the final straw for Cloutier.'

Beauvoir was nodding now. Following the logic. 'She could see that Vivienne wasn't just ruining their lives but now was bleeding her dad dry. So she arranges to meet her.'

'To kill her?' asked Lacoste.

'No, probably not. But to have it out with her, finally.'

'Why would Vivienne agree to that?'

'Maybe Cloutier told her she had the money,' suggested Beauvoir. 'Vivienne chose a spot close by, where she'd had private meetings before.'

'The bridge,' said Lacoste.

'The bridge,' he said.

Despite her affection for the woman, Lacoste could see it now. Could see how an uncomfortable confrontation could spiral out of control.

'Only Cloutier was lying,' said Beauvoir. 'She didn't really have the cash, of course. When Vivienne realized that, she'd be furious. Might've even attacked Cloutier, who pushed her away.'

And through the railing.

'But if it was all triggered by that twenty thousand, why would she tell us about it now?' asked Lacoste.

'She'd have no choice,' said Gamache. 'The information was in the email about all the finances. She'd know we'd work it out. What I'm still wondering is why Homer didn't say anything about that loan.'

'He might've worried that it made Vivienne look bad,' said Beauvoir. 'And it does. Taking so much money from her father, then running away with a married lover.'

'No. It makes her look like a woman who's been beaten for years and was now desperate to save herself and her unborn child,' snapped Lacoste. 'Was it a series of decisions a healthy person would make? Probably not. But who can say what any of us would do to survive? You want to know what I think actually happened?'

She looked at her two colleagues.

'Please,' said Gamache.

'I think we were right all along, and this's just complicating things. I think Carl Tracey killed his wife. Maybe he knew about that secret account, maybe he didn't. Either way, he wanted to get rid of her. With Pauline Vachon's help, they came up with the plan to throw her into the river. And you know what?'

'What?' said Beauvoir.

'He might be a moron, but it looks like it worked. We can't get him. He's going to walk free.'

'Oh, shit,' said Jean-Guy, hanging his head.

Isabelle was right.

'I think we need to speak to Homer,' said Gamache. 'Find out about the money. At least this's new, and admissible.'

'Yeah,' said Beauvoir, getting up. 'Untainted by that goddamned poisonous tree. But before we do, I want to go back over the evidence one more time.'

'Again?' asked Lacoste. 'I have it memorized.'

'Again,' said Beauvoir. 'I'm not giving up on Tracey yet. There's something in there we've missed.'

They spent the next hour sifting through evidence. Testimony. Events. They knew it by heart. They knew it was futile. That the search would prove fruitless.

And it did.

Finally Beauvoir stood up and yanked his coat from the back of his chair.

'Nothing. Let's go speak to Homer about this money. Maybe something will come up.'

They had nowhere else to turn. Just this one slender thread to follow.

Reine-Marie greeted them at the door, and when Armand asked about Homer, she pointed upstairs.

'He went to his room right after you left.'

Jean-Guy climbed the stairs, and from the living room they heard him knock. Then knock again.

'Monsieur Godin, it's Jean-Guy Beauvoir. I'm afraid we have some more questions.'

There was silence.

Armand and Isabelle looked at each other, then started up the stairs. But only got halfway before Jean-Guy appeared on the landing.

'It's empty. He's not there.'

'Bathroom?' asked Gamache, taking the stairs two at a time.

They searched the upstairs, but there was no Homer.

'When was the last time you saw him?' Armand asked Reine-Marie.

'Right after you left. He went straight to his room.'

Gamache looked at his watch. 'Over an hour ago.'

'Cloutier! Cameron!' Beauvoir shouted as he walked quickly toward the kitchen. The two agents came out. 'Where's Monsieur Godin?'

'In his bedroom,' said Cloutier.

'He's not.'

'Could he have slipped out?' said Gamache. 'Taken Fred for a walk? There's a heavy fog, so we might not have seen him.'

But on hearing his name, the dog appeared at the kitchen door. His tail slowly swishing back and forth.

'I'm sorry,' said Reine-Marie. 'I thought he was in his bedroom.'

'It's not your fault at all,' said Armand. 'Your—'

Anticipating the question, she put her hand in the pocket of her cardigan and brought out her car keys. 'I made sure I had them on me.'

'Well done,' he said with a smile. 'That's a relief. That means he's on foot.'

Beauvoir was in the study, using the landline to warn the agents guarding Carl Tracey's home.

'How long will it take him to get there?' asked Cloutier.

'At least half an hour, walking along the road, in good conditions,' said Gamache, going to the kitchen as he spoke.

The others followed him.

'He's not there, *patron*,' said Cameron.

445

But Gamache didn't answer him, choosing to answer Cloutier instead.

'He probably took the woods at first, so we wouldn't see him, then cut back onto the road. Once he sees the Sûreté car at Tracey's place, he'll head into the forest, to avoid being seen.'

As he spoke, he opened and closed drawers.

'I've been through those woods – it's not easy going. I'd think it'll take him a good hour or more.' Once again he looked at his watch.

Homer would be arriving right about now.

'Damn.' Armand turned to Reine-Marie. 'The carving knife's gone.'

She paled, visualizing the large, sharp knife.

'I just called Tracey's home,' Lacoste reported. 'No answer.'

'We've gotta go,' said Beauvoir.

CHAPTER 39

—

'Anything?' asked Beauvoir.

He'd slammed the car door, not trying to be discreet. Just the opposite. He wanted to make noise. Let Homer know they were there.

'Nothing,' said one of the agents.

'Did you speak to Tracey?' asked Beauvoir. 'Warn him?'

'We knocked on the door, but there was no answer,' said the other agent. 'Without a warrant, we didn't think we should break in. But we've been watching closely, and no one's approached the house.'

He looked at his colleague, who nodded agreement.

'You did the right thing,' said Beauvoir.

Homer had been gone for just under an hour and a half. He should be there soon. If he wasn't already.

Beauvoir looked around and considered the options.

They could go into the woods and hope to find Homer.

They could go into the house and take Tracey into protective custody.

They could leave him there as bait, stake out the house, and arrest Homer when he appeared.

Or they could do nothing. And let Homer do what he came to do.

Jean-Guy Beauvoir knew he'd never do that. But still . . .

'I'm going to get Tracey,' he said. 'Bring him into protective custody. We'll knock down the door if we have to.'

'I'll come with you,' said Lacoste. 'You two come with us.' She indicated the agents who'd been on duty. 'You two' – she pointed to Cloutier and Cameron – 'stay here and watch the road.'

While clearly not happy about being left behind, they had no choice.

Beauvoir looked at Gamache, who was scanning the tree line. '*Patron?*'

'I'll stay out here.'

His eyes returned to Beauvoir, briefly, before coming to rest on the two officers. Cloutier and Cameron.

Beauvoir couldn't make out what Gamache was thinking.

'Monsieur Godin isn't armed, is he?' asked one of the agents.

'He has a kitchen knife,' said Gamache.

She gave a snort. An old man with a kitchen knife.

'Not much good against . . .' The agent placed her hand on her gun.

'You're not to use that,' said Beauvoir. 'Unless there's absolutely no other option. Understand?'

'*Oui, patron,*' she said, immediately dropping her hand to her side.

'And don't be fooled by his weapon,' said Gamache.

The agent looked unconvinced. But she was young and didn't understand that Homer Godin wasn't an old man with a kitchen knife. He was a father with nothing to lose.

Isabelle Lacoste studied Gamache as he scanned the

terrain, his eyes narrow as he tried to penetrate the mist rising from the snow in the fields.

She'd asked him a few weeks back, over drinks at the bistro one Saturday when she and her husband and children were visiting Three Pines, why he wanted to return to the Sûreté.

He was still on suspension at the time. He could easily just quit and get on with his life.

The Chief had smiled broadly. 'I could ask you the same thing. You have even more reason to leave the Sûreté.'

He'd glanced over her shoulder, to the door between Myrna's bookstore and the bistro. And saw, yet again, Isabelle Lacoste crumple to the floor. Shot. Her last act had saved all their lives. She'd done it knowing full well it would cost her her own.

Fortunately, she didn't remember it, so great was the trauma.

And Gamache could never forget, so great was the trauma.

But she'd recovered. Fought her way back, one excruciating step at a time.

Things are strongest where they're broken. If ever there was a person who proved that, it was Isabelle Lacoste.

'Honestly?' Isabelle said. 'I didn't think I would, but then I realized I missed it. So?' she'd pressed. 'Why do you want to go back? We both know you could name your job outside the Sûreté. You could run for Premier and probably win.'

'Now there's a terrifying thought,' he'd said. But she'd earned the right to a truthful answer. And so, after a pause, he gave it to her.

'It's where I belong. We're all handed a cup. This's mine.'

Lacoste stared at him. Seeing the ghosts in his eyes.

The horrific decisions, the terrible orders conceived and carried out.

The consequences of leadership.

As long as Armand Gamache carried the burden, no one else had to. He was already shattered. The damage done. The cup to his lips.

On seeing the sadness in her face, he smiled. 'Not to worry, Isabelle. Maybe I'm being selfish.' He leaned toward her and lowered his voice. 'After all, it's how the light gets in.'

That conversation flashed through her mind, more as a feeling than actually verbatim, as they stood on the side of the road, the icy mist seeping into their bones.

Beauvoir started down the drive.

Lacoste turned to Gamache. 'You sure?'

'I'm sure,' he said. 'Be careful. Tracey has knives, too.'

As Beauvoir and the others approached the house, Gamache signaled to Cameron to walk to the far side of the field and hold the position.

'And me?' asked Cloutier.

'You stay here, by the car. We'll need you when we find Homer.'

'He won't listen to me.'

'I think you'd be surprised.'

Gamache walked along the slushy road, in the opposite direction to Cameron, who was now barely visible through the mist.

Gamache heard Beauvoir on the other side of the house, knocking on the door.

'Tracey, it's the Sûreté. Chief Inspector Beauvoir.'

Gamache took a few steps off the road, onto the soft grass, soaked by melting snow.

There was a door back there. Closed. It led, he knew, into Tracey's studio.

As he got closer, he saw the boot prints.

He stopped. And stood absolutely still.

He heard pounding now. Beauvoir. At the door. Trying to get a response.

But there was no one there to respond, Gamache knew. At least no one alive.

He turned and shouted to Cloutier. 'Homer's already been here and gone. Beauvoir needs to get inside and find Tracey.'

'Yessir.'

She ran down the drive, sliding slightly in the mud but keeping her footing.

'He's here,' she shouted. 'Homer's here.'

At the door, everyone turned.

'How'd you know?' demanded Beauvoir.

'Chief Inspector Gamache told me. Said to tell you to go inside. Tracey might be—'

'*Merde*,' said Beauvoir, and reached for the door handle as the two agents reached for their guns.

'Holster them,' said Lacoste.

The door was locked, and solid. They threw themselves against it, just as Cameron arrived. The human battering ram.

When he put his shoulder to it, the door burst open.

As he rushed in, Beauvoir wondered, very briefly, where Gamache was.

CHAPTER 40

'Tell him I'm following Homer,' Gamache shouted after Cloutier, as she ran to warn Beauvoir.

Then he turned back to the prints.

One set arriving.

One set returning.

Gamache followed the boot prints into the forest.

After a few steps, he paused and looked around. He knew then where Homer was heading.

No longer needing to follow the prints, Gamache moved through the woods as fast as he could, weaving between trees. Brittle branches scraped his coat, his hands, his face.

Once he had to stop as the mist grew thick and he lost his bearings. But he reoriented himself and pressed on.

It took ten minutes of slipping and slogging through mud and ankle-deep slush before he broke through to what was little more than an overgrown path.

He could hear labored breathing ahead of him, but it wasn't until he turned the corner that he saw.

Homer. On the bridge. The mist rising from the Bella Bella almost enveloping him.

But he wasn't alone.

Carl Tracey's body was slung over his shoulder.

'Homer!'

Godin turned.

———

'Here,' shouted Cameron from the back of the house. 'In the studio.'

Beauvoir hurried back there, expecting to find Tracey, either cowering behind his pots or dead. Instead he found Cameron standing by the back door.

'Godin must've gotten in this way,' said Cameron.

'No sign of Tracey?' said Beauvoir, pushing past Cameron. 'Jesus, there're footprints coming and going.'

'There's blood on the floor,' said Lacoste, pointing to the stains. 'Not a lot. Someone's hurt, but doesn't look like a fatal stabbing. There'd be lots more blood.'

'And a body,' said Beauvoir.

He stepped outside and saw what Gamache had seen. Not just two sets of prints, but one was deeper than the other.

'Homer must've taken Tracey with him.'

'And the Chief's following them,' said Lacoste, pointing to another set of prints.

'Oh, God,' said Cloutier, and when they turned to her, she said, 'He shouted something I didn't hear. I should've stopped and asked, but I just kept running.'

Lacoste turned to Beauvoir. 'He thinks we're right behind him. He thinks he'll get backup.'

Cameron started past Beauvoir to follow the prints, and the man, into the forest, but Beauvoir stopped him.

'Wait.'

Every fiber in his body wanted to run into the woods. He could feel the others straining to do the same thing.

But he remembered the Chief's advice.

Think. Take a breath. Take a moment. Just a moment. To think.

So now, almost vibrating with the need to act, Jean-Guy Beauvoir thought.

'Godin's taking Tracey to the bridge.' Turning to Lacoste, he said, 'Take the car. You two go with her.' He pointed to Cameron and Cloutier.

'You?' she asked.

But Jean-Guy Beauvoir was already doing exactly what he always did. He was following Armand Gamache.

By the time Lacoste reached the car, Jean-Guy Beauvoir and the other two agents were well into the forest. Racing through the mist and trees.

'Drop him, Homer.'

Godin, twenty paces ahead, was heaving for breath.

'Put him down.' As he spoke, Gamache approached, reaching into his pocket as he walked toward the bridge. Not for the gun still resting there but for his phone. As Homer watched, Gamache stopped, pressed a button, and placed the phone on the ground, propped against a rock.

There was no reception there, he knew. It couldn't send, but it could record.

Homer, with Tracey unconscious and slung over his shoulder like a sack of potatoes, said nothing. Did nothing. Except stare at Gamache and gasp for breath.

Gamache approached, slowly. His hands out in front of him. He couldn't see the knife. It was possible Homer had already used it. And dropped it.

Was Carl Tracey dead?

But Gamache, who'd seen many, many bodies, didn't think so. There was still a pink hue to Tracey's hands as they hung limp. And there was no trail of blood, no sopping stain on Homer's coat, as there would be if he'd stabbed Tracey to death.

Homer backed up a step. Two. Toward the gap in the railing, mended only with yellow police tape.

And Armand knew what he planned to do. What he'd planned all along.

He would follow his daughter into the water. And take Tracey with him. Only parting ways in the afterlife. As Tracey went to hell, and Homer went . . . ?

'Fred,' said Armand.

For a moment Homer looked confused. Then spoke. 'Keep him. He's yours.'

'No, I mean, why didn't Vivienne take Fred with her when she left?'

He glanced behind him. Nothing.

He'd expected Beauvoir and Lacoste to be there by now.

He was running out of time, and Homer was running out of bridge. Gamache's only hope was to distract him long enough.

'It doesn't make sense,' said Gamache as he stepped onto the bridge. 'She wouldn't leave without her dog. I don't understand. Do you?'

Tracey made a sound, and Homer tightened his grip on him.

If Gamache had hoped to engage Homer, break his focus, he'd failed.

Homer looked blank. But not confused. He was certain about the only thing that mattered now.

Gamache tried again. Anything to stop Homer's slow progress toward the edge.

'There's something else bothering me,' he said. 'Tracey was at the art-supply shop Saturday morning. Why didn't Vivienne go to you then? Why didn't she leave earlier?'

Again, nothing. Just the vacant stare.

Tracey moved now, groggy, and again Homer tightened his grip.

Stay still, Gamache begged the rousing man. *Don't move.*

'You took twenty thousand dollars out of the bank. To give to Vivienne?'

'Yes.'

Simple question. Simple answer. But at least an answer. It gave Gamache information, but, equally important, it created a tiny crack in Homer's focus. And, maybe, time for Jean-Guy and Isabelle and the others to arrive. If he could just engage Homer.

Though Armand was far from sure that it would matter.

Homer took another step backward.

'She asked for the money?' he said.

'Yes.'

'To raise it, you had to take a mortgage out against your home.'

Homer gave one curt nod.

Gamache took another step. Farther onto the bridge.

'Did you ask Lysette Cloutier about that? About how to do it? Did she know about the money?'

'I don't know, I might have. It doesn't matter.'

Homer still looked dazed, but now something else had crept into his eyes. It wasn't quite fear, but he was wary.

Now, what, thought Gamache, *could a man willing to kill himself be wary of?* Something to do with Cloutier?

'What is it, Homer? What do you want to tell me? What do you need to tell me?'

'I loved Vivienne.'

'I know you did.'

'I have to do this. It's my fault. I have to make it right.'

'It's not your fault, and this won't make anything right, Homer. You must know that. Following one terrible act with another doesn't balance the books.'

'All those years of hurt. All the pain.' Homer was pleading with him now, trying to get Armand to see. To understand. 'All the times I should've stopped it but didn't. Kathy begged me, but—'

'There was nothing you could do. You sent Vivienne money, you mortgaged your home. You tried to see her, to help—'

Annie's father stared at Vivienne's father. His mind racing. Trying to get a hold of something, anything, that would penetrate Homer's resolve.

But everything he said seemed to be making it worse, if that was possible.

Homer hefted Tracey further onto his shoulder. Tightening his grip.

'You're wrong,' said Homer. 'About everything. This isn't a terrible act. It's the one decent thing I can do for Vivienne. To make up for all the damage. All the pain I caused her. I owe her this. You're right. This might not ... what did you call it? Balance the books? Not even close. But it's all I have left.'

Armand heard a car door slam and saw Homer's eyes flicker over his shoulder.

'*Patron?*'

*

457

The sight that met Isabelle Lacoste was chilling. But not surprising.

Vivienne's father was about to make good on his promise. He was about to throw Vivienne's killer off the bridge. The only question was whether he'd go over with him.

But that really wasn't in doubt, she knew, as she looked at his face.

Beauvoir could see light through the trees. The opening. The road.

They were almost there.

He couldn't hear anything from up ahead, for all his crashing through the branches and undergrowth.

But as soon as he broke through, he saw the Sûreté vehicles and, racing around the corner, saw immediately what was happening. He skidded to a stop.

Armand felt the heft of Cameron's gun in his pocket and considered drawing it out. Considered using it, to wound the man. Bring him down.

But decided against it.

Homer was too close to the edge. In every way. It would propel him over.

And the threat of being shot wouldn't make him drop Tracey. It was no threat at all to a man about to do something far worse. It might even be a kindness.

A coup de grâce. A battlefield execution. To end his agony.

Beauvoir had moved to one side of the road while Lacoste took the far side. They inched along the soft shoulder, where the forest met the road. Once or twice, Homer's eyes

flicked in his direction. The man clearly saw what Beauvoir was doing. And didn't care.

Beauvoir's breathing settled, but he remained taut, prepared to move fast. Though, like Lacoste and Gamache, he suspected it would not be nearly fast enough.

Gamache had an idea.

Wild. Desperate. And maybe the only thing that would stop Homer Godin from throwing Carl Tracey off the bridge.

'He didn't kill your daughter.'

'What?'

'Tracey. He didn't kill Vivienne.'

The words, like a soft bullet, entered Vivienne's father. And he stopped.

Beauvoir and Lacoste glanced at each other. They were on either side of the narrow road, with Gamache between them, up ahead. On the bridge.

They knew what he was doing. And it seemed to be working.

Homer Godin was a decent man. Driven mad by grief and despair. But he had no desire to kill anyone, except the person who'd murdered his daughter.

If Gamache could convince him that Carl Tracey was innocent, at least of the murder ...

'Who?' was all Homer could say. All he needed to say.

His eyes wide, fixed on Gamache.

Armand had no idea what to say. Though he knew it didn't matter.

He just had to come up with a name. Someone. Anyone. Would do.

Anything to get Homer to drop Tracey and step away from the edge.

He was just about to say the name of the one suspect not actually on the bridge, Pauline Vachon, when from behind him came a voice.

'I did.'

Homer shifted his gaze. And while Gamache was tempted to look behind him, he didn't.

Didn't have to. He knew who'd spoken.

———

'I'm sorry, Homer.'

Lysette Cloutier had walked to just a few paces behind Gamache. And now she stepped forward, until she was beside him.

Beauvoir moved swiftly forward until he had one foot on the bridge. His hand on the rickety railing. He was just a few paces from Homer, could almost, almost reach out and touch him.

Homer was staring so intently at Cloutier, standing in the middle of the road, that he didn't notice Beauvoir off to the side.

Now Beauvoir stopped. Not wanting to spook the man.

'Lysette?' whispered Homer.

'I'm sorry,' she repeated, her words coming out on a sigh. 'It was an accident. I didn't mean to. It just happened.'

'Why're you saying this?' he asked.

'Because it's the truth. I was her godmother. I'd promised to look after her. You'd told me about Carl, about the abuse. She needed support. Needed money. To get away. I felt awful that I hadn't done more, done anything, to protect her. I'd promised Kathy ... promised you ...'

'Stay back,' Gamache whispered as Lysette took a step toward Homer.

'I'd saved up some money. I called her a week ago. Told her I'd like to give it to her. She said she needed time to get things in order but that she'd meet me here, on Saturday night. She'd sneak away after her husband was drunk and passed out.'

Homer was staring at her. He looked confused, and Gamache wondered how much he was taking in. Out of the corner of his eye, he saw Beauvoir almost within reach of Homer.

The mist rising from the Bella Bella was burning off in the early-morning sun.

They could see clearly now. Finally.

'I got here first. Those boot prints were mine. When she arrived, she got out of her car. She had her duffel bag over her shoulder. I was about to give her the money when she said she was pregnant. A girl. A daughter.'

Lysette looked down.

No one moved. No one breathed.

They were there now. At the end.

Lysette mumbled something, and Homer shouted, 'What's that? I can't hear. What're you saying?'

'She was so happy to tell me that. About the baby. I don't

461

know what came over me, Homer.' Lysette's eyes and voice both rose. 'I said something I shouldn't have. I told her I hoped her daughter was kinder to her than she'd been to her mother.'

There was silence then, except for the Bella Bella rushing beneath them.

'She was standing about where you are,' said Lysette. 'She got upset. Started yelling at me that I didn't know. It just ...' she searched for words. 'It just all came out, of both of us. She started screaming that it was all her mother's fault and how dare I ...' She heaved and caught her breath. 'And I shouted back. Defending Kathy, even though I knew, I knew Viv was right. Oh, God.'

They were frozen in place. A tableau. Waiting for the rest.

'She came at me, and I pushed her away. And ...'

And.

Homer, perhaps in shock, maybe intentionally, loosened his grip on Carl Tracey.

And Tracey, coming to, flailed as he fell to the ground.

Kicking. Twisting.

Hitting Homer in the chest and sending him backward.

Gamache jumped forward, but Beauvoir got there first.

Homer's arms pinwheeled as he stumbled. He reached behind him. Desperate for something to grab, to stop his fall.

But there was nothing there. Just air.

His eyes wide with terror, Homer Godin began to go over the edge. Beauvoir got a handful of Homer's coat and for a moment the momentum stopped. But Homer was too far gone.

Beauvoir, still clinging to his coat, felt an almighty yank as Homer disappeared.

Dragging Jean-Guy with him.

Time seemed to stand still.

Jean-Guy felt, for a moment, as though he were hanging in midair. Neither flying nor falling.

He'd let go of Homer. The man was gone. Vivienne's father was gone, into the river. And Jean-Guy was turned to the bridge. Reaching for it. But it was just beyond his grasp.

He was falling.

Annie. Annie. Honoré.

And then he fell.

It all happened so fast it seemed in slow motion.

Gamache leaped off after him. Following Beauvoir over the edge.

With one hand, he grasped the post. With the other, he reached out.

Reaching, reaching.

Jean-Guy's hand was stretching out toward him. Jean-Guy's eyes, pleading.

Then their hands touched, and gripped.

There was a yank, as Jean-Guy's fall was stopped. But not for long, Gamache knew. His arm and shoulder had been wrenched. Slivers from the rotten wood were pushing into his palm. Making it slippery with blood. He was losing his grip, on the post. On Jean-Guy.

Jean-Guy was staring up at him. Eyes wide with terror.

Neither spoke. Neither could.

In a moment they'd both be in the river. The freezing

463

water closing over them. Not able to breathe for the shock, the cold, the turbulence. The roiling. Turning them over and over. Their bodies hitting rocks and tree trunks.

Until all struggle left them. All breath left them. And finally all life left them, as their bodies bobbed and thumped down the Bella Bella. Past St. Thomas's Church. Past Miss Jane Neal's home. Past Clara's. Past the old railway station.

Under the stone bridge they'd go. And come to rest at the bend in the river.

He held Jean-Guy's frantic eyes and saw his lips move. Annie.

And Armand could see what Jean-Guy was about to do.

'Don't,' he rasped. 'You. Dare.'

But Jean-Guy did.

Knowing Armand could not hold him and keep a grip on the bridge, Jean-Guy opened his grip. Released his hand.

Jean-Guy Beauvoir let go.

But Armand did not. He closed his hand even tighter, even as he felt Jean-Guy's fingers squeezing through his own.

All this took just moments but felt like an eternity.

Just as his hold slipped completely, Armand twisted and heaved. Throwing Jean-Guy as far as he could. Toward the shore.

The effort pulled his hand from the bridge and turned his body onto its back, so that for a moment Armand was looking up. At the sky. Into the April sunshine.

Reine-Marie. Reine-Marie.

He heard a splash as Jean-Guy hit the water.

Then his back arched and arms spread out, and he saw the river roiling below.

Armand had managed to throw Jean-Guy clear of the worst of the torrent, but still he'd splashed down in deep water. Arms flailing, trying to get his head above the bone-chilling water, he felt the current grab him, sweeping him out into the river.

Just as he was about to go under, hands gripped him. Water washing over him, retching and coughing, he felt himself pulled to shore.

He looked up, through the brilliant sunshine and cascading water, to where he'd come from.

Afraid to see a void where Armand had been.

Eyes screwed shut, Armand prepared to hit the water, then fight for his life.

But instead he was jerked to a stop.

The blood rushed to his head, mixing with the rush of the river below, until the sounds were indistinguishable. Water into blood. Blood into water.

Then he looked up, into the smashed face of Bob Cameron. The tackle. Penalized for holding, too often and too tight.

Holding on, tight.

As Armand hung there, suspended. Between the bridge and the water.

CHAPTER 41

R eine-Marie hugged him.
   And he held her.

Finally letting go, Armand asked, 'Is he all right?'

She nodded. 'Hot bath, warm clothing. He's in the kitchen by the fire. Annie's on her way down. Homer?'

Armand shook his head.

Reine-Marie sighed. 'God.' Then she turned and embraced Isabelle.

When they entered the kitchen, Jean-Guy got to his feet. He was clutching a blue blanket around his shoulders and looked a little, though Armand would never ever say it to his face, like Ruth. From Clara's portrait.

Jean-Guy would not appreciate being told he looked like the old poet. Never mind the Virgin Mary.

When he'd gotten to the rocky shore, gagging and heaving, Jean-Guy had first made sure Armand was safe. Only then did he focus on the person bending over him.

Wiping the Bella Bella from his eyes, Jean-Guy looked at Isabelle Lacoste.

Through chattering teeth he managed, 'Thank you. Thank you.'

'Don't thank me,' she said, putting her warm coat over Jean-Guy's shoulders. 'I just arrived. He got to you first.'

She pointed to the person collapsed next to him.

Soaking and shivering, there was Carl Tracey. He'd seen Beauvoir fall and had slithered quickly down the embankment to the river.

'You?' said Beauvoir.

'Yeah, well,' mumbled Tracey through blue lips, 'sometimes ya gotta do something stupid.'

Hands trembling, Jean-Guy took off the warm coat and gave it to Carl Tracey.

Safe now, warm and dry in the familiar kitchen, Jean-Guy walked over to Armand and, without a word, embraced him, then took the bandaged hand.

'*Merci.*'

They'd said the word together.

'Homer?' Jean-Guy asked as they subsided with groans into comfortable chairs by the woodstove.

'Found at the bend in the river,' said Isabelle.

Where the Bella Bella left Three Pines.

'Where Vivienne was found?'

Armand nodded.

He'd stood on the banks of the river and waited for the divers to bring Homer ashore.

The coroner, Dr Harris, also waiting, noticed Armand's hand wrapped in a scarf. She'd taken the splinters out and put on disinfectant and a bandage.

Lysette Cloutier had asked if she could be there when Homer's body was brought in. They'd agreed, and while

Lacoste directed the recovery efforts, Lysette had stood next to Gamache, squinting into water that now gleamed and danced with reflected sunlight.

Finally, when Homer was back, Gamache turned to her and asked, 'Why did you do it?'

'Is she arrested?' Reine-Marie asked.

'Not yet,' said Isabelle. 'She's outside with Cameron, waiting for the coroner's car to take the body away. I wanted to speak with you.' She turned to Jean-Guy. 'I think you should be the one to lay the charges and take her in, if you're up to it. Your last arrest. It was manslaughter, of course.'

'No it wasn't,' said Armand. 'She was lying.'

'It was premeditated?' asked Jean-Guy. 'She planned it?'

'We'll let her explain,' said Armand. 'She wants to talk. I've asked Cameron to bring her here, once she's seen Homer off.'

They'd get the truth this time, with or without malice. But first, Armand wanted to tell them what Homer had said to him on the bridge.

After the coroner's car drove away, Lysette Cloutier and Bob Cameron joined them around the woodstove.

Reine-Marie, having heard what happened, gave Bob Cameron a bear hug. As he accepted the embrace, he breathed in the subtle scent of rose. And below that, barely there, a hint of sandalwood.

'*Merci*,' she'd whispered into his ear. '*Merci*.'

Lysette was trembling so badly with cold and shock that Armand did up a hot-water bottle while Reine-Marie wrapped her in a heavy Hudson's Bay blanket.

'Better?' she asked, and got a small nod. Warmer, if not better.

When they'd settled in again, hands around mugs of hot sweet tea, all eyes turned to Lysette Cloutier, who sat staring into the fire.

'I have a few questions, Agent Cloutier,' Beauvoir said, pulling the blanket tighter as another wave of shivers passed through him. 'To get things straight.'

She nodded. No more fight left. Nothing to fight for anymore.

'If you killed Vivienne, why did you get us involved? Why tell us she was missing in the first place?'

'I had to. How could I explain to Homer if I didn't? Besides, this way I could see what was happening.'

'Not just see but influence?'

'If necessary, *oui*.'

'That Saturday night she was killed, you said you met Vivienne on the bridge. How did you arrange that?'

'Like I said, I called and we set it up.'

'But there're no records of your calling their home in the days before her death.'

'I called from another line.'

'*Non*. Every number is accounted for. Every call. There weren't many, so it didn't take long. There were no calls from an unidentified number.' Beauvoir put his tea down and leaned toward her, lowering his voice. 'So how did you do it?'

'I called,' she repeated.

'Why're you lying?' asked Beauvoir. 'You know you didn't do it.'

'What?' said Cameron, looking from Beauvoir to Cloutier. Then back to Beauvoir. 'Didn't do what?'

'Agent Cloutier didn't kill Vivienne,' said Chief Inspector Beauvoir.

'So it was Tracey,' said Cameron. 'We were right all along.'

He turned to Gamache. 'You told Homer that Tracey didn't do it, but that was a lie. You just wanted him to drop Tracey.'

'*Non*,' said Gamache, holding the gaze of the man who'd saved his life. 'I wasn't lying. We were wrong all along. I was wrong. I'd warned you not to assume Tracey was guilty, and then I fell into the same trap. The evidence against Tracey was strong but circumstantial. He was vile, but he was also telling the truth. Those posts between himself and Pauline Vachon were about the clay. That night, after their fight, he left Vivienne bruised but alive. Carl Tracey did not murder his wife. She'd arranged to meet someone else on that bridge.'

His gaze was so prolonged, so considered, that Cameron shifted in his seat. His large body tensing. His damaged face alert. It felt like that moment just before the quarterback called out the last number. That moment, suspended in time, just before they passed the point of no return.

Gamache turned back to the others.

'Before you arrived, I tossed things out to Homer, trying to break his concentration. Anything that came into my head. And what did were the two nagging questions. Why didn't Vivienne take Fred with her when she left home?'

Once again, on hearing his name, Fred raised his head. Not looking at the one who'd spoken. He was looking for someone who still hadn't returned.

'The other was, why didn't she leave earlier that day?' said Gamache. 'When Tracey was at the art shop.'

'There's only one answer,' said Beauvoir. 'She didn't leave in the morning and she didn't take Fred with her to the bridge that night because she didn't intend to go. Not yet, anyway. Her plan was always to leave with her lover.'

He stared at Cameron, who sat up straighter. The scars on his face turning white against his flushed face.

'But the call to her father,' Cameron said, his voice raised. 'She told him she was leaving that night. Coming to him. Not to me. Him.'

'No,' said Beauvoir. 'Vivienne never planned to go to her father.'

'She lied to him?' asked Cameron.

'No,' said Beauvoir.

'So what does that mean?' said Cameron. Then his face cleared. His eyes opened wider.

'Her father lied?' He looked from one to the other of the senior officers. 'I don't understand. Why would he lie?'

'Did you know?' Isabelle Lacoste asked Cloutier.

Lysette Cloutier was very still for what felt like a long time. Balancing on the knife edge.

'I suspected. Not right away, but there were things I knew.'

'Like what?'

'On her deathbed Kathy didn't just ask, she begged me to protect Vivienne. Not guide her, not watch over her, but to protect her. This was before Vivienne had even met Carl Tracey. So who was I supposed to protect her from? It didn't occur to me at the time to wonder. I was so upset I didn't think more about it, about the wording. But later—'

'Last summer. When Homer said Vivienne told him to break it off with you,' said Gamache.

'I began to wonder.'

'What?' asked Cameron, trying to catch up.

'Why she'd do that. Again, at the time I was so hurt I just accepted it. Accepted that Vivienne was jealous and controlling and demanding of all her father's attention. But then I got to wondering if it was more than that.'

'What?' demanded Cameron. 'I don't get it.'

'Don't you?' asked Gamache. 'The money from Homer

471

to his daughter. His decision to break off a relationship not with just anyone, but Vivienne's godmother. Who is also a Sûreté officer.'

'The payments into Vivienne's account started last July,' said Lysette. 'Exactly when he ended the relationship. When I saw that, I wanted to believe it was a coincidence. But things started adding up.'

'What was the money?' asked Cameron. 'What're you saying?'

'Why did Vivienne marry Carl Tracey?' Beauvoir asked. 'Several people asked that question. We asked it. Why would a supposedly smart young woman marry a man so clearly violent, abusive? Madame Fleury gave us the answer.'

'The devil she knew,' said Gamache. 'The damage done. Homer talked about that on the bridge. I didn't understand at the time, I was so focused on just trying to stop him. But when we were waiting on the shores of the Bella Bella for his body to be brought in, I went back over what he'd said. And then I realized something. He actually confessed.'

'Oh, my God,' said Cameron. 'He beat her, too? When she was growing up?'

'I think you saw it, without realizing,' said Gamache. 'When she opened the door the first time. Last summer. You saw the look in her eyes. You recognized in them what you see in the mirror. It was, I think, one of the things that drew you to her. A mutual hurt that went back to the earliest memories. Of course she'd marry an abusive man. It was all she knew, all she thought she deserved.'

Gamache looked at Cloutier. 'When did you begin to suspect?'

'I didn't, not really. Not until I saw those payments.'

'What were they?' asked Cameron. 'Blackmail?'

'Restitution,' said Lacoste. 'Vivienne was already planning her escape last summer. About the time she miscarried. She probably suspected that Tracey had something to do with it. She knew she needed to get out, but she also needed money. So she contacted her father and demanded payment, for all the pain.'

'And if he didn't pay,' said Beauvoir, 'she'd tell her god-mother all about it. I doubt Vivienne even knew that you and her father had grown close.'

'So Homer broke it off with you and paid,' said Gamache. 'Over and over again on the bridge, he told us about the pain he'd caused Vivienne. The hurt. He even said that his wife had begged him to stop it. I thought he meant stop Tracey abusing their daughter. But standing by the river, quietly, going back over it, I remembered that Kathy had never met Tracey. She couldn't have meant him. So who did she mean? There was only one answer.'

'She was begging me to protect Vivienne from her father,' said Cloutier. 'From Homer. And I didn't. Worse, I'd fallen in love with him. I didn't see it. Didn't want to see it.'

'None of us did,' said Gamache.

'But you couldn't have saved Vivienne if you had.' Cloutier's voice rose. 'I could've. You didn't promise to protect her. I did. But instead I actually blamed Vivienne for being cruel to her father. For cutting him out of her life.'

'So that's why Tracey killed Vivienne,' said Cameron. 'He knew about that money.'

'But how would he?' asked Beauvoir. 'Would she really have told him? I think if she was going to confide in anyone about the money, it would be someone she trusted. A lover, for example. Don't you?'

His voice had grown quiet. Almost a whisper. As he locked eyes with Cameron across the fire.

Cameron flushed red, almost purple. And closed his hands into fists.

'There was something else Homer said on the bridge,' said Gamache. 'Before you all arrived. Or, actually, something he didn't say.'

He looked at the circle of faces, all of them focused on him. Even Cameron broke contact with Beauvoir and shifted his gaze.

'When he was preparing to take Tracey with him, he said it was punishment for all the years Tracey had hurt Vivienne.'

'Yes,' said Cameron. 'Exactly.'

'You're not listening,' said Beauvoir.

'Wait,' said Lysette Cloutier, who understood what Gamache was saying. 'Wait. That can't be true.'

'Yes it is,' said Lacoste.

'What?' said Cameron, looking from one to the other.

'Homer Godin was punishing Tracey for abusing his daughter,' Beauvoir explained. 'But not for killing her.'

He let that sink in.

'He never once said that, not on the bridge anyway,' said Gamache. 'Before, yes. I think he'd convinced himself Vivienne's death was Tracey's fault. If Tracey hadn't been abusing her, she'd never have needed to get away. Never have needed to demand the money. Never have needed to meet her father on the bridge.'

'And Homer would not have killed her,' said Beauvoir.

The words sat there. No one protesting. No one denying them.

It was, finally, the truth.

Lysette Cloutier hung her head, dropping it toward her heart. While Bob Cameron, wide-eyed, absorbed what had been said.

'I should've seen it sooner,' said Beauvoir quietly. 'Only two numbers were called from the house that day. One a wrong number. The other was to her father. Vivienne was on that bridge to meet someone, and it could only be the one person she'd spoken to that day. Her father.'

Finally it was that simple. That obvious.

'But what about Fred?' asked Reine-Marie. And once again the dog raised his head. Then lowered it to his paws. 'Why did she leave him behind?'

'Her plan was never to go away that night,' said Armand. 'She wanted to get the money from her father, then return home and talk to you.' He turned to Cameron. 'That's why she didn't leave when Tracey was at the art store, and that's why she didn't take Fred to the bridge. You didn't break off the affair last fall, did you?'

'No. I broke it off just after Christmas. I couldn't do that to my family.'

Gamache nodded. 'I think she genuinely believed the child was yours.'

'She wanted to tell you,' said Beauvoir, 'and see if maybe—'

'I'd go with her,' he said.

He didn't tell them what his answer would have been, nor did they ask.

'She called over and over, trying to get through to you,' said Beauvoir. 'She finally gave up and went to the bridge to meet her father.'

'But if she'd refused to see him since she left home, why agree to meet him that night?' asked Cameron.

'Yes,' said Cloutier. 'The money could've been wired into her account, like all the rest. No need to see him at all.'

'The baby,' said Beauvoir. 'That changed everything. The idea of being a parent changes you.'

Cameron nodded. Remembering his own mounting terror as his first child grew in his wife's womb. That maybe he'd be his father. Maybe he'd be impatient. Cruel. Violent.

Maybe he'd lash out. With fists. With a belt. With a baseball bat.

'She needed to face her abuser,' said Cameron. 'Look him in the eye. Confront him.'

As he'd confronted his own father. Before his son was born.

Only then did he know, in his heart, that he would love his children, protect his children. He would never hit them. And he had not.

'Yes,' said Beauvoir. 'Vivienne met her father on the bridge for one reason. To look him in the eye and tell him what he'd done to her. She had to do it for her own sake, but also for her daughter's.'

'It wasn't about the money,' said Lacoste. 'That was the excuse to get him there.'

There was silence as some looked down at the floor, some stared into the fire, and others looked out the window, at the bright, cheerful day. At the three huge trees, swaying, playing in the breeze.

'Do you think her plan was to kill him?' asked Cameron.

'No,' said Gamache. 'If it was, she'd have taken Tracey's rifle. She had no weapon. I think it was as Chief Inspector Beauvoir says. She wanted her freedom. Not another burden. Killing her father would've bound him to her for the rest of her life.'

But oh, thought Armand, the courage it must have taken to face him. And in doing that, turn her back on all the justified rage. All that had maddened and tormented her her entire life.

To rid herself of all the subtle demonisms of life and

thought, Vivienne had to stand on that bridge and face them. Face him.

Her courage was almost unimaginable.

And once free ...

'Something went wrong,' Beauvoir said quietly. 'Maybe she tripped. Maybe he pushed her away. If he did, I don't think he meant to kill her.'

But maybe that was wishful thinking.

'I realize now that he almost told me what happened,' said Armand. 'That afternoon, when the case was thrown out. We stood out there' – he nodded toward the path along the Bella Bella – 'and I told him how sorry I was. He talked about forgiveness and asked if some things were too horrible to forgive. I thought he was talking about Tracey's acquittal. He asked if a sincere apology really helped.' Armand looked into the fire, remembering Homer's worn face. The exhaustion in those eyes. 'I think he told her, on the bridge that night, how sorry he was. And asked forgiveness.'

'Do you think he meant it?' Reine-Marie asked.

'I want to believe he did. Yes.'

Mostly, though, Armand hoped and prayed that the last thing Vivienne Godin saw wasn't the monster, coming at her out of the dark again. But her father, reaching out. Trying to save her.

They'd never know the full truth. But they could hope.

CHAPTER 42

'So I'm confused,' said Gabri.

'We know you are,' said Ruth, patting his hand. 'And so's Olivier. Gays and confused.'

'Homer killed his own daughter?' said Gabri, ignoring her.

'It looks like it,' said Olivier.

They were sitting in the bistro over after-dinner drinks.

Gabri was shaking his head. 'It's all so sad.'

'And confusing?' asked Ruth.

'Yes. Why would he do it?'

'Those cops explained it all,' said Ruth. 'Weren't you listening?'

'By "those cops," you mean Armand, Jean-Guy, and Isabelle?' asked Olivier.

'Whoever. But yes, that's what they said. Homer did it.'

They, of course, had said slightly more than that.

The villagers had seen Armand and Jean-Guy, Isabelle and the other officers return to Three Pines that morning.

Jean-Guy, wet, cold, bruised, had gone straight to the Gamache home.

While Armand, disheveled, slightly wild-eyed, hand wrapped in a scarf, had walked with Isabelle and the others

to the path through the woods. That took them to the bend in the river, where the Bella Bella left Three Pines.

A few minutes later, an ambulance, Sûreté cars, the coroner returned.

Homer was discovered exactly where Vivienne had been found. Knocking gently up against a huge tree trunk.

Only then did Armand and Isabelle return home, watched by Clara, Gabri, Olivier. By Billy Williams and Myrna. By Ruth, with Rosa, who was silent for once. Though she did watch Armand with sad eyes. But then, ducks were often sad.

By that afternoon the sun was out in full force. Snowdrops and fragrant, delicate lily of the valley were beginning to appear. Crocuses broke through the grass of the village green.

Life had not just been restored, it had burst forth, as Isabelle and Jean-Guy, Armand and Reine-Marie walked into the bistro.

They joined Clara and Ruth and Rosa by the fieldstone fireplace. Billy Williams sat at a distance from Myrna but stole glances at her. Catching her eyes once, he smiled. And when Myrna smiled back, he blushed and looked away.

Olivier brought them cafés au lait and warm almond croissants, then perched on the arm of the large chair, next to Gabri.

The fire crackled in the background as they heard what had happened.

Ruth looked down at her thin, veined hand, holding Gabri's pink, pudgy one.

You would have a different body by then,
An old murky one, a stranger's body you could
Not even imagine, and you would be lost and alone.

But not lost, she thought.

And not alone.

That evening, Clara was in her studio. Ruth's final comment as she left to head home ringing in her ears.

'Maybe there's a reason they call it a stool,' she'd said, nodding to where Clara sat in front of the easel. 'Something to think about.'

Fuck, fuck, fuck. But this time it didn't come from the duck.

Once she stopped muttering, Clara turned to Myrna, who was sitting on the sofa, her bottom resting on the concrete floor. Her knees up around her ears.

'Homer kept saying he was going to kill Tracey,' said Clara. 'He even tried. Why would he do that if he knew Tracey hadn't killed his daughter? Was it an act?'

'I don't think so,' said Myrna.

'You think Armand and the others might be wrong, and Tracey really did kill Vivienne?'

'No. I think Homer was mad with grief, with guilt. I think he couldn't bear to accept what he'd done. All those years of abuse and then being responsible for Vivienne's death.'

'And his granddaughter's.'

'Yes. I think his own self-loathing and his anger at Tracey for his abuse of Vivienne got all mixed up. He saw himself in Tracey and decided both must die. It's pretty obvious by what Armand said that Homer meant to take his own life, along with Tracey's. Both must go into the river.'

'To be cleansed?' asked Clara.

'To be punished.'

'You think his grief was real? It sure seemed real. Fooled everyone, including Armand.'

'I don't think anyone was fooled. I think Vivienne's death destroyed Homer. I doubt it was on purpose. I want to believe he went to the bridge to try to make amends.'

'I don't understand,' said Clara. 'He beat her. His own daughter. A child. God knows what else he did to her. And now what? You're saying he really did love her?'

'I'm saying people change.' She held up her hands to ward off Clara's protests. 'I know, it's easy to say. And it doesn't undo the damage. But we've seen changes of heart. Changes of perception. It happens. Racists, homophobes, misogynists, they can change. And some do.'

'Truth and reconciliation,' said Clara.

'Yes. The truth must come first. And then, maybe, reconciliation. Maybe.'

'You think Vivienne and her father might've reconciled?'

'Maybe. I think getting the courage to confront him was the first step. If not to forgiveness, at least to healing. And I think Homer's willingness to meet her, and to take the money, shows that maybe he wanted that, too. Maybe.'

'He killed her,' Clara reminded Myrna. 'Then he was willing to see Carl Tracey tried and convicted for something he himself did. Hardly the acts of a contrite man.'

'True.' Myrna pushed herself out of the sofa. 'I guess I just want to believe.'

Just as she'd wanted to believe, desperately, that Clara's miniatures were brilliant.

But that had proved a delusion. Dominica Oddly had made that clear. And had, with a few well-turned phrases on her site, destroyed Clara's credibility as an artist.

Her gallery had dropped her. Collectors were returning paintings. Social media was on a feeding frenzy.

Myrna looked at the tiny paintings, nailed to the wall

where Clara had put them. Where she could always see them. A reminder. A warning.

Oddly had been right about them. But she'd also been wrong. She might have a duty to tell the truth, but there was no need to be so cruel.

'Are you going to do a portrait of her?' asked Myrna.

'Her who? Vivienne? I never met her.'

'No, you know who I mean.'

Myrna waited for the answer. That would reveal so much about her friend's state of mind.

But Clara didn't answer. Or maybe she did, thought Myrna, as she watched her friend stare into the vast, white, empty expanse of canvas in front of her. And put down her brush.

Jean-Guy Beauvoir pulled the car in to the now-familiar yard, and he and Armand got out.

The donkeys noticed first. Coming over to the fence to greet them.

'What do you want?' demanded Carl Tracey, once again standing at the barn door with a pitchfork. 'Come to arrest me? I keep telling you, I didn't kill Vivienne.'

Jean-Guy looked at the man and felt a wave of revulsion. He might not have killed his wife, but he beat her. Isolated her. Tormented her.

But Carl Tracey had also done something else.

'Non,' said Beauvoir. 'I've come to thank you. For saving my life.'

He didn't offer his hand. Couldn't take it that far. But he did look Carl Tracey, his unexpected savior, in the eyes. And saw there surprise. And even, maybe, a softening? A hint of what this man could have been, might still become. Might actually be, deep inside.

Carl Tracey's actions on the bridge had been instinctive. Maybe, below all the rot, there existed some timid decency.

'Yeah, well, a blow to the head'll do that.'

Was there, as he said it, the smallest possible smile?

'And I came to apologize,' said Gamache. 'For having you arrested, charged. I was wrong, and I'm sorry.'

'You're kidding,' said Tracey, scanning the woods, the road, behind the Sûreté officers. 'This's a trap, right?'

Did Carl Tracey go through life looking for, seeing, manufacturing traps set by others, for him? How, Gamache wondered, must that affect how he sees the world?

It didn't forgive the abuse, the violence. It wasn't Gamache's to forgive. But it might help explain it.

'No, no trap. An apology.'

While Jean-Guy backed the car up, Armand watched through the windshield as Tracey fed the donkeys carrots and scratched their long noses.

Superintendent Lacoste crossed her legs and smoothed her slacks. And looked across the coffee table at Chief Superintendent Toussaint.

It had been a week since the events in Three Pines, and her leave was coming to an end.

She was meeting with Toussaint to tell the head of the Sûreté which job she'd accept.

'I saw your tweets, Isabelle,' said Madeleine Toussaint as they settled into the comfortable armchairs in the sitting area of the office. 'Defending Chief Inspector Gamache. You didn't hide your identity.'

'Why should I?'

'Because you used your rank. You were posting not as a

private citizen but as a senior officer in the Sûreté. Making it look like the official Sûreté position.'

'As it should have been. I waited, you know, for someone more senior to defend him.' She glared at Toussaint. 'And when that didn't happen . . .'

'There're issues you're not aware of.'

'What issues exactly make it okay to attack our own?'

'I didn't attack him.'

'Oh, no? You think I don't know where that video came from?' Lacoste demanded.

'What video?'

But Lacoste had seen the surprise in Toussaint's eyes. The tensing of her body. A spasm of alarm. Of fear even.

'When the shit was flying, he made sure it didn't stick to you,' said Lacoste, leaning forward. 'You do know that Monsieur Gamache was the one who recommended you for this job.'

'He's not the only reason I got it.'

'True. You got it because the Premier asked you not to defend Monsieur Gamache in the hearings and you agreed.'

'That's a lie.'

'It's the truth.'

Toussaint's jaw clamped shut, and her eyes hardened. The problem with going up against Isabelle Lacoste was that she was a hero. Unassailable.

And a die-hard defender of Gamache.

'Be careful, Isabelle. It's never a good idea to catch a falling knife.'

Toussaint knew that while Superintendent Lacoste might be beyond reach, Gamache was not.

When the smoke had cleared on that final, fateful raid and Isabelle Lacoste lay in her own blood, Chief Superintendent Gamache had to answer for his decisions.

Madeleine Toussaint had known, even as she stood in those woods surveying the wreckage, that he could never really explain his actions to anyone who wasn't there. Even as they made sweeping arrests, in the most successful raid in decades, the vultures were circling.

Politicians desperate to rid themselves of this inconvenient person. A vicious and ravenous social media, desperate for fodder.

On his last day in command, before being suspended, he'd recommended Toussaint for his job. A black woman, a Haitian. They'd stood in this office. He shook her hand and told her she'd be great. But he had one request.

'Don't defend me, Madeleine. You won't win, and they'll come after you.'

'But—'

'Promise me.'

When the board of review took their shot, no one in power had stepped in front of Armand Gamache to stop it.

Chief Superintendent Gamache had gone down.

And Superintendent Toussaint had risen up.

But what no one expected, was that Gamache would actually return. Would accept such a demotion.

With the departure that evening of Jean-Guy Beauvoir to Paris, Gamache once again took over the homicide department. Respected by colleagues and subordinates, he was viewed with suspicion and worse by those who feared the power he wielded. No matter his official rank.

And Madeleine Toussaint had grown used to her own power. Used to the office. The deferential looks. The salutes. The respect of her community.

She wasn't about to give it up. But to hold on to it, she had to diminish Gamache. And that meant one thing. A purge of his most powerful supporters.

'I've been looking at your health records, Isabelle.' She nodded at the dossier on the table between them. 'The Sûreté demands a certain level of fitness, especially in its leaders. We have to act as role models.'

'Yes,' said Lacoste. 'I know. I also know there are different sorts of fitness.'

The words hit home, but Toussaint tried not to show it. 'I'm sorry to say we'll have to pension you off. While you'll keep most of your salary and your benefits, I'll have to ask for your ID and your weapon back. Your security code will no longer be valid.'

If she'd expected an argument, Toussaint was disappointed. Isabelle Lacoste just nodded and put her hand in her pocket to bring out her Sûreté ID.

But instead what she brought out was her cell phone. Propping it against some books on the table, she hit play.

Chief Superintendent Toussaint watched with thin lips and narrow eyes.

She watched Jean-Guy Beauvoir dive across the screen. Reaching for the falling man.

She watched as he grabbed a handful of the man's coat and hung on, even as he himself was dragged over the edge.

Her eyes widened as she watched Gamache leap forward. No time to think. He reacted instinctively.

She no longer saw him. He'd disappeared over the edge of the bridge. But she did see his hand. White-knuckled. Gripped onto the foot of the post.

As she watched, the hand began to slip.

Her mouth opened a little as the finger slid off. Isabelle Lacoste leaped forward to grab the hand. But someone was there before her. The former tackle, Cameron, was on his belly, reaching over the side.

There were shouts for help. Cries for help. A splash.

All this the Chief Superintendent knew. She'd read the report. But knowing and seeing were two different things.

Lacoste picked up her phone and turned it off.

Then she took an envelope out of her pocket and, placing it on the table, slid it toward the Chief Superintendent.

Isabelle Lacoste knew that the doctored video purporting to show Gamache killing unarmed kids had come from Toussaint.

It was done to discredit her predecessor, not expecting the real video to be found and released by some crazy old woman in a village that didn't even, officially, exist.

And now it was gaining ground. Overtaking the fake.

Gamache's own reputation was not only being restored, it was growing.

And this video, if released, would put the final lie to Toussaint's doctored effort to show Gamache as a psychotic coward.

'What do you want?' Toussaint asked.

'That' – Lacoste gestured toward the envelope – 'is the job I want. The job I will have.'

Toussaint nodded. Knowing, of course, what it said.

While Gamache could not be made Chief Superintendent, Isabelle Lacoste could.

Toussaint picked up the envelope, tore it open, and read. Then she looked across the table at Isabelle Lacoste. Perplexed at first, then realization growing.

'You must be kidding.'

CHAPTER 43

⌒

'W e need to go,' said Annie. 'They've almost finished boarding.'

Armand's Sûreté credentials had gotten him and Reine-Marie past security. They stood with Annie and Jean-Guy by the gate at Trudeau International Airport.

Honoré was in Reine-Marie's arms while Armand and Jean-Guy struggled with the travel stroller.

'Here,' said Reine-Marie. She handed the child to Annie, walked over to them, pressed a button, lifted some nylon, and up it folded.

The two men nodded to each other, Laurel and Hardy style. *Hm, hm, hm.*

'Can I leave him here and bring you to Paris, Maman?'

'Oh, don't ask me twice,' said Reine-Marie, taking Honoré back.

Dropping her face to his hair, she took a deep breath, then handed him to his grandfather.

The Air Canada representative approached. 'I'm sorry, but we're closing the gate.'

'*Merci*,' said Annie, and looked at her father.

'See you soon, buddy,' Armand whispered to the tired

child, almost asleep in his arms. 'You'll love Paris. What an adventure you'll have. And you'll see your cousins Florence and Zora.'

He held Honoré in the pocket of his shoulder, resting his cheek on the little head, for a moment. Then he kissed his forehead and whispered, 'I love you.'

The boy put his small hand on his grandfather's large one. Holding it there.

'Dad?' said Annie, putting out her arms.

Armand handed Honoré back to his mother.

'Before I go, I want to give you this,' said Jean-Guy, holding out an envelope.

'Money?' asked Armand, as he took it.

Jean-Guy laughed. '*Non*. A name. The person I'm recommending as your second-in-command.'

'Hope they're better than your last one,' said Armand.

'Hard to be worse,' agreed Jean-Guy. 'It is, of course, your decision.'

'Does this person know?'

'They applied. And yes, they do know about the recommendation.' He nodded to the envelope. 'I used one of the things you taught me, when making my decision about your second-in-command.'

'You mean the four statements that lead to wisdom?' asked Armand.

Jean-Guy shook his head.

'The three questions to ask yourself before speaking?'

Again, Jean-Guy shook his head.

'Then what?'

'Sometimes you just have to do something stupid.'

Armand raised his brows, and Annie turned to her mother.

'Oh, dear God, don't tell me that's the lesson he's taken from Dad?'

'I thought your dad got it from him.'

Armand put the envelope in his pocket. He knew the name it contained. Bob Cameron. A lowly agent. Not even an inspector.

Gamache hadn't considered him. Cameron had potential, but still, giving him such a promotion would be a hard sell to his superiors, and the rest of the unit. But if someone can drop far, maybe he can also rise fast.

Armand put out his hand to Jean-Guy, who took it and held it. And looked into those familiar eyes. And saw that, after all these years, after all that had happened, after all the pain and hurt, one thing had not changed.

In those eyes he still saw kindness.

And Armand, looking deep into Jean-Guy's, saw below all the pain, all the hurt, all the ghosts, a gleam. A beam. Of kindness.

'I'll find a way to be useful,' Jean-Guy whispered. *'Patron.'*

'And so will I. *Patron.'*

Then he embraced Annie. 'I love you. Take care of yourself. If you need anything, anything at all . . .'

'I know, Dad. I love you, too.'

The young family disappeared through the door, Honoré holding up his hand to wave goodbye.

It was the secret wave he and his grandfather had worked out after Great-aunt Ruth had shown the boy the one-finger wave. Papa had explained that really, three fingers were even better. For the three pines.

Armand raised his hand and waved back.

Then they were gone.

To start their new life in the City of Light.

*

Once home, Reine-Marie poured them each a scotch while Armand walked Henri and Gracie. And Fred. Slowly around the village green.

He looked up as a plane moved overhead. Among the stars.

The next morning the villagers gathered to dismantle the wall of sandbags. All danger was past.

Then, led by Myrna, they walked down the path beside the Bella Bella, past young fiddleheads and lily of the valley and crocuses in the woods, to the bend in the river.

Lighting candles and a stick of dried sage, they smudged the area, blessed the area, said a prayer for the dead and the living. Then all walked back to the bistro for breakfast.

But Armand and Reine-Marie stopped at the bench on the village green. A peaceful place in the bright sunshine. They watched robins hop on the grass. They smelled woodsmoke and mud. And sweet pine.

Armand put his hand into his coat pocket and felt the envelope there. He'd forgotten it but now brought it out.

'What's that?' Reine-Marie asked.

'From Jean-Guy. His suggestion for my second-in-command.'

After he'd opened it, he smiled and put it back in his pocket. Beside him, Reine-Marie closed her eyes and tilted her face up.

Then they walked back to the bistro to join the others.

Unheard by anyone else, Armand bent down and whispered to Ruth. 'I forgive you, but don't ever do it again.'

'Do what?'

'You know.' While he couldn't bring himself to say the words, especially to the elderly woman, even this elderly woman, he brought out his phone and showed her. The

Twitter handle @dumbass. And the link to the real Sûreté video of the raid on the factory. There were other posts by @ dumbass, defending Gamache. But when the video went up, they'd stopped.

There was no longer any need to defend him once that vile video went viral.

'How did you find it?' he asked.

'I didn't. You think I'd defend you?'

'I do.'

'I would,' the old poet admitted. 'I did. But that's not me.'

Armand stepped back and stared at Ruth. He knew her to be many things, but never a liar.

So if she wasn't @dumbass, who was?

Madeleine Toussaint sat at her desk and opened her computer.

Putting in her Sûreté code, she went back over her posts, aimed at Gamache, and deleted them all. Pausing just a moment at the final one.

Then Chief Superintendent Toussaint hit delete. And @ dumbass disappeared. Never, she prayed, to be found. Because if anyone knew ... If the Premier found out she'd defied him, and defended Gamache by posting the real video ...

It was an act of contrition. An amend. And now they were even, and she owed her former mentor nothing.

Looking across the room, her eyes fell on the last remnant of the last occupant. Something she kept meaning to take down. But had kept up. The framed poster, nailed to the wall by the door. The first, and last, thing seen each day.

Noli timere.

Armand sat on the sofa beside Reine-Marie and reached for the café au lait Olivier had brought them.

He seemed distracted, but now he reached into his pocket and handed Reine-Marie the envelope. 'You might want to read this.'

'Jean-Guy's recommendation?' She put on her reading glasses. 'Will you take it?'

'I think so.'

Armand watched her face as Reine-Marie read. He saw the smile. And relief. As she stared at Jean-Guy's familiar hand and the name he'd so carefully written.

Armand's new second-in-command.

Isabelle Lacoste.

Reine-Marie lowered the paper to her lap and looked into the fireplace. Everything might be all right, after all, she thought.

ACKNOWLEDGEMENTS

—

This book was initially going to be dedicated to my wonderful agent of fifteen years, Teresa Chris, in thanks for her own dedication to the books. She was the first publishing professional to believe in Gamache and Three Pines.

But, having said that, I decided to dedicate *A Better Man* not to my agent, but to a dog. (Sorry, Teresa . . .)

Bishop, the golden retriever who shared Michael's and my life for many years, died while I was writing this book. In fact, I almost changed the name of the dog in the book from Fred to Bishop, but for some reason, 'Fred' just worked better. Besides, that was the name of my assistant Lise's dog, who also died while I was writing *A Better Man*. He deserved to be remembered, too.

Bishop is the last in a long line of golden retrievers who have shared, and improved, our lives. Who taught us how to be more generous, more kind, way more forgiving. More patient. More human.

Our first golden was Bonnie.

I'd wanted a dog for a long time. Michael did not. Just before we got married I somehow convinced him that a puppy would be the perfect wedding gift to each other. It was, for

Michael, the same as giving each other razor-sharp teeth, pee, poop, and tumbleweeds of hair.

He was not enthusiastic.

After our honeymoon we picked up Bonnie, all eight weeks of her, and brought her home.

She immediately peed. Then cried all night.

In the morning I came down to find Michael cradling her, and Bonnie curled, asleep, in his arms.

She was forever his. And he was hers.

Each successive dog, over twenty years, tolerated me and bonded to Michael. Which, I must say, was fine with me. I loved seeing the joy in both their eyes when they spotted each other.

Not long after Michael was diagnosed with dementia, our last golden, Trudy, passed away. Michael came with me to the vet, and watched, befuddled by what was happening. Upset that I was upset, but not quite grasping why.

For weeks, Michael looked for Trudy. And asked where she was. It broke my already fragile heart.

A month or so later, knowing our distress, Kirk came by and said he'd heard about an old dog, a golden, whose family could no longer care for him. Would we like to meet him?

Michael was doing his ever-present jigsaw puzzle when Bishop arrived, just for a visit. Bishop took one look at Michael, walked over, placed his teddy chew toy on Michael's lap, sat down, and barely left Michael's side, until the day Michael died.

Bishop was our miracle dog. Our gift from a loving Higher Power.

He was dedicated to Michael. And so, after Bishop's passing this spring, at the grand age of fourteen, it seemed only right to return the favor, and dedicate *A Better Man* to a wonderful dog.

Indeed, to all our dogs.

To all the cats, horses, birds, gerbils, fish, and animals who make our lives so much better. Who give up their freedom, for us.

I now live apparently alone, but in reality I live with Bonnie, Maggie, Seamus, Trudy, Bishop. And Michael. Ever-present and immortal.

There are also some humans I want to acknowledge.

Of course, Teresa Chris, my patient (dear God, let that be true) literary agent.

My wonderful editors, Kelley Ragland, Hope Dellon, Ed Wood. My publishers, especially Andy Martin with Minotaur/St. Martin's Press in the U.S., and Louise Loiselle with Flammarion Québec. Thank you to Paul Hochman and Sarah Melnyk.

To Jamie Broadhurst and everyone at Raincoast Books.

Two people in particular, both lawyers, helped with ideas for *A Better Man*. Thank you to Laura Marr and Mike Conway.

Thank you to my family, Rob and Audi, Doug and Mary, to the nieces and nephews, for all your support and patience. For being happy for (though no doubt kinda surprised by) my success. For cheering me on, especially when things got tough. All this would be hollow, meaningless, without you to share it with.

To Kirk Lawrence and Walter Marinelli, Rocky and Steve Gottlieb. To Jon and Cotton and Betsy and Tom and Oscar and Brendan. To Hillary and Bill and Chelsea and Marc. To Danny and Lucy. Normand and Peter. Robert Bathurst, Ann Cleeves, Rhys Bowen. To Rosemary and Will and David. Kim and Deanna and Sylvie and Nathalie and Erin, Guy, and Jackie, and my neighbors in Knowlton, and, and . . .

Special thanks to Linda 'In Scotland' Lyall, who manages the website and now answers, with Lise's help, most of the mail, though I read it all and do answer some. I met Linda face to face for the first time in fifteen years this summer. She's as beautiful as she is kind.

And finally, to my assistant, and great friend, Lise. Without her, there would be no books. Lise does so much for me it's impossible to list it all. But mostly, she's my friend. My confidante.

These books are about community. About love and belonging. About the great gift of friendship.

How lucky I am to live in Three Pines. In every way. With you.

We are never alone.

Louise Penny